# THE
# MUTINY
# ON THE BOUNTY
## TRILOGY

# THE
# MUTINY
# ON THE BOUNTY
## TRILOGY

*Comprising the Three Volumes*

MUTINY ON THE BOUNTY
MEN AGAINST THE SEA
& PITCAIRN'S ISLAND

By Charles Nordhoff
& James Norman Hall

KONECKY & KONECKY

KONECKY & KONECKY
72 AYERS PT. ROAD
OLD SAYBROOK, CT 06475

ISBN: 1-56852-537-0
MANUFACTURED IN THE UNITED STATES OF AMERICA

# PREFACE

On the twenty-third of December, 1787, His Majesty's armed transport *Bounty* sailed from Portsmouth on as strange, eventful, and tragic a voyage as ever befell an English ship. Her errand was to proceed to the island of Tahiti (or Otaheite, as it was then called), in the Great South Sea, there to collect a cargo of young breadfruit trees for transportation to the West Indies, where, it was hoped, the trees would thrive and thus, eventually, provide an abundance of cheap food for the negro slaves of the English planters.

The events of that voyage it is the purpose of this tale to unfold. *Mutiny on the Bounty,* which opens the story, is concerned with the voyage from England, the long Tahiti sojourn while the cargo of young breadfruit trees was being assembled, the departure of the homeward-bound ship, the mutiny, and the fate of those of her company who later returned to Tahiti, where the greater part of them were eventually seized by *H. M. S. Pandora* and taken back to England, in irons, for trial.

The authors chose as the narrator of this part of the tale a fictitious character, Roger Byam, who tells it as an old man, after his retirement from the Navy. Byam had his actual counterpart in the person of Peter Heywood, whose name was, for this reason, omitted from the roster of the *Bounty's* company. Midshipman Byam's experience follows closely that of Midshipman Heywood. With the license of historical novelists, the authors based the career of Byam upon that of Heywood, but in depicting it they did not, of course, follow the latter in every detail. In the essentials, relating to the mutiny and its aftermath, they have adhered to the facts preserved in the records of the British Admiralty.

*Men Against the Sea,* the second part of the narrative, is the story of Captain Bligh and the eighteen loyal men who, on the morning of the mutiny, were set adrift by the mutineers in the *Bounty's* launch, an open boat twenty-three feet long, with a beam of six feet, nine inches. In this small craft Captain Bligh carried his men a voyage of 3600 miles, from the island of Tofoa (or Tofua, as it is now called), in the Friendly, or Tongan Group, to Timor, in the Dutch East Indies. The wind and weather of *Men Against the Sea* are those of Captain Bligh's own log, a series of brief daily notes which formed the chief literary source of this part of the tale. The voyage is described in the words of one of those who survived it — Thomas Ledward, acting surgeon of the *Bounty,* whose medical knowledge and whose experience in reading men's sufferings would qualify him as a sensitive and reliable observer.

*Pitcairn's Island,* which concludes the tale, is perhaps the strangest and most romantic part of it. After two unsuccessful attempts to settle on the island of Tupuai (or Tubuai, as the name is now more commonly spelled), the mutineers returned to Tahiti, where they parted company. Fletcher Christian, acting lieutenant of the *Bounty* and instigator of the mutiny, once more embarked in the ship for an unknown destination. With him were eight of his own men and eighteen Polynesians (twelve women and six men). They sailed from Tahiti in September 1789, and for a period of eighteen years nothing more was heard of them. In February 1808, the American sealing vessel *Topaz,* calling at Pitcairn, discovered on this supposedly uninhabited crumb of land a thriving community of mixed blood: a number of middle-aged Polynesian women and more than a score of children, under the benevolent rule of a white-haired English seaman, Alexander Smith, the only survivor of the fifteen men who had landed there so long before.

Various and discrepant accounts have been preserved concerning the events which took place on Pitcairn during the eighteen years preceding the visit of the *Topaz.* The source of them all, direct or indirect, was Alexander Smith (or John Adams, as he later called himself). He told the story first to Captain Folger, of the *Topaz;* then, in 1814, to Captains Staines and Pipon, of the English frigates *Briton* and *Tagus;* then to Captain Beechey, of *H. M. S. Blossom,* in 1825; and finally, in 1829, to J. A. Moerenhout, author of *Voyages aux Îles du Grand Océan.* Later accounts were recorded by Walter Brodie, who set down, in 1850, a narrative obtained from Arthur, Matthew Quintal's son; and by Rosalind Young, in her *Story of Pitcairn Island,* which gives certain details retained in the memory of Eliza, daughter of John Mills, who reached the advanced age of ninety-three.

Each of these accounts is remarkable for its differences from the others. The authors, therefore, after careful study of every existing account, adopted a chronology and selected a sequence of events which seemed to them to render more plausible the play of cause and effect.

The history of those early years on Pitcairn was tragic, perhaps inevitably so. Fifteen men and twelve women, of two widely different races, were set down on a small island, one of the loneliest in the world. At the end of a decade, although there were many children, only one man and ten women remained; of the sixteen dead, fifteen had come to violent ends. These are the facts upon which all the accounts agree. If, at times, in the Pitcairn narrative, blood flows overfreely, and horror seems to pile on horror, it is not because the authors would have it so: it *was* so, in Pitcairn history.

But the outcome of those early turbulent years was no less extraordinary than the threads of chance which led to the settlement of the island. All who were fortunate enough to visit the Pitcairn colony during the first quarter of the nineteenth century agree that it presented a veritable picture of the Golden Age.

Those who are interested in the source material concerning the *Bounty* mutiny will find an exhaustive bibliography of books, articles, and unpublished manuscripts in the Appendix to Mr. George Mackaness's *Life of Vice-Admiral William Bligh,* published by Messrs. Angus and Robertson, of Sydney, Australia. Among the principal sources consulted by the authors were the following: "Minutes of the Proceedings of a Court-Martial on Lieutenant William Bligh and certain members of his crew, to investigate the cause of the loss of *H. M. S. Bounty*"; *A Narrative of the Mutiny on Board His Majesty's Ship "Bounty,"* by William Bligh; *A Voyage to the South Sea,* by William Bligh; *The Mutiny and Piratical Seizure of H. M. S. "Bounty,"* by Sir John Barrow; *Pitcairn Island and the Islanders,* by Walter Brodie; *Mutineers of the "Bounty" and Their Descendants in Pitcairn and Norfolk Islands,* by Lady Belcher; *Bligh of the "Bounty,"* by Geoffrey Rawson; *Voyage of H. M. S. "Pandora,"* by E. Edwards and G. Hamilton; *The Life of Vice-Admiral William Bligh,* by George Mackaness; *The Story of Pitcairn Island,* by Rosalind Young; *Captain Bligh's Second Voyage to the South Seas,* by I. Lee; *Pitcairn Island Register Book; New South Wales Historical Records;* Cook's *Voyages;* Hawkesworth's *Voyages;* Beechey's *Voyages;* Ellis's *Polynesian Researches; Ancient Tahiti,* by Teura Henry; and *A Memoir of Peter Heywood.* Two excellent studies of the present-day descendants of the

*Bounty* mutineers, from the point of view of an anthropologist, have been made by Dr. Harry Shapiro in his *Descendants of the Bounty Mutineers* and *The Heritage of the Bounty*.

We wish to express our cordial thanks to Mr. N. C. Wyeth, whose illustrations lend so much colour and vividness to the story of the *Bounty* and her men.

*June, 1940.*

J. N. H.
C. N.

# CONTENTS

THE
# MUTINY
# ON THE BOUNTY
## TRILOGY

*To*
Captain Viggo Rasmussen, *Schooner Tiaré Taporo*, Rarotonga
*and*
Captain Andy Thomson, *Schooner Tagua,* Rarotonga
Old friends who sail the seas the *Bounty* sailed

# OFFICERS AND CREW OF H. M. S. BOUNTY

Lieutenant William Bligh, *Captain*
John Fryer, *Master*
Fletcher Christian, *Master's Mate*
Charles Churchill, *Master-at-Arms*
William Elphinstone, *Master-at-Arms's Mate*
"Old Bacchus," *Surgeon*
Thomas Ledward, *Acting Surgeon*
David Nelson, *Botanist*
William Peckover, *Gunner*
John Mills, *Gunner's Mate*
William Cole, *Boatswain*
James Morrison, *Boatswain's Mate*
William Purcell, *Carpenter*
Charles Norman, *Carpenter's Mate*
Thomas McIntosh, *Carpenter's Crew*
Joseph Coleman, *Armourer*

## Midshipmen

Roger Byam          Robert Tinkler
Thomas Hayward      Edward Young
John Hallet         George Stewart

John Norton    } *Quartermasters*
Peter Lenkletter }

George Simpson, *Quartermaster's Mate*
Lawrence Lebogue, *Sailmaker*
Mr. Samuel, *Clerk*
Robert Lamb, *Butcher*
William Brown, *Gardener*

John Smith    } *Cooks*
Thomas Hall   }

## Able Seamen

Thomas Burkitt      John Williams
Matthew Quintal     Thomas Ellison
John Sumner         Isaac Martin
John Millward       Richard Skinner
William McCoy       Matthew Thompson
Henry Hillbrandt    William Muspratt
Alexander Smith     Michael Byrne

# I · LIEUTENANT BLIGH

THE British are frequently criticized by other nations for their dislike of change, and indeed we love England for those aspects of nature and life which change the least. Here in the West Country, where I was born, men are slow of speech, tenacious of opinion, and averse — beyond their countrymen elsewhere — to innovation of any sort. The houses of my neighbours, the tenants' cottages, the very fishing boats which ply on the Bristol Channel, all conform to the patterns of a simpler age. And an old man, forty of whose three-and-seventy years have been spent afloat, may be pardoned a not unnatural tenderness toward the scenes of his youth, and a satisfaction that these scenes remain so little altered by time.

No men are more conservative than those who design and build ships save those who sail them; and since storms are less frequent at sea than some landsmen suppose, the life of a sailor is principally made up of the daily performance of certain tasks, in certain manners and at certain times. Forty years of this life have made a slave of me, and I continue, almost against my will, to live by the clock. There is no reason why I should rise at seven each morning, yet seven finds me dressing, nevertheless; my copy of the *Times* would reach me even though I failed to order a horse saddled at ten for my ride down to Watchet to meet the post. But habit is too much for me, and habit finds a powerful ally in old Thacker, my housekeeper, whose duties, as I perceive with inward amusement, are lightened by the regularity she does everything to encourage. She will listen to no hint of retirement. In spite of her years, which must number nearly eighty by now, her step is still brisk and her black eyes snap with a remnant of the old malice. It would give me pleasure to speak with her of the days when my mother was still living, but when I try to draw her into talk she wastes no time in putting me in my place. Servant and master, with the churchyard only a step ahead! I am lonely now; when Thacker dies, I shall be lonely indeed.

Seven generations of Byams have lived and died in Withycombe;

the name has been known in the region of the Quantock Hills for five hundred years and more. I am the last of them; it is strange to think that at my death what remains of our blood will flow in the veins of an Indian woman in the South Sea.

If it be true that a man's useful life is over on the day when his thoughts begin to dwell in the past, then I have served little purpose in living since my retirement from His Majesty's Navy fifteen years ago. The present has lost substance and reality, and I have discovered, with some regret, that contemplation of the future brings neither pleasure nor concern. But forty years at sea, including the turbulent period of the wars against the Danes, the Dutch, and the French, have left my memory so well stored that I ask no greater delight than to be free to wander in the past.

My study, high up in the north wing of Withycombe, with its tall windows giving on the Bristol Channel and the green distant coast of Wales, is the point of departure for these travels through the past. The journal I have kept, since I went to sea as a midshipman in 1787, lies at hand in the camphor-wood box beside my chair, and I have only to take up a sheaf of its pages to smell once more the reek of battle smoke, to feel the stinging sleet of a gale in the North Sea, or to enjoy the calm beauty of a tropical night under the constellations of the Southern Hemisphere.

In the evening, when the unimportant duties of an old man's day are done, and I have supped alone in silence, I feel the pleasant anticipation of a visitor to Town, who on his first evening spends an agreeable half-hour in deciding which theatre he will attend. Shall I fight the old battles over again? Camperdown, Copenhagen, Trafalgar — these names thunder in memory like the booming of great guns. Yet more and more frequently I turn the pages of my journal still further back, to the frayed and blotted log of a midshipman — to an episode I have spent a good part of my life in attempting to forget. Insignificant in the annals of the Navy, and even more so from an historian's point of view, this incident was nevertheless the strangest, the most picturesque, and the most tragic of my career.

It has long been my purpose to follow the example of other retired officers and employ the too abundant leisure of an old man in setting down, with the aid of my journal and in the fullest possible detail, a narrative of some one of the episodes of my life at sea. The decision was made last night; I shall write of my first ship, the *Bounty,* of the mutiny on board, of my long residence on the island of Tahiti in the South Sea, and of how I was conveyed home in irons, to be tried by court-martial and condemned to death. Two natures clashed on the stage of that drama of long ago, two men as strong and enigmatical as any I have known—Fletcher Christian and William Bligh.

When my father died of a pleurisy, early in the spring of 1787, my mother gave few outward signs of grief, though their life together, in an age when the domestic virtues were unfashionable, had been a singularly happy one. Sharing the interest in the natural sciences which had brought my father the honour of a Fellowship in the Royal Society, my mother was a countrywoman at heart, caring more for life at Withycombe than for the artificial distractions of town.

I was to have gone up to Oxford that fall, to Magdalen, my father's college, and during that first summer of my mother's widowhood I began to know her, not as a parent, but as a most charming companion, of whose company I never wearied. The women of her generation were schooled to reserve their tears for the sufferings of others, and to meet adversity with a smile. A warm heart and an inquiring mind made her conversation entertaining or philosophical as the occasion required; and, unlike the young ladies of the present time, she had been taught that silence can be agreeable when one has nothing to say.

On the morning when Sir Joseph Banks's letter arrived, we were strolling about the garden, scarcely exchanging a word. It was late in July, the sky was blue, and the warm air bore the scent of roses; such a morning as enables us to tolerate our English climate, which foreigners declare, perhaps with some justice, the worst in the world. I was thinking how uncommonly handsome my mother looked in black, with her thick fair hair, fresh colour, and dark blue eyes. Thacker, her new maid,—a black-eyed Devon girl,—came tripping down the path. She dropped my mother a curtsey and held out a letter on a silver tray. My mother took the letter, gave me a glance of apology, and began to read, seating herself on a rustic bench.

"From Sir Joseph," she said, when she had perused the letter at length and laid it down. "You have heard of Lieutenant Bligh, who was with Captain Cook on his last voyage? Sir Joseph writes that he is on leave, stopping with friends near Taunton, and would enjoy an evening with us. Your father thought very highly of him."

I was a rawboned lad of seventeen, lazy in body and mind, with overfast growth, but the words were like a galvanic shock to me. "With Captain Cook!" I exclaimed. "Ask him by all means!"

My mother smiled. "I thought you would be pleased," she said.

The carriage was dispatched in good time with a note for Mr. Bligh, bidding him to dine with us that evening if he could. I remember how I set out, with the son of one of our tenants, to sail my boat at high tide on Bridgwater Bay, and how little I enjoyed the sail. My thoughts were all of our visitor, and the hours till dinner-time seemed to stretch ahead interminably.

I was fonder, perhaps, of reading than most lads of my age, and the book I loved best of all was one given me by my father on my tenth birthday — Dr. Hawkesworth's account of the voyages to the South Sea. I knew the three, heavy, leather-bound volumes almost by heart, and I had read with equal interest the French narrative of Monsieur de Bougainville's voyage. These early accounts of discoveries in the South Sea, and of the manners and customs of the inhabitants of Otaheite and Owhyhee (as those islands were then called), excited an interest almost inconceivable to-day. The writings of Jean Jacques Rousseau, which were to have such lamentable and far-reaching results, preached a doctrine which had made converts even among people of consequence. It became fashionable to believe that only among men in a state of nature, freed from all restraints, could true virtue and happiness be found. And when Wallis, Byron, Bougainville, and Cook returned from their voyage of discovery with alluring accounts of the New Cytheræa, whose happy inhabitants, relieved from the curse of Adam, spent their days in song and dance, the doctrines of Rousseau received new impetus. Even my father, so engrossed in his astronomical studies that he had lost touch with the world, listened eagerly to the tales of his friend Sir Joseph Banks, and often discussed with my mother, whose interest was equal to his, the virtues of what he termed "a natural life."

My own interest was less philosophical than adventurous; like other youngsters, I longed to sail unknown seas, to raise uncharted islands, and to trade with gentle Indians who regarded white men as gods. The thought that I was soon to converse with an officer who had accompanied Captain Cook on his last voyage — a mariner, and not a man of science like Sir Joseph — kept me woolgathering all afternoon, and I was not disappointed when the carriage drew up at last and Mr. Bligh stepped out.

Bligh was at that time in the prime of life. He was of middle stature, strongly made and inclining to stoutness, though he carried himself well. His weather-beaten face was broad, with a firm mouth and very fine dark eyes, and his thick powdered hair grew high on his head, above a noble brow. He wore his three-cornered black hat athwartships; his coat was of bright blue broadcloth, trimmed with white, with gold anchor buttons and the long tails of the day. His waistcoat, breeches, and stockings were white. The old-fashioned uniform was one to set off a well-made man. Bligh's voice, strong, vibrant, and a little harsh, gave an impression of uncommon vitality; his bearing showed resolution and courage, and the glance of his eye gave evidence of an assurance such as few men possess. These symptoms of a strong and aggressive nature were tempered by the lofty brow of a man of intellect, and the agreeable and unpretentious manner he assumed ashore.

The carriage, as I said, drew up before our door, the footman sprang down from the box, and Mr. Bligh stepped out. I had been waiting to welcome him; as I made myself known, he gave me a handclasp and a smile.

"Your father's son," he said. "A great loss — he was known, by name at least, to all who practise navigation."

Presently my mother came down and we went in to dinner. Bligh spoke very handsomely of my father's work on the determination of longitude, and after a time the conversation turned to the islands of the South Sea.

"Is it true," my mother asked, "that the Indians of Tahiti are as happy as Captain Cook believed?"

"Ah, ma'am," said our guest, "happiness is a vast word! It is true that they live without great labour, and that nearly all of the light tasks they perform are self-imposed; released from the fear of want and from all salutary discipline, they regard nothing seriously."

"Roger and I," observed my mother, "have been studying the ideas of J. J. Rousseau. As you know, he believes that true happiness can only be enjoyed by man in a state of nature."

Bligh nodded. "I have been told of his ideas," he said, "though unfortunately I left school too young to learn French. But if a rough seaman may express an opinion on a subject more suited to a philosopher, I believe that true happiness can only be enjoyed by a disciplined and enlightened people. As for the Indians of Tahiti, though they are freed from the fear of want, their conduct is regulated by a thousand absurd restrictions, which no civilized man would put up with. These restrictions constitute a kind of unwritten law, called *taboo,* and instead of making for a wholesome discipline they lay down fanciful and unjust rules to control every action of a man's life. A few days among men in a state of nature might have changed Monsieur Rousseau's ideas." He paused and turned to me. "You know French, then?" he asked, as if to include me in the talk.

"Yes, sir," I replied.

"I'll do him justice, Mr. Bligh," my mother put in; "he has a gift for languages. My son might pass for a native of France or Italy, and is making progress in German now. His Latin won him a prize last year."

"I wish I had his gift! Lord!" Bligh laughed. "I'd rather face a hurricane than translate a page of Cæsar nowadays! And the task Sir Joseph has set me is worse still! There is no harm in telling you that I shall soon set sail for the South Sea." Perceiving our interest, he went on:—

"I have been in the merchant service since I was paid off four years ago, when peace was signed. Mr. Campbell, the West India merchant, gave me command of his ship, *Britannia,* and during my voyages, when I frequently had planters of consequence as passengers on board, I was many times asked to tell what I knew of the breadfruit, which flourishes in Tahiti and Owhyhee. Considering that the breadfruit might provide a cheap and wholesome food for their negro slaves, several of the West India merchants and planters petitioned the Crown, asking that a vessel be fitted out suitably to convey the breadfruit from Tahiti to the West Indian islands. Sir Joseph Banks thought well of the idea and gave it his support. It is due largely to his interest that the Admiralty is now fitting out a small vessel for the voyage, and at Sir Joseph's suggestion I was recalled to the Service and am to be given command. We should sail before the end of the year."

"Were I a man," said my mother, whose eyes were bright with interest, "I should beg you to take me along; you will need gardeners, no doubt, and I could care for the young plants."

Bligh smiled. "I would ask no better, ma'am," he said gallantly, "though I have been supplied with a botanist — David Nelson, who served in a similar capacity on Captain Cook's last voyage. My ship, the *Bounty,* will be a floating garden fitted with every convenience for the care of the plants, and I have no fear but that we shall be able to carry out the purpose of the voyage. It is the task our good friend Sir Joseph has enjoined on me that presents the greatest difficulty. He has solicited me most earnestly to employ my time in Tahiti in acquiring a greater knowledge of the Indians and their customs, and a more complete vocabulary and grammar of their language, than it has hitherto been possible to gather. He believes that a dictionary of the language, in particular, might prove of the greatest service to mariners in the South Sea. But I know as little of dictionaries as of Greek, and shall have no one on board qualified for such a task."

"How shall you lay your course, sir?" I asked. "About Cape Horn?"

"I shall make the attempt, though the season will be advanced beyond the time of easterly winds. We shall return from Tahiti by way of the East Indies and the Cape of Good Hope."

My mother gave me a glance and we rose as she took leave of us. While he cracked walnuts and sipped my father's Madeira, Bligh questioned me, in the agreeable manner he knew so well how to assume, as to my knowledge of languages. At last he seemed satisfied, finished the wine in his glass, and shook his head at the man who would have filled it. He was moderate in the use of wine, in an age when nearly all the officers of His Majesty's Navy drank to excess. Finally he spoke.

"Young man," he said seriously, "how would you like to sail with me?"

I had been thinking, ever since his first mention of the voyage, that I should like nothing better, but his words took me aback.

"Do you mean it, sir?" I stammered. "Would it be possible?"

"It rests with you and Mrs. Byam to decide. It would be a pleasure to make a place for you among my young gentlemen."

The warm summer evening was as beautiful as the day that had preceded it, and when we had joined my mother in the garden, she and Bligh spoke of the projected voyage. I knew that he was waiting for me to mention his proposal, and presently, during a pause in the talk, I summoned up my courage.

"Mother," I said, "Lieutenant Bligh has been good enough to suggest that I accompany him."

If she felt surprise, she gave no sign of it, but turned calmly to our guest. "You have paid Roger a compliment," she remarked. "Could an inexperienced lad be of use to you on board?"

"He'll make a seaman, ma'am, never fear! I've taken a fancy to the cut of his jib, as the old tars say. And I could put his gift for languages to good use."

"How long shall you be gone?"

"Two years, perhaps."

"He was to have gone up to Oxford, but I suppose that could wait." She turned to me half banteringly. "Well, sir, what do you say?"

"With your permission, there is nothing I would rather do."

She smiled at me in the twilight and gave my hand a little pat. "Then you have it," she said. "I would be the last to stand in the way. A voyage to the South Sea! If I were a lad and Mr. Bligh would have me, I'd run away from home to join his ship!"

Bligh gave one of his short, harsh laughs and looked at my mother admiringly. "You'd have made a rare sailor, ma'am," he remarked — "afraid of nothing, I'll wager."

It was arranged that I should join the *Bounty* at Spithead, but the storing, and victualing, and fitting-out took so long that the autumn was far advanced before she was ready to sail. In October I took leave of my mother and went up to London to order my uniforms, to call on old Mr. Erskine, our solicitor, and to pay my respects to Sir Joseph Banks.

My clearest memory of those days is of an evening at Sir Joseph's house. He was a figure of romance to my eyes — a handsome, florid man of forty-five, President of the Royal Society, companion of the immortal Captain Cook, friend of Indian princesses, and explorer of Labrador, Iceland, and the great South Sea. When we had dined, he led me to his study, hung with strange weapons and ornaments from distant lands. He took up from among the papers on his table a sheaf of manuscript.

"My vocabulary of the Tahitian language," he said. "I have had this copy made. It is short and imperfect, as you will discover, but may prove of some service to you. Please observe that the system of spelling Captain Cook and I adopted should be changed. I have given the matter some thought, and Bligh agrees with me that it will be better and simpler to set down the words as an Italian would spell them — particularly in the case of the vowels. You know Italian, eh?"

"Yes, sir."

"Good!" he went on. "You will be some months in Tahiti, while they are gathering the young breadfruit plants. Bligh will see to it that you are given leisure to devote yourself to the dictionary I hope to publish on your return. Dialects of the Tahitian language are spoken over an immense space of the South Sea, and a dictionary of the commoner words, with some little information as to the grammar, will be in demand among mariners before many years have passed. At present we think of the South Sea as little less remote than the moon, but depend on it, the rich whale fisheries and new lands for planting and settlement will soon attract notice, now that we have lost the American Colonies.

"There are many distractions in Tahiti," he went on after a pause; "take care that you are not misled into wasting your time. And, above all, take care in the selection of your Indian friends. When a ship drops anchor in Matavai Bay the Indians come out in throngs, each eager to choose a friend, or *taio,* from amongst her company. Bide your time, learn something of politics on shore, and choose as your *taio* a man of consideration and authority. Such a man can be of infinite use to you; in return for a few axes, knives, fishhooks, and trinkets for his women, he will keep you supplied with fresh provisions, entertain you at his residence when you step ashore, and do everything in his power to make himself useful. Should you make the mistake of choosing as your *taio* a man of the lower orders, you may find him dull, incurious, and with an imperfect knowledge of the Indian tongue. In my opinion they are not only a different class, but a different race, conquered long ago by those who now rule the land. Persons of consequence in Tahiti are taller, fairer, and vastly more intelligent than the *manahune,* or serfs."

"Then there is no more equality in Tahiti than amongst ourselves?"

Sir Joseph smiled. "Less, I should say. The Indians have a false appearance of equality from the simplicity of their manners and the fact that the employments of all classes are the same. The king may be seen heading a fishing party, or the queen paddling her own canoe, or beating out bark cloth with her women. But of real equality there is none; no action, however meritorious, can raise a man above the position to which he was born. The chiefs alone, believed to be descended from the gods, are thought to have souls." He paused, fingers drumming on the arm of his chair. "You've everything you will need?" he asked. "Clothing, writing materials, money? Midshipmen's fare is not the best in the world, but when you go on board, one of the master's mates will ask each of you for three or four pounds to lay in a few small luxuries for the berth. Have you a sextant?"

"Yes, sir — one of my father's; I showed it to Mr. Bligh."

"I'm glad Bligh's in command; there's not a better seaman afloat. I am told that he is a bit of a tartar at sea, but better a taut hand than a slack one, any day! He will instruct you in your duties; perform them smartly, and remember — discipline's the thing!"

I took my leave of Sir Joseph with his last words still ringing in my ears — "Discipline's the thing!" I was destined to ponder over them deeply, and sometimes bitterly, before we met again.

## II · SEA LAW

Toward the end of November I joined the *Bounty* at Spithead. It makes me smile to-day to think of the box I brought down on the coach from London, packed with clothing and uniforms on which I had laid out more than a hundred pounds: blue tail-coats lined with white silk, with the white patch on the collar known in those days as a "weekly account"; breeches and waistcoats of white nankeen, and a brace of "scrapers" — smart three-cornered reefer's hats, with gold loops and cockades. For a few days I made a brave show in my finery, but when the *Bounty* sailed it was stowed away for good, and worn no more.

Our ship looked no bigger than a longboat among the tall first-rates and seventy-fours at anchor near by. She had been built for the merchant service, at Hull, three years before, and purchased for two thousand pounds; ninety feet long on deck and with a beam of twenty-four feet, her burthen was little more than two hundred tons. Her name — *Bethia* — had been painted out, and at the suggestion of Sir Joseph Banks she was rechristened *Bounty*. The ship had been many months at Deptford, where the Admiralty had spent more than four thousand pounds in altering and refitting her. The great cabin aft was now rigged as a garden, with innumerable pots standing in racks, and gutters running below to allow the water to be used over and over again. The result was that Lieutenant Bligh and the master, Mr. Fryer, were squeezed into two small cabins on either side of the ladderway, and forced to mess with the surgeon, in a screened-off space of the lower deck, aft of the main hatch. The ship was small to begin with; she carried a heavy cargo of stores and articles for barter with the Indians, and all hands on board were so cramped that I heard mutterings even before we set sail. I believe, in fact, that the discomfort of our life, and the bad humour it brought about, played no small part in the unhappy ending of a voyage which seemed ill-fated from the start.

The *Bounty* was copper-sheathed, a new thing in those days, and with her bluff, heavy hull, short masts, and stout rigging, she looked more like a whaling vessel than an armed transport of His Majesty's Navy. She carried a pair of swivel guns mounted on stocks forward, and six swivels and four four-pounders aft, on the upper deck.

All was new and strange to me on the morning when I presented myself to Lieutenant Bligh, the ship was crowded with women, — the sailors' "wives," — rum seemed to flow like water everywhere, and sharp-faced Jews, in their wherries, hovered alongside, eager to lend money at interest against pay day, or to sell on credit the worthless trinkets on their trays. The cries of the bumboat men, the shrill scolding of the women, and the shouts and curses of the sailors made a pandemonium stunning to a landsman's ears.

Making my way aft, I found Mr. Bligh on the quarter-deck. A tall, swarthy man was just ahead of me.

"I have been to the Portsmouth observatory, sir," he said to the captain; "the timekeeper is one minute fifty-two seconds too fast for mean time, and losing at the rate of one second a day. Mr. Bailey made a note of it in this letter to you."

"Thank you, Mr. Christian," said Bligh shortly, and at that moment, turning his head, he caught sight of me. I uncovered, stepping forward to present myself. "Ah, Mr. Byam," he went on, "this is Mr. Christian, the master's mate; he will show you your berth and instruct you in some of your duties. . . . And, by the way, you will dine with me on board the *Tigress;* Captain Courtney knew your father and asked me to bring you when he heard that you would be on board." He glanced at his large silver watch. "Be ready in an hour's time."

I bowed in reply to his nod of dismissal and followed Christian to the ladderway. The berth was a screened-off space of the lower deck, on the larboard side, abreast of the main hatch. Its dimensions were scarcely more than eight feet by ten, yet four of us were to make this kennel our home. Three or four boxes stood around the sides, and a scuttle of heavy discoloured glass admitted a dim light. A quadrant hung on a nail driven into the ship's side, and, though she was not long from Deptford, a reek of bilge water hung in the air. A handsome, sulky-looking boy of sixteen, in a uniform like my own, was arranging the gear in his box, and straightened up to give me a contemptuous stare. His name was Hayward, as I learned when Christian introduced us briefly, and he scarcely deigned to take my outstretched hand.

When we regained the upper deck, Christian lost his air of preoccupation, and smiled. "Mr. Hayward has been two years at sea," he remarked; "he knows you for a Johnny Newcomer. But the *Bounty* is a little ship; such airs would be more fitting aboard a first-rate."

He spoke in a cultivated voice, with a trace of the Manx accent, and I could barely hear the words above the racket from the forward part of the ship. It was a calm, bright winter morning, and I studied my companion in the clear sunlight. He was a man to glance at more than once.

Fletcher Christian was at that time in his twenty-fourth year, — a fine figure of a seaman in his plain blue, gold-buttoned frock, — handsomely and strongly built, with thick dark brown hair and a complexion naturally dark, and burned by the sun to a shade rarely seen among the white race. His mouth and chin expressed great resolution of character, and his eyes, black, deep-set, and brilliant, had something of hypnotic power in their far-away gaze. He looked more like a Spaniard than an Englishman, though his family had been settled since the fifteenth century on the Isle of Man. Christian was what women call a romantic-looking man; his moods of gaiety alternated with fits of black depression, and he possessed a fiery temper which he controlled by efforts that brought the sweat to his brow. Though only a master's mate, a step above a midshipman, he was of gentle birth — better born than Bligh and a gentleman in manner and speech.

"Lieutenant Bligh," he said, in his musing, abstracted way, "desires me to instruct you in some of your duties. Navigation, nautical astronomy, and trigonometry he will teach you himself, since we have no schoolmaster on board, as on a man-of-war. And I can assure you that you will not sup till you have worked out the ship's position each day. You will be assigned to one of the watches, to keep order when the men are at the braces or aloft. You will see that the hammocks are stowed in the morning, and report the men whose hammocks are badly lashed. Never lounge against the guns or the ship's side, and never walk the deck with your hands in your pockets. You will be expected to go aloft with the men to learn how to bend canvas and how to reef and furl a sail, and when the ship is at anchor you may be placed in charge of one of the boats. And, last of all, you are the slave of those tyrants, the master and master's mates."

He gave me a whimsical glance and a smile. We were standing by the gratings abaft the mainmast, and at that moment a stout elderly man, in a uniform much like Bligh's, came puffing up the ladderway. His bronzed face was at once kindly and resolute, and I should have known him for a seaman anywhere.

"Ah, Mr. Christian, there you are!" he exclaimed as he heaved himself on deck. "What a madhouse! I'd like to sink the lot of those Jews, and heave the wenches overboard! Who's this? The new reefer, Mr. Byam, I'll be bound! Welcome on board, Mr. Byam; your father's name stands high in our science, eh, Mr. Christian?"

"Mr. Fryer, the master," said Christian in my ear.

"A madhouse," Fryer went on. "Thank God we shall pay off tomorrow night! Wenches everywhere, above decks and below." He turned to Christian. "Go forward and gather a boat's crew for Lieutenant Bligh — there are a few men still sober."

"There's discipline on a man-of-war at sea," he continued; "but give me a merchant ship in port. The captain's clerk is the only sober man below. The surgeon . . . Ah, here he is now!"

Turning to follow Fryer's glance, I saw a head thatched with thick snow-white hair appearing in the ladderway. Our sawbones had a wooden leg and a long equine face, red as the wattles of a turkey cock; even the back of his neck, lined with deep wrinkles like a tortoise's, was of the same fiery red. His twinkling bright blue eyes caught sight of the man beside me. Holding to the ladder with one hand, he waved a half-empty bottle of brandy at us.

"Ahoy there, Mr. Fryer!" he hailed jovially. "Have you seen Nelson, the botanist? I prescribed a drop of brandy for his rheumatic leg; it's time he took his medicine."

"He's gone ashore."

The surgeon shook his head with mock regret. "He'll give his good shillings to some Portsmouth quack, I'll wager. Yet here on board he might enjoy free and gratis the advice of the most enlightened medical opinion. Away with all bark and physic!" He flourished his bottle. "Here is the remedy for nine tenths of human ills. Aye! Drops of brandy! That's it!" Suddenly, in a mellow, husky voice, sweet and true, he began to sing: —

> "And Johnny shall have a new bonnet
> And Johnny shall go to the fair,
> And Johnny shall have a blue ribbon
> To tie up his bonny brown hair."

With a final flourish of his bottle, our surgeon went hopping down the ladderway. Fryer stared after him for a moment before he followed him below. Left to myself in the midst of the uproar on deck, I looked about me curiously.

Lieutenant Bligh, an old hand in the Navy, was nowhere to be seen. On the morrow the men would receive two months' wages in advance, and on the following day we should set sail on a voyage to the other side of the world, facing the hardships and dangers of seas still largely unexplored. The *Bounty* might well be gone two years or more, and now, on the eve of departure, her crew was allowed to relax for a day or two of such amusements as sailors most enjoy.

While I waited for Bligh in the uproar, I diverted myself in studying the rigging of the *Bounty*. Born and brought up on the west coast of England, I had loved the sea from childhood and lived amongst men who spoke of ships and their qualities as men gossip of horses elsewhere. The *Bounty* was ship-rigged, and to a true landsman her rigging would have seemed a veritable maze of ropes. But even in my inexperience I knew enough to name her sails, the different parts of her standing rigging, and most of the complex system of halliards, lifts, braces, sheets, and other ropes for the management of sails and yards. She spread two headsails — foretopmast-staysail and jib; on fore and main masts she carried courses, topsails, topgallants, and royals, and the mizzenmast spread the latter three sails. That American innovation, the crossjack, had not in those days been introduced. The crossjack yard was still, as the French say, a *vergue sèche,* — a barren yard, — and the *Bounty's* driver, though loose at the foot, was of the gaff-headed type, then superseding the clumsy lateen our ships had carried on the mizzen for centuries.

As I mused on the *Bounty's* sails and ropes, asking myself how this order or that would be given, and wondering how I should go about obeying were I told to furl a royal or lend a hand at one of the braces, I felt something of the spell which even the smallest ship casts over me to this day. For a ship is the noblest of all man's works — a cunning fabric of wood, and iron, and hemp, wonderfully propelled by wings of canvas, and seeming at times to have the very breath of life. I was craning my neck to stare aloft when I heard Bligh's voice, harsh and abrupt.

"Mr. Byam!"

I gathered my wits with a start and found Lieutenant Bligh, in full uniform, at my side. He gave a faint quizzing smile and went on: "She's small, eh? But a taut little ship — a taut little ship!" He made me a sign to follow him over the *Bounty's* side.

Our boat's crew, if not strictly sober, were able to row, and put their backs into it with a will. We were soon alongside Captain Courtney's tall seventy-four. The *Tigress* paid Mr. Bligh the compliment of piping the side. Side boys in spotless white stood at attention by the red ropes to the gangway; the boatswain, in full uniform, blew a slow and solemn salute on his silver whistle as Bligh's foot touched the deck. Marine sentries stood at attention, and all was silent save for the mournful piping. We walked aft, saluting the quarter-deck, where Captain Courtney awaited us.

Courtney and Bligh were old acquaintances; he had been with Bligh on the *Belle Poule,* in the stubborn and bloody action of Dogger Bank six years before. Captain Courtney was a member of a great family — a tall, slender officer, with a quizzing glass and a thin-lipped ironic mouth. He greeted us pleasantly, spoke of my father, whom he had known more by reputation than otherwise, and led us to his cabin aft, where a red-coated sentry stood at the bulkhead, a drawn sword in his hand. It was the first time I had been in the cabin of a man-of-war, and I gazed about me curiously. Its floor was the upper gun-deck and its ceiling the poop; so the apartment seemed very lofty for a ship. The ports were glazed, and a door aft gave on the stern-walk, with its carvings and gilded rail, where the captain might take his pleasure undisturbed. But the cabin itself was furnished with Spartan bareness: a long settee under the ports, a heavy fixed table, and a few chairs. A lamp swung in gimbals overhead; there were a telescope in a bracket, a short shelf of books, and a stand of muskets and cutlasses in a rack about the mizzenmast. The table was laid for three.

"A glass of sherry with you, Mr. Bligh," said the captain, as a man handed the glasses on a tray. He smiled at me in his courtly way, and raised his glass. "To the memory of your father, young man! We seamen owe him a lasting debt."

As we drank, I heard a great stir and shuffling of feet on deck, and the distant sound of a drum. Captain Courtney glanced at his watch, finished his wine, and rose from the settee.

"My apologies. They're flogging a man through the fleet, and I hear the boats coming. I must read the sentence at the gangway — a deuced bore. Make yourselves at home; should you wish to be spectators, I can recommend the poop."

Next moment he passed the rigid marine at the bulkhead and was gone. Bligh listened for a moment to the distant drumming, set down his glass, and beckoned me to follow him. From the quarter-deck a short ladder led up to the poop, a high point of vantage from which all that went on was visible. Though the air was crisp, the wind was the merest cat's-paw and the sun shone in a blue and cloudless sky.

The order to turn all hands aft to witness punishment was being piped by the boatswain and shouted by his mates. The marines, with muskets and side-arms, were hastening aft to fall in before us on the poop. Captain Courtney and his lieutenants stood on the weather quarter-deck, and the junior officers were gathered to leeward of them. The doctor and purser stood further to leeward, under the break of the poop, behind the boatswain and his mates. The ship's company was gathered along the lee bulwarks — some, to see better, standing in the boats or on the booms. A tall ninety-eight and a third-rate like the *Tigress* lay at anchor close by, and I saw that their ports and bulwarks were crowded with silent men.

The half-minute bell began to sound, and the noise of drumming grew louder — the doleful tattoo of the rogue's march. Then, around the bows of the *Tigress,* came a procession I shall never forget.

In the lead, rowed slowly in time to the nervous beat of the drum, came the longboat of a near-by ship. Her surgeon and master-at-arms stood beside the drummer; just aft of them a human figure was huddled in a posture I could not make out at first. Behind the longboat, and rowing in time to the same doleful music, came a boat from every ship of the fleet, manned with marines to attend the punishment. I heard an order "Way enough!" and as the rowing ceased the longboat drifted to a halt by the gangway. I glanced down over the rail. My breath seemed to catch in my throat, and without knowing that I spoke, I exclaimed softly, "Oh, my God!" Mr. Bligh gave me a side-long glance and one of his slight, grim smiles.

The huddled figure in the bows of the boat was that of a powerful man of thirty or thirty-five. He was stripped to his wide sailor's trousers of duck, and his bare arms were bronzed and tattooed. Stockings had been bound around his wrists, which were stoutly lashed to a capstan bar. His thick yellow hair was in disorder and I could not see his face, for his head hung down over his chest. His trousers, the thwart on which he lay huddled, and the frames and planking of the boat on either side of him were blotched and spattered with black blood. Blood I had seen before; it was the man's back that made me catch my breath. From neck to waist the cat-o'-nine-tails had laid the bones bare, and the flesh hung in blackened, tattered strips.

Captain Courtney sauntered placidly across the deck to glance down at the hideous spectacle below. The surgeon in the boat bent over the mutilated, seized-up body, straightened his back, and looked at Courtney by the gangway.

"The man is dead, sir," he said solemnly. A murmur faint as a stir of air in the treetops came from the men crowded on the booms. The Captain of the *Tigress* folded his arms and turned his head slightly with raised eyebrows. He made a gallant figure, with his sword, his rich laced uniform, his cocked hat and powdered queue. In the tense silence which followed he turned to the surgeon again.

"Dead," he said lightly, in his cultivated drawl. "Lucky devil! Master-at-arms!" The warrant officer at the doctor's side sprang to attention and pulled off his hat. "How many are due?"

"Two dozen, sir."

Courtney strolled back to his place on the weather side and took from his first lieutenant's hand a copy of the Articles of War. As he swept off his cocked hat gracefully and held it over his heart, every man on the ship uncovered in respect to the King's commandments. Then, in his clear, drawling voice, the captain read the Article which prescribes the punishment for striking an officer of His Majesty's Navy. One of the boatswain's mates was untying a red baize bag, from which he drew out the red-handled cat, eyeing it uncertainly, with frequent glances to windward. The captain concluded his reading, replaced his hat, and caught the man's eye. Again I heard the faint sighing murmur forward, and again deep silence fell before Courtney's glance. "Do your duty," he ordered calmly; "two dozen, I believe."

"Two dozen it is, sir," said the boatswain's mate in a hollow voice as he walked slowly to the side. There were clenched jaws and gleaming eyes among the men forward, but the silence was so profound that I could hear the faint creak of blocks aloft as the braces swayed in the light air.

I could not turn my eyes away from the boatswain's mate, climbing slowly down the ship's side. If the man had shouted aloud, he could not have expressed more clearly the reluctance he felt. He stepped into the boat, and as he moved among the men on the thwarts they drew back with set stern faces. At the capstan bar, he hesitated and looked up uncertainly. Courtney had sauntered to the bulwarks and was gazing down with folded arms.

"Come! Do your duty!" he ordered, with the air of a man whose dinner is growing cold.

The man with the cat drew its tails through the fingers of his left hand, raised his arm, and sent them whistling down on the poor battered corpse. I turned away, giddy and sick. Bligh stood by the rail, a hand on his hip, watching the scene below as a man might watch a play indifferently performed. The measured blows continued — each breaking the silence like a pistol shot. I counted them mechanically for what seemed an age, but the end came at last — twenty-two, a pause, twenty-three . . . twenty-four. I heard a word of command; the marines fell out and trooped down the poop ladder. Eight bells struck. There were a stir and bustle on the ship, and I heard the boatswain piping the long-drawn, cheery call to dinner.

When we sat down to dine, Courtney seemed to have dismissed the incident from his mind. He tossed off a glass of sherry to Bligh's health, and tasted his soup. "Cold!" he remarked ruefully. "Hardships of a seaman's life, eh, Bligh?"

His guest took soup with a relish, and sounds better fitted to the forecastle than aft, for his manners at table were coarse. "Damme!" he said. "We fared worse aboard the old *Poule!*"

"But not in Tahiti, I'll wager. I hear you are to pay the Indian ladies of the South Sea another call."

"Aye, and a long one. We shall be some months in getting our load of breadfruit trees."

"I heard of your voyage in Town. Cheap food for the West Indian slaves, eh? I wish I were sailing with you."

"By God, I wish you were! I could promise you some sport."

"Are the Indian women as handsome as Cook painted them?"

"Indeed they are, if you've no prejudice against a brown skin. They are wonderfully clean in person, and have enough sensibility to attract a fastidious man. Witness Sir Joseph; he declares that there are no such women in the world!"

Our host sighed romantically. "Say no more! Say no more! I can see you, like a Bashaw under the palms, in the midst of a harem the Sultan himself might envy!"

Still sickened by what I had seen, I was doing my best to make a pretense of eating, silent while the older men talked. Bligh was the first to mention the flogging.

"What had the man done?" he asked.

Captain Courtney set down his glass of claret and glanced up absently. "Oh, the fellow who was flogged," he said. "He was one of Captain Allison's foretopmen, on the *Unconquerable*. And a smart hand, they say. He was posted for desertion, and then Allison, who remembered his face, saw him stepping out of a public house in Portsmouth. The man tried to spring away and Allison seized him by the arm. Damme! Good topmen don't grow on every hedge! Well, this insolent fellow blacked Allison's eye, just as a file of marines passed. They made him prisoner, and you saw the rest. Odd! We were only the fifth ship; eight dozen did for him. But Allison has a boatswain's mate who's an artist, they say — left-handed, so he lays them on crisscross, and strong as an ox."

Bligh listened with interest to Courtney's words, and nodded approvingly. "Struck his captain, eh?" he remarked. "By God! He deserved all he got, and more! No laws are more just than those governing the conduct of men at sea."

"Is there any need of such cruelty?" I asked, unable to keep silent. "Why did they not hang the poor fellow and have done with it?"

"Poor fellow?" Captain Courtney turned to me with eyebrows raised. "You have much to learn, my lad. A year or two at sea will harden him, eh, Bligh?"

"I'll see to that," said the Captain of the *Bounty*. "No, Mr. Byam, you must waste no sympathy on rascals of that stripe."

"And remember," put in Courtney, with a manner of friendly admonishment, "remember, as Mr. Bligh says, that no laws are more just than those governing the conduct of men at sea. Not only just, but necessary; discipline must be preserved, on a merchantman as well as on a man-of-war, and mutiny and piracy suppressed."

"Yes," said Bligh, "our sea law is stern, but it has the authority of centuries. And it has grown more humane with time," he continued, not without a trace of regret. "Keel-hauling has been abolished, save among the French, and a captain no longer has the right to condemn and put to death one of his crew."

Still agitated by the shock of what I had seen, I ate little and took more wine than was my custom, sitting in silence for the most part, while the two officers gossiped, sailor-like, as to the whereabouts of former friends, and spoke of Admiral Parker, and the fight at Dogger Bank. It was mid-afternoon when Bligh and I were pulled back to the *Bounty*. The tide was low, and I saw a boat aground on a flat some distance off, while a party of men dug a shallow grave in the mud. They were burying the body of the poor fellow who had been flogged through the fleet — burying him below tide mark, in silence, and without religious rites.

## OFFICERS AND CREW OF H. M. S. BOUNTY

Lieutenant William Bligh, *Captain*
John Fryer, *Master*
Fletcher Christian, *Master's Mate*
Charles Churchill, *Master-at-Arms*
William Elphinstone, *Master-at-Arms's Mate*
Thomas Huggan, *Surgeon*
Thomas Ledward, *Acting Surgeon*
David Nelson, *Botanist*
William Peckover, *Gunner*
John Mills, *Gunner's Mate*
William Cole, *Boatswain*
James Morrison, *Boatswain's Mate*
William Purcell, *Carpenter*
Charles Norman, *Carpenter's Mate*
Thomas McIntosh, *Carpenter's Crew*
Joseph Coleman, *Armourer*

Roger Byam
Thomas Hayward
John Hallet
Robert Tinkler        } *Midshipmen*
Edward Young
George Stewart

John Norton ⎫ *Quartermasters*
Peter Lenkletter ⎬

George Simpson, *Quartermaster's Mate*
Lawrence Lebogue, *Sailmaker*
Mr. Samuel, *Clerk*
Robert Lamb, *Butcher*
William Brown, *Gardener*

John Smith ⎫ *Cooks*
Thomas Hall ⎬

Thomas Burkitt ⎫
Matthew Quintal
John Sumner
John Millward
William McCoy
Henry Hillbrandt
Alexander Smith
John Williams ⎬ *Able Seamen*
Thomas Ellison
Isaac Martin
Richard Skinner
Matthew Thompson
William Muspratt
Michael Byrne ⎭

# III · AT SEA

AT daybreak on the twenty-eighth of November we got sail on the *Bounty* and worked down to St. Helen's, where we dropped anchor. For nearly a month we were detained there and at Spithead by contrary winds; it was not until the twenty-third of December that we set sail down the Channel with a fair wind.

A month sounds an age to be crowded with more than forty other men on board a small vessel at anchor most of the time, but I was making the acquaintance of my shipmates, and so keen on learning my new duties that the days were all too short. The *Bounty* carried six midshipmen, and, since we had no schoolmaster, as is customary on a

man-of-war, Lieutenant Bligh and the master divided the duty of instructing us in trigonometry, nautical astronomy, and navigation. I
shared with Stewart and Young the advantage of learning navigation
under Bligh, and in justice to an officer whose character in other respects
was by no means perfect, I must say that there was no finer seaman and
navigator afloat at the time. Both of my fellow midshipmen were men
grown: George Stewart of a good family in the Orkneys, a young man
of twenty-three or four, and a seaman who had made several voyages
before this: and Edward Young, a stout, salty-looking fellow, with a
handsome face marred by the loss of nearly all his front teeth. Both of
them were already very fair navigators, and I was hard put to it not
to earn the reputation of a dunce.

The boatswain, Mr. Cole, and his mate, James Morrison, instructed
me in seamanship. Cole was an old-style Navy salt, bronzed, taciturn,
and pigtailed, with a profound knowledge of his work and little other
knowledge of any kind. Morrison was very different — a man of good
birth, he had been a midshipman, and had shipped aboard the *Bounty*
because of his interest in the voyage. He was a first-rate seaman and
navigator; a dark, slender, intelligent man of thirty or thereabouts,
cool in the face of danger, not given to oaths, and far above his station
on board. Morrison did not thrash the men to their work, delivering
blows impartially in the manner of a boatswain's mate; he carried a
colt, a piece of knotted rope, to be sure, but it was only used on obvious
malingerers, or when Bligh shouted to him: "Start that man!"

There were much irritation and grumbling at the continued bad
weather, but at last, on the evening of the twenty-second of December,
the sky cleared and the wind shifted to the eastward. It was still dark
next morning when I heard the boatswain's pipe and Morrison's call:
"All hands! Turn out and save a clue! Out or down here! Rise and
shine! Out or down there! Lash and carry!"

The stars were bright when I came on deck, and the grey glimmer
of dawn was in the East. For three weeks we had had strong southwesterly winds, with rain and fog; now the air was sharp with frost,
and a strong east wind blew in gusts off the coast of France. Lieutenant
Bligh was on the quarter-deck with Mr. Fryer, the master; Christian
and Elphinstone, the master's mates, were forward among the men.
There was a great bustle on deck and the ship rang with the piping of
the bos'n's whistle. I heard the shouting of the men at the windlass,
and Christian's voice above the din: "Hove short, sir!"

"Loose the topsails!" came from Fryer, and Christian passed the order on. My station was the mizzen-top, and in a twinkling we had the gaskets off and the small sail sheeted home. The knots in the gaskets were stiff with frost, and the men setting the fore-topsail were slow at their work. Bligh glanced aloft impatiently.

"What are you doing there?" he shouted angrily. "Are you all asleep, foretop? The main-topmen are off the yard! Look alive, you crawling caterpillars!"

The topsails filled and the yards were braced up sharp; the *Bounty* broke out her own anchor as she gathered way on the larboard tack. She was smartly manned in spite of Bligh's complaints, but he was on edge, for a thousand critical eyes watched our departure from the ships at anchor closer inshore. With a "Yo! Heave ho!" the anchor came up and was catted.

Then it was: "Loose the forecourse!" and presently, as she began to heel to the gusts: "Get the mainsail on her!" There was a thunder of canvas and a wild rattling of blocks. When the brace was hove short, Bligh himself roared: "Board the main tack!" Little by little, with a mighty chorus at the windlass: "Heave ho! Heave and pawl! Yo, heave, hearty, ho!" the weather clew of the sail came down to the waterway. Heeling well to starboard, the bluff-bowed little ship tore through the sheltered water, on her way to the open sea.

The sun rose in a cloudless sky — a glorious winter's morning, clear, cold, and sparkling. I stood by the bulwarks as we flew down the Solent, my breath trailing off like thin smoke. Presently we sped through the Needles and the *Bounty* headed away to sea, going like a race horse, with topgallants set.

That night the wind increased to a strong gale, with a heavy sea, but on the following day the weather moderated, permitting us to keep our Christmas cheerfully. Extra grog was served out, and the mess cooks were to be heard whistling as they seeded the raisins for duff, not, as a landsman might suppose, from the prospect of good cheer, but in order to prove to their messmates that the raisins were not going into their mouths.

I was still making the acquaintance of my shipmates at this time. The men of the *Bounty* had been attracted by the prospect of a voyage to the South Sea, or selected for their stations by the master or Bligh himself. Our fourteen able-bodied seamen were true salts, not the scum of the taverns and jails impressed to man so many of His Majesty's ships; the officers were nearly all men of experience and tried character, and even our botanist, Mr. Nelson, had been recommended by Sir. Joseph Banks because of his former voyage to Tahiti under Captain Cook. Mr. Bligh might have had a hundred midshipmen had he obliged all those who applied for a place in the *Bounty's* berth; as it was, there were six of us, though the ship's establishment provided for only two. Stewart and Young were seamen and pleasant fellows enough; Hallet was a sickly-looking boy of fifteen with a shifty eye and a weak, peevish mouth; Tinkler, Mr. Fryer's brother-in-law, was a year younger, though he had been to sea before — a monkey of a lad, whose continual scrapes kept him at the masthead half the time. Hayward, the handsome, sulky boy I had met when I first set foot in the berth, was only sixteen, but big and strong for his age. He was something of a bully and aspired to be cock of the berth, since he had been two years at sea aboard a seventy-four.

I shared with Hayward, Stewart, and Young a berth on the lower deck. In this small space the four of us swung our hammocks at night and had our mess, using a chest for a table and other chests for seats. On consideration of a liberal share of our grog, received each Saturday night, Alexander Smith, able-bodied, acted as our hammock man, and for a lesser sum of the same ship's currency, Thomas Ellison, the youngest of the seamen, filled the office of mess boy. Mr. Christian was caterer to the midshipmen's mess; like the others, I had paid him five pounds on joining the ship, and he had laid out the money in a supply of potatoes, onions, Dutch cheeses (for making that midshipman's dish called "crab"), tea, coffee, and sugar, and other small luxuries. These private stores enabled us to live well for several weeks, though a more villainous cook than young Tom Ellison would be impossible to find. As for drink, the ship's allowance was so liberal that Christian made no special provision for us. For a month or more every man aboard received a gallon of beer each day, and when that was gone, a pint of fiery white *mistela* wine from Spain — the wine our seamen love and call affectionately "Miss Taylor." And when the last of the wine was gone we fell back on an ample supply of the sailor's sheet anchor — grog. We had a wondrous fifer on board — a half-blind Irishman named Michael Byrne. He had managed to conceal his blindness till the *Bounty* was at sea, when it became apparent, much to Mr. Bligh's annoyance. But when he struck up "Nancy Dawson" on the first day he piped the men to grog, his blindness was forgotten. He could put more trills and runs into that lively old tune than any man of us had heard before — a cheeriness in keeping with this happiest hour of the seaman's day.

We lost a good part of our beer in a strong easterly gale that overtook the *Bounty* the day after Christmas. Several casks went adrift from their lashings and were washed overboard when a great sea broke over the ship; the same wave stove in all three of our boats and nearly carried them away. I was off watch at the time, and below, diverting myself in the surgeon's cabin on the orlop, aft. It was a close, stinking little den, below the water line — reeking of the bilges and lit by a candle that burned blue for lack of air. But that mattered nothing to Old Bacchus. Our sawbones's name was Thomas Huggan and it was so inscribed on the ship's articles, but he was known as Old Bacchus to all our company. His normal state was what sailors call "in the wind" or "shaking a cloth," and the signal that he had passed his normal state earned him the name by which all hands on the *Bounty* knew him. When he had indiscreetly added a glass of brandy or a tot of grog to the carefully measured supply of spirits demanded at close intervals by a stomach which must have been copper-sheathed, it was his custom to rise, balancing himself on his starboard leg, place a hand between the third and fourth buttons of his waistcoat, and recite with comic gravity a verse which begins: —

Bacchus must now his power resign.

With his wooden leg, his fiery face, snow-white hair, and rakish blue eyes, Old Bacchus seemed the veritable archetype of naval surgeons. He had been afloat so long that he could scarcely recollect the days when he had lived ashore, and viewed with apprehension the prospect of retirement. He preferred salt beef to the finest steak or chop to be obtained ashore, and confided to me one day that it was almost impossible for him to sleep in a bed. A cannon ball had carried away his larboard leg when his ship was exchanging broadsides, yardarm to yardarm, with the *Ranger,* and he had been made prisoner by John Paul Jones.

The cronies of Old Bacchus were Mr. Nelson, the botanist, and Peckover, the *Bounty's* gunner. The duties of a gunner, onerous enough on board a man-of-war, were of the very lightest on our ship, and Peckover — a jovial fellow who loved a song and a glass dearly — had some leisure for conviviality. Mr. Nelson was a quiet, elderly man with iron-grey hair. Though devoted to the study of plants, he seemed to derive great pleasure from the surgeon's company, and could spin a yarn with the best when in the mood. The great event in his life had been his voyage to the South Sea with Captain Cook, whose memory he revered.

Mr. Nelson's cabin was forward of the surgeon's, separated from it by the cabin of Samuel, the captain's clerk, and he was to be found more often in the surgeon's cabin than in his own. All of the cabins were provided with standing bed places, built in by the carpenters at Deptford, but Bacchus preferred to sling a hammock at night, and used his bed as a settee and the capacious locker under it as a private spirit room. The cabin was scarcely more than six feet by seven; the bed occupied nearly half of this space, and opposite, under the hammock battens, were three small casks of wine, as yet unbroached. On one of them a candle guttered and burned blue.

Another cask served as a seat for me, and Bacchus and Nelson sat side by side on the bed. Each man held a pewter pint of flip — beer strongly laced with rum. The ship was on the larboard tack and making heavy weather of it, so that at times my cask threatened to slide from under me, but the two men on the settee seemed to give the weather no thought.

"A first-rate man, Purcell!" remarked the surgeon, glancing down admiringly at his new wooden leg; "a better ship's carpenter never swung an adze! My other leg was most damnably uncomfortable, but this one's like my own flesh and bone! Mr. Purcell's health!" He took a long pull at the flip and smacked his lips. "You're a lucky man, Nelson! Should anything happen to your underpinning, you've me to saw off the old leg and Purcell to make you a better one!"

Nelson smiled. "Very kind, I'm sure," he said; "but I hope I shall not have to trouble you."

"I hope not, my dear fellow — I hope not! But never dread an amputation. With a pint of rum, a well-stropped razor, and a crosscut saw, I'd have your leg off before you knew it. Paul Jones's American surgeon did the trick for me.

"Let's see — it must have been in seventy-eight. I was on the old *Drake,* Captain Burden, and we were on the lookout for Paul Jones's *Ranger* at the time. Then we learned that she was hove-to off the mouth of Belfast Lough. An extraordinary affair, begad! We actually had sight-seers on board — one of them was an officer of the Inniskilling

Fusileers in full uniform. We moved out slowly and came up astern of the American ship. Up went our colours and we hailed: 'What ship is that?' 'American Continental ship *Ranger!*' roared the Yankee master, as his own colours went up. 'Come on — we're waiting for you!' Next moment both ships let go their broadsides. . . . Good God!"

The *Bounty* staggered with the shock of a great sea which broke into her at that moment. "Up with you, Byam!" ordered the surgeon; and, as I sprang out of his cabin toward the ladderway, I heard, above the creaking and straining of the ship and the roar of angry water, a faint shouting for all hands on deck. Then I found myself in an uproar and confusion very strange after the peace of the surgeon's snuggery.

Bligh stood by the mizzenmast, beside Fryer, who was bawling orders to his mates. They were shortening sail to get the ship hove-to. The men at the clew lines struggled with might and main to hoist the stubborn thundering canvas to the yards.

My own task, with two other midshipmen, was to furl the mizzen topsail — a small sail, but far from easy to subdue at such a time. The men below brailed up the driver and made fast the vangs of its gaff. Presently the *Bounty* was hove-to, all snug on the larboard tack, under reefed fore and main topsails.

The great wave which had boarded us left destruction in its wake. All three of our boats were stove in; the casks of beer which had been lashed on deck were nowhere to be seen; and the stern of the ship so damaged that the cabin was filled with water, which leaked into the bread room below, spoiling a large part of our stock of bread.

In latitude 39°N. the gale abated, the sun shone out, and we made all sail for Teneriffe with a fine northerly wind. On the fourth of January we spoke a French merchant vessel, bound for Mauritius, which let go her topgallant sheets in salute. The next morning we saw the island of Teneriffe to the southwest of us, about twelve leagues distant, but it fell calm near the land and we were a day and a night working up to the road of Santa Cruz, where we anchored in twenty-five fathoms, close to a Spanish packet and an American brig.

For five days we lay at anchor in the road, and it was here that the seeds of discontent, destined to be the ruin of the voyage, were sown among the *Bounty's* people. As there was a great surf on the beach, Lieutenant Bligh bargained with the shore boats to bring off our water and supplies, and kept his own men busy from morning to night repairing the mischief the storm had done our ship. This occasioned much grumbling in the forecastle, as some of the sailors had hoped to be employed in the ship's boats, which would have enabled them at least to set foot on the island and to obtain some of the wine for which it is famous, said to be little inferior to the best London Madeira.

During our sojourn the allowance of salt beef was stopped, and fresh beef, obtained on shore, issued instead. The *Bounty's* salt beef was the worst I have ever met with at sea, but the beef substituted for it in Teneriffe was worse still. The men declared that it had been cut from the carcasses of dead horses or mules, and complained to the master that it was unfit for food. Fryer informed Bligh of the complaint; the captain flew into a passion and swore that the men should eat the fresh beef or nothing at all. The result was that most of it was thrown overboard — a sight which did nothing to soothe Bligh's temper.

I was fortunate enough to have a run ashore, for Bligh took me with him one day to wait upon the governor, the Marquis de Brancheforté. With the governor's permission Mr. Nelson ranged the hills every day in search of plants and natural curiosities, but his friend the surgeon only appeared on deck once during the five days we lay at anchor. Old Bacchus had ordered a monstrous supply of brandy for himself — enough to do the very god of wine, his namesake, for a year. Not trusting the shore boats with such precious freight, he had obtained the captain's permission to send the small cutter to the pier, and when a man went below to inform him that his brandy was alongside, the surgeon came stumping to the ladderway and clambered on deck. The cutter was down to the gunwales with her load; as there was a high swell running, Old Bacchus stood by the bulwarks anxiously. "Easy with it!" he ordered with tender solicitude. "Easy now! A glass of grog all around if you break nothing!" When the last of the small casks was aboard and had been sent below, the surgeon heaved a sigh. I was standing near by and saw him glance at the land for the first time. He caught my eye. "One island's as like another as two peas in a pod," he remarked indifferently, pulling out a handkerchief to mop his fiery face.

When we sailed from Teneriffe, Bligh divided the people into three watches, making Christian acting lieutenant, and giving him charge of the third watch. Bligh had known him for some years in the West India trade, and believed himself to be Christian's friend and benefactor. His friendship took the form of inviting Christian to sup or dine one day, and cursing him in the coarsest manner before the men the next; but in this case he did him a real service, since it was ten to one that, if all went well on the voyage, the appointment would be confirmed by the Admiralty, and Christian would find himself the holder of His Majesty's commission. He now rated as a gentleman, with the midshipmen and Bligh; and Fryer was provided with a grievance both against the captain, and — such is human nature — against his former subordinate.

Nor were grievances wanting during our passage from Teneriffe to Cape Horn. The people's food on British ships is always bad and always scanty — a fact which in later days caused so many of our seamen to desert to American vessels. But on the *Bounty* the food was of poorer quality, and issued in scantier quantities, than any man of us had seen before. When Bligh called the ship's company aft to read the order appointing Christian acting lieutenant, he also informed them that, as the length of the voyage was uncertain, and the season so far advanced that it was doubtful whether we should be able to make our way around Cape Horn, it seemed necessary to reduce the allowance of bread to two thirds of the usual amount. Realizing the need for economy, the men received this cheerfully, but continued to grumble about the salt beef and pork.

We carried no purser. Bligh filled the office himself, assisted by Samuel, his clerk — a smug, tight-lipped little man, of a Jewish cast of countenance, who was believed, not without reason, to be the captain's "narker" or spy among the men. He was heartily disliked by all hands, and it was observed that the man who showed his dislike for Mr. Samuel too openly was apt to find himself in trouble with Lieutenant Bligh. It was Samuel's task to issue the provisions to the cooks of the messes; each time a cask of salt meat was broached, the choicest pieces were reserved for the cabin, and the remainder, scarcely fit for human food, issued out to the messes without being weighed. Samuel would call out "Four pounds," and mark the amount down in his book, when anyone could perceive that the meat would not have weighed three.

Seamen regard meanness in their own kind with the utmost contempt, and that great rarity in the Service, a mean officer, is looked upon with loathing by his men. They can put up with a harsh captain, but nothing will drive British seamen to mutiny faster than a captain suspected of lining his pockets at their expense.

While the *Bounty* was still in the northeast trades, an incident occurred which gave us reason to suspect Bligh of meanness of this kind.
The weather was fine, and one morning the main hatch was raised and
our stock of cheeses brought up on deck to air. Bligh missed no detail
of the management of his ship; he displayed in such matters a smallness
of mind scarcely in accord with his commission. This unwillingness to
trust those under him to perform their duties is apt to be the defect of
the officer risen from the ranks, — or "come in through the hawse-hole,"
as seamen say, — and is the principal reason why such officers are rarely
popular with their men.

Bligh stood by Hillbrandt, the cooper, while he started the hoops
on our casks of cheese and knocked out the heads. Two cheeses, of
about fifty pounds weight, were found to be missing from one of the
casks, and Bligh flew into one of his passions of rage.

"Stolen, by God!" he shouted.

"Perhaps you will recollect, sir," Hillbrandt made bold to say, "that
while we were in Deptford the cask was opened by your order and
the cheeses carried ashore."

"You insolent scoundrel! Hold your tongue!"

Christian and Fryer happened to be on deck at the time, and Bligh
included them in the black scowl he gave the men near by. "A damned
set of thieves," he went on. "You're all in collusion against me — officers
and men. But I'll tame you — by God, I will!" He turned to the cooper.
"Another word from you and I'll have you seized up and flogged to the
bone." He turned aft on his heel and bawled down the ladderway.
"Mr. Samuel! Come on deck this instant."

Samuel came trotting up to his master obsequiously, and Bligh went
on: "Two of the cheeses have been stolen. See that the allowance is
stopped — from the officers too, mind you — until the deficiency is
made good."

I could see that Fryer was deeply offended, though he said nothing
at the time; as for Christian, — a man of honour, — his feelings were
not difficult to imagine. The men had a pretty clear idea of which way
the wind blew by this time, and on the next banyan day, when butter
alone was served out, they refused it, saying that to accept butter without cheese would be a tacit acknowledgment of the theft. John Williams, one of the seamen, declared publicly in the forecastle that he
had carried the two cheeses to Mr. Bligh's house, with a cask of vinegar

and some other things which were sent up in a boat from Long Reach.

As the private stocks of provisions obtained in Spithead now began to run out, all hands went "from grub galore to the King's own," as seamen say. Our bread, which was only beginning to breed maggots, was fairly good, though it needed teeth better than mine to eat the central "reefer's nut"; but our salt meat was unspeakably bad. Meeting Alexander Smith one morning when he was cook to his mess, I was shown a piece of it fresh from the cask — a dark, stony, unwholesome-looking lump, glistening with salt.

"Have a look, Mr. Byam," he said. "What'll it be, I wonder? Not beef or pork, that's certain! I mind one day on the old *Antelope* — two years ago, that was — the cooper found three horseshoes in the bottom of a cask!" He shook his pigtail back over his shoulder and shifted a great quid of tobacco to his starboard cheek. "You've seen the victualing yards in Portsmouth, sir? Pass that way any night, and you'll hear the dogs bark and the horses neigh! And I'll tell you something else you young gentlemen don't know." He glanced up and down the deck cautiously and then whispered: "It's as much as a black man's life is worth to pass that way by night! They'd pop him into a cask like that!" He snapped his fingers impressively.

Smith was a great admirer of Old Bacchus, whom he had known on other ships, and a few days later he handed me a little wooden box. "For the surgeon, sir," he said. "Will you give it to him?"

It was a snuffbox, curiously wrought of some dark, reddish wood, like mahogany, and very neatly fitted with a lid; a handsome bit of work, carved and polished with a seaman's skill. I found leisure to visit the surgeon the same evening.

Christian's watch was on duty at the time. Young Tinkler and I were in Mr. Fryer's watch, and the third watch had been placed in charge of Mr. Peckover, a short, powerful man of forty or forty-five, who could scarcely remember a time when he had not been at sea. His good-humoured face had been blackened by the West Indian sun, and his arms were covered with tattooing.

I found Peckover with the doctor and Nelson — squeezed together on the settee.

"Come in," cried the surgeon. "Wait a bit, my lad — I think I can make a place for you."

He sprang up with surprising agility and pushed a small cask into the doorway. Peckover held the spigot open while the wine poured frothing into a pewter pint. I delivered the snuffbox before I sat down on my cask, pint in hand.

"From Smith, you say?" asked the surgeon. "Very handsome of him! Very handsome indeed! I remember Smith well on the old *Antelope* — eh, Peckover? I have a recollection that I used to treat him to a drop of grog now and then. And why not, I say! A thirsty man goes straight to my heart." He glanced complacently about his cabin, packed to the hammock battens with small casks of spirits and wine. "Thank God that neither I nor my friends shall go thirsty on this voyage!"

Nelson stretched out his hand for the snuffbox and examined it with interest. "I shall always marvel," he remarked, "at the ingenuity of our seamen. This would be a credit to any craftsman ashore, with all the tools of his trade. And a fine bit of wood, handsomely polished, too! Mahogany, no doubt, though the grain seems different."

Bacchus looked at Peckover quizzically, and the gunner returned the look, grinning.

"Wood?" said the surgeon. "Well, I have heard it called that, and worse. Wood that once bellowed — aye, and neighed and barked, if the tales be true. In plain English, my dear Nelson, your mahogany is old junk, more politely called salt beef — His Majesty's own!"

"Good Lord!" exclaimed Nelson, examining the snuffbox in real astonishment.

"Aye, salt beef! Handsome as any mahogany and quite as durable. Why, it had been proposed to sheathe our West India frigates with it — a material said to defy the attacks of the toredo worm!"

I took the little box from Nelson's hand, to inspect it with a new interest. "Well, I'm damned!" I thought.

Old Bacchus had rolled up his sleeve and was pouring a train of snuff along his shaven and polished forearm. With a loud sniffing sound it disappeared up his nose. He sneezed, blew his nose violently on an enormous blue handkerchief, and filled his tankard with *mistela*.

"A glass of wine with you gentlemen!" he remarked, and poured the entire pint down his throat without taking breath. Mr. Peckover glanced at his friend admiringly.

"Aye, Peckover," said the surgeon, catching his eye, "nothing like a nip of salt beef to give a man a thirst. Let the cook keep his slush. Give me a bit of the lean, well soaked and boiled, and you can have all the steaks and cutlets ashore. Begad! Just suppose, now, that we were all wrecked on a desert island, without a scrap to eat. I'd pull out my snuffbox and have one meal, at any rate, while the rest of you went hungry!"

"So you would, surgeon, so you would," said the gunner in his rumbling voice, grinning from ear to ear.

## IV · TYRANNY

ONE sultry afternoon, before we picked up the southeast trades, Bligh sent his servant to bid me sup with him. Since the great cabin was taken up with our breadfruit garden, the captain messed on the lower deck, in an apartment on the larboard side, extending from the hatch to the bulkhead abaft the mainmast. I dressed myself with some care, and, going aft, found that Christian was my fellow guest. The surgeon and Fryer messed regularly with Bligh, but Old Bacchus had excused himself this evening.

There was a fine show of plate on the captain's table, but when the dishes were uncovered I saw that Bligh fared little better than his men. We had salt beef, in plenty for once, and the pick of the cask, bad butter, and worse cheese, from which the long red worms had been hand-picked, a supply of salted cabbage, believed to prevent scurvy, and a dish heaped with the mashed pease seamen call "dog's body."

Mr. Bligh, though temperate in the use of wine, attacked his food with more relish than most officers would care to display. Fryer was a rough, honest old seaman, but his manners at table put the captain's to shame; yet Christian, who had been a mere master's mate only a few days before, supped fastidiously despite the coarseness of the food. Christian was on the captain's right, Fryer on his left, and I sat opposite, facing him. The talk had turned to the members of the *Bounty's* company.

"Damn them!" said Bligh, his mouth full of beef and pease, which he continued to chew rapidly as he spoke. "A lazy, incompetent lot of scoundrels! God knows a captain has trials enough without being cursed with such a crew! The dregs of the public houses. . . ." He swallowed violently and filled his mouth once more. "That fellow I had flogged yesterday; what was his name, Mr. Fryer?"

"Burkitt," replied the master, a little red in the face.

"Yes, Burkitt, the insolent hound! And they're all as bad. I'm damned if they know a sheet from a tack!"

"I venture to differ with you, sir," said the master. "I should call Smith, Quintal, and McCoy first-class seamen, and even Burkitt, though he was in the wrong . . ."

"The insolent hound!" repeated Bligh violently, interrupting the master. "At the slightest report of misconduct, I shall have him seized up again. Next time it will be four dozen, instead of two!"

Christian caught my eye as the captain spoke. "If I may express an opinion, Mr. Bligh," he said quietly, "Burkitt's nature is one to tame with kindness rather than with blows."

Bligh's short, harsh laugh rang out grimly. "La-di-da, Mr. Christian! On my word, you should apply for a place as master in a young ladies' seminary! Kindness, indeed! Well, I'm damned!" He took up a glass of the reeking ship's water, rinsing his mouth preparatory to an attack on the sourcrout. "A fine captain you'll make if you don't heave overboard such ridiculous notions. Kindness! Our seamen understand kindness as well as they understand Greek! Fear is what they *do* understand! Without that, mutiny and piracy would be rife on the high seas!"

"Aye," admitted Fryer, as if regretfully. "There is some truth in that."

Christian shook his head. "I cannot agree," he said courteously. "Our seamen do not differ from other Englishmen. Some must be ruled by fear, it is true, but there are others, and finer men, who will follow a kind, just, and fearless officer to the death."

"Have we any such paragons on board?" asked the captain sneeringly.

"In my opinion, sir," said Christian, speaking in his light and courteous manner, "we have, and not a few."

"Now, by God! Name one!"

"Mr. Purcell, the carpenter. He . . ."

This time Bligh laughed long and loud. "Damme!" he exclaimed, "you're a fine judge of men! That stubborn, thick-headed old rogue! Kindness. . . . Ah, that's too good!"

Christian flushed, controlling his hot temper with an effort. "You won't have the carpenter, I see," he said lightly: "then may I suggest Morrison, sir?"

"Suggest to your heart's content," answered Bligh scornfully. "Morrison? The gentlemanly boatswain's mate? The sheep masquerading as a wolf? Kindness? Morrison's too damned kind now!"

"But a fine seaman, sir," put in Fryer gruffly; "he has been a midshipman, and is a gentleman born."

"I know, I know!" said Bligh in his most offensive way; "and no higher in my estimation for all that." He turned to me, with what he meant to be a courteous smile. "Saving your presence, Mr. Byam, damn all midshipmen, I say! There could be no worse schools than the berth for the making of sea officers!" He turned to Christian once more, and his manner changed to an unpleasant truculence.

"As for Morrison, let him take care! I've my eye on him, for I can see that he spares the cat. A boatswain's mate who was not a gentleman would have had half the hide off Burkitt's back. Let him take care, I say! Let him lay on when I give the word or, by God, I'll have him seized up for a lesson from the boatswain himself!"

I perceived, as the meal went on, that the captain's mess was anything but a congenial one. Fryer disliked the captain, and had not forgotten the incident of the cheeses. Bligh made no secret of his dislike for the master, whom he often upbraided before the men on deck; and he felt for Christian a contempt he was at no pains to conceal.

I was not surprised, a few days later, to learn from Old Bacchus that Christian and the master had quitted the captain's mess, leaving Bligh to dine and sup alone. We were south of the line by this time.

At Teneriffe, we had taken on board a large supply of pumpkins, which now began to show symptoms of spoiling under the equatorial sun. As most of them were too large for the use of Bligh's table, Samuel was ordered to issue them to the men in lieu of bread. The rate of exchange — one pound of pumpkin to replace two pounds of bread — was considered unfair by the men, and when Bligh was informed of this he came on deck in a passion and called all hands. Samuel was then ordered to summon the first man of every mess.

"Now," exclaimed Bligh violently, "let me see who will dare to refuse the pumpkins, or anything else I order to be served. You insolent rascals! By God! I'll make you eat grass before I've done with you!"

Everyone now took the pumpkins, not excepting the officers, though the amount was so scanty that it was usually thrown together by the men, the cooks of the different messes drawing lots for the whole. There was some murmuring, particularly among the officers, but the grievance might have ended there had not all hands begun to believe that the casks of beef and pork were short of their weight. This had been suspected for some time, as Samuel could never be prevailed on to weigh the meat when opened, and at last the shortage became so obvious that the people applied to the master, begging that he would examine into the affair and procure them redress. Bligh ordered all hands aft at once.

"So you've complained to Mr. Fryer, eh?" he said, shortly and harshly. "You're not content! Let me tell you, by God, that you'd better make up your minds to *be* content! Everything that Mr. Samuel does is done by my orders, do you understand? My orders! Waste no more time in complaints, for you will get no redress! I am the only judge of what is right and wrong. Damn your eyes! I'm tired of you and your complaints! The first man to complain from now on will be seized up and flogged."

Perceiving that no redress was to be hoped for before the end of the voyage, the men resolved to bear their sufferings with patience, and neither murmured nor complained from that time. But the officers, though they dared make no open complaints, were less easily satisfied and murmured frequently among themselves of their continual state of hunger, which they thought was due to the fact that the captain and his clerk had profited by the victualing of the ship. Our allowance of food was so scanty that the men quarreled fiercely over the division of it in the galley, and when several men had been hurt it became necessary for the master's mate of the watch to superintend the division of the food.

About a hundred leagues off the coast of Brazil, the wind chopped around to north and northwest, and I realized that we had reached the southern limit of the southeast trades. It was here, in the region of variable westerlies, that the *Bounty* was becalmed for a day or two, and the people employed themselves in fishing, each mess risking a part of its small allowance of salt pork in hopes of catching one of the sharks that swam about the ship.

The landsman turns up his nose at the shark, but, to a sailor craving fresh meat, the flesh of a shark under ten feet in length is a veritable luxury. The larger sharks have a strong rank smell, but the flesh of the small ones, cut into slices like so many beefsteaks, parboiled first and then broiled with plenty of pepper and salt, eats very well indeed, resembling codfish in flavour.

I tasted shark for the first time one evening off the Brazilian coast. It was dead calm; the sails hung slack from the yards, only moving a little when the ship rolled to a gently northerly swell. John Mills, the gunner's mate, stood forward abreast of the windlass, with a heavy line coiled in his hand. He was an old seaman, one of Christian's watch —a man of forty or thereabouts who had served in the West Indies on the *Mediator,* Captain Cuthbert Collingwood. I disliked the man, — a tall, rawboned, dour old salt, — but I watched with interest as he prepared his bait. Two of his messmates stood by, ready to bear a hand — Brown, the assistant botanist, and Norman, the carpenter's mate. The mess had contributed the large piece of salt pork now going over the side; they shared the risk of losing the bait without results, as they would share whatever Mills was fortunate enough to catch. A shark about ten feet long had just passed under the bows. I craned my neck to watch.

Next moment a small striped fish like a mackerel flashed this way and that about the bait. "Pilot fish!" cried Norman. "Take care — here comes the shark!"

"Damn you!" growled Mills. "Don't dance about like a monkey — you'll frighten him off!"

The shark, an ugly yellowish blotch in the blue water, was rising beneath the bait, and all eyes were on him as he turned on his side, opened his jaws, and gulped down the piece of pork. "Hooked, by God!" roared Mills as he hove the line short. "Now, my hearties, on deck with him!" The line was strong and the messmates hove with a will; in an instant the shark came struggling over the bulwarks and thumped down on deck. Mills seized a hatchet and struck the fish a heavy blow on the snout; next moment six or seven men were astride of the quivering carcass, knives out and cutting away for dear life. The spectacle was laughable. Mills, to whom the head belonged by right of capture, was seated at the forward end; each of the others, pushing himself as far aft as possible, to enlarge his cut of shark, was slicing away within an inch of the next man's rump. There were cries of "Mind what you are about, there!" "Take care, else I'll have a slice off your backside!" And in about three minutes' time the poor fish had been severed into as many great slices as there had been men bestriding him.

The deck was washed, and Mills was picking up the several slices into which he had cut his share of the fish, when Mr. Samuel, the captain's clerk, came strolling forward.

"A fine catch, my good man," he remarked in his patronizing way. "I must have a slice, eh?"

In common with all of the *Bounty's* people, Mills disliked Samuel heartily. The clerk drank neither rum nor wine, and it was suspected that he hoarded his ration of spirits for sale ashore.

"So you must have a slice," growled the gunner's mate. "Well, I must have a glass of grog, and a stiff one, too, if you are to eat shark to-day."

"Come! Come! My good man," said Samuel pettishly. "You've enough fish there for a dozen."

"And you've enough grog stowed away for a thousand, by God!"

"It's for the captain's table I want it," said Samuel.

"Then catch him a shark yourself. This is mine. He gets the best of the bread and the pick of the junk cask as it is."

"You forget yourself, Mills! Come, give me a slice — that large one there — and I'll say nothing."

"Say nothing be damned! Here — take your slice!" As he spoke, Mills flung the ten or twelve pounds of raw fish straight at Samuel's face, with the full strength of a brawny, tattooed arm. He turned on his heel to go below, growling under his breath.

Mr. Samuel picked himself up from the deck, not forgetting his slice of shark, and walked slowly aft. The look in his eye boded no good fortune to the gunner's mate.

The news spread over the ship rapidly, and for the first time aboard the *Bounty* Mills found himself a popular man, though there was little hope that he would escape punishment. As Old Bacchus put it that night, "The least he can hope for is a red-checked shirt at the gangway. Samuel's a worm and a dirty worm, but discipline's discipline, begad!"

I believe that a day will come when flogging will be abolished on His Majesty's ships. It is an over-brutal punishment, which destroys a good man's self-respect and makes a bad man worse. Landsmen have little idea of the savagery of a flogging at the gangway. The lashes are laid on with the full strength of a powerful man's arm, with such force that each blow knocks the breath clean out of the delinquent's body. One blow takes off the skin and draws blood where each knot falls. Six blows make the whole back raw. Twelve cut deeply into the flesh and leave it a red mass, horrible to see. Yet six dozen are a common punishment.

As had been predicted, Mills spent the night in irons. The kind hearts of our British seamen were evident next morning when I was told that his messmates had saved their entire allowance of grog for Mills, to fortify him against the flogging they considered inevitable. At six bells Mr. Bligh came on deck, and bade Christian turn the hands aft to witness punishment. The weather had grown cooler, and the *Bounty* was slipping southward with all sail set, before a light northwest breeze. The order was piped and shouted forward; I joined the assembly of officers aft, while the people fell in on the booms and along the ship's side. All were silent.

"Rig the gratings," ordered Mr. Bligh, in his harsh voice.

The carpenter and his mates dragged aft two of the wooden gratings used to cover the hatches. They placed one flat on the deck, and the other upright, secured to the bulwarks by the lee gangway.

"The gratings are rigged, sir," reported Purcell, the carpenter.

"John Mills!" said Bligh. "Step forward!"

Flushed with the rum he had taken, and dressed in his best, Mills stepped out from among his messmates. His unusual smartness was designed to mollify the punishment, yet there was in his bearing a trace of defiance. He was a hard man, and he felt that he had been hardly used.

"Have you anything to say?" asked Bligh of the bare-headed seaman before him.

"No, sir," growled Mills sullenly.

"Strip!" ordered the captain.

Mills tore off his shirt, flung it to one of his messmates, and advanced bare-shouldered to the gratings.

"Seize him up," said Bligh.

Norton and Lenkletter, our quartermasters — old pigtailed seamen who had performed this office scores of times in the past — now advanced with lengths of spun yarn, and lashed Mills's outstretched wrists to the upright grating.

"Seized up, sir!" reported Norton.

Bligh took off his hat, as did every man on the ship, opened a copy of the Articles of War, and read in a solemn voice the article which prescribes the punishments for mutinous conduct. Morrison, the boat-swain's mate, was undoing the red baize bag in which he kept the cat.

"Three dozen, Mr. Morrison," said Bligh as he finished reading. "Do your duty!"

Morrison was a kindly, reflective man. I felt for him at that moment, for I knew that he hated flogging on principle, and must feel the injustice of this punishment. Yet he would not dare, under the keen eye of the captain, to lighten the force of his blows. However unwilling, he was Bligh's instrument.

He advanced to the grating, drew the tails of the cat through his fingers, flung his arm back, and struck. Mills winced involuntarily as the cat came whistling down on his bare back, and the breath flew out of his body with a loud "Ugh!" A great red welt sprang out against the white skin, with drops of blood trickling down on one side. Mills was a burly ruffian and he endured the first dozen without crying out, though by that time his back was a red slough from neck to waist.

Bligh watched the punishment with folded arms. "I'll show the man who's captain of this ship," I heard him remark placidly to Christian. "By God, I will!" The eighteenth blow broke the iron of Mills's self-control. He was writhing on the grating, his teeth tightly clenched and the blood pouring down his back. "Oh!" he shouted thickly. "Oh, my God! Oh!"

"Mr. Morrison," called Bligh, sternly and suddenly. "See that you lay on with a will."

Morrison passed the tails of the cat through his fingers to free them of blood and bits of flesh. Under the eye of the captain he delivered the remaining lashes, taking a time that seemed interminable to me. When they cut Mills down he was black in the face and collapsed at once on the deck. Old Bacchus stumped forward and ordered him taken below to the sick bay, to be washed with brine. Bligh sauntered to the ladder-way and the men resumed their duties sullenly.

Early in March we were ordered to lay aside our light tropical clothing for warm garments which had been provided for our passage around Cape Horn. The topgallant masts were sent down, new sails bent, and the ship made ready for the heavy winds and seas which lay ahead. The weather grew cooler each day, until I was glad to go below for my occasional evenings with Bacchus and his cronies, or to my mess in the berth. The surgeon messed with us now, as well as Stewart and Hayward, my fellow midshipmen, Morrison, and Mr. Nelson, the botanist. We were all the best of friends, though young Hayward never forgot that I was his junior in service, and plumed himself on a knowledge of seamanship certainly more extensive than my own.

Those were days and nights of misery for every man on board. Sometimes the wind hauled to the southwest, with squalls of snow, forcing us to come about on the larboard tack; sometimes the gale increased to the force of a hurricane and we lay hove-to under a rag of staysail, pitching into the breaking seas. Though our ship was new and sound, her seams opened under the strain and it became necessary to man the pumps every hour. The hatches were constantly battened down, and when the forward deck began to leak, Bligh gave orders that the people should sling their hammocks in the great cabin aft. At last our captain's iron determination gave way, and to the great joy and relief of every man on board he ordered the helm put up to bear away for the Cape of Good Hope.

The fine weather which followed and our rapid passage east did much to raise the spirits of the men on board. We had caught great numbers of sea birds off Cape Horn and penned them in cages provided by the carpenter. The pintado and the albatross were the best; when penned like a Strasburg goose and well stuffed with ground corn for a few days, they seemed to us as good as ducks or geese, and this fresh food did wonders for our invalids.

With the returning cheerfulness on board, the *Bounty's* midshipmen began to play the pranks of their kind the world over, and none of us escaped penance at the masthead — penance that was in general richly deserved. No one was oftener in hot water than young Tinkler, a monkey of a lad, beloved by every man on the ship. Bligh's severity to Tinkler, one cold moonlight night, when we were in the longitude of Tristan da Cunha, was a warning to all of us, and the cause of much murmuring among the men.

Hallet, Hayward, Tinkler, and I were in the larboard berth. The gunner's watch was on duty, and Stewart and Young on deck. We had supped and were passing the time at Ablewhackets — a game I have never seen played ashore. It is commenced by playing cards, which must be named the Good Books. The table is termed the Board of Green Cloth, the hand the Flipper; the light the Glim, and so on. To call a table a table, or a card a card, brings an instant cry of "Watch," whereupon the delinquent must extend his Flipper to be severely firked with a stocking full of sand by each of the players in turn, who repeat his offense while firking him. Should the pain bring an oath to his lips, as is more than likely, there is another cry of "Watch," and he undergoes a second round of firking by all hands. As will be perceived, the game is a noisy one.

Young Tinkler had inadvertently pronounced the word "table," and Hayward, something of a bully, roared, "Watch!" When he took his turn at the firking, he laid on so hard that the youngster, beside himself with pain, squeaked, "Ouch! Damn your blood!" "Watch!" roared Hayward again, and at the same moment we heard another roar from aft — Mr. Bligh calling angrily for the ship's corporal. Tinkler and Hallet rushed for their berth on the starboard side; Hayward doused the glim in an instant, kicked off his pumps, threw off his jacket, and sprang into his hammock, where he pulled his blanket up to his chin and began to snore, gently and regularly. I wasted no time in doing the same, but young Tinkler, in his anxiety, must have turned in all standing as he was.

Next moment, Churchill, the master-at-arms, came fumbling into the darkened berth. "Come, come, young gentlemen; no shamming, now!" he called. He listened warily to our breathing, and felt us to make sure that our jackets and pumps were off, before he went out, grumbling, to the starboard berth. Hallet had taken the same precautions as ourselves, but poor little Tinkler was caught red-handed — pumps, jacket, and all. "Up with you, Mr. Tinkler," rumbled Churchill. "This'll mean the masthead, and it's a bloody cold night. I'd let you off if I could. You young gentlemen keep half the ship awake with your cursed pranks!" He led him aft, and presently I heard Bligh's harsh voice, raised angrily.

"Damme, Mr. Tinkler! Do you think this ship's a bear garden? By God! I've half a mind to seize you up and give you a taste of the colt! To the masthead with you!"

Next morning at daylight Tinkler was still at the main topgallant crosstrees. The sky was clear, but the strong west-southwest wind was icy cold. Presently Mr. Bligh came on deck, and, hailing the masthead, desired Tinkler to come down. There was no reply, even when he hailed a second time. At a word from Mr. Christian, one of the topmen sprang into the rigging, reached the crosstrees, and hailed the deck to say that Tinkler seemed to be dying, and that he dared not leave him for fear he would fall. Christian himself then went aloft, sent the topman down into the top for a tailblock, made a whip with the studding-sail halliards, and lowered Tinkler to the deck. The poor lad was blue with cold, unable to stand up or to speak.

We got him into his hammock in the berth, wrapped in warm blankets, and Old Bacchus came stumping forward with a can of his universal remedy. He felt the lad's pulse, propped his head up, and began to feed him neat rum with a spoon. Tinkler coughed and opened his eyes, while a faint colour appeared in his cheeks.

"Aha!" exclaimed the surgeon. "Nothing like rum, my lad! Just a sip, now. That's it! Now a swallow. Begad! Nothing like rum. I'll soon have you right as a trivet! And that reminds me — I'll have just a drop myself. A corpse reviver, eh?"

Coughing as the fiery liquor ran down his throat, Tinkler smiled in spite of himself. Two hours later he was on deck, none the worse for his night aloft.

On the twenty-third of May we dropped anchor in False Bay, near Cape Town. Table Bay is reckoned unsafe riding at this time of year, on account of the strong northwest winds. The ship required to be caulked in every part, for she had become so leaky that we had been obliged to pump every hour during our passage from Cape Horn. Our sails and rigging were in sad need of repair, and the timekeeper was taken ashore to ascertain its rate. On the twenty-ninth of June we sailed out of the bay, saluting the Dutch fort with thirteen guns as we passed.

I have few recollections of the long, cold, and dismal passage from the Cape of Good Hope to Van Diemen's Land. Day after day we scudded before strong westerly to southwesterly winds, carrying only the foresail and close-reefed maintopsail. The seas, which run for thousands of miles in these latitudes, unobstructed by land, were like mountain ridges; twice, when the wind increased to a gale, Bligh almost drove his ship under before we could get the sails clewed up and the *Bounty* hove-to. I observed that as long as the wind held southwest or west-southwest great numbers of birds accompanied us, — pintados, albatross, and blue petrels, — but that when the wind chopped around to the north, even for an hour or two, the birds left us at once. And when they reappeared their presence was always the forerunner of a southerly wind.

On the twentieth of August we sighted the rock called the Mewstone, which lies near the southwest cape of Van Diemen's Land, bearing northeast about six leagues, and two days later we anchored in Adventure Bay. We passed a fortnight here — wooding, watering, and sawing out plank, of which the carpenter was in need. It was a gloomy place, hemmed in by forests of tall straight trees of the eucalyptus kind, many of them a hundred and fifty feet high and rising sixty or eighty feet without a branch. Long strips of bark hung in tatters from their trunks, or decayed on the ground underfoot; few birds sang in the bush; and I saw only one animal — a small creature of the opossum sort, which scuttled into a hollow log. There were men here, but they were timid as wild animals — black, naked, and uncouth, with hair growing in tufts like peppercorns, and voices like the cackling of geese. I saw small parties of them at different times, but they made off at sight of us.

Mr. Bligh put me in charge of a watering party, giving us the large cutter and instructing me to have the casks filled in a gully at the west end of the beach. Purcell, the carpenter, had rigged his saw pit close to this place, and was busy sawing out plank, with his mates, Norman and McIntosh, and two of the seamen detailed to the task. They had felled two or three of the large eucalyptus trees, but the carpenter, after inspecting the wood, had declared it worthless, and instructed his men to set to work on certain smaller trees of a different kind, with a rough bark and firm reddish wood.

I was superintending the filling of my casks one morning when Bligh appeared, a fowling piece over his arm and accompanied by Mr. Nelson. He glanced toward the saw pit and came to a halt.

"Mr. Purcell!" he called harshly.

"Yes, sir."

The *Bounty's* carpenter was not unlike her captain in certain respects. Saving the surgeon, he was the oldest man on board, and nearly all of his life had been spent at sea. He knew his trade as well as Bligh understood navigation, and his temper was as arbitrary and his anger as fierce and sudden as Bligh's.

"Damme, Mr. Purcell!" exclaimed the captain. "Those logs are too small for plank. I thought I instructed you to make use of the large trees."

"You did, sir," replied Purcell, whose own temper was rising.

"Obey your orders, then, instead of wasting time."

"I am not wasting time, sir," said the carpenter, very red in the face.

"The wood of the large trees is useless, as I discovered when I had cut some of them down."

"Useless? Nonsense. . . . Mr. Nelson, am I not right?"

"I am a botanist, sir," said Nelson, unwilling to take part in the dispute. "I make no pretense to a carpenter's knowledge of woods."

"Aye — that's what a carpenter *does* know," put in old Purcell. "The wood of these large trees will be worthless if sawn into plank."

Bligh's temper now got the better of him. "Do as I tell you, Mr. Purcell," he ordered violently. "I've no mind to argue with you or any other man under my command."

"Very well, sir," said Purcell obstinately. "The large trees it is. But I tell you the plank will be useless. A carpenter knows his business as well as a captain knows *his*."

Bligh had turned away; now he spun about on his heel.

"You mutinous old bastard — you have gone too far! Mr. Norman, take command of the work here. Mr. Purcell, report yourself instantly to Lieutenant Christian for fifteen days in irons."

It was my task to ferry Purcell out to the ship. The old man was flushed with anger; his jaw was set and his fists clenched till the veins stood out on his forearms. "Calls me a bastard," he muttered to no one in particular, "and puts me in irons for doing my duty. He hasn't heard the last of this, by God! Wait till we get to England! I know my rights, I do!"

We were still on the shortest of short rations, and Adventure Bay offered little in the way of refreshment for our invalids, or food for those of us who were well. Though we drew the seine repeatedly, we caught few fish and those of inferior kinds, and the mussels among the rocks, which at first promised a welcome change in our diet, proved poisonous to those who partook of them. While Mr. Bligh feasted on the wild duck his fowling piece brought down, the ship's people were half starved and there was much muttering among the officers.

The whole of our fortnight in Adventure Bay was marred by wrangling and discontent. The carpenter was in irons; Fryer and Bligh were scarcely on speaking terms, owing to the master's suspicions that the captain had lined his pockets in victualing the ship; and just before our departure, Ned Young, one of the midshipmen, was lashed to a gun on the quarter-deck and given a dozen with a colt.

Young had been sent, with three men and the small cutter, to gather shellfish, crabs, and whatever he might find for our sick, who lived in a tent pitched on the beach. They pulled away in the direction of Cape Frederick Henry and did not return till after dark, when Young reported that Dick Skinner, one of the A.B.'s and the ship's hairdresser, had wandered off into the woods and disappeared.

"Skinner saw a hollow tree," Young told Mr. Bligh, "which, from the bees about it, he believed to contain a store of honey. He asked my permission to smoke the bees out and obtain their honey for our sick, saying that he had kept bees in his youth and understood their ways. I assented readily, knowing that you, sir, would be pleased if we could obtain the honey, and an hour or two later, when we had loaded the cutter with shellfish, we returned to the tree. A fire still smouldered at its foot, but Skinner was nowhere to be seen. We wandered through the woods and hailed till nightfall, but I regret to report, sir, that we could find no trace of the man."

I chanced to know that Bligh had called for the hairdresser, requiring his services that very afternoon, and had been incensed at Young when it was learned that Skinner had accompanied him. Now that the man was reported missing, Mr. Bligh was thoroughly enraged.

"Now damn you and all other midshipmen!" roared the captain. "You're all alike! If you had gotten the honey, you would have eaten it on the spot! Where the devil is Skinner, I say? Take your boat's crew this instant and pull back to where you saw the man last. Aye, and bring him back this time!"

Young was a man grown. He flushed at the captain's words, but touched his hat respectfully and summoned his men at once. The party did not return till the following forenoon, having been nearly twenty-four hours without food. Skinner was with them this time; he had wandered off in search of another honey tree and become lost in the thick bush.

Bligh paced the quarter-deck angrily as the boat approached. By nature a man who brooded over grudges till they were magnified out of all proportion to reality, the captain was ready to explode the moment Young set foot on deck.

"Come aft, Mr. Young!" he called harshly. "I'm going to teach you to attend to your duty, instead of skylarking about the woods. Mr. Morrison!"

"Yes, sir!"

"Come aft here and seize up Mr. Young on that gun yonder! You're to give him a dozen with a rope's end."

Young was an officer of the ship and rated as a gentleman, a proud, fearless man of gentle birth. Though Bligh was within his powers as captain, the public flogging of such a man was almost without precedent in the Service. Morrison's jaw dropped at the order, which he obeyed with such evidence of reluctance that Bligh shouted at him threateningly, "Look alive, Mr. Morrison! I've my eye on you!"

I shall not speak of the flogging of Young, nor tell how Skinner's back was cut to ribbons with two dozen at the gangway. It is enough to say that Young was a different man from that day on, performing his duties sullenly and in silence, and avoiding the other midshipmen in the berth. He informed me long afterwards that, had events turned out differently, it was his intention to resign from the Service on the ship's arrival in England, and call Bligh to account as man to man.

On the fourth of September, with a fine spanking breeze at northwest, we weighed anchor and sailed out of Adventure Bay. Seven weeks later, after an uneventful passage made miserable by an outbreak of scurvy and the constant state of starvation to which we were reduced, I saw my first South Sea island.

We had gotten our easting in the high southern latitudes, and once in the trade winds we made a long board to the north on the starboard tack. We were well into the tropics now and in the vicinity of land. Man-of-war hawks hovered overhead, their long forked tails opening and shutting like scissor-blades; shoals of flying fish rose under the ship's cutwater to skim away and plunge into the sea like whiffs of grapeshot. The sea was of the pale turquoise blue only to be seen within the tropics, shading to purple here and there where clouds obscured the sun. The roll of the Pacific from east to west was broken by the labyrinth of low coral islands to the east of us, — the vast cluster of half-drowned lands called by the natives *Paumotu,* — and the *Bounty* sailed a tranquil sea.

I was off watch that afternoon and engaged in sorting over the articles I had laid in, at the suggestion of Sir Joseph Banks, for barter with the Indians of Tahiti. Nails, files, and fishhooks were in great demand, as well as bits of cheap jewelry for the women and girls. My mother had given me fifty pounds for the purchase of these things, and Sir Joseph had added another fifty to it, advising me that liberality

to the Indians would be amply repaid. "Never forget," he had remarked, "that in the South Sea the Seven Deadly Sins are compounded
into one, and that one is meanness." I had taken this advice to heart,
and now, as I looked over my store of gifts, I felt satisfied that I had
laid out my hundred pounds to good effect. I had been a lover of fishing
since childhood, and my hooks were of all sizes and the best that money
could buy. My sea chest was half filled with other things — coils of brass
wire, cheap rings, bracelets, and necklaces; files, scissors, razors, a
variety of looking-glasses, and a dozen engraved portraits of King
George, which Sir Joseph had procured for me. And down in one
corner of the chest, safe from the prying eyes of my messmates, was a
velvet-lined box from Maiden Lane. It contained a bracelet and necklace, curiously wrought in a design like the sinnet seamen plait. I was
a romantic lad, not without my dreams of some fair barbarian girl
who might bestow her favours on me. As I look back over the long
procession of years, I cannot but smile at a boy's simplicity, but I would
give all my hard-earned worldly wisdom to recapture if only for an
hour the mood of those days of my youth. I had returned them to my
chest when I heard Mr. Bligh's harsh, vibrant voice. His cabin was
scarcely fifteen feet aft of where I sat.

"Mr. Fryer!" he called peremptorily. "Be good enough to step into
my cabin."

"Yes, sir," replied the master's voice.

I had no desire to eavesdrop on the conversation that followed,
but there was no way to avoid it without leaving my open chest in
the berth.

"To-morrow or the day after," said Bligh, "we shall drop anchor in
Matavai Bay. I have had Mr. Samuel make an inventory of the stores
on hand, which has enabled him to cast up an account of the provisions expended on the voyage so far. I desire you to glance over this
book, which requires your signature."

A long silence followed, broken at last by Fryer's voice. "I cannot
sign this, sir," he said.

"Cannot sign it? What do you mean, sir?"

"The clerk is mistaken, Mr. Bligh. No such amounts of beef and
pork have been issued!"

"You are wrong!" answered the captain angrily. "I know what was
taken aboard and what remains. Mr. Samuel is right!"

"I cannot sign, sir," said Fryer obstinately.

"And why the devil not? All that the clerk has done was done by my orders. Sign it instantly! Damme! I am not the most patient man in the world."

"I cannot sign," insisted Fryer, a note of anger in his voice; "not in conscience, sir!"

"But you *can* sign," shouted Bligh in a rage; "and what is more, you *shall!*" He went stamping up the ladderway and on to the deck. "Mr. Christian!" I heard him shout to the officer of the watch. "Call all hands on deck this instant!"

The order was piped and shouted forward and, when we assembled, the captain, flushed with anger, uncovered and read the Articles of War. Mr. Samuel then came forward with his book and a pen and ink.

"Now, sir!" Bligh ordered the master, "sign this book!"

There was a dead silence while Fryer took up the pen reluctantly.

"Mr. Bligh," he said, controlling his temper with difficulty, "the ship's people will bear witness that I sign in obedience to your orders, but please to recollect, sir, that this matter may be reopened later on."

At that moment a long-drawn shout came from the man in the foretop. "Land ho!"


# V · TAHITI

THE lookout had sighted Mehetia, a small, high island forty miles to the southeast of Tahiti. I stared ahead, half incredulously, at the tiny motionless projection on the horizon line. The wind died away toward sunset and we were all night working up to the land.

I went off watch at eight bells, but could not sleep; an hour later, perched on the fore-topgallant crosstrees, I watched the new day dawn. The beauty of that sunrise seemed ample compensation for all of the hardships suffered during the voyage: a sunrise such as only the seaman knows, and then only in the regions between the tropics, remote from home. Saving the light, fluffy "fair-weather clouds" just above the vast ring of horizon which encircled us, the sky was clear. The stars paled gradually; as the rosy light grew stronger, the velvet of the heavens faded and turned blue. Then the sun, still below the horizon, began to tint the little clouds in the east with every shade of mother-of-pearl.

An hour later we were skirting the reef, before a light air from the south. For the first time in my life I saw the slender, graceful trunk and green fronds of the far-famed coconut tree, the thatched cottages of the South Sea Islanders, set in their shady groves, and the people themselves, numbers of whom walked along the reef not more than a cable's length away. They waved large pieces of white cloth and shouted what I supposed were invitations to come ashore, though their voices were drowned in the noise of a surf which would have made landing impossible even had Mr. Bligh hove-to and lowered a boat.

Mehetia is high and round in shape, and not more than three miles in its greatest extent. The village is at the southern end, where there is a tolerably flat shelf of land at the base of the mountain, but else-where the green cliffs are steep-to, with the sea breaking at their feet. The white line of the breakers, the vivid emerald of the tropical vegeta-tion covering the mountains everywhere, the rich foliage of the bread-fruit trees in the little valleys, and the plumed tops of the coconut palms growing in clusters here and there, made up a picture which enchanted me. The island had the air of a little paradise, newly created, all fresh and dewy in the dawn, stocked with everything needful for the comfort and happiness of man.

The men walking along the shelf of reef at the base of the cliffs were too far away for inspection, but they seemed fine stout fellows, taller than Englishmen. They were dressed in girdles of bark cloth which shone with a dazzling whiteness in the morning sunlight. They were naked except for these girdles, and they laughed and shouted to one another as they followed us along, clambering with great agility over the rocks.

As we rounded the northern end of the island, Smith hailed me from the top. "Look, Mr. Byam!" he shouted, pointing ahead eagerly. There, many leagues away, I saw the outlines of a mighty mountain rising from the sea, — sweeping ridges falling away symmetrically from a tall central peak, — all pale blue and ghostly in the morning light.

The breeze was making up now, and the *Bounty,* heeling a little on the larboard tack, was leaving a broad white wake. When I reached the deck I found Mr. Bligh in a rarely pleasant mood. I bade him good morning, standing to leeward of him on the quarter-deck, and he saluted me with a clap on the back.

"There it is, young man," he said, pointing to the high ghostly outlines of the land ahead. "Tahiti! We have made a long passage of it, a long hard passage, but, by God, there is the island at last!"

"It looks a beautiful island, sir," I remarked.

"Indeed it is — none more so. Captain Cook loved it only next to England; were I an old man, with my work done and no family at home, I should ask nothing better than to end my days under its palms! And you will find the people as friendly and hospitable as the land they inhabit. Aye — and some of the Indian girls as beautiful. We have come a long way to visit them! Last night I was computing the distance we have run by log since leaving England. To-morrow morning, when we drop anchor in Matavai Bay, we shall have sailed more than twenty-seven thousand miles!"

Since that morning, so many years ago, I have sailed all the seas of the world and visited most of the islands in them, including the West Indies, and the Asiatic Archipelago. But of all the islands I have seen, none approaches Tahiti in loveliness.

As we drew nearer to the land, with the rising sun behind us, there was not a man on board the *Bounty* who did not gaze ahead with emotions that differed in each case, no doubt, but in which awe and wonder played a part. But I am wrong — there was one. Toward six bells, when we were only a few miles off the southern extremity of the island, Old Bacchus came stumping on deck. Standing by the mizzenmast, with a hand on a swivel-stock, he stared indifferently for a moment at the wooded precipices, the waterfalls and sharp green peaks, now abeam of the ship. Then he shrugged his shoulders.

"They're all the same," he remarked indifferently. "When you've seen one island in the tropics, you've seen the lot."

The surgeon went stumping to the ladderway, and, as he disappeared, Mr. Nelson ceased his pacing of the deck to stand at my side. The botanist was a believer in exercise and kept his muscles hard and his colour fresh by walking two or three miles on deck each morning the weather permitted.

"Well, Byam," he remarked, "I'm glad to be back! Many a time, since my voyage with Captain Cook, I've dreamed of revisiting Tahiti, without the faintest hope that the dream might come true. Yet here we are! I can scarcely wait to set foot on shore!"

We were skirting the windward coast of Taiarapu, the richest and

loveliest part of the island, and I could not take my eyes off the land.
In the foreground, a mile or more offshore, a reef of coral broke the
roll of the sea, and the calm waters of the lagoon inside formed a
highway on which the Indians travel back and forth in their canoes.
Behind the inner beach was the narrow belt of flat land where the
rustic dwellings of the people were scattered picturesquely among their
neat plantations of the *ava* and the cloth plant, shaded by groves of
breadfruit and coconut. In the background were the mountains —
rising fantastically in turrets, spires, and precipices, wooded to their
very tops. Innumerable waterfalls plunged over the cliffs and hung
like suspended threads of silver, many of them a thousand feet or
more in height and visible at a great distance against the background
of dark green. Seen for the first time by European eyes, this coast is like
nothing else on our workaday planet; a landscape, rather, of some
fantastic dream.

Nelson was pointing ahead to a break in the line of reef. "Captain
Cook nearly lost his ship yonder," he said, "when the current set him
on the reef during a calm. One of his anchors lies there to this day —
there where the sea breaks high. I know this part of the island well.
As you can see, Tahiti is made up of two lands, connected by the
low isthmus the Indians call Taravao. This before us is the lesser,
called Taiarapu or Tahiti Iti; the great island yonder they call Tahiti
Nui. Vehiatua is the king of the smaller one — the most powerful of
the Indian princes. His realm is richer and more populous than those
of his rivals."

All through the afternoon we skirted the land, passing the low
isthmus between the two islands, coasting the rich verdant districts of
Faaone and Hitiaa, and toward evening, as the light breeze died away,
moving slowly along the rock-bound coast of Tiarei, where the reef
ends and the sea thunders at the base of cliffs.

There was little sleeping aboard the *Bounty* that night. The ship
lay becalmed about a league off the mouth of the great valley of
Papenoo, and the faint land breeze, wandering down from the heights
of the interior, and out to sea, brought with it the sweet smell of the
land and of growing things. We sniffed it eagerly, our noses grown
keen from the long months at sea, detecting the scent of strange flowers,
of wood smoke, and of Mother Earth herself — sweetest of all smells
to a sailor. The sufferers from scurvy, breathing deep of the land
breeze, seemed to draw in new life; their apathy and silence left them

as they spoke eagerly of the fruits they hoped to eat on the morrow, fruits they craved as a man dying of thirst craves water.

We sighted Eimeo a little before sunset: the small lofty island which lies to the west of Tahiti, four leagues distant. The sun went down over the spires and pinnacles of Eimeo's sky line, and was followed into the sea by the thin golden crescent of the new moon. There is little twilight in these latitudes and, almost immediately it seemed to me, the stars came out in a cloudless dome of sky. One great planet, low in the west, sent a shimmering track of light over the sea. I saw the Cross and the Magellanic Clouds in the south, and constellations unknown to dwellers in the Northern Hemisphere, all close and warm and golden against the black sky. A faint burst of song came from the surgeon's cabin below, where he was carousing with Peckover; every other man on the ship, I believe, was on deck.

All along shore we could see the flare of innumerable torches, where the Indians went about their fishing or traveled from house to house along the beach. The men of the *Bounty* stood by the bulwarks or on the booms, speaking in low voices and gazing toward the dark loom of the land. A change seemed to come over all of us that night: all unhappiness, all discontent, seemed banished, giving way to a tranquil content and the happiest anticipation of what the morrow would bring. Mr. Bligh himself, walking the deck with Christian, was rarely affable; as they passed me from time to time I overheard snatches of his talk: "Not a bad voyage, eh? . . . Only four down with scurvy, and we'll have them right in a week ashore. . . . The ship's sound as a walnut. . . . Bad anchorage. . . . We'll soon shift out of Matavai Bay. . . . A fine place for refreshments. . . ."

I was in the master's watch, and toward midnight Mr. Fryer chanced to notice me stifling a yawn, for it was many hours since I had slept.

"Take a caulk, Mr. Byam," he said kindly. "Take a caulk! All's quiet to-night. I'll see that you are waked if we need you."

I chose a place in the shadow of the bitts, just abaft of the main hatch, and lay down on deck, but, though I yawned with heavy eyes, it was long before sleep came to me. When I awoke, the grey light of dawn was in the East.

We had drifted some distance to the west during the night, and now the ship lay off the valley of Vaipoopoo, from which runs the river that empties into the sea at the tip of Point Venus, the most northerly point of Tahiti Nui. It was here that the *Dolphin*, Captain Wallis, had approached the newly discovered land, and here on this long, low point Captain Cook had set up his observatory to study the transit of the planet which gave the place its name. Far off in the interior of the island, its base framed in the vertical cliffs bordering the valley, rose the tall central mountain called Orohena, a thin sharp pinnacle of volcanic rock which rises to a height of seven thousand feet and is perhaps as difficult of ascent as any peak in the world. Its summit was now touched by the sun, and as the light of day grew stronger, driving the shadows from the valley and illuminating the foothills and the rich smiling coastal land, I fancied that I had never gazed on a scene more pleasing to the eye. The whole aspect of the coast about Matavai Bay was open, sunny, and hospitable.

The entrance to the bay bore southwest by west, little more than a league distant, and a great number of canoes were now putting out to us. Most of them were small, holding only four or five persons; strange-looking craft, with an outrigger on the larboard side and a high stern sweeping up in a shape almost semicircular. There were two or three double canoes among them, each holding thirty or more people. The Indian craft approached us rapidly. Their paddlers took half a dozen short quick strokes on one side, and then, at a signal from the man astern, all shifted to the other side. As the leading canoes drew near, I heard questioning shouts: *"Taio? Peritane? Rima?"* which is to say: "Friend? British? Lima?" In the latter case, they were asking whether the *Bounty* was a Spanish ship from Peru. *"Taio!"* shouted Bligh, who knew some words of the Tahitian language. *"Taio! Peritane!"* Next moment the first boatload of Indians came springing over the bulwarks, and I had my first glimpse at close quarters of this far-famed race.

Most of our visitors were men — tall, handsome, stalwart fellows, of a light copper colour. They wore kilts of figured cloth of their own manufacture, light fringed capes thrown over their shoulders and joined at the throat, and turbans of brown cloth on their heads. Some of them, naked from the waist up, displayed the arms and torsos of veritable giants; others, instead of turbans, wore on their heads the little bonnets of freshly plaited coconut leaves they call *taumata*. Their countenances, like those of children, mirrored every passing mood, and when they smiled, which was often, I was astonished at the whiteness and perfection of their teeth. The few women who came on board at this time were all of the lower orders of society, and uncommonly diminutive as compared with the men. They wore skirts of white cloth falling in graceful folds, and cloaks of the same material to protect their shoulders from the sun, draped to leave the right arm free, and not unlike the toga of the Romans. Their faces were expressive of good nature, kindness, and mirth, and it was easy to perceive why so many of our seamen in former times had formed attachments among girls who seemed to have all the amiable qualities of their sex.

Mr. Bligh had given orders that the Indians were to be treated with the greatest kindness by everyone on board, though watched closely to prevent the thefts to which the commoners among them were prone. As the morning breeze freshened and we worked in toward the entrance with yards braced up on the larboard tack, the hubbub on the ship was deafening. At least a hundred men and a quarter as many women overran the decks, shouting, laughing, gesticulating, and addressing our people in the most animated manner, as if taking for granted that their unintelligible harangues were understood. The seamen found the feminine portion of our visitors so engaging that we had difficulty in keeping them at their stations. The breeze continued to freshen, and before long we sailed through the narrow passage between the westerly point of the reef before Point Venus and the sunken rock called the Dolphin Bank, on which Captain Wallis so nearly lost his ship. At nine in the forenoon we dropped anchor in Matavai Bay, in thirteen fathoms.

A vast throng of visitors set out immediately from the beach in their canoes, but for some time no persons of consequence came on board. I was joking with a party of girls to whom I had given some trifling gifts, when Mr. Bligh's servant came on deck to tell me that the captain desired to see me below. I found him alone in his cabin, bending over a chart of Matavai Bay.

"Ah, Mr. Byam," he said, motioning me to sit down on his chest. "I want a word with you. We shall probably lie here for several months while Mr. Nelson collects our young breadfruit plants. I am going to release you from further duties on board so that you may be free to carry out the wishes of my worthy friend, Sir Joseph Banks. I have given the matter some thought and believe that you will best accomplish your task by living ashore amongst the natives. Everything now depends on your choice of a *taio,* or friend, and let me advise you to go slowly. Persons of consequence in Tahiti, as elsewhere, do not wear their hearts on their sleeves, and should you make the mistake of choosing a friend among the lower orders of their society, you will find yourself greatly handicapped in your work."

He paused and I said, "I think I understand, sir."

"Yes," he went on. "By all means go slowly. Spend as much time as you wish on shore for a day or two, and when you have found a family to your liking inform me of the fact, so that I may make inquiries as to their standing. Once you have settled on a *taio* you can move your chest and writing materials ashore. After that I expect to see no more of you except when you report your progress to me once each week."

He gave me a curt but friendly nod, and perceiving that the interview was at an end, I rose and took leave of him. On deck, Mr. Fryer, the master, beckoned me to him.

"You have seen Mr. Bligh?" he asked, raising his voice to make the words audible in the din. "He informed me last night that on our arrival here you were to be relieved of duty on board the ship. There is nothing to fear from the Indians. Go ashore at any time you wish. You are free to make gifts of your own things to the Indians, but remember — no trading. The captain has placed all of the trading in the hands of Mr. Peckover. You are to make a dictionary of the Indian tongue, I understand?"

"Yes, sir — at the desire of Sir Joseph Banks."

"A praiseworthy task — a praiseworthy task! Some slight knowledge of the language will no doubt be of great service to future mariners in this sea. And you're a lucky lad, Mr. Byam, a lucky lad! I envy you, on my word I do!"

At that moment a double canoe, which had brought out a handsome gift of pigs from some chief ashore, cast off from the ship. I was all eagerness to set foot on land. "May I go with those people if they'll have me?" I asked the master.

"Off with you, by all means. Give them a hail."

I sprang to the bulwarks and shouted to catch the attention of a man in the stern of one of the canoes, who seemed to be in a position of authority. As I caught his eye, I pointed to myself, then to the canoe, and then to the beach a cable's length away. He caught my meaning instantly and shouted some order to his paddlers. They backed water so that the high stern of one of the canoes came close alongside, rising well above the *Bounty's* bulwarks. As I sprang over the rail and slid down the hollowed-out stern into the canoe, the paddlers, glancing back over their shoulders and grinning at me, raised a cheer. The Indian captain gave a shout, a score of paddles dug into the water simultaneously, and the canoe moved away toward the land.

From One Tree Hill to Point Venus a curving beach of black volcanic sand stretches for about a mile and a half. We were heading for a spot about midway between these two boundaries of Matavai Bay, and I saw that a considerable surf was pounding on the steep beach. As we drew near the breakers the man in the stern of the other canoe snatched up a heavy steering paddle and shouted an order which caused the men to cease paddling while four or five waves passed under us. A dense throng of Indians stood on the beach, awaiting our arrival with eagerness. Suddenly the man beside me began to shout, gripping the haft of his steering paddle strongly.

"*A hoe!*" he shouted. "*Teie te are rahi!*" (Paddle! Here is the great wave!) I recollect the words, for I was destined to hear them many times.

The men bent to their work, all shouting together; the canoe shot forward as a wave larger than the others lifted us high in the air and sent us racing for the sands. While the steersman held us stern-on, with efforts that made the muscles of his arms bulge mightily, we sped far up the beach, where a score of willing hands seized our little vessel to hold her against the backwash of the sea. I sprang out as the wave receded and made my way to high-water mark, while rollers were fetched and the double canoe hauled ashore with much shouting and laughter, to be housed under a long thatched shed.

Next moment I was surrounded by a throng so dense that I could scarcely breathe. But the crowd was good-natured and civil as no crowd in England could be; all seemed desirous to welcome me with every sign of pleasure. The clamour was deafening, for all talked and shouted at once. Small children with bright dark eyes clung to their mothers' skirts and stared at me apprehensively, while their mothers and fathers pushed forward to shake my hand, a form of greeting, as I was to learn with some surprise, immemorially old among the Tahitians.

Then, suddenly as the clamour of voices had begun, it ceased. The people fell back deferentially to make way for a tall man of middle age, who was approaching me with an air of easy authority and good-natured assurance. A murmur ran through the crowd: "*O Hitihiti!*"

The newcomer was smooth-shaven, unlike most of the Indian men, who wore short beards. His hair, thick and sprinkled with grey, was close-cropped, and his kilt and short fringed cloak were of the finest workmanship and spotlessly clean. He was well over six feet in height, lighter-skinned than the run of his countrymen, and magnificently proportioned; his face, frank, firm, and humorous, attracted me instantly.

This gentleman — for I recognized at a glance that he was of a class different from any of the Indians I had seen hitherto — approached me with dignity, shook my hand warmly, and then, seizing me by the shoulders, applied his nose to my cheek, giving several loud sniffs as he did so. I was startled by the suddenness and novelty of the greeting, but I realized that this must be what Captain Cook and other navigators had termed "nose-rubbing," though in reality it is a smelling of cheeks, and corresponds to our kiss. On releasing me, my new friend stepped back a pace while a loud murmur of approval went through the crowd. He then pointed to his broad chest and said: "Me Hitihiti! You midshipman! What name?"

I was so taken aback at these words of English that I stared at him for a moment before I replied. The people had evidently been waiting to see what effect the marvelous accomplishment of their compatriot would produce, and my display of astonishment turned out to be precisely what they were hoping for. There were nods and exclamations of satisfaction on all sides, and Hitihiti, now thoroughly pleased with himself and with me, repeated his question, "What name?"

"Byam," I replied; and he said, "Byam! Byam!" nodding violently, while "Byam, Byam, Byam," echoed throughout the crowd.

Hitihiti again pointed to his chest. "Fourteen year now," he said with an air of pride, "me sail Captain Cook!" "*Tuté! Tuté!*" exclaimed a little old man close by, as if afraid that I might not understand.

"Could I have a drink of water?" I asked, for it was long since I had tasted any but the foul water aboard ship. Hitihiti started, and seized my hand.

He shouted an order to the people about us, which sent some of the boys and young men scampering off inland. He then led me up the steep rise behind the beach to a rustic shed where several young women made haste to spread a mat. We sat down side by side, and the crowd, increasing rapidly as parties of Indians arrived from up and down the coast, seated themselves on the grass outside. A dripping gourd, filled to the brim with clear sparkling water from the brook near by, was handed me, and I drank deep, setting it down half empty with a sigh of satisfaction.

I was then given a young coconut to drink — my first taste of this cool, sweet wine of the South Sea — and a broad leaf was spread beside me, on which the young woman laid ripe bananas and one or two kinds of fruit I had not seen before. While I set to greedily on these delicacies, I heard a shout go up from the crowd, and saw that the *Bounty's* launch was coming in through the surf, with Bligh in the stern sheets. My host sprang to his feet. *"O Parai!"* he exclaimed, and, as we waited for the boat to land, "You, me, *taio,* eh?"

Hitihiti was the first of the Indians to greet Bligh, whom he seemed to know well. And the captain recognized my friend at once.

"Hitihiti," he said as he shook the Indian's hand, "you've grown little older, my friend, though you've some grey hairs now."

Hitihiti laughed. "Ten year, eh? Plenty long time! By God! Parai, you get fat!"

It was now the captain's turn to laugh, as he touched his waist, by no means small in girth.

"Come ashore," the Indian went on emphatically. "Eat plenty pig! Where Captain Cook? He come Tahiti soon?"

"My father?"

Hitihiti looked at Bligh in astonishment. "Captain Cook your father?" he asked.

"Certainly — didn't you know that?"

For a moment the Indian chief stood in silent amazement; then, with extraordinary animation, he raised a hand for silence and addressed the crowd. The words were unintelligible to me, but I perceived at once that Hitihiti was a trained orator, and I knew that he was telling them that Bligh was the son of Captain Cook. Mr. Bligh stood close beside me as the chief went on with his harangue.

"I have instructed all of the people not to let the Indians know that Captain Cook is dead," he said in a low voice. "And I believe that we shall accomplish our mission the quicker for their belief that I am his son."

While I was somewhat taken aback by this piece of deception, I knew the reverence in which the people of Tahiti held the name of Cook, and perceived that, according to the Jesuitical idea that the end justifies the means, Mr. Bligh was right.

As Hitihiti ceased to speak there was a buzz of excited talk among the Indians, who looked at Bligh with fresh interest, not unmixed with awe. In their eyes, Captain Cook's son was little less than a god. I took the opportunity to inform Mr. Bligh that Hitihiti had offered to become my *taio,* and that with his approval I thought well of the idea, since I should be able to communicate to some extent with my Indian friend.

"Excellent," said the captain with a nod. "He is a chief of consequence on this part of the island, and nearly related to all of the principal families. And, as you say, the English he picked up on board the *Resolution* should be of great assistance to you in your work." He turned to the Indian. "Hitihiti!"

"Yes, Parai."

"Mr. Byam informs me that you and he are to be friends."

Hitihiti nodded. "Me, Byam, *taio!*"

"Good!" said Bligh. "Mr. Byam is the son of a chief in his own land. He will have gifts for you, and in return I want you to take him to your house, where he will stop. His work, while we are here, is to learn your language, so that British seamen may be able to converse with your people. Do you understand?"

Hitihiti turned to face me and stretched out an enormous hand. "*Taio,* eh?" he remarked smilingly, and we shook hands on the bargain.

Presently a canoe was launched to fetch my things from the ship, and that night I slept in the house of my new friend — Hitihiti-Te-Atua-Iri-Hau, chief of Mahina and Ahonu, and hereditary high priest of the temple of Fareroi.

## VI · AN INDIAN HOUSEHOLD

I CAN still recall vividly our walk that afternoon — from the landing place to Point Venus, and eastward, behind a second long curving beach of sand, on which the sea broke high, to the house of my *taio,* set on a grassy point, sheltered from the sea by a short stretch of coral reef which supported a beautiful little islet called Motu Au. The islet was not more than half a cable's length from shore; its beaches were of snowy coral sand, contrasting with the rich dark green of the tall trees that grew almost to the water's edge. Between the beach and the islet lay the lagoon — warm blue water, two or three fathoms deep and clear as air.

We walked in constant shade, under groves of breadfruit trees on which the fruit was beginning to ripen. Many of these trees must have been of immense age, from their girth and height; with their broad glossy leaves, smooth bark, and majestic shape, they are among the noblest of all shade trees, and certainly the most useful to mankind. Here and there the slender bole of an old coconut palm rose high in the air; scattered picturesquely, as if at random, among the groves I saw the houses of the Indians, thatched with bright yellow leaves of the palmetto and surrounded by fences of bamboo.

My host, though no more than forty-five, was already many times a grandfather, and as we approached his house, after a walk of little more than half an hour, I heard joyful shouts and saw a dozen sturdy children skipping out to greet him. They halted at sight of me, but soon lost their fear and began to climb up Hitihiti's legs and examine, inquisitively as monkeys, the strange garments I wore. By the time we came to the door the chief had a small boy on each of his shoulders, and his eldest granddaughter was leading me by the hand.

The house was a fine one — sixty feet long by twenty wide, with a lofty, newly thatched roof, and, instead of gables, semicircular extensions at each end, giving the whole an oval shape. Such houses were built only for chiefs. The ends, supported by pillars of old polished coconut wood, were open, and the sides were walled by vertical lathes of bright yellow bamboo, through which the air filtered freely. The floor was of fresh white coral sand, spread with mats at one end on a thick bed of sweet-smelling grass called *aretu*. Of furniture there was scarcely any: small wooden pillows on the family bed, like tiny tables with four short legs; two or three of the seats used only by chiefs, carved from a single log of hard red wood; and a stand of weapons hanging on one of the pillars which supported the ridgepole, including my host's ponderous war club.

Hitihiti's daughter — mother of two of the younger children accompanying us — met us at the door. She was a young woman of twenty-five, with a stately figure and carriage, and the pale golden skin and auburn hair which are not uncommon among this people. These fair Indians were termed *ehu;* I have seen men and women of this strain — unmixed with European blood — whose eyes were blue. My host smiled at his daughter and then at me.

"O Hina," he said in introduction. He said something to her in which I distinguished the word *taio* and my own name. Hina stepped forward with a grave slow smile to shake my hand, and then, taking me by the shoulders as her father had done, she laid her nose to my cheek and sniffed. I reciprocated this Indian kiss, and smelled for the first time the perfume of the scented coconut oil with which the women of Tahiti anoint themselves.

There are perhaps no women in the world — not even the greatest ladies of fashion in Europe — more meticulous in the care of their persons than were the Indian women of the upper class. Each morning and evening they bathed in one of the innumerable clear cool streams, not merely plunging in and out again, but stopping to be scrubbed from head to foot by their serving women with a porous volcanic stone, used as we use pumice in our baths. Their servants then anointed them with *monoi* — coconut oil, perfumed with the petals of the Tahitian gardenia. Their hair was dried and arranged, a task which required an hour or more; their eyebrows were examined in a mirror which consisted of a blackened coconut shell filled with water, and plucked or shaven with a shark's tooth, to make the slender arch which was the fashion among them. A servant then brought a supply of powdered charcoal with which the teeth were scrubbed. When they were ready to dress, the skirt, or *pareu,* which reached from waist to the knees and was of snow-white bark cloth, was adjusted so that each fold hung in a certain fashion. Then came the cloak, which was worn to protect the upper part of the body from sunburn, which the ladies of Tahiti dreaded quite as much as the ladies of the English Court. Each fold of the cloak was arranged just so, and it was ridiculous — to a man, at least — to watch the long efforts of a tirewoman to please her mistress in this respect.

Hina's manners were as handsome as her person. She had the smiling dignity and perfect assurance only to be found among the highest circles of our own race, a poised urbanity, neither forward nor shy. And this is, perhaps, a fitting place to say a word for the Indian ladies, so often and so shamelessly slandered by the different navigators who have visited their island. Captain Cook alone, who knew them best and was their loyal friend, has done them justice, saying that virtue was perhaps as common and as highly prized among them as among our own women at home, and that to form an impression of the ladies of Tahiti from the women who visited his ships would be like judging the virtue of Englishwomen from a study of the nymphs of Spithead. In Tahiti, as in other lands, there are people given over to vice and lewdness, and women of this kind naturally congregated upon the arrival of a ship; but, so far as I know, there was also as great a proportion of faithful wives and affectionate mothers as elsewhere, many of whom were a veritable honour to their sex.

The house which was to be my dwelling for many months stood, as I have said, on a grassy point, about a mile to the eastward of Point Venus. Either by accident or by design, the site was one that commanded in all directions prospects an artist might have traveled many miles to paint. On the northern side were the beach, the lagoon, and the beautiful little island already mentioned; to the south, or directly inland, was the great valley of Vaipoopoo and a distant glimpse of Orohena, framed in the cliffs of the gorge; to the west lay Point Venus, with the sea breaking high on the protecting reefs; and to the east, facing the sunrise, was a magnificent view of the rocky, unprotected coast of Orofara and Faaripoo, where the surges of the Pacific thundered and spouted at the base of stern black cliffs. No doubt because of the beauty of the easterly view at dawn, the name of our point was Hitimahana — the rising of the sun.

A little crowd of the chief's retainers gathered about us, regarding their patron's friend with respectful curiosity, and, while Hina gave some order to the cooks, an exceedingly handsome young girl came out of the house and, at a word from my *taio,* greeted me as his daughter had done. Her name was Maimiti, and she was a niece of my host's — a proud, shy girl of seventeen.

With a nod to Hina my *taio* led me to his rustic dining room — a thatched shed in the shade of a clump of ironwood trees, about a hundred yards distant. The floor of coral sand was spread with mats, on which a dozen of the broad fresh leaves of the plantain served as our tablecloth. The men of Tahiti were uncommonly fond of the company of their women, whose position in society was perhaps as high as that of women anywhere. They were petted, courted, permitted no share in any hard labour, and allowed a liberty such as only our own great ladies enjoy. Yet in spite of all this, the Indians believe that Man was sky-descended, and Woman earth-born: Man *raa,* or holy; Woman *noa,* or common. Women were not permitted to set foot in the temples of the greater gods, and among all classes of society it was forbidden — unthinkable in fact — for the two sexes to sit down to a meal together. I was surprised to find that Hitihiti and I sat down alone to our dinner, and that no woman had a hand either in the cooking or in the serving of the meal.

We sat facing each other across the cloth of fresh green leaves. A pleasant breeze blew freely through the unwalled house, and the breakers on the distant reef made a murmuring undertone of sound. A serving man brought two coconut shells of water, in which we washed our hands and rinsed our mouths. I felt a sharp hunger, augmented by savoury whiffs of roasting pork from the cookhouse not far off.

We were given baked fish with cooked plantains and bananas; pork fresh from the oven, and certain native vegetables which I had never tasted before; and a great pudding to finish with, served with a sauce of rich, sweet coconut cream. I was only a lad, with the appetite of a midshipman, and I had been many months at sea, but though I did my best to maintain the honour of England by eating enough for three men, my host put me to shame. Long after repletion forced me to halt, Hitihiti continued his leisurely meal, devouring quantities of fish, pork, plantains, and pudding I can only describe as fabulous. At last he sighed and called for water to wash his hands.

"First eat — now sleep," he said, as he rose. A wide mat was spread for us under an old branching *purau* tree on the beach. We lay down side by side for the siesta which in Tahiti always follows the midday meal.

This was the beginning of a period of my life on which I look back with nothing but pleasure. I had not a care in the world, save the making of my dictionary, in which I took the keenest interest, and which gave me sufficient occupation to prevent ennui. I lived on the fat of the land, amongst affectionate friends and amid surroundings of the most exquisite beauty. We rose at dawn, plunged into the river which ran within pistol shot of Hitihiti's door, ate a light breakfast of fruits, and went about our occupations until the fishing canoes returned from the sea at eleven or twelve o'clock. Then, while the meal was preparing, I had a bath in the sea, swimming across to the islet or sporting in the high breakers further west. After dinner the whole household slept till three or four in the afternoon, when I frequently joined them in excursions to visit their friends. After sundown, when the strings of candlenuts were lit, we lay about on mats, conversing or telling stories till one after another dropped off to sleep.

During the voyage out from England I had gone through Dr. Johnson's dictionary, which had been provided for me, marking such words as seemed to me in most common usage in everyday speech. I had then set these down alphabetically — nearly seven thousand in all. My present task was to discover and set down their equivalents in the Indian tongue. I have always loved languages; the study of them has been one of the chief interests of my life, and in my younger days I could pick up a new tongue more readily, perhaps, than most men. If I am blessed with any talent, it is the humble one of the gift of tongues.

The language of Tahiti appealed to me from the first, and with the help of my *taio,* his daughter, and young Maimiti, I made rapid progress and was soon able to ask simple questions and to understand the replies. It is a strange language and a beautiful one. Like the Greek of Homer, it is rich in words descriptive of the moods of Nature and of human emotions; and, like Greek again, it has in certain respects a precision that our English lacks. To break a bottle is *parari;* to break a rope, *motu;* to break a bone, *fati.* The Indians distinguish with the greatest nicety between the different kinds of fear: fear of a scolding or of being shamed is *matau;* fear of a dangerous shark or of an assassin, *riaria;* fear of a spectre must be expressed with still another word. They have innumerable adjectives to express the varying moods of sea and sky. One word describes the boundless sea without land in sight; another the deep blue sea off soundings; another the sea in a calm with a high oily swell. They have a word for the glance which passes between a man and a woman planning an assignation, and another word for the look exchanged by two men plotting to assassinate a third. Their language of the eyes, in fact, is so eloquent and so complete that at times they seem scarcely to need a spoken tongue. They are masters of the downcast eye, the sidelong glance, the direct glance, the raising of the eyebrow, the lift of the chin, and all the pantomime with which they can communicate without those about them being aware of the fact.

I think I may say, in all truth, that I was the first white man to speak fluently the Tahitian tongue, and the first to make a serious attempt to reduce the language to writing. Sir Joseph Banks had provided me with a brief vocabulary, compiled from his own notes and from Captain Cook's, but as soon as I heard the Indian tongue spoken

I realized that, as he had suggested, a new system of orthography must be devised. Since my work was to be done for the benefit of mariners, it seemed better to aim at simplicity than at a high degree of academic perfection, so I devised an alphabet of thirteen letters — five vowels and eight consonants — with which the sounds of the language could be set down fairly well.

Hitihiti spoke the Tahitian language as only a chief could, for the lower orders, as in other lands, possessed vocabularies of no more than a few hundred words. He was interested in my work and of infinite use to me, though, as with all his countrymen, mental effort fatigued him if sustained for more than an hour or two. I overcame this difficulty by making myself agreeable to the ladies, and dividing my work into two parts. From Hitihiti I learned the words pertaining to war, religion, navigation, shipbuilding, fishing, agriculture, and other manly pursuits; from Hina and Maimiti I obtained vocabularies concerning the pursuits and amusements of women.

I opened my chest on the day of my arrival at their house and made my host a present of what I thought would please him and the ladies most. This was the seal on our pledged friendship, but though my files, fishhooks, scissors, and trinkets were received with appreciation, I had the satisfaction of learning, as time went on, that the friendship of an Indian like Hitihiti was not for sale. He and his daughter and his niece were sincerely fond of me, I believe, showing their affection in many unmistakable ways. I must have been an infinite nuisance to them, with my pen and ink and endless questions, but their patient good-humour was equal to my demands. Sometimes Maimiti would throw up her hands in mock despair, and exclaim laughingly: "Let me be! I can think no more!" or the old chief, after an hour's patient answering of my questions, would say: "Let us sleep, Byam! Take care, or you will crack your head and mine with too much thinking!" But on the next morning they were always ready to help me once more.

Each Sunday I gathered my manuscript together and reported myself on board the *Bounty* to Mr. Bligh. I must say, in justice to him, that whatever task he undertook was thoroughly performed. He showed the greatest interest in my work, and never failed to run over with me the list of words I had set down during the week. Had his character in other respects been equal to his courage, his energy, and his understanding, Bligh would to-day have his niche in history, among the great seamen of England.

Shortly after the arrival of the *Bounty,* Mr. Bligh had ordered a

large tent pitched near the landing place, and Nelson and his assistant, a young gardener named Brown, were now established on
shore, with seven men to help them gather and pot the breadfruit
plants.

This tree cannot be propagated from seeds, since it produces none.
Mr. Nelson informed me that in his opinion the breadfruit had
been cultivated and improved from time immemorial, until — as in
the case of the banana — seeds had been entirely eliminated from the
fruit. It seems to thrive best when tended by man, and in the neigh-
bourhood of his dwellings. When well grown, the breadfruit tree sends
out lateral roots of great length, within a foot or two of the surface of the ground. Should an Indian desire a young tree to plant elsewhere, he has only to dig down and cut one of these roots, which, when
separated from the parent tree, immediately sends up a vigorous
young plant. When the shoot has reached the height of a man, it is
ready to be transplanted, which is done by first cutting it back to a
height of about a yard, and then digging down to cut off a small section
of the root. Planted in suitable soil and watered from time to time, not
one in a hundred of the young trees will fail to grow.

Nelson took long walks daily, scouring the districts of Mahina and
Pare for young plants already well grown. The chiefs had ordered their
subjects to give Nelson all he asked for, as a present to be sent to
King George in return for the gifts the *Bounty* had brought from
England.

The *Bounty's* people who remained on board seemed to have forgotten for the time being their captain's severities and the hardships
of our long voyage. Discipline was relaxed; the men were allowed to
go frequently on shore; and except for the surgeon every man of them
had his Indian *taio,* and nearly every one his Indian lass. Tahiti was in
those days a veritable paradise to the seaman — one of the richest
islands in the world, with a mild and wholesome climate, abounding
in every variety of delicious food, and inhabited by a race of gentle
and hospitable barbarians. The humblest A. B. in the forecastle might
enter any house on shore, assured of a welcome. And as regards the
possibilities of dissipation, to which seamen are given in every port,
the island could only be described as a Mohammedan paradise.

When I had been about a fortnight at my *taio's* house I was agreeably
surprised one morning to receive a visit from some of my shipmates,
who came around from Matavai Bay in a double canoe. She was

paddled by a dozen or more Indians, and three white men sat in the stern. My host had gone aboard the *Bounty* that day to dine with Bligh, and I stood on the beach as the canoe approached, with Hina, Maimiti, and Hina's husband, a young chief named Tuatau. As the canoe rose on a wave I saw that the two white men facing me were Christian and Peckover, and a moment later I was amazed to see Old Bacchus on the thwart aft of them. A wave reared up behind the little vessel, the Indians dashed their paddles into the water, and the canoe swept forward and ran far up the beach.

The surgeon sprang over the gunwale and came stumping up to greet me, his wooden leg sinking deep into the sand. I had on only a girdle of the native cloth, and my shoulders were burned brown by the sun.

"Well, Byam," said Bacchus as he shook my hand, "damme if I didn't think you an Indian at first! Time I was going ashore, I thought, and where should I go if not to pay you a visit, my lad! So I bottled off a dozen of Teneriffe wine." He turned to the gunner, who stood by the canoe. "Hey, Peckover," he called solicitously, "tell them to be easy with that hamper — should any of the bottles be broken, it would mean another trip to the ship."

Christian gave me a handshake, with a glint of amusement in his eyes, and we waited while the surgeon and Peckover superintended the unloading of a large hamper of wine. Presently a native came staggering up the beach with it, and I introduced my shipmates to my Indian friends. Hina and her husband led the way to the house, and we followed, Maimiti walking with Christian and me. I had liked Christian from the moment when I first set eyes on him, but it was not until we reached Tahiti that I came to know him well. He was a stalwart, handsome man, and more than once, during the short walk to the house, I saw young Maimiti give him a sidelong glance.

When we were seated on mats on Hitihiti's cool verandah, Old Bacchus motioned the men to set down the hamper of wine. Still panting from the exertion of his walk, he fumbled for his snuffbox, pulled up his sleeve, laid a train of snuff on his polished forearm, and sniffed it up in a twinkling. Then, after a violent sneeze or two and a flourish of his enormous handkerchief, he reached into his coat tails and produced a corkscrew.

He and Peckover were soon well under way on a morning's carouse, and Tuatau loth to leave them while the wine held out, so Christian,

Maimiti, Hina, and I walked away up the beach, leaving the preparations of our dinner to Hitihiti's numerous cooks. The morning was
warm and calm, and we were glad to walk in the shade of the tall
ironwood trees that fringed the sands. A river little larger than an
English brook flowed into the sea about a mile east of the house, ending
in a clear deep pool close to the beach. Gnarled old hibiscus trees arched
together overhead, and the sun, filtering through their foliage, cast
changing patterns of light and shade on the still water. The two girls
retreated into the underbrush and soon stepped out clad in light girdles
of glazed native cloth, which is nearly waterproof. No women in the
world are more modest than the ladies of Tahiti, but they bare their
breasts as innocently as an Englishwoman shows her face. Standing
beside me on the bank, clad in a native kilt which showed his own
stalwart figure to the best advantage, Christian glanced up at them
and caught his breath.

"My God, Byam!" he said in a low voice.

Slenderly and strongly made, in the first bloom of young womanhood, and with her magnificent dark hair unbound, Maimiti made a
picture worth traveling far to behold. She stood for a moment with a
hand on the elder woman's shoulder, and then, gathering her kilt
about her, she ran nimbly up a gnarled limb that overhung the deep
water. Poising herself for an instant high above the pool, she sprang
into the water with a merry shout, and I saw her swimming with slow
easy strokes along the bottom, two fathoms deep. Christian, a capital
swimmer, went in head first, and Hina followed him with a great
splash. For an hour or more we frolicked in the pool, startling shoals
of small speckled fish like trout, and making the cool green tunnel
overhead echo with laughter.

The Indians of Tahiti rarely bathe in the sea except when a great
surf is running. At such times the more daring among the men and
women delight in a sport they call *horue* — swimming out among
the great breakers with a light board about a fathom long, and choosing their moment to come speeding in, a quarter of a mile or more,
on the crest of a high feathering sea. Their daily bathing is done in
the clear cool streams which flow down from the mountains everywhere, and though they bathe twice, and often three times each day,
they look forward to the next bath as though it were the first in a
month. Men, women, and children bathe together with a great hubbub
of shouting and merriment, for this is the social hour of their day,

when friends are met, courtships carried on, and gossip and news exchanged.

After our bath we dried ourselves in the sun, while the girls combed out their hair with combs of bamboo, curiously carved. Christian was a gentleman, and very far from a rake, though of a warm and susceptible temperament. He lagged behind with young Maimiti while we walked back to the house, and once, turning my head by chance, I saw that the two were walking hand in hand. They made a handsome couple — the young English seaman and the Indian girl. The kindly fate which veils the future from us gave me no inkling of what lay in store for these two — destined to face together, hand in hand as I saw them now, long wanderings and suffering, and tragedy. Maimiti cast down her eyes, while a blush suffused her clear olive cheeks with crimson, and strove gently to release her hand; but Christian held her fast, smiling at me.

"Every sailor must have his sweetheart," he said, half lightly and half in earnest, "and I've found mine. I'll stake my life there's not a truer lass in all these islands!"

Hina smiled gravely and touched my arm as a hint to leave Christian to his courting. She had liked him at first sight, and knew his rank on board. And thanks to the uncanny fashion in which news of every sort spreads among the people of Tahiti, she knew that he had had no traffic with the women who infested the ship.


## VII · CHRISTIAN AND BLIGH

From the day of his meeting with Maimiti, Christian missed no opportunity of visiting us, arriving by day or by night as his duties on board the *Bounty* permitted. The Indians, who felt no need of unbroken sleep, were frequently up and about during the night, and often made a meal at midnight when the fishers returned from the reef. Old Hitihiti oftentimes awakened me merely from a desire to converse, or when he suddenly recollected some word which had escaped his memory during the day. I grew accustomed to this casual and broken sleep, and learned, like my host, to make up during the afternoon for what was lost at night.

Christian was soon accepted by the household as the avowed lover of Maimiti. He seldom came without some little gifts for her and the others, and his visits were anticipated with eager pleasure. He was a man of moods; at sea I had seen him stern, reticent, and almost intimidating for a fortnight at a time. Then all at once he would unbend, shake off his preoccupation, and become the heartiest and gayest of companions. No man knew better how to make himself agreeable to others when he chose; his sincerity, his education, which went beyond that of most sea officers of the time, and the charm of his manner combined to win the respect of men and women alike. And the ardour of his nature, his handsome person and changing moods, made him what women call a romantic man.

One night, when I had been about six weeks at the house of Hitihiti, I was awakened gently in the Indian fashion by a hand on my shoulder. The flare of a candlenut made a dim light in the house, and I saw Christian standing over me, with his sweetheart at his side.

"Come down to the beach, Byam," he said; "they have built a fire there. I have something to tell you."

Rubbing the sleep from my eyes, I followed them out of the house, to where a fire of coconut husks burned bright and ruddy. The night was moonless and the sea so calm that the breakers scarcely whispered on the sand. Mats were spread around the fire, and Hitihiti's people lay about, conversing in low voices while fish roasted on the coals.

Christian sat down, his back to the bole of a coconut palm and an arm about Maimiti's waist, while I reclined near by. I knew at the first glance that his gaiety of the weeks past had been succeeded by one of his sombre moods.

"I must tell you," he said slowly, at the end of a long silence, "Old Bacchus died last night."

"Good God!" I exclaimed . . . "What . . ."

"He died, not of drink, as might have been supposed, but of eating a poisonous fish. We purchased about fifty pounds of fish from a canoe that came in from Tetiaroa, and your mess had a string of them fried for dinner yesterday. They were of a bright red colour and different from the others. Hayward, Nelson, and Morrison were close to death for six hours, but they are better now. The surgeon died at eight bells, four hours ago."

"Good God!" I repeated stupidly and mechanically.

"He will be buried in the morning, and Mr. Bligh bids you to be on hand."

At first the news dazed me and I did not realize the full extent of the loss; little by little the fact that Old Bacchus was no longer of the *Bounty's* company came home to me.

"A drunkard," said Christian musingly, as if to himself, "but beloved by all on board. We shall be the worse off for his death."

Maimiti turned to me, and in the ruddy firelight I saw glistening in her eyes the easy tears of her race. "*Ua mate te ruau avae hoe,*" she said sorrowfully. (The old man with one leg is dead.)

"I have been many years at sea," Christian went on, "and I can tell you that the welfare of men on shipboard depends on things which seem small. A joke at the right moment, a kind word, or a glass of grog is sometimes more efficacious than the cat-of-nine-tails. With the surgeon gone, life on the *Bounty* will not be what it was."

Christian spoke no more that night, but sat gazing into the fire, a sombre expression in his eyes. Maimiti, a silent girl, laid her head on his shoulder and fell asleep, while he stroked her hair tenderly and absently. I lay awake for a long time, thinking of Old Bacchus and of the trick of fate which had so abruptly closed his career, on a heathen island, twelve thousand miles from England. Perhaps his jovial shade would be well content to haunt the moonlit groves of Tahiti, where the sea he loved was only a pistol shot away — its salt smell in the air and the thunder of its breakers sounding day and night. And he had died on shipboard, as he would have desired, safe from the dreaded years of retirement on shore. Christian was right, I thought; without Old Bacchus, life on the *Bounty* could not be the same.

We buried him on Point Venus, close to where Captain Cook had set up his observatory twenty years before. There was some delay in getting the consent of Teina, the great chief whom the English had believed to be king of Tahiti, and who was the first of the Pomares. At last all was arranged, and the Indians themselves dug the grave, laying it out very exactly east and west. It was not until four o'clock in the afternoon that Old Bacchus was laid to rest, Bligh reading the burial service and a great crowd of Indians — silent, attentive, and respectful — surrounding us. When the captain and the *Bounty's* people had gone on board to see to the auctioning of the dead man's effects, Nelson and Peckover remained on shore, the former still pale and shaken from fish poisoning. The Indians had dispersed, and only the three of us lingered by the new grave, covered with slabs of coral in the Indian style.

Nelson cleared his throat and drew from a bag he carried three glasses and a bottle of Spanish wine. "We were his best friends on board," he said to Peckover, "you and Byam and I. I think it would please him if we added one small ceremony to the burial service Captain Bligh read so well." The botanist cleared his throat once more, handed us the glasses, and uncorked his bottle of wine. Then, baring our heads, we drank in silence to Old Bacchus, and when the bottle was empty we broke our glasses on the grave.

The relaxation of discipline which had followed the hardships of the *Bounty's* long voyage now came to an end as Bligh's harsh and ungovernable temper once more began to assert itself. I saw something of what was going on during my visits to the ship, and learned more from Hitihiti and Christian, who gave me to understand that there was much murmuring on board.

Each man on the ship, as I have said, had his Indian friend, who felt it his duty to send out to his *taio* frequent gifts of food. The seamen quite naturally regarded this as their own property, to be disposed of as they wished, but Bligh soon put an end to such ideas by announcing that all that came on board belonged to the ship, to be disposed of as the captain might direct. It was hard for a seaman whose *taio* had sent out a fine fat hog of two or three hundredweight to see it seized for ship's stores, and to be forced to dine on a small ration of poor pork issued by Mr. Samuel. Even the master's hogs were seized, though Bligh had at the moment forty of his own.

I witnessed unpleasant scenes of this kind one morning when I had gone on board to wait upon Mr. Bligh. The captain had gone ashore and was not expected for some time, so I loitered by the gangway, watching the canoes put out from shore. Young Hallet, the petulant and sickly-looking midshipman whom I liked least of those in the berth, was on duty to see that no provisions were smuggled on board, and he stepped to the gangway as a small canoe, paddled by two men, came alongside. Tom Ellison, the youngest of the seamen and the most popular with all hands, was in the bow of the canoe. He dropped his paddle, clambered up the ship's side, touched his forelock to Hallet, and leaned down to take the gifts his *taio* handed up to him. They were a handful of the Indian apples called *vi,* a fan, with a handle made of a whale's tooth, curiously carved, and a bundle of the native cloth. The Indian grinned up at Ellison, waved his hand, and paddled away. Hallet stooped to take up the apples laid on deck, and began to eat one, saying, "I must have these, Ellison."

"Right, sir," said Ellison, though I could see that he regretted his fruit. "You'll find them sweet!"

"And this fan," said the midshipman, taking it from Ellison's hand. "Will you give it to me?"

"I cannot, sir. It comes from a girl. You've a *taio* of your own."

"He pays me no attention these days. What have you there?"

"A bundle of tapa cloth."

Hallet stooped to feel the thick bundle and gave the seaman an evil smile. "It feels uncommonly like a sucking pig. Shall I call Mr. Samuel?" Ellison flushed and the other went on, without giving him time to reply, "See here! A bargain — the fan's mine, and I say nothing about the pig."

Without a word, the young seaman snatched up his bundle and strode off to the forecastle in a rage, leaving the fan in his superior's hands. I was about to utter angry words when Samuel, the captain's clerk, walked aft. Hallet stopped him. "Do you want a bit of tender pork?" he asked in a low voice. "Then go to the forecastle. I suspect that Ellison has a sucking pig wrapped up in a bale of the Indian cloth!" Samuel gave him a nod and a knowing leer, and passed. I stepped forward.

"You little swine!" I said to Hallet.

"You've been spying on me, Byam!" he squeaked.

"And if you were not such a contemptible little sneak, I'd do more than that!"

The captain's boat was approaching, and, swallowing my anger, I began to prepare the manuscript of my week's work for his inspection. Half an hour later, when the interview with Bligh was over and we came on deck, I found Christian at the gangway, to receive a gift of provisions and other things sent out by Maimiti, a great landowner in her own right.

There were a brace of fat hogs, as well as taro, plantains, and other vegetables; fine mats, Indian cloaks, and a pair of very handsome pearls from the Low Islands. Bligh strolled to the gangway, and, seeing the hogs, called for Samuel and ordered him to take them over for ship's stores. Christian flushed.

"Mr. Bligh," he said, "I meant these hogs for my own mess."

"No!" answered the captain harshly.

He glanced at the mats and cloaks, which Christian was about to send below. "Mr. Samuel," he went on, "take charge of these Indian curiosities, which may be useful for trading in other groups."

"One moment, sir," protested Christian. "These things were given me for members of my family in England."

Instead of replying, the captain turned away contemptuously toward the gangway. Maimiti's servant was handing up to Christian a small package done up in the tapa cloth. "Pearls," said the man in the Indian tongue. "My mistress sends them to you, to be given your mother in England." Still deeply flushed with anger, Christian took the package from the man's hand.

"Did he say pearls?" put in Bligh. "Come — let me see them!"

Samuel craned his neck and I admit that I did the same. Reluctantly, and in angry silence, Christian unwrapped the small package to display a matched pair of pearls as large as gooseberries, and of the most perfect orient. Samuel, a London Jew, permitted himself an exclamation of astonishment. After a moment's hesitation, Bligh spoke.

"Give them to Mr. Samuel," he ordered. "Pearls are highly prized in the Friendly Islands."

"Surely, sir," exclaimed Christian angrily, "you do not mean to seize these as well! They were given me for my mother!"

"Deliver them to Mr. Samuel," Bligh repeated.

"I refuse!" replied Christian, controlling himself with a great effort.

He turned away abruptly, closing his hand on the pearls, and went below. A glance passed between the captain and his clerk, but though Bligh's hands were clasping and unclasping behind his back, he said no more.

It was not hard to imagine the feelings of the *Bounty's* people at this time — rationed in the midst of plenty, and treated like smugglers each time they returned from shore. There must have been much angry murmuring in the forecastle, for the contrast between life on shore and life on the ship was oversharp. I had a home and my mother to return to, but the seamen could look forward to nothing in England save the prospect of the press gang, or begging on the Portsmouth streets. It seemed to me that if Mr. Bligh continued as he had begun, we should soon have desertions or worse.

Going on board to report myself one morning in mid-January, I found the captain pacing the quarter-deck in a rage. I stood to leeward of him for some time before he noticed me, and then, catching his eye, I saluted him and said, "Come on board, sir."

"Ah, Mr. Byam," he said, coming to a halt abruptly. "I cannot run over your work to-day; we'll put it off till next week. The ship's corporal and two of the seamen — Muspratt and Millward — have deserted. The ungrateful scoundrels shall suffer for this when I get my hands on them! They took the small cutter and eight stand of arms and ammunition. I have just learned that they left the cutter not far from here and set out for Tetiaroa in a sailing canoe." Mr. Bligh paused, his face set sternly, and seemed to reflect. "Has your *taio* a large canoe?" he asked.

"Yes, sir," I replied.

"In that case I shall put the pursuit in your hands. Ask for Hitihiti's canoe and as many of his men as you think necessary, and sail for Tetiaroa to-day. The wind is fair. Secure the men without using force if you can, but secure them! Churchill may give you some trouble. Should you find that they are not on the island, return to-morrow if the wind permits."

When I had taken leave of the captain, I found Stewart and Tinkler in the berth.

"You've heard the news, of course," said Stewart.

"Yes; Mr. Bligh told me, and I've the task of catching the men."

Stewart laughed. "By God! I don't envy you!"

"How did they make off with the cutter?" I asked.

"Hayward was mate of the watch, and was fool enough to take a caulk. The men stole away with the cutter while he slept. Bligh was like a madman when he learned it. He's put Hayward in irons for a month, and threatens to have him flogged on the day of his release!"

An hour later I found Hitihiti at the house, and told him of my orders and of the captain's request for the loan of his large sailing canoe. He agreed at once to let me have her, with a dozen of his men, and insisted on accompanying the expedition himself.

My host's vessel was of the kind called *va'a motu* — a single sailing canoe, about fifty feet long and two foot beam. On the larboard side, at a distance of about a fathom from the hull, was a long outrigger, or float, made fast to cross booms fore and aft, which crossed the gunwales and were lashed fast to them. Her mast was tall and strongly stayed, and her great sail of closely woven matting was bordered with a light frame of saplings.

I watched idly while Hitihiti's retainers rolled the vessel out from her shed where she was kept, carefully oiled and chocked high above the ground. They fetched the mast and stepped it, and set up the standing rigging all ataut. Then, in their leisurely fashion, the women of the household fetched bunches of newly husked drinking nuts and other provisions for the voyage. The men seemed to look forward eagerly to the expedition — a break in the dreamy monotony of their lives. Counting on taking the deserters by surprise, they seemed to have no fear of the muskets, but Hitihiti asked me with some concern if I were sure that Churchill and his companions had no pistols. When I assured him that the deserters were not provided with pistols, he brightened at once, and began to speak of the voyage.

We sailed at two o'clock in the afternoon, with a fresh easterly breeze on the beam. Tetiaroā lies almost due north of Matavai, about thirty miles distant. It is a cluster of five low coral islands, set here and there on the reef which encircles a lagoon some four miles across, and is the property of what mariners call the royal family — that of the great chief Teina, or Pomare. It is the fashionable watering place for the chiefs of the north end of Tahiti; they repair to its shady groves to recover from the ravages of the *ava* with which they constantly intoxicate themselves, and to live on a light wholesome diet of coconuts and fish. And to Tetiaroa also repair the *pori* — the young girls, one from each district of Tahiti, who are placed on stone platforms at certain times of the year, where they may be admired and compared with their competitors by passers-by. In Tetiaroa, these *pori* are fed on a special diet, kept in the shade to bleach their skins, and constantly rubbed with the perfumed mollifying oil called *monoi;* and I must do the old women who care for them the justice to remark that the whole of Europe might be searched without finding a score of young females lovelier than the *pori* I saw on one small coral island.

As we bore away for Tetiaroa I began to appreciate the qualities of Hitihiti's canoe. Amidships, a long, heavy plank, adzed out of a breadfruit tree, extended from the outrigger float, across the gunwales, and well outboard on the weather side. Four or five of the heaviest men of our crew now took their places on this plank, well out to windward, to prevent us from capsizing in the gusts. Two other men were employed constantly in bailing, as the canoe tore through the waves at a speed of not less than twelve knots. The *Bounty* sailed well, as ships went in those days, but Hitihiti's little vessel would have sailed two miles to her one. The chief and I sat side by side on a seat in her high stern, well above the spray which flew over hei bows as she sliced through the waves.

At considerable hazard we ran our canoe over the reef and into the calm waters of the Tetiaroa lagoon. There we were soon surrounded by small canoes and swimmers, all eager to impart some information of importance: the deserters, fearing pursuit, had set sail two or three hours before, some thought for Eimeo, others for the west side of Tahiti. The wind was dying away, as it does toward sunset in this region, and since darkness would soon set in and we had no certain knowledge of Churchill's destination, Hitihiti deemed it best to spend the night on Tetiaroa, and return to Bligh with our news when the morning breeze made up.

I shall not forget the night I spent on the coral island. The Indians of Tahiti are by nature a people given over to levity, passionately devoted to pleasure, and incapable of those burdens of the white man — worry and care. And in Tetiaroa, their watering place, they seemed to cast aside whatever light cares of family and state they feel when at home, and pass the time in entertainments of every kind, by night and by day. Relieved of his mission, which I am convinced he would have done his utmost to accomplish under other circumstances, Hitihiti now seemed to forget everything but the prospects of entertainment ashore, directing his paddlers to make at once for the nearest islet, called Rimatuu.

Three or four chiefs and their retinues were on the islet at the time, and, as its area was no more than five hundred acres, the place seemed densely populated. We were lodged at the house of a famous warrior named Poino, whose recent excesses in drinking the *ava* had nearly cost him his life. He lay on a pile of mats, scarcely able to move, his skin scaling off and green as verdigris, but Hitihiti informed me that in a month he would be quite restored. Several of Poino's relatives had accompanied him to Tetiaroa, and among them was a young girl, a member of the great Vehiatua family of Taiarapu, in charge of two old women. I had a glimpse of her in the distance as we supped, but thought no more of the young lady till after nightfall, when I was invited to see a *heiva,* or Indian entertainment.

Strolling with Hitihiti through the groves, we saw the flare of torch-light some distance ahead, and heard the beating of the small drums — a hollow, resonant sound with a strange measure. My friend's head went up and his step quickened. Ahead of us, in a large clearing, there was a raised platform of hewn blocks of coral, about which no less than two or three hundred spectators were seated on the ground. The scene was brightly illuminated by torches of coconut leaves, bound in long bundles and held aloft by serving men, who lighted fresh ones as fast as the old burned out. As we took our places, two clowns, called *faaata*, were finishing a performance which raised a gale of laughter, and as they stepped off the platform six young women, accompanied by four drummers, trooped on to perform. These girls were of the lower order of society, and their dance was believed by the Indians to ensure the fertility of the crops. The dress of the dancers consisted of no more than a wreath of flowers and green leaves about their waists, and the dance itself, in which they stood in two lines of three, face to face, was of a nature so unbelievably wanton that no words could convey the least idea of it. But if the clowns had raised a gale of laughter, the dance raised a hurricane. Hitihiti laughed as heartily as the rest — the antics of one girl, in fact, brought the tears to his eyes and caused him to slap his thigh resoundingly. Presently the dance was over and, in the pause that followed, my *taio* informed me that we were now to see a dance of a very different kind.

The second group of dancers came through the crowd, which parted right and left before them, each girl escorted by two old women and announced by a herald, who shouted her name and titles as she stepped on to the platform. All were dressed alike and very beautifully, in flowing draperies of snow-white Indian cloth, and the curious head-dresses called *tamau*. They carried fans, with handles curiously carved, and over their breasts they wore plates of pearl shell, polished till they gleamed like mirrors, and tinted with all the colors of the rainbow. Selected for their beauty, nurtured with the greatest care, kept constantly in the shade, and beautified with the numerous Indian cosmetics, these girls were of the most exquisite loveliness. Poino's young relative, the second to be announced, caused a murmur of admiration among the spectators.

Like all the Indians of the upper class, she was a full head taller than the commoners. Her figure was of the most perfect symmetry, her skin smooth and blooming as an apricot, and her dark lustrous eyes set wide apart in a face so lovely that I caught my breath at sight of her. While the herald announced her long name, and longer list of titles, she stood facing us, her eyes cast down proudly and modestly. Judging that the announcement was unintelligible to me, Hitihiti leaned over and whispered the girl's household name.

"Tehani," he announced in my ear, which is to say "The Darling," a name by no means inappropriate, I thought. The *hura* is danced in couples, and next moment Tehani and the first girl began to dance. The measure is slow, stately, and of great beauty, the movements of the arms, in particular, being wonderfully graceful and performed in the most exact time. When Tehani and her companion retired from the stage, amid hearty applause, they were succeeded by a brace of clowns, whose antics kept us laughing till the next pair of girls was ready to dance. But I scarcely noticed the other performers, for I was eager to return to the house, whither I knew Tehani had been led. It was fortunate for my work and my peace of mind, I thought somewhat ruefully, that she was not a member of Hitihiti's household, yet I knew that I would have given anything I possessed to have had her there. But I was not destined to see her again in Tetiaroa, for her two old duennas guarded her closely in a small separate house.

We sailed about two hours after sunrise, with the east wind abeam, and I was able to make my report to Mr. Bligh the same afternoon. The deserters were not apprehended till nearly three weeks later, when they gave themselves up, worn out by guarding against the constant attempts of the Indians to capture them. Churchill was given two dozen lashes, and Muspratt and Millward four dozen each.

The *Bounty* had at this time been shifted to a new anchorage in the harbour of Toaroa, where she was moored close to the shore. It had been Bligh's intention to have Hayward flogged with the deserters, and on the morning of the punishment, happening to be on board, I saw Hayward's *taio,* a chief named Moana, standing on deck with a sullen and gloomy face. But at the last moment the captain changed his mind and ordered Hayward below, to serve out the balance of his month in irons. On the same night an incident occurred which might have caused the loss of the ship and left us marooned among the Indians without the means of returning to England. The wind blew fresh from northwest all night, directly on shore, and at daybreak it was discovered that two strands of the small bower cable had been cut through, and that only one strand was holding the *Bounty* off the rocks. Mr. Bligh made a great to-do about the affair, but it was not till sometime afterwards that I learned the truth of it.

Hitihiti told me that Moana, Hayward's *taio,* was so incensed at the prospect of seeing the midshipman flogged that he had gone aboard that morning with a loaded pistol concealed under his cloak, planning to shoot Mr. Bligh through the heart before the first stroke of the cat could be delivered. Seeing his *taio* escape a flogging, but sent below to be confined, Moana conceived the idea of releasing his friend by wrecking the ship. He sent one of his henchmen to sever the cable under cover of night, and had the man performed his task properly the ship would infallibly have been lost.

I reflected for some time on Hitihiti's words, and finally, considering the incident closed and knowing that the cables were now watched with extra care throughout the night, I came to the conclusion that it was not necessary to inform Mr. Bligh of what I had learned. To tell him would only have increased his harshness to Hayward, and caused trouble with Moana, a powerful chief.

Toward the end of March it became evident to all hands that the *Bounty* would soon set sail. More than a thousand young breadfruit trees, in pots and tubs, had been taken on board, and the great cabin aft resembled a botanical garden with the young plants standing thick in their racks, all in a most flourishing condition, their foliage of the richest dark green. Great quantities of pork had been salted down, under the captain's direction, and a large sea store of yams laid in. Only Mr. Bligh knew when we would sail, but it was clear that the day of departure could not be far off.

I confess that I felt no eagerness to leave Tahiti. No man could have lived with so kind a host as Hitihiti without becoming deeply attached to the old man and his family, and my work on the Indian language interested me more each day. I was now able to carry on ordinary conversations with some fluency, though I knew enough to realize that a real mastery of this complex tongue would require years. The vocabulary I had planned was now complete and had been many times revised as I perceived mistakes, and I had made good progress on the grammar. Leading a life of the most delightful ease and tranquillity, and engaged on a congenial task in which I felt that I was making some headway, it is not to be wondered at that for days at a time I scarcely gave England a thought. Had it not been for my mother, I believe that I might have been content to settle down to a long period of the Indian life, and had I been assured that another vessel would touch at Tahiti within six months or a year, I should certainly have asked Mr. Bligh's permission to stop over and complete my work.

Christian, whom I had grown to know well, disliked the thought of departure as much as I. His attachment to Maimiti was of the tenderest description, and I knew how he must dread the final parting from her. Of the midshipmen, Stewart was as deeply attached to his Indian sweetheart as Christian himself. Young was constantly in the company of a girl called Taurua, the Indian name for the evening star. Stewart called his sweetheart Peggy; she was the daughter of a chief of some consequence on the north end of the island, and devotedly attached to him.

A day or two before the *Bounty* sailed, Christian, Young, and Stewart strolled up the beach to call on me, accompanied by Alexander Smith, my hammock man. Smith had formed an alliance with a short, dark, lively girl of the lower orders, who loved him in the robust fashion of a sailor's lass. He called her Bal'hadi, which was as close as his honest English tongue could twist itself to Paraha Iti, her true name.

We had been so long in Tahiti, and my shipmates had been so constantly in the company of the natives, that many of them were able to make themselves understood to some extent in the Indian language. Both Stewart and Ellison spoke it remarkably well, and Young and Smith had likewise made considerable progress in it. Smith, nevertheless, was of the opinion that, if English were spoken slowly and in a loud voice, it must be a stupid foreigner indeed who could fail to understand.

As my visitors from the *Bounty* approached the house I knew instinctively that Christian had news for me, but he had been so much among the Indians that he had acquired some notion of their ceremonial ideas of politeness, which demand a decent interval of light conversation before any important announcement is made.

Maimiti greeted her lover affectionately, and old Hitihiti had mats spread for us in the shade and ordered drinking coconuts to be fetched. My host had asked me, as a last favour, to have made for him a model of the *Bounty's* launch, which he admired greatly. He believed that with the aid of this model his native shipwrights would be able to build a boat, since I had explained to him the process of warping a plank. I had entrusted the model making to Smith, who had completed the task in less than a week, with every dimension true to scale. He walked behind the others, followed by Bal'hadi, who carried the model on her shoulder. Hitihiti's face lit up at sight of it.

"Now I shall start my boat," he said to me in the native tongue. "You have kept your word and I am well content!"

"Let him remember," said Smith, "a foot to the inch and he can't go wrong, I'll warrant!"

He handed the model to Hitihiti, who took it with every sign of pleasure and gave me an order to one of his servants, who soon appeared leading a pair of fine hogs.

"They are for you, Smith," I explained, but my hammock man shook his head regretfully.

"No use, sir," he said. "Mr. Bligh won't let us keep the pigs our *taios* send on board. But if the old chief would give me a sucking pig, me and my lass could cook and eat it in no time." He smacked his lips and gave me a hopeful glance.

Hitihiti smiled with pleasure at the request and directed that Smith should go with one of the Indians to pick out the pig that pleased him best. A few minutes later the seaman passed us, his sweetheart at his side and a squealing young porker under his arm. They disappeared into a thicket near the beach, and presently we heard louder squeals, followed by silence, and saw a column of smoke rising above the trees. I have a fancy that the Indian law which prohibited women from dining with men was broken that day.

Reclining in the shade and drinking the sweet milk of young coconuts, we had been gossiping idly with the girls, and presently Christian glanced up and caught my eye.

"I have news for you, Byam," he said. "We are to set sail on Saturday. Mr. Bligh bids you come on board on Friday night."

As if she understood the words, Maimiti looked at me sorrowfully, took her lover's hand and held it tight. "Bad news for me, at any rate," Christian went on. "I have been very happy here."

"And for me," put in Stewart, with a glance at his Peggy.

Young yawned. "I'm not sentimental," he remarked. "Taurua here will soon find another fancy man." The lively brown-eyed girl at his side understood his words perfectly. She tossed her head in denial and gave him a playful slap on the cheek. Christian smiled.

"Young is right," he said; "when the true seaman leaves one sweetheart he is already looking forward to the next! But I find it hard to practise what I preach!"

Toward evening our guests left us to return to the ship, and I was forced to follow them the next day. I took leave of Hitihiti and his household with sincere regret, fully convinced that I should never see any one of them again.

I found the *Bounty* crowded with Indians, and loaded with coconuts, plantains, hogs, and goats. The great chief Teina and his wife were the captain's guests and slept on the ship that night. At daybreak we worked out through the narrow Toaroa passage, and stood off and on all day, while Bligh took leave of Teina and made up his parting gifts to the chief. Just before sunset the launch was sent ashore with Teina and Itea, while we manned the ship with all hands and gave them three hearty cheers. An hour later the helm was put up and the *Bounty* stood off shore with all sail set.

## VIII · HOMEWARD BOUND

Now that we were at sea again, I had time to observe the change that had come over the ship's company as a result of our long island sojourn. In colour we were almost as brown as the Indians, and most of us were tattooed on various parts of our bodies with strange designs that added to our exotic appearance. The Tahitians are wonderfully skilled at tattooing, and although the process of acquiring it is both slow and painful, there were few of the men who had not been willing to undergo the torture for the sake of carrying home such evidence of their adventures in the South Sea. Edward Young was the most completely decorated of the midshipmen. On either leg he carried the design of a coconut tree, the trunk beginning at the heel and the foliage spreading out over the fleshy part of the calf. Encircling the thighs were wide bands of conventionalized design, and on his back he had the picture of a breadfruit tree, done with such spirit that one could all but hear the rustle of the wind through its branches.

In addition to such pictures, there was scarcely a man on the ship who had not acquired some words and phrases of the Tahitian language, which they took care to use in their talk with one another. A few had become remarkably proficient, and could carry on conversations in which scarcely a word of English was to be heard. All of them had pieces of the Indian cloth, and it was a curious sight, in the early mornings when they were washing down the decks, to see them at their work dressed only in turbans of tapa, with a strip of the same material about their loins, and jabbering away with great fluency in the Indian tongue. An Englishman fresh from home would hardly have recognized them as fellow countrymen.

There was an inward change as noticeable to any thoughtful observer as these outward ones. Duties were performed as usual, but there was little heartiness displayed, and this applied to some of the officers as well as to the men. Never, I fancy, has one of His Majesty's ships been worked homeward, after long absence, with less enthusiasm.

I was talking of this matter one day with Mr. Nelson, who was always to be found during the daylight hours in the great cabin, looking after his beloved breadfruit plants. I felt vaguely uneasy at this time, and it was always a comforting experience to talk with Mr. Nelson. He was one of those men who are truly called the salt of the earth, and was a rock of peace in our somewhat turbulent ship's company. I confessed that I was disturbed, without knowing exactly why, at the way the ship's work was going on. Nelson thought there was nothing to be concerned about.

"Does it seem strange to you, my dear fellow, that we should all feel a little let down after our idyllic life at Tahiti? I am surprised that the men show as much willingness as they do. My own feelings as I think of England ahead of us and Tahiti behind are decidedly mixed ones. Yours must be, too."

"I admit that they are," I replied.

"Imagine, then, how the men must feel, who have so little to go home to. What have they to expect at the end of the voyage? Before they have been a week ashore most of them may be seized by some press gang as recruits for another of His Majesty's ships. Who knows what the situation may be by the time the *Bounty* reaches England? We may be at war with France, or Spain, or Holland, or heaven knows what power; and in that case, alas for any poor seamen arriving in a home port! They won't even be given the chance to spend their back pay. The sailor leads a dog's life, Byam, and no mistake."

"Do you think war with France is likely?" I asked.

"War with France is always likely," he replied, smiling. "If I were an A.B. I should curse the thought of any war. Think what a paradise Tahiti has been for our men. For once in their lives they have been treated as human beings. They have had abundant food, easy duties, and unlimited opportunities for the sailor's chief distraction, women.

I confess that I was surprised, before we left Tahiti, that the lot of them didn't take to the hills. Certainly I should have done so had I been in any of their places."

As the days passed, and we left Tahiti farther and farther astern, the memory of our life there seemed like that of a dream, and gradually, one by one, we fell into the old routine. No unhappy incidents occurred to mar the peace of that period. Captain Bligh took his regular turns on the quarter-deck, but he rarely spoke to anyone, and most of his time was spent in his cabin, where he was busy working on his charts of the islands. So all went quietly enough until the morning of April 23, when we sighted the island of Namuka, in the Friendly Archipelago. Bligh had been here before, with Captain Cook, and it was his intention to replenish our wood and water before proceeding in the direction of Endeavour Straits.

The wind being to the southward, we had some difficulty in making the land, and it was not until late afternoon that we came to anchor in the road, in twenty-three fathoms. The island was much less romantic in appearance than Tahiti or any of the Society Islands that we had seen, but I was conscious of the same feeling of awe and wonder I had experienced elsewhere as I looked upon lands which only a handful of white men had ever seen, and whose very existence, to say nothing of their names, was unknown to people at home.

On the morning of the twenty-fourth we weighed and worked more to the eastward, and again anchored a mile and a half from shore, at a more convenient place for our watering parties. By this time the arrival of the ship was known far and wide on shore, and the Indians were arriving not only from various parts of Namuka, but from neighbouring islands as well. We had scarcely come to our new anchorage before we were surrounded with canoes, and our decks were so filled with people that we had difficulty in performing our duties. At first the confusion was great, but order was established when two chiefs came aboard whom Bligh remembered from his visit in 1777. We were able to make them understand that the decks must be cleared, and they set about it in so resolute and impetuous a manner that soon all of the Indians, except those in the chiefs' retinues, were again in their canoes. Captain Bligh then called me to him to act as interpreter, but I found that my study of the Tahitian language was of little service here. The Friendly Island speech, although it has points of resemblance, differs greatly from the Tahitian. However, with the aid of signs and an occasional word or phrase, we explained our purpose in coming, and, the chiefs having shouted some orders to their people, most of the canoes made speedily for shore.

It was Captain Cook who had given the name, "The Friendly Islands," to this archipelago, but my own impressions of its inhabitants were far from favourable. They resembled the Tahitians in stature, the colour of the skin and hair, and it was plain that they belonged to the same great family; but there was an insolent boldness in their behaviour lacking in the deportment of the Tahitians. They were thieves of the worst order and, if offered the slightest opportunity, would seize whatever loose article lay nearest and leap overboard with it. Christian was strongly of the opinion that they were not to be trusted in any respect, and suggested that a strong guard accompany the parties to be sent ashore for wood and water. Captain Bligh laughed at the notion.

"Surely you're not afraid of the beggars, Mr. Christian?"

"No, sir, but I think we have reason to be cautious in our dealings with them. In my opinion . . ."

He was not permitted to finish.

"And who's asked you for your opinion? Damme! If I haven't an old woman for my second-in-command! Come, Mr. Nelson, we must do something to reassure these timid souls," and he went down the ladder to the cutter that was waiting to row him ashore. Mr. Nelson followed — he was to collect some breadfruit plants to replace several that had died during the voyage — and the party, including the two chiefs, set out for the beach.

This little scene had taken place before many of the ship's company, and I could see that Christian had controlled his temper with difficulty. Mr. Bligh had the unfortunate habit of making such humiliating remarks to his officers, no matter who might be within hearing. It may be said in his defense, perhaps, that, being a thick-skinned man, he had no conception of how galling such remarks could be, particularly to a man like Christian.

As it chanced, nothing unusual happened that day. The fact that Mr. Bligh had gone off with two of the chiefs was a guarantee that his party would not be molested. Later in the day the natives came off to trade, bringing the usual island produce — pigs, fowls, coconuts, yams, and plantains. The afternoon and the whole of the following day were given up to this business, and the third morning the wood and watering parties were sent ashore in Christian's charge. It was then that his distrust of the Indians proved fully justified, for we had no sooner set foot on the beach than they began to make trouble for us. Mr. Bligh had not refused to send a guard with the ship's boats, but he had given strict orders that the arms were not to be used. Hayward was in charge of the cutter and I of the launch, and Christian went with the shore parties. The Indians thronged to the watering place, several hundred yards from the beach. Every effort was made to keep them at a distance, but they became increasingly bold as the work went on, and we had not been half an hour ashore before several of the sailors, who were cutting wood, had had their axes snatched from their hands. Christian performed his work admirably, in the opinion of all the shore party, and it was thanks to his coolness that we were not rushed and overwhelmed by the savages. They outnumbered us fifty to one. We managed to get down our wood and water without coming to a pitched battle, but when we were getting off, toward sundown, they rushed us and managed to make off with the grapnel of the cutter.

When we arrived on board and our losses were reported by Christian, Captain Bligh flew into a rage, cursing him in language that would have been out of place had he been speaking to a common sailor.

"You are an incompetent cowardly rascal, sir! Damn me if you're not! Are you afraid of a crowd of bloody savages whilst you have arms in your hands?"

"Of what service are they, sir, when you forbid their use?" Christian asked quietly. Bligh ignored this question and continued to pour out such a flood of abuse that Christian turned abruptly and left him, going down to his cabin. When in one of his rages Bligh seemed insane. I had never before met a man of this kind, and my conclusion was, having observed him so often in this state, that he had little recollection, afterward, of what he had said or done. I observed that he frequently worked himself into these passions over matters for which he was really to blame. Being unwilling to admit a fault in his own conduct, it seemed necessary to convince himself, through anger, that the blame lay elsewhere.

Usually, after Bligh had given vent to a fit of this sort, we could promise ourselves several days of calm, during which time he would have little or nothing to say to us, but it chanced that the following day a similar incident occurred which was to have the gravest consequences for all of us. I am no believer in fate. Men's actions, in so far as their relationships with one another are concerned, are largely under their own control; but there are times when malicious powers seem to order our small human affairs for their own amusement, and one of these occasions must surely have been on the twenty-seventh day of April, in the year 1789.

We had sailed from Namuka on the evening of the twenty-sixth and, the wind being light, had made but little progress during the night. All of the following day we were within seven or eight leagues of the land. The supplies we had received from the Indians were being stored away, and the carpenters were making pens for the pigs and crates for the fowls not intended for early use. Mr. Bligh had kept to his cabin all the morning, but early in the afternoon he appeared on deck to give some instructions to Mr. Samuel, who was in charge of the work of sorting over our purchases at Namuka. A great many coconuts had been piled up on the quarter-deck between the guns, and Bligh, who knew to the last ounce how many yams we had purchased, and the exact number of coconuts, discovered that a few of the latter were missing. He may have been told of this by Samuel, but at any rate he knew it.

He ordered all the officers to come on deck immediately, and questioned each of them as to the number of coconuts he had bought on his own account, and whether or not he had seen any one of the men helping himself to those on the quarter-deck. All denied having any such knowledge, and Bligh, doubtless thinking that the officers were shielding the men, became more and more angry. At length he came to Christian.

"Now, Mr. Christian, I wish to know the exact number of coconuts you purchased for your own use."

"I really don't know, sir," Christian replied, "but I hope you don't think me so mean as to be guilty of stealing yours?"

"Yes, you bloody hound! I *do* think so! You must have stolen some of mine or you would be able to give a better account of your own. You're damned rascals and thieves, the lot of you! You'll be stealing my yams next, or have the men steal them for you! But I'll make you suffer! I'll teach you to steal, you dogs! I'll break the spirit of every man of you! You'll wish you'd never seen me before we reach Endeavour Straits!"

Of all the humiliating scenes that had taken place up to that time, this was the worst; and yet, considering the nature of the offense com-

mitted, there was something meanly comic about it. Christian, however, could not see this side of the matter, and small wonder that he
could not. No other captain in His Majesty's service would have made
such an accusation against his second-in-command, to say nothing
of his other officers. Bligh stamped up and down the quarter-deck,
his face distorted with passion, shaking his fists and shouting at us as
though we were at the other end of the ship. Of a sudden he stopped.

"Mr. Samuel!"

"Yes, sir," said Samuel, stepping forward.

"You'll stop the villains' grog until further orders. And instead of a
pound of yams per man you'll issue half a pound to all the messes.
Understand?"

"Yes, sir."

"And, by God, I'll reduce you to a quarter of a pound if I find
anything else missing, and make you crawl on your bellies for that!"

He then gave orders that all of the coconuts, belonging to officers
and men alike, be carried aft to add to the ship's stores. When this
had been done he returned to his cabin.

I never remember the ship to have been more silent than she was
that evening. Most of us, doubtless, were thinking of the long voyage
ahead. Another year might pass before the *Bounty* could reach England. Meanwhile we should be under the heavy hand of a captain who
could do with us as he pleased; against whose tyranny there could be
no appeal. My own mess was particularly silent, for at this time Samuel
was a member of it, and we knew that anything we might say would
be quickly carried to Captain Bligh. Peckover ate his salt junk and
his half a pound of yams in a few savage bites, and withdrew. The rest
of us were not long in following.

Mr. Fryer's watch came on at eight o'clock. Most of the ship's
company were on deck during the early hours, owing to the fineness
of the evening. The breeze had been light all day and remained so; we
had no more than steerageway, but the air was refreshingly cool. The
moon was in its first quarter, and by its light we could dimly see, far
ahead, the outline of the island of Tofoa.

Between ten and eleven Bligh came on deck to leave his orders for
the night. He paced up and down the quarter-deck for some time,
paying no attention to anyone. Presently he stopped near Fryer, who
ventured to say: "Sir, I think we shall have a fine breeze by and by.

This moon coming on will be fortunate for us when we approach the coast of New Holland."

"Yes, Mr. Fryer, so it will," he replied. A few minutes later he gave his orders as to the course to be steered, and returned to his cabin.

Fryer's prediction of wind was not to be fulfilled. At midnight, when our watch went off duty, the sea was like a mill pond, with a glassy sheen upon the water, reflecting the Southern constellations. Going below, I found it much too hot for sleep. Tinkler and I came on deck together and stood for a while by the rail aft, talking of home and what we would choose for our first meal on shore. Presently, looking around cautiously, he said: "Byam, do you know that I am a double-dyed villain? I stole one of Mr. Bligh's missing coconuts."

"So it's you we have to thank for our dressing-down, you little rascal," I replied.

"Alas, yes. I'm one of the damned rogues and thieves. I could tell you the names of two others, but I forbear. We were thirsty and too lazy to go to the main top for the gun barrel. And there were the coconuts, such a tempting sight, a great heap of them between the guns on the quarter-deck. I wish they were there now; I'd steal another. There's nothing more refreshing than coconut water. Curse old Nelson's breadfruit garden! It keeps a man thirsty all the time."

We were all, in fact, envious of our breadfruit plants. Whatever happened, they had to be watered regularly, and in order to cut down the amount drunk by the ship's company Bligh had thought of a very excellent and ingenious arrangement to prevent us from quenching our thirst too often. Any man who wanted a drink had first to climb to the main top to fetch a gun barrel left there. He then climbed down with this to the scuttle butt, outside the galley, inserted the gun barrel into the bunghole, and, having sucked up his drink, he was required to carry the drinking tube to the main top again. No man, no matter how thirsty he might be, was permitted to make more than two of these gun-barrel climbs during his watch, and a lazy man did without his drink until thirst got the better of him.

"God be thanked! For once I wasn't suspected," Tinkler went on. "How do you explain that? If he had asked me I should have denied, of course, that I'd had anything to do with his rotten coconuts. But I'm afraid my guilty conscience might have given me away this time. I was so damned sorry for Christian."

"Did Christian know that you had taken some of the nuts?"

"Not some — only one, mind you! As I've told you, there were fellow conspirators. Of course he did. In fact, he saw me do it and looked the other way, as any decent officer was bound to do. It wasn't as though we were endangering the safety of the vessel. Four coconuts missing, that's all — I give you my word. Four out of how many thousands? And I was responsible for only one. Well, if I sleep over my sins, perhaps they won't seem so black to-morrow."

Tinkler was like the ship's cat; he could curl up anywhere for a nap. He now lay down by one of the quarter-deck guns, with his arm for a pillow, and, as I thought, was soon fast asleep.

It was then about one o'clock, and with the exception of the watch there was no one on deck but Tinkler and myself. Mr. Peckover was standing at the rail on the opposite side of the deck. I could make out his form dimly in the starlight. Someone appeared at the after ladderway. It was Christian. After half a dozen turns up and down the deck, he observed me standing between the guns.

"Oh, it's you, Byam?" He came and stood beside me, his elbows on the rail. I had not seen him since the affair of the afternoon.

At length he asked, "Did you know that he had invited me to sup with him? Why? Can you tell me that? After spitting on me, wiping his feet on me, he sent Samuel to ask me to eat at his table!"

"You didn't go?"

"After what had happened? God in heaven, no!"

I had never before seen a man in a mood of such black despair. He seemed at the last extremity of endurance. I was glad to be there, to be of service as a confidant, for it was plain that he was in desperate need of unburdening himself. That Bligh should have asked him to supper was, in truth, all but incredible, after the events of the afternoon. I suggested that it might be taken as evidence of an unsuspected delicacy of conscience in Bligh, but I believed this no more than did Christian himself.

"We're in his power. Officers and men alike, he considers us so many dogs to be kicked or fondled according to his whim. And there can be no relief. None. Not till we reach England. God knows when that will be!"

He was silent for some time, staring gloomily out over the starlit sea. At length he said, "Byam, there's something I wish you would do for me."

"What is it?"

"The chances are there'll be no occasion, but on a long voyage like this one never knows what may happen. If, for any reason, I should fail to reach home, I'd like you to see my people in Cumberland. Would that be too much trouble for you?"

"Not at all," I replied.

"During the last conversation I had with my father, just before I joined the ship, he asked that I make such an arrangement with some-one aboard the *Bounty*. In case anything should happen, he said that it would be a comfort to him to talk with one of my friends. I promised, and I've let half the voyage pass without fulfilling it. I feel better now that I have spoken."

"You can count on me," I said, shaking his hand.

"Good! That's settled, then."

"Well, Mr. Christian! You're up late."

We turned quickly to find Bligh standing a yard away. He was bare-foot and dressed only in his shirt and trousers. Neither of us had heard him approach.

"Yes, sir," Christian replied, coldly.

"And you, Mr. Byam. Can't you sleep?"

"It's very warm below, sir."

"I hadn't noticed it. A true sailor can sleep in an oven if the case requires. Or on a cake of ice."

He stood there for a moment as though expecting us to make some reply; then he turned abruptly and walked to the ladderway, halting to glance at the trim of the sails before going below again. Christian and I talked in desultory fashion for a brief time; then he bade me good-night and went forward somewhere.

Tinkler, who had been lying in deep shadow by one of the guns, sat up and stretched his arms with a deep yawn.

"Go below, Byam, and show that you are a true seaman. Damn you and Christian and your gabble! I was just getting drowsy when he came along."

"Did you hear what he said?" I asked.

"About notifying his father in case anything happened? Yes; I couldn't help eavesdropping. My father made no such request of me — which only goes to show that he has no hope of my not coming back. . . I must have a drink. I've been thinking of nothing but water this past hour, and I'm not entitled to one before morning. What would you do, in my case?"

"Mr. Peckover has just gone below for a moment," I said. "You might chance it."

"Has he?" Tinkler leaped to his feet. He ran up the shrouds for the gun barrel and had carried it aloft again before Peckover returned. As we went below together I heard three bells strike, and the far-off call of the lookout in the foretop: "All's well!" I settled myself in my hammock and was soon asleep.

## IX · THE MUTINY

SHORTLY after daybreak I was awakened by someone shaking me roughly by the shoulder, and at the same time I was aware of loud voices, Mr. Bligh's among them, and the heavy trampling of feet on deck. Churchill, the master-at-arms, stood by my hammock with a pistol in his hand, and I saw Thompson, holding a musket with the bayonet fixed, stationed by the arms chest which stood on the gratings of the main hatch. At the same time two men, whose names I do not remember, rushed into the berth, and one of them shouted, "We're with you, Churchill! Give us arms!" They were furnished with muskets by Thompson and hurried on deck again. Stewart, whose hammock was next to mine in the larboard berth, was already up and dressing in great haste. Despite the confused tumult of voices overhead, Young was still asleep.

"Have we been attacked, Churchill?" I asked; for my first thought was that the *Bounty* must have drifted close to one of the islands there-about, and that we had been boarded by the savages.

"Put on your clothes and lose no time about it, Mr. Byam," he replied. "We have taken the ship and Captain Bligh is a prisoner."

Aroused suddenly from the deepest slumber, I did not even then grasp the meaning of what he said, and for a moment sat gazing stupidly at him.

"They've mutinied, Byam!" said Stewart. "Good God, Churchill! Are you mad? Have you any conception of what you're doing?"

"We know very well what we're doing," he replied. "Bligh has brought all this on himself. Now, by God, we'll make him suffer!"

Thompson shook his musket in menacing fashion. "We're going to shoot the dog!" he said; "and don't you try any of your young gentlemen's tricks on us, or we'll murder some more of you! Seize 'em up, Churchill! They're not to be trusted."

"Hold your tongue and mind the arms chest," Churchill replied. "Come, Mr. Byam, hurry into your clothes. Quintal, stand fast by the door there! No one's to come forward without my orders — understand?"

"Aye, aye, sir!"

Turning my head, I saw Matthew Quintal at the rear entrance to the berth. Even as I looked, Samuel appeared behind him, dressed only in his trousers, his thin hair standing awry and his pale face considerably paler than its wont. "Mr. Churchill!" he called.

"Go back, you fat swine, or I'll run you through the guts!" Quintal shouted.

"Mr. Churchill, sir! Allow me to speak to you," Samuel called again.

"Drive him back," Churchill said, and Quintal made so fierce a gesture with his musket that Samuel vanished without waiting to hear more. "Give him a prod in the backside, Quintal," someone shouted, and, looking up, I saw two more armed men leaning over the hatchway.

Without weapons of any sort, there was nothing that Stewart and I could do but obey Churchill's orders. Both he and Thompson were powerful men and we should have been no match for them even had they been unarmed. I immediately thought of Christian, a man as quick in action as in decision, but I knew there could be no hope of his still being at liberty. He was the officer of the morning watch and had doubtless been rushed and overwhelmed at the very outset of the mutiny, even before Bligh had been secured. Catching my eye, Stewart shook his head slightly, as much as to say, "It's useless. There's nothing to be done."

We dressed in short order, and Churchill then ordered us to precede him along the passage to the fore ladderway. "Keep the others in the berth, Thompson," he called back. "Leave 'em to me; I'll mind 'em!" Thompson replied. There were several armed guards at the fore-hatch, among them Alexander Smith, my hammock man, whose loyalty in whatever situation I should have thought unquestionable. It was a shock to see him in Churchill's party, but the scene that presented itself as we came on deck made me forget the very existence of Smith.

Captain Bligh, naked except for his shirt, and with his hands tied behind his back, was standing by the mizzenmast. Christian stood before him, holding in one hand the end of the line by which Bligh was bound and in the other a bayonet, and around them were several of the able seamen, fully armed, among whom I recognized John Mills, Isaac Martin, Richard Skinner, and Thomas Burkitt. Churchill then said to us, "Stand by here. We mean no harm to either of you unless you take part against us." He then left us.

Stewart and I had taken it for granted that Churchill was the ringleader of the mutineers. As already related, after his attempted desertion at Tahiti he had been severely punished by Bligh. I knew how deeply he hated him, and it was conceivable that such a man could goad himself even to the point of mutiny. But that Christian could have done so, no matter what the provocation, was beyond anything I could have dreamed of as possible. Stewart's only comment was, "Christian! Good God! Then there's no hope."

The situation looked hopeless indeed. At this time the only unarmed men I saw on deck were Captain Bligh and ourselves. The ship was entirely in the hands of the mutineers. Evidently we had been brought up to divide the party of midshipmen below, thus preventing any opportunity for our taking concerted action. In the confusion we made our way aft a little way, and as we approached the spot where Bligh was standing, I heard Christian say, "Will you hold your tongue, sir, or shall I force you to hold it? I'm master of this ship now, and, by God, I'll stand no more of your abuse!" Sweat was pouring down Bligh's face. He had been making a great outcry, shouting, "Murder! Treason!" at the top of his voice.

"Master of my ship, you mutinous dog!" he yelled. "I'll see you hung! I'll have you flogged to ribbons! I'll . . ."

"*Mamu*, sir! Hold your tongue or you are dead this instant!"

Christian placed the point of his bayonet at Bligh's throat with a look in his eye there was no mistaking. "Slit the dog's gullet!" someone shouted; and there were cries of "Let him have it, Mr. Christian!" "Throw him overboard!" "Feed the bastard to the sharks!" and the like. It was only then, I think, that Captain Bligh realized his true situation. He stood for a moment breathing hard, looking about him with an expression of incredulity on his face.

"Mr. Christian, allow me to speak!" he begged hoarsely. "Think what you do! Release me — lay aside your arms! Let us be friends again, and I give you my word that nothing more shall be said of this matter."

"Your word is of no value, sir," Christian replied. "Had you been a man of honour things would never have come to this pass."

"What do you mean to do with me?"

"Shoot you, you bloody rogue!" cried Burkitt, shaking his musket at him.

"Shooting's too good for him! Seize him up at the gratings, Mr. Christian! Give us a chance at him with the cat!"

"That's it! Seize him up! Give him a taste of his own poison!"

"Flay the hide off him!"

"Silence!" Christian called, sternly; and then, to Bligh: "We'll give you justice, sir, which is more than you have ever given us. We'll take you in irons to England . . ."

A dozen protesting voices interrupted him.

"To England? Never! We won't have it, Mr. Christian!"

Immediately the deck was again in an uproar, all the mutineers clamouring against Christian's proposal. Never was the situation with respect to Bligh so critical as at that moment, and it was to his credit that he showed no sign of flinching. The men were in a savage mood, and it was touch and go as to whether he would be shot where he stood; but he glared at each of them in turn as though challenging them to do so. Luckily a diversion was created when Ellison came dashing up flourishing a bayonet. There was no real harm in this lad, but he loved mischief better than his dinner, and, being thoughtless and high-spirited, he could be counted upon to get himself into trouble whenever the opportunity presented itself. Evidently he considered joining in a mutiny nothing more than a fine lark, and he now came dancing up to Bligh with such a comical expression upon his face that the tension was relieved at once. The men broke into cheers. "Hooray, Tommy! Are you with us, lad?"

"Let me guard him, Mr. Christian!" he cried. "I'll watch him like a cat!" He skipped up and down in front of Bligh, brandishing his weapon. "Oh, you rogue! You old villain! You'd flog us, would you? You'd stop our grog, would you? You'd make us eat grass, would you?"

The men cheered him wildly. "Lay on, lad!" they shouted. "We'll back you! Give him a jab in the guts!"

"You and your Mr. Samuel! A pair of swindlers, that's what you are!

Cheating us out of our food! You've made a pretty penny between you! You old thief! You should be a bumboat man. I'll lay you'd make your fortune in no time!"

It was a bitter experience for Bligh to be baited thus by the least of his seamen, but as a matter of fact nothing more fortunate for him could have happened. His life at that moment hung in the balance, and Ellison, in giving vent to his feelings, relieved the pent-up emotions of men who were not glib of speech and could express their hatred of Bligh only in action. Christian realized this, I think, and permitted Ellison to speak his mind, but he soon cut him short and put him in his place.

"Clear the cutter!" he called. "Mr. Churchill!"

"Aye, aye, sir!"

"Fetch up Mr. Fryer and Mr. Purcell! Burkitt!"

"Here, sir!"

"You and Sumner and Mills and Martin — stand guard here over Mr. Bligh!"

Burkitt took the end of the line in one of his huge hairy fists.

"We'll mind him, sir! I'll lay to that!"

"What's your plan, Mr. Christian? We've a right to know," said Sumner. Christian turned quickly and looked at him. "Mind what you're about, Sumner!" he said quietly. "I'm master of this ship! Lively, men, with the cutter."

Several men climbed into the boat to clear out the yams, sweet potatoes, and other ship's stores which were kept there, while others unlashed it and got ready the tackle for hoisting it over the side. Burkitt stood directly in front of Captain Bligh, holding the point of a bayonet within an inch of his breast. Sumner stood behind him with his musket at ready, and the other men on either side. Thompson excepted, they were the hardest characters among the sailors, and Bligh wisely said nothing to arouse them further. Others of the mutineers were stationed about the decks, and there were three at each of the ladderways. I wondered how the affair had been so well and secretly planned. I searched my memory, but could recall no incident of a character in the least suspicious.

I had been so intent in watching the scene of which Bligh was the centre that I had forgotten Stewart. We had become separated, and while I was searching for him Christian saw me for the first time. He came at once to where I was standing. His voice was calm, but I could see that he was labouring under great excitement.

"Byam, this is my affair," he said. "Not a man shall be hurt, but if any take part against us it will be at the peril of the entire ship's company. Act as you think best."

"What do you mean to do?" I asked.

"I would have carried Bligh to England as a prisoner. That is impossible; the men won't have it. He shall have the cutter to go where he chooses. Mr. Fryer, Hayward, Hallet, and Samuel shall go with him."

There was no time for further talk. Churchill came up with the master and Purcell. The carpenter, as usual, was surly and taciturn. Both he and Fryer were horror-stricken at what had happened, but they were entirely self-possessed. Christian well knew that these two men would seize the first opportunity, if one presented itself, for retaking the ship, and he had them well guarded.

"Mr. Byam, surely you are not concerned in this?" Fryer asked.

"No more than yourself, sir," I replied.

"Mr. Byam has nothing to do with it," said Christian. "Mr. Purcell . . ."

Fryer interrupted him.

"In God's name, Mr. Christian! What is it you do? Do you realize that this means the ruin of everything? Give up this madness, and I promise that we shall all make your interest our own. Only let us reach England . . ."

"It is too late, Mr. Fryer," he replied, coldly. "I have been in hell for weeks past, and I mean to stand it no longer."

"Your difficulties with Captain Bligh give you no right to bring ruin upon the rest of us."

"Hold your tongue, sir," said Christian. "Mr. Purcell, have your men fetch up the thwarts, knees, and gear bolts for the large cutter. Churchill, let the carpenter go below to see to this. Send a guard with him."

Purcell and Churchill went down the forward ladderway.

"Do you mean to set us adrift?" Fryer asked.

"We are no more than nine leagues from the land here," Christian replied. "In so calm a sea Mr. Bligh will have no difficulty in making it."

"I will stay with the ship."

"No, Mr. Fryer; you will go with Captain Bligh. Williams! Take the master to his cabin while he collects his clothes. He is to be kept there until I send word."

Fryer requested earnestly to be allowed to remain with the vessel, but Christian well knew his reason for desiring this and would not hear to the proposal. He put an end to the matter by sending the master below.

Purcell now returned, followed by Norman and McIntosh, his mates, carrying the gear for the cutter. Purcell came up to me at once.

"Mr. Byam, I know that you have no hand in this business. But you are, or have been, a friend to Mr. Christian. Beg him to give Captain Bligh the launch. The cutter is rotten and will never swim to the land."

This, I knew, was the case. The cutter was riddled with worms and leaked so badly as to be almost useless. The carpenters were to have started repairing her that same morning. Purcell would not come with me to speak of the matter, giving as a reason Christian's dislike of him. "He would not care to grant any request of mine," he said. "If the cutter is hoisted out, it will be almost certain death for Captain Bligh and all who are permitted to go with him."

I wasted no time, but went to Christian at once. Several of the mutineers gathered round to hear what I had to say. Christian agreed at once. "He shall have the launch," he said. "Tell the carpenter to have his men fit her." He then called, "Leave off with the cutter, my lads! Clear the launch."

There were immediate protests, led by Churchill, against this new arrangement.

"The launch, Mr. Christian?"

"Don't let him have it, sir! The old fox'll get home in her!"

"She's too bloody good for him!"

There was an argument over the matter, but Christian forced his will upon the others. In fact, they made no determined stand. All were eager to be rid of the captain, and they had little reason to fear that he would ever see England again.

The mutineers were in such complete control of the situation that Christian now gave orders for the rest of those who were not of his party to be brought on deck. Samuel, Bligh's clerk, was among the first to appear. He was anything but a favourite with the ship's company, and was greeted with jeers and threats by his particular enemies. I had supposed that he would make a poor showing in such a situation. On the contrary, he acted with spirit and determination. Disregarding the insults of the sailors, he went directly to Captain Bligh to receive his orders. He was permitted to go to Bligh's cabin with John Smith, the captain's servant, to fetch up his clothes. They helped him on with his boots and trousers and laid his coat over his shoulders.

I saw Hayward and Hallet standing aft by the rail. Hallet was crying, and both of them were in a state of great alarm. Someone touched my shoulder and I found Mr. Nelson standing beside me.

"Well, Byam, I'm afraid that we're even farther from home than we thought. Do you know what they plan to do with us?"

I told him the little I knew. He smiled ruefully, glancing toward the island of Tofoa, now a faint blur on the horizon.

"I suppose that Captain Bligh will take us there," he said. "I don't much relish the prospect of meeting any more Friendly Islanders. Their friendliness is of a kind that we can well dispense with."

The carpenter appeared at the ladderway, followed by Robert Lamb, the butcher, who was helping to bring up his tool chest.

"Mr. Nelson," he said, "we know whom we have to thank for this."

"Yes, Mr. Purcell, our unlucky stars," Nelson replied.

"No, sir! We have Captain Bligh to thank for it, and him alone! He has brought it upon us all by his damnable behaviour!"

Purcell had the deepest hatred for Bligh, which was returned with interest. The two men had not spoken for months save when absolutely necessary. Nevertheless, when Mr. Nelson suggested that he might be permitted to stay with the ship if he chose, the carpenter was horrified.

"Stop aboard? With rogues and pirates? Never, sir! I shall follow my commander."

At this moment Churchill, who was everywhere about the decks, caught sight of us.

"What are you about there, Purcell? Damn your blood! You'd steal our tools, would you?"

"Your tools, you scoundrel? They're mine, and they go where I go!"

"You shan't take a nail from the ship if I have my way," Churchill replied. He then called out to Christian, and there was another argument, not only with respect to the tool chest, but as to the carpenter himself. Christian was partly in the mind to keep him on the vessel, knowing his value as a craftsman, but all the others urged against it. Purcell had a violent temper and was regarded by the men as a tyrant second only to Bligh.

"He's a damned old villain, sir!"

"Keep the carpenter's mates, Mr. Christian. They're the men for us."

"Make him go in the boat!"

"Make me go, you pirates?" he cried. "I'd like to see the man who'll *stop* me!"

Unfortunately, Purcell was as thick-headed as he was fearless, and he now so far forgot the interests of Bligh's party as to boast of what we would do as soon as we should be clear of the mutineers.

"Mark my word, you rogues! We'll bring every man of you to justice! We'll build a vessel to carry us home . . ."

"So he will, Mr. Christian, if we give him his tools," several men shouted.

"The old fox could build a ship with a clasp knife!"

Purcell realized too late what he had done. I believe that Christian would have given him many of his tools, of which there were duplicates on board, but having been reminded of what he might do with them, he now ordered the tool chest to be examined, and Purcell was permitted to have nothing but a hand saw, a small axe, a hammer, and a bag of nails. Bligh, who had overheard all that was said, could contain himself no longer. "You infernal idiot!" he roared at Purcell, and was prevented from saying more by Burkitt, who placed a bayonet at his throat.

The decks were now filled with people, but Christian took good care that those not of his party should be prevented from coming together in any numbers. As soon as the launch had been cleared, he ordered the boatswain to swing her out. "And mind yourself, Mr. Cole! If you spring a yard or carry anything away it will go hard with you!" Fifteen or more of us were ordered to assist him, for the mutineers were too canny to lay aside their arms and bear a hand.

"Foresail and mainsail there! All ready?"

"Aye, aye, sir!"

"Let go sheets and tacks!"

"All clear, sir!"

"Clew garnets — up with the clews!"

The breeze was still so light as barely to fill the sails, and the clews of the mainsail and foresail went smoothly up to the quarters of the yards. The yards were now squared and the braces made fast, and with half a dozen men holding the launch inboard she was hoisted, swung out over the bulwarks, and lowered away.

One of the first men ordered into her was Samuel. Hayward and Hallet followed next. Both were shedding tears and crying for mercy, and they were half carried to the gangway. Hayward turned to Christian, clasping his hands imploringly.

"Mr. Christian, what have I ever done that you should treat me so?" he exclaimed. "In God's name, permit me to stay with the ship!"

"We can dispense with your services here," Christian replied, grimly. "Into the boat, the pair of you!"

Purcell went next. He required no urging. I think he would have died rather than remain in the ship now that she had been seized by mutineers. His few tools were handed down to him by the boatswain, who followed. Christian ordered Bligh to be brought to the gangway, and his hands were freed.

"Now, Mr. Bligh, there is your boat, and you are fortunate to have the launch and not the cutter. Go into her at once, sir!"

"Mr. Christian," said Bligh, "for the last time I beg you to reflect! I'll pawn my honour — I pledge you my word never to think of this again if you will desist. Consider my wife and family!"

"No, Mr. Bligh. You should have thought of your family long before this, and we well know what your honour is worth. Go into the boat, sir!"

Seeing that all pleading was useless, Bligh obeyed, and was followed by Mr. Peckover and Norton, the quartermaster. Christian then handed down a sextant and a book of nautical tables.

"You have your compass, sir. This book is sufficient for every purpose, and the sextant is my own. You know it to be a good one."

With his hands freed and once more in command, though only of his ship's launch, Bligh became his old self again.

"I know you to be a bloody scoundrel!" he shouted, shaking his fist in Christian's direction. "But I'll have vengeance! Mind that, you ungrateful villain! I'll see you swinging at a yardarm before two years have passed! And every traitor with you!"

Fortunately for Bligh, Christian's attention was engaged elsewhere, but several of the mutineers at the bulwarks replied to him in language as forceful as the captain's, and it was a near thing that he was not fired upon.

In the confusion I had lost sight of Stewart. We had been hauling together at one of the braces when the launch was hoisted out, but now I could find him nowhere. It soon became clear that many were to be allowed to go with Bligh, and Mr. Nelson and I, who had been standing together by the bulwarks, were hastening toward the after ladderway when we were stopped by Christian.

"Mr. Nelson, you and Mr. Byam may stay with the ship if you choose," he said.

"I have sympathy with you for the wrongs you have suffered, Mr. Christian," Nelson replied, "but none whatever with this action to redress them."

"And when have I asked you for sympathy, sir? Mr. Byam, what is your decision?"

"I shall go with Captain Bligh."

"Then make haste, both of you."

"Have we permission to fetch our clothes?" Nelson asked.

"Yes, but look sharp!"

Nelson's cabin was on the orlop deck directly below that of Fryer. Two guards stood by the ladderway on the lower deck. We parted there and I went to the midshipmen's berth, where Thompson was still on guard over the arms chest. I had seen nothing of Tinkler and Elphinstone, and was about to look into the starboard berth to see if they were still there. Thompson prevented me.

"Never you mind the starboard berth," he said. "Get your clothes and clear out!"

The berth was screened off from the main hatchway by a canvas-covered framework. To my surprise, I found Young still asleep in his hammock. He had been on watch from twelve to four, and this was his customary time for rest, but it was strange that he could have slept through such a turmoil. I tried to rouse him, but he was a notoriously heavy sleeper. Finding the matter hopeless, I left off and began to ransack my chest for things I should most need. Stacked in the corner of the berth were several Friendly Island war clubs that we had obtained from the savages of Namuka. They had been carved from the *toa,* or ironwood tree, which well deserved its name, for in weight and texture the wood was indeed like iron. At the sight of them the thought flashed into my mind, "Could I strike Thompson down with one of these?" I glanced quickly out the doorway. Thompson was now seated on the arms chest with his musket between his knees, facing the passageway leading aft. But he saw me thrust out my head and, with an oath, ordered me to "look sharp and clear out of there."

At this moment Morrison came along the passageway, and as luck would have it Thompson's attention was attracted by someone calling him from above. I beckoned Morrison into the berth, and he dodged in without having been seen. There was no need for words. I handed him one of the war clubs and took another for myself; then, together, we made a last effort to waken Young. Not daring to speak, we nearly shook him out of his hammock, but we might have spared ourselves the trouble. I heard Thompson call out, "He's getting his clothes, sir. I'll have him up at once." Morrison drew back by the door and raised his club, and I stood at ready on the other side, for we both expected Thompson to come in for me. Instead of that he shouted, "Out of there, Byam, and be quick about it!"

"I'm coming," I called, and again looked out of the doorway. My heart sank as I saw Burkitt and McCoy coming along from the fore hatchway. They stopped by the arms chest to speak to Thompson. Both had muskets, of course. Our chance to get at Thompson and the arms chest was lost unless they should pass on. Fortune was against us. We waited for at least two minutes longer and the men remained where they were. I heard Nelson's voice calling down the hatchway: "Byam! Lively there, lad, or you'll be left behind!" And Tinkler's: "For God's sake, hasten, Byam!"

It was a bitter moment for Morrison and me. The opportunity had been a poor one at best, but had there been time something might have come of it. We quickly put the war clubs aside and rushed out, colliding with Thompson, who was coming to see what I was about.

"Damn your blood, Morrison! What are you doing here?"

We didn't wait to explain, but ran along the passage to the ladderway. Morrison preceded me, and in my haste to reach the deck, cumbered as I was with my bag of clothes, I slipped and fell halfway down the ladder, giving my shoulder a wrench as I struck the gratings. I clambered up again and was rushing toward the gangway when Churchill seized me. "You're too late, Byam," he said. "You can't go." "Can't go? By God, I *will!*" I exclaimed, giving him a shove which loosened his hold and all but toppled him over. I was frantic, for I saw the launch being veered astern, one of the mutineers carrying the painter aft. Burkitt and Quintal were holding Coleman, the armourer, who was begging to go into the boat, and Morrison was struggling with several men who were keeping him back from the gangway. We were, in fact, too late; the launch was loaded almost to the point of foundering, and I heard Bligh shouting: "I can take no more of you, lads! I'll do you justice if ever we reach England!"

When the launch had drifted astern, the man holding the painter took a turn with it around the rail and threw the free end to someone in the boat. Those left in the ship now crowded along the rail, and I had difficulty in finding a place where I could look over the side. I was sick at heart, and appalled at the realization that I was, indeed, to be left behind among the mutineers. Norton was in the bow of the launch holding the end of the painter. Bligh was standing on a thwart, astern. Of the others, some were seated and some were standing, and the boat was so heavily loaded as to have no more than seven or eight inches of freeboard. There was a great deal of shouting back and forth, and Bligh was contributing his full share to the tumult by bellowing out orders to those in the boat, and curses and imprecations against Christian and his men.

Some of the mutineers looked on silently and thoughtfully, but others were jeering at Bligh, and I heard one of them shout: "Go and see if you can live on half a pound of yams a day, you bloody villain!" Fryer called out, "In God's name, Mr. Christian, give us arms and ammunition! Think where we go! Let us have a chance to defend our lives!" Others, the boatswain among them, joined earnestly in this plea.

"Arms be damned!" someone shouted back.

"You don't need 'em."

"Old Bligh loves the savages. He'll take care of you!"

"Use your rattan on 'em, boatswain!"

Coleman and I sought out Christian, who was standing by one of the cabin gratings, out of sight of the launch. We begged him to let Bligh have some muskets and ammunition.

"Never!" he said. "They shall have no firearms."

"Then give them some cutlasses at least, Mr. Christian," Coleman urged, "unless you wish them to be murdered the moment they set foot on shore. Think of our experience at Namuka!"

Christian consented to this. He ordered Churchill to fetch some cutlasses from the arms chest, and a moment later he returned with four, which were handed into the boat. Meanwhile, Morrison had taken advantage of this opportunity to run below for some additional provisions for the launch. He and John Millward brought up a mess kid filled with pieces of salt pork, several calabashes of water, and some additional bottles of wine and spirits, which they lowered into the boat.

"You cowards!" Purcell shouted, as the cutlasses were handed in. "Will you give us nothing but these?"

"Shall we lower the arms chest, carpenter?" Isaac Martin asked, jeeringly. McCoy threatened him with his musket. "You'll get a bellyful of lead in a minute," he shouted.

"Bear off and turn one of the swivels on 'em!" someone else called. "Give 'em a whiff of grape!"

Burkitt now raised his musket and pointed it at Bligh. Alexander Smith, who was standing beside him, seized the barrel of the musket and thrust it up. I am convinced that Burkitt meant to shoot Bligh, but Christian, observing this, ordered him to be dragged back, deprived of his arms, and placed under guard. He made a terrific struggle, and it required four men to disarm him.

Meanwhile, Fryer and others were urging Bligh to cast off lest they should all be murdered. This Bligh now ordered to be done, and the launch dropped slowly astern. The oars were gotten out, and the boat, so low in the water that she seemed on the point of foundering, was headed toward the island of Tofoa, which bore northeast, about ten leagues distant. Twelve men made a good load for the launch. She now carried nineteen, to say nothing of the food and water and the gear of the men.

"Thank God we were too late to go with her, Byam!"

Morrison was standing beside me.

"Do you mean that?" I asked.

He was silent for a moment, as though considering the matter carefully. Then he said, "No, I don't. I would willingly have taken my chance in her — but it's a slim chance indeed. They'll never see England again."

Tinkler was sitting on a thwart. Mr. Nelson, and Peckover, Norton, Elphinstone, the master's mate, Ledward, the acting surgeon — all were as good as dead, more than a thousand miles from any port where they might expect help. About them were islands filled with the cruelest of savages, who could be held at bay only by men well armed. Granted that some might escape death at the hands of the Indians, what chance had so tiny a boat, so appallingly loaded, to reach any civilized port? The possibility was so remote as to be not worth considering.

Sick at heart, I turned away from the sight of the frail craft, looking so small, so helpless, on that great waste of waters. There had been a cheer from some of the mutineers: "Huzza for Tahiti!" as Christian had ordered, "Get sail on her!" Ellison, McCoy, and Williams had run aloft to loose the fore-topgallant sail. Afterward a silence had fallen over the ship, and the men stood by the bulwarks, gazing at the launch growing smaller and smaller as we drew away from her. Christian, too, was watching, standing where I had last seen him, by the cabin grating. What his thoughts were at this time it would be impossible to say. His sense of the wrongs he had suffered at Bligh's hands was so deep and overpowering as to dominate, I believe, every other feeling. In the course of a long life I have met no others of his kind. I knew him, I suppose, as well as anyone could be said to know him, and yet I never felt that I truly understood the workings of his mind and heart. Men of such passionate nature, when goaded by injustice into action, lose all sense of anything save their own misery. They neither know nor care, until it is too late, what ruin they make of the lives of others.

It was getting on toward eight o'clock when the launch had been cast off. Shortly afterward the breeze, from the northeast, freshened, and the *Bounty* gathered way quietly, slipping through the water with a slight hiss of foam. The launch became a mere speck, seen momentarily as she rose to the swell or as the sunlight flashed from her oars. Within half an hour she had vanished as though swallowed up by the sea. Our course was west-northwest.

## X · FLETCHER CHRISTIAN

OUR company was divided, and, though linked together by a common disaster, we were not to share a common fate. I doubt whether a ship has ever sailed from England whose numbers, during the course of her voyage, were to be so widely scattered over the face of the earth, and whose individual members were to meet ends so strange and, in many cases, so tragic.

There had gone with Bligh, in the launch: —

> John Fryer, *Master*
> Thomas Ledward, *Acting Surgeon*
> David Nelson, *Botanist*
> William Peckover, *Gunner*
> William Cole, *Boatswain*
> William Elphinstone, *Master's Mate*
> William Purcell, *Carpenter*
>
> Thomas Hayward ⎫
> John Hallet ⎬ *Midshipmen*
> Robert Tinkler ⎭
>
> John Norton ⎫ *Quartermasters*
> Peter Lenkletter ⎭
>
> George Simpson, *Quartermaster's Mate*
> Lawrence Lebogue, *Sailmaker*
> Mr. Samuel, *Clerk*
> Robert Lamb, *Butcher*
>
> John Smith ⎫ *Cooks*
> Thomas Hall ⎭

Of those who remained in the *Bounty,* the following had taken an active part in the mutiny: —

> Fletcher Christian, *Acting Lieutenant*
> John Mills, *Gunner's Mate*
> Charles Churchill, *Master-at-Arms*
> William Brown, *Gardener*
>
> Thomas Burkitt ⎫
> Matthew Quintal ⎪
> John Sumner ⎪
> John Millward ⎪
> William McCoy ⎪
> Henry Hillbrandt ⎪
> Alexander Smith ⎬ *Able Seamen*
> John Williams ⎪
> Thomas Ellison ⎪
> Isaac Martin ⎪
> Richard Skinner ⎪
> Matthew Thompson ⎭

Those in the *Bounty* with, but not of, Christian's party, were:—

Edward Young ⎱ *Midshipmen*
George Stewart ⎰

James Morrison, *Boatswain's Mate*
Joseph Coleman, *Armourer*
Charles Norman, *Carpenter's Mate*
Thomas McIntosh, *Carpenter's Crew*
William Muspratt, *Able Seaman*

Also Michael Byrne, the half-blind seaman, and myself. William Muspratt had, for a moment, pretended to be of the mutineers' party and had accepted a musket offered to him by Churchill. He had overheard Fryer say that he hoped to form a party to retake the vessel, and I am certain he had taken the musket for no other reason than to assist Fryer. When he saw that the matter was hopeless, he immediately laid aside his arms. Coleman, Norman, and McIntosh had been prevented from going in the launch because the mutineers had need of their services as artificers. Smiths and carpenters can no more be dispensed with on a ship at sea than can seamen themselves.

It was but natural that those who had taken no part in the mutiny should be looked upon with suspicion by those who had. Most of the seamen, however, showed no active hostility against us. Churchill ordered us to remain on deck, but forward of the mizzenmast, and there we awaited Christian's pleasure. Burkitt, who had been deprived of his musket and placed under arms, lest he should shoot Captain Bligh, was again set at liberty. He and Thompson now began baiting and jeering at us, and McCoy and John Williams joined with them. For a moment it seemed likely that there would be a pitched battle between us, and there is no doubt that the non-mutineers would have had the worst of it. Fortunately for us, Christian soon restored order. He came forward, his eyes blazing with anger.

"Get about your work, Thompson," he ordered. "Burkitt, if I have any more trouble from you, I'll put you in irons and keep you there!"

"That's how it is to be, is it?" Thompson replied. "Well, we won't have it, Mr. Christian. We ain't mutinied to have you come the Captain Bligh over us!"

"No, by God, we haven't!" Martin added; "and that you'll find!"

Christian looked at them for a moment without speaking, and there was that in his eyes to relieve any apprehensions one might have had as to his ability to cope with the situation. The four turbulent men dropped their glances sullenly. Several of the seamen were standing by, Alexander Smith among them. "Order all hands aft, Smith," said Christian. He returned to the quarter-deck and paced up and down while the men collected. Then he turned and faced them.

"There is one matter we will decide once for all," he began, quietly, "and that is who is to be captain of this ship. I have taken her with your help, in order to be rid of a tyrant who has made life a burden to all of us. Make no mistake about our status from this time on. We are mutineers, and if we should be discovered and taken by one of His Majesty's vessels, not a man of us but will suffer death. That possibility is not so remote as some of you may think. Should Mr. Bligh succeed in reaching England, immediately upon his arrival there a ship of war will be sent in search of us. Should the *Bounty* not be reported in a year's time, or, at the latest, two years, a ship will be sent, nevertheless, to discover, if possible, the reason for her disappearance. Bear this in mind, all of you. We are not only mutineers but pirates as well, for we have run away with one of His Majesty's armed vessels. We are cut off from England forever, except as prisoners whose fate, if taken home, is certain.

"The Pacific is wide, and still so little known that we need never be taken except as the result of our own folly. In our situation a leader is essential, one whose will is to be obeyed without question. It should be needless to tell British seamen that no ship, whether manned by mutineers or not, can be handled without discipline. If I am to command the *Bounty* I mean to be obeyed. There shall be no injustice here. I shall punish no man without good cause, but I will have no man question my authority.

"I am willing that you shall decide who is to command the *Bounty*. If there is some man most of you prefer in my place, name him, and I will resign my authority. If you wish me to lead you, mind what I have said. I mean to be obeyed."

Churchill was the first to speak. "Well, men, what have you to say?"

"I'm for Mr. Christian!" Smith called out.

There was an immediate hearty agreement with Smith on the part of all the mutineers with the exception of Thompson and Martin; but when Christian called for a show of hands, even these two raised theirs with the others.

"We have another matter to decide," Christian went on. "There are a number of men with us who took no part in seizing the vessel. They would have gone with Mr. Bligh had opportunity permitted . . ."

"Put 'em in irons, sir," Mills called out. "They'll do us a mischief if they can."

"On this ship, there shall be no putting of anyone in irons without good cause," Christian replied. "These men are not to be blamed for taking no part with us. They decided as seemed best to them, and I respect their decisions; but I shall know how to act if they show toward us any sign of treachery. It is for them to decide now what their treatment with us shall be."

He then called each of us in turn, beginning with Young, and asked whether he could count upon our coöperation, as members of the ship's company, so long as we remained in the *Bounty*. Young decided, then and there, to throw in his lot with the mutineers.

"Chance has decided this matter for me, Mr. Christian," he said. "I will not say that I would have helped you take the ship had I been awake at the time of the mutiny, but now that you have taken her, I am content that it should be so. I have no great desire to see England again. Wherever you may go you can count on me to go with you."

Of the neutral party, he was alone in this decision. The rest of us promised to obey orders, to assist in every way in working the ship, and to refrain from all treachery so long as we should remain aboard of her. Our numbers being what they were, this was the only thing we could do. Christian neither asked, nor, I think, expected, that we should not desert if an opportunity presented itself.

"That is sufficient," he said when he had heard us out. "I require from you no more than that. But you will understand that I must protect myself and these men from capture. In doing so I shall consider our interests before your own. You could not expect me to do otherwise."

He then appointed his officers. Young was made master, Stewart the master's mate, myself quartermaster, Morrison boatswain, and Alexander Smith boatswain's mate. Churchill was master-at-arms, as before. Burkitt and Hillbrandt were appointed quartermaster's mates. Millward and Byrne were to be the cooks. We were divided into three watches.

These matters being decided, we went about our duties. A part of the great cabin was fitted up as Christian's quarters, and as soon as they were ready the arms chest was removed there. He used it for his bed, and kept the keys always on his own person. One of the mutineers stood on guard, day and night, at the doorway to the cabin. As for Christian himself, he messed alone, and rarely spoke to anyone except to give an order. The captain of a vessel lives, of necessity, a solitary existence, but never could there have been one more lonely than Fletcher Christian. Despite the bitterness I felt toward him at this time, my heart softened as I watched him pacing the quarter-deck hour after hour, by day and by night. All the gaiety had gone out of him; there was never the hint of a smile on his face — only an expression of sombre melancholy.

Stewart, Young, and I messed together, as usual, but our meals were not the jolly affairs they had so often been in the past. It was impossible to become accustomed to the emptiness and silence of the ship. We avoided speaking of those who had gone in the launch, as one avoids speaking of the recently dead, but we were reminded of them at every turn; and the thought of their probable fate, and our own, put a damp upon our spirits hard to overcome. But this applied to Stewart and me rather than to Young. He seemed to have few regrets for the turn our fortunes had taken; indeed, he looked forward with pleasure, rather than otherwise, to the prospect of spending the remainder of his life on some island in the South Sea.

"We may as well make the best of it, lads," he said one evening when we were discussing the future. "It's far from a bad best, if you look at the matter sensibly. I've always wanted a life of ease. Ever since reading Captain Wallis's and Captain Cook's accounts of their discoveries in the Pacific, I've dreamed of nothing but tropical islands. When the chance came to ship with the *Bounty* I was the happiest man in England. I'm willing to confess now that, had it been possible, I would have deserted the ship at Tahiti."

"We shall never see Tahiti again, that is certain," said Stewart, gloomily. "It will be the last place Mr. Christian will consider as a refuge. He knows only too well that a ship of war will turn up there, sooner or later, in search of us."

"What does it matter?" asked Young. "There are scores, hundreds of other islands where we can live as happily. I advise the pair of you to put all thoughts of home out of your minds. The chances of your ever seeing England again are very remote. Make the most of what life offers you here."

Remote indeed they seemed then. After parting with the launch we had followed the course the ship was then on, west-northwest, until well into the afternoon; then we bore off to the eastward, since which time our general course had been east by south. We were now in unknown seas, in so far as I knew, off the track of any ship that had explored the Pacific. It was clear that Christian was in search of undiscovered islands, for we hove-to at night lest we should pass any in the darkness. Those days and nights were as peaceful as any that I remember. The absence of Bligh was a godsend to all of us, mutineers and non-mutineers alike. There was no more of the continual feeling of tension, of uncertainty as to what would happen, whenever the captain appeared upon deck. Christian maintained the strictest discipline, but no one had cause to complain of his justice. He was a born leader of men, and knew how to rule them without the perpetual floggings and abuse which Bligh considered so essential. After the turbulent events of the mutiny the men seemed glad of the tranquillity which had settled over the ship. The breeze blew steadily from the northeast, and the *Bounty* nosed her way quietly along as though she had mastered the task of sailing herself and required no further help from us. The moon waxed and was on the wane when, one morning shortly after sunrise, land was descried bearing west by north.

Late in the afternoon we approached to within a mile of the reef which seemed to enclose the island, forming a shallow lagoon where we saw many canoes plying back and forth. The island appeared to be about eight miles long. The interior was mountainous like that of Tahiti, although the land was not so high, and the lowlands surrounding it were covered with the same luxuriance of vegetation. As in most of the islands in that part of the Pacific, deep water came directly up to the reef, and we coasted along, close inshore. Several canoes, with ten or a dozen men in each, put off from the beach and soon came up with us. The Indians resembled the Tahitians in colour, stature, and the manner of their dress, and it was evident that they had never seen a European vessel before. We tried to persuade them to come alongside, and at last one of them paddled abreast of us at a distance of about thirty yards.

The men were strongly made, with handsome features and well-formed bodies. At Christian's order I spoke to them in the Tahitian language, asking them the name of their land. This they understood, and replied that it was Rarotonga. They seemed utterly astonished at my words. One of them replied at some length, but his speech was largely unintelligible. For all our friendly gestures we could not persuade them to approach more closely. Some trinkets Christian wished to give them were wrapped in a cloth and lowered over the side on a piece of planking. When we had let this drift well astern, they approached and took the parcel and the plank as well, which they put into their canoe without unwrapping the cloth to see what it contained.

Having failed in our efforts to persuade any of them to come on board, Christian gave orders to make sail, much to the regret of all of us, for this island was scarcely less beautiful than Tahiti, and, judging by the actions of the men in the canoes, the people would not have opposed our landing. It has always remained a puzzle to me why Christian did not choose this island as his hiding-place; for Rarotonga lies nearly seven hundred miles southwest of Tahiti, and at this time he had no reason to believe that its existence was known to any Europeans save ourselves. His reason may have been that, in coasting the entire length of one side of the island, no possible anchorage was to be seen; or perhaps, at this time, he was so disturbed in mind as to have no definite plans for the future.

One evening, greatly to my surprise, he sent for me to sup with him. The afterpart of the great cabin had been partitioned off for his use, and there I found him, seated at his table, with a copy of one of Captain Cook's charts outspread before him. He greeted me with formal politeness, but when he had dismissed the sentinel stationed outside and had closed the door, he fell back into the old friendly manner customary between us before the mutiny.

"I have asked you to sup with me, Byam," he said, "but you need not accept unless you choose."

I responded, against my inclination, to his friendly overtures. I had come to resent bitterly the ruin he had brought upon us all; but under the influence of his appealing kindly manner I found my indignation melting away. I stood before Fletcher Christian, my friend, not the mutineer who had cast nineteen men adrift in a small boat thousands of miles from home. To those who blame me I can merely say that they never knew the man.

He was in great need of someone to whom he could unburden his thoughts, and I had not been five minutes in his cabin before he was speaking of the mutiny.

"When I think of Bligh," he said, "I have no regrets. None whatever. I have suffered too much at his hands ever to care what his fate may be. But for those who went with him . . ."

He shut his eyes tightly and pressed his knuckles against them, as though to blot from his mind the picture of the small open boat, filled, almost to the point of foundering, with innocent men. Such desolation of heart was apparent in his voice and the expression on his face that I pitied him deeply. I knew that he would never know peace again — never until his last day. He begged me to profit by his example and never act upon impulse, and for all my sympathy I could not avoid saying that a mutiny so carefully and secretly planned could hardly be called an act of impulse.

"Good God!" he exclaimed. "Did you think it was planned? Ten minutes before Bligh was seized I had no more thought of mutiny than you yourself. Had it been an act of deliberation . . . Is it possible that you could have believed it?"

"What else could I think?" I replied. "It happened in your watch. When I was awakened by Churchill I found you in complete possession of the ship, with armed men stationed at the hatchways and all about the decks. It is inconceivable to me that all this could have happened without prearrangement."

"And yet it did," Christian replied, earnestly. "It was all the work of five minutes. Let me tell you. . . . Do you remember the talk we had the night before, during Peckover's watch?"

"Perfectly."

"I asked that, in case anything happened to me during the voyage home, you would explain the circumstances to my people when you reached England. My reason for speaking of this matter was that I planned to leave the ship before the morning watch. I had taken no one into my confidence except the quartermaster, John Norton, a man whom I knew I could trust. I was not willing that you should know. I wanted to spare your feelings until I had gone, and it was certain that you would have tried to dissuade me. Norton had managed to make, secretly, a tiny raft upon which I hoped to reach the island of Tofoa. With the sea as calm as it was, I had every reason to think that I could make the land."

"You really meant to cut yourself off for all time from home and friends?"

"Yes. I was in hell, Byam! I had suffered from Bligh's tyranny to the limit of my endurance. When he accused me, that same afternoon, with stealing his coconuts, I felt that I could bear no more."

"I know," I said; "you were sorely tried, but we were all in the same sorry situation with you."

"I didn't think of that. I thought only of the shame of the accusation; of the contemptible, sordid meanness of the man who could bring such a charge against his officers. I thought as well of the long voyage ahead of us, and I knew that I could not and would not endure another year of such torment.

"But luck was against me. The calmness and beauty of the night, so favourable otherwise to my purpose, were against me. As you know, most of the ship's company were on deck and, almost becalmed as we were, it would have been impossible to slip away unseen. At last I decided that the plan would have to be abandoned, temporarily at least. I should have to wait until we passed some other island farther to the westward.

"Even at four o'clock, when I took charge of the deck from Peckover, the thought of mutiny had not occurred to me. Believe this; I assure you that it is true. I paced up and down for some time, brooding over the repeated insults I had received from Bligh. I don't defend myself; I merely relate the facts. I was in a mood to kill the man. Yes, that thought crossed my mind more than once: why not murder him and be done with it? The temptation was all but overpowering. This will give you an indication of the state of my feelings at that time. I was, in sober truth, out of my mind.

"As you know, Hayward was the mate of my watch. In order to regain control of myself I went in search of him, and found him stretched out in the lee of the cutter, asleep. At another time such neglect of duty would have aroused my anger. We were in unknown waters, and Bligh had rightly given orders that the strictest watch should be kept, no matter how far we might be from land. Hayward was in charge of the forward deck, and three of the men, taking their cue from him, were asleep. I stood for a moment looking down at Hayward, and then, as plainly as though they had been spoken, I heard the words, 'Seize the ship.'

"From that moment my brain worked with the utmost clearness and precision. It appeared to function outside of me; I had only to obey its commands. I realized what an opportunity had presented itself, but not at all the wrong I should be doing the rest of you. Burkitt was awake, standing in the waist by the bulwarks on the larboard side. He had been frequently punished by Bligh and I knew that I could count on his help, but I didn't reveal my plan then — for I now had a plan. I asked him to come below with me and waken Churchill, Martin, Thompson, and Quintal, without disturbing anyone else, and to tell them I wanted to see them at the fore ladderway. Meanwhile I went to Coleman's hammock, roused him quietly, and asked for the key to the arms chest, saying that I wanted a musket to shoot a shark. He gave it to me, turned over in his hammock, and fell asleep again.

"I found Hallet asleep on the arms chest. As he was also of my watch, I roused him with a show of anger and set him on deck by the after ladderway. He was badly frightened at being caught, and begged me in a low voice to say nothing of the matter to Captain Bligh. Burkitt and the men he had awakened were awaiting me. They fell in at once with my plan. We provided ourselves with muskets and pistols, and I placed Thompson sentinel over the arms chest. We then roused McCoy, Williams, Alexander Smith, and others, every man of them promising his hearty support. They were given arms, and when I had placed sentinels at the hatchways we went to Bligh's cabin. The rest you know."

He fell silent and sat for some time with his head in his hands, staring at the deck between his feet. At length I forced myself to say, "What chance do you think Bligh has of reaching England?"

"Little enough. Timor is the nearest place where they could expect help. It is twelve hundred leagues from the place where the launch was cast adrift. . . . When I seized the ship my only thought was that I would carry Bligh home in irons. The men wouldn't have it; you saw that for yourself. I was forced to give way on that point. Then came the question of who was to go with him. My plan was, at first, to send only Fryer, Samuel, Hallet, and Hayward, but I could not refuse to let any others go with him who wished to; in fact, not to have done so would have been highly dangerous. Fryer, Purcell, Cole, and Peckover would, I knew, make every effort to form a party for retaking the ship, if kept with us. . . . Well, enough of this. What is done can't be undone. I now have to think of the men who are with me. The least I can do is to prevent them from being taken."

"And what of the rest of us?"

"I have been expecting that question. You have every right to ask it. I can't hope that any of you will give up all thoughts and hope of home and throw in your lot with us as Young has done. My predicament is only less hard than the one I have brought you into."

He rose and stood by one of the stern ports, looking out to westward, where the sun had just set. Presently he turned to me again.

"If I should take you to Tahiti and allow you to part company from us, none of you would feel bound to keep silence about the mutiny. For the present, much as I regret it, I must keep you with us. I can say no more. You must be content with that."

Of his immediate plans Christian said nothing, although he gave me to understand that we should be making land within a few days. On the morning of May 28, precisely four weeks after the mutiny, an island was seen dead to windward, distant about six leagues. We spent most of that day in beating up to it, and were becalmed toward nightfall about three miles off the western end. At dawn, when the trade wind made up again, we coasted along the barrier reef which lay a great way offshore, in places as far as two miles. Stewart, who had a perfect memory for latitudes and longitudes and for any chart he had seen, was convinced that this island was Tupuai, which had been discovered by Captain Cook. After nearly two months at sea, the place seemed a Garden of Eden to all of us and, mutineers and nonmutineers alike, we were eager to go ashore. There were various small islands scattered along the reef, and between them, across the lagoons, we had entrancing glimpses of the main island. All along the coast we saw evidences of a numerous population.

Christian now informed us that there was a pass through the reef into the lagoon, and that he meant to take the ship inside; but when we came abreast of the entrance we found a formidable array of Indians awaiting us. The entire male population of the island must have gathered there. We estimated their numbers at eight or nine hundred. All were armed with spears, clubs, and canoe loads of stones for repelling our entrance. There was no doubt of the hostility of their intentions; they would have none of our friendly overtures, but brandished their spears and sent such showers of stones on our decks from their slings that several of our men were hurt. We were forced to draw off the land, and from the masthead it was clear that the passage into the lagoon and the lagoon itself was scattered with coral shoals which would make navigation of the ship difficult, even granted that we were unmolested by the Indians. With them in opposition all hope of a landing had to be abandoned. Some of the mutineers were for turning the guns on the Indians, and had we done so we could have killed hundreds of them and brought the remainder under subjection; but Christian would have none of this plan. He was resolved that, wherever we went, we would make a peaceful settlement or none at all.

He now called a conference on the quarter-deck of the men of his own party, and the rest of us, with the exception of Young, were sent forward, out of hearing. At the end of a quarter of an hour the men dispersed to their duties, and it was plain that some decision had been reached pleasing to all of them. The ship was headed north.

Young was bound to say nothing of what had taken place at the meeting, and we refrained from asking him embarrassing questions. But, knowing our position, we also knew that north, if that course were to be held for several days, could mean only one thing: our destination was Tahiti. Morrison, Stewart, and I talked in whispers in the berth that evening. We scarcely dared hope for such good fortune as a return to Tahiti. There, if anywhere, we stood some chance of meeting any vessel that might be sent out to search for the *Bounty*. We might have to wait for several years, but a vessel was certain to come at last. We resolved that, if the *Bounty* called there, we would never come away in her. We would escape, somehow, and conceal ourselves until the ship had put to sea again.

## XI · THE LAST OF THE BOUNTY

On the day following our decision to escape, should the ship put in at Tahiti, Christian sent for me once more. I found him with Churchill in his cabin, and when he had motioned me to the settee he dismissed the sentinel and closed the door. Christian looked stern, sad, and careworn, but Churchill, who stood by the door with folded arms, greeted me with a smile. He was a tall, powerful fellow, in middle life, with cold blue eyes and a determined reckless face.

"I have sent for you, Mr. Byam," said Christian formally, "to acquaint you with our decision regarding you and your companions who had no hand in the taking of the ship. We bear you no ill-will, yet circumstances oblige us to take every precaution for our own safety. We are now steering for Tahiti, where we shall stop for a week or more while we load livestock and stores."

My face must have betrayed my thoughts, for Christian shook his head. "My first thought," he went on, "was to leave you there, where sooner or later you might hope for a ship to take you home. But the men would have none of it, and I fear that they are right."

He glanced at Churchill, who nodded, still standing with folded arms. "No, Mr. Byam," said the master-at-arms, "we had it out in the forecastle last night — a regular Dover-court. Not a man on the ship but wishes you well, but we can't allow it."

"They are right," said Christian gloomily; "we can neither leave you on Tahiti nor let you set foot on shore. The men were for keeping the lot of you below decks, under guard, but I persuaded them that if you and Mr. Stewart and Mr. Morrison would give parole not to mention the mutiny to the Indians, nor to say anything which might prejudice our interests, we might safely permit you to come on deck while we are at anchor in Matavai."

"I think I understand, sir," I replied, "though I must admit that we had hoped to be left in Tahiti, whither we supposed the ship to be bound."

"Impossible!" Christian said. "I hate to carry you away against your will, but it is essential to the safety of your shipmates. None of us will ever see England again — we must make up our minds to that. You may tell the others that it is my intention to search out one of the many unknown islands in this sea, land our stores and livestock, destroy the ship, and settle there for good, hoping never again to see a strange white face."

"Aye, Mr. Christian," put in Churchill approvingly. "It is the only way."

Christian stood up, to notify me that the interview was at an end, and I went on deck with a sinking heart. With the fresh east wind abeam, the *Bounty* was sailing fast on the starboard tack, rolling slowly and regularly to the lift of the swell. I stood by the lee gangway, watching the blue water swirl past the ship's side, and striving to collect my thoughts. Stewart and I had often discussed in privacy our hopes and fears for the future, and now, unless we found means to escape during the ship's sojourn in Matavai, our hopes seemed destined to come to naught. It was true that the parole demanded of us, if we were to be allowed on deck, contained no mention of escape, but I had no doubt that we should be closely watched. And even if we were lucky enough to escape, I realized that the chances were a hundred to one we should be retaken. Christian would have invented some plausible tale to account for the absence of Bligh and the others, and, as captain of the ship, the chiefs would be on his side. For the reward of a musket or two, they would have the mountains and valleys of the interior scoured by men certain to find us, no matter how distant and secret our hiding-place. Our only chance — a slender one, indeed — would be to get possession of a fast sailing canoe and make for the islands to leeward of Tahiti, whither the authority of Teina and the other great chiefs of north Tahiti did not extend. Once there, even though Christian learned our destination and gave pursuit, we might be able to dodge from island to island till he wearied of the chase.

To leave the ship under the eyes of the mutineers would be hard indeed; to set sail at once, in a fast and seaworthy canoe, watered and provisioned for a voyage across the open sea, would be harder still. Yet hardest of all was the thought of the alternative: "England — home, lost to us forever."

As I stood by the gangway, deep in these disquieting reflections, Stewart touched my arm. "Look," he said; "they are throwing the plants overboard!" Directed by Young, a line of men had formed on the ladderway, and they were beginning to pass the pots from hand to hand. A man by the rail, aft, pulled up each young plant by the roots and flung it overboard, while others emptied the earth into the sea and carried the pots to the forehatch. We carried more than a thousand young breadfruit trees, all in flourishing condition, and now the *Bounty* left a wake of their rich green foliage tossing on the blue swell. They had been gathered and cared for with infinite pains; to obtain them we had suffered hardships, braved unknown seas, and sailed more than twenty-seven thousand miles, in fair weather and foul. And now the plants, eagerly awaited in the West Indies, were going overboard like so much unwanted ballast.

"Waste!" remarked Stewart presently. "Futility and waste! And, like a good Scot, I hate both!"

It was sad to reflect on the results of the expedition: the plants thrown overboard; Bligh and his companions probably drowned or killed by savages; the mutineers, desperate and unhappy, planning to hide away forever from the face of mankind; ourselves forced to share the same hard fate.

Later, in the privacy of the berth, I told Stewart of my interview with Christian and of the gloomy prospect ahead of us. "We must tell Morrison as soon as possible," he said.

He was silent for some time, his thin, bronzed face expressionless. At last he looked up. "At least I'll see Peggy."

"That's certain, if you give your parole."

"I'd give that, and more, for a glimpse of her!" He rose abruptly and began to pace back and forth nervously. I said nothing, and presently he went on in a low voice: "Forgive me for inflicting my thoughts on you — seamen are sentimental, and I have been long at sea. But Peggy might be the means of effecting our escape — I can think of no other."

"That she might!" I exclaimed, for I had given the subject much anxious thought. "She could obtain a canoe for us — a favour we could ask of no other person in Matavai. Since we must give our parole we cannot make known the true state of affairs, nor why we desire to leave the ship. You will have to tell Peggy that we are planning to desert, as Churchill and the others deserted, in order to live among the Indians after the ship is gone. The chiefs alone own vessels large enough to take us to the Leeward Islands, and both Teina and Hitihiti feel themselves too much indebted to the friendship of King George to take part in what they would regard as a conspiracy against him. Peggy's father is under no such obligation."

Stewart seated himself once more. His mind was quicker than my own, and he had perceived in an instant what had taken me some time to puzzle out.

"Precisely," he said. "Peggy is our only chance. I could arrange everything in ten minutes alone with her. It must be on a night when the wind holds from the east. The canoe will be paddled past the ship as if outbound on one of their night passages to Tetiaroa, and her crew must make some disturbance which will draw the men of the watch to that side of the *Bounty*. We can then slip overboard on the other side and swim to Peggy's vessel, which will lie hove-to while they get sail on her. With good luck, no one will observe us in the dark."

"By God, Stewart! I believe it can be done!"

"Must be done, rather! Morrison and I are Navy men, and we have our careers to think of. But there have been many times when I have longed to stay here."

On the evening of the fifth of June we raised the highlands of Tahiti, far ahead and ghostly among the clouds, and on the following afternoon we sailed into Matavai Bay and dropped anchor close to Point

Venus. Every man on board had been instructed what to tell the Indians of his acquaintance who might make inquiries: at Aitutaki we had fallen in with Captain Cook, Bligh's father, who was forming an English settlement on that island. Bligh, Nelson, and others of the *Bounty's* crew had been taken aboard Cook's ship, and he had ordered the *Bounty* to leave the breadfruit plants with him, and return to Tahiti to trade for further stores and whatever livestock it might be possible to obtain. The ship was then to set sail in search of another island suitable for settlement.

The Indians flocked out to the ship — Teina, Hitihiti, and the other chiefs curious to know why we had returned so soon and what had become of the absent members of the ship's company. The story invented by Christian satisfied them completely, and since he was popular — much more so than Bligh — the natives promised to furnish everything we desired, and the trading was friendly and brisk.

I dined with Christian that evening; his sweetheart and old Hitihiti, my *taio,* were the other guests. With the girl — who would eat nothing — at his side, Christian seemed to have shaken off for the moment the sombre mood from which he had not emerged since the mutiny. He raised his glass and smiled at me across the table.

"To our sweethearts," he said lightly. "You can drink to mine, Byam, since you have none of your own." Maimiti smiled gravely and touched the glass with her lips, but my *taio* drained his wine at a gulp.

"Stop ashore my house, Byam," he said.

I could feel Christian's eyes on me as I replied. "I'm sorry," I said; "but we shall be here only a few days, and Mr. Christian has informed me that I shall be needed on board."

Hitihiti was evidently surprised at this. He turned to Christian, who nodded.

"Yes," he said. "He will be needed on board during the whole time we are at anchor here." The old chief understood enough of discipline on a British ship to let the subject drop.

Peggy had come on board during the afternoon, and when I went on deck after dinner I saw the couple seated by the mainmast, in the shadow of the pumps. Stewart's arm was about her waist and they were speaking together in the Indian tongue. When she had gone ashore, Stewart, Morrison, and I met by agreement on the main hatch. Young was the officer of the watch, and since we were at anchor and the night was calm, he had given his men permission to sleep on deck. He was a carefree, unsuspicious fellow, and now he lolled on the poop, his head turned toward the dark loom of the land. Taurua, his Indian sweetheart, kept the watch with him — a slender ghostly figure, shrouded in white tapa. The night was chilly, for it was winter in Tahiti, and Matavai Bay was a black mirror to reflect the stars.

"I have talked with Peggy," said Stewart in a low voice, "and explained our determination to desert the ship. She thinks that I am leaving for her sake — a half-truth, at least. As for you two, she believes that you are enamoured of the Indian life, or of some of the young ladies on shore. Peggy will aid us with her whole heart. Unfortunately, the only large canoe her family possesses is at Tetiaroa. She will send a small vessel to fetch it to-morrow if the wind is fair."

"Then let us pray for a fair wind," said Morrison seriously.

"I wish we could take the others," I said.

"There will be no chance of that," Morrison replied. "Christian means to keep them confined below till the ship sails."

"In any case there would be too many," said Stewart. "Their very numbers would make escape impossible."

Morrison shrugged his shoulders. "No — we can think only of ourselves. I have only one desire, one thought — to return to England. A ship will come, you may count on that, though we may have to wait two or three years for her. We shall have to be patient, that is all."

"Patient?" Stewart remarked. "Well, I could put up with three years here — or with four or five! And Byam is a lover of the Indian life."

"Damn the Indian life," said Morrison without a smile. "Who knows what wars are going on, what chances for prize-money and promotion we are missing!"

I went to sleep with a light heart that night, for our escape seemed a certainty, and the prospect of a year or two among the Indians was far from displeasing. At dawn I saw Peggy's light double canoe, paddled by half-a-dozen stalwart fellows, set out for Tetiaroa, and all through the forenoon I watched every sign of the weather anxiously. Nature herself now took a hand against us. The day turned chilly and films of cloud began to stream seaward off the mountains. We were in the lee of the high land, and Matavai Bay remained still as a lake, but the wind had chopped around to the south and was blowing up one of the boisterous southerly storms the Indians call *maraai*. Gazing out to sea,

I perceived the line of whitecaps at the end of the lee, and knew that as long as the south wind held, no canoe would even attempt to return from the island north of us.

Day after day the strong south wind blew, while we traded for our strange cargo. Hogs, fowls, dogs, and cats came on board till the ship resembled a menagerie, and finally the bull and the cow left on Tahiti by Captain Cook. Goats skipped about comically on deck, among mounds of taro, sweet potatoes, and yams. And little by little our hope, which had run so high, began to change to fear. There were signs that Christian was nearly ready to sail, and Peggy's face, when she visited her lover on board, grew haggard with anxiety. I shall not dwell on our suspense. It is enough to say that on the ninth day the wind shifted to northeast and brought our sailing canoe in, four hours after the shift. This was at noon and all was arranged for our escape the same night, but now at the last moment fate turned against us once more. At two o'clock in the afternoon Christian ordered the anchor up and, close-hauled on the starboard tack, the *Bounty* sailed out of Matavai Bay.

The months from June to September of that year, 1789, are a night-mare in my memory, and since they have little to do with the main thread of this narrative, I shall give them no more space than they deserve.

In spite of our hostile reception when we first visited Tupuai, Chris-tian had determined to settle on that island. We were now southbound, like modern Noahs on our Ark, with livestock of various kinds to increase and multiply on the island, and even a few Indian Eves to be-come the grandmothers of a new race — half white, half brown. Chris-tian's Maimiti was on board, and Young's Taurua; and Alexander Smith, distrustful of the ladies of Tupuai, had persuaded Bal'hadi to accompany him. Nor was any great degree of persuasion necessary, for the Indians were passionately fond of travel and adventure of any sort. Long after Tahiti had disappeared below the horizon north of us, it was discovered that we had on board nine Indian men, twelve women, and eight boys, most of them stowaways.

Our reception on Tupuai was at first friendly, owing to the Tahitian passengers, who explained our desire to settle on the island. With incredible labour we hauled the ship up on land and built thatched shelters to protect her decks from the sun. We then built a fort, on a point of land purchased from one of the chiefs, and surrounded it with a moat twenty feet deep and twice as wide, all hands, including Christian himself, taking part in the work. The men murmured much at this truly Herculean labour, but Christian's foresight was soon evident. Our goats, loosed to increase among the mountains of the interior, descended on the taro gardens of the Indians, which they cultivate and water with infinite pains. Unable to capture or kill the wary animals, the people came to us, asking us to shoot them with our muskets. When we refused, explaining that the progeny of the marauders would provide an important supply of food, the Indians at first murmured and then broke out in open hostility, declaring that they would never cease their efforts until we were either exterminated or driven from the island for good. Time after time they attacked our fortress furiously, only to be driven off by the fire of our four-pounders and swivels, and before long it became impossible to venture outside save in strong parties, heavily armed. Our lives grew insupportable; even the hardiest among us wearied of the constant fighting, and early in September, perceiving that all hands were heartily sick of the place, Christian assembled the lot of us and called for a show of hands. All were for leaving Tupuai; sixteen expressed a desire to be left on Tahiti, and the rest wished to sail away with the *Bounty* to search for some uninhabited island where they might settle in peace. On being informed of our decision to leave Tupuai, the Indians agreed to cease hostilities while we launched and watered the ship, and after a week of labour such as falls to the lot of few men, we got the *Bounty* launched, her sails bent, and water and stores aboard. At the last moment, on the verge of leaving this ill-omened place, we nearly lost the ship in a tremendous squall which made up unperceived during the night. As it was, we lost the spare gaff of the driver and all our spare topgallant yards.

At daybreak, with a fresh breeze at east, we weighed and sailed out through the narrow passage, heartily glad to be clear of a place where we had met with nothing but misfortune and strife, and five days later, after an agreeable voyage, we were at anchor once more in Matavai Bay. The following men had decided to remain on the ship: — Fletcher Christian, Acting Lieutenant; John Mills, Gunner's Mate; Edward Young, Midshipman; William Brown, Gardener; Isaac Martin, William McCoy, John Williams, Matthew Quintal, and Alexander Smith, Able Seamen.

The rest of the *Bounty's* company had elected to remain on Tahiti. I was overjoyed at this sudden change in my fortunes, as were Stewart and Morrison. My old friend Hitihiti was among the first of the Indians to come off to us, and when I informed him that I hoped to go ashore and make my home at his house, his face beamed with smiles. As he had come out in a double canoe large enough to freight all my belongings ashore, I lost no time in asking Christian's permission to leave the ship. I found him at the main hatch, superintending the division of the muskets, cutlasses, pistols, and ammunition, of which each man was to have his share.

"By all means," he said, looking up from the paper in his hand. "Go ashore whenever you like. And take a musket with you and a supply of lead to mould bullets. We are so short of powder that I can give only a few charges to each man. You will stop with Hitihiti, of course?"

"That is my intention, sir."

"I shall see you to-night, then. I wish to speak to you and to Stewart — I shall ask him to be there an hour after sundown."

My hammock man and his lusty Indian wench lent me a hand to get my things out of the berth, and after a farewell glance about the *Bounty's* decks, and a silent handshake with Edward Young, I followed my belongings into Hitihiti's canoe.

It was like a homecoming to return once more to the house of my *taio,* to greet Hina and her husband, and to see Hitihiti's grandchildren running to welcome me. I had lived so long among these kind people that they seemed joined to me by ties closer than those of mere friendship.

When I had stowed my belongings and precious manuscript I became at once the centre of a circle of all ages, eager to hear the story of our adventures. I recounted at length, in the Indian tongue, the history of our attempt to settle on Tupuai, and ended by expressing some sympathy with the people of that island, who, after all, had done no more than repel what they considered an invasion of their home. Hina shook her head indignantly.

"No!" she exclaimed; "you are wrong. I have seen some of those people, who came here in a large canoe five years ago. They are savages! You should have killed them all and taken their island!"

"You are fierce, Hina," I said with a smile. "Why should we kill innocent men, whose only fault was love of their land? Had we desired to kill them, Christian would not have allowed it."

"He was foolish, then. Did they not try to kill him, and you? But what will you do, now that you have returned? Shall you be long among us?"

"To-morrow or the day after, Christian and eight of the others will set sail for Aitutaki to rejoin Captain Cook. The rest of us, who love your island, have permission to settle here."

All of us who were to be left on Tahiti had given our words to tell the same story, and, little as I liked the task, I lied with a brazen face. Hina leaned towards me and seized me in a strong embrace, smelling at my cheek affectionately.

"Ah, Byam," she said, "we are delighted, all of us! The house has been empty since you sailed away!"

"Aye," said her husband heartily. "You are one of us, and we shall not let you go!"

Early in the evening Stewart appeared on the path from Matavai, accompanied by Peggy and her father, old Tipau. Hitihiti had returned to the ship, to fetch Christian and his niece. I walked down to the beach with Stewart and his sweetheart, leaving the old chief to gossip with the others in the house.

The calm Pacific nuzzled lazily at the sands, and we sat quietly, as if the beauty of the evening had cast upon us a spell of silence and immobility.

Twilight was fading to night when Stewart started slightly and gazed out to sea. "There they come!" he said. Rising and falling on the gentle swell outside the reef, I saw the double canoe — a moving shadow on the waters. She came on rapidly, and before long her prows grounded on the sand and Christian sprang out, turning to help Maimiti over the high gunwale. He nodded to us, saying only, "Wait for me here," and followed Hitihiti to the house to take leave of his sweetheart's family. At a word from Stewart, Peggy followed him.

The sight of Christian on the twilit beach had moved me deeply. It was not hard to imagine his feelings on the eve of this final departure from Tahiti. Presently I heard a rustle in the bushes behind us, and his step falling softly on the sand. We rose, but he motioned us to seat ourselves, and sank down cross-legged beside us, casting aside his hat and running his fingers through his thick dark hair.

"This is the last time I shall see you," he said abruptly, after a long silence. "We shall sail in the morning, as soon as the wind makes up.

"I have told you the story of the mutiny," he went on; "remember that I, and I alone, am responsible. In all probability, Bligh and those with him are long since dead — drowned or killed by savages. In the case of Bligh, I have no regrets; the thought of the others, innocent men, lies heavy on my conscience. You know the circumstances; they may explain, even to some extent excuse, the action I took, but they can never exonerate me. I am a mutineer and, since I made off with one of His Majesty's ships, a pirate as well. It is my duty to guide and protect those who have chosen to follow me. You know my plans. This is the greatest ocean in the world, set with innumerable islands. On one of them — north, or south, or east, or west of here — we shall settle, and destroy the ship. You shall see us no more — I promise you that."

Again silence fell upon us. The stillness of the night was broken only by the faint lap and wash of the sea, and far down the beach, where a fire of coconut husks made a ruddy point of light, I heard the wail of an awakening child.

"Sooner or later," Christian went on, after a long pause, "a British man-of-war will drop anchor here. If Bligh, or any of his men, succeed in reaching England, the Admiralty will dispatch a ship at once, to apprehend the mutineers. If, as I fear, all those in the *Bounty's* launch are lost, a vessel will be sent out, after a reasonable period of waiting, in search of us. When she comes, I desire you earnestly to go out to her at once and give yourselves up to the officer in command — you two, and the others who had no hand in the mutiny. You are innocent, and no harm can come to you. As for the others, let them behave as they think best. Since they refuse to follow me, I am forced to wash my hands of them.

"Once before, Byam, in a moment of desperation, I requested you to communicate with my father, in the event of my not reaching home. Fate was against me that night! Had I succeeded in leaving the ship . . . My father is Charles Christian, of Mairlandclere, in Cumberland. Will one of you, the first to reach England, go to him and explain the circumstances of the mutiny? Tell him the story as I have told it to you, and explain particularly that my design was only to relieve Bligh of his command and take him home in irons. A full acquaintance with the truth may extenuate in my father's eyes, though never justify, the crime I have committed. Will you do this for me?"

Christian stood up and Stewart and I sprang to our feet. I was the first to seize Christian's hand.

"Yes," I said, too moved for further speech.

A moment later Christian turned to hail the house. "Maimiti!" he called, in his strong seaman's voice. She must have been awaiting the call, for she appeared almost instantly, a slender white figure flitting under the palms. The paddlers followed her, seized the canoe, and dragged it into the wash of the sea. The Indian girl came to me without a word and embraced me tenderly in the fashion of her people. Still in silence she embraced Stewart, and sprang into the canoe. Christian shook our hands for the last time. "God bless you both!" he said.

We stood on the beach, watching the double canoe fade into the night. At dawn, when I walked out of the house for a plunge in the sea, the *Bounty* was standing offshore with all sail set, heading north, with the light easterly breeze abeam.

## XII · TEHANI

THOUGH I had reason to congratulate myself on my present situation, the week following the *Bounty's* departure was an unhappy time for me. For the first time in my life, I think, I began to question the doctrines of the Church in which I had been brought up, and to ask myself whether human destiny was ordered by divine law or ruled by chance. If God were all-powerful and good, I thought, with a lad's simplicity, why had He permitted one man, in a moment of not unrighteous anger against oppression and injustice, to ruin his own life and the lives of so many others? Many a good and innocent man had accompanied Bligh in the launch: where were they now? The majority of the mutineers themselves were simple fellows with a grievance that might have led better men to revolt. Held in subjection by the iron law of the sea, they had endured with little complaint the hardships of the long voyage and the temper of a man considered brutal in a brutal age. Had Bligh not goaded his junior officer beyond endurance, no other man on the ship would have raised the cry of mutiny, and the voyage would have been completed peacefully. But one moment of passion had changed everything. Out of the whole ship's company, only seven of us — those who had had no hand in the mutiny and were now awaiting the first English ship — had come out of the affair scot-free. And our fate could scarcely be termed enviable — marooned for an indefinite time among Indians, on an island at the very ends of the earth. As for the mutineers who had chosen to remain on Tahiti, I knew only too well what their fate was likely to be. Young Ellison, who had been our mess boy, was often in my thoughts at this time. He had no realization of the gravity of the part he had played. Yet I knew that unless he quitted Tahiti before the arrival of a British man-of-war, our sea law would infallibly condemn him to death.

During those days of doubt and depression at Hitihiti's house, when Hina strove to divert my thoughts and my good old *taio* tried fruitlessly to cheer me up, I ceased to be a boy and became a man. Morrison was settled with Poino, the famous warrior who lived not far off, and Stewart was living with Peggy, in the house of Tipau, at the foot of One Tree Hill. I went frequently to pass the time of day with these two friends, and from their example learned to be ashamed of my fruitless depression. Morrison and Millward, who lived with Stewart at Poino's house, were already planning the little schooner they eventually built, and in which, without awaiting the arrival of a ship from home, they hoped to sail to Batavia, whence they might get passage to England. Stewart, who loved gardening, worked daily at beautifying the grounds about the new house old Tipau was building for him. When I mentioned my thoughts to him, he only smiled and said: "Never worry about what you cannot change," and went on with his digging, and planting, and laying out of paths. Perceiving at last that hard work was the remedy for my greensickness, I set to once more on my dictionary and was soon absorbed in the task.

One morning, about ten days after the departure of the *Bounty*, I found myself unable to sleep and set out for a walk on the long curving beach that led to Point Venus. It was still an hour before dawn, but the stars were bright and the northerly breeze blowing from the region of the equator made the air warm and mild. A dog barked at me as I passed an encampment of fishermen asleep on the sands under blankets of bark cloth. Their great net, hung on stakes to dry, stretched for a quarter of a mile along my path. At the very tip of the point, sheltered by the reef and provided with a deep, safe entrance, lies one of the most beautiful little harbours on the island, resorted to by travelers in sailing canoes who wish to pass the night on shore. The water is always calm and beautifully clear, and a good-sized vessel can be moored so close in shore than a man may leap from her stern to the beach.

The point was a favourite resort of mine at this hour, for the view up the coast at sunrise was one I loved. I was pleased to find the cove deserted, and, settling myself comfortably on one of the high sand dunes, I gazed eastward, where the first faint flush of dawn was beginning to appear. At that moment a slight sound caught my ear, and, glancing seaward, I perceived that a large sailing canoe was stealing in through the passage. Her great brown sails of matting were ghostly blots on the sea, and presently I could hear the low commands of the man at the masthead, conning her in. She came on fast under her press of sail, rounded-to smartly inside, and dropped her stone anchor with a resounding plunge. The sails were furled while paddlers brought her stern to the land, and a man sprang ashore to make fast her stern-line to a coconut stump.

From the size of the vessel and the number of her crew, I judged that she carried passengers of consequence, but whoever they were, they still slept under the little thatched awning aft. Several of the crew came on land to build a fire of coconut husks and prepare food for the morning meal, and I saw two women helped ashore, who strolled away westward along the point and disappeared.

It was full daylight, with the rim of the sun just above the horizon, when I rose, unperceived by the travelers, and walked across to the large river which emptied into the sea on the west side of the point. It was called Vaipoopoo, and close to the mouth there was a long reach of deep clear water in which I loved to swim — a quiet and beautiful spot, distant from the habitations of the Indians. The water was a good twenty yards across and so deep that a boat of twelve tons burthen might have entered to a distance of a quarter of a mile. Tall old *mape* trees arched overhead, their buttressed roots forming many a rustic seat along the banks.

I had long since chosen such a seat for myself, high above the still water and at a distance of about a cable's length from the beach. Frequently in the late afternoon I spent an hour or two alone at this place, listening to the rustling of the trees high overhead, and watching the small speckled fresh-water fish as they rose for their evening meal of flies. In my fancy I had named this spot Withycombe, after our home in England, for indeed there were moments when the place seemed English to the core, when I fancied myself in the warm summer twilight at home, watching the trout rise in one of our West Country streams.

To Withycombe, then, I repaired for my morning bath. I threw off the light mantle of Indian cloth from my shoulders and girded up the kilt about my waist. Next moment I slipped into the deep clear water and swam leisurely downstream, drifting with the gentle flow of the current. High in a tree overhead a bird was singing — an *omaomao,* whose song is sweeter than that of our English nightingale.

As I drifted downstream I perceived suddenly, seated among the buttressed roots of an old tree, a young girl lovely as a water-sprite. I must have made some slight splashing sound, for she turned her head with a little start and gazed full into my eyes. I recognized her at once — she was Tehani, whom I had seen in Tetiaroa long before. She gave no sign of shyness or embarrassment, for a girl of her position had in those days nothing to fear by day or by night, alone or in company. A rude word to her would have been the cause of instant death to the offender; an act of violence to her person might easily have brought on a devastating war. This sense of security imparted to the girls of Tehani's class an innocent assurance of manner which was by no means the least of their charms.

"May you live!" I said, Indian-fashion, rounding-to against the current.

"And you!" replied Tehani, with a smile. "I know who you are! You are Byam, the *taio* of Hitihiti!" .

"True," said I, eager to prolong the conversation. "Shall I tell you who *you* are? You are Tehani, Poino's relative! I saw you in Tetiaroa, when you danced there."

She laughed aloud at this. "Ah, you saw me? Did I dance well?"

"So beautifully that I have never forgotten that night!"

"*Arero mona!*" she exclaimed mockingly, for the Indians call a flatterer "sweet tongue."

"So beautifully," I went on as if I had not heard, "that I said to Hitihiti: 'Who is yonder girl, lovelier than any girl in Tahiti, who might be the young goddess of the dance herself?'"

"*Arero mona!*" she mocked again, but I could see the blush mantling her smooth cheeks. She had just come out of the river and her brown hair lay in damp ringlets on her shoulders. "Come — let us see which can swim further under water, you or I!" Tehani slipped into the stream, and dived so smoothly that she scarcely rippled the still water. Clinging to the great root which had been her seat, I watched for what seemed an interminable time. The river turned in a bend about fifty yards below me, and at last, from out of sight beyond the bend, I heard Tehani's voice. "Come," she called gaily. "It is your turn to try!"

I dove at the words and began to swim downstream, about a fathom deep. The water was clear as air and I could see the shoals of small bright fish scatter before me and seek refuge among the shadowy boulders below. On and on I went, determined that no girl should excel me in the water, an element I have always loved. Aided by the current, my progress was swift, and finally, when my lungs would endure no more and I felt satisfied that I had won, I came to the surface with a gasp. A chuckle musical as the murmur of the stream greeted me, and shaking the water from my eyes I saw the girl seated on a long root, flush with the water, a full ten yards beyond.

"You came up there?" I asked in some chagrin.

"I have not cheated."

"Let us rest for a little while, and then I shall try again."

Tehani patted the root beside her. "Come and rest here," she said.

I pulled myself up beside her, shaking the wet hair back from my eyes. Moved by common impulse, our two heads turned, and Tehani's clear brown eyes smiled into mine. She turned away suddenly and all at once I felt my heart beating fast. Her hand was close to mine on the rough gnarled root; I took it gently, and since it was not withdrawn I locked my fingers in hers. She bent her head to gaze into the clear water, and for a long time neither of us spoke.

I gazed, not at the water, but at the beautiful girl at my side. She wore only a light kilt of white cloth, and her bare shoulder and arm, turned to me, were smooth as satin and of the most exquisite proportions. Her feet and hands, small and delicately made, might have been envied by a princess, and Phidias himself could have produced in cold marble nothing one half so lovely as her young breasts, bared in all innocence. In her face I saw sweetness and strength.

"Tehani!" I said, and took her hand in both of mine.

She made no answer, but raised her head slowly and turned to me. Then all at once, and without a word between us, she was in my arms. The faint perfume of her hair intoxicated me, and for a time the beating of my heart made speech impossible. It was the girl who spoke first.

"Byam," she asked, stroking my wet hair caressingly, "have you no wife?"

"No," I replied.

"I have no husband," said the girl.

At that moment I heard a woman's voice calling from downstream: "Tehani! Tehani O!" The girl hailed back, bidding the caller to wait, and turned to me.

"It is only my servant who came ashore with me. I bade her wait at the mouth of the stream while I bathed."

"You came from Tetiaroa?" I asked, with her head on my shoulder and my arm about her waist.

"No, I have been to Raiatea with my uncle. We have been two days and two nights at sea."

"Who is your uncle?"

The girl turned to me in real astonishment. "You do not know?" she said incredulously.

"No."

"Yet you speak our tongue like one of us! Strange men, you English — I have never talked with one of you before. My uncle is Vehiatua, of course, high chief of Taiarapu."

"I have often heard of him."

"Are you a chief in your own land?"

"A very small one, perhaps."

"I knew it! Knew it the moment I laid eyes on you! Hitihiti would not take as his *taio* a common man."

Again we fell silent, both conscious that our words reflected only the surface of our minds. "Tehani!" I said.

"Yes."

She raised her head and I kissed her in the English fashion, full on the lips. We walked back to the cove hand in hand, while the servant followed us, her eyes round with wonder.

Vehiatua had come ashore and was at breakfast when we came to the cove. He was a nobly proportioned old man, with thick gray hair and a manner of cheerful, good-natured dignity. His retainers were grouped about him as he ate, serving him with breadfruit, grilled fish fresh from the coals, and bananas from a great bunch they had brought ashore. The old chief's tattooing, which covered every portion of his body save his face, was the most beautiful and intricate I have ever seen. I was glad that I wore only my kilt, for it is discourteous to approach the great Indian chiefs with covered shoulders. Vehiatua gave no sign of surprise at sight of me.

"Eh, Tehani," he called out affectionately to his niece. "Your breakfast is ready for you on board. And who is the young man with you?"

"The *taio* of Hitihiti — Byam is his name."

"I have heard of him." And then, turning to me courteously, Vehiatua asked me to join him at his meal. I sat down beside him, nothing loth, and answered his questions regarding Hitihiti and the *Bounty*, of which he had heard much. He expressed surprise at my knowledge of the Indian tongue, and I told him of my mission and how my *taio* had aided me.

"And now you and the others are settling on Tahiti to remain among us?" Vehiatua asked.

"For a long time, at any rate," I replied. "It is possible that when the next British ship arrives, in two years or three, King George may send word that one or all of us must go home."

"Aye," said the old aristocrat, "one must obey one's king!"

Presently Tehani came ashore, her breakfast over and her toilet made, very different from the young tomboy who had beaten me at diving so short a time before. Her beautiful hair, dried in the sun, combed out and perfumed, was dressed in the Grecian fashion, low on the nape of her neck. Her mantle of snow-white cloth was draped in classic folds, and she walked ahead of her little band of women with an air of dignity few English girls of sixteen could have assumed. The chief gave me a nod and rose to his feet.

"Let us go to the house of my kinsman," he said.

A stout muscular fellow crouched before Vehiatua, hands braced on his knees. The chief vaulted to his shoulders with the ease of long practice, and the human horse stood upright with a grunt. Vehiatua, Teina, and two or three other great chiefs of those days were never permitted to walk, for the touch of their feet rendered a commoner's land theirs. Wherever they went, save in their own domains, they were borne on the backs of men trained to the task.

With Tehani at my side, I followed her uncle down the beach, walking on the hard moist sand at the water's edge. As we passed the encampment of fishermen they hastened to throw off the mantles from their shoulders and seat themselves on the sand. To remain standing while a high chief passed would have been the greatest of insults.

"*Maeva te arii!*" was their greeting. (Hail to the chief!)

"May you live," said Vehiatua affably; "and may your fishing prosper!"

Old Hitihiti met us before his door, throwing off his mantle and stepping forward with bare shoulders to greet his friend. A meal was being prepared, and though our visitor had just eaten a prodigious quantity of food, he expressed his willingness to share in a second breakfast. Tehani and Hina knew each other well and seemed to have much to talk over. From the glances Hina cast at me from time to time, I suspected that Tehani was telling her of our meeting in the stream.

Toward noon, when the others had sought out shady places in which to spread their mats for a nap, I found my *taio* awake. He was alone, under his favourite hibiscus tree close to the beach, and I told him of my meeting with the girl, and that I loved her too dearly for my peace of mind.

"Why not marry her, if she is willing?" asked Hitihiti, when I had done.

"I think she might be willing, but what would her parents say?"

"She has none; both are dead."

"Vehiatua then."

"He likes you."

"Very well. But suppose we were married, and an English ship came with orders that I must go home."

My *taio* shrugged his great shoulders in despair. "You English are all alike," he said impatiently; "you make yourselves miserable by thinking of what may never happen! Is not to-day enough, that you must think of to-morrow and the day after that? The thought of an English ship makes you hesitate to marry the girl you fancy! And ten years, or twenty, might pass before another ship arrives! Enough of such talk! Yesterday is gone; you have to-day; to-morrow may never come!"

I could not help smiling at my old friend's philosophic outburst, not without its grain of sound common sense — called "common" because it is so rare. Worry over the future is without doubt the white man's greatest strength and greatest weakness in his quest of happiness — the only conceivable object in life. To the people of Tahiti, worry over the future was unknown; their language indeed contained no word with which to express such an idea.

No doubt Hitihiti was right, I reflected; since I was destined to live a long time among the Indians, I was justified in adopting their point of view. "You are my *taio*," I said. "Will you intercede for me with Vehiatua? Tell him that I love his niece dearly, and desire to marry her?"

The old chief clapped me on the back. "With all my heart!" he exclaimed. "You have been too long without a wife! Now let me sleep."

Tehani was awake before the others had finished their siesta, and I found her strolling on the beach. We were alone, and she came to me swiftly. "Sweetheart," I said, "I have spoken to my *taio,* and he has promised to ask Vehiatua for your hand. I have not done wrong?"

"I spoke to my uncle before he lay down to sleep," Tehani replied, smiling. "I told him I wanted you for my husband and must have you. He asked if you were willing, and I said that I must have you, willing or not! 'Do you want me to make war on Hitihiti and kidnap his friend?' he asked. 'Yes,' said I, 'if it comes to that!' He looked at me affectionately and then said: 'Have I ever denied you anything, my little pigeon, since your mother died? This Byam of yours is English, but he is a man nevertheless, and no man could resist you!' Tell me, do you think that is true?"

"I am sure of it!" I answered, pressing her hand.

When we returned to the house the sun was low, and the two chiefs, who had dismissed their followers, were conversing earnestly. "Here they are!" said Vehiatua, as we came in hand in hand.

"And well content with one another," remarked my *taio* smilingly.

"Vehiatua gives his consent to the marriage," he went on to me. "But he makes one condition — you are to spend most of your time in Tautira. He cannot bear to be separated from his niece. You will sympathize with him, Byam, and I too can understand. But you must come often to visit old Hitihiti, you two!"

"You are to be married at once, Tehani says, and in my house," said the chief of Taiarapu. "You can sail with me to-morrow, and Hitihiti and Hina will follow in their single canoe. They will represent your family at the temple. You two may consider yourselves betrothed."

I rose at these words and went into the house to open my box. When I returned, I carried the bracelet and the necklace purchased in London so long before. I showed them first to Vehiatua, who turned them admiringly in his hands.

"My gift to Tehani," I explained. "With your permission."

"She should be happy, for no girl in these islands possesses such things. I have seen gold, and know that it is very precious and does not rust like iron. A royal gift, Byam! What may we give you in return?"

"This!" I said, clasping the necklace about Tehani's neck, and taking her by the shoulders as if I would carry her off.

Vehiatua chuckled approvingly. "Well answered!" he said. "A royal gift in truth. For three and seventy generations she can count her ancestors back to the gods! Look at her! Where in all these islands will you find her like?"

Early the next morning, Vehiatua's men carried my belongings to the cove, and presently we went on board and the paddlers drove the vessel out through the passage, in the morning calm. She was the finest of all the Indian ships I had seen — her twin hulls each well over a hundred feet long, and twelve feet deep in the holds. Her two masts, well stayed and fitted with ratlines up which the sailors could run, spread huge sails of matting, edged with light frames of wood. On the platform between the two hulls was the small house in which the chief and his women slept, and it was here, sheltered from the rays of the sun, that I was invited to recline during our forty-mile voyage.

We paddled westward, skirting the long reefs of Pare, till the wind made up, and then, spreading our sails, we raced down the channel between Tahiti and Eimeo, with a fresh breeze at north-northeast. Toward noon, when we were off the point of Maraa, the wind died away and presently made up strong from the southeast, so that we were obliged to make a long board out to sea. I perceived at this time that the large Indian canoes, like Vehiatua's, could outpoint and outfoot any European vessel of their day. With the wind abeam they would have left our best frigates hull-down in no time, and, close-hauled, they would lay incredibly close to the wind.

The sea was rough off shore, and nearly all of the women on board were sick, but I was delighted to observe that Tehani was as good a sailor as I. She was *tapatai,* as the Indians said — fearless of wind and sea. As we approached the southern coast of Tahiti Nui, she pointed out to me the principal landmarks on shore, and on Taiarapu, beyond the low isthmus toward which we were steering. The southeast wind fell away an hour before sunset, as we were entering a wide passage through the reefs. The sails were furled and, with a score of paddlers on each side, we rowed into a magnificent landlocked bay, where the fleets of all the nations of Europe might have cast anchor, secure from any storm. This bay is on the south side of the Isthmus of Taravao, and is one of the finest and most beautiful harbours in the world.

The isthmus was uninhabited and overgrown with jungle, for the Indians believed it to be the haunt of evil spirits and unfit to be inhabited by men. We slept on board Vehiatua's vessel that night, and next morning — since the passage around the southeast extremity of Taiarapu was judged dangerous, owing to the violent currents and sunken reefs extending far out to sea — our vessel was dragged on rollers across the isthmus, a distance of about a mile and a half, by a great company of people from the near-by district of Vairao, summoned for the purpose. The principal chiefs and landowners of Tahiti, on their voyages around the island, always have their canoes dragged across this low land, and in the course of centuries a deep smooth path has been worn in the soil. The Vairao people performed their task with remarkable order and cheerfulness, and in less than three hours' time our vessel was launched on the north side. At Pueu we entered a passage through the reef and traveled the rest of the distance in the smooth sheltered water close along shore. It was mid-afternoon when we reached Tautira, where Vehiatua resided most of the time.

The chief was received ceremoniously by the members of his household, by the priest of the temple, who offered up a long prayer of thanks that Vehiatua had been preserved from the dangers of the sea, and by a vast throng of his subjects, to whom his justice and good nature had endeared him.

A meal had been prepared, for news of our coming had preceded us, and when Vehiatua, Taomi, the old priest, Tuahu, Tehani's elder brother, and I sat down to eat on the great semicircular verandah of the house, I caught my breath at the magnificence of the prospect. The house, shaded by old breadfruit trees, stood on high land, close to the deep clear river of Vaitepiha. To the east, the blue plain of the Pacific stretched away to the horizon; to the north and west, across ten miles of calm sea, Tahiti Nui swept up in all its grandeur to the central peaks; and to the west I gazed into the heart of the great valley of Vaitepiha, where cascades hung from cliffs smothered in vegetation of the richest green, and ridges like knife-blades ran up to peaks like turrets and spires. No man in the world, perhaps, save Vehiatua, possessed a house commanding such a view.

Hitihiti and his daughter arrived next day, and the ceremonies of my marriage with Tehani began on the day following. Vehiatua's first act was to present me with a fine new house, on the beach, about a cable's length distant from his own. It had been built for the under chief of the district, a famous warrior. This good-natured personage moved out cheerfully when informed that Vehiatua desired the house for his son-in-law — for so he was kind enough to consider me.

Into my new house I moved at once, with Hitihiti, his daughter, her husband, and the people of their household who had accompanied them from Matavai. Early in the morning my party and I set out for Vehiatua's house, carrying with us numerous gifts. These were termed the *o* — which is to say, with truly extraordinary brevity, "insurance of welcome." When these presents had been formally received, both families joined in a slow and stately parade to my house, while servants in the rear brought the bride's gifts — livestock, cloth, mats, furniture, and other things which would be useful to the new household. A throng of Vehiatua's subjects lined the path, and a band of strolling players caused constant laughter with their antics and songs.

In the house, Hina, who represented the female side of my "family," spread a large new mat, and on it a sheet of new white cloth. Vehiatua was a widower, and his older sister, a thin, white-haired old lady, straight and active as a girl, acted for his clan. Her name was Tetuanui, and she now spread upon Hina's cloth, half overlapping it, a snow-white sheet of her own. This symbolized the union of the two families, and Tehani and I were at once ordered to seat ourselves on the cloth, side by side. To the right and left of us were arrayed a great quantity of gifts — mats, capes, and wreaths of bright featherwork. We were then enjoined to accept these gifts in formal phrases, and when we had done so Hina and Tetuanui called for their *paoniho*. Every Indian woman was provided with one of these barbarous little implements — a short stick of polished wood, set with a shark's tooth keen as any razor. They were used to gash the head, causing the blood to flow down copiously over the face, on occasions of mourning and of rejoicing. While the spectators gazed at them in admiration, the two ladies now did us the honour of cutting their heads till they bled in a manner which made me long to protest. Taomi, the priest, took them by the hands and led them around and around us, so that the blood dripped and mingled on the sheet on which we sat. We were then directed to rise, and the sheet, stained with the mingled blood of the two families, was carefully folded up and preserved.

Vehiatua had dispatched to the mountains, the night before, a brace of his *piimato*, or climbers of cliffs. The office of these men was heredi-

tary, and every chief kept one or two of them to fetch the skulls of his
ancestors when required for some religious ceremony, and to return
them afterwards to the secret caves, high up on the cliffs, where they
were kept secure from desecration by hostile hands. The *piimato* carried
in each hand a short pointed stick of ironwood, and with the aid of these
they climbed up and down vertical walls of rock to which a lizard could
scarcely cling. The skulls of Vehiatua's ancestors were to be witnesses
of the religious ceremony presently to take place.

When the ceremony of the bride's reception in my house was over,
we paraded slowly back to the house of Vehiatua, and went through a
precisely similar ceremony there, even to the bloodletting and the folded
sheets. This marked my reception into the house of Tehani's family.
We next sat down to a feast, the men apart from the women, which
lasted till mid-afternoon.

The social part of the marriage was now over; the religious remained. It was performed in Vehiatua's family *marae,* or temple, on
the point not far from his house. Old Taomi, the priest, led the solemn
procession. The temple was a walled enclosure, shaded by huge banyan
trees and paved with flat stones. Along one side a pyramid thirty
yards long and twenty wide rose in four steps to a height of about forty
feet, and on top of it I perceived the effigy of a bird, curiously carved in
wood. Accompanied by Hitihiti and his daughter, I was led to one
corner of the enclosure, while Tehani, with Vehiatua and other relatives, took her place opposite me. The old priest then approached me
solemnly and asked: —

"You desire to take this woman for your wife; will not your
affection for her cool?"

"No," I replied.

Taomi next walked slowly across to where my young bride awaited
him, and put the same question to her, and when she answered, "No,"
he made a sign to the others, who advanced from their respective
corners of the *marae* and unfolded the two sheets of white cloth, on
which the blood of the two families was mingled. Other priests now
came forward, bearing very reverently the skulls of Vehiatua's ancestors, some of them so old that they seemed ready to crumble at a
touch. These silent witnesses to the ceremony were placed carefully in
a line on the pavement, so that their sightless eyes might behold the
marriage of their remote descendant.

The girl and I were told to seat ourselves on the bloodstained sheets of cloth, hand in hand, while our relatives grouped themselves on either side. The priest then called upon the mighty chiefs and warriors whose skulls stood before us, giving each man his full name and resounding titles, and calling upon him to witness and to bless the union of Tehani with the white man from beyond the sea. When this was done, old Taomi turned to me.

"This woman will soon be your wife," he said seriously. "Remember that she is a woman, and weak. A commoner may strike his wife in anger, but not a chief. Be kind to her, be considerate of her." He paused, gazing down at me, and then addressed Tehani: "This man will soon be your husband. Bridle your tongue in anger; be patient; be thoughtful of his welfare. If he falls ill, care for him; if he is wounded in battle, heal his wounds. Love is the food of marriage; let not yours starve." He paused again and concluded, addressing us both: "*E maitai ia mai te mea ra e e na reira orua!*" This set phrase might be translated: "It will be well, if thus it be with you two!"

The solemnity of old Taomi's words and manner impressed the girl beside me so deeply that her hand trembled in mine, and, turning my head, I saw that there were tears in her eyes. In the dead silence following his words of admonition, the priest began a long prayer to Taaroa, the god of the Vehiatua clan, beseeching him to bless our union and to keep us in bonds of mutual affection. At last he finished, paused, and then called suddenly: "Bring the *tapoi!*"

A neophyte came running from the rear of the temple, carrying a great sheet of the sacred brown cloth made by men. The priest seized it, spread it wide, and flung it over us, covering Tehani and me completely. Next moment it was flung aside and we were told to rise. The marriage was over, and we were now embraced in the Indian fashion by the members of both clans. Of the days of feasting and merrymaking that followed our wedding there is no need to speak.

## XIII · THE MOON OF PIPIRI

IT means little to say that I was happy with Tehani. It may mean more to state that only two women have left their mark on my life — my mother and the Indian girl. Long before the birth of our daughter I had resigned myself to the prospect of a life of tranquil happiness in Tautira; the sense of my immense remoteness from England grew stronger with the passage of time, and the hope that a ship might come faded into the background of my thoughts. Had it not been for my mother, who alone seemed to lend reality to memories of England, I am by no means certain that the arrival of a ship would have been welcome to me. And since I felt assured that neither Bligh nor any of those with him in the launch would ever reach home, I knew that my mother would be in no distress on my account until it became evident that the *Bounty* was long overdue. Adopting old Hitihiti's tropical philosophy, I put the past and the future out of mind, and for eighteen months — the happiest period of my entire life — I enjoyed each day to the full.

With her marriage, Tehani seemed to take on a new dignity and seriousness, though in the privacy of our home she showed at times that she was still the same wild tomboy who had beaten me at swimming in Matavai. I was working on my dictionary every day, and Sir Joseph Banks himself could not have entered into these labours with greater enthusiasm than did my wife. She directed our household with a firmness and skill that surprised me in so young a girl, leaving me free to do my writing and to divert myself with fishing parties, or with hunting wild boars in the hills. But I preferred excursions in which Tehani could accompany me, and missed many a boar hunt in order to take my wife on short voyages in our sailing canoe.

About a month after our marriage, Tehani and I sailed down to Matavai for a visit to my *taio*. I was eager to see old Hitihiti, as well as Stewart, Morrison, and other friends among the *Bounty's* people settled there. The distance is about fifty miles, and with the strong trade wind abaft the beam we made the passage in less than five hours, arriving early in the afternoon.

"Your friends are building a ship," Hitihiti informed me as we dined. "Morrison and Millward, the man with him at the house of Poino, are directing the task, and several others are helping. They have laid the keel and made fast the stem and stern. They are working on the point, not far from the sea."

Toward evening we strolled across to the little shipyard — Hina, her father, Tehani, and I. Morrison had chosen a glade about a hundred yards from the beach, an open grassy spot shaded by tall breadfruit trees. A crowd of Indians sat about on the grass, watching the white

men at work. Their interest was intense, and in return for the privilege
of being spectators they kept the shipbuilders more than supplied with
food. The great chief Teina, to whom the land belonged, was there,
with his wife Itea. They greeted us affably, and at that moment
Morrison glanced up and caught my eye. He laid down his adze,
wiped the sweat from his eyes, and took my hand heartily.

"We have heard of your marriage," he said. "Let me wish you happiness."

I made him known to Tehani, and as he pressed her hand young
Tom Ellison came up to me. "What do you think of our ship,
Mr. Byam?" he asked. "She's only thirty feet long, but Mr. Morrison
hopes to sail her to Batavia. We've christened her already: *Resolution's*
to be her name. By God, it takes resolution to build a ship without
nails, or proper tools, or sawn-out plank!"

I shook hands with old Coleman, the *Bounty's* armourer, and with
the German cooper, Hillbrandt. Norman and McIntosh, the carpenter's mates, were there, and Dick Skinner, the hairdresser who had
been flogged in Adventure Bay. All worked with a will, under Morrison's direction; some impelled by a desire to reach England, others,
conscious of their guilt, by the fear that a British ship might take them
before their little vessel could set sail.

At sunset the shipwrights laid down their tools, and, leaving Tehani
to return to the house with Hina and my *taio*, I accompanied Morrison to his residence at the foot of One Tree Hill. He and Millward
lived with the warrior Poino, their friend, a stone's throw from Stewart's house.

I found Stewart pottering about his garden in the dusk. He had
made Tipau's wild glen a place of ordered beauty, with paths leading
this way and that, bordered with flowering shrubs, and shaded rockeries where he had planted many kinds of ferns. He made me welcome,
straightening his back and shaking the earth from his hands.

"Byam, you'll stop to sup, of course? And you too, Morrison?"

Ellison passed us at that moment on his way over the hill, for he
lived in Pare, a mile to the west. Stewart liked the lad and called out
to him: "I say, Tom! Won't you stop the night? It will be like old
times."

"With all my heart, Mr. Stewart!" he said, grinning. "I'm half afraid
to go home, anyhow."

"What's wrong?" asked Morrison.

"That wench of mine again. Last night she caught me giving her sister a kiss. I swear there was no harm intended, but do you think she would listen to reason? She knocked her sister down with a tapa mallet, and would have done the same for me if I had not run for it."

Stewart laughed. "I've no doubt you deserved it."

Peggy was calling us into the house, and half an hour later we sat down to our evening meal, served by old Tipau's slaves. Stewart's dining room was a large thatched house open to the air, and decorated with hanging baskets of ferns. A man stood at one end, holding aloft a torch which illuminated the place with a flickering glare. Peggy had gone off to sup with her women, and Tipau preferred to eat his meal alone.

"How long will it take you to complete your vessel?" I asked Morrison.

"Six months or more. The work goes slowly with so few tools."

"You hope to reach Batavia in her?"

"Yes. From there we can get passage home on a Dutch ship. Five of us are to make the attempt — Norman, McIntosh, Muspratt, Byrne, and I. Stewart and Coleman prefer to wait here for an English ship."

"I feel the same," I remarked. "I am happy in Tautira, and glad of the chance to work on my Indian dictionary."

"As for me," said Stewart, "I find Tahiti a pleasant place enough. And I have no desire to be drowned!"

"Drowned be damned!" exclaimed Morrison impatiently. "Our little schooner will be staunch enough to sail around the world!"

"You haven't told Mr. Byam about *us*," put in Ellison. "We are going to start a little kingdom of our own. Desperate characters we are — not one but would swing at the yardarm if taken by a British ship! Mr. Morrison has promised to set us down on some island west of here."

"It is the best thing they can do," said Morrison. "I shall try to find an island where the people are friendly. Tom is coming, as are Millward, Burkitt, Hillbrandt, and Sumner. Churchill intends to stay here, though he's certain to be taken and hanged. Dick Skinner believes it his duty to give himself up and suffer for his crime. As for Thompson, he is more of a beast than a man, and I would not have him on board."

"Where is Burkitt?" I asked.

"He and Muspratt are living in Papara," said Stewart, "with the chief of the Teva clan."

"They offered to join us in the work," Morrison added, "but neither man has any skill."

I was glad to have news of the *Bounty's* people, most of whom I liked. We talked late into the night, while Tipau's man lit torch after torch from the bundle at his side. The moon was rising when I took leave of my friends and trudged home along the deserted beach.

I had occasion, the next morning, to recall what Morrison had said of Thompson, the most stupid and brutal of the *Bounty's* crew. He and Churchill had struck up an oddly assorted friendship, and spent most of their time sailing about the island in a small canoe, fitted with a sail of canvas. Thompson disliked the Indians as much as he distrusted them, and on shore was never without a loaded musket in his hand.

Going down to the beach for an early bath in the sea, I found the pair encamped by their canoe, with a sucking pig roasting on the coals near by. "Come — join us at breakfast, Mr. Byam," called Churchill, hospitably.

Thompson looked up, scowling. "Damn you, Churchill," he growled — "Let him find his own grub. We've no more than enough for ourselves."

Churchill flushed. "Hold your tongue, Matt," he exclaimed, "Mr. Byam's my friend! Go and learn manners from the Indians, before I knock them into your head!"

Thompson rose and stalked off to a sandhill, where he seated himself sulkily, his musket between his knees. I had already breakfasted, and as I turned away I saw a dozen men pulling a large sailing canoe up on the beach, and the owner and his wife approaching us. The man carried in his arms a child of three or four years. They stopped by Churchill's canoe to admire its sail of canvas, and turned to wish us good day. The Indian woman leaned over the boom to examine the stitching of the bolt rope, and at that moment I heard Thompson's harsh voice.

"Get out of it!" he ordered abruptly.

The Indians glanced up courteously, not understanding the words, and Thompson shouted again: "Grease off, damn you!" The Indian couple glanced at us in bewilderment, and Churchill was opening his mouth to speak when suddenly, without further warning, the seaman leveled his musket and fired. The ball passed through the child and through the father's chest; both fell dying on the beach, staining the sand with their blood. The woman shrieked and people began to run toward us from the house.

Churchill sprang to his feet and bounded to where Thompson sat, with the smoking musket in his hand. One blow of his fist stretched the murderer on the sand; he snatched up the musket, seized Thompson's limp body under the arms, and ran, dragging him, to where the canoe lay in the wash of the sea. Setting the musket carefully against a thwart, he tossed his companion into the bilges as if he had been a dead pig, then sprang into the canoe, pushing off as he did so. Next moment he had sail on her; the little vessel was making off swiftly to the west before the gathering crowd understood what had occurred.

I rushed to the dying father and his small daughter, but perceived at once that there was nothing to be done for them. Within five minutes both expired. The moment it was ascertained that they were dead the frantic mother seized her *paoniho* and gashed her head in a shocking manner, while blood covered her face and shoulders. The crew of her vessel armed themselves with large stones and were beginning to gather about me threateningly when Hitihiti appeared. He grasped the situation, and the sullen murmur of the people died away as he held up an arm for silence.

"This man is my *taio*," he said; "he is as innocent as yourselves! Why do you stand there chattering like women? You have weapons! Launch your canoe! I know the man who killed your master; he is an evil-smelling dog, and not one of the Englishmen will lift a hand to protect him!"

They set off at once in pursuit, but, as I learned afterwards, they were unable to come up with the fugitives. The dead were buried the same night, and Hina and Tehani did their best to comfort the poor woman, whose home was on the neighbouring island of Eimeo. The sequel to this tragedy came a fortnight later, when Tehani and I returned to our home.

Fearing to land on the west side of Tahiti, and wishing to put the greatest possible distance between themselves and Matavai, Churchill had steered his canoe through the dangerous reefs at the south end of Taiarapu and sailed on to Tautira, where Vehiatua, supposing him to be one of my friends, had welcomed him. But Thompson's reputation had preceded him, and he found himself shunned and abhorred by all. Churchill was by this time heartily sick of his companion and desired nothing better than to be rid of him. He told me as much when he came to my house on the evening of our arrival, musket in hand.

"I've half a mind to shoot the fellow!" he remarked. "Hanging's too good for him! But damn me if I can shoot a man in cold blood! I was a fool not to leave him to be dealt with by the Indians in Matavai!"

"They'd have made short work of him," I said.

"And a bloody good job! I'm done with him. I told him to-day he could have the canoe if he'd get out of here and not come back."

"Leave him to the Indians," I suggested. "They'd have killed him long since had he not been with you."

"Aye. Look — there he is now."

Thompson was seated alone on the beach, half a cable's length from us, with the air of a man brooding over his wrongs, as he nursed the musket between his knees.

"The man's half mad," growled Churchill. "You've a musket, Byam; best load it and keep it handy till he's gone."

"Are you planning to stop in Tautira?" I asked after a pause.

"Yes. I like the old chief — your father-in-law, whatever he is — and he seems to like me. He's a fighting man, and so is the other chief, Atuanui. We were planning a bit of a war last night. He says if I'll help him he'll give me a piece of land, with a fine young wife thrown in. But come — it is time we went to his house."

Vehiatua had bidden us to witness a *heiva* that evening — a night dance of the kind I had seen in Tetiaroa long before. We found the grounds bright with torchlight and thronged with spectators, and when we had greeted our friends, Tehani and I seated ourselves with Churchill on the grass, on the outer fringe of the audience.

The drums had scarcely struck up when I heard an Indian shout warningly behind us, followed instantly by the report of a musket. Churchill attempted to spring to his feet, but sank down coughing beside me, the musket dropping from his nerveless hand. Women were shrieking and men shouting on all sides, and I heard Vehiatua's voice boom out above the uproar: "Aye! Kill him! Kill him!" In the flickering torchlight I saw Thompson break away from the scuffle behind me and begin to run toward the beach with ungainly bounds, still clinging to his musket. Atuanui, the warrior chief, snatched up a great stone and hurled it with his giant's arm. It struck the murderer between the shoulders, and sent him sprawling. Next moment the Indian warrior was upon him, beating out his brains with the same stone that had brought him down. When I returned to the house, Churchill was dead.

Since the Indians made war, and abandoned plans for war, for reasons which struck me as frivolous in the extreme, the loss of Churchill was accepted as an unfavourable omen by Vehiatua's priests, and the expedition planned against the people of the south coast of Eimeo was given up. I was secretly glad to be freed from the duty of taking up arms against men to whom I bore no ill-will, and settled down with relief to a tranquil domestic life and my studies of the Indian tongue.

I shall not cumber this narrative with my observations on the life and customs of the Indians — their religion, their intricate system of *tapu,* their manner of making war, their *arioi* society, and their arts and sciences, all of which have been fully described by Cook, Bougainville, and other early visitors to Tahiti. But I shall do the people of Tahiti the justice to mention two of their customs, shocking in themselves, but less so when the reasons for them are made clear. I allude to infanticide and human sacrifice.

Nowhere in the world are children cherished more tenderly than in the South Sea, yet infanticide was considered by the Indians a praiseworthy act of self-sacrifice. The object of the *arioi* society — the strolling players whose chiefs were of the most considerable families in Tahiti — was to set an example both to chiefs and to commoners, as a warning against overpopulating the island. Should a member of the society give birth to a female child, it was killed at once, in the quickest and most painless manner, and their greatest term of contempt was *vahine fanaunau* — a fertile woman. The Indians had a perfect understanding of the dangers of overpopulation, and guarded against them by making large families unfashionable. Cruel as the method seems, it should not be criticized without reflecting that men increase, while the amount of habitable land on a small island remains the same.

As for human sacrifice, the ceremony was rarely performed, and then only on the altar of Oro, god of war. The victim was taken unaware and killed mercifully, by a sudden blow from behind, and he was without exception a man who, in the opinion of the chiefs, deserved death for the public good. In a land where courts, judges, and executioners were unknown, the prospect of being sacrificed to the god of war restrained many a man from crimes against society.

The people of Tahiti were fortunate in many respects — the climate, the fertility of their island, and the abundance of food to be obtained with little effort; yet they were still more fortunate, perhaps, in their lack of money or any other general medium of exchange. Hogs, mats, or bark cloth might be given as a reward for building a house or the tattooing of a young chief, but such property was perishable, and considered a gift rather than an exchange. Since there was nothing that a miser might hoard, avarice, that most contemptible of human failings, was unknown, and there was little incentive to greed. To be accused of meanness was dreaded by chief and commoner alike, for a mean man was considered an object of ridicule. By our introduction of iron, and inculcation of the principles of barter, there is no doubt that we have worked the Indians infinite harm.

On the fifteenth of August, 1790, our daughter Helen was born. The child was given Tehani's name and long title, which in truth I cannot recollect, but I gave her my mother's name as well. She was a lovely little creature, with strange and beautiful eyes, dark blue as the sea, and since she was our first-born, or *matahiapo,* her birth was the occasion for ceremonies religious and political.

A large enclosure had been fenced on the sacred ground behind Vehiatua's family temple, and three small houses built within. The first was called "The House of Sweet Fern," in which the mother was to be delivered of her child; the second was known as "The House of the Weak," where mother and child would pass a fortnight afterwards; the third was called "The Common House" and had been built to shelter Tehani's attendants. For six days after our little Helen was born, silence reigned on sea and land along the coast of Tiarapu; all of the commoners retiring into the mountain fastnesses, where they might converse, build fires for their cooking, and live in comfort till the restriction was over.

On the seventh day I was admitted into the House of the Weak, and saw my daughter for the first time. Vehiatua and I went together, for no man save Taomi, the priest, had set foot within the enclosure till that time. It was dark in the house, and for a moment I could scarcely make out Tehani on her couch of soft mats and tapa, nor the tiny newcomer, waving chubby fists at me.

Our child was three months old when Stewart and Peggy sailed around the island to visit us. They had a small daughter of their own, as I had learned some time before, and the two young mothers found in their children an inexhaustible subject of conversation. Stewart spent a week with us, and one day of the seven stands out in my memory.

It was still dark when I rose that morning, but when I emerged from my plunge into the river the fowls were beginning to flutter down from the trees. As I stood on the bank, breathing deep of the cool morning air, I felt a touch on my shoulder and found my wife beside me.

"They are still asleep," she said; "you should see Helen and little Peggy, side by side! Look, there is not a cloud in the sky! Let us take a small canoe and paddle to Fenua Ino — the four of us, and the children, and Tuahu."

We had often spoken of spending a day on the islet of Fenua Ino, a place I had never visited, and, knowing that Stewart would enjoy the trip, I assented readily. We chose a single canoe, stocked her with provisions and drinking-nuts, and installed the two sleeping babies on soft tapa, side by side in the shell of a large sea-turtle, well polished and cleaned, and shaded with green coconut fronds. Tuahu, my brother-in-law, was a tall, powerful young man, a year older than I, and as pleasant a companion as I have ever known. He took his place in the stern, to steer us through the reefs, and set us a lively stroke. Stewart and I had long since become accomplished hands in a canoe, and our wives were strong active girls, able to wield a paddle with any man.

For five miles south from Tautira, the coast is sheltered by a reef at some distance from the land, and is perhaps the richest and most densely populated district in all Tahiti. This was the coast I had seen when the *Bounty* first approached the island, so long before. Then the reef ceases, and the Pacific thunders against the tall green cliffs called Te Pari — a wild region, uninhabited and believed to be the haunt of evil spirits. At the beginning of the cliffs, where the reef ended, was the small coral island, about half a mile from shore, where we planned to spend the day.

We spread our mats in the shade of a great unfamiliar tree, and Tuahu fetched our lunch and the turtle shell. Stewart called to his wife: "Bring the children, Peggy. Byam and I will keep an eye on them, and have a yarn while you and Tehani explore the island."

Stewart and I stretched ourselves out comfortably in the shade. Our daughters slept in their odd cradle, starting a little from time to time as babies do, but never opening an eye.

"Byam, what do you suppose has become of Christian?" Stewart asked. "Sometimes I think that he may have killed himself."

"Never! He felt too deeply his responsibility toward the others."

"Perhaps you are right. By this time they must have settled on some island — I wonder where!"

"I have often puzzled over that question," I replied. "They might have gone to one of the Navigators' Islands, or to any of the coral islands we passed on the voyage north."

Stewart shook his head. "I think not," he said; "those places are too well known. There must be scores of rich islands still uncharted in this part of the sea. Christian would be more apt to search for some such place, where he would be safer from pursuit."

I made no reply and for a long time we lay sprawled in the shade, our hands behind our heads. I felt deeply the lonely peace and beauty of the islet. Beyond the long white curve of the reef, a northerly breeze ruffled the Pacific gently. I groped in memory for a phrase of Greek and at last it came to me — "wine-dark sea." Stewart spoke, half to himself, as if putting his thoughts into words: "What a place for a hermit's meditations!"

"Would you like to live here?" I asked.

"Perhaps. But I would miss the sight of English faces. You, Byam, living alone among the Indians, do you never miss your own kind?"

I thought for a moment before I replied: "Not thus far."

Stewart smiled. "You are half Indian already. Dearly as I love Peggy, I would be less happy at Matavai without Ellison. I've grown fond of the lad, and he spends half his time at our house. It's a damned shame he had to meddle in the mutiny."

"There's not an ounce of harm in the young idiot," I said; "and now he must sail away with Morrison and pass the rest of his days in hiding, on some cannibal island to the west. All for the pleasure of waving a bayonet under Bligh's nose!"

"They'll be launching the *Resolution* in another six weeks," remarked

Stewart. "Morrison has done wonders! She's a staunch little ship, fit to weather anything."

Our wives were approaching us, followed by Tuahu, who carried a mass of sweet-scented flowers which they had woven into wreaths for us.

One flower in particular, in long sprays and wonderfully fragrant, took my fancy. It was unknown on Tahiti, and our companions were trying to recall its name.

"It is common in the low islands east of here, where the people eat man," said Tuahu; "I saw hundreds of the trees in Anaa, when I was there last year. They have a name for it in their language, as we have in ours, but I forget both."

"*Tafano!*" exclaimed Tehani, suddenly.

"Aye, that's it!" said her brother, and I made a note of the word for my dictionary.

We fetched the baskets of food for the girls, and retired to a little distance, Indian fashion, to eat our own lunch. When it was over and we were together once more, in the shade, Tuahu recounted the legend of the islet.

"Shall I tell you why no men live here?" he began. "It is because of the danger at night. Several times in the past men have tried to sleep here, out of bravado, or because they did not know. All have crossed to Tahiti in the morning silent and dejected, and died soon after, raving mad. Since the very beginning, a woman has come here each night when the sun has set. She is more lovely than any mortal, with a melodious voice, long shining hair, and eyes no man can resist. Her pleasure is to seduce mortal men, knowing that her embraces mean madness and death."

Stewart winked at me. He plucked two blades of coarse grass, a long and a short, and held them out. "Come," he said banteringly, with a glance at the girls, "we'll draw to see who stops the night."

But Tehani snatched the grass from his hand. "Stop the night if you like," she said to Stewart, "but Byam goes ashore! I want no demon-woman for him, nor mortal girls who would swim out to impersonate her!"

Stewart sailed for Matavai on the day after our picnic, and four months passed before I saw him again. Yet as I review those months in memory, they seem no longer than so many weeks. It has often been observed — with a justice for which I can vouch — that in the South Sea men lose their sense of the passage of time. In a climate where perpetual summer reigns and there is little to distinguish one week from another, the days slip by imperceptibly.

That year of 1790 was the happiest and seemed the shortest of my entire life. And 1791 began happily enough; January passed, and February, and toward the middle of March Tehani sailed with Vehiatua to the other side of the island, to take part in some religious ceremony. The Indian ceremonies of this nature were wearisome to me, and I decided to remain in Tautira, with my brother-in-law. My wife had been gone a week or more when the ship came.

Tuahu and I had been amusing ourselves at a *heiva* the night before, and, returning late to bed, I slept till the sun was up. Tuahu woke me with a hand on my shoulder. "Byam!" he said in a voice breathless with excitement. "Wake up! A ship! A ship!"

Rubbing the sleep from my eyes, I followed him to the beach, where numbers of people were already gathering. All were staring out to the east, into the dazzling light of the morning sun. There was a light breeze at east by north, and far offshore, so far that she was hull-down and her courses hidden by the curve of the world, I saw a European ship. Topsails, topgallants, and royals — looking small, dark, and weatherbeaten in the level light — were visible, though the distance was still too great to guess at her nationality. The Indians were in great excitement.

"If a Spanish ship," I heard one man say, "she will put in here."

"And if French, she will go to Hitiaa!"

"British ships always go to Matavai," said Tuahu, glancing at me for confirmation.

"Do you think she is British?" asked Tetuanui, my wife's old aunt.

I shrugged my shoulders, and an Indian said: "She is not Spanish, anyway. They are standing off too far."

The vessel was approaching the land on the starboard tack, and it was clear that she was not steering for the Spanish anchorage at Pueu. She might have been a French frigate making for Bougainville's harbour, or a British vessel bound for Matavai. We seated ourselves on the grass, and presently, as she drew slightly nearer and the light increased, I was all but convinced, from the shape of her topsails, that she was British. I sprang to my feet.

"Tuahu," I said, "I believe she's British! Let us take your small sailing canoe and run down to Matavai."

My brother-in-law sprang up eagerly. "We shall beat them there by hours," he exclaimed; "this wind always blows strongest close to land. They will be becalmed offshore."

We made a hasty breakfast on cold pork and yams, left over from the night before, had the canoe well stocked with provisions and drinking nuts, and set sail within the hour, accompanied by one man. As Tuahu had predicted, the wind blew strong alongshore, while the vessel four or five miles distant lay almost becalmed. With the fresh breeze abeam, our canoe tore through the sheltered water within the reefs, headed out into the open sea at Pueu, and sailed past Hitiaa and Tiarei. It was mid-afternoon when we ran through the gentle breakers before Hitihiti's house. The place was deserted, for news of the ship had preceded us, and my *taio,* with all his household, had repaired to the lookout point on One Tree Hill.

## XIV · THE PANDORA

THROUGHOUT the day the Indians had been coming to Matavai in great numbers, and many canoes were drawn up on the beach, belonging to those who had arrived from remote parts of the island. When I climbed One Tree Hill, late in the afternoon, I found it thronged with people keeping a lookout for the vessel. The excitement was intense. It was such a scene as must have presented itself twenty-four years earlier when Captain Wallis arrived in the *Dolphin,* the first European vessel to visit the island. The crowd was so great that I had difficulty in finding Stewart. Presently I spied him with some of the Matavai people, standing near the ancient flowering tree which gave the hill its name. He made his way to me at once.

"I've been expecting you all day, Byam," he said. "What can you tell me of the ship? You must have seen her as you were coming round the coast."

"Yes," I replied. "She's an English frigate, I should say."

"I thought as much," he replied, sadly. "I suppose I should be glad. In one sense, I am, of course. But fate has played a sorry trick upon us. You must feel that, too?"

I did feel it, profoundly. The first sight of the vessel had given me a moment of keen happiness. I knew that it meant home; but after all these months Tahiti was home as well, and I realized that I was bound to the island by ties no less strong than those which drew me from it. Either to go or to stay seemed a cruel choice; but we well knew that there would be no choice. Our duty was plain. We should have to go aboard as soon as the ship came to anchor and report the mutiny.

We had little doubt that the vessel had been sent out in search of the *Bounty*. The Indians, of course, had no inkling of this. They believed that the awaited ship probably belonged to Captain Cook, coming for additional supplies of young breadfruit trees, and that Captain Bligh, his supposed son, would be with him. While Stewart and I were talking, a messenger from Teina was sent in search of us. He wished to see us at his house. We sent back word that we would come shortly.

"What of our wives and children?" Stewart asked gloomily. "It may seem strange to you, Byam, but the truth is that I have never before realized that we should have to go. England seems so far away, as though it were on another planet."

"I know," I replied. "My feeling has been the same."

He shook his head mournfully. "Let's not talk of it. You are certain the ship is English?"

"All but certain."

"In that case, I'm sorry for poor Morrison. He left in the schooner four days ago. They may be well on their way westward by this time."

Morrison's plans, he told me, had not changed. All the mutineers remaining on Tahiti, with the exception of Skinner, had decided to go with him in the *Resolution*. They had agreed among themselves to go ashore at some island to the westward where there would be little chance of their ever being discovered. Morrison, Norman, McIntosh, Byrne, and Muspratt would then try to make their way to Batavia, on the island of Java, where they hoped to sell the schooner and take passage in some ship bound to Europe.

"It's a desperate venture for all of them," Stewart continued. "There are Ellison, Hillbrandt, Burkitt, Millward, and Sumner to be left at some island yet to be decided upon. God knows what their fate will be! They have firearms and think they will be able to defend themselves until they can establish friendly relations with the people. But what can five men do against hundreds of savages? We know what the islanders to the westward are like; our experiences at Namuka taught us that. They are as good as dead, in my opinion."

"They will have a fighting chance at least," I said. "In any event it will be better than being taken home to be hung."

"Yes, they were wise to go, no doubt. What chance do you think Morrison has of reaching Batavia?"

We discussed the matter at length. Morrison was an excellent navigator, and five men were ample to work the little schooner. They were provided with a compass and one of Captain Bligh's charts of the passage through Endeavour Straits; but looked at in the most hopeful light, it seemed doubtful indeed that the *Resolution* would ever reach Batavia. Stewart told me that the schooner had first gone to the district of Papara, on the southern side of Tahiti, to pick up McIntosh, Hillbrandt, and Millward. It was possible, he thought, that the schooner might still be there.

Presently a great shout went up from the watchers on the hill. The frigate had been sighted as she emerged from behind a distant headland. She was four or five miles offshore, and the dying wind was so light that we knew she could not make the land before dark. Evidently her captain realized this, for shortly afterward the ship hove-to under her topsails.

Some of the Indians remained on the hill, but most of them, seeing that the vessel did not intend to come in that night, descended with us. On our way to Teina's house we met Skinner and Coleman, who had been on an excursion into the mountains and had only just heard the news of the frigate. Coleman was deeply moved when I told him that the ship was, almost certainly, English. More than any of us, with the exception of Morrison, had he longed for home. He had a wife and children there and had formed no alliance with any of the Tahitian women. Tears of joy dimmed his eyes, and without waiting for further information he rushed up the hill for a sight of the vessel that would take him to England.

Stewart and I were concerned for Skinner. He had long since repented of the part he had taken in the mutiny, and was, in fact, the only one of the mutineers who had done so. His sense of guilt had grown stronger as the months had passed. A deeply religious man, he had brooded over his disloyalty to the Crown and was determined to give himself up at the first opportunity. We knew that repentance, however sincere, would have no weight with a court-martial. His doom was certain if he surrendered himself. Guilty though he undoubtedly was, we had no desire to see the poor fellow clapped into irons and taken to England to be hung. But he would not listen to our suggestions that he try to hide himself while there was yet time.

"I have no wish to escape," he said. "I know what will happen when I surrender myself, but my death will be a warning to others who may be tempted to mutiny."

We pleaded with him for some time, but it was useless, so we left him and proceeded to Teina's house. We found the chief at supper, which he asked us to share with him, and while we ate he plied us with questions concerning the vessel. How many guns was she likely to carry? How many men? Would King George be aboard? And the like. All the Tahitians had a great desire to see the King of England, and Bligh, as well as the British captains who had visited the island before him, had played upon their credulity to the extent of giving them reason to hope that the King might some day visit Tahiti.

We explained to Teina that King George had great dominions, and was so occupied with affairs at home, particularly in wars with neighboring nations, that he had little opportunity for voyaging to such far places.

"But Tuté will come," Teina said, with conviction. (Tuté was the universal name for Captain Cook, the nearest they could come to the sound of it; and Bligh was called Parai.) "Parai promised that Tuté would come. This must be his ship." He went on to conjecture what the purpose of this visit might be. He believed that Cook and Bligh, if the latter chanced to be with him, would now decide to remain permanently at Tahiti. He would urge them to do so, and would set aside great tracts of land for their use and provide them with as many servants as they might want. With their help he would bring the whole of Tahiti under subjection; then we would all proceed to the island of Eimeo, and on to Raiatea and Bora Bora, conquering each of these islands in turn. And he promised that Stewart and I should be made great chiefs, and that our children should grow in power after us.

It must have been well past midnight when we left Teina's house, but none of the people there or elsewhere thought of sleep that night. Those who had come from distant parts were encamped along the beach and among the groves inland, and the light of their fires illuminated the entire circle of the bay. Canoes were still arriving, most of them small craft containing ten or a dozen men, bringing island produce to be bartered for the trade goods of the vessel. As we walked down the beach we saw one huge canoe, containing fifty or more paddlers, just entering the bay. Her men were singing as they urged her forward, and the blades of the paddles flashed in the firelight as they approached. It was an interesting sight to watch them berth her. With her great curved stern rising high above the water, she looked like some strange sea monster. She was heavily loaded and grounded at some distance from the beach, whereupon all the men leaped out and brought her farther along. There must have been one hundred people in her, to say nothing of the cargo of pigs and fowls. When these had been unloaded, rollers were placed under her keel, and with twenty or thirty men on each side she was quickly run up the long slope of the beach to level ground.

We went to Stewart's house, which stood just under One Tree Hill, on the western side of the bay. Here, too, everyone was astir. Peggy, Stewart's wife, with their little daughter asleep on the mat beside her, was sorting over great rolls of tapa cloth, selecting the finest pieces as gifts for her husband's friends on the ship. She took it for granted that we must know everyone aboard, and it was plain that she had no suspicion of what the arrival of the vessel might mean to us both. Presently I went off to seek Tuahu and my other friends from Tautira who were encamped near by. By this time dawn was not far off, and Tuahu suggested that we should take a canoe and paddle out to sea to meet the vessel.

"If it is a strange ship, Byam, the captain will be glad of a pilot into the bay. But I think it is Parai coming back to see us. We shall be the first to met him."

I agreed to the proposal at once, and taking old Paoto, Tuahu's servant, with us, we hauled our canoe to the water, and a few moments later had rounded Point Venus and were well out to sea.

Tahiti had never seemed so beautiful as on that morning, in the faint light of dawn. The stars were shining brightly when we set out, but they faded gradually, and the island stood out in clear, cold silhouette against the sky. We paddled steadily for half an hour before we caught sight of the ship, and then drifted to wait for her to come up with us. The breeze was of the lightest, and an hour later she was still at a considerable distance. She was a frigate of twenty-four guns, and, although I was convinced that she was British, my heart leaped when at last I saw the English colours.

In my first eagerness to go off to her, I had forgotten that I was dressed as an Indian and not as an English midshipman. My only remaining uniform had come to grief at Tautira. I had not worn it from the day I left the *Bounty,* but had kept it carefully wrapped in a piece of tapa cloth hanging from a rafter in my house. Thinking it safe there, I had not examined the parcel in many months, and when at last I did so I found that it had been nearly devoured by rats, and was past all hope of repair. This mattered nothing then, for I had long since adopted the Tahitian costume, and for the most part wore nothing but a girdle of tapa and a turban of the same material. Reminded now of my half-naked condition, I was tempted to turn back, but it was too late to reconsider. The vessel was only a few hundred yards distant and had altered her course to pick us up.

The larboard bulwarks were crowded with men, and I saw the captain on the quarter-deck with his spyglass leveled at us, and a group of officers standing behind him. As the ship came alongside we paddled with her, and a line was thrown to us from the gangway. I clambered aboard and Tuahu after me. Paoto remained in the canoe, which was veered astern and towed after us.

My skin was as brown as that of the Indians themselves, and, with my arms covered with tattooing, it is not strange that I should have been mistaken for a Tahitian. A lieutenant stood at the gangway, and as we reached the deck sailors and marines alike crowded close for a better view. The lieutenant smiled ingratiatingly and patted Tuahu on the shoulder. "Maitai! Maitai!" (Good! Good!) he said. This was evidently the only Indian word he knew.

"You can address him in English, sir," I said, smiling. "He understands it very well. My name is Byam, Roger Byam, late midshipman of His Majesty's ship *Bounty*. If you like, I shall be glad to pilot you in to the anchorage."

The expression on the lieutenant's face altered at once. Without replying he glanced me up and down, from head to foot.

"Corporal of marines!" he called.

The corporal advanced and saluted.

"Fall in a guard and take this man aft."

To my astonishment four men with muskets and bayonets fixed were told off, and I was placed in the midst of them, and in this manner marched to the captain, who awaited us on the quarter-deck. The lieutenant preceded us. "Here's one of the pirates, sir," he said.

"That I am not, sir!" I replied. "No more than you yourself!"

"Silence!" the captain ordered. He regarded me with an expression of cold hostility, but I was too incensed at the accusation to hold my tongue.

"Allow me to speak, sir," I said. "I am not one of the mutineers. My name is . . ."

"Did you hear me, you scoundrel? I ordered you to be silent!"

I was hot with shame and anger, but I had self-possession enough not to give way further to it, and I was certain that the misunderstanding with respect to me would soon be cleared up. I saw Tuahu regarding me with an expression of utter amazement. I was not permitted to speak to him.

The most humiliating treatment was yet to come. The armourer was sent for, and a few moments later handcuffs were placed upon me and I was taken under guard to the captain's cabin, there to await his pleasure. Two hours passed, during which time I was kept standing by the door. I saw no one except the guards, who refused to speak to me. Meanwhile the ship had been worked into Matavai Bay and came to anchor at the same spot where the *Bounty* had lain upon her arrival nearly three years earlier. Through the ports I could see the throngs of Indians along the shore and canoes putting off to the frigate. In one of the first of these were Coleman and Stewart. Stewart was dressed in his midshipman's uniform, and Coleman in an old jacket and a pair of trousers patched with pieces of tapa cloth, all that remained of his European clothing. Their canoes passed under the counter and I saw no more of them for some time.

The frigate was called the *Pandora,* and she was commanded by Captain Edward Edwards, a tall spare man with cold blue eyes and pale bony hands and face. As soon as the ship was safely anchored he came to his cabin, followed by one of his lieutenants, Mr. Parkin. He seated himself at his table and ordered me to be brought before him. I protested at once against the treatment I had received, but he ordered me to be silent, and sat for some time regarding me as though I were a curiosity brought to him for examination. Having finished his scrutiny, he leaned back in his chair and gazed sternly at my face.

"What is your name?"

"Roger Byam."

"You were a midshipman on His Majesty's armed vessel, the *Bounty?*"

"Yes, sir."

"How many of the *Bounty's* company are now on the island of Tahiti?"

"Three, I believe, not counting myself."

"Who are they?"

I gave him their names.

"Where is Fletcher Christian, and where is the *Bounty?*"

I told him of Christian's departure with eight of the mutineers, and of all the events that had taken place at Tahiti since that time. I told him of the building of the schooner, under Morrison's supervision, and of Morrison's intention to sail with her to Batavia, where he hoped to find a homeward-bound ship.

"A likely story!" he said grimly. "In that case, why did not you go with him?"

"Because the schooner was not well found for so long a voyage. It seemed to me wiser to wait here for the arrival of an English ship."

"Which you never expected to see, no doubt. You will be surprised to learn that Captain Bligh, and the men who were driven from his ship with him, have succeeded in reaching England?"

"I am profoundly glad to hear it, sir."

"And you will be equally surprised to learn that all the facts of the mutiny, including that of your own villainy, are known."

"My villainy, sir? I am as free from guilt in that affair as any member of your own ship's company!"

"You dare to deny that you plotted with Christian to seize the *Bounty?*"

"Surely, sir, you must know that some of us who were left in the ship were compelled to remain for lack of accommodation in the launch? There were nine of us who took no part whatever in the mutiny. The launch was so overloaded that Captain Bligh himself begged that no more men should be sent into her; and he promised, if ever he reached England, to do justice to those of us who were forced to remain behind. Why, then, am I treated as though I were a pirate? If Captain Bligh were here . . ."

Edwards cut me short.

"That will do," he said. "You will meet Captain Bligh in good time, when you have been taken to England to suffer the punishment you so richly merit. Now then, will you or will you not tell me where the *Bounty* is to be found?"

"I have told you all that I know, sir."

"I shall find her and those who went with her, be sure of that. And I promise that neither you nor they shall gain by an attempt to shield them."

I was too angry and sick at heart to reply. Never, during all the months that had passed since the mutiny, had I suspected that I might be considered a member of Christian's party. Although I had not been able to speak with Bligh on the morning the ship was seized, Nelson, and others who went in the launch, knew of my loyalty and of my intention to leave with them. I had supposed that Bligh himself must have known, and I could not imagine what might have happened to cause me to be listed among the mutineers. I was eager to know the fate of those who had gone with Bligh, and how many of them had reached England safely, but Edwards would not permit me to inquire.

"You are here to be questioned, not I," he said. "You still refuse to tell me where Christian is?"

"I know no more than you do, sir," I replied.

He turned to the lieutenant.

"Mr. Parkin, have this man sent below, and see to it that he has no communication with anyone. . . . Wait a moment. Ask Mr. Hayward to step in."

My surprise at the mention of Hayward's name must have been apparent. A moment later the door opened, and Thomas Hayward, my former messmate on the *Bounty,* appeared. Forgetting my shackles, I stepped forward to greet him, but he gazed at me with a look of contempt, at the same time putting his hands behind his back.

"You know this man, Mr. Hayward?"

"Yes, sir. He is Roger Byam, a former midshipman on the *Bounty*."

"That will do," said Edwards. With another cool glance at me, Hayward went out, and I was taken by the guard to the orlop deck, to a place evidently prepared for prisoners, next to the bread room. It was a foul situation, below the water line, and nauseating with the stench of the bilges. The only means of ventilation was a ladderway some distance forward. Irons were now placed on my legs as well as on my wrists, and here I was left, with two guards outside the door at either end of the compartment. About an hour later, Stewart, Coleman, and Skinner were brought down and ironed in the same manner. No one, save the guard who brought our food, was permitted to enter the place, and we were forbidden to speak to each other. There we lay the whole of that interminable day, as wretched in mind and body as men could well be.

## XV · DOCTOR HAMILTON

DURING the next four days, Stewart, Coleman, Skinner, and I were conscious of little save our own misery. A frigate's orlop deck is a foul place in which to be confined at any time, and with the ship at anchor, in the lee of a tropical island, the heat and stench were scarcely to be endured. Our sentinels were changed every two hours, and I remember with what longing we watched the departing guard returning to the freshness of the open air. Food was brought to us morning and evening, and only thus were we able to distinguish night from day, for no sunlight penetrated to our quarters. Our victuals were the rancid salt beef and hard bread which the *Pandora* had carried all the way from England, with never an addition of the fresh meat, fruit, and vegetables which the island furnished in such abundance. But more than food we craved fresh air and the luxury of movement. Our leg irons were made fast to ringbolts in the planking, and although we could rise to our feet, we could take no more than one short step in either direction.

On the fifth morning of our confinement, the corporal of marines appeared with an extra guard. My leg irons were removed and I was taken up the ladderway and aft along the gundeck to a cabin on the starboard side of the vessel. It was the surgeon's cabin, and the surgeon himself, Dr. Hamilton, was awaiting me there. He dismissed the guard and then, observing that I was in handcuffs, recalled the corporal and requested that these be removed. The man was reluctant to comply.

"Lieutenant Parkin's orders were . . ."

"Nonsense," the doctor interrupted. "Take them off. I'll answer for this man's safety." The irons were then removed and once more the corporal retired. The surgeon turned the key in the lock, smiling as he did so.

"I'm not taking this precaution against yourself, Mr. Byam," he said. "I wish our conversation to be uninterrupted. Please to be seated."

He was a sturdily built man of forty, or thereabout, with a pleasant voice and manner. He looked like a ship's surgeon and a capable one. I felt drawn to him immediately. After the treatment accorded us by Edwards and Parkin, mere courtesy seemed, by contrast, the highest of virtues. I seated myself on his clothes chest and waited for him to speak.

"First," he said, "about your studies of the Tahitian language. You will wonder how I know of them. Of that, presently. Have you continued them during your sojourn here?"

"I have, sir," I replied. "Not a day has passed that I have not added to my dictionary. I have also compiled a grammar for the use of those who may wish to study the language hereafter."

"Good! Sir Joseph Banks was not mistaken, I see, in the confidence he placed in you."

"Sir Joseph! You know him, sir?" I asked, eagerly.

"Not as intimately as I could wish. In fact, I met him only shortly before the *Pandora* sailed; but he is an esteemed friend of friends of mine."

"Then you can tell me whether he believes me guilty in this affair of the mutiny. Do you yourself, sir, think I could have been so mad as to have joined it? And yet I have been treated by Captain Edwards as though I were one of the ringleaders."

The surgeon regarded me gravely for a moment.

"I will say this, Mr. Byam, if it will afford you comfort. You have not the look of a guilty man. As for Sir Joseph, despite all that has been said against you, he still believes in your innocence. . . .

"Wait! Allow me to continue," he went on as I was about to interrupt him. "I am as ready to hear what you have to say as you are to speak; but let me first inform you how serious the charges laid against you seem to be. I have been informed on this matter by Sir Joseph, who has not only talked with Captain Bligh, but has read the sworn statement concerning the mutiny which he has furnished to the Admiralty. I will not give the details. One will suffice to show how deeply you are implicated. On the night before the *Bounty* was seized, Captain Bligh himself, coming on deck during the middle watch, surprised you and Mr. Christian in earnest conversation. And Captain Bligh, so he insists, overheard you say to Mr. Christian: 'You can count on me, sir,' or words to that precise effect."

I was so taken aback as to be speechless for a moment. However strange it may seem, although I had the clearest recollection of the conversation with Christian, this vastly important detail had quite slipped from memory. The excitement of the events immediately following had, I suppose, driven it from my mind. Now that it had been recalled to me, I realized at once how black the appearances against me must be, and that Bligh was justified in placing the most damning construction upon what I had said. What could he have believed except that I was pledging my allegiance to Christian in his plan to seize the ship?

Dr. Hamilton sat with his hands clasped, his elbows on the arms of his chair, waiting for me to speak.

"It is plain from your manner, Mr. Byam, that you have a recollection of such a conversation."

"I have, sir. I said those very words to Mr. Christian, and under the circumstances described by Captain Bligh." I then proceeded to tell him the whole story of the mutiny, omitting nothing. He heard me through without comment. When I had finished he gazed at me keenly; then he said, "My boy, you have convinced me, and here's my hand on it!" I shook it warmly. "But I must tell you that my conviction is due to your manner rather than to the matter you have related. You must see for yourself that the very plausibility of your story is against it."

"How is that, sir?" I asked.

"Understand — I believe you; but put yourself in the place of the ships' captains who will sit at the court-martial. Your sincerity of manner in telling the story will have weight with them too, but they will be justified in ascribing this to your longing to escape death. As to the story, could you blame them for thinking it a little too perfect to fit the facts? It meets your necessities so well. The damning words to Christian are completely explained. And your going below, on the morning of the mutiny, just before the launch was cast off, is perfectly explained as well. There is not one of those captains who will not say to himself: 'This is such a tale as one would expect an intelligent midshipman, eager to save his life, to invent.'"

"But, as I have told you, sir, Robert Tinkler overheard the conversation with Christian. He can corroborate every word of my testimony."

"Yes; Tinkler, I think, saves you. Your life is in his hands. He reached England safely with the rest of Captain Bligh's party. To return to your story, you see how difficult it will be to convince a court-martial that Mr. Christian, presumably a man of intelligence and one capable of reflection, would have considered the mad plan of casting himself adrift on a tiny raft, for the purpose of making his way, alone, to an island peopled with savages?"

"It would not seem improbable if they knew Christian's character and the abuse he had received from Captain Bligh."

"But these officers will know nothing of Christian's character, and their sympathies will all be with Captain Bligh. You will have to prove your story of that conversation beyond the shadow of a doubt. Was there no one at that time to whom he revealed his plan to leave the ship? Such a man would be a most important witness for you."

"Yes; John Norton, one of the quartermasters. He prepared the raft for Christian."

The surgeon opened a drawer in his table and brought forth a paper.

"I have here a list of the men who went with Captain Bligh in the launch. Twelve of the party survived to reach England."

He glanced down the list, and then looked at me gravely.

"Norton, I am sorry to say, is not one of them. According to this record he was killed by the savages on the island of Tofoa."

It was a shock to me to learn of Norton's death, and I realized what a misfortune the lack of his evidence would be for me. Mr. Nelson, too, was dead, having succumbed to a fever when the party reached Coupang. Mr. Nelson was not only my friend; he was also a witness who could have vouched for my intention to leave the ship. With these two gone, my chance for acquittal seemed much less hopeful. Dr. Hamilton took a more encouraging view of the situation.

"You must not be disheartened," he said. "Tinkler's evidence is vastly more important to you than that of Norton and Mr. Nelson, and you may be sure that he will be summoned. Sir Joseph Banks will see to it that every scrap of evidence in your favour is brought to bear. No, take my word for it, your case is far from hopeless."

His quiet confident manner reassured me, and for the time I put aside all thought of what my fate might be. Mr. Hamilton then related, briefly, what I was most eager to hear: the story of what had happened to Bligh and his party after the launch had been cast adrift. They had first called at the island of Tofoa, for water and other refreshment, but the savages, seeing that the party lacked the means of defending themselves, attacked them in such numbers that a massacre of the entire company was barely averted. As it happened, Norton was the only man to be killed. Their subsequent adventures made up a record of appalling hardships, and had any one but Bligh been in command, there is little doubt that the launch would never have been heard of again. On the fourteenth of June, forty-seven days after the mutiny, they reached the Dutch settlement at Coupang Bay, on the island of Timor, a distance of more than twelve hundred leagues from Tofoa. After recuperating for two months among the kindly inhabitants of Coupang, a small schooner was purchased and fitted out for the voyage to Batavia, where they arrived on October 1, 1789. Here three more of the party died: Elphinstone, Lenkletter, the remaining quartermaster, and Thomas Hall, a seaman. Ledward, the acting surgeon, was left behind at Batavia, and the rest of the party embarked in ships of the Dutch East India Company for the voyage home. Robert Lamb, the butcher, died on the passage, leaving but twelve of the nineteen men who had set out from the *Bounty's* side.

"In all the annals of our maritime history there has never been such an open-boat voyage as this," Dr. Hamilton continued. "You will understand the excitement and interest aroused when Bligh reached England. I was then in London, and for weeks the story of the mutiny and the voyage of the launch were the chief topics of conversation everywhere. The whole country rang with Bligh's praises, and the sympathy for him is universal. It would be useless to deny the fact, Mr. Byam — those who remained in the *Bounty* are all considered scoundrels of the blackest description."

"But did Captain Bligh say nothing," I asked, "of the men who were kept against their inclination? I fully understand, now, his bitterness toward me, but there are others whom he knows to be innocent, and he pledged himself to do them justice if ever he reached England. Stewart and Coleman are in irons at this moment, as you may know. They are as guiltless as any of those who went with Captain Bligh."

"I have read the instructions furnished to Captain Edwards by the Admiralty," he replied. "They contain a list of the names of those who remained in the *Bounty,* and you are all considered mutineers. No distinction is made amongst you, and Captain Edwards is instructed to keep you so closely confined as to preclude all possibility of escape."

"Does this mean that we shall be confined where we are now until the *Pandora* reaches England?"

"Not if Captain Edwards will follow my advice. His instructions also say that, in confining you, he is to have a proper regard for the preservation of your lives. In this matter I am equally responsible with him, and I would not answer for the life of a pig kept for months on end on the orlop deck. I shall do my best to persuade him to remove you to more healthful quarters."

"And if possible, sir," I urged, "persuade him to permit us to speak with one another."

"God bless my soul! Do you tell me that he has denied you that small privilege?" The surgeon regarded me with a grim smile. "Captain Edwards is a just man, Mr. Byam. You will understand, perhaps, what I mean by this? He will carry out his instructions to the letter, and if ever he errs, it will not be on the side of leniency. But I think that I can promise you relief in some small matters. At any rate, be assured that I shall try. To return to the matter of your studies: you have your manuscripts at your house, I presume?"

All of my personal belongings had been left at Tautira. I told the surgeon of my friend, Tuahu, and that, if I might send him word, he would bring my chest to the ship. Dr. Hamilton asked that I write his name on a slip of paper.

"I will find him," he said. "Sir Joseph is extremely anxious that these manuscripts of yours should not be lost."

"It would be a godsend to me, sir, if I might continue my work on the voyage home."

"Sir Joseph had requested this very thing, in case you should be found," the surgeon replied. "Captain Edwards will, I believe, grant permission."

This news cheered me greatly. I should have an occupation that would suffice to make the long confinement endurable, and as Stewart, Coleman, and Skinner were all proficient in the Indian tongue, if we were permitted to converse my studies could be carried on with their help.

Mr. Hamilton glanced at his timepiece.

"I must send you below soon," he said. "I had Captain Edwards's consent to this interview that I might question you with respect to the manuscripts. He is ashore this morning. I have taken advantage of the fact to enlarge upon my privilege."

He rose, unlocked the door of his cabin, glanced out, and closed it again.

"I shall enlarge upon it still more," he said. "Sir Joseph has charged me with another commission. In case you could be found, he asked me to deliver this letter to you."

Dr. Hamilton busied himself with some papers of his own while I read my letter. It was from my mother, of course. I still have it to this day, but I need not consult it to refresh my memory. For all the years that have passed, I can recall it, word for word: —

MY DEAR SON: —

I have only just learned that I may have this precious opportunity to write to you. I must make every moment count, and waste none in unnecessary words.

When Captain Bligh returned with the news of the dreadful fate of the *Bounty,* I wrote to him at once, and received from him the letter which I enclose. What may have happened to turn him against you, I cannot conceive. After the receipt of so cruel a message I did not again write to him, but you must not believe that I have been greatly distressed. I know you too well, dear Roger, to have the least doubt of your innocence.

I know what your anxiety, on my account, will be upon the arrival of the *Pandora,* when you learn that you are counted among the mutineers. Imagine then, dear son, that you have been able to write to me, explaining fully the circumstances, and imagine that your letter has reached me. I am as certain as though I had this letter before me that events over which you had no control caused you to remain in the *Bounty,* and I await with perfect confidence your homecoming and the clearing of your name from this infamous charge.

My only concern for you is at the thought of the hardships you may have to suffer as a prisoner on the long voyage to England. But they can be borne, and remember, my son, that home is beyond them.

Sir Joseph has talked with Captain Bligh, and you will be gratified to know that he does not share Mr. Bligh's belief that you were one of his enemies. I have not been told upon what ground you are charged with conspiracy, but in closing his letter to me, Sir Joseph said: 'I confidently expect that the proof of your son's innocence only awaits the day when the *Pandora* returns and all the facts shall be known.' I not only expect it. I am as sure of it as I am of the light of to-morrow's sun.

Good-bye, my dear Roger. I may not write more. The *Pandora* is to sail within three or four days, and my letter must go to London by this night's coach. God bless you, my son, and bring you safely home! Believe me, my dear boy, I can smile at the thought of the preposterous charge against you. May England breed many such villains as you are supposed to be.

Dr. Hamilton was kindness itself. Our quarters on the orlop deck were as dark as a cave and I could never have read my letter there. He permitted me to go over it again and again in his cabin until I knew it by heart. The enclosed letter from Bligh to my mother was, surely, the most cruel and heartless message that has ever been sent to the mother of an absent son: —

LONDON, *April 2nd,* 1790.

MADAME: —

I received your letter this day, and feel for you very much, being perfectly sensible of the extreme distress you must suffer from the conduct of your son, Roger Byam. His baseness is beyond all description, but I hope you will endeavour to prevent the loss of him, heavy as the misfortune is, from affecting you too severely. I imagine he is, with the rest of the mutineers, returned to Otaheite.

I am, Madame,

WILLIAM BLIGH.

I returned to our dark hole in a vastly different frame of mind than when I left it. As we passed along the lower deck I caught glimpses through the scuttles of the Matavai beach, and the canoes and the boats from the frigate plying back and forth between the ship and the shore. Those brief bright glimpses brought home to me the preciousness of freedom, the inestimable boon of being merely alive and at liberty. I made no attempt to compute the length of time that must pass before it could be mine again.

## XVI · THE ROUNDHOUSE

THE following morning our prison was cleaned for the first time since we had been confined there, and lighted with two additional candles. A bucket of sea water was then furnished us and we were permitted to wash our hands and faces. We were in a truly deplorable condition, only less filthy than the prison itself, and we begged the master-at-arms to allow us a complete bath.

"I have been ordered to give you one bucket of water and no more," he said. "Make haste, for the captain is coming directly."

We had no sooner finished our hurried toilet than Captain Edwards entered, followed by Lieutenant Parkin. The master-at-arms called out, "Prisoners! Stand!" We rose to our feet, and Edwards glanced around the compartment and from one to another of us. The stench of the place was frightful, and our naked bodies gleamed with sweat in the dim light. From the appearance of my fellow prisoners I knew what a disgusting appearance I myself must present. My intention had been to protest against the inhumanity of such a place of confinement; but believing that conditions would speak eloquently enough for themselves, I decided to say nothing. Edwards turned to the master-at-arms.

"Command them to hold out their hands," he said.

"Prisoners, hold out your hands!"

We obeyed, and Edwards examined our handcuffs and leg irons. It chanced that Stewart's manacles fitted somewhat loosely to his wrists, and Edwards noticed this.

"Mr. Parkin, see to it that the armourer inspects all of these irons," he said. "I shall hold him responsible if any prisoner shall be able to free himself."

"I shall attend to the matter immediately, sir," Parkin replied.

Edwards continued to regard us coldly for a moment or two.

"Inform the prisoners that, in future, they may converse with one another. But let them understand this: they shall speak only in English. If I hear of as much as a single word passing between them in the Indian language, the permission I have granted shall be withdrawn."

This information was conveyed to us through the proper channel.

"And under no circumstances whatever is any prisoner to speak to a sentinel or to any member of the ship's company except Mr. Parkin or the corporal in charge of the guard. I shall severely punish any infringement of this order."

Parkin was in general charge of us. I felt an instinctive aversion for this man. He was short, thickset, and excessively hairy, with eyebrows that met in an irregular line over his nose. The vice of cruelty was written plain on his face, and we had not been long in discovering the character of the man in whose power we were. Thus far he had displayed it in various small ways, but Edwards had now given him the kind of opportunity he craved. No sooner had the captain left us than Parkin himself made an inspection of our irons, beginning with Stewart, whom he ordered to lie down and stretch up his hands. He then grasped the chain connecting the handcuffs, and, placing his foot against Stewart's chest, he strained and tugged with all his strength, succeeding at length in wrenching off the irons, taking the skin from Stewart's knuckles and the backs of both hands as he did so. As the handcuffs came away he nearly fell over backward. In his anger, Stewart forgot his helpless position. He sprang to his feet, and had Parkin been within reach Stewart would have knocked him down.

"You filthy beast!" he said. "Do you call yourself an officer?"

Parkin had a high soft voice, almost feminine in quality, in strange contrast to his swarthy, hairy appearance.

"What did you say?" he asked. "Repeat that."

"I called you a filthy beast," said Stewart, "and so you are!"

He was as near to Parkin as his irons would permit him to go. The lieutenant took care to keep beyond reach.

"You will regret that," he said. "I promise that you will repent of it more than once before you're hung."

I am unable to say whether he would have tried the irons of the rest of us in the same manner. I was resolved that he should not test mine in that fashion; but at that moment the armourer appeared and Parkin ordered him to carry on the examination. It would have been impossible for any of us to have freed ourselves from the leg irons, but Parkin ordered all the handcuffs to be altered so that they should fit more tightly. When they had been repaired and brought back, it was only with great difficulty that they could be fastened upon us.

Meanwhile, I told the others of my conversation with the surgeon. We forgot our wretched situation in the pleasure of being permitted to converse again, and the day passed more rapidly than the previous five had done. Realizing now that we had nothing to hope for until we reached England, we resolved to make the best of things, and to devise methods of passing the time. Of the four of us, Skinner alone had nothing to hope for, and yet he was the most cheerful of us all. I began to suspect, at this time, that the man was not wholly right in his mind. He said more than once that, if the decision were again to be made, he would give himself up to justice as he had done, and he seemed to look forward with pleasure to the day when he would be hung.

We were careful to obey Edwards's order with respect to the sentinels. We had no desire to make trouble for them, and Parkin was spying about at all hours. But there was a seaman, James Good, whose name was an indication of his kindly nature. He was the man usually sent with our food, and he never failed to whisper to us welcome bits of news as he handed round our plates. "Mr. Parkin's gone ashore, sir," he would say; "you won't be bothered this morning." Or, "I'll fetch you a bit of fresh meat for your supper." Whenever possible he would bring us morsels of fresh pork or breadfruit or sweet potatoes wrapped in a handkerchief inside his blouse. This he did with the connivance of the cooks. Had any of these men been discovered, they would have been severely flogged, and yet they cheerfully ran the risk in order to lighten the misery of our situation.

But never had Good brought us such welcome news as on the evening when he informed us that we were to be moved to other quarters.

"Have you heard the knockin' and 'ammerin' on deck, sir?" he whispered to me. "The carpenters are makin' a proper 'ouse for you up there."

We had heard, at times, the sounds of hammering, and now that we knew it concerned us, it was music to our ears. The following day we were unshackled from the filthy planking of our dungeon, marched up the ladderway, along the lower deck, and up a second ladderway to the pure air of the upper deck. At first our eyes were so dazzled by the brilliance of the sunshine that we could scarcely see, and so lost half the pleasure of our moment in the open. It was, in fact, no more than a moment. Edwards was present, and the master-at-arms ordered us into our new prison at once. We mounted the ladder to the top of the box, which stood on the quarter-deck. There was a scuttle about eighteen inches square through which we descended inside.

This place was to be our prison for as long as we remained on the *Pandora*. It was called "the roundhouse," but more often we prisoners referred to it as "Pandora's Box." It was eleven feet long at the deck and eighteen feet wide at the bulkhead. There were two scuttles, nine inches square, in the bulkhead, and these, with the one in the roof, were heavily barred and gave us what light we had. Across the deck midway between the walls was a line of fourteen heavy ringbolts to which the leg irons were to be attached. We were now made fast in the corners of the compartment, Stewart and Skinner next the bulkhead, and Coleman and I on the after side. Our leg irons were cylindrical bands three inches wide with a twelve-inch length of chain which passed through a ringbolt. One key unlocked all the leg irons and another the handcuffs. The keys were carried by the master-at-arms.

As in our former prison, we could stand up and move half a pace in either direction, and we had full headroom. The floor was the deck itself, and on either side were small scupper holes. In fair weather the roof scuttle was left open save for the iron grating, and two sentries continually paced the roof. The monotonous, everlasting tread of their feet so close overhead became a sound as wearisome to us as the clinking of our chains through the ringbolts.

We could not suppose that so large a prison had been prepared for four men, and by each of the unoccupied ringbolts lay a pair of leg irons ready for use. Evidently Captain Edwards had reason to believe that he would soon take others of the *Bounty's* company. That Christian and his party had returned was so improbable as not to be worth considering. The only remaining possibility was that the departure of the *Resolution* from Papara had been delayed, and that she was either captured or about to be. We were not long kept in doubt. Two days later, the grating over the roof scuttle was raised, and Morrison, Norman, and Ellison were brought down and chained beside us.

This was a meeting such as none of us had hoped for. Morrison and Norman had not yet recovered from their astonishment at being treated as pirates. Ellison was the same scatter-brained youngster he had always been. Excitement in any form was the breath of life to him, and to be considered a desperate character, chained up like a wild beast, was his conception of a lark. Fortunately he had no sense of the gravity of his situation, and we did nothing to remind him of it. Of all those who had taken part in the mutiny, he was the one I most hoped would escape capture.

The armourer, supervised by Parkin, fitted handcuffs to the new captives, and Ellison being no more than a boy, Parkin tried upon him the same measures he had used with Stewart. Ordering him to lie down, he placed one foot on his chest and tried to draw the handcuffs over his hands. For a moment Ellison endured this treatment in silence; then he said, smiling, "Leave off, sir. I'll give you these things if you want them, but you can't get them that way."

Parkin's only reply was to let go the chain so suddenly that Ellison fell back, striking his head heavily on the deck. Parkin's eyes shone with delight as Ellison sat up, rubbing his head. He ordered him to stretch up his hands again, but this time Ellison was prepared, and when Parkin let go the chain the boy fell back on one shoulder and avoided striking his head.

"That's one for me, sir," he said with a grin.

The lieutenant was breathing heavily, not so much from exertion as from emotion. The fact that a common seaman and a mutineer beside had dared to speak to him was more than he could endure.

"Lie down!" he ordered.

A look of fear came into Ellison's eyes as he obeyed. He stretched up his arms, expecting Parkin to grasp the chain again. Instead of that he kicked Ellison in the side, as cruel a blow as was ever given a defenseless man.

"That will teach you how to speak to an officer," he said, in his soft bland voice. The armourer was a witness of this foul proceeding. "Good God, sir!" he exclaimed in spite of himself. By a happy chance Parkin stood within reach of Morrison, who drew back his manacled fists and gave him a blow which sent him staggering in my direction. I had barely time to fetch him another that knocked him off his balance, and as he fell he struck his head against one of the ringbolts. He got up slowly and looked from one to another of us without speaking. Presently he turned to the armourer.

"You may go, Jackson," he said. "I shall know how to deal with this." The armourer went up the ladder, and Parkin stood looking down at Ellison, who was lying on his belly with his hands pressed against his side.

"Oh, you dogs!" he exclaimed softly, as though speaking to himself. "I could have you flogged to death for this. But I'm to see you hung! Remember that — I'm to see you hung!" He then went up the ladder, the grating was lifted for him, and he climbed out.

Had not the armourer witnessed the brutal assault upon Ellison, I have no doubt that we should have suffered for our rebellious conduct. But evidently Parkin feared that the truth would come out if complaint should be made to the captain. At any rate, no action was taken, and for several days we saw no more of the man. Ellison suffered great pain, but youth and natural toughness of body were in his favour, and he quickly recovered.

As soon as we were alone again, Morrison gave us an account of the taking of the schooner. Having called at Papara to pick up McIntosh, Hillbrandt, and Millward, they had decided to take advantage of the fine weather to salt down some extra casks of pork. Several days were spent in this work, and on the morning of what was to have been their last day on the island, most of the men made an excursion far up the Papara Valley for a supply of mountain plantains. Morrison, Ellison, and Norman remained with the schooner, and toward noon word reached the district of the arrival of a vessel at Matavai. Before any action could be taken, a ship's launch filled with marines appeared.

"Norman and I could have danced for joy at sight of the English uniforms," Morrison went on; "but when we thought of the others we felt less happy. They were certain of capture now and I had no time to send them warning. The launch was upon us five minutes after she had rounded the point. She came alongside and you can imagine our astonishment when we saw that Thomas Hayward, in a lieutenant's uniform, was in charge of her."

"I suppose you fell on each other's necks, Morrison," Stewart put in.

"He didn't condescend to speak to me, but ordered his men to clap me in irons. He remained with the schooner with most of the marines. We were sent back with the launch."

"Mr. Hayward is in a difficult position; we must remember that," said Coleman.

"In a position that precisely suits the little cad," said Stewart, hotly. "He knows that we are as innocent as he himself."

"Do you remember how he whimpered when Christian ordered him into the launch?" asked Morrison.

"So he did, Coleman," said Norman. "Him and Mr. Hallet both begged to stay with the ship, and that's something none of us was guilty of."

Hayward's superior, contemptuous attitude was naturally resented by all of us who had taken no part in the mutiny. Making all possible allowances for him, we still found it inexcusable.

The other men were soon brought in from Papara. There were seven of them: McIntosh, Hillbrandt, Burkitt, Millward, Sumner, Muspratt, and Byrne. The roundhouse was none too large, now, for our accommodation. Eight men were chained so that they slept with their heads at the bulkhead, and six on the opposite side. I was in the corner, on the starboard side aft, with Muspratt on my left. I had reason to be grateful for my chance position in the roundhouse. Two or three days after we had been confined there, I discovered in one of the wall planks a knot that had become loosened as the green lumber dried in the sun. I tried for several nights, without success, to draw it out. James Good, our steward, came to my assistance. He pushed the knot in to me, and thereafter I had a tiny window through which I had a glimpse of the bay and the shore line beyond. Sometimes, as the *Pandora* shifted her position with the current, I had Stewart's house directly opposite my window, and although we were too far distant to enable me to distinguish the people moving about there, I could easily imagine who they were.

I watched canoes and the ship's boats coming and going. Many of the people in the canoes I knew; they were old friends of one or another of us. As they approached, I could see them more and more distinctly until they were cut off from view by the side of the vessel. Several times I saw Peggy, Stewart's wife, being paddled around the ship by her father or one of her brothers. With what longing she gazed in our direction! Her father, wisely, never brought her within earshot. She would have been certain to cry out to her husband had she thought him within hearing, only adding to the misery of them both. I said nothing to Stewart of the matter. I had no desire to harrow his feelings any more than was already the case with him.

One morning while I was standing on lookout, Muspratt, who was keeping watch for me, gave the warning, "Hatchway!" and I had barely time to thrust in the knot before the master-at-arms descended the ladder, followed by Edwards. It was an unexpected visit, the first we had had from the captain since our confinement in the roundhouse. Our prison had not been cleaned in all that time, and I will say no more of its condition than that fourteen chained men were obliged to obey the calls of nature in that close-walled space.

Edwards halted at the foot of the ladder.

"Master-at-arms, why is this place in such a filthy state?"

"Mr. Parkin's orders were that it was to be cleaned once a week, sir."

"Have it washed out immediately, and report to me when it is done."

"Very good, sir."

Edwards lost no time in leaving the place; then, to our great joy, swabs were handed down to us, and bucket after bucket of salt water. When we had scoured our quarters thoroughly, passing the swabs from hand to hand, we scrubbed each other. To be clean once more had a wonderful effect upon our spirits. Some of the men sang and whistled at the work, sounds that contrasted strangely with the clinking of manacles, but these cheerful noises were cut short by a curt order from the master-at-arms. In half an hour we had the place as clean as salt water and good will could make it, whereupon the master-at-arms returned, followed, this time, by Dr. Hamilton. The surgeon threw a quick glance in my direction, and there was a friendly glint in his eyes; otherwise he gave no indication that we had met before. He passed along the line, glancing over our bodies in a professional manner, and stopped before Muspratt.

"That needs attention, my man," he said, indicating a great boil on

Muspratt's knee. "Have him sent to the sick-bay at ten, Mr. Jackson."

"Yes, sir."

Dr. Hamilton had fully as much dignity as the captain, but he did not feel it necessary to address us through an inferior officer.

"Are any of the rest of you suffering from boils or other humours?" he asked. "If so, speak up, and I'll attend to you at the same time. Remember, it is my duty to care for your health as well as that of the ship's company. You must not hesitate to inform me when you need my services."

"May I speak, sir?" Stewart asked.

"Certainly."

"Would it be possible, while the ship remains here, for us to be supplied now and then with fresh food?"

Morrison eagerly seconded this request.

"We have friends among the Indians, sir, who would be only too glad to send us fruit and cooked vegetables if this could be permitted."

"And it would save the ship's stores, sir," Coleman added.

Dr. Hamilton glanced from one to another of us.

"But you're having fresh food," he said.

"No, sir, begging your pardon," said Coleman. "Only salt beef and hard bread."

Dr. Hamilton looked at the master-at-arms.

"That's been their victuals, sir. Mr. Parkin's orders."

"I see," the surgeon replied. "I'll look into the matter. Perhaps it can be arranged."

We thanked him warmly, and he went on deck again.

It was plain from the events of that morning that Parkin's treatment of us had been without the knowledge of the captain or of Dr. Hamilton. Edwards was willing to be ignorant of the lieutenant's cruelty, but from that day forth Dr. Hamilton made us frequent visits. We were never again compelled to lie in our own filth, and our food was the same as that given to the seamen of the *Pandora*.

## XVII · THE SEARCH FOR THE BOUNTY

ONE morning early in May, Stewart and I were freed from our leg irons and conducted to the place used as the sick-bay on the lower deck.

We found Dr. Hamilton awaiting us in the passageway outside. He said nothing, but motioned us to enter. We went in, not knowing what to expect, and the door was closed behind us. Tehani and Peggy were there, with our little daughters.

Tehani came close and put her arms around me, speaking in a low voice directly into my ear, lest she should be heard by those outside.

"Listen, Byam. I have no time for weeping. I must speak quickly. Atuanui is here with three hundred Tautira men, his best warriors. They have been coming around the coast from both sides, five or ten each time. For many days I have been trying to see you. There was no chance. At last it comes. They will attack the ship at night. In the darkness the great guns will do us little harm. What we fear is that you may be killed by the soldiers before we can reach you. That is why the attack has not yet been made. Are you all in the house they have built on the deck? Are you chained? Atuanui wishes to know how you are guarded there."

I was so overcome with joy at seeing Tehani and our little daughter that I was unable to speak for a moment.

"Tell me, Byam, quickly! We shall not have long to speak."

"How long have you been at Matavai, Tehani?"

"Three days after you left Tautira, I came. Did you think I would desert you? It is Atuanui and I who have made this plan. All of your friends are eager to attack."

"Tehani," I said, "you must tell Atuanui that there is no chance to save us. He and all of his men would be killed."

"No, no, Byam! We will club them to death before they can use their guns. We will save you from these evil men. Atuanui wishes to attack to-morrow night. There is no moon. It must be done quickly, for the ship is soon to go."

It was useless trying to explain to Tehani the reason for our imprisonment. She could not understand; and, indeed, we had only ourselves to blame, for, as already related, the fact of the mutiny had been kept a secret from all the Tahitians.

"We know. That captain, Etuati, has told Hitihiti that you are bad men. He says he must take you to England to be punished. Hitihiti does not believe this. No one believes it."

Meanwhile, Stewart's wife had told him what Tehani had told me. There was but one way of preventing an attack upon the frigate. We explained that all of the prisoners were chained, hand and foot; that we were entirely helpless and would undoubtedly be killed before the ship could be taken. I told Tehani, which was true, that Captain Edwards was prepared for such an attack, and our guards under orders to shoot us at the first sign of any attempt at rescue on the part of our friends on shore. We succeeded at last in convincing our wives of the hopelessness of the plan.

Until this moment Tehani and Peggy had kept their emotions under control. Realizing now that nothing could be done, Peggy broke down in a flood of passionate weeping heart-rending to see. Stewart tried in vain to comfort her. Tehani sat on the floor at my feet, her head buried in her arms, making no sound. Had she wept I would have been better able to bear it. I knelt beside her with our child in my arms. For the first time in my life I tasted to the full the bitterness of true misery.

Presently Stewart could endure no more. He opened the door. Dr. Hamilton and the guards were waiting outside. He motioned them to come in. Peggy clung to him desperately, and it was only with the greatest difficulty that he could disengage her fingers. Had it not been for Tehani she would have had to be carried from the ship. Tehani's grief was beyond tears, as mine was. We held each other close, for a moment, without speaking. Then she lifted up Peggy, and supported her as we went out. Stewart and I followed, carrying our children. At the gangway we gave them to the servants who had come with our wives. Stewart begged to be taken to the roundhouse at once. I was conducted to Dr. Hamilton's cabin and was deeply grateful for the privilege he gave me of being alone there for a few moments. Through the port I saw the canoe, with my friend Tuahu and Tipau, Peggy's father, at the paddles, leave the side of the ship. One of the servants held Peggy's child. Tehani sat on a thwart in the bow, holding our little Helen in her arms. I watched the canoe growing smaller and smaller, with such despair in my heart as I had never known till then.

I was still standing at the port when Dr. Hamilton entered.

"Sit down, my boy," he said. His eyes were moist as he looked at me. "I persuaded Captain Edwards to consent to this meeting. My intentions were of the best, but I didn't realize how cruel a trial it would be for all of you."

"I can speak for Stewart as well as for myself, sir. We are deeply grateful to you."

"Would you mind telling me your wife's name?"

"Tehani. She is the niece of Vehiatua, the chief of Taiarapu."

"She is a noble woman, Mr. Byam. I was greatly impressed by her dignity and poise. I don't mind confessing that my ideas of the Indian women have altered greatly, now that I have seen them. My conception had been gained from the stories about them that circulate in England. I had supposed them all wanton little creatures without character or depth of feeling. I see more clearly every day how mistaken this conception was. We call these people savages! I realize now that in many respects we are the savages, not they."

"You have not seen my wife before?" I asked.

"On the contrary, I have seen her every day this past month. She has been moving heaven and earth in her attempts to see you. Stewart's wife has been doing the same. Until yesterday, Captain Edwards refused all requests of the Indians for permission to visit the prisoners. He fears that they may attempt to rescue you."

"He has reason to fear it, sir."

"Reason to fear it? How is that?"

I would gladly have avoided speaking of what Tehani had told me, and could I have been certain that Atuanui would abandon his plan, I would have said nothing. But I knew his fearless impetuous nature, and neither he nor Tehani had any conception of the murderous effect of great guns loaded with grape. They had never seen them fired, and it was more than possible that Atuanui might yet be persuaded of the feasibility of his plan. Therefore I told the surgeon of the plan to attack the frigate, and of what I had done to prevent its being carried out. He was astonished at the news.

"We have had no suspicion that anything of the sort was afoot," he said. "You have done well to tell me of this. An attack would mean the death of scores, if not hundreds, of the Indians."

"Captain Edwards can easily avoid all danger," I said. "He will have only to keep a strong guard on shore and to prohibit any gathering of canoes near the ship."

The surgeon then told me that he had received from Tuahu the manuscripts of my dictionary and grammar.

"I have your private Journal as well," he added. "Would you permit me to look into this latter sometime, or does it contain matters which you wish no one to see?"

I told him that it contained nothing but a day-to-day account of my experiences from the time of leaving England until the arrival of the *Pandora,* which he was welcome to read, if he chose.

"I shall appreciate that privilege," he replied. "Your Journal will be of great value to you in later years. If you like, I will take care of all these papers for you. They can go into the bottom of my small medicine chest, and there they will be certain of reaching England safely. With respect to the dictionary, Captain Edwards knows of the great interest Sir Joseph Banks takes in it, and you are to be permitted to work on it during the passage home."

This was a welcome assurance indeed. I had looked forward with dread to our long voyage. I now mentioned the captain's prohibition against our speaking in Tahitian among ourselves. "If this could be removed, sir, I could be given much help by the other prisoners, and perform a service to them at the same time, by giving them something to occupy their minds."

The surgeon promised to intercede with the captain on this account, and as soon as the *Pandora* sailed the permission was granted.

All the next day the ship's boats were kept busy bringing off provisions, and the tents and implements of the carpenters and armourers which had been set up on the beach near our anchorage. Our steward, James Good, told us that the frigate was to sail within twenty-four hours. Edwards had gained no information with respect to Christian and the *Bounty,* and apparently had come to the conclusion that we had told the truth in saying that we knew nothing of Christian's possible destination. All that day I gazed my fill at the green land where I had been so happy, and during the night I heard every bell strike, followed by the clear calls of the sentinels in various parts of the ship. Fortunately, no attempt was made to seize the frigate. At dawn we were under way. At ten o'clock, looking from my knot-hole window, I saw nothing but empty sea.

There followed a weary time for the fourteen men confined in "Pandora's Box." My dictionary proved a blessing to nearly all of us. On our second day at sea it was brought to me by Dr. Hamilton himself, together with writing materials, and the surgeon had had the carpenter make me a small table which rested on the floor across my lap as I sat in my corner. The green island timber of which the roundhouse had been made was beginning to shrink in the hot sun, and sufficient light streamed through the cracks between the planks to enable me to write without straining my eyes greatly. The prohibition against speaking in the Indian tongue was lifted, and the other men entered with pleasure into my studies. Stewart, Morrison, and Ellison were accomplished linguists, only a little less proficient in Tahitian than in English. Ellison surprised me. He spoke the language with a purer accent than any of us, and seemed to have absorbed his knowledge of it without the least effort. He pointed out many fine distinctions between words that had escaped me. This poor lad had never known who his parents were. He had been kicked from larboard to starboard ever since he could remember, and it had never occurred to him that he had a good mind. It saddened me to think that such a youngster, with an excellent capacity for education, had received none, while many a dull-witted son of wealthy parents was offered advantages he was not equipped to profit by.

There were grey days of continual violent squalls when it was impossible to work on the dictionary. The frigate laboured heavily through the seas, rolling and pitching, and we rolled with her, each man clinging to his ringbolt in an attempt to maintain his position. Often we were thrown to the extent of our chains, and our wrists and ankles were terribly galled by the bands of iron around them. To add to our misery in seasons of bad weather, the rain trickled down upon us day and night through the uncaulked seams in the roof of our prison, and we slept, or, better, tried to sleep, on boards slimy wet.

We had been several days at sea when we learned that the *Pandora* was not alone on this voyage. She was accompanied by the *Resolution,* the little schooner which Morrison and the others had built. Edwards had fitted her out as a tender to the frigate, and she was commanded by Mr. Oliver, the master's mate of the *Pandora,* with a crew of a midshipman, a quartermaster, and six seamen. She was a beautiful little craft and outsailed the frigate in any kind of weather. Many and many a time poor Morrison, and the men who were to have gone with him in the *Resolution,* had occasion to lament their fate in being captured at Papara. Whatever hardships they might have suffered would have seemed light indeed compared with the misery of existence in "Pandora's Box."

Henry Hillbrandt soon began to show signs of breaking under the strain of confinement. By nature he was a man of brooding, melancholy disposition, and it was evident that thoughts of the court-martial ahead of us were preying upon his mind. I remember well the evening when he first gave evidence of this. The sea was dead calm, but a fine cold rain had been falling since morning, and we were cold, wet, and miserable. It must have been toward midnight that I was wakened from a doze by the sound of Hillbrandt's voice. It was pitch-dark in the roundhouse. Hillbrandt was praying in low monotonous tones that went on interminably. Seamen, however irreverent some of them may be, invariably respect those of a religious temperament, and rarely interfere with another man's prayers. Although I could see nothing in the darkness, I knew that the other men were awake, listening to Hillbrandt. He continued for at least half an hour, praying God to save him from being hanged. It was the same thing over and over again. At last I heard Millward's voice: "Hillbrandt! For God's sake, *mamu!*" (Be quiet!)

Hillbrandt broke off.

"Who was that? Was it you, Millward?"

"Yes. We want no more of your praying."

"No," someone else put in. "Pray to yourself if you must, Hillbrandt, but give us a rest."

Of a sudden Hillbrandt broke out in a violent fit of sobbing. "We're doomed, men," he said; "doomed, every one of us! We're to be hanged, think of that! Choked to death at the end of a rope!"

"Damn your blood! Hold your tongue, will you?" I heard Burkitt say. "Choke him off, Sumner, if he says another word!"

Sumner was chained next to Hillbrandt. "That I will!" he replied. "I'll save the hangman one dirty job if he don't let up!"

One topic, our possible fate when we reached England, was never mentioned in the roundhouse. With the exception of Hillbrandt and Skinner, present misery was enough for all of us, without anticipating events to come.

The events of that dreary time are only less unpleasant to recall than they were to endure. We had no knowledge of whither we were bound, except that it was in the general direction of home. James Good, our only source of information, told us that Captain Edwards was making a zigzag course to westward, calling at every island raised, in search of the *Bounty*. We had to form our own conclusions as to where we were from the little I could see through my knothole window. Some of the others could also see something of what was taking place outside through the cracks that began to appear in the walls as the planking shrunk under the tropical sun. I kept a record of the days. We left Tahiti on May 9, 1791. On the nineteenth of May we sighted an island which all who could view it recognized at once. It was Aitutaki, discovered by Captain Bligh after the departure of the *Bounty* from Tahiti, and shortly before the mutiny. There was great excitement in the roundhouse that morning. The ship came close inshore and hove-to on the larboard tack while the cutter was being lowered. We saw one of the lieutenants and fifteen men go off in the boat.

"We'll have Christian and the others here before nightfall; I'll venture my day's rations on it," said Coleman.

"Nonsense, Coleman," said Stewart. "Christian would never be so foolish as to choose any hiding-place known to Captain Bligh."

"What of Tupuai, Mr. Stewart?" Norman asked. "Christian would have stayed there if the Indians had been friendly, and that island was known to Captain Bligh."

"What do you think, Byam?" Stewart asked.

My opinion was, and Morrison and most of the others agreed, that Christian would never again seek an asylum on a known island, more particularly on any island that Bligh had visited. Nevertheless, we waited with impatience for the return of the cutter. The frigate stood off and on all day, and toward sunset we saw the cutter putting off from shore. I had an excellent view of her as she approached, and when I could say, with certainty, that none of Christian's party was in her, Ellison gave a cheer, and clapped his manacled hands together. We all felt as he did: we wanted Christian and the men with him to escape. As soon as the cutter was hoisted on board we stood out to sea, and that is the last we saw of Aitutaki.

Every day or two we had glimpses of the *Resolution* and knew that she was following us from island to island. She came up with us again when we were within sight of a low island, or atoll, which consisted of a number of small islands connected by long stretches of barren reef, the whole enclosing a lagoon of considerable extent. We saw the schooner being revictualed from the frigate, and then she stood in for shore with a cutter and one of the yawls in tow. The schooner was proving of great service to Edwards in his search. Owing to her light draft, she could examine, close inshore, the various islands at which we touched. The following day James Good brought us most interesting news. The boats' crews had gone ashore at the atoll, and had discovered on the beach of one of the islands a spar marked "Bounty's Driver Gaff."

This discovery caused no less excitement in the roundhouse than it did, presumably, in Captain Edwards's cabin. The captain evidently considered the find as proof that the *Bounty* had called at this island, or had passed near it. We knew better, but we took good care to keep the information to ourselves. This driver gaff was, unquestionably, one of the missing spars that had gone adrift at Tupuai, and had been carried by winds and currents these many miles to leeward.

During the next two months we cruised north and south among the islands of the Union Group, the Navigator and the Friendly Archipelagoes, still searching for some trace of the *Bounty*. On the twenty-first of June, in a night of very thick weather, we lost the *Resolution*. The frigate cruised about in that vicinity for several days, but the schooner was seen no more, whereupon Captain Edwards proceeded to Namuka, in the Friendly Islands, the appointed place of rendezvous in case the vessels should become separated. Namuka, it will be remembered, was the island where the *Bounty* had put in for refreshment only a few days before the mutiny. The *Pandora* anchored where the *Bounty* had lain, and from my knot-hole I could see the familiar scene: the scattered thatched houses of the Indians among the groves, the watering place where the grapnel had been stolen, and the same throngs of thieving savages crowding about the ship in their canoes.

The *Pandora* remained here from July 28 until the second of August, waiting for the *Resolution,* and during that time the Indians proved as troublesome to the frigate's watering parties as they had to those of the *Bounty*. The schooner having failed to appear, she was given up as lost, and Captain Edwards now decided to proceed on the homeward voyage without further loss of time. Accordingly, we sailed from Namuka, and the following afternoon passed within view of the island of Tofoa, and within a few miles of the very spot where the mutiny had taken place so many months before. The interest of the men in the roundhouse, as we peered through the cracks at the blue outline of Tofoa, may be imagined. To me, the events of that melancholy morning, and all that had since passed, seemed unreal, and our present misfortunes the experiences of a nightmare from which I should wake, presently, to find myself still at home, in England. I had the strange feeling that I had traveled backward in time and was living again through the events of the night preceding the mutiny.

## XVIII · THE LAST OF THE PANDORA

I WILL pass briefly over the events of August. They were, no doubt, interesting enough to the members of the *Pandora's* company. To the prisoners in the roundhouse they passed with interminable slowness. Islands were raised and left behind as we proceeded toward Endeavour Straits. We were sailing much the same course as that followed by Captain Bligh in his open-boat voyage to Timor, and as we ploughed through that vast ocean scattered with islands and shoals all but unknown to white men, I gained a truer conception of the remarkable nature of Bligh's achievement. That he should have succeeded in bringing seventeen men, without arms, and so meagrely provided with food and water, through fair weather and foul, to a destination nearly four thousand miles from his point of departure seemed in the nature of a miracle. This achievement was our principal topic of conversation in the roundhouse. Whatever our personal feelings toward Bligh, there was not one of us who did not feel proud, as Englishmen, of his voyage in the *Bounty's* launch.

We saw little of Edwards. Three or four times, perhaps, in the course of the voyage thus far, he had made an official inspection, merely stopping at the foot of the ladder, glancing coldly from one to another of us, and going out again. We were at the mercy of Parkin, who made existence as wretched for us as he dared. As we approached Endeavour Straits even Parkin ceased to visit us, this duty being left to the master-at-arms. The lieutenants as well as the captain himself were continually occupied with the navigation of the ship. Every day one, and sometimes two, of the ship's boats were sent out in advance of the frigate, for we had now reached the northern extremity of the Great Barrier Reef which extends along the eastern coast of Australia, as treacherous an extent of shoal-infested ocean as any on the surface of the globe. Our course was extremely tortuous, among reefs and sand-bars innumerable, and all day long we could hear the calls of the men heaving the lead as we worked our way slowly along. Not even the prisoners suffered from boredom at this time. Those of us who could see something of what was taking place outside kept constant watch, reporting to others the dangers sighted or passed.

The twenty-eighth of August was a dismal day of alternate calms and black squalls which greatly increased the dangers of navigation. Looking from my knot-hole at dawn, I saw that we were in the midst of a labyrinth of reefs and shoals upon which the sea broke with great violence. The frigate had been hove-to during the night, and now one of the boats, with Lieutenant Corner in command, had gone ahead to seek for a possible passage. We could see little of what was taking place, but the orders continually shouted from the quarter-deck indicated only too clearly the difficulties in which the ship found herself. Once, as we wore about, we passed within half a cable's length of as villainous a reef as ever brought a sailor's heart into his mouth.

So it went all that day, and as evening drew on it was apparent that we were in greater danger than we had been at dawn. The launch was still far in advance of us, and a gun was fired as a signal for her to return. Darkness fell swiftly. False fires were burned and muskets fired to indicate our position to the launch. The musket fire was answered from the launch, and as the reports became more distinct we knew that she was slowly approaching. All this while the leadsmen were continually sounding, finding no bottom at one hundred and ten fathoms; but soon we heard them calling depths again: fifty fathoms, forty, thirty-six, twenty-two. Immediately upon calling this latter depth the ship was put about, but before the tacks were hauled on board and the sails trimmed, the frigate struck, and every man in the roundhouse was thrown sprawling to the length of his chain.

Before we could recover ourselves the ship struck again, with such force that we thought the masts would come down. It was now pitch-dark, and to make matters worse another heavy squall bore down upon us. Above the roaring of the wind we could hear the voices of the men, sounding faint and thin as orders were shouted. Every effort was made to get the ship free by means of the sails, but, this failing, they were furled and the other boats put over the side for the purpose of carrying out an anchor. The squall passed as suddenly as it had come, and we now heard distinctly the musket shots of the men in the returning launch.

The violence of the shocks we had received left no doubt in our minds that the ship had been badly damaged. I heard Edwards's voice: "How does she do, Mr. Roberts?" and Roberts's reply: "She's making water fast, sir. There's nearly three feet in the hold."

The effect upon the prisoners of this dreadful news may be imagined. Hillbrandt and Michael Byrne began to cry aloud in piteous voices, begging those outside to release us from our irons. All our efforts to quiet them were useless, and the clamour they made, with the tumult of shouting outside and the thunder of the surf on the reef where we lay, added to the terror and gloom of the situation.

Hands were immediately turned to the pumps, and orders were given that other men should bail at the hatchways. Presently the grating over the roundhouse scuttle was unlocked and the master-at-arms entered with a lantern. He quickly unshackled Coleman, Norman, and McIntosh, and ordered them on deck to lend a hand. We begged the master-at-arms to release all of us, but he gave no heed, and when he had gone out with the three men the iron grating was replaced and locked as before.

Some of the prisoners now began to rave and curse like madmen, wrenching at their chains in the vain effort to break them. At this time Edwards appeared at the scuttle and sternly ordered us to be silent.

"For God's sake, unshackle us, sir!" Muspratt called. "Give us a chance for our lives!"

"Silence! Do you hear me?" Edwards replied; then, to the master-at-arms, who stood beside him by the scuttle: "Mr. Jackson, I hold you responsible for the prisoners. They are not to be loosed without my orders."

"Let us bear a hand at the pumps, sir," Morrison called, earnestly.

"Silence, you villains!" Edwards called, and with that he left us.

Realizing now that pleading was useless, the men quieted down, and we resigned ourselves to the situation in that mood of hopeless apathy that comes over men powerless to help themselves. Within an hour another tempest of wind and rain struck us, and again the frigate was lifted by the seas and battered with awful violence on the reef. These repeated shocks threw us from side to side and against the walls and each other, so that we were dreadfully cut and bruised. As nearly as we could judge, the ship was being carried farther and farther across the reef. At length she lay quiet, down by the head, and we heard Lieutenant Corner's voice: "She's clear, sir!"

It must then have been about ten o'clock. The second squall had passed, and in the silence that followed the screaming of the wind we could plainly hear the orders being given. The guns were being heaved over the side, and the men who could be spared from bailing and pumping were employed in thrumbing a topsail to haul under the ship's bottom, in an endeavor to fother her. But the leak gained so fast that this plan had to be abandoned, and every man on board, with the exception of our guards and ourselves, fell to bailing and pumping.

Edwards's conduct toward us is neither to be explained nor excused. The reef upon which the *Pandora* had struck was leagues distant from any land, with the exception of a few small sand-bars and stretches of barren rock. Had we been free, there would have been no possibility of escape; and yet Edwards doubled the guard over the roundhouse and gave orders to the master-at-arms to keep us chained hand and foot. Fortunately, we did not realize the imminence of our danger. The roundhouse being on the quarter-deck, we were high above the water, and while we knew that the ship was doomed, we did not know that the leak was gaining so rapidly. It was, in fact, a race between the sea and daylight, and had the frigate gone down in the night, every man on board of her must have perished.

In the first grey light of dawn, we realized that the end was a matter, not of hours, but of minutes. The frigate's stern was now high out of water, and the pitch of the deck made it impossible to stand. The boats were lying close by, and the officers were busy getting supplies into them. In the forward part of the vessel the water was fast approaching the gun-ports. Men swarmed on top of the roundhouse and were going into the boats by the stern ladders. We called to those outside, begging and pleading that we might not be forgotten, and some of the men began wrenching at their leg irons with the fury of despair. What the orders respecting us were, or whether any had been given, I know not, but our entreaties must have been heard by those outside. Joseph Hodges, the armourer's mate, came down to us and removed the irons of Byrne, Muspratt, and Skinner; but Skinner, in his eagerness to get out, was hauled up with his handcuffs on, the two other men following close behind. Then the scuttle was closed and barred again. This was done, I believe, by the order of Lieutenant Parkin, for a moment before I had seen him peering down at us.

Hodges had not noticed that the scuttle had been closed. He was unlocking our irons as rapidly as possible when the ship gave a lurch and there was a general cry of "There she goes!" Men were leaping into the water from the stern, for the boats had pushed off at the first appearance of motion in the ship. We shouted with all our strength, for the water was beginning to flow in upon us. That we were not all drowned was due to the humanity of James Moulter, the boatswain's mate. He had scrambled up on the roof of the roundhouse in order to leap into the sea, and, hearing our cries, he replied that he would either set us free or go to the bottom with us. He drew out the bars that fastened the scuttle to the coamings, and heaved the scuttle overboard. "Hasten, lads!" he cried, and then himself leaped into the sea.

In his excitement and fear, the armourer's mate had neglected to remove the handcuffs of Burkitt and Hillbrandt, although they were free of their leg irons. We scrambled out, helping each other, and not a moment too soon. The ship was under water as far as the mainmast, and I saw Captain Edwards swimming toward the pinnace, which was at a considerable distance. I leaped from the stern and had all I could do to clear myself from the driver boom before the ship went down. I swam with all my strength and was able to keep beyond the suction of the water as the stern of the frigate rose perpendicularly and slid into the sea. Few seamen know how to swim, and the cries of drowning men were awful beyond the power of words to describe. All hatch covers, spare booms, the coops for fowls, and the like, had been cut loose, and some of the men had succeeded in reaching floating articles; but others went down almost within reach of planks or booms that might have saved them. I swam to one of the hatch covers and found Muspratt at the other end. He was unable to swim, but told me that he could hang on until he should be picked up. I swam to a short plank, and, with this to buoy me, started in the direction of one of the boats. I had been in the water nearly an hour before I was taken up by the blue yawl. Of the prisoners, Ellison and Byrne had been rescued by this boat, which was now filled with men, and we set out for a small sandy key on the reef at a distance of about three miles from where the ship went down. This was the only bit of land above water anywhere about, although there were shoals on every side near enough to the surface for the sea to break over them.

There was quiet water at the key, which was nearly encircled by reef, and we had no difficulty in landing. As soon as the men were disembarked, with such provision as the boat contained, the yawl was sent back to the scene of the wreck. Ellison, Byrne, and I were kept at the oars, and Bowling, the master's mate, was at the tiller. We made a wide search among floating wreckage, and so strong were the currents thereabout that we took up men as far as three miles from the reef where the ship had struck. We rescued twelve in all, among them Burkitt, clinging to a spar with his handcuffs still on his wrists.

It was nearly midday before we returned to the key, and by that time the other boats had assembled there. The sand-bar, for it was no more than that, was about thirty paces long by twenty wide. Nothing grew there — not a sprig of green to relieve the eyes from the blinding glare of the sun. Captain Edwards ordered a muster of the survivors, and it was found that thirty-three of the ship's company and four of the prisoners had been drowned. Of the prisoners, Stewart, Sumner, Hillbrandt, and Skinner were missing.

Morrison told me that he had seen Stewart go down. He had not been able to get clear of the ship as she foundered. A heavy spar had shot up from the broken water, and as it fell Stewart was struck on the head and sank instantly. Of all the events that had happened since the *Bounty* left England, excepting only my parting from my wife and little daughter, Stewart's death was the one that cast the deepest gloom upon my spirit. A better companion and a truer friend, in good fortune and bad, never lived.

Captain Edwards ordered tents to be erected with the sails from the ship's boats, one for the officers and one for the men. We prisoners were sent to the windward end of the sand-bar, and, as there was no possibility of escape, we were not guarded in the daytime; but two sentinels were placed over us at night, lest ten of us should attack a ship's company nearly ten times our strength. Nor were we permitted to speak to anyone save each other. During our five months' confinement in the frigate, our bodies, which had become inured to tropical sunlight at the time of our capture, had bleached, and were almost as white as that of any counting-house clerk in London. Most of us were stark naked, and our skin was soon terribly blistered by the sun. We begged to be allowed to erect a shelter for ourselves with one of the sails not in use, but Edwards was so lacking in humanity as to refuse this request. Our only recourse was to wet the burning sand at the water's edge and bury ourselves in it up to the neck.

The suffering from thirst was scarcely to be endured. Nearly all of us had swallowed quantities of salt water before we had been rescued by the boats, which added to our torture. The provision that had been saved was so scanty that each man's allowance on the first day spent on the key was two musket-balls' weight of bread and a gill of wine. No water was issued that day. Lieutenant Corner made a fire with some bits of driftwood, placed a copper kettle over it, and, by saving the drops of steam condensed in the cover, got about a wine-glass full of water, which was issued to the ship's company, a tea-spoonful per man, until the supply was exhausted. One of the seamen, a man named Connell, went out of his senses from drinking salt water.

We prisoners were far too miserable to converse. We lay by the water's edge, covered by sand and longing for darkness; and when it came we were only a little less wretched than before. Our raging thirst and our burned and blistered bodies made sleep impossible. The following morning the *Pandora's* master was sent in the pinnace to the scene of the wreck to learn whether anything else might be recovered from it. He returned with a part of the topgallant masts which were above water, and with a cat which he had found perched on the cross-trees. This poor animal was saved only to be sacrificed to the needs of shipwrecked seamen. It was cooked and eaten that same day, and a cap was made from its fur to cover the bald head of one of the officers who had lost his wig.

The following day was a repetition of the preceding one. In the early morning a search was made in the shallow water along the sand-bar for shellfish, and a number of giant cockles were discovered; but the thirst of every man was so great that these could not be eaten and had to be thrown away. The carpenters were employed in pre-paring the boats for the long voyage ahead of us. The floor boards were cut into uprights which were fastened to the gunwales, and around these canvas was stretched to prevent the sea from breaking into the boats, for they would all be so heavily loaded as to leave very little freeboard.

On the morning of August 31, the repairs to the boats having been completed, Captain Edwards mustered the company. We prisoners were herded together, under guard, a little to one side of the others. Officers, seamen, and prisoners alike, we were as gaunt and woebegone a crowd as had ever been cast ashore from a shipwrecked vessel. Edwards was clad in his shirt, trousers, and pumps, without stockings. Dr. Hamilton was in a like costume except that he had lost his shoes; but he had saved his medicine chest, and he took an opportunity to whisper to me that my Journal and manuscripts had been saved with it. Most of the sailors were naked to the waist, but had managed to come ashore in their trousers, and, with the exception of three or four, wore turbans made of large red or yellow handkerchiefs twisted about their heads, a common article of dress among the men at sea. Of the prisoners, four of us were stark naked, and the others had only rags of pulpy Indian bark cloth about their waists. We were all without hats and our bodies were seared and blistered by the sun. Muspratt in particular suffered terribly from his burns. Our condition spoke eloquently for us, but Edwards would have done nothing had it not been that Dr. Hamilton urged him to allow the naked men to have some remnants of canvas. It was owing to the surgeon that they had some slight covering from the pitiless sun.

Edwards walked up and down in front of the company for some time. We were gathered in a half-circle before the boats, which were ready to be launched. The sky was cloudless and the sea of the deepest blue, save where it broke over the reefs and shoals that stretched away before us. We waited in silence for the captain to speak. Presently he turned and faced us.

"Men," he said, "we have a long and dangerous voyage ahead of us. The nearest port at which we can expect help is the Dutch settlement on the island of Timor, between four and five hundred leagues from this place. We shall pass various islands on our way, but they are inhabited by savages from whom we have nothing to expect but the barbarity common to such people. Our supply of provision is so scant that each man's allowance will be small indeed; but it will be sufficient to maintain life even though we are unable to add to it during the passage. Each of us, officers, men, and prisoners alike, will receive the following allowance, which will be issued each day at noon: two ounces of bread, half an ounce of portable soup, half an ounce of essence of malt, two small glasses of water, and one of wine. It is to be hoped that we shall be able to add to our supplies during the voyage, but this cannot be counted upon.

"With favouring winds and weather we may be able to reach Timor in fourteen or fifteen days, but I must warn you that we can scarcely expect such good fortune. But within three weeks, if we meet with no accidents on the way, we shall be approaching our destination. Most of our provision must be carried in the launch, and for this reason, as well as for support and defense, the boats must keep together.

"I expect implicit obedience from every man, and cheerful and immediate compliance with the orders issued by your officers. Our safety depends upon this, and any infringement of discipline will be severely dealt with.

"Captain William Bligh, in a boat laden more deeply than any of ours, and with provision even more scanty, has made the same voyage that we are to make. He must have passed near this spot, and at that time he and his men had sailed and rowed their boat between six and seven hundred leagues. And he arrived at Timor with the loss of only one man. What he has done, we can do."

Edwards now turned to us.

"As for you," he continued, "you are not to forget that you are pirates and mutineers being taken to England to suffer the punishment you so richly merit. I am ordered by His Majesty's Government to have a proper regard for the preservation of your lives. This duty I shall continue to fulfill."

This was the first, indeed the only, time he condescended to address us directly.

The boats were now dragged into the water, and our company was distributed among them. Morrison, Ellison, and I were assigned to the captain's pinnace.

We were delayed in starting owing to the condition of the seaman Connell, the man who had drunk salt water to allay his thirst. All through the previous night he had been raving mad, and it was plain that he had only a few hours to live. In his condition it was impossible to take him into any of the boats. His sufferings were horrible, and offered an object lesson to anyone who might have been tempted to follow his example. Death came mercifully at about ten o'clock in the morning, and in his haste to embark Edwards read no burial service over the body. A shallow grave was scooped in the sand, and it was the work of no more than five minutes to bury him there. A lump of sun-blackened coral was placed as a headstone. No British seaman, I imagine, has had a lonelier grave.

We now quickly embarked, and, with the pinnace in the van, set out on our voyage to Timor.

## XIX · TEN WEARY MONTHS

WE had a fair wind and a calm sea, and the sail was hoisted directly we left the key. Edwards sat at the tiller. He looked as gaunt and ill-kempt as any of his men, but his lips were set in their usual thin line, and from the expression on his face he might have been walking the quarter-deck of the *Pandora*. One of the men cried, "Ho for Timor, lads!" but there was no response. We were so tortured by thirst that scarcely a word passed among the company.

Morrison, Ellison, and I had been placed in the bow of the pinnace. Her burden of twenty-four men brought her low in the water and made it impossible for Edwards to separate us from the seamen; but lest we should somehow contaminate them, he took the precaution of placing Hayward, and Rickards, the master's mate, next to us. When it was necessary for either of them to take the tiller, Packer, the gunner or Edmonds, the captain's clerk, took his place. When the wind failed we took our turns at the oars with the others, but we were never permitted to forget that we were pirates on the way to a rope's end on some ship of war in Portsmouth Harbour. Hayward evidently felt the awkwardness of his situation in being placed directly beside us in a small boat; but under Edwards's watchful eye he managed to maintain toward us his usual manner of contemptuous aloofness.

The calm sea was less than half a dozen miles in extent; then we found ourselves, as before the wreck, in the midst of a maze of sand-bars and half-drowned reefs, leagues distant from any land. The currents and tide-rips were as strong as they were treacherous, and it was necessary to take in sail and trust to the oars; but with the boat so heavily laden it was heart-breaking work keeping clear of the shoals. The floor of the sea was a miracle of vivid colouring, but its beauty became hateful to us, and I remember with what longing we looked ahead for the deep blue water that meant safety.

At midday our allowance of food and water was issued. Edwards had devised a pair of scales, using two musket balls for weights, and the water and wine were measured in a small glass. We had but two of these glasses, and it was necessary for each man to drink his allowance at once so that others might be served; but later we provided ourselves with clam shells which enabled us to sip as slowly as we pleased.

All the morning the four boats had kept within a mile of one another, and the work at the oars had increased our thirst to the point of agony. Most of us were without hats, and the heat of the tropical sun was like a heavy weight upon the brain. The only relief from it was to wet such garments as we had and place them on our heads, and many sponged their bodies, as well, with sea water, but the absorption through the skin of the salts in the water increased thirst and gave a nauseating taste to the saliva. Some of the men, made reckless by suffering, begged or demanded an increased allowance of water, and one of them, in the launch, after he had drunk his own allowance, tried to seize the glass of another as it was being passed from hand to hand, and the precious liquid was spilled. The man was immediately knocked senseless by Bowling, one of the master's mates, who clubbed him over the head with an emptied bottle. Under the circumstances, it was a well-deserved punishment. Edwards now spoke to the company.

"It is my purpose," he said, "to bring every man of you safe to Timor; but if we have another incident of this kind, the one responsible for it shall be shot. Let each man remember that his sufferings are shared by all of the others. To-morrow we shall be close in with the coast of Australia. Somewhere along that coast we shall undoubtedly find water; I promise that we shall not leave it until we do. Meanwhile, bear in mind what I have said."

From the condition of my own parched lips and swollen tongue, I was able to appreciate what an effort it must have cost Edwards to make even so brief an address to the company. We proceeded on our way, the four boats keeping within view of each other during the afternoon, and before sunset we had passed through the worst of the reefs and had more open water before us. The pinnace, which was still in the van, lay-to to allow the other boats to come up with her, and we made fast, bow and stern, lest we should become separated during the night. Never, I imagine, have men welcomed the coming of darkness more gratefully. The breeze was cool, and carried us smoothly on the way we would go. Oars were laid over the thwarts, and by this means we were able to stow two tiers of men, which gave us room to stretch our limbs a little.

At dawn the lines were again cast off, and each boat proceeded as best it could. We were now close in with the northernmost coast of Australia, but whether it was the continent itself or one of the innumerable islands adjoining it, no one of us knew. The land had an arid look, and we gazed at it with hopeless eyes, for it seemed unlikely that we should find water there. The pinnace and the red yawl were close together at this time. For several hours we coasted along within half a mile of the shore. We saw no signs of man or beast, and the vegetation was nothing more than scattered trees and hardy shrubs that looked as tortured with thirst as ourselves.

We came to an inlet that deeply indented the coast. The breeze died down, the oars were gotten out, and we rowed into the bay. Here the water was like a sheet of glass, reflecting the sky and the brown shore line. It was about three miles to the head of the bay, but, eager though we were to reach it, we made but slow progress in our enfeebled condition. As we approached we saw a narrow valley where the vegetation was of a much richer green, which made it all but certain that water was to be found there. At last we brought up within wading distance of the beach, and in their eagerness some of the men leaped into the water; but Edwards ordered them back until a guard had been told off in each of the boats to watch over the prisoners. The rest of the company were then permitted to go ashore, and we watched with feverish eyes as they spread out along the bay and proceeded inland. Then a shout was heard, and all of them rushed like madmen to one spot. An excellent spring had been found within fifty yards of the beach. It was all that our guards could do to prevent themselves from rushing after the others.

The delay was torture, but our turn came at last. We drank and drank and drank again until we could hold no more. Nothing mattered now. Having been relieved from the most terrible of all man's bodily sufferings, we were content. Those whose thirst was quenched crawled into the shade of the trees and fell asleep at once. They lay sprawled like dead men, around the spring. Edwards would gladly have remained here, but the launch and the blue yawl had, somehow, missed the bay and, shut in by land as we were, it was impossible to signal them. Therefore the men were kicked or buffeted awake by the officers, and having filled our small keg, the teakettle, two bottles, and even a pair of water-tight boots belonging to the gunner, we re-embarked. Several of the seamen were so exhausted that it was impossible to waken them. They were carried aboard and dropped into the bottom of the boats.

When we had emerged from the bay we saw the launch and the blue yawl far ahead of us. We made all haste to come up with them and signalled by musket fire; but the signals were not heard, and it was not until mid-afternoon that we managed to get abreast of them. They had found no water and we were now too far to leeward to permit them to return to the bay where the spring was. Edwards issued three wineglasses of water to each man in the two boats, and we made sail again.

At daybreak the following morning we were not far from an island that proved to be inhabited. It looked much less desolate than the mainland. The white sandy beach soon gave way to rising ground where there was abundant vegetation. We searched eagerly for a landing place; but we had been seen from afar, and as we proceeded the Indians gathered in ever greater numbers, following us along the beach. They were jet-black in colour and stark naked, and armed with spears and bows and arrows. Finding a break in the reef, we entered a narrow lagoon and approached to within half a cable's length of the shore. In a moment the place was thronged with savages in a state of great excitement, and it was evident that they had never before seen white men. We made signs to them that we wanted water, and after much persuasion half a dozen of them were coaxed near enough to the boats to enable us to give them some buttons cut from various articles of clothing. They took the keg of the pinnace, the only container of any size that we had for water, and presently returned with it filled. The eager, desperate haste with which we drank would have offered a pitiful sight to any civilized observer, but the savages laughed and yelled with delight as they watched us. The keg was soon emptied and again given to them, but upon bringing it back a second time they placed it on the beach and made signs for us to come and fetch it. This Edwards would not allow to be done, suspecting treachery, and he ordered the boats to push off to a safer distance. At this sign of timidity on our part the natives rushed forward to the water's edge and discharged a shower of arrows at us. Fortunately no one was hit, although there were many narrow escapes. One arrow struck a thwart in our boat, piercing an oak plank an inch thick. A volley was then fired over their heads, and the sound and the smoke so frightened them that all ran for their lives, and in an instant the beach was deserted. The pinnace pushed in to recover the keg. We got it, and none too soon, for the savages rushed out again, but we made off before any harm was done.

The savages were so numerous and so hostile that Edwards abandoned hope of refreshment here. Other islands were in view at this time, and rather than risk the loss of any of the company, we were ordered to proceed to the nearest of these. About two o'clock in the morning we entered a small bay which I still remember with the keenest pleasure. It was a cool cloudless night, with a late moon casting a glamorous light over the glassy surface of the water. The four boats entered in complete silence as a precaution against the presence of savages. We disembarked upon a beach of coral sand, packed hard and firm, and delightfully cool to our bare feet. The prisoners were taken aside under a guard, and two parties were told off to make an exploration of the place. The rest of the company remained by the boats with their arms in readiness. In about an hour's time the search parties returned with the welcome news that the place was deserted, and that they had found water. Every man had his thirst quenched that night. Sentinels were then posted, and all of the others stretched out on the cool sand for the sleep so desperately needed.

I awoke shortly after dawn, feeling completely refreshed and very hungry. The bay was still in shadow, but the light was streaming up from behind the green hills enclosing it. Morrison was awake, but the rest of the prisoners, as well as the *Pandora's* company, were sleeping as though they would never have done. Edwards let them have their sleep out, but as the men awakened they were sent out in small parties to search for food. A pleasanter refuge than this bay afforded could scarcely have been found, except for the fact that no food-bearing trees could be discovered, nor did those searching the shallows of the bay have any better success. Morrison and I proposed to the master-at-arms that the prisoners be permitted to forage for the ship's company. The request was carried to Edwards, who granted it with great reluctance. To be indebted to a group of pirates and mutineers for benefits of any kind was opposed to all his ideas of fitness; but, his own men having failed to discover anything save a few sea snails, we were sent out, well guarded, to see what we could do.

We made fishlines of bark cut into thin strips and braided, and we devised fish hooks with some nails furnished us by the carpenter. With other nails and long slender poles cut from the bush, we made fish spears, and, thus provided, we set out with the ever-present marines accompanying us in one of the ship's boats.

During our long sojourn at Tahiti we had learned how and where to search for shellfish, and within two hours we returned with the boat loaded with fish, lobsters, mussels, and the like, enough for two good meals for the whole company. We received no word of thanks from Edwards, and immediately we had returned we had the guard round us as before; but it was enough for us to see with what relish all hands partook of the meal.

We remained at this place, which Edwards named "Laforey's Island," all of that day and the following night. We found no Indians, but it was plainly used by them as a place of frequent resort. The ground in the vicinity of the spring was much footworn, and two or three well-used paths led over the hills toward the interior. Near the shore we found some heaps of sun-bleached human bones which gave us reason to believe that the people were cannibals. On the morning of September 2 we again embarked, greatly refreshed, and before night-fall had reached the open sea beyond Endeavour Straits.

For all the years that have passed, I still have a clear recollection of the feeling of horror and gloom that, at this time, seized the greater part of the men in the pinnace. Timor was still a thousand miles distant, and not many of us had more than a dim hope of reaching it. We had far more than our share of faint-hearts, for the *Pandora's* crew had been made up largely of landsmen, with no sense of the traditions of the sea, unaccustomed to the dangers and hardships which sailors take as a matter of course. Above all, they were ignorant of what a good ship's boat can do when ably handled. Luckily, most of the *Pandora's* officers were thorough seamen, and there was a saving leaven of the same type among the men.

Now that we were once more in the open sea, new dangers presented themselves. There was a heavy westerly swell running, and with our boats so deep in the water we were kept bailing constantly. Our only vessels were some giant mussel shells we had found at Laforey's Island, and they were heavy and ill-adapted to the purpose. During the first day we had not a moment of rest. The wind had come round to the east and, running counter to the swell, made a dangerous sea. There were times when every man of us was bailing who could be spared for the purpose, and at midday it was only with great difficulty that the food and water could be issued.

At nightfall the boats were again fastened to each other, but the towlines broke repeatedly, and we were in such danger of being dashed to pieces against each other that we were obliged to cast off and trust to Providence that we should be able to keep together. Muskets were fired in each of the boats at two-hour intervals, but these signals could not always be made, owing to our powder being wetted. At dawn we found ourselves widely scattered, and the blue yawl was so far to windward that for an hour or two we thought we had lost her; but at last we caught sight of her masthead as she rose to the crest of a sea.

By midday we had again assembled, and the meagre allowance of food and water was passed around. Those noonday meetings have left a series of indelible pictures in my mind. I see the blue yawl or the launch slowly approaching, looking inconceivably small and lonely, now lost to view in the trough of the sea, now clearly outlined against the sky as it rose to the swell. At last it is near enough so that we can make out the figures of the men, bailing, bailing, bailing, without respite. Now we are within half a cable's length of each other, and I see the faces, gaunt and hollow-eyed, and the expression of unutterable weariness upon each of them. We would stare at each other like so many spectres. Sometimes Edwards would call across to one of his officers: "How do you prosper, Mr. Corner?" or, "Is it well with your company, Mr. Passmore?" And the reply would come back, "We're not doing badly, sir." Then we would approach each other as closely as we dared while the precious food and water were being passed from boat to boat.

Dr. Hamilton was a tower of strength to the men in the red yawl. He suffered as much as the rest of us, but he heartened and encouraged everyone at these midday meetings. I was glad for the sake of Muspratt and Burkitt that the surgeon was with them, for Parkin was in charge of the red yawl, and he would have found the means to increase the misery of the prisoners had it not been for the doctor.

A curious incident occurred in the pinnace at one of these noonday assemblies. An elderly sailor named Thompson had carried with him from the wreck of the *Pandora* a small bag of dollars, his savings during many years. When the day's allowance of water was being issued, a wineglass was passed to the man sitting next him, a Scot named McPherson. Prompted by his raging thirst, Thompson offered the whole of his savings for this small glass of water. McPherson's struggle was a bitter one. His desire for the dollars — and it was a goodly sum, sewed up in a canvas bag — was almost equally balanced by his desire for the two or three mouthfuls of water the glass contained. The rest of us forgot our misery for a moment as we waited to see the result. Presently the master's mate said: "Do one thing or the other and be quick about it." "Give me the bag," said McPherson, but while Thompson was loosening the cord which held it to his waist, the Scot thought better of the matter and drank his allowance of water at a gulp.

The sufferings of the older men were, naturally, greater than those of the younger ones. A midshipman, who was no more than a boy, sold his allowance of water two days running for another man's allowance of bread. So terrible is thirst that several of the men drank their own urine. They died, without exception, in the sequel of the voyage.

We again attempted to keep the boats together by towing, during the nights of the fifth and sixth of September, but the lines broke as usual, and the strain on the boats was so great that we were obliged to abandon this method of keeping together during the night. Edwards had given his officers the exact latitude of Timor, and the longitude by the timekeeper on that date. This in case we should become separated. Fortunately, we managed to keep within sight of each other during the whole of the following week. In the pinnace we caught one booby, and the blood and flesh were divided into twenty-four shares and distributed in the old seaman's manner of "Who shall have this?" This good fortune came on the eleventh of September, at a time when we were sorely in need of it.

On the morning of the thirteenth land was sighted, a faint bluish blur on the Western horizon. At first we could not believe it possible that Timor was within view, but as the morning wore on even the skeptics were convinced that it was land and not cloud that we saw. We were so wretched in mind and body that we could not even summon up the strength to cheer when Rickards said, "It's Timor, lads. No doubt of it."

To add to our misery, it fell dead calm about the middle of the afternoon. The oars were gotten out and we proceeded wearily on. The boats now separated, each one being in haste to make the land. Some of the older men in the pinnace were by now so helpless that they lacked the strength to sit upright. They lay huddled in the bottom of the boat, moaning and crying out for water.

By noon of the following day we were close in with the land. The other boats were not in sight. The torture of thirst had become so great that Edwards decided to pass out our remaining supply of water, which came to half a bottle per man. This greatly refreshed us and we proceeded along the coast, seeking a possible landing place.

I remember nothing of the hinterlands of Timor. I have in mind only a dim picture of green hills and distant mountains. Every man's gaze, like my own, was fixed on the foreshore. There was a high surf running, and for several hours we found no place at which a boat could be landed without risk of its being dashed to pieces. Toward sunset we came to a more sheltered part of the coast, and two of the sailors swam ashore with bottles fastened about their necks. They proceeded along the beach, the boat following, until it was almost dark, without finding so much as a muddy creek where we might have refreshed ourselves. Having taken them aboard again, we stood off the land. We had the breeze again and made good progress during the night. The next morning we found an excellent landing place, and near it the water so urgently needed. I doubt whether some of the men could have survived another day without it, for we had been upon short rations so long that all the bodily juices were dried up.

About twelve o'clock on the night of September 15, the pinnace came to a grapnel off the float by the fort in Coupang Bay. It was a calm night with the sky ablaze with stars. The settlement was asleep. A ship was anchored not far from where we lay, and two or three smaller craft, but in the darkness we were unable to see whether any of the other boats of the *Pandora* had arrived. The night was profoundly still. On the high rampart of the fort a dog stood, barking mournfully. That was our welcome to Coupang. Worn out with our long journey, we remained where we were until daylight, sleeping huddled in our places, and never, I imagine, have men slept more soundly.

I shall give only a brief account of our experiences from the morning of our arrival at Coupang until the day when we sighted the cliffs of Old England. Captain Edwards and his men doubtless enjoyed the stay at Coupang, where they were the guests of the Dutch East India Company. As for the prisoners, we were guests of another sort. We were taken at once to the fort and placed in stocks in the guardroom, a dreary place with a bare stone floor, and lighted by two small barred windows high in the wall. Parkin took charge of us again, and he saw to it that we lacked even the most primitive means for comfort. Edwards never once visited us, but we were not forgotten by Dr. Hamilton. During the first week at Timor, he was kept busy attending the *Pandora's* sick, several of whom died within a few days of our arrival; but as soon as he was free to do so he paid us a visit, accompanied by the Dutch surgeon of the place. So foul was our prison by that time that before they could enter it the place had to be scrubbed out by slaves, and ourselves with it. We begged Dr. Hamilton to use his influence so that Lieutenant Corner might be placed in charge of us; but Corner being a decent and humane man, Edwards would not consent to this. We remained in Parkin's care, and he made our life so wretched that we wished ourselves dead a dozen times over before we reached the Cape of Good Hope.

On October 6 the entire company was embarked on the *Rembang,* a Dutch East India ship, for the passage to Batavia, on the island of Java. The *Rembang* was an ancient vessel, and leaked so badly that it was necessary to work the pumps every hour in the twenty-four. We prisoners were kept at this work, and, exhausting though it was, we preferred it to confinement below decks. Near the island of Flores a great storm arose, which struck us so suddenly that every sail on the ship was torn to ribbons. The Dutch sailors believed the vessel lost, and there was reason to think so, for the pumps became choked and useless at the time when we most needed them, and the ship was fast driving on a lee shore only seven miles distant. It was due to Edwards, who took command, and the exertion of some of our British tars, that we weathered the storm.

We arrived at Samarang on October 30, and here, to the amazement and delight of everyone, we found the schooner *Resolution,* from which we had become separated among the Navigators' Islands four months earlier. After losing sight of the *Pandora,* Oliver, the master's mate in charge of the *Resolution,* had cruised about for several days in search of us, and had then proceeded to the Friendly Islands. Namuka was the island appointed for a rendezvous in case of such an emergency, but Oliver had gone to Tofoa, mistaking this island for Namuka, and so had missed us. He and his crew of nine had undergone dangers and hardships equal to, if not greater than, our own. Upon reaching the great reef that stretches between New Guinea and the coast of Australia, they had searched in vain for an opening, and then formed the desperate resolve of running over the reef on the crest of a sea. It was a chance in a hundred, but they succeeded, and were later saved from death by thirst when they met a small Dutch vessel beyond Endeavour Straits. Having been supplied with food and water, they pursued their voyage to Samarang, where we found them.

Edwards sold the *Resolution* at Samarang, and the money was divided among the *Pandora's* crew for the purchase of clothing and other necessities. This seemed hard upon Morrison and the other prisoners who had built the schooner. Not a shilling did they receive, but they at least had the satisfaction of knowing that they had built a staunch little ship, as good as any turned out by the shipwrights of England. After her sale at Samarang she had a long and honourable career in the western Pacific, and made the record passage between China and the Sandwich Islands.

At Samarang the *Rembang* was reconditioned and we proceeded to Batavia, where the company was divided and transshipped to four vessels of the Dutch East India Company for the long voyage to Holland. Captain Edwards, with Lieutenant Parkin, the master, purser, gunner, clerk, two midshipmen, and the ten prisoners from the *Bounty,* embarked on the *Vreedenburg,* and on January 15, 1792, we arrived at the Cape of Good Hope, where we found *H.M.S. Gorgon* awaiting orders for England. Edwards therefore left the *Vreedenburg* and took passage for all of his party on the *Gorgon.* We remained at the Cape for nearly three months, during which time we were confined on the *Gorgon.* Mr. Gardner, first lieutenant of that vessel, treated us with great humanity. We were chained by one leg only, instead of having both feet and both hands in irons as heretofore, and we were given an old sail to lie upon at night, a luxury we had not enjoyed during the previous twelve months. On the long passage to England we were permitted to remain on deck for several hours each day to enjoy the fresh air. This circumstance was galling to Edwards, who would have kept us below during all that weary time; but as the ship was not his, he was not in a position to protest.

On the nineteenth of June we arrived off Spithead, and before dark had anchored in Portsmouth Harbour. Four years and six months had passed since the *Bounty's* departure from England, during which time we had spent nearly fifteen months in irons.

## XX · SIR JOSEPH BANKS

EVERY vessel in Portsmouth Harbour knew of the arrival of the *Gorgon,* and that she had brought home with her some of the notorious *Bounty* mutineers. The harbour was crowded with shipping at this time, merchant vessels and ships of war. Among the latter was *H.M.S. Hector,* and on the morning of June 21, 1792, we were transferred to this vessel to await court-martial. It was a cloudy day, threatening rain, with a fresh breeze blowing, and the choppy waves slapped briskly against the bow of the boat. As we passed ship after ship we saw rows of heads looking down at us from the high decks, and groups of men crowded at the gun-ports for a view of us. We knew only too well what they were thinking and saying to each other: "Thank God I'm not in any of those men's boots!"

We were received with impressive solemnity on board the *Hector*. A double line of marines with fixed bayonets were drawn up on either side of the gangway. There was a deep silence as we passed between them and down to the lower gundeck. No doubt we looked like pirates in our nondescript clothing acquired here and there all the way from Timor to England. Some of us were without hats, others without shoes, and none of us had anything resembling a uniform. The rags that we wore consisted of cast-off garments given us by various kind-hearted English sailors at Batavia and at Table Bay, — chiefly by men of the *Gorgon*, — and they were in a wretched state indeed by the time we reached home. We were conducted to the gun room which lay right aft, and it was a great relief to find that the treatment to which Edwards had so long accustomed us was now a thing of the past. We were regarded, not as condemned men, but as prisoners awaiting trial, and what a world of difference this made can be appreciated only by men who have been placed in a similar situation. Neither leg irons nor handcuffs were placed upon us, and we had the freedom of the gun room, which was guarded by marines. We had decent food, hammocks to sleep in, and were granted all privileges comportable with our position as prisoners.

Considering our hardships and the fact that we had been so long in irons, it is remarkable that we were all in good health. None of us had been ill in all that time, and yet many of the *Pandora's* company had been continually ailing, and more than a dozen of them had died at Timor and Samarang and Batavia. No doubt Edwards took credit to himself for our condition, but he deserved none. We were well, not because of his treatment, but in spite of it.

We had not been above an hour on board the *Hector* when I was summoned to the cabin of Captain Montague, who commanded the vessel. He dismissed the guard and bade me, in a most kindly fashion, to be seated. No mention was made of the mutiny. For a quarter of an hour he chatted with me in the courteous, affable manner he might have used toward one of his officers whom he had asked to dine with him. He questioned me at length concerning the wreck of the *Pandora,* and our subsequent adventures on the voyage to Timor. He was evidently interested in the story, but I was sure that I had not been summoned merely to entertain him with an account of our experiences. At length he opened a drawer in his table and drew forth a small packet which he handed to me.

"I have some letters for you, Mr. Byam. You may have as much time as you like here, alone. When you are ready to return to your quarters. you have only to open the door and inform the guard."

He then left me, and I opened the packet with trembling hands. It contained a letter from Sir Joseph Banks, written only a few days earlier, upon his receipt of the news of the *Gorgon's* arrival. He informed me that my mother had died six weeks before, and enclosed a letter to me written the night before her death, forwarded to him by our old servant, Thacker.

I was grateful indeed to Captain Montague for the privilege of half an hour's privacy in his cabin; but there was no relief, then or later, for the desolation of heart I felt. Scarcely a day had passed, in the years since the *Bounty* had left England, that I had not thought of my mother and longed for her, and the consciousness of her love had sustained me through all the weary months of our imprisonment. There was never any question of her belief in my innocence, but she was as proud in spirit as she was gentle and kind-hearted, and the slur cast upon our good name by the event of the mutiny — above all, the fact that Bligh considered me among the guiltiest of the mutineers — was a shock beyond her strength to withstand. There was nothing of this in her letter; I had the facts, later, from Thacker, who told me that my mother's health had begun to fail from the day when she had received the letter from Bligh. I have made all possible allowances for him. He had reason to believe that I was an accomplice of Christian; but a man with a spark of humanity would never have written the letter he sent to my mother. I no more forgive him the cruelty of it now than I did when I first read it.

It was the irony of my fate that, having been blessed with the steadfast love of two women, I should now — at a time when I most needed them — be separated from my mother by death and from my Indian wife by half the circumference of the globe. Upon these two I had centred all my affections. Now that my mother was gone, I clung to the memory of Tehani more tenderly than ever before.

What might now happen seemed a matter of little consequence. I could not imagine life in England without my mother; the thought that I might lose her had never occurred to me. But when I became calmer, I realized that, for her sake at least, it was necessary to clear our name from the stigma attached to it. I must prove my innocence beyond all question.

Sir Joseph Banks came to see me only a few days after I had received his letter. My own father could not have been kinder. He had seen my mother only a few weeks before her death, and he gave me all of the small details of that visit. He remembered everything she had said, and he allowed me to question him to my heart's content. I felt immeasurably comforted and strengthened. Sir Joseph was one of those men who seem members of a race apart; who find themselves equally at home among all kinds and conditions of people. In appearance he was a typical John Bull, solidly made, with the clear ruddy complexion our English climate gives. He seemed to radiate energy, and no man could be five minutes in his presence without being the better for it. At this time he was President of the Royal Society, and his name was known and honoured, not only in England, but on the Continent as well. I doubt whether there was a busier man in London, and yet, during those anxious weeks before the court-martial, one would have thought that his only concern was to see to it that all of us were given justice and fair play.

He quickly roused me from my despairing mood, and I found myself talking with interest and enthusiasm of my Tahitian dictionary and grammar. I told him that my manuscripts had been saved from the wreck of the *Pandora* and were in the care of Dr. Hamilton, now on his way home with the rest of the *Pandora's* survivors.

"Excellent, Byam! Excellent!" he said. "There is one gain, at least, from the voyage of the *Bounty*." He had the faculty of entering with enthusiasm into another man's work, and of making him feel that there was nothing more important. "I shall see Dr. Hamilton the moment he arrives in England. But enough of this for the present. Now I want your story of the mutiny — the whole of it — every detail."

"You have heard Captain Bligh's account, sir? You know how black the case against me appears to be?"

"I do," he replied, gravely. "Captain Bligh is my good friend, but I know his faults of character as well as his virtues. His belief in your guilt is sincerely held; yet allow me to say that I have never for a moment doubted your innocence."

"Is Captain Bligh now in England, sir?" I asked.

"No. He has again been sent to Tahiti to fulfill the task of conveying breadfruit plants to the West Indies. This time, I hope, the voyage will be successfully completed."

This was serious news for me. I felt certain that, if I could confront Bligh, I could convince him of my innocence, force him to acknowledge that he had been mistaken in jumping to the conclusion that the conversation with Christian had concerned the mutiny. With him gone, only his sworn deposition at the Admiralty would confront me, and there was no possibility of its being retracted.

"Put all that aside, Byam," said Sir Joseph. "There is no help for it, and all your desire to confront Bligh won't bring him back in time for the court-martial. Now proceed with your story, and remember that I am completely in the dark with respect to the part you played."

I then gave him, as I had given Dr. Hamilton, a complete account of the mutiny, and of all that had happened since. He allowed me to finish with scarcely an interruption. When I had done so I waited anxiously for him to speak.

"Byam, we may as well face the facts. You are in grave danger. Mr. Nelson, who knew of your intention to go in the launch with Bligh, is dead. Norton, the quartermaster, who could have corroborated your story of Christian's intention to escape from the *Bounty* on the night before the mutiny, is dead."

"I know it, sir. I had the information from Dr. Hamilton."

"Your chance of acquittal depends almost entirely upon the testimony of one man: your friend Robert Tinkler."

"But he returned safely to England."

"Yes, but where is he now? . . . He must be found at once. You say that he is a brother-in-law of Fryer, the master of the *Bounty?*"

"Yes, sir."

"In that case I should be able to get trace of him. I can learn, at the Admiralty, on what ship Fryer is now serving."

I had, somehow, taken it for granted that Tinkler would know of the need I should have for him if ever I returned home; but Sir Joseph pointed out to me the fact that Tinkler would be quite ignorant of this.

"It is not at all likely," he said, "that he will know of Bligh's depositions at the Admiralty. And it will no more have occurred to him than it did to you that your conversation with Christian could be construed as evidence against you. The chances are that Tinkler will have forgotten that Bligh overheard it. No; take my word for it, he will have no fears on your account. Not a moment must be lost in finding him."

"How soon will the court-martial take place, sir?" I asked.

"That rests with the Admiralty, of course. But this matter has been hanging fire for so long that they will wish to dispose of it as soon as possible. It will be necessary to wait until the rest of the *Pandora's* company arrive, but they should be nearing England by this time."

Sir Joseph now left me. He was to return to London by that night's coach.

"You shall hear from me shortly," he said. "Meanwhile, rest assured that I shall find your friend Tinkler if he is to be found in England."

Our conversation had taken place in Captain Montague's cabin. The other prisoners were anxiously awaiting my return to the gun room. Sir Joseph was the first visitor we had had; in fact, we were not permitted to see anyone except persons officially connected with the forthcoming court-martial. Sir Joseph was not, perhaps, so connected, but his interest in the *Bounty* and his influence at the Admiralty gave him access to us.

I gave the others an account of my conversation with him, omitting only his opinion of the fate in store for Millward, Burkitt, Ellison, and Muspratt. These men were, he thought, doomed past hope, with the possible exception of Muspratt. Byrne was entirely innocent of any part in the mutiny, but the poor fellow had been treated as a condemned man for so long that he had more than half come to believe himself guilty. As for Coleman, Norman, and McIntosh, it was inconceivable to any of us that they would be convicted. Morrison was in a situation only less dangerous than my own, and it grieved me to think that I was responsible for it. Our delay below decks on the morning of the mutiny, in the hope of getting possession of the arms chest, was known only to ourselves, and the chances were that the story would be regarded as a fiction invented afterward to explain our absence at the time the launch put off.

We had talked of the forthcoming court-martial so often during the long passage to England that we had little more to say to each other now that the event loomed so ominously near. At times, as a relief from anxiety, we spoke of our happy life at Tahiti, but for the most part we spent our days silently, each man engaged in his own reflections; or we stood at the gun-room ports looking out at the busy

life of the harbour. There were times when I was seized with a sense
of the unreality of this experience, like that one feels upon waking
from some dream in which the events have been more than usually
disconnected and fantastic. Hardest of all to realize was the fact that
we were indeed at home again, lying at anchor only a few miles from
Spithead, whence the *Bounty* had sailed so long ago.

Meanwhile, owing to the kindness of Sir Joseph, we were provided
with decent clothing in which to appear before the court-martial. This
small diversion was a most welcome one, and to be properly clothed
again had an excellent effect upon our spirits.

Ten days passed before I had further word from Sir Joseph. The
letter I then received I still have in my possession, although it is now
faded and worn with age. To reread it is to recall vividly the emotion
I felt on the morning when it was handed to me by the corporal of
the guard at the gun-room door.

My dear Byam: —

I can imagine with what anxiety you are awaiting word from me. I regret
that I cannot go to Portsmouth at this time, for I should much prefer to
give you my news by word of mouth. This being impossible, a letter must
serve.

Upon returning to London I went directly to the Admiralty office, where
I learned that Fryer is now at his home in London, awaiting summons to
testify at the court-martial. I sent for him at once and learned that Tinkler,
shortly after his return to England, was offered a berth as master's mate on
the *Carib Maid,* a West India merchantman. The captain of the vessel was
a friend of Fryer's, and as it was a good berth for the lad, offering opportunity for advancement, he accepted it.

Tinkler returned from his first voyage a year ago, and shortly afterward
set out on a second one. Fryer received word, not three months since, that
the *Carib Maid* was lost with all hands in a hurricane near the island
of Cuba.

It would be useless to deny the fact that this is a great misfortune for you.
Even so, your situation, I believe, is not hopeless. I have had a long conversation with Fryer, who speaks of you in the most friendly terms. He is
convinced that you had no hand in the mutiny, and his testimony will be
valuable.

Cole, Purcell, and Peckover I have also seen. They are now stationed at
Deptford, awaiting summons to the court-martial. They all speak highly
of you, and Purcell tells me that you yourself told him of your intention
to leave in the launch with Bligh. They all know of Bligh's conviction that

you were an accomplice of Christian, and it speaks well for your character among them that they all believe you innocent.

My good friend, Mr. Graham, who has been Secretary to different admirals on the Newfoundland Station these past twelve years, and who has, consequently, acted as Judge Advocate at courts-martial all of that time, has offered me to attend you. He has a thorough knowledge of the service, uncommon abilities, and is a good lawyer. He already has most of the evidences with him.

Farewell, my dear Byam. Keep up your spirits, and rest assured that I shall be watchful for your good. I shall certainly attend the court-martial, and now that my friend, Graham, has consented to go down, I shall be more at ease than if you were attended by the first counsel in England.

My feeling upon reading this letter may be imagined. Sir Joseph had done what he could to soften the blow to me, but I was under no doubt as to the seriousness of my position. I knew that, without Tinkler's evidence, my case was all but desperate, no matter how ably it might be presented. Nevertheless, I clung to hope as a man will. I resolved to fight for my life with all the energy I possessed. In one sense, the stimulus of danger was a blessing in disguise, for it kept me from brooding over my mother's death. I put out of mind every thought not connected with the approaching trial.

Sea officers, as I had been informed by Sir Joseph, have a great aversion to lawyers. I was well content, therefore, to have Mr. Graham, a Navy man himself, as my representative. Morrison resolved to conduct his own case. Coleman, Norman, McIntosh, and Byrne, who had every reason to hope that they would be cleared of the charges against them, secured the services of a retired sea officer, Captain Manly, to represent and advise all four of them; and an officer from the Admiralty, Captain Bentham, was appointed by the Crown to care for the interests of the other men.

We were visited by these gentlemen during the following week, but the first to come was Mr. Graham. He was a tall spare man in his late fifties, of distinguished bearing, and with a quiet voice and manner that inspired confidence. From the moment of seeing him I was sure that my fortunes could not be in better hands. None of us had any knowledge of court-martial proceedings, and at my request Mr. Graham permitted us to question him with respect to these matters.

"I have the morning at your disposal, Mr. Byam," he said, "and I shall be glad to be of what assistance I can to any of you."

"I mean to conduct my own case, sir," Morrison said. "I should like particularly to know the exact wording of the Article under which we are to be tried."

"I can give you that precisely, from memory," Mr. Graham replied. "It is Article Nineteen, of the Naval Articles of War, which reads as follows: 'If any person, in or belonging to the Fleet, shall make, or endeavour to make, any mutinous assembly, upon any pretense whatsoever, every person offending herein, being convicted thereof by the sentence of the Court-Martial, shall suffer death.'"

"Has the Court no alternative course?" I asked.

"None. It must acquit, or convict and condemn to death."

"But supposing, sir, that there are extenuating circumstances," Morrison added. "Supposing that a mutiny arises in a ship, as it did in ours, where a part of the company have no knowledge of any intention to seize the vessel, and who take no part in the seizure?"

"If they remain in the vessel with the mutinous party, the law considers them equally guilty with the others. Our martial law is very severe in this matter. The man who stands neuter is considered an offender with him who lifts his hand against his captain."

"But there were some of us, sir," Coleman added, earnestly, "who would gladly have gone with Captain Bligh when his party was driven from the ship into the launch. We were retained against our will by the mutineers, who had need of our services."

"Such a situation calls for special consideration by the Court and will doubtless receive it," Mr. Graham replied. "If the men so retained can prove their innocence of any complicity, they stand in no danger."

"Sir, may I speak?" asked Ellison.

"Certainly, my lad."

"I was one of the mutineers, sir. I'd no hand in starting the trouble, but like all the rest of us I had no love for Captain Bligh, and I joined in when I was asked to. Is there any hope for me?"

Mr. Graham regarded him gravely for a moment.

"I prefer not to give an opinion on that," he said. "Suppose we let the question be decided by the court-martial itself."

"I'm not afraid of the truth, sir. If you think there's no chance, I'd be obliged if you'd tell me so."

But Mr. Graham would not commit himself. "Let me advise all of you not to prejudge your cases," he said. "I have sat through many a court-martial, and, as in any civil court of law, one is not justified in forming an opinion as to a possible verdict until all the evidence is in.

And so you see, young man," he added, turning to Ellison, "how mistaken I should be in attempting to tell you what I think."

The days dragged by with painful slowness. Before this time most of the men had received letters from their families. Some of them were many months old, but they were read none the less eagerly for that. With the exception of the letter received from my mother, at Tahiti, no news from families or friends had reached any of us during the more than four years we had been absent from home. Poor Coleman's family lived in Portsmouth, but he was not permitted to see them. Of all the married members of the *Bounty's* company, he was, I suspect, the only man who had remained faithful to his wife during our sojourn at Tahiti. To be prevented from seeing her and his children after all these years was a cruel blow.

July passed, and August, and still we waited.

## XXI · H.M.S. DUKE

ON the morning of September 12, the ten prisoners on board the *Hector* were ordered to hold themselves in readiness to proceed to *H.M.S. Duke*. It was a grey, chilly, windless day, so still that we could hear ships' bells from far and near striking the half-hours and the hours. The *Duke* was anchored abreast of the *Hector* and about a quarter of a mile distant. Shortly before eight o'clock we saw a longboat, with a guard of marines in dress uniform, put off from the great ship's side and approach the *Hector,* and on the stroke of the hour a solitary gun was fired from the *Duke*. It was the signal for the court-martial. Our time had come.

I cannot speak of the emotions of my fellow prisoners at that solemn moment, but I know that my own feeling was one of profound relief. We had waited too long and endured too much to be capable of intense emotion — at least, that was the case with me. I felt unutterably weary, in body and mind, and if I desired anything it was peace — the peace of certainty as to my fate, whatever it might be. I remember how impatient I was to arrive on board the *Duke*. One's sense of time is largely a matter of mood, and the voyage from the *Hector* to the gangway of the larger ship, brief as it was, seemed all but interminable.

The court-martial was held in the great cabin of the *Duke,* which extended the width of the vessel, from the forward limit of the poop to the stern gallery. The quarter-deck was thronged with people, chiefly officers in full-dress uniform who had assembled from the many ships of war in the harbour to attend the proceedings. There were also a number of civilians, Sir Joseph Banks among them. Dr. Hamilton, whom I had last seen at the Cape of Good Hope, was standing with the other officers of the *Pandora* by the bulwarks on the larboard side of the deck. Edwards was there, of course, with his satellite, Parkin, beside him. He glanced us over with his habitual air of cold hostility, and he appeared to be thinking: "These scoundrels freed from their irons? What gross neglect of duty!"

On the other side of the deck were gathered the officers of the *Bounty,* looking self-conscious and ill at ease in that company of ships' captains and admirals and rear admirals. It was a strange meeting for old shipmates, and many were the silent messages that passed back and forth as we looked eagerly at each other. Mr. Fryer, the master, was there, and Cole, the boatswain, and Purcell, the carpenter, and Peckover, the gunner. A clear picture flashed into mind of the last view we had had of them as they looked up at us from the launch across the widening space of blue water. Little any of us thought then that we should ever meet again.

The hum of conversation died away to silence as the door of the great cabin opened. Audience was admitted. The spectators filed into the room; then we were marched in with a guard, a lieutenant of marines with a drawn sword in his hand preceding us. We were ranged in a line by the bulkhead on the right-hand side of the door. During the first day's proceedings we were compelled to stand, but owing to the length of the trial, a bench was later provided for us.

A long table stood fore and aft in the middle of the cabin, with a chair at the head for the President of the Court; the other members sat along the sides at his right and left. A little to the right and to the rear of the President's seat was a small table for the Judge Advocate, and another, on the opposite side, for the writers who were to transcribe the proceedings. At still another table sat the advisors to the prisoners. On either side of the door leading to the stern gallery, and along the walls, were settees occupied by the sea officers and civilians who attended as spectators.

At nine o'clock precisely, the door opened again and the members of the Court filed in to their places. At the order of the master-at-arms the audience rose, and when the members of the Court were in their places, all were seated again. The names of the twelve men who held over us the power of life and death were as follows: —

The Right Honourable Lord Hood, Vice Admiral of the Blue, and Commander-in-Chief of His Majesty's ships and vessels at Portsmouth Harbour, *President*

> Captain Sir Andrew Snape Hammond, Bart.
> "      John Colpoys
> "      Sir George Montague
> "      Sir Roger Curtis
> "      John Bazeley
> "      Sir Andrew Snape Douglas
> "      John Thomas Duckworth
> "      John Nicholson Inglefield
> "      John Knight
> "      Albemarle Bertie
> "      Richard Goodwin Keats

My lethargy of the earlier part of the morning left me as I gazed at the impressive scene before me. At first my attention was fully engaged with our judges, whose faces I examined one by one as the opportunity presented itself. They were, for the most part, men in middle life, and one would have known them anywhere, in any dress, for officers in His Majesty's Navy. As I looked at their stern, wind-roughened, impassive faces, my heart sank. I recalled Dr. Hamilton's words: "But these men will know nothing of Christian's character, and their sympathies will all be with Captain Bligh. You will have to prove your story of that conversation with Christian beyond the shadow of a doubt." The only one of the twelve men who might, I thought, be willing to give a prisoner the benefit of a doubt was Sir George Montague, captain of the *Hector*.

Our names were called, and we stood before the Court while the charges against us were read. This document was of considerable length, and recapitulated the history of the *Bounty* from the time of her departure from England until she was seized by the mutineers. Then followed Bligh's sworn statement, his own account of the mutiny, a document of great interest to all of us, and to me in particular. The statement, which follows, was read by the Judge Advocate: —

I respectfully beg to submit to the Lords Commissioners of the Admiralty the information that His Majesty's armed vessel, *Bounty,* under my command, was taken from me by some of the inferior officers and men on the 28th of April, 1789, in the following manner.

A little before sunrise, Fletcher Christian, who was mate of the ship and officer of the watch, Charles Churchill, master-at-arms, Thomas Burkitt, seaman, and John Mills, gunner's mate, came into my cabin, and, while I was asleep, seized me in my bed and tied my hands behind my back with a strong cord; and, with cutlasses and bayonets fixed at my breast, threatened me with instant death if I spoke or made the least noise. I nevertheless called out so loud for help that everyone heard me and were flying to my assistance; but all of my officers except those who were concerned in the mutiny found themselves secured by armed sentinels.

I was now hauled upon deck in my shirt and without a rag else, and secured by a guard abaft the mizzenmast, during which the mutineers expressed much joy at my position.

I demanded of Christian the cause of such a violent act, but no answer was given but, "Hold your tongue, sir, or you are dead this instant!" He held me by the cord which tied my hands, and threatened to stab me with the bayonet he held in his right hand. I, however, did my utmost to rally the disaffected villains to a sense of their duty, but to no effect.

The boatswain was ordered to hoist the launch out, and while I was kept under a guard with Christian at their head, the officers and men not concerned in the mutiny were ordered into the boat. This being done, I was told by Christian: "Sir, your officers and men are now in the boat and you must go with them," and the guard carried me across the deck with their bayonets presented on every side. Upon attempting to make some resistance, one of the villains said to another: "Damn his eyes, the dog! Blow his brains out!" I was at last forced into the boat and we were then veered astern, in all, nineteen souls.

While the boat was yet alongside, the boatswain and carpenter and some others collected several necessary things, and with some difficulty a compass and quadrant were got, but no arms of any kind and none of my maps or drawings. The size of the boat was 23 feet from stem to stern, and rowed six oars. We were cast adrift with the following provision: 25 gallons of water, 150 pounds of bread, 30 pounds of pork, 6 quarts of rum, and 6 bottles of wine.

The boat was so lumbered and deep in the water that it was believed we could never reach the shore, and some of the pirates made their joke of this. I asked for arms, but the request was received with the greatest abuse and insolence. Four cutlasses were, however, thrown into the boat at the last moment, and in this miserable situation we set out for the island of Tofoa, one of the Friendly Islands, ten leagues distant from where the ship then was. This island we reached at seven o'clock the same evening, but the shore being very steep and rocky, we could find no chance of landing till the following day.

During our search for water at this island we were attacked by the savages and barely escaped with our lives, one of our number, John Norton, a quartermaster, being killed as he attempted to recover the launch's grapnel.

After considering our melancholy situation, I was earnestly solicited by all hands to take them toward home; and when I told them that no hope of relief remained for us until we came to Timor, a distance of 1200 leagues, they all agreed to live upon one ounce of bread per man each day, and one gill of water. Therefore, after recommending this promise forever to their memory, I bore away for New Holland and Timor, across a sea but little known, and in a small boat laden with 18 souls, without a single map of any kind, and nothing but my own recollection and general knowledge of the situation of places to direct us.

After enduring dangers and privations impossible to describe, we sighted Timor on the 12th of June, and on the morning of the 15th, before daylight, I anchored under the fort at the Dutch settlement at Coupang. This voyage in an open boat I believe to be unparalleled in the history of Navigation.

At Timor my boat's company were treated with the greatest humanity by the Governor and the officers of the Dutch East India Company. Here, for 1000 Rix dollars — for which I gave bills on His Majesty's Government — I purchased a small schooner, thirty-four feet long, which I fitted for sea under the name of His Majesty's schooner, *Resource*. In this vessel we proceeded by way of Surabaya and Samarang to the Dutch settlement of Batavia, where I sold the *Resource* and, with my people, embarked for Europe in ships of the Dutch East India Company.

The lists, which I herewith submit, of those who were cast adrift with me in the launch and those who remained in the *Bounty* will show the strength of the pirates.

I beg leave to inform their Lordships that the secrecy of the mutiny was beyond all conception, so that I cannot discover that any who were with me had the least knowledge of it.

It is of great importance to add that, on the night preceding the mutiny, coming upon deck during the middle watch, according to my custom, I discovered Fletcher Christian, the ringleader of the pirates, in earnest conversation with Roger Byam, one of the midshipmen. In the darkness of the deck I was not observed by these men, who were standing on the starboard side of the quarter-deck between the guns; nor had I any apprehension at that time that their conversation was not innocent. But as I approached, unseen, I saw Roger Byam shake hands with Christian, and I distinctly heard him say these words: "You can count on me," to which Christian replied:

"Good! That's settled, then." The moment they discovered me they broke off their talk. I have not the slightest doubt that this conversation concerned the forthcoming mutiny.

A moment of deep silence followed the reading of Captain Bligh's statement. I was conscious of the gaze of many pairs of eyes directed upon me. No more damning statement could have been brought forward, and it was only too plain how deep an impression it had made upon the Court. How, without Tinkler's evidence, could it possibly be refuted? A sense of the hopelessness of my situation came over me. I knew that had I been in the place of any of my judges, I should have felt certain of the guilt of at least one of the prisoners.

The Judge Advocate asked: "Do you wish me to read the names on the appended lists, my lord?"

Lord Hood nodded. "Proceed," he said.

The lists were then read — first the names of those who had gone in the launch with Bligh, then of those who remained with Christian's party. One thing that astonished me was Bligh's silence with respect to Coleman, Norman, and McIntosh. He well knew of their desire to go with him in the launch, and that they had been prevented from doing so by the mutineers. The barest justice demanded that he should have acknowledged their innocence; yet he made no distinction between them and the guiltiest members of Christian's party. To this day I am unable to account for his injustice to these men.

John Fryer, master of the *Bounty,* was now called. He had not changed in the least since I had last seen him, on the morning of the mutiny. He glanced quickly in our direction, but there was time for no more than a glance. He was directed to stand at the end of the table, opposite Lord Hood, and was sworn.

The Court said: "Inform the Court of all the circumstances within your knowledge concerning the running away with His Majesty's ship, *Bounty.*"

I shall give Fryer's testimony with few omissions, for it provides a clear picture of what was seen by the *Bounty's* master on the day of the mutiny.

"On the 28th of April, 1789, we tacked and stood to the south'ard and westward until the island of Tofoa bore north; then we steered west-northwest. In the first part of the evening we had little wind. I had the first watch. The moon was at that time in its first quarter. Between ten and eleven o'clock, Mr. Bligh came on deck agreeable to his usual custom, to leave his orders for the night. After he had been on deck some little time, I said, 'Sir, we have got a moon coming on which will be fortunate for us when we come on the coast of New Holland.' Mr. Bligh replied, 'Yes, Mr. Fryer, so it will,' which was all the conversation that passed between us. After leaving his orders, he went off the deck.

"At twelve o'clock everything was quiet on board. I was relieved by Mr. Peckover, the gunner. Everything remained quiet until he was relieved, at four o'clock, by Mr. Christian. At the dawn of day I was much alarmed, whether from the noise Mr. Bligh said he made or by the people coming into my cabin, I cannot tell. But when I attempted to jump up, John Sumner and Matthew Quintal laid their hands upon my breast and desired me to lie down, saying, 'You are a prisoner, sir. Hold your tongue or you are a dead man, but if you remain quiet, there is no person on board that will hurt a hair of your head.'

"I then, by raising myself on the locker, which place I always slept on for coolness, saw Mr. Bligh in his shirt, with his hands tied behind him, going up the ladder, and Mr. Christian holding him by the cord. The master-at-arms, Charles Churchill, then came to my cabin and took a brace of pistols and a hanger, saying, 'I will take care of these, Mr. Fryer.' I asked what they were going to do with their captain. 'Damn his eyes!' Sumner said. 'Put him into the boat and let the dog see if he can live on half a pound of yams a day.' 'Into the boat!' I said. 'For God's sake, what for?' 'Sir,' Quintal said, 'hold your tongue. Christian is captain of the ship, and recollect that Mr. Bligh has brought all this upon himself.'

"I then said, 'What boat are they going to put Captain Bligh into?' They said, 'The large cutter.' 'Good God!' I said, 'the cutter's bottom is almost out of her, being very much eaten with worms.' 'Damn his eyes,' Sumner and Quintal said, 'it is too good for him even so!' I said, 'I hope they are not going to set Captain Bligh adrift by himself?' They answered, 'No. Mr. Samuel, his clerk, and Mr. Hayward and Mr. Hallet are going with him.'

"At last I prevailed on them to call on deck to Christian to give me permission to go up, which, after some hesitation, he granted. Mr. Bligh was standing by the mizzenmast with his hands tied behind his back, and there were several men guarding him. I said, 'Mr. Christian, consider what you are about.' 'Hold your tongue, sir,' he replied. 'I have been in hell for weeks past. Captain Bligh has brought all this on himself.'

"Mr. Purcell, the carpenter, had been permitted to come on deck at the same time with myself, and Mr. Christian now ordered him to have the gear for the large cutter brought up. When we came to Mr. Christian, Mr. Byam was talking with him. I said, 'Mr. Byam, surely you are not concerned in this?' He appeared to be horrified at such a thought. Mr. Christian said, 'No, Mr. Fryer, Mr. Byam has no hand in this business.' I then said, 'Mr. Christian, I will stay with the ship,' thinking that, if permitted to do so, a chance might offer for retaking the vessel. Christian replied, 'No, Mr. Fryer, you will go with Captain Bligh.' He then ordered Quintal, one of the seamen under arms, to conduct me to my cabin while I collected such things as I should need.

"At the hatchway I saw James Morrison, the boatswain's mate. I said to him, 'Morrison, I hope you have no hand in this?' He replied, 'No, sir, I have not.' 'If that's the case,' I replied, in a low voice, 'be on your guard. There may be an opportunity for recovering ourselves.' His answer was, 'I'm afraid it is too late, Mr. Fryer.'

"I was then confined to my cabin, and a third sentinel was put on, John Millward, who, I thought, seemed friendly. Mr. Peckover, the gunner, and Mr. Nelson, the botanist, were confined in the cockpit, to which place I persuaded the sentinels to let me go. Mr. Nelson said, 'What is best to be done, Mr. Fryer?' I said to them, 'If we are ordered into the boat, say that you will stay on board, and I flatter myself that we shall recover the ship in a short time.' Mr. Peckover said, 'If we stay we shall all be deemed pirates.' I told them not; that I would answer for them and everyone that would join with me. At the time we were talking, Henry Hillbrandt, the cooper, was in the bread room, getting some bread to be put into the boat for Captain Bligh. I suppose he must have heard our conversation and had gone on deck to tell Mr. Christian, as I was immediately ordered up to my cabin. I heard from the sentinels that Christian had consented to give Mr. Bligh the launch, not for his own sake but for the safety of those who were going with him. I asked if they knew who was to go with Captain Bligh, and they said they believed a great many.

"Soon after this, Mr. Peckover, Mr. Nelson, and myself were ordered upon deck. Captain Bligh was then at the gangway. He said, 'Mr. Fryer, stay with the ship.' 'No, by God!' Christian replied. 'Go into the boat or I will run you through,' pointing his bayonet at my breast. I then asked Christian to permit Mr. Tinkler, my brother-in-law, to go with me. Christian said, 'No,' but after much solicitation he permitted him to go.

"I cannot say who was in the boat first, Mr. Bligh or myself; however, we were both on the gangway together. All of this time there was very bad language made use of by the people to Captain Bligh. We begged that they would give us two or three muskets into the boat, but they would not consent to it. The boat was then ordered astern. After lying astern for some time, four cutlasses were handed in, the people at the same time making use of very abusive language. I heard several of them say, 'Shoot the dog!' meaning Captain Bligh. Mr. Cole, the boatswain, said, 'We had better cast off and take our chance, for they will certainly do us a mischief if we stay much longer.' Captain Bligh very readily agreed. There was little wind. We got out the oars and rowed directly astern. Our reason for so doing was that we should sooner be out of reach of the guns.

"As soon as the boat was cast off I heard Christian give orders to loose the topgallant sails. They steered the same course as Captain Bligh had ordered, and continued to do so for the time we saw them.

"The confusion that prevailed on board was so great, and our attention, from that time to our arrival at Timor, so much taken up by regard for the preservation of our lives, that it was not possible for me to make any note or memorandum, even if I had had the means to do so, which I had not. This account is an exact statement of the case to the best of my recollection.

"The following is the list of persons that I observed under arms: Fletcher Christian, Charles Churchill, the master-at-arms, Thomas Burkitt, one of the prisoners, Matthew Quintal, John Millward, one of the prisoners, John Sumner and Isaac Martin. Joseph Coleman, armourer, one of the prisoners, wished to come into the boat and called several times to us to recollect that he had no hand in the business. Charles Norman, one of the prisoners, and Thomas McIntosh, another of the prisoners, also wished to come with us, but were prevented by the mutineers, who had need of their services on the ship. Michael Byrne, another of the prisoners, wished, I think, to come with us as well, but feared to do so lest the boat should be lost."

Fryer here ended his testimony.

The Court asked: "You have named seven persons who were under arms. Did you believe that these were the only persons under arms?"

Fryer: No.

The Court: What was your reason for so believing?

Fryer: From hearing the people in the boat say so, but I did not see any more, to the best of my recollection.

The Court: Inform the Court of the time you remained on deck at each of the times when you went on deck.

Fryer: About ten minutes or a quarter of an hour.

The Court: When you were upon the quarter-deck, did you see any of the prisoners active in obeying any orders from Christian or Churchill?

Fryer: I saw Burkitt and Millward under arms as sentinels.

The Court: When the launch was veered astern, did you observe any of the prisoners join in the bad language which you say passed upon that occasion?

Fryer: Not to the best of my recollection. I saw Millward upon the taffrail with a musket in his hand. There was so much noise and confusion that I could not hear one man from another.

The Court: You also say that when the cutlasses were handed into the boat, very bad language was used by the mutineers. Did any of the prisoners join in it upon that occasion?

Fryer: Not to my recollection. It was a general thing among the whole.

The Court: Did you see Thomas Ellison, one of the prisoners, upon the morning of the mutiny?

Fryer: Not at first. Later I did.

The Court: What was he doing?

Fryer: He was standing near Captain Bligh, but I cannot charge my memory as to what he was doing.

The Court: Did he have arms in his hands?

Fryer: I am not certain whether he had or no.

The Court: Did you see William Muspratt?

Fryer: No.

The Court: When Mr. Bligh and you were ordered into the boat, did any person assist, or offer to assist Mr. Christian in putting those orders into execution?

Fryer: Yes. Churchill, Sumner, Quintal, and Burkitt.

The Court: Were you near enough, when you heard Christian order the topgallant sails to be loosed, to know any of the people who went upon the yards?

Fryer: I saw only one, who was a boy at that time — Thomas Ellison.

The Court: How many men did it require to hoist out the launch?

Fryer: It might be done with ten men.

The Court: Did you see any of the prisoners assist in hoisting her out?

Fryer: Yes. Mr. Byam, Mr. Morrison, Mr. Coleman, Norman and McIntosh all assisted; but this was done at Mr. Cole's, the boatswain's, orders, passed through him by Mr. Christian.

The Court: Did you consider these men as assisting the mutineers or as assisting Captain Bligh?

Fryer: I considered them as assisting Captain Bligh, as giving him a chance for his life.

The Court: What reason had you to imagine that John Millward was friendly toward you at the time he was placed sentinel over you?

Fryer: He appeared to be very uneasy in his mind, as though he had taken arms reluctantly.

The Court: You say that you obtained permission for Tinkler to join the boat with you. Had he been compelled to remain in the ship?

Fryer: He had been told by Churchill that he was to stay aboard to be his servant, and came to tell me in my cabin.

The Court: In what part of the ship were the youngsters berthed?

Fryer: On the lower deck, on either side of the main hatchway.

The Court: Did you observe whether there was a sentinel over the main hatchway?

Fryer: Yes. I omitted to mention that Thompson was stationed there by the arms chest, with a musket and a bayonet fixed.

The Court: Did you consider him to have been a sentinel over the midshipmen's berth?

Fryer: Yes; over the berth and the arms chest at the same time.

The Court: Do you know that, on that day, any effort was made by any person in the ship to recover her?

Fryer: No.

The Court: What time elapsed from the first alarm to the time of your being forced into the boat?

Fryer: About two hours and a half, or three hours, to the best of my recollection.

The Court: What did you suppose to be Mr. Christian's meaning when he said that he had been in hell for weeks past?

Fryer: I suppose he meant on account of the abuse he had received from Captain Bligh.

The Court: Had there been any very recent quarrel?

Fryer: The day before the mutiny, Mr. Bligh charged Christian with stealing his coconuts.

The prisoners were now permitted to question the witness, and I was ordered to speak first. Fryer must have felt the strangeness of our situation as much as did I, myself. He had been more than kind to me during our long association on the *Bounty,* and to meet for the first time since the mutiny under those circumstances, when our conversation could be only of the most formal kind, was a strain upon the self-control of both of us. I was certain that he considered me as innocent as himself, and that he felt nothing but good will toward me. I asked three questions.

Myself: When you came upon deck the first time, and found me in conversation with Mr. Christian, did you overhear anything that was said?

Fryer: No, Mr. Byam. There was . . .

Lord Hood interrupted.

"You must reply to the prisoner's questions by addressing the Court," he said. The master therefore turned to the President.

Fryer: I cannot recollect that I overheard any of the conversation.

Myself: Had you any reason to believe that I was a member of Mr. Christian's party?

Fryer: None whatever.

Myself: If you had been permitted to remain in the ship, and had you endeavoured to form a party to retake the vessel, would I have been among those to whom you would have opened your mind?

Fryer: He would have been among the very first to whom I would have spoken of the matter.

The Court: You say that you had no reason to believe Mr. Byam a member of Christian's party. Did you not consider the fact that when you came upon deck he was in conversation with Mr. Christian a suspicious circumstance?

Fryer: I did not; for Mr. Christian spoke to many of those, during the mutiny, who were not members of his party.

The Court: During your watch, on the night before the mutiny, did you observe Mr. Christian and the prisoner, Byam, together on deck?

Fryer: No. To the best of my recollection, Mr. Byam was on deck during the whole of my watch, and Mr. Christian did not appear at all.

The Court: Did you speak to Mr. Byam at this time?

Fryer: Yes, upon several occasions.

The Court: Did he appear to be disturbed, or nervous, or anxious in mind?

Fryer: Not in the least.

I felt deeply grateful to Fryer, not only for the matter of his testimony concerning myself, but even more for the manner of it. It must have been plain to all the Court that he considered me innocent.

Morrison asked: "Did you observe any part of my conduct, particularly on that day, which would lead you to believe that I was one of the mutineers?"

Fryer: I did not.

The other prisoners questioned him in turn, and poor Burkitt only made his case appear even worse than it had before, for Fryer was obliged to repeat and enlarge upon the details of Burkitt's activity as one of the mutineers.

The master then withdrew and Mr. Cole, the boatswain, was called to the stand. His testimony necessarily covered much the same ground; but while this was true in the case of each of the witnesses, there were important points of difference in their evidence. Each man had witnessed events from different parts of the ship, and their interpretation of what they saw, as well as their recollection of it after so long an interval of time, varied considerably.

I learned from Cole's evidence that he had seen Stewart and me dressing in the berth on the early morning of the mutiny, with Churchill standing guard over us. His testimony was of melancholy importance to Ellison, and the more damaging because of the evident reluctance with which he gave it. Cole had a great liking for Ellison, as had most of the ship's company. Nevertheless, being a man of strict honesty and a high sense of duty, he was obliged to say that he had seen Ellison acting as one of the guards over Bligh. He passed lightly and quickly over the mention of his name, hoping that the Court might not notice it. His evident struggle between the desire to spare all of the prisoners as much as possible, and the necessity for telling the truth, was apparent to all, and won him the sympathy of the Court but no mercy. When he had finished he was at once probed for further information concerning Ellison.

The Court: You say that when you were allowed upon deck, you

saw the prisoner, Ellison, among the other armed men. How was he
armed?

Cole: With a bayonet.

The Court: Was he one of the guards over Captain Bligh?

Cole: Yes.

The Court: Did you hear the prisoner, Ellison, make any remarks?

Cole: Yes.

The Court: What were they?

Cole: I heard him call Captain Bligh an old villain.

I then asked: "When you saw Stewart and me dressing in the
berth, with Churchill standing over us with a pistol, did you hear any
of the conversation that passed between us and Churchill and Thompson?"

Cole: No, I heard nothing of the conversation. There was too much
noise and confusion.

Ellison: You say that I was armed with a bayonet, Mr. Cole. Did you
see me use it in any way?

Cole: By no means, lad. You . . .

"Address your replies to the Court."

Cole: He never once offered to use his bayonet. He merely flourished
it in Captain Bligh's face.

At this reply I saw the hint of a grim smile on the faces of some of
the members of the Court. Cole added, earnestly: "There was no real
harm in this lad. He was only a boy at that time, and full of mischief
and high spirits."

The Court: Do you think this in any way excuses him for taking
part in a mutiny?

Cole: No, sir, but . . .

"That will do, Boatswain," Lord Hood interrupted. "Are there any
further questions from the prisoners?"

Morrison: Do you recollect, when I came on deck after you had called
me out of my hammock, that I came to you abaft the windlass and
said, 'Mr. Cole, what is to be done?' and that your answer was, 'By
God, James, I do not know, but go and help them with the cutter'?

Cole: Yes, I do remember it.

Morrison: Do you remember that, in consequence of your order, I
went about clearing the cutter? And afterward the launch, when
Mr. Christian ordered that boat to be hoisted out instead of the cutter?

Cole: Yes.

Morrison: Do you remember that I brought a towline and grapnel out of the main hold and put them into the launch? And do you remember calling me to assist you to hoist a cask of water out of the hold, and at the same time threatening John Norton, the quartermaster, that he should not go in the boat if he was not more attentive in getting things into her?

Cole: I have every reason to believe that he was employed in this business under my direction. I remember telling Norton that, for he was frightened out of his wits.

Morrison: Do you recollect that I assisted you when you were getting your own things, which were tied up in part of your bedding, into the boat?

Cole: I had forgotten this, but it is strictly true. I had no reason at any time to suppose that he was concerned in the mutiny.

Morrison: After I had helped you put your things into the boat, did I not then run below to get my own, hoping to be allowed to go with Captain Bligh?

Cole: I know that he went below, and I make no doubt that it was for the purpose of getting his clothes to come with us.

The Court: Did the prisoner, Morrison, seem eager to go into the boat?

Cole: None of us was eager, for we never expected to see England again. But he was willing to go, and I make no doubt he would have gone had there been room.

Burkitt then asked: "When you came aft to get the compass out of the binnacle, did not Matthew Quintal come and say he would be damned if you should have it? And you then said, 'Quintal, it is very hard you'll not let us have a compass when there's plenty more in the storeroom'? Then did you not look hard at me, and did I not say, 'Quintal, let Mr. Cole have it, and anything else that will be of service to him'?"

Cole: I know that Quintal objected to letting the compass go, though I do not remember that Burkitt said anything, but he was standing near by. The confusion was so great that it was impossible I could take notice of everything particularly.

Burkitt: During the time that you say I was under arms, do you recollect hearing me give any orders, or making use of bad language?

Cole: I only observed that he was under arms.

Millward: Can you say whether I took a musket willingly, or only because of Churchill's orders?

Cole: I do not know whether it was by Churchill's order or not. He took the musket.

The Court: Were all the people who were put into the boat bound, or were they at liberty in going into her?

Cole: They were not bound, but they marched them who were below on deck with sentinels at different times.

The Court: Were there no other arms in the ship but those in the arms chest in the main hatchway?

Cole: Not to my knowledge.

The Court: At what time did day break on that morning?

Cole: I suppose about a quarter before five, or half-past four.

The Court put many other questions to the boatswain beside those given here. He was examined closely, as Fryer had been, concerning the men in Christian's watch, those he saw under arms, my own relationship with Christian, and the like. His evidence made it plain that, although Morrison, Coleman, Norman, McIntosh, and myself all assisted in hoisting out the launch, this was done at the boatswain's orders, and could not be construed as evidence that we were of the mutineers' party.

At the conclusion of Cole's testimony, the Court adjourned for the day, and we were again conveyed to the gun room of the *Hector*. Mr. Graham came, bringing a brief note from Sir Joseph, which read: "Now you know the worst, Byam. Keep up a good heart. Both Fryer and Cole have struck excellent blows for you to-day. It is evident that their opinion of your character made an impression upon the Court."

Mr. Graham talked with me for half an hour, going over the evidence in detail, instructing me further as to the questions I should ask of the witnesses yet to be heard. He refused to give an opinion as to what he thought of my chances. "If you can, keep your mind from dwelling upon the outcome," he said. "It is not my part either to hearten or discourage you unduly, but I think it well that you have no illusions about your situation. It is grave but not hopeless. Meanwhile, be assured that I shall do everything in my power to help you."

"May I ask one more question, Mr. Graham?" I said.

"Certainly. As many as you like."

"In your heart, do you believe me innocent or guilty?"

"I can answer that without a moment's hesitation. I believe you innocent."

This heartened me greatly, and gave me reason to hope that some, at least, of the members of the Court might feel as he did.

There was little conversation in the gun room that evening. As long as daylight served, Morrison sat by a port, with his Bible on his knee, reading aloud to Muspratt, who had requested this. Ellison turned into his hammock early and was asleep within five minutes. Four men among us had little to fear. The events of the first day's hearing made it increasingly plain that Coleman, Norman, McIntosh, and Byrne were all but certain of acquittal. Burkitt and Millward paced up and down the room in their bare feet. The soft padding of Burkitt's feet was the last sound I heard before I went to sleep.


## XXII · THE CASE FOR THE CROWN

At nine o'clock the following morning the hearing was resumed. As we were marched into the great cabin I noticed that it was even more closely packed with spectators than it had been the previous day. The same solemnity marked the proceedings, and Court and spectators alike attended the examination of the witnesses with the same air of absorbed interest.

William Peckover, gunner of the *Bounty,* was called in and sworn. The remarkable thing about his testimony was that he claimed to have seen but four men under arms during the whole of the mutiny — Christian, Burkitt, Sumner, and Quintal. I do not believe that he deliberately falsified his testimony. I think he must have reasoned in this way: "The mutiny took place so long ago, how can I be certain as to whom I saw under arms? I have a clear recollection of only four. The other lads shall have the benefit of the doubt. God knows they need it!" Immediately he had finished, he was questioned on this point.

The Court: How many people did the *Bounty's* company consist of?
Peckover: Forty-three, I believe, at this time.
The Court: State again how many of those you saw under arms.
Peckover: Four.
The Court: Was it your opinion that four people took the ship from nine and thirty?

Peckover: Not by any means.

The Court: Give your reasons for thinking so.

Peckover: There certainly must have been more concerned or they would not have taken the ship from us. But these are all I can say, positively, that I saw under arms.

The Court: What were your particular reasons for submitting when you saw but four men under arms?

Peckover: I came naked upon the deck, with only my trousers on, and there I saw Burkitt with a musket and a bayonet, and Mr. Christian alongside of Captain Bligh, and a sentry at the gangway, but who he was I do not remember.

The Court: Did you expostulate with Mr. Christian on his conduct?

Peckover: I did not.

The Court: Did you see Mr. Byam that morning?

Peckover: Yes. I saw him standing by the booms talking with Mr. Nelson, the botanist. Then he went below, and I did not again see him until the launch had been ordered astern.

The Court: Where was he then?

Peckover: I saw him for a moment at the taffrail.

The Court: What are your reasons for believing that Coleman, Norman, McIntosh, and Byrne were averse to the mutiny?

Peckover: When they were looking down upon us from the stern they appeared to wish to come into the boat, what slight view I had of them. I was busy stowing things in the boat, so that I remember only Coleman calling to me.

The Court: You have said that, in talking with Mr. Purcell, he said to you that he knew whose fault the business was, or words to that effect. Do you apprehend that Mr. Purcell alluded to any of the prisoners?

Peckover: No. I think he alluded to Captain Bligh, owing to the abuse so many of the ship's company had received from him.

The Court: What was the nature of this abuse?

Peckover: Many severe punishments for slight offenses, and foul and abusive language to all hands. Try as they would, neither officers nor men could ever do anything to please him.

Morrison then questioned the gunner, and brought out even more clearly, not only that he had never been under arms, but also that he had done everything in his power to supply the launch with provision and much-needed articles so that the men in her might have a better chance for their lives. Morrison conducted his case remarkably well. Unfortunately, the questions I put were to little purpose. Peckover had been officer of the middle watch on the night before the mutiny. He had seen Christian and me upon deck at that time, but had heard nothing of our conversation; nor had he heard any of the conversation that passed between Nelson and me the following morning.

Purcell, the carpenter, next took the stand. He was the same burly, heavy-jowled man whom I had heard say to Nelson on the morning of the mutiny: "Stop aboard? With rogues and pirates? Never, sir! I shall follow my commander." I had great respect for the old fellow. No one could have hated Bligh more, but there was never any hesitation in Purcell's decisions when it came to a matter of duty. His evidence was of great importance to me, but whether it helped or prejudiced my case it was difficult to say. Purcell gave the names of seventeen men whom, he stated with conviction, he had seen armed; among them, Ellison, Burkitt, and Millward. Muspratt he omitted to name.

The Court asked: "In the former part of your evidence you say that you asked Mr. Byam to intercede with Christian for the launch instead of the cutter. Why did you speak of this matter to Byam? Did you consider him one of the mutineers?"

Purcell: By no means. But I knew him to be a friend of Mr. Christian. I also knew that Christian had no liking for me and would have listened to no request I might have made.

The Court: Do you believe that it was owing to the prisoner Byam's intercession that Christian permitted the launch to be hoisted out instead of the cutter?

Purcell: Yes; and had we not been given the launch none of us would ever have seen England again.

The Court: What had been the relations between Christian and Byam throughout the voyage of the *Bounty* to Tahiti and during the sojourn there?

Purcell: Most friendly.

The Court: Name any others whom you believe to have been particularly friendly with Mr. Christian.

Purcell: Mr. Stewart was one. I can think of no others that I could say were intimate with him. Mr. Christian was not an easy man to know.

The Court: Do you think it likely that Mr. Christian would not have divulged his plans for the mutiny to Mr. Byam, his most intimate friend?

Purcell was taken aback by this question, put to him by Captain Hammond, who sat on Lord Hood's right. He lowered his head like an old bull at bay.

Purcell: Yes, I do think it likely. Mr. Christian was not a man to involve his friends in trouble, and he must have known that Mr. Byam would remain loyal to his commander.

The Court: Where was Byam just before the launch was veered astern?

Purcell: I do not know. I had seen him upon deck a few moments before, and he had told me of his intention to go with Captain Bligh. I think he must have gone to the midshipmen's berth for his clothes.

The Court: Did you see Morrison at this time?

Purcell: No.

The Court: Do you think it possible that the prisoners, Byam and Morrison, may have feared to go into the boat and that they went below to avoid the necessity of leaving the ship?

Purcell: No, I do not. They must have been prevented from coming. They were not cowards as both Mr. Hayward and Mr. Hallet were . . .

Lord Hood interrupted, sternly admonishing the carpenter to reply only to the questions asked of him.

The Court: Putting every circumstance together, declare to this Court, upon the oath you have taken, how you considered Mr. Byam's behaviour, whether as a person joined in the mutiny or as a person wishing well to Captain Bligh.

Purcell: I by no means considered him as a person concerned in the mutiny.

The Court: Did you consider Morrison as a mutineer?

Purcell: I did not.

A pause followed. Lord Hood said: "The prisoners may now question the witness."

Myself: How deep in the water was the launch when the last of the people went into her?

Purcell: We had seven and one-half inches of freeboard, amidships.

Myself: Do you think others might have come into her without endangering the safety of all?

Purcell: Not one more could have entered her. Captain Bligh himself begged that no more should be sent off. When we lost Norton, the quartermaster, who was killed by the savages at Tofoa, for all our regret at the poor fellow's death we were glad to have the boat lightened of his weight. It gave the rest of us so much more chance of life.

The following morning, Friday, September 14, Thomas Hayward gave his evidence. We had awaited this most eagerly. Hayward was the mate of Christian's watch and on deck at the time the mutiny started. I, in particular, was curious to know whether his story would corroborate the account given me by Christian on the day he had called me into his cabin. Hayward made no mention whatever of having been asleep on watch at the time the ship was seized. He said that he was standing aft at that moment, looking over the side at a shark, and that Christian had told him to oversee the vessel while he went below to lash his hammock.

"A moment later," he went on, "to my unutterable surprise, I saw Christian, Charles Churchill, Thomas Burkitt, one of the prisoners, John Sumner, Matthew Quintal, William McCoy, Isaac Martin, Henry Hillbrandt, and Alexander Smith coming aft, armed with muskets and bayonets. On my going forward to prevent their proceedings, I asked Christian the cause for such an act, and he told me to hold my tongue, instantly. Martin was left as a sentinel on deck, and the rest of the party proceeded to Mr. Bligh's cabin.

"I heard the cry of 'Murder!' from Mr. Bligh, and heard Christian call for a rope. John Mills, contrary to all orders, cut the deep-sea line and carried a piece of it to them. Thomas Ellison, who was at the helm, quitted it and armed himself with a bayonet. The ship's decks now began to be thronged with men. I saw George Stewart, James Morrison, one of the prisoners, and Roger Byam, another of the prisoners, standing by the booms.

"As soon as the launch was out, John Samuel, the captain's clerk, John Hallet, midshipman, and myself were ordered into her. We requested time sufficient to collect a few clothes, which was granted. About this time I spoke to either Stewart or Byam, I cannot be positive which, but I think it was Byam. I told him to go into the boat, but in my hurry I cannot remember to have received an answer. When I came upon deck again I saw Ellison standing as one of the sentries over Captain Bligh. We were then forced into the boat. I remember hearing Robert Tinkler, who was not yet in the launch, call out, 'Byam, for

God's sake, hasten!' A moment later Tinkler himself came into the launch. He was among the last to enter. When we were towing astern of the ship, I saw the prisoners, Byam and Morrison, standing at the taffrail among the other mutineers. They seemed well content to be there. I remember hearing Burkitt use very abusive language, and I distinctly heard Millward jeering at Captain Bligh. This is all that I know of the mutiny in His Majesty's ship *Bounty*."

The Court asked: "You say that Burkitt used very abusive language while the launch lay astern. To whom did it seem to be addressed?"

Hayward: To the boat's people generally, I should say.

The Court: Can you recall what Millward said when he jeered at Captain Bligh?

Hayward: Yes, precisely. He said, "You bloody villain! See if you can live on half a pound of yams a day."

The Court: What number of armed men did you perceive on the *Bounty* on the morning of the mutiny?

Hayward: Eighteen.

The Court: Did you hear any of the conversation that passed between Christian and Byam with respect to having the launch in the place of the cutter?

Hayward: No.

The Court: Were you on deck during the middle watch on the night before the mutiny?

Hayward: No.

The Court: Do you know at what time the prisoner, Byam, came down to the berth on that night?

Hayward: Yes. I chanced to be awake at that time and I heard the ship's bell strike half-past one.

The Court: How do you know that it was Byam who came in?

Hayward: His hammock was next to mine on the larboard side of the berth.

The Court: Relate everything you remember with respect to Morrison.

Hayward: I remember seeing Morrison assisting to clear the yams and other supplies out of the launch before she was hoisted out, but I am doubtful whether he was at first under arms or not.

The Court: Do you mean by this that he was later under arms?

Hayward: I believe that he was, but I cannot say positively.

The Court: Did he appear to you, by his conduct, to be assisting the mutineers, or was he merely obeying the orders that were given to get the boat out?

Hayward: If I were to give it as my opinion, I should say that he was assisting the mutineers. He perhaps might wish to get the boat out to get quit of us as soon as possible.

The Court: Relate all you know of Ellison.

Hayward: Ellison was at the helm at the outbreak of the mutiny. Soon after the people had gone below to secure Captain Bligh, he quitted the helm and armed himself with a bayonet. Before going into the boat I saw him as a sentinel over Captain Bligh, and I remember him saying, "Damn him, I will be sentinel over him!"

The Court: Relate all you remember of Muspratt.

Hayward: I remember seeing Muspratt on the larboard side of the waist with a musket in his hand.

The Court: Relate all you remember of Burkitt.

Hayward: I saw Thomas Burkitt come aft, following Christian and Churchill when they went to Captain Bligh's cabin, and I saw him descend the after ladder with them. He was armed with a musket and a bayonet. After the launch was astern I saw him at the taffrail, and heard him using very abusive language to us in the boat.

The Court: Relate what you remember of Millward.

Hayward: I saw him armed as one of the sentinels, and after the boat was veered astern, I saw him at the taffrail, where he jeered at Captain Bligh, as I have said.

The Court: Have you any reason to believe that the prisoner, Byam, would have been prevented from going in the boat at the time you did, had he desired to do so?

Hayward: No.

The Court: Where was he at the time the launch was veered aft?

Hayward: I cannot say, but a moment later I saw him at the taffrail, looking down at us with the other mutineers.

The Court: Did you hear him make any remarks at that time?

Hayward: I am doubtful whether I did or not.

The Court: You have given it as your opinion that Morrison was assisting the mutineers so as to get Captain Bligh and his party out of the ship as soon as possible. In the former part of your evidence you have said that the prisoner, McIntosh, was also assisting to hoist the launch out, and that you did not look upon him as a mutineer. What is the reason for your thinking differently of them?

Hayward: The difference was in the countenances of the two. The countenance of Morrison seemed to be rejoiced and that of McIntosh depressed.

Morrison then asked: "You say that you observed joy in my countenance, and you have given it as your opinion that I was one of the mutineers. Can you declare, before God and this Court, that such evidence is not the result of a private pique?

Hayward: No, it is not the result of a private pique. It is an opinion I formed after quitting the ship, from the prisoners not coming with us when they had as good an opportunity as the rest, there being more boats than one.

Morrison: One of the boats, as you know, was badly eaten with worms. Are you certain that we might have had the other?

Hayward: Not having been present at any conference among you, I cannot say.

Morrison: Can you deny that you were present when Captain Bligh begged that the boat might not be overloaded; and can you deny that he said, "I'll do you justice, lads"?

Hayward: I was present at the time Mr. Bligh made such a declaration, but understood it as respecting the clothes and other heavy articles with which the boat was already too full.

Ellison now put a question which brought into this grimly serious trial the only touch of humour that attended it.

Ellison: You know that Captain Bligh used these words: "Don't let the boat be overloaded, lads. I'll do you justice." And you say you think this alluded to the clothes and other heavy articles in the launch. Do you honestly think that the words, "I'll do you justice," alluded to the clothes? Or did they allude to Coleman, McIntosh, Norman, Byrne, Mr. Stewart, Mr. Byam, and Mr. Morrison, who would have gone in the launch if there had been room?

Ellison scored a point here, for us, not for himself. Even the members of the Court maintained with difficulty their expressions of dignified severity.

Hayward: If Captain Bligh made use of the words, "My lads," it was to the people already in the boat and not to those in the ship.

The Court: Your opinion, then, is that Captain Bligh was not alluding to any of the people remaining in the ship?

Hayward, realizing that the Court itself considered his opinion preposterous, then acknowledged that Bligh might have been referring to those in the ship.

The malicious manner in which he had testified astonished me. This was particularly true in his evidence concerning Morrison and me. He must have known, in his heart, that we were as innocent as himself; yet he lost no opportunity to throw what doubt he could upon the purity of our intentions. Morrison he had never liked, and this ill-will was heartily returned; but my relations with Hayward on the *Bounty,* although never cordial, had not been unfriendly. I had the clearest recollection of the events of the mutiny. Hayward had never once spoken to me on that morning, and Stewart had told me that he had only seen Hayward at a distance. And yet Hayward had testified that he had told one or the other of us to go into the boat. The true facts were that he was so terrified throughout the whole of this time as to be ignorant of what he did, or said. It was my opinion at the time of the court-martial, and it is so still, that he arranged his recollections of what had taken place so as to put his own actions in the most favourable possible light. He was a man easily dominated by others of stronger character, and I believe that his long association with Captain Edwards, of the *Pandora,* who considered all of us piratical scoundrels, had completely coloured Hayward's own opinions.

John Hallet was called next. He was now in his twentieth year, and I scarcely recognized the thin, frightened-looking boy I had known on the *Bounty* in the grown man who stood before us. He was dressed in a handsome lieutenant's uniform — a long-tailed coat of bright blue, with white cuffs and lapels and gold anchor buttons. He wore white silk breeches and stockings, and his black pumps shone like mirrors. As he entered the great cabin he removed his cocked hat and placed it under his arm, halting to make a sweeping bow to the President as he did so. Upon taking the stand he glanced at us with an air that said only too plainly: "You see how I have risen in the world? And what are you? Pirates and mutineers!"

His story was the briefest of any of those yet given, but it was of grave importance to Morrison and myself. He stated with conviction that when the launch was about to leave the *Bounty,* he had seen Morrison at the taffrail, armed with a musket. He also named Burkitt, Ellison, and Millward as having been armed. His evidence with respect to myself came when he was being questioned by various members of the Court.

The Court: Did you see Roger Byam on the morning of the mutiny?

Hallet: I remember to have seen him once.

The Court: What was he doing at that time?

Hallet: He was on the platform on the larboard side, upon deck, standing still and looking attentively toward Captain Bligh.

The Court: Was he armed?

Hallet: I cannot say that he was.

The Court: Had you any conversation with him?

Hallet: No.

The Court: Do you know whether he was or was not prevented from coming into the boat?

Hallet: I do not know that he ever offered to go into the boat.

The Court: Did you hear any person propose to him to go into the boat?

Hallet: No.

The Court: Do you know any other particulars respecting him on that day?

Hallet: While he was standing as I have before related, Captain Bligh said something to him, but what, I did not hear; upon which Byam laughed, and turned and walked away.

The Court: Relate all you know of the conduct of James Morrison on that day.

Hallet: When I first saw him he was unarmed; but he shortly afterward appeared under arms.

The Court: How was he armed?

Hallet: With a musket.

The Court: At what part of the ship was he when you saw him so armed?

Hallet: It was when the boat was veered astern. He was leaning over the taffrail, calling out in a jeering manner, "If my friends inquire for me, tell them I am somewhere in the South Sea."

The Court: Relate all you know respecting Thomas Ellison.

Hallet: He appeared early under arms, and came up to me and insolently said, "Mr. Hallet, you need not mind this. We are only going to put the Captain on shore, and then you and the others may return."

The Court: Describe to the Court the situation of Captain Bligh when the prisoner, Byam, laughed and walked away, as you have described.

Hallet: He was standing with his arms bound, Christian holding the cord in one hand, and a bayonet to his breast with the other.

Upon the advice of Mr. Graham, I refrained from questioning Hallet at this time.

"This is the gravest accusation that has been made against you," he whispered, "excepting only Bligh's. Do not examine Hallet upon it now. It will be best to wait until the Court hears your defense. At that time you will have the opportunity to recall any of the witnesses you choose."

Morrison asked: "You say that you saw me armed at the taffrail. Can you declare, positively, before God and this Court, that it was I and no other person whom you saw under arms?"

Hallet: I have declared it.

Morrison: You have sworn that I did jeeringly say, "Tell my friends, if they inquire for me, that I am somewhere in the South Sea." To whom did I address this sneering message?

Hallet: I did not remark that it was addressed to anyone in particular.

Morrison: Do you remember that I did, personally, assist you to haul one of your chests up the main hatchway, and whether or not I was armed then?

Hallet: The circumstances concerning the chest I do not remember. I have before said that I did not see you under arms till after the launch had been veered astern.

The witness withdrew, and John Smith, who had been Captain Bligh's servant, was called. He was the last witness, and the only one of the *Bounty's* seamen who gave evidence. In fact, there were only three of the able seamen of the *Bounty's* company, John Smith, Thomas Hall, and Robert Lamb, who had not been of Christian's party; and of these both Lamb and Hall were dead. Smith's evidence was not of importance to any of us who were before the Court. He testified that, at Christian's orders, he had served out rum to all those under arms; also that he had gone to Captain Bligh's cabin to fetch up his clothes and other articles which were put into the launch.

This concluded the evidence given by members of the *Bounty's* company who went into the launch. Captain Edwards and the lieutenants of the *Pandora* were then called in turn, to testify as to the *Pandora's* sojourn at Tahiti when the fourteen prisoners were taken. At the sight of Edwards and Parkin, I was conscious of the same feeling of hot anger experienced how many times during the dreary months when we were in their power. Nevertheless, I must do them the justice to say that their evidence as to the proceedings at Tahiti was scrupulously exact. Edwards told how I had come off to the ship when she was still several miles out at sea, explaining who I was and giving him exact information with respect to the other *Bounty* men then on the island. He also acknowledged that the other men had given themselves up voluntarily. We should have liked to question him with respect to the inhuman treatment we had received at his hands, but this did not concern the mutiny, so we said nothing.

These were the last of the Crown witnesses, and the Court adjourned until the following day, when we were to be heard in our own defense.

## XXIII · THE DEFENSE

BEING the only midshipman among the prisoners, I should, as a matter of course, have been the first to be called for my defense; but when the Court met on the Saturday morning, I requested, and was granted, permission to defer presenting my case until Monday morning. Coleman, whose acquittal was a foregone conclusion, was ready to be heard, and was therefore called. His statement was brief, and, having given it, he questioned Fryer, Cole, Peckover, Purcell, and others, all of whom testified as to Coleman's innocence, and that he had been detained in the *Bounty* against his will. The Court then adjourned.

Nearly the whole of Sunday I spent with my advisor, Mr. Graham. Captain Manly and Captain Bentham, advisors to the other prisoners, came with him, and the three groups separated to various parts of the gun room so as not to disturb one another.

I had already prepared, in writing, a rough copy of my defense. Mr. Graham went over this with great care, pointing out various omissions and making suggestions as to the arrangement of the matter. He instructed me as to the witnesses I should call and examine, after my defense had been read, and the questions I should ask each one. Hayward had testified that he had been awake on the night before the mutiny and had heard me come down to the berth at half-past one.

"This evidence is of importance to you, Mr. Byam," Mr. Graham said. "You have told me that Tinkler went down with you at that time and that you bade each other good-night?"

"Yes, sir."

"Then Hayward must have heard you speak. We must see to it that he acknowledges this. If we can prove that Tinkler was with you it will bear out your account of the conversation with Christian, which Tinkler overheard. Hallet struck you a heavy blow in saying that you turned away laughing after Captain Bligh had spoken to you."

"There was not a word of truth in the statement, sir," I said, hotly.

"I am sure there was not. In my opinion neither Hayward nor Hallet made a favourable impression upon the Court. But their evidence cannot be disregarded. Together, it is enough to condemn Morrison; his situation now is much more grave than it was. Did you have an opportunity to observe the actions of Hayward and Hallet on the morning of the mutiny?"

"Yes, I saw them a number of times."

"What can you say of them? Were they cool and self-possessed?"

"On the contrary, they were both frightened out of their wits the whole time, and both were crying and begging for mercy when they were ordered into the launch."

"It is extremely important that you should bring this out. When you question the other *Bounty* witnesses, you must examine each of them upon this point. If they agree with you, that Hallet and Hayward were much alarmed, it will throw doubt upon the reliability of their testimony."

It was late in the afternoon when Mr. Graham rose to go.

"I think we have covered everything, Mr. Byam," he said. "Do you wish to read your defense, or would you prefer that I read it for you?"

"What do you think I should do, sir?"

"I advise you to read it, unless you think you may be too nervous."

I told him that I had no apprehensions on that score.

"Good!" he replied. "Your story will make a deeper impression if given in your own voice. Read it clearly and slowly. You must have noticed that several members of the Court seem to be all but convinced of your guilt? It is apparent in the questions they have asked the witnesses."

"I have noticed it, sir."

"I suggest that, as you read, you keep these particular men in mind. If you do this the manner of your reading will take care of itself. It is unnecessary to remind you that you are fighting for your life. This is certain to make your words sufficiently impressive."

By this time the advisors to the other prisoners had completed their work, and they left the *Hector* with Mr. Graham. No day, in all the interminable months we had passed as prisoners, had slipped by so quickly as this one.

On Monday morning, September 17, the solitary gun boomed from the *Duke,* the signal for assembling the court-martial. We were conveyed on board with the usual guard of marines, and arrived a good half-hour before the opening of the Court. Although I had told Mr. Graham that he need have no fears about my coolness, I felt anything but self-possessed as the minutes slowly passed. As we were marched across the quarter-deck, I caught a glimpse of Sir Joseph and Dr. Hamilton among the crowd of officers and civilians waiting there. I dreaded that daily ordeal of mounting the gangway of the *Duke,* and the march, two by two, along the deck to the great cabin. We were objects of curiosity to everyone, and many of the officers stared at us as though we were wild animals. At least, so it seemed to me, but no doubt I was unusually sensitive at that time, and imagined insolence and hostility on faces which revealed nothing more than natural curiosity.

A few minutes before nine the spectators were all in their places, and on the stroke of the hour the members of the Court filed in. All in the room rose and remained standing until Lord Hood and the other officers had taken their places.

A moment of silence followed; then the master-at-arms called: "Roger Byam, stand forth!"

I rose and waited, facing Lord Hood.

"You have been accused, with others, of the mutinous and piratical seizure of His Majesty's armed vessel, *Bounty.* You have heard the Crown's witnesses. The Court is now ready to receive whatever you may have to say in your own defense. Are you prepared?"

"Yes, sir."

"Raise your right hand."

I was then sworn, and I remember how my hand trembled as I held it up. I looked toward Sir Joseph for comfort, but he sat with his hands clasped around his knee, gazing straight before him. The Court waited for me to proceed. For a moment, panic seized me. The eyes of everyone in the room were turned toward me, and their faces became a blur before my own. Then, as though it were someone else, a long distance away, I heard my own voice speaking: —

"My lord, and gentlemen of this Honourable Court: The crime of mutiny, for which I am now arraigned, is one of so grave a nature as to awake the horror and indignation of all men, and he who stands accused of it must appear an object of unpardonable guilt.

"In such a character it is my misfortune to appear before this Tribunal. I realize that appearances are against me, but they are appearances only, and I declare before God and the members of this Court that I am innocent; that I have never been guilty, either in thought or in deed, of the crime with which I am charged."

Once I was fairly started, I regained my self-control, and, bearing in mind Mr. Graham's advice, I read on, slowly and deliberately. I explained fully the conversation with Christian on the night before the mutiny, showing that it had nothing to do with that event. I then told the story of the ship's seizure as it concerned myself. I told of my conversation with Mr. Purcell and Mr. Nelson, both of whom knew that I meant to leave the ship. I told of going below, at the same time with Mr. Nelson, to fetch my clothes, preparatory to going into the launch, and how, in the midshipmen's berth, an opportunity seemed to present itself for seizing the arms chest from Thompson. I told how Morrison and I, with Friendly Island war clubs in our hands, waited for a chance to attack Thompson, and how that chance was thwarted; and how Morrison and I then rushed upon deck, only to find that we were too late to go with Captain Bligh.

"My lord and gentlemen," I concluded, "it is a heavy misfortune for me that the three men are dead whose evidence would prove, beyond all doubt, the truth of what I say. John Norton, the quartermaster, who knew of Christian's intention to leave the *Bounty* on the night before the mutiny, and who prepared for him the small raft upon which Christian meant to embark, is dead. Mr. Nelson died at Batavia; and Robert Tinkler, who overheard all of my conversation with Christian, has been lost at sea with the vessel upon which he was serving. Fortune, I realize, has been against me. Lacking the evidence of these three men, I can only say, I entreat you to believe me! My good name is as precious to me as life itself, and I beg of you, my lord and gentlemen, to consider the situation in which I am placed; to remember that I lack those witnesses whose evidence would, I am certain, convince you of the truth of every statement I have made.

"To the mercy of this Honourable Court I now commit myself."

It was impossible to guess how my words had impressed the Court. Lord Hood sat with his chin propped upon one hand, listening with grave attention. I glanced hastily at the others. Two or three of them were making memoranda of points in my story. One captain, with a long cadaverous face, sat with eyes lowered, and one might have thought him asleep. I had observed him before. He had maintained the same position throughout the hearing, and the same air of apparent inattention; but he was among the keenest of the questioners. No point that might throw light upon the events of the mutiny, or the trustworthiness of the witnesses, escaped him. He addressed his questions without lifting his eyes, as though he had the witness pinned down to the table between his elbows.

Another of the captains whom I feared most sat on Lord Hood's left, the farthest from him on that side, and the nearest to the stand for the witnesses. Hour after hour he sat as rigid as though he were made of bronze. Once he had taken his seat at the table, only his eyes were permitted freedom of movement; his glances were keen and swift, like the thrust of a rapier. When I had finished, the eyes of this latter captain were directed upon me for a moment, and, brief as the glance had been, it chilled me to the heart. I again recalled what Dr. Hamilton had said at the time of our first conversation on the *Pandora*: "There is not one of those captains who will not say to himself, 'This is such a tale as one would expect an intelligent midshipman, eager to save his life, to invent.'"

It seemed to me, judging by the faces of the men before me, that, with the exception of Captain Montague, each of them was thinking those very words. I felt utterly weary, physically and spiritually. Then I saw Sir Joseph looking straight at me in his kindly, heartening manner, as much as to say: "Well done, my lad! Never say die!" His glance gave me new reserves of strength and courage.

"My lord," I said, "may I now call what witnesses are available to me?"

Lord Hood nodded. The master-at-arms went to the door and called, "John Fryer! This way!"

The *Bounty's* master took the stand, was again sworn, and awaited my questions.

Myself: What watch had I on the day of the mutiny?

Fryer: He was in my watch, the first watch of the preceding evening.

Myself: Had you stayed in the ship, in the expectation of retaking her, was my conduct, from the time when you first knew me to this, in which you are to answer the question, such that you would have entrusted me with your design, and do you believe that I would have favoured it? (I had been instructed by Mr. Graham to ask this question again.)

Fryer: I should not have hesitated in opening my design to him, and I am sure that he would have favoured it.

Myself: Did you consider those people who assisted in hoisting out the launch as helping Captain Bligh or the mutineers?

Fryer: Those without arms, as assisting Captain Bligh.

Myself: How many men, including Captain Bligh, went into the launch?

Fryer: Nineteen.

Myself: What height from the water was the gunwale of the launch when she put off from the ship?

Fryer: Not more than eight inches, to the best of my knowledge and remembrance.

Myself: Would the launch have carried more people?

Fryer: Not one more, in my opinion, without endangering the lives of all who were in her.

Myself: Did you, at any time during the mutiny, see me armed?

Fryer: No.

Myself: Did Captain Bligh speak to me at any time on the morning of the mutiny?

Fryer: Not to my knowledge.

Myself: Did you observe, on that morning, that I was guilty at any time of levity of conduct?

Fryer: I did not.

Myself: Did you see Mr. Hayward on deck during the time of the mutiny?

Fryer: Yes; several times.

Myself: In what state was he? Did he appear to be composed, or was he agitated and alarmed?

Fryer: He was greatly agitated and alarmed, and crying when he was forced into the boat.

Myself: Did you see Mr. Hallet on that morning?

Fryer: Yes; upon several occasions.

Myself: In what state did he appear to be?

Fryer: He was greatly frightened and crying when he went into the boat.

Myself: What was my general character on the *Bounty?*

Fryer: Excellent. To the best of my recollection he was held in high esteem by everyone.

The Court asked: "After the launch had left the ship, and during the voyage to Timor, was the subject of the mutiny often discussed among you?"

Fryer: No, not often. Our sufferings were so great, and the efforts necessary for the preservation of our lives so constant, that we had little time or inclination to speak of the mutiny.

The Court: Did you, during that voyage, or at any time thereafter, hear Captain Bligh refer to a conversation he had overheard between Christian and the prisoner, Byam, which took place in the middle watch on the night before the mutiny?

Fryer: I did not.

The Court: Did you, at any time, hear him refer to the prisoner, Byam?

Fryer: Yes; upon more than one occasion.

The Court: Can you recall what he said?

Fryer: On the day of the mutiny, after the launch had been cast off and we were rowing toward the island of Tofoa, I heard Mr. Bligh say, referring to Mr. Byam, "He is an ungrateful scoundrel, the worst of them all except Christian." He later repeated this opinion several times, in much the same words.

The Court: Did anyone in the boat speak in Byam's defense?

Fryer: Yes, I did, as well as various others. But Captain Bligh bade us hold our tongues. He would allow nothing to be said in Mr. Byam's favour.

The Court: Did you at any time hear Robert Tinkler refer to a conversation between Christian and Byam which took place in the middle watch on the night before the mutiny?

Fryer: I cannot recall that I did.

The Court: Did Robert Tinkler ever speak in defense of Byam?

Fryer: Yes. He never believed him implicated in the mutiny. On the occasion I have mentioned, when Captain Bligh first accused Mr. Byam, Tinkler, forgetting himself, said, warmly: "He is *not* one of the mutineers, sir. I would stake my life upon it!" Captain Bligh silenced him instantly.

The Court: Robert Tinkler was your brother-in-law, was he not?

Fryer: He was.

The Court: He has been lost at sea?

Fryer: He has been reported lost with his ship, the *Carib Maid,* among or near the West Indies.

The Court: Were your relations with Captain Bligh cordial or the reverse?

Fryer: They were far from cordial.

Cole, the boatswain, was summoned next, and was followed by Mr. Purcell. I put to each of them the same questions I had asked of the master, and they replied to them as he had done. The questions asked by the members of the Court were much the same, and both men were examined particularly as to whether either Bligh or Tinkler had ever referred to my conversation with Christian, upon which the fact of my guilt or innocence so strongly depended. Neither of them could remember having heard any reference made to this conversation. I had strongly hoped that Mr. Peckover, the gunner, and officer of the middle watch, might have overheard something of this conversation, but he could say only what further incriminated me, that he had seen Christian and me in conversation on the quarter-deck during that watch.

The Court asked: "At what time did you observe Christian and the prisoner, Byam, in conversation?"

Peckover: It might have been at about one o'clock.

The Court: Was it the prisoner's, Byam's, custom to remain on deck at night after the end of his watch?

Peckover: I cannot say that it was.

The Court: Was it Mr. Christian's habit to be much on deck at night, when not on duty?

Peckover: No, not as a general thing, but it was not unusual for him to come up at night to observe the state of the weather.

The Court: What, in your opinion, was their reason for remaining so long on the deck on this particular night?

Peckover: I suppose they wished to enjoy the coolness of the upper deck.

The Court: When Captain Bligh came on deck, during your watch, what did he do?

Peckover: He paced up and down for a few moments.

The Court: Did Christian and the prisoner, Byam, perceive him?

Peckover: I cannot say. The moon had set before that time and it was dark upon deck.

The Court: Did Captain Bligh speak with Christian and Byam?

Peckover: I believe he did, but I did not hear what he said.

The Court: At what time did Byam go below to the berth?

Peckover: It may have been about half-past one.

The Court: Did Christian go below at that time?

Peckover: I cannot be certain. I believe he remained on deck.

The Court: Did you, at any time during your watch on that night, see John Norton, one of the quartermasters?

It was Sir George Montague, captain of the *Hector,* who put this question. I do not know why it had not occurred to me to ask it, or how Mr. Graham could have failed to suggest it to me. The reason may have been that Norton, being dead, seemed as out of the matter as Mr. Nelson himself, or any of the others who had died. Immediately Captain Montague had spoken I realized how important the question was.

Peckover: Yes; I saw Norton at about two o'clock.

The Court: Upon what occasion?

Peckover: I had heard the sound of hammering by the windlass, and myself went forward to see what the cause of it was. I found Norton at work upon something, and asked him what he was about at that hour of the night. He told me that he was repairing a hencoop for some fowls we had bought of the savages at Namuka.

The Court: Did you see at what work he was engaged?

Peckover: No, not clearly. It was quite dark, but I made no doubt that he was engaged as he said.

The Court: Did you have any further conversation with him?

Peckover: I told him to leave off; that there was time enough for making hencoops in the daytime.

The Court: Was not such work the business of the carpenters of the *Bounty?*

Peckover: Yes; but it was not uncommon for Norton to assist them when there was much carpenter's work to be done.

The Court: Had you ever known Norton to be so employed at night before?

Peckover: Never before, that I can remember.

The Court: Do you think it might have been a small raft upon which the quartermaster was working?

Peckover: Yes, it might have been. As I have said, it was dark and I took no particular notice of what the object was.

The Court, particularly in the person of Captain Montague, questioned the gunner carefully on this matter, but Peckover could not remember that he had seen Christian and Norton in conversation during that evening. Nevertheless, here was a ray of hope for me — a bit of evidence, and the only one, to bear out my story that Christian had intended to desert the ship during that night, and that he had taken Norton into his confidence.

Hayward followed on the witness stand, but for all my questioning he would not acknowledge that Tinkler had come down to the berth with me on the night before the mutiny. And yet he must have heard us bid each other good-night. At that time we were standing within two paces of his hammock, and he had said that he heard me come in. Hallet clung to his story that I had laughed and turned away when, as he said, Captain Bligh spoke to me. But I could see that his sullen, insolent manner of clinging to it had made an unfavourable impression upon the Court.

My case rested here, and Morrison was next called for his defense. He was cool and self-possessed. His story was perfectly clear, well presented, and, I thought, wholly convincing. He confirmed my story as to the reason we had been below at the time the launch was veered astern. Of the witnesses he called, Fryer, Cole, Purcell, and Peckover bore out all that he said, with the exception of his reason for not being on deck in time to go with the launch; for of this matter, of course, they could know nothing. Hallet and Hayward were the only witnesses who had testified to having seen him under arms, and he forced both of them to admit that they might have been mistaken.

The Court adjourned for lunch. At one o'clock it reassembled, and Norman, McIntosh, and Byrne were quickly heard. Their innocence had already been clearly established and, advisedly, they had made their pleas brief.

Burkitt, Millward, and Muspratt came next. The guilt of the first two was so evident that little could be said in extenuation of it. Both men had been willing mutineers from the beginning.

Ellison was the last to be heard. He had written his own defense, and Captain Bentham let it stand as it was, believing that the naïve boyish way in which Ellison had explained his actions would make the only appeal for clemency the poor lad could hope for. I well remember the conclusion of his plea: "I hope, honourable gentlemen, you'll be so kind as to take my case under consideration, as I was only a boy at the time, and I leave myself to the clemency and mercy of this Honourable Court."

By this time it was nearly 4 P.M. The Court adjourned, and we were taken back to the *Hector* to await its verdict.

## XXIV · CONDEMNED

TUESDAY, the eighteenth of September, 1792, was a typically English autumn day, with a grey sea and a grey sky. It had rained during the early morning, but by the time the gun was fired from the *Duke,* assembling the court-martial, the downpour had changed to a light drizzle through which the many ships of war at anchor could be seen dimly. At length the sky lightened perceptibly, and the sun shone wanly through. The *Duke's* quarter-deck was thronged with people awaiting the opening of the Court. Sir Joseph and Dr. Hamilton were there. On the other side of the deck were the *Bounty* witnesses and the officers of the *Pandora.*

Throughout the court-martial no relatives or friends of the prisoners had been permitted to attend the hearings. Even had such permission been granted, now that my mother was dead, I had no relatives who might have come. This was a consolation to me. Whatever my fate, it was good to be certain that none of my kin was waiting that morning for the verdict that would either clear me or condemn me to death.

But as my glance went over the crowd my pulse quickened at seeing Mr. Erskine, my father's solicitor and the old friend of both of my parents. He was then well into his seventies. He had stopped with us at Withycombe many a time, and the great treats of my life, as a youngster, had been my rare visits to London with my father, when I had seen much of Mr. Erskine. He had often taken me to view the sights of London, and his kindnesses upon these occasions made them among the happiest of my boyhood recollections. For the first time since the beginning of the court-martial I was deeply stirred, and I could see that Mr. Erskine controlled his own emotion with difficulty. His association with my parents and Withycombe was so close that he seemed like a near and deeply loved relative.

Presently the door of the great cabin was opened and the spectators filed in to their places. The prisoners followed, and we stood waiting while the members of the Court took their seats. The master-at-arms called, "Roger Byam!"

I stood in my place.

The President asked, "Have you anything further to say in your defense?"

"No, my lord."

The same question was put to each of us. The spectators were then asked to leave the room, the prisoners were marched out, and the door of the great cabin closed behind us. We were taken into the waist, by the foremast. The spectators stood in groups about the quarter-deck, or walked up and down, talking together. We could hear nothing they said; indeed, a silence seemed to have fallen over the ship. There were seamen going about routine duties, but they performed them in a subdued, soundless manner as though they were officiating at church.

Mr. Graham had visited me on the previous evening. He had told me how I might know, the moment I entered the room to learn my fate, what that fate was to be. A midshipman's dirk would be lying on the table before the President. If the dirk were placed at right angles to me, I should know that I had been acquitted. If it lay with the point toward the foot of the table where I was to stand, I should know that I had been condemned.

I felt strangely indifferent as to which it might be. Presently I fell into a kind of stupor, a waking dream, in which blurred images passed over the surface of consciousness, stirring it but little more than the ghost of a breeze disturbs the surface of a calm sea.

It must have been at about half-past nine that the Court had been cleared. When I roused myself from my reverie, an immeasurable period of time seemed to have elapsed; and indeed, the sun had passed the meridian. I heard the ship's bells strike one o'clock. The clouds had vanished, the sky was pale blue, and the sunlight had that golden quality which beautifies whatever it touches, giving a kind of splendour to familiar, common objects. The *Duke's* great guns looked magical in that light, and the throng on the quarter-deck, in their varicoloured uniforms, with sudden gleams of light flashing from epaulettes or sword hilts, seemed like figures out of some romantic tale rather than officers of His Majesty's Navy.

The door of the great cabin reopened at last. The master-at-arms appeared, announcing that audience was admitted; then I heard my name called. The sound of the syllables seemed strange to me; it was as though I had never heard them before.

I was accompanied by a lieutenant with a drawn sword and a guard of four men with muskets and bayonets fixed. I found myself standing at the end of the long table, facing the President. The midshipman's dirk was lying on the table before him. Its point was toward me.

The entire Court rose. Lord Hood regarded me in silence for a moment.

"Roger Byam: having heard the evidence produced in support of the charges made against you; and having heard what you have alleged in your own defense; and having maturely and deliberately weighed the whole of the evidence, this Court is of the opinion that the charges have been proved against you. It doth, therefore, judge that you shall suffer death by being hanged by the neck on board such of His Majesty's ships of war, and at such a time and such a place as the Commissioners for executing the office of Lord High Admiral of Great Britain and Ireland, or any three of them for the time being, shall, in writing, under their hands, direct."

I waited, expecting to hear more, knowing at the same time that there was nothing more to be said. Then a voice — whose, I do not know — said, "The prisoner may retire." I turned about and was marched out of the great cabin, back to where the others were waiting.

I felt little emotion; only a sense of relief that the long ordeal was over. A true conception of all the horror and ignominy of this end was to come later. At the time sentence was pronounced I was merely stunned and dazed by the finality of it. Evidently the expression on my face told the others nothing, for Morrison asked, "What is it, Byam?" "I'm to be hung," I said, and I shall never forget the look of horror on Morrison's face. He had no time to reply, for he was called next. We watched as the door of the cabin closed behind him. Coleman, Norman, McIntosh, and Byrne stood in a group, waiting their turns, and I remember how the others drew closer to me, as though for mutual protection and comfort. Ellison touched my arm and smiled, without speaking. Burkitt stood clasping and unclasping his huge hairy hands.

The door opened again and Morrison was marched back to us. His face was pale, but he had himself well under control. He turned to me with a bitter smile. "We must enjoy life while we can, Byam." A moment later he added, "I wish to God *my* mother were dead."

I felt a welcome surge of anger. Morrison had, unquestionably, been convicted upon the evidence of two men, Hayward and Hallet. They alone of the witnesses had testified to having seen him under arms. Having heard the evidence of the other witnesses, I had never for a moment doubted that Morrison's name would be cleared; nor, I think, had he himself doubted. I could find nothing to say to comfort him.

Coleman followed. When he came out of the courtroom again, the guard stood to one side and Coleman walked, a free man, to one side of the quarter-deck. Norman, McIntosh, and Byrne were escorted in in turn, and as they came out the guard stood aside in each case, and they joined Coleman. Byrne was sobbing with joy and relief. The poor chap was almost blind, and groped his way to the others, his hands outstretched and the tears streaming down his face. Although their acquittal had been all but certain, now that they were actually at liberty their dazed manner and their bewilderment as to what to do with themselves would have touched any man's heart.

Burkitt, Ellison, Millward, and Muspratt were called in quick succession. All were found guilty and condemned to death. Immediately after sentence had been pronounced upon Muspratt, the spectators came out into the sunshine of the quarter-deck. We expected to see the members of the Court follow, but when the room had been cleared the door was closed again. Something, evidently, was to follow. The strain of waiting during the next half-hour was hardly to be borne.

Audience was again admitted, and the master-at-arms appeared at the door.

"James Morrison!"

Again Morrison was marched in. When he returned, he came as near to giving way to his emotion as I had ever seen him do. He had been recommended to His Majesty's mercy. This meant, almost certainly, that the recommendation of the Court would be followed and Morrison pardoned. A moment later Lord Hood came out, followed by the captains who had sat with him. The court-martial was at an end.

Muspratt looked at me in such a desolate manner that my heart went out to him. I put my hand on his shoulder, but there was nothing to be said. In the silence of the ship, I could hear the faint hum of conversation from the quarter-deck. I saw Sir Joseph, Mr. Erskine, and Dr. Hamilton standing together by the larboard bulwarks. They were not permitted to come to us at that time, a circumstance for which I was deeply grateful.

Mercifully, we were not compelled to wait long on the *Duke*. The guard was drawn up; we were escorted to the gangway and clambered down the side into the longboat waiting to convey us back to the *Hector*. Another boat was lying alongside. There were no marines in her — only six seamen at the oars. Directly we had pushed off, we saw the freed men descending the side to be taken ashore. We had no opportunity to bid them good-bye and Godspeed, and when their boat put off from the side of the *Duke*, ours had almost reached the *Hector*. Ellison stood and waved his hat, and they waved back as they passed around the *Duke* and turned toward the shore. A moment later they were cut off from view. I never saw any man of them again.

During the whole time of our confinement on board the *Hector* we had been treated with great kindness by Captain Montague. We were, of course, carefully guarded, with marines stationed in the gun room as well as outside the door, but aside from that there had been little to remind us of the fact that we were prisoners. Now that we had been condemned and were awaiting execution of sentence, Captain Montague did all he could to make our situation endurable. He granted me the privilege of being confined in a cabin belonging to one of his lieutenants who was absent on leave. After eighteen months of imprisonment, during which time I had had not a moment of privacy, I was able to appreciate this courtesy at its full value. Twice daily I was permitted to go to the gun room for the purpose of exercise and to see the others.

Sir Joseph Banks, the most considerate of men, did not come to see me until the second day after we had been condemned, so that when he did come, late in the afternoon, I was prepared to meet him. I was then most eager to see him, and when I opened the door of my cabin to find him standing there, my heart leaped with pleasure.

He gripped my hand in both of his, then turned to take a bulky parcel from the seaman who had brought him to the cabin.

"Sit down, Byam," he said. He laid the parcel on the small table and proceeded to remove the wrappings.

"I've brought you an old companion and friend. Do you recognize it?" he added, as he laid aside the last of the wrappings. It was the manuscript of my Tahitian dictionary and grammar.

"Allow me to say this," he went on. "I have gone over your manuscripts with great interest, and I know enough of the Tahitian language to appreciate the quality of the work you've done. It is excellent, Byam; precisely what is needed. This book, when it is published, will be of great value, not only practically but philosophically. Now tell me this: how much time would you require to put it into final shape, ready for the printers?"

"Do you mean that I may work on it here?"

"Would you care to do so?"

I was in need, heaven knows, of something to occupy my mind. Sir Joseph's thoughtfulness touched me deeply.

"Nothing would please me more, sir," I replied. "I am under no illusions as to the importance of this work . . ."

"But it *is* important, my dear fellow," he interrupted. "Make no mistake about that. I've brought your manuscripts not merely out of consideration for you. This task must be completed. The Royal Society is greatly interested, and it has been suggested to me that an introductory essay accompany the volume, in which the Tahitian language shall be discussed generally, and its points of difference to any of our European tongues pointed out. Such an essay is quite beyond me. I had only a superficial knowledge of the Tahitian speech, acquired during my sojourn on the island with Captain Cook, and I have forgotten most of what I learned at that time. Only you can write this essay."

"I shall be glad to attempt it," I replied, "if there is sufficient time . . ."

"Could you complete it in a month?"

"I think so."

"Then a clear month you shall have. I have enough influence at the Admiralty to be able to promise you that."

"I shall make the most of it, sir."

"Do you prefer not to talk of the events of the . . . of the past week?" he asked, after a brief silence.

"It doesn't matter, sir. If there is something you wish to say . . ."

"Only this, Byam. It is needless to tell you what my feelings are. There has never been a more tragic miscarriage of justice in the history of His Majesty's Navy. I know how embittered you must be. You understand why you have been condemned?"

"I believe I do, sir."

"There was no alternative, Byam. None. All the palliating circumstances — the fact that no man had seen you under arms, the testimony as to the excellent character you bore, and all the rest — were not sufficient to offset Bligh's damning statement as to your complicity with Christian in planning the mutiny. That statement stood unchallenged, except by yourself, throughout the court-martial. Only your friend Tinkler could have challenged and disproved it. Lacking his evidence . . ."

"I understand, sir," I replied. "Let us say no more about it. What seems to me not only a tragic but a needless miscarriage of justice applies to poor Muspratt. There is no more loyal-hearted seaman afloat than Muspratt, and he is to be hung solely upon the evidence of one man — Hayward. Muspratt's testimony as to why he took arms is strictly true. It was for the purpose of helping Fryer in case he was able to form a party for retaking the ship. The instant he saw that the party could not be formed, he put down the musket."

"I agree with you, and you will be glad to know that there is still hope for Muspratt. Say nothing, of course, to the poor fellow about this, but I have it upon good authority that he may yet be reprieved."

That same afternoon, when I saw Muspratt in the gun room, I was tempted, for the first time in my life, to betray a matter entrusted to me in confidence. It would be impossible to say how badly I wanted to give Muspratt a glimmer of hope, the merest hint of what might happen in his case. I refrained, however.

Those September days were as beautiful as any that I remember. A transparent film of vapour hung high in the air, diffusing the light of the sun, so that the very atmosphere seemed to be composed of a golden dust transforming every object it fell upon. So it was, day after day, without change. The *Hector* was moored, bow and stern, and the view from my cabin was always the same, but I never tired of it. I had a prospect of the harbour looking toward the Channel and the Isle of Wight, with a great first-rate and three seventy-fours anchored not far distant. I saw boats passing back and forth, their oars dipped in gold, and the men in them seemed transfigured in the pale light. Knowing how brief a time remained to me, I found nothing unworthy of interest and attention. Even the common objects in my small cabin, — the locker, the table, and the inkwell before me, — seen in various lights at different hours of the day, I found beautiful and wondered that I had failed to notice such things before.

I was not wholly wretched at this time. A man who knows that he is to die, that his fate is fixed and irrevocable, seems to be endowed, as a recompense, with the faculty of benumbed acquiescence. The thing is there, slowly or swiftly approaching, but for the most part he is mercifully spared the full realization that it must and will come. There are moments, however, when he is not spared. Now and then, particularly at night, I would be gripped by a sense of horror that struck me to the heart. I would feel the rope about my throat, and see the faces of the brawny seamen who were waiting the order to hoist me to the yardarm; and I would hear the last words that would ever strike my ear: "And may God have mercy upon you." At such times I would pray silently for the courage to meet that moment when it should come.

Of the other condemned men, Ellison best endured the cruel waiting. He had lost his old gaiety of manner, but it was replaced by a quiet courage to face the facts that was beyond praise. Burkitt became more and more like a wild beast at bay. Every time that I was taken to the gun room for exercise I would find him pacing up and down, turning his head from side to side with the same expression of dazed incredulity on his face. He had the mighty chest of a Viking and his limbs would have made those of three ordinary men. He had never known an ache or a pain in his life save those inflicted by some boatswain's mate with a cat-o'-nine-tails. To men with such a power of life in them, death has no reality until it is at hand. Even now, I could see that Burkitt had not entirely given up hope. There was always the possibility of escape. He was narrowly watched by the guards; the eyes of one or another of them were upon him constantly.

Millward and Muspratt were sunk in moods of hopeless apathy, and rarely spoke to anyone. No one knew on what day the execution would be carried out. Not even the captain of the *Hector* would know until the Admiralty order had been received. Meanwhile, Morrison was kept in a state of what would have been, for me, the most harrowing anxiety. Although recommended to the King's clemency, there was always the possibility that mercy would be refused. The days passed and no pardon came, but Morrison was his usual calm self, and he discussed my work on the dictionary as though he had no other interest in the world. Had he been condemned to die with the rest of us, Morrison would have awaited the ordeal with the same fortitude.

Mr. Graham came to bid me farewell before leaving Portsmouth. He told me, as Sir Joseph had done, that the Court had no alternative in imposing sentence upon me; and, although he did not say so directly, he gave me to understand that I could not hope for a reprieve. The following afternoon Mr. Erskine came, remaining until dusk, during which time I settled my affairs and made my will. My only living relative was a cousin on my mother's side, a lad of fifteen who lived in India with his father. It was strange to think that our old home at Withycombe and the rest of our family fortune would go to this boy whom I had never seen.

I shall not venture to say how I would have passed those days without work to engross my thoughts. Once again my dictionary proved to be the greatest of blessings, and it was not long before I was able to give it the whole of my attention. Every one of those manuscript pages was fragrant with Tahiti and memories of Tehani and our little Helen. Some of them the baby had torn or finger-marked, and I could plainly hear her mother's voice as she took them quickly from her, scolding her lovingly: "Oh, you little mischief! Is this the way you help your father?"

Scarcely a word but brought memories thronging back. "Tafano" —I well remembered the circumstances which added that to my lexicon. The sweet poignant odour of the flower seemed to rise from the page where I had written it, and I lived again the happy day that Stewart and Peggy and Tehani and I had spent on the little island in the Tautira lagoon.

I worked all day long, and every day, and by the middle of October my task was completed, in so far as the dictionary and grammar were concerned. I proceeded at once to write the introductory essay, for I knew that the time remaining to me must be short.

The strain of waiting was telling upon all of us. Although he failed to show it, Morrison must have found it hardest to bear. To me, it seemed the refinement of cruelty to keep him so long in doubt as to his fate. A month had passed, and still he received no word.

I had received several letters from Sir Joseph, but there was no mention of Admiralty news; nor did I expect any. He himself would not know the day set for the execution.

On the twenty-fifth of October, I was revising, for the fourth or fifth time, the introductory essay for my dictionary, when there came a knock at the door. Every summons of this sort brought a cold sweat to my forehead, but this one was immediately followed by a well-remembered voice: "Are you there, Byam?" and I opened the door to Dr. Hamilton.

I had not seen him since the closing day of the court-martial. He informed me that he had just been appointed surgeon to the *Spitfire,* then stationed at Portsmouth. It was one of the ships I could see from my cabin window. She was on the eve of sailing for the Newfoundland station, and the doctor had come to bid me good-bye.

We talked of the *Pandora,* the shipwreck, the voyage to Timor, and of those two monsters of inhumanity, Edwards and Parkin. Dr. Hamilton was no longer under the necessity of concealing his feelings concerning either of these men. Parkin he loathed, of course, but his opinion of Edwards was, naturally, more fair and just than my own.

"I quite understand your feeling toward him, Byam," he said; "but the truth is that Edwards is not the beast you think him."

"Have you forgotten the morning of the wreck, Doctor, when we were chained hand and foot until the very moment when the ship went down?" I asked. "That our lives were saved was due entirely to the humanity of Moulter, the boatswain's mate. And have you forgotten how later, when we were on the sand-bar, Edwards refused to give us a sail that was not in use, so that we might protect our naked bodies from the sun?"

"I agree with you there; that *was* cruelty of the monstrous sort; no excuse whatever can be made for it. But otherwise, Byam . . . Well, you must remember the character of the man. He has a high sense of what he considers his duty, but not a grain of imagination — nothing remotely resembling what might be called uncommon sense. You will remember my telling you of his Admiralty instructions? He was ordered to confine his prisoners in such a manner as to preclude all possibility of escape, and at the same time to have a due regard for the preservation of their lives. Captains of the Edwards kind should never be given truly responsible positions; they are fitted to carry out only the letter and never the spirit of Admiralty orders. One can at least say this for him: he acted in accordance with what he considered his duty."

"I'm afraid, sir," I replied, "that I can never take so lenient a view of him. I have suffered too much at his hands."

"I don't wonder, Byam. I don't wonder at all. You have . . ."

The doctor was in the very midst of a sentence when the door was flung open and Sir Joseph entered. He was breathing heavily as though he had been running, and I could see that he was labouring under great emotion.

"Byam, my dear lad!"

He broke off, unable to say more. I felt an icy chill at my heart. Dr. Hamilton rose hastily, and looked from Sir Joseph to me and back again.

"No . . . Wait . . . It's not what you think. . . . One moment. . . ."

He took a stride into the tiny cabin and gripped me by the shoulders.

"Byam. . . . Tinkler is safe. . . . He is found. . . . He is in London now; at this moment!"

"Sit you down, lad," said Dr. Hamilton. I needed no urging. My legs felt as weak as though I had been lying in bed for months. The surgeon took a small silver flask from his pocket, unscrewed the top, and offered it to me. Sir Joseph sat in the chair at my table and mopped his forehead with a large silk handkerchief. "Will you prescribe for me as well, Doctor?" he asked.

"Please forgive me, sir," I said, handing him the flask.

"Good heaven, Byam, don't apologize!" he replied. "Necessity knows no laws of deportment." He took a pull at the flask and returned it to the surgeon. "Damn fine brandy, sir. I'll wager it has never done better service than here, this day. . . . Byam, I came from London as fast as a light chaise would bring me. Yesterday, at breakfast, I was glancing through my *Times*. In the shipping news I chanced to see an item announcing the arrival of the West Indiaman *Sapphire* with the survivors of the crew of the *Carib Maid*, lost on a passage between Jamaica and the Havannah. I need not tell you that I left my breakfast unfinished. When I arrived at the dock I found the *Sapphire* already discharging her cargo. The *Carib Maid* people had gone ashore the evening before. I traced them to an inn near by. Tinkler was there, on the point of setting out to the house of his brother-in-law, Fryer. Like the other *Carib Maid* survivors, he was still dressed in various articles of clothing furnished by the *Sapphire's* company. He looked the part of a shipwrecked mariner, but I gave him no time for excuses. I bundled him into my carriage and carried him straight to Lord Hood. As luck would have it, the Admiral was in Town; he had dined with me the night before. Tinkler, of course, was in the greatest bewilderment at all this. I said nothing of my reason for wanting him — not a word. At half-past ten Lord Hood and I were at the Admiralty with Tinkler between us, dressed just as he had come ashore, in a seaman's jersey and boots three sizes too large for him.

"Now what has happened, or what will happen, is this: Tinkler will be examined before the Admiralty Commissioners, who alone have the power to hear his evidence. By the grace of God and my copy of yesterday's *Times,* that evidence cannot be impeached as biased or prejudiced. Tinkler knows nothing of the court-martial. He has not seen Fryer, and he does not know that you are within ten thousand miles of London. I left him at the Admiralty, in proper charge, and came in all haste to Portsmouth."

I could think of nothing to say. I merely sat, staring like a dumb man, at Sir Joseph.

"Will the court-martial be reconvened to pass upon this evidence?" Dr. Hamilton asked.

"No, that cannot be done; it is unnecessary that it should be done. The Admiralty Commissioners who will receive Tinkler's evidence have the power, in case the new testimony warrants it, of reversing the verdict of the court-martial in Byam's case, and completely exonerating him. We shall have their decision within a few days, I hope."

My heart sank at this. "Will it require days, sir, for the decision to be made?" I asked.

"You must bear up, lad," Sir Joseph replied. "I understand, God knows, how hard the waiting will be; but official wheels turn slowly."

"And my ship, the *Spitfire,* sails to-morrow," said Dr. Hamilton, ruefully. "I shall have to leave England without knowing your fate, Byam."

"Perhaps it's just as well, Doctor," I replied.

Sir Joseph opened his mouth to speak, and then gazed blankly at me.

"Byam, I'm afraid I've made an unpardonable mistake! The realization has only this moment come to me! Good God, what have I done! You should have been told nothing of all this until the decision of the Commissioners has been given!"

"Not at all, sir," I replied. "You shan't be allowed to condemn yourself. You have given me reason to hope. Even though the hope prove unfounded, I shall be none the less grateful."

"You truly mean that?"

"Yes, sir."

He gave me a keen, scrutinizing glance. "I see that you do. I am glad I came." He rose. "And now I must leave you again. I shall go back to London at once. I must be there to expedite matters as much as possible for you." He shook my hand. "If it is good news, Byam, Captain Montague shall receive it for you by messenger riding the best horses that ever galloped the Portsmouth road."

## XXV · TINKLER

SIR JOSEPH BANKS carried my completed manuscripts back to London with him. Having finished my work, I asked permission to take up my quarters in the gun room again, and returned the same evening. The strain of waiting was less hard to endure in company. I told only Morrison of Tinkler's return; it would have been cruel to have informed the others, men deprived of all hope of life.

Morrison's Bible proved a resource to all of us during those last days. It was the same copy he had carried with him on the *Bounty,* and had been preserved even through the wreck of the *Pandora.* We read aloud. in turn, to the others, and we continued for hours so as to prevent ourselves from thinking of what was soon to come. Millward and Muspratt had aroused themselves from their stupor of despair. My liking and respect for these men increased greatly at this time. Tom Ellison had never for a moment lost his courage. It was a bitter thought that this lad, who had not an ounce of harm in him, was to lose his life as the result of a boyish indiscretion, at a time when he was most fitted to live. Only Burkitt remained as he had been from the day when sentence was pronounced. Except for brief intervals at mealtime, he paced up and down, hour after hour. Occasionally he would sit down for a moment, his head between his hands, staring dully at the floor; then he would lift his great shaggy head and glance around the room as though he had never seen it before, and a moment later spring to his feet and resume his pacing.

On the morning of October 26, we watched the *Spitfire* getting up her anchors. It was a windless day, and boats' crews from the *Hector* and the *Brunswick* were sent to assist in towing her out of the harbour. We saw, or thought we saw, Dr. Hamilton standing on the poop as the ship moved slowly out toward Spithead. Whether or not it was the surgeon, we knew that he was thinking of us that morning as we were thinking of him and wishing him Godspeed.

We welcomed every diversion, however slight; not a ship's boat crossing our line of vision escaped us. We criticized the way her men handled the oars, and conjectured as to where she was going and why. And every time the door of the gun room opened, every time the guard was changed or food was brought, I felt the cold chill about my heart that every condemned man must have known. Many a time during those weeks did I wish that the Admiralty Commissioners might have stood in our places for one day. The needless cruelty inflicted upon six men, prolonged during a period of more than a month, gave me a disgust for official routine which I retain to this day.

On the Sunday afternoon, Morrison was reading aloud to the rest of us. It was a cold day of drizzling rain, and Morrison was sitting close to one of the ports, holding his Bible on a level with his eyes that he might benefit by what dim light there was. All of us, excepting Burkitt, were gathered around him as we listened to that most beautiful of all the Psalms: —

The Lord is my shepherd; I shall not want.

Morrison read on in his clear musical voice, choosing those psalms that had comforted many generations of men in time of trouble. Of a sudden he halted in the midst of a sentence, and turned his head quickly toward the door. In so far as I remember we had heard nothing, — no sound, no voice, no tread of feet, — and yet we rose together and stood waiting, our eyes turned in the same direction. Burkitt stopped short and looked from the guards to us and back again. "What's up?" he asked, hoarsely. There was no need to reply. The door opened and a lieutenant of marines entered, followed by the master-at-arms and a guard of eight men.

It was all but dark in the room and we could scarcely distinguish the faces of the men who had entered. The master-at-arms carried a paper in his hand. He crossed to one of the ports and held it up to the dim light.

"Thomas Burkitt — John Millward — Thomas Ellison."

"The prisoners named step forward," the lieutenant ordered.

The three men moved to the centre of the room. Handcuffs were snapped upon their wrists, and they were placed in the centre of the guard, four men in front and four behind.

"Forward, march!"

They were gone in an instant without a word of farewell being said. Morrison, Muspratt, and I stood where we were, and the door was closed and locked once more. A moment later, as we peered from the ports, we saw one of the *Hector's* cutters put off from the gangway, and in the last grey light of the autumn afternoon we could distinguish the three shackled men on a thwart astern. Moored abreast of the *Hector* and about four hundred yards distant was *H.M.S. Brunswick*. We saw the cutter pass under her counter and disappear.

The anxiety of the night that followed is painful to recall. Morrison, Muspratt, and I made no pretense of sleeping. We sat by one of the ports, now and then peering out into the darkness toward the *Brunswick*, talking in low voices of the men who had gone. We knew well enough that it was their last night of life. The fact that we had been left behind gave us reason to hope that their fate was not to be ours. My heart went out to poor Muspratt, whose anguish of mind may be imagined. I did not dare hint, even now, at what Sir Joseph had told me concerning him, but I was glad that Morrison encouraged him to hope.

"Your case has been taken under consideration, Muspratt; I am sure of it," he said. "I have never doubted that it would be. The fact that we have been left here proves that there is something in the wind concerning us."

"What do you think, Mr. Byam?" asked Muspratt.

"That Morrison is right," I replied. "He has been recommended to the King's clemency. The Court's appeal on his behalf must have been granted. You and I have been left here with him. Don't you see, Muspratt? If they intended to hang us, we would have been sent to the *Brunswick* with the rest."

"But maybe they want to hang them first? Or what if they're going to hang us on the *Hector*?"

So we talked the night long, and God knows it was long. We considered every possibility, every conceivable reason for our separation from the others. And the minutes and the hours dragged by, and at last the darkness was suffused with the ashy light of dawn, through which the huge mass of the *Brunswick* grew more and more distinct.

Our guard was changed with the watch, at eight bells. No news came. One of the few prohibitions imposed upon us — and a quite just one — was that we should not speak to the guards, so we had no means of knowing what news was current on the ship. At nine o'clock, Morrison, who was standing by a port, turned and said, "They've run up the signal for punishment on the *Brunswick*."

On all British ships, eleven o'clock in the morning was the hour for inflicting punishment. We had no doubt as to whom the *Brunswick's* signal concerned. Ellison, Burkitt, and Millward had but two hours to live.

At half-past ten we saw one of the *Hector's* longboats, filled with seamen, put off to the *Brunswick*. Boats from other vessels in the harbour followed; the men in them, we knew, were being sent to witness the execution. Muspratt remained at the port, gazing toward the *Brunswick* as though fascinated by the sight of her lofty yards. Morrison and I paced the room together, talking in the Indian tongue of Teina and Itea and other friends at Tahiti, in a desperate attempt to occupy our minds. It was getting on toward the hour when Captain Montague entered, followed by the lieutenant who had come the night before. A glance at the captain's face told us all we needed to know, but if there was still doubt in our minds it was banished when the lieutenant ordered the guard to dismiss. The men filed quickly out, glancing back at us with friendly smiles. Captain Montague unfolded the paper in his hand.

"James Morrison — William Muspratt," he called.

The two men stepped forward. Captain Montague glanced at them over the top of the paper he held, a kindly gleam in his blue eyes. He then read, solemnly: —

"In response to the earnest appeal of Lord Hood (Admiral of the Blue, and President of the Court-Martial by which you have been tried, convicted, and condemned to death for the crime of mutiny on His Majesty's armed transport, *Bounty*), who, by reason of certain extenuating circumstances, has begged that you may not be compelled to suffer the extreme penalty prescribed by our just laws, His Majesty is graciously pleased to grant to you, and each of you, a free and unconditional pardon."

"Roger Byam."

I took my place beside my two comrades.

"The Commissioners for executing the Office of Lord High Admiral of Great Britain and Ireland, having received and heard the sworn testimony of Robert Tinkler, former midshipman of His Majesty's armed transport, *Bounty,* are convinced of your entire innocence of the crime of mutiny, for which you have been tried, convicted, and condemned to death. The Lord's Commissioners do, therefore, annul the verdict of the Court-Martial as it respects your person, and you stand acquitted."

Captain Montague then stepped forward and shook each of us warmly by the hand.

"I have no doubt," he said, "that three loyal subjects have been spared to-day for further usefulness to His Majesty."

My heart was too full for words. I could only mutter, "Thank you, sir!" but Morrison would not have been Morrison had he not been prepared even for such a moment as this.

"Sir," he said, earnestly, "when the sentence of the law was passed upon me, I received it, I trust, as became a man; and if it had been carried into execution, I should have met my fate, I hope, in a manner becoming a Christian. I receive with gratitude my Sovereign's mercy, for which my future life shall be faithfully devoted to His service."

Captain Montague bowed gravely.

"Are we now at liberty, sir?" I asked, doubtingly.

"You are free to go this moment if you choose."

"You will understand, sir, that we desire, if possible, to avoid . . ."

The captain turned to the lieutenant. "Mr. Cunningham, will you see to it that a boat is ordered at once?"

Captain Montague accompanied us to the upper deck, and a few moments later we were informed that the boat was waiting at the gangway. As I bade farewell to the captain he said, "I hope, Mr. Byam, to have the pleasure of meeting you again soon, under more fortunate circumstances." We climbed hastily down the side, and the midshipman in charge of the boat's crew gave orders to push off. We were in no position to enjoy the sweetness of those first moments of freedom. Six bells had struck while we were waiting on deck. Within two cables' lengths of us lay the *Brunswick,* her lofty masts and yards clearly outlined against the grey sky, and on our way to the wharf at Portsmouth we had to pass directly under her carved and gilded stern. Three men on her upper deck were standing at the very brink of death. Well we knew what was happening there. We sat with averted faces. We drew away from her, the seamen pulling at their oars steadily and in silence, but I saw that their eyes were all turned in the same direction, toward the tall ship now astern.

Of a sudden a great gun broke the silence with a reverberating roar. Against my will I turned my head. A cloud of smoke half hid the vessel, but as it billowed out and drifted slowly away I saw three small black figures suspended in mid-air, twitching as they swayed slowly from side to side.

Captain Montague had given me a letter from Sir Joseph, written at the Admiralty immediately after the decision of the Commissioners was known. He had taken inside places for us on that night's London coach. As a postscript he had written: "Mr. Erskine expects you at his house. You must not disappoint the old gentleman, Byam. You will want to see no one for several days; I quite understand that. When you have had the time you need alone, will you send me word? I have something of importance to communicate."

Nothing could have been more characteristic of Sir Joseph than this postscript. With all his bluff, hearty, manly qualities, he combined the delicacy and thoughtfulness of a woman.

The three of us were too shaken in mind for conversation — too sore in spirit, too bewildered at the change in our fortunes. We sat gazing out at the fields of home gradually fading from view as the autumn evening closed in. Opposite me in the coach there was a vacant place, and it remained unoccupied all the way to London, which we reached at daylight the following morning. But for me, all through the night, Tom Ellison sat there. I heard his laughter, his cheery voice. I saw him peering eagerly out of the window, missing nothing, enjoying everything, engaging in conversation the old gentleman who sat next to me. "Yes, sir, we've been away from home five long years, lacking one month. If you've ever been a sailor you'll know what this journey means to us. . . . What's that, sir? . . . No, no; much farther than that. Ever hear of an island called Tahiti? Well, that's where we've been. If you was to dig a hole straight through the earth you'd come out somewhere near it."

Sea Law. Just — yes; just, savage, and implacable. I would have given the whole of the Articles of War and all those who wrote them to have had Tom Ellison sitting, in the flesh, opposite me in that seat in the London coach.

It saddens me to think of our brief, casual farewells. There was reason for this. We three had been together so long, it was inconceivable that we could drift apart. We stood outside the booking office at the Angel, St. Clements, Strand, watching foot passengers, carts, chaises, and hackney coaches passing by. Morrison and I were both well provided with money, he by his family and I by Mr. Erskine, but Muspratt, we knew, had not two ha'pence to rub together in his pocket. His home was in Yarmouth, where he had lived with his mother and two younger sisters. Morrison was bound to the North Country.

"See here, Muspratt," he said, "how are you off for rhino?"

"Oh, I'll manage, Mr. Morrison," he replied. "I've ridden shanks' mare to Yarmouth before now."

"And your mother's waiting for you there? He's not to ride shanks' mare this time, eh, Byam?"

"That he is not!" I replied, heartily. We pressed five pounds each upon him, and it did our hearts good to see the expression of amazement and delight on Muspratt's face. We shook his hand warmly and he hurried away at once to book his seat in the Yarmouth coach. We stood looking after him as he made his way down the crowded street. He turned and waved to us from the corner, and disappeared.

"Well, Byam?" said Morrison. I gripped his hand.

"God bless you, lad!" he said. "We must never lose track of each other." A moment later I was alone, among strangers, for the first time in five years.

I could not have wished for a kinder, more considerate host than Mr. Erskine, my father's old friend. He had long been a widower, and still lived, with three elderly servants, in the house in Fig-Tree Court, near the Temple, where I had last visited him on my way to join the *Bounty*. The silence of that well-ordered house, where I had no appointments to keep and might do as I pleased from morning till night, was as healing to my spirit as the breath of the sea to a man at the end of a long illness. I wandered about the quiet streets in the vicinity of the Temple, or sat for hours by the window in my pleasant room overlooking Fig-Tree Court, where scarcely a dozen passers-by were to be seen in the course of an afternoon. And I thought of nothing. I had to accustom myself by degrees to the business of living — to the very thought that the gift of life was still mine to enjoy. Meanwhile, I was scarcely more animate than the two old trees that cast faint shadows on the pavement in the wan autumnal sun.

I had gone for my usual walk that day. When I returned, at five o'clock, Mr. Erskine had not yet come in, but Clegg, his butler, met me in the hallway.

"There's a gentleman waiting to see you, sir. He's in the library."

I took the stairs three at a time. I knew that my letter would bring him at the earliest possible moment. I flung open the door. There was Tinkler, standing with his back to the sea-coal fire.

Mr. Erskine was engaged that evening. At least, he sent word by Clegg to that effect; but my belief is that, upon coming home and learning that Tinkler was there, he had retired to his own room for no other reason than that we might have the evening together, alone. We had dinner in the library, in front of the fire. There was so much to be said that we scarcely knew how or where to begin. Tinkler had not yet recovered from his astonishment at the manner in which he had been pounced upon and kidnapped by Sir Joseph Banks.

"Remember, Byam, that I still thought of you as being somewhere on the other side of the world. When I had returned from my first voyage to the West Indies, I had heard that a ship, the *Pandora,* had been sent out to search for the *Bounty*. That was the extent of my information about you, and months had passed since that time. I had heard nothing of Edwards's return, and not a word of the court-martial. I had come ashore the previous evening, in clothing borrowed from men on the *Sapphire,* the ship that had rescued us. Another time I'll tell you the story of the *Carib Maid* and how she was lost. Only ten of us survived, — the other boats were lost, — and there we were at an inn about a stone's throw from the dock where the *Sapphire* was berthed. I'd had a glorious breakfast of eggs and bacon, and was just on the point of setting out for my brother-in-law's house when a fine carriage and pair drove up, and before I could say How-do-you-do or God bless me I found myself inside, sitting opposite Sir Joseph Banks.

"I had never laid eyes on him until that moment. He gave not even a hint of what he required of me, but I imagined that it must, somehow, concern the *Bounty*. 'Possess your soul in patience, Mr. Tinkler,' he said. 'I shall see to it that Mr. Fryer is notified of your arrival. I will merely say this, now: Mr. Fryer will strongly approve of my taking you in charge in this high-handed fashion.' With that I had to be content. Sir Joseph gave some instructions to his coachman and we drove westward at more than a smart clip. Presently we stopped before a very splendid house. Sir Joseph leaped out, strode up to the door, vanished, and ten minutes later out he came again with Admiral Hood in tow! Naturally, I was more mystified than ever, but I felt highly flattered at having two such guardians. We drove straight to the Admiralty.

"I shan't go into the details. Sir Joseph and the Admiral left me in charge of a Captain Maxon — Matson — some such name. He was a very courteous, pleasant, and vigilant companion, and didn't let me out of his sight for a moment. I spent the rest of that day, the following night, and until ten o'clock the next morning in his company. We told each other the stories of our lives, but all I gathered from him as to the business in hand was that it concerned the *Bounty*.

"Promptly at ten that morning, I was taken before the Board of Admiralty Commissioners. Picture me, still dressed in the cast-off clothing of three men, standing before that august assembly! I was sworn, and then graciously permitted to sit down.

" 'Mr. Tinkler, will you please to inform the Commissioners of anything you may know concerning Roger Byam, former midshipman of His Majesty's armed transport, *Bounty*.'

"You can imagine, Byam, how the mention of your name affected me. I felt a cold shiver of apprehension running with considerable speed up my spine and on to the roots of my hair. I had by no means forgotten how often Bligh had damned you as a piratical scoundrel without permitting any of us to say a word in your defense. Believe me, I had tried; and the second time I attempted it I thought he meant to throw me out of the boat. Now I thought, 'By God, old Byam's caught! He's in trouble, here or somewhere.' I looked from one to another of the Commissioners for a hint of what was expected of me.

" 'Do you mean, sir, concerning his present whereabouts?' I asked.

" 'No. Perhaps the question was a little vague. You are quite naturally mystified. We wish to know the particulars, if you recall them, of a conversation said to have taken place on the quarter-deck of the *Bounty* between Mr. Fletcher Christian and Mr. Byam on the night previous to the mutiny on that ship. Did you overhear such a conversation?'

"I remembered it at once, and it was at that moment, Byam, that light began to dawn upon me.

" 'Yes, sir,' I replied; 'I remember it quite well.'

" 'Reflect carefully, Mr. Tinkler. A man's life depends upon what you shall now depose concerning that conversation. Take as much time as you need to collect your thoughts. Omit no smallest detail.'

"The whole business came clear to me, Byam. I knew then precisely what was wanted, and you may thank God that my memory is as yet unimpaired by old age. But here's the extraordinary thing: from the night when you and Christian were talking between the larboard guns on the quarter-deck until the moment when I stood before the Commissioners, I'd forgotten the immensely important fact that Bligh had overheard a part of what you said. Wouldn't you think that might have stuck in my mind? There's a reasonable explanation, of course: during the boat voyage to Timor, and afterward, old Bligh never once, to my knowledge, explained why he considered you of Christian's party. We all believed that the reason was your failing to appear on deck before the launch was veered astern. And we knew that Christian had spoken to you a number of times on the morning of the mutiny. Furthermore, you were Christian's friend. That was more than enough to make the old rascal damn you straight out.

"You may believe that I took my time in proceeding. I told the story from the moment when we went on deck together during Peckover's watch. I'd forgotten nothing. I even told them how I'd confessed to you that I was one of the culprits who had stolen Bligh's invaluable coconuts. I told them how I lay down to take a caulk between the guns just before Christian came along and engaged you in conversation. But above everything, Byam, thank heaven and Robert Tinkler for this: I remembered how Bligh came up at the very moment you were shaking Christian's hand, when you said, 'You can count on me.'

"The Commissioners sat leaning forward in their chairs. One old fellow sat with a hand cupped behind his ear. On his behalf I spoke with particular slowness and distinctness. 'Mr. Christian replied: "Good, Byam," or "Thank you, Byam," I cannot be certain which, and they shook hands upon it. At this moment Mr. Bligh interrupted them; they had not heard him approach. He made some remark about their being up late, and . . .'"

"'That will do, Mr. Tinkler,' I was told. I was ushered out of the room, and . . . well, old lad, here we are!"

"You know, Byam," Tinkler went on, after a moment of silence, "I've often wondered whether that affair of the coconuts was not the actual cause of the mutiny. Do you remember how Bligh abused Christian?"

"I'm not likely to forget that," I replied.

"I can recall Bligh's very words: 'Yes, you bloody hound! I *do* think so! You must have stolen some of mine or you would be able to give a better account of your own!' What a thing to say to his second-in-command! I more than half believe that was what goaded Christian to desperation. What do you think?"

"Let's not talk of it, Tinkler," I said. "I'm sick to death of the business."

"Forgive me, lad. Of course you are."

"But I'd like nothing better than to hear about your voyage in the launch to Timor."

"I'll say this, Byam: in that situation, Bligh was beyond all praise. He was the same old blackguard, and he ruled us with an iron hand, but, by God, he brought us through! I don't believe there's another man in England who could have done it."

"What prevented him and Purcell from murdering each other, cooped up as they were in a small boat?"

"It was a near thing, a very near thing. Matters came to a head at a small island on the Great Barrier Reef. We were in a desperate situation and had put in there for the night. I've forgotten how the dispute started, but I remember Bligh and Purcell standing on a sandy beach facing each other like a couple of old bulls. We were damn near dead of hunger and thirst, but these two still had fight in 'em. Bligh made a stride to the boat, took two of our four cutlasses, and handed one to the carpenter. 'Now, sir,' he said, 'defend yourself or forever hold your peace!' The rest of us scarecrows stood looking on; we were too wretched to care what might happen. And Purcell backed down. He apologized. That was the only time there was ever a question of Bligh's authority."

"Do you remember Coupang, Tinkler?"

"Coupang! That heaven on earth! Let me tell you how we came in. It was about three in the morning . . . but wait a minute! How about filling my glass? As a host, Byam, you leave something to be desired."

And so it went the night through.


## XXVI · WITHYCOMBE

I HAD spent a week at Fig-Tree Court when I sent Sir Joseph the message he had asked for. I supposed that he wished to see me for some reason connected with my Indian dictionary, and now that the first numbness of mind succeeding my acquittal had passed, I looked forward with pleasure to the interview; and it would give me an opportunity to ask whether I might render any services to him, or to the Royal Society, upon my return to the South Sea.

The death of my mother had severed my last tie with England, and I had been through so much that all ambition, all a young man's craving for a life of action, seemed dead in me. I may, perhaps, be excused for my feeling of bitterness at this time. English faces seemed strange to me, and English ways harsh and even cruel. I longed only for Tehani and the tranquil beauty of the South Sea.

It was my intention to inform Sir Joseph of my plan to leave England for good. I was possessed of ample means to do as I pleased — even to purchase a vessel, should that prove necessary. Ships would be sailing from time to time for the newly formed settlement at Port Jackson, in New South Wales, and, once there, I might find it possible to buy or charter a small ship to take me to Tahiti. I knew that, for my mother's sake, I could not leave England without paying a visit to Withycombe, and I both dreaded and longed to see our old house, so filled with memories.

Sir Joseph's reply to my message was an invitation to dinner on the same evening, and I found him in company with Captain Montague, of the *Hector*. We discussed for a time the events taking place in Europe, which pointed to an early outbreak of war. Presently Sir Joseph turned to me.

"What are your plans, Byam?" he asked. "Shall you return to the Navy, or go up to Oxford, as your father hoped?"

"Neither, sir," I replied. "I have decided to return to the South Sea."

Montague set down his glass at my words, and Sir Joseph looked at me in astonishment, but neither man spoke.

"There is nothing, now, to keep me in England," I added.

Sir Joseph shook his head slowly. "It had not occurred to me that you were considering Tahiti," he said. "I feared that, in your present state, you might intend to give up the sea for the seclusion of an academic career. But the islands . . . no, my lad!"

"Why not, sir?" I asked. "I am free of obligations at home, and I should be happy there. Saving yourself and Captain Montague and a handful of other friends, there is no one in England I wish to see again."

"I understand — I understand," Sir Joseph remarked kindly. "You have suffered much, Byam; but remember, time will heal the deepest wounds. And remember another thing: if I may say so, you *have* obligations, and weighty ones."

"To whom, sir?" I inquired.

My host paused, thoughtfully. "I see that it has not even occurred to you," he said. "It is a delicate matter to explain. Montague, suppose I leave it to you?"

The captain sipped his wine as if pondering how to begin. Presently he looked up. "Sir Joseph and I have spoken of you more than once, Mr. Byam. You have obligations, as he says."

"To whom, sir?" I asked once more.

"To your name; to the memory of your father and mother. You have been imprisoned and tried for mutiny, and though you were acquitted and are as innocent as Sir Joseph or myself, something — a little unpleasant something — may cling to your name. *May* cling, I say; whether or not it shall, rests with you. If you choose to follow some career ashore, or, worst of all, decide to bury yourself in the South Sea, men will say, when your name is spoken of: 'Roger Byam? Yes, I remember him well; one of the *Bounty* mutineers. He was tried by court-martial and acquitted at the last moment. A near thing!' Public opinion is a mighty force, Mr. Byam. No man can afford to disregard it."

"If I may speak plainly, sir," I replied, warmly, "damn public opinion! I am innocent, and my parents — if there is a life beyond death — know of my innocence. Let the others believe what they will!"

"You were a victim of circumstance and have been hardly used," said Captain Montague, kindly. "I understand very well how you feel; but Sir Joseph and I are right. You owe it to the honourable name you bear to continue the career of a sea officer. War is in the air; your part in it will soon silence the whispers. Come, Byam! To speak plainly, I want you on the *Hector,* and have saved a place in the berth for you."

Sir Joseph nodded. "That's what you should do, Byam."

I was still in a nervous condition as the result of my long imprisonment and the suspense I had been through. Captain Montague's kindness moved me deeply.

"Uncommonly good of you, sir," I muttered. "Indeed I appreciate the offer, but . . ."

"There's no need for an immediate decision," he interrupted. "Think over what I have said. Let me know your decision within a month. I can hold the offer open until then."

"Yes, take your time," said Sir Joseph. "We'll say no more of it to-night."

Captain Montague took leave of us early; afterward Sir Joseph led me to his study, hung with weapons and ornaments from distant lands.

"Byam," he said, when we had settled ourselves before the fire, "there is a question I have long desired to ask you. You know me for a man of honour; if you see fit to answer, you have my word that I will never divulge the reply."

He paused. "Proceed, sir," I said; "I will do my best."

"Where is Fletcher Christian — can you tell me?"

"Upon my word, sir," I replied, "I do not know, nor could I hazard a guess."

He looked at me for a moment with his shrewd blue eyes, rose briskly, and pulled down a great chart of the Pacific from its roller on the wall. "Fetch the lamp, Byam," he said.

Side by side, while I held the lamp, we scanned the chart of the greatest ocean in the world. "Here is Tahiti," he said. "What course was the *Bounty* steering when last seen?"

"Northeast by north, I should say."

"It might have been a blind, of course, but the Marquesas lie that way. The Spaniard, Mendaña, discovered them long ago. Rich islands, too, and only a week distant with the wind abeam. See, here they are."

"I doubt it, sir," I replied. "Christian gave us to understand that it was his intention to seek out an island as yet unknown. He would not have risked settling on a place likely to be visited."

"Perhaps not," he replied, musingly. "Edwards touched at Aitutaki, I believe?"

"Yes, sir," I replied, and as I glanced at the dot of land in the immense waste of waters, a sudden thought struck me. "By God!" I exclaimed.

"What is it, Byam?"

"I must tell you in confidence, Sir Joseph."

"You have my word."

"I told you that I could not even hazard a guess, but I had forgotten one possibility. After the mutiny, when we were sailing eastward from Tofoa, we raised a rich volcanic island not marked on any chart. It lies to the southwest of Aitutaki, distant not more than one hundred and fifty miles, I believe. We did not land, but the Indians came out in their canoes, and seemed friendly enough. I questioned one man in the language of Tahiti, and he told me the name of the place was Rarotonga. The mutineers were eager to go ashore, but Christian would have none of it. Yet, when he left Tahiti for the last time, he must have thought of this rich unknown island, so close to the west. If I were to search for Christian now, I should go straight to Rarotonga and be pretty sure of finding him there."

Eighteen years were to pass before I learned how mistaken I was in this opinion. Sir Joseph listened attentively. "That's interesting," he said. "Captain Cook had no idea there was land so close to Aitutaki. A high island, you say?"

"Two or three thousand feet, at least. The mountains are rugged and green to the very tops. There is a broad belt of coastal land; it looked rich and populous."

"The very place for them! Is the island large?"

"Nearly the size of Eimeo, I should say."

"Gad, Byam!" he exclaimed, regretfully; "I'd like to report the discovery. But have no fear — the secret is safe with me. . . . Christian . . . poor devil!"

"You knew him, sir?"

He nodded. "I knew him well."

"He was my good friend," I said. "There was provocation, God knows, for what he did."

"No doubt. It's strange . . . I had supposed that Bligh was his best friend."

"I am sure that Captain Bligh thought so, too. . . . I've a sad task ahead of me. I promised Christian that I would see his mother if ever I reached England."

"His people are gentlefolk; they live in Cumberland."

"Yes, sir; I know."

Sir Joseph rolled up the chart. I glanced at the tall clock against the wall. "Time I was getting home, sir," I said.

"Aye, bedtime, lad. But one word before you go. Let me advise you, most earnestly, to consider Captain Montague's offer. You are sore in spirit, but that will pass. Montague and I are older men. We know this sorry old world better than you. Give up the idea of burying yourself in the South Sea!"

"I'll think it over, sir," I said.

Day after day I put off my visit to Withycombe. I dreaded leaving the quiet old house in Fig-Tree Court, and when at last I took leave of Mr. Erskine I had already been to Cumberland and back on Christian's errand. Of my interview with his mother I shall not speak.

On a chill winter evening, with a fine rain drizzling down, I alighted from the coach in Taunton, and found our carriage awaiting me. Our old coachman was dead, and his son, the companion of many a boyhood scrape, was on the box. The street was ankle-deep in mud, with pools of water glimmering in the faint gleam of the lamps. I stepped into the carriage, and we went swaying down the rutty, dimly lighted street.

The faint musty smell of leather was perfume to me, and brought back a flood of memories — of rainy Sundays in the past when we had driven to church. Here, in the door, was the pocket into which my mother used to slip her prayer book, nearly always forgotten until we were about to enter our pew. I could hear the very tones of her voice, humorous and apologetic: "Oh, Roger! My prayer book! Run back and fetch it, dear." And there seemed to linger in the old coach the fragrance of English lavender, which she preferred to all the scents of France.

The rain fell steadily, and the horses trotted on, splashing through pools, slowing to a walk on the hills. Tired with my long journey from London, I fell into a doze. When I awoke, the wheels were crunching on the gravel of the Withycombe drive, and ahead of us I could see the lights of the house. For a moment, five years were blotted from my mind; I was returning from school for the Christmas holidays, and my mother would be listening for the carriage, ready to run to the door to welcome me.

Thacker was standing under the portico, and the butler and the other servants — a forlorn little group, it seemed to me. Never, save on that night, have I seen tears in Thacker's eyes.

A few moments later I was seated alone in the high-ceilinged dining-room, filled with shadows and memories. The candles on the table burned without a flicker, and in their yellow light our old butler moved noiselessly about, filling my glass and setting before me food that I ate without knowing what it was. It had been my privilege to dine here on Sundays, as a small boy, and on other evenings to come in to say good-night when my father and mother were at dessert — a good-night enriched by a walnut, or a handful of raisins or Spanish figs. Here I had dined with my mother, after my father's death; here Bligh had dined with us on that night so long ago. Save for him and his letter my mother might be opposite me now. . . . I rose and went upstairs.

In my father's study, high up in the north wing, I stretched out in a long chair under the chandelier. His spirit seemed to fill the place: his collection of sextants in the cabinet, the astronomical charts on the wall, the books in their tall shelves — all were eloquent of him. I took down a leather-bound volume of Captain Cook's *Voyages,* but found it impossible to read. I was listening for my mother's light footstep in the passage outside, and her voice at the door: "Roger, may I come in?" At last I took up a candle and made my way along the hallway, passing the door of my mother's room on the way to my own. Into her room I dared not go that night. I fancied her there, as I had seen her a hundred times in the past, reading in bed, with her thick hair tumbled on the pillow, and a candle on the table at her side.

West winds, blowing off the Atlantic, made that December a warm and rainy month, and I took many a long walk along the muddy lanes, with the rain in my face and the wind moaning through the leafless trees. A change, so gradual as to be almost imperceptible, was coming over me; I was beginning to realize that my roots, like those of my ancestors, were deep in this West Country soil. Tehani, our child, the South Sea — all seemed to lose substance and reality, fading to the ghostliness of a beautiful, half-remembered dream. Reality lay here — in the Watchet churchyard, in Withycombe, among the cottages of our tenants. And the solid walls of our old house, the order preserved within, through death and distress, brought home to me the sense of a continuity it was my duty to preserve. Little by little my bitterness dissolved.

Toward the end of the month my decision was made. It cost me dear at the time, but I have since had no cause to regret it. I wrote to Captain Montague that I would join his ship, and enclosed a copy of the letter in a longer one to Sir Joseph Banks. Two days later, on a grey windless morning, I stood under the portico, waiting for the carriage which was to take me to Taunton to catch the London coach.

The Bristol Channel lay like polished steel under the low clouds, and the air was so still that I could hear the cawing of the rooks from far and near. Two fishing boats were working out to sea, their sails hanging slack, and the men at the sweeps. I was watching them creeping laboriously toward the Atlantic when I heard Tom's chirrup to the horses, and the sound of wheels on the drive.

## XXVII · EPILOGUE

I JOINED Captain Montague's ship in January, 1793, and hostilities broke out in the following month, the beginning of our wars with the allied nations of Europe — the stormiest and most critical period of British naval history, which was to culminate, after twelve years of almost constant actions, in the great sea fight off the coast of Spain. I had the honour of fighting the Dutch at Camperdown, the Danes at Copenhagen, and the Spanish and French at Trafalgar, and it was after that most glorious of victories that I was promoted to the rank of captain.

Throughout the period of the wars I had many a dream of being stationed in the Pacific upon the establishment of peace, but a sea officer in time of war has little leisure for reflection, and as the years passed my longing to return to the South Sea grew less painful, and the sufferings I had endured less bitter in memory. It was not until the summer of 1809, when in command of the *Curieuse,* a smart frigate of thirty-two guns, captured from the French, that my dream came true. I received orders to set sail for Port Jackson, in New South Wales, and thence to Valparaiso, touching at Tahiti on the way.

I had on board a half-company of the Seventy-third Regiment, sent out to relieve the New South Wales Corps; the remainder of the regiment had gone ahead, on board the ships *Dromedary* and *Hindostan.* Four years before, through the influence of Sir Joseph Banks, Lord Camden had appointed Captain Bligh governor of New South Wales; now the notorious Rum Rebellion had run its course, and a new governor, Colonel Lachlan Macquarie, had been sent to take charge of the troubled colony. Accusing Bligh of harsh and tyrannical misuse of his powers, Major Johnston, the senior officer of the New

South Wales Corps, and a Mr. MacArthur, the most influential of the settlers, had seized the reins of government and kept Bligh a prisoner in Government House for more than a year.

During the long voyage out, by the Cape of Good Hope and through Bass Straits, Bligh was often in my thoughts. For his belief that I was one of the mutineers, and my sufferings as a prisoner, I had never blamed him at heart. But the letter to my mother, which had certainly been the cause of her death, was another matter. I had no desire to affront him in public, yet I knew I could never take his hand. He had played the part of a brave captain in the wars; at Copenhagen, Nelson had congratulated him on the quarter-deck of the *Elephant*. But now, as his career was drawing to a close, the history of the *Bounty* was repeating itself, and Bligh was once more the central figure in a mutiny. I had no means of determining the justice of the case, but the fact was strange, to say the least.

We left Spithead in August, and it was not until February, 1810, that the *Curieuse* entered the magnificent harbour of Port Jackson, and cast anchor in Farm Cove, exchanging salutes with the three British ships of war moored close by — the *Porpoise,* the *Dromedary,* and the *Hindostan.* While we were making all snug, a boat put off from the latter ship, bringing her captain, John Pascoe, on board. Pascoe had had the honour of serving as Nelson's flag-lieutenant at Trafalgar, and was an old friend of mine. It was a hot day of the antipodean summer, and a blistering sun shone down from a cloudless sky. I ushered my guest into the cabin, where it was cooler than on deck, and ordered the steward to make a pitcher of claret punch. Pascoe sank down on a settee, mopping his face with a large silk handkerchief.

"Whew! I'll wager hell is no hotter than Sydney just now!" he exclaimed. "And, by God, their climate is no hotter than their politics! What have you heard of all this in England?"

"Only rumours; we know nothing of the truth."

"The truth is hard to get at, even here. No doubt there is justice on both sides. The rum traffic has been the ruin of the colony, and it was in the hands of the military officers. Bligh perceived the evil and attempted to stop it, using the same famous tact and consideration which brought on the *Bounty* mutiny. As governor, he was invested with far more power than the King enjoys at home, but his only means of enforcing it was the Rum Puncheon Corps, as they are called.

You know at least the result: Bligh a prisoner in Government House, and the administration in the hands of Major Johnston, a puppet for Mr. MacArthur, the richest settler in the colony. A pretty mess!"

"What will happen now?"

"The Seventy-third stays here and the Corps returns to England. Johnston, MacArthur, and Bligh will have it out at home. Colonel Macquarie, whom I brought out, remains as governor."

Pascoe was eager for news from home, and we gossiped for a time. Presently he rose. "I must be pushing off, Byam," he said: "Bligh has ordered us to sail this afternoon."

When I had taken leave of him at the gangway, I ordered a boat and went ashore to arrange for the debarkation of the troops, and wait upon the governor. It was indeed a fiery day, and as I trudged up the path that led to Government House I sank ankle-deep in dust. The anteroom in which I was asked to take a chair was dark and cool.

"His Excellency is occupied for the moment, Captain Byam," said the A.D.C. who received me. He bowed and sat down to continue his writing, and next moment, from beyond the closed door, I heard a strident voice raised angrily. In an instant I felt myself twenty years younger, transported as if by magic to the deck of the *Bounty* on the afternoon before the mutiny. The same harsh voice, unchanged by a score of years, rang out in memory, as if repeating the words which had goaded Christian to madness: "Yes, you bloody hound! I *do* think so. You must have stolen some of mine or you would be able to give a better account of your own. You're damned rascals and thieves, the lot of you!"

The voice in the cabinet ceased and I heard the deep, conciliatory murmur of the governor. Then Bligh broke out again. His grievances had lost nothing in the two years he had brooded over them.

"Major Johnston, sir? By God! The man should be taken out and shot! As for MacArthur, I took his measure the first time I laid eyes on him. 'What, sir?' I said, 'are you to have such flocks of sheep and cattle as no man ever heard of before? No, sir! I have heard of you and your concerns, sir! You have got five thousand acres of the finest land, but, by God, you shan't keep it!' 'I have received the land by order of the Secretary of State,' replied MacArthur, coolly, 'and on the recommendation of the Privy Council.' 'Damn the Privy Council!'

said I, 'and the Secretary of State, too! What have they to do with me?'"

Again I heard the deep conciliatory murmur of the Governor's voice, interrupted by Bligh's strident tones: "Sydney, sir? A sink of iniquity! A more depraved, licentious lot of rascals don't exist! The settlers? God save the mark! They're worse than the convicts — the very scum of the earth! You must know how open I am to mercy and compassion, but, by God, sir, such qualities are wasted here! Rule them with a hand of iron! Rule them by fear!"

There was a scraping of chairs and the door was flung open. A stout burly man in captain's uniform stood in the doorway, his face purple with emotion and heat. Without a glance at me, he strode truculently across the room, while the A.D.C. sprang up and hastened to open the outer door. Captain Bligh gave him neither word nor glance as he brushed past. Next moment he was gone. The tired young A.D.C. closed the door, and turned to me with a faint smile. "Thank God!" he murmured devoutly, under his breath.

We came in sight of Tahiti on a morning in early April, passing to the north of Eimeo with a fine breeze at west by north. But the wind chopped around to the east as we approached the land, and we were all day long working up to Matavai Bay. My lieutenant, Mr. Cobden, must have had some inkling of what was passing in my mind, for he and the master saw to it that I was disturbed by no detail of the working of the ship.

Communication with Tahiti was all but impossible in those days, and not once, during the twenty years that had passed since I had embraced Tehani in the *Pandora's* sick bay, had I had word of her, or of our child. In 1796, having learned that the ship *Duff* was to sail for Tahiti with a cargo of missionaries, — the first in the South Sea, — I had been at some pains to make the acquaintance of one of those worthy men, and received his promise to search out my Indian wife and child, and send me word of them when the ship returned to England. But no letter came back to me. In Port Jackson, I had met and talked with some of these same missionaries, and told them of my orders to visit Tahiti and report on the condition of the people. Their accounts of the island were of a most melancholy nature. Considering their lives and those of their wives and children in danger, the missionaries had embarked for Port Jackson on a vessel providentially lying at anchor in Matavai Bay. They had spent twelve years on Tahiti, learned the language (they were kind enough to say that my dictionary had·been of the greatest aid to them), and worked unremittingly at their task of preaching the Gospel. Yet not a single convert had been made. War, and the diseases introduced by the visits of European ships, had destroyed four fifths of the people, I was told, and the future of the island appeared dark indeed. As for Tehani, not one of the worthy missionaries had ever heard of her, nor set foot on Taiarapu, where I supposed her still to reside.

As my ship approached the land on that April afternoon, Tahiti wore the green and smiling aspect I remembered so well, and it was hard to believe that an island so fair to the eye could be the scene of war and pestilence. A flood of memories overwhelmed me as Point Venus came in sight, and One Tree Hill, and the pale green of the shoal called Dolphin Bank. Yonder was the islet, Motu Au, opposite Hitihiti's house; close at hand I saw Stewart's shady glen, and the mouth of the small valley where Morrison and Millward had resided with Poino. And closer still was the mouth of the river in which I had first met Tehani, so long ago. I was only forty years old,—robust and in the prime of life,—yet as I conned the frigate through the narrow passage I knew so well, I had the feeling which comes to very old men, of having lived too long. Centuries seemed to have elapsed since I had looked last on the scene now before me. I dreaded setting foot on shore.

It was strange as we dropped anchor to see that no canoes put out. A few people were discernible along the beach, watching us apathetically, but they were pitifully few beside the throngs of former days, and where once the thatched roofs of their dwellings had been clustered thick under the trees, there was scarcely a house to be seen. Even the trees themselves had a withered, yellow look, for, as I was to learn, the victorious party had hacked and girdled nearly every breadfruit tree in Matavai.

At last a small patched canoe put out to us with two men on board. They were dressed in cast-off scraps of European clothing and were no more than beggars, for they had nothing to exchange for what we gave them. They addressed us in broken English. I was pleased, when they spoke together in their own tongue, to find that I understood pretty well what they said. I inquired for Tipau, Poino, and Hitihiti, but received only shrugs and blank stares in reply.

It lacked an hour of sunset when my boat's crew landed me on Hitihiti's point. I ordered them to await my coming on the Matavai beach, and turned inland alone, at the very spot where the surgeon had stumped through the sand twenty years before. Not a human being was to be seen, nor could I find a trace of my *taio's* house. The point, formerly covered with a well-kept lawn, was now grown over with rank weeds, and the path leading to the temple of Fareroi, once trodden by countless feet, was scarcely discernible. On my way to the still reach of river where I had met Tehani, I halted at sight of an old woman, squatting motionless on the sand as she gazed out to sea. She looked up at me dully, but brightened when she found that I addressed her in her own tongue, though haltingly. Hitihiti? She had heard of him, but he was dead long since. Hina? She shook her head. She had never heard of Tipau, but remembered Poino well. He was dead. She shrugged her shoulders. "Once Tahiti was a land of men," she said; "now only shadows fill the land."

The river was unchanged, and though the bank was overgrown with vegetation, I found my way to my seat among the roots of the ancient *mapé* tree. The noble tree stood firmly rooted and flourishing, and the river ran on with the same faint murmuring sound. But my youth was gone, and all my old friends dead. For a moment anguish gripped me; I would have renounced my career and all I possessed in the world to have been twenty years younger, sporting in the river with Tehani.

I dared not think of her, nor of our child. I had resolved to sail to Tautira on the morrow and dreaded what I might discover there. Presently I rose, crossed the river at a shallow place, and walked toward One Tree Hill. The groves of breadfruit trees which had once provided food for innumerable people were now hacked, yellow, and drooping; in place of scores of neat Indian cottages, only a few filthy hovels were to be seen; and where a thousand people had lived only twenty years before I met scarce a dozen on my walk.

Proceeding down the eastern slope of One Tree Hill I soon reached Stewart's glen where I had passed so many happy hours. There I sat me down on a flat stone, close to the spot where his house had once stood. Not a trace of the house remained, nor of the garden he had tended with such care, though I found what I took to be the remains of one of his rockeries for ferns. Stewart's bones, overgrown with coral, lay mingled with the *Pandora's* rotting timbers on a reef off the

Australian coast. Where was Peggy? Where was their child? The sun had set, and the shadows were deepening in the glen. Sadly I rose and made my way over the steep rocky trail that led to Matavai.

Next morning I took the pinnace and a dozen men and sailed around the east side of Tahiti Nui to Taiarapu. The eastern coast seemed in a more flourishing state than Matavai, and I was agreeably surprised to find that Vehiatua's former realm had not been desolated by war. But pestilence had done its work, and scarce one man was to be found where five had lived in my time. As we approached Tautira, I strained my eyes for the sight of Vehiatua's tall house on the point. It was gone, but presently I perceived with emotion that my own house, or one like it, stood on the spot where I had lived. The boat grounded on the sand, while a score of people, with brighter faces than those of Matavai, stood on the beach to welcome us. I scanned their countenances while my heart beat painfully, but there was no man or woman I knew. I dared not ask for Tehani, and the missionaries in Port Jackson had informed me that Vehiatua was dead, so, telling my people to bargain for a supply of coconuts, I set off in search of someone known to me. The little crowd of Indians stopped by the boat. I was glad to be left alone.

I took the well-remembered path, and before I had walked halfway to the house I met a middle-aged man of commanding presence, who halted at sight of me. Our eyes met, and for an instant neither spoke.

"Tuahu?" I said.

"Byam!" He stepped forward to clasp me in the Indian embrace. There were tears in his eyes as he looked at me. Presently he said, "Come to the house."

"I was on my way there," I replied, "but let us stop a moment where we can be alone."

He understood perfectly what was in my mind, and waited with downcast eyes while I mustered up courage to ask a question his silence answered only too eloquently.

"Where is Tehani?"

"*Ua mate* — dead," he replied quietly. "She died in the moon of Paroro, when you were three moons gone."

"And our child?" I asked after a long silence.

"She lives," said Tuahu. "A woman now, with a child of her own.

Her husband is the son of Atuanui. He will be high chief of Taiarapu one day. You shall see your daughter presently."

Tuahu waited in considerate silence for me to speak. "Old friend and kinsman," I said at last, "you know how dearly I loved her. All these years, while my country has been engaged in constant wars, I have dreamed of coming back. This place is a graveyard of memories, and I have been stirred enough. I wish to see my daughter; not to make myself known to her. To tell her that I am her father, to embrace her, to speak with her of her mother, would be more than I could endure. You understand?"

Tuahu smiled sorrowfully. "I understand," he said.

At that moment I heard a sound of voices on the path, and he touched my arm. "She is coming, Byam," he said in a low voice. A tall girl was approaching us, followed by a servant, and leading a tiny child by the hand. Her eyes were dark blue as the sea; her robe of snow-white cloth fell from her shoulders in graceful folds, and on her bosom I saw a necklace of gold, curiously wrought like the sinnet seamen plait.

"Tehani," called the man beside me, and I caught my breath as she turned, for she had all her dead mother's beauty, and something of my own mother, as well. "The English captain from Matavai," Tuahu was saying, and she gave me her hand graciously. My granddaughter was staring up at me in wonder, and I turned away blindly.

"We must go on," said Tehani to her uncle. "I promised the child she should see the English boat."

"Aye, go," replied Tuahu.

The moon was bright overhead when I reëmbarked in the pinnace to return to my ship. A chill night breeze came whispering down from the depths of the valley, and suddenly the place was full of ghosts,— shadows of men alive and dead,—my own among them.

# MEN AGAINST THE SEA

*To the memory of*

CAPTAIN JOSIAH MITCHELL

*of the Clipper Ship "Hornet"*

who, in the year 1866, after his vessel had been lost by
fire, in Lat. 2° N., 110° 10′ W., safely carried fourteen
of his men, in a small open boat, to the Hawaiian Islands,
a distance of 4000 miles, after a passage of
43 days and 8 hours

# THE COMPANY OF THE BOUNTY'S LAUNCH

Lieutenant William Bligh, *Captain*
John Fryer, *Master*
Thomas Ledward, *Acting Surgeon*
David Nelson, *Botanist*
William Peckover, *Gunner*
William Cole, *Boatswain*
William Elphinstone, *Master's Mate*
William Purcell, *Carpenter*

Thomas Hayward  
John Hallet  } *Midshipmen*
Robert Tinkler

John Norton  } *Quartermasters*
Peter Lenkletter

George Simpson, *Quartermaster's Mate*
Lawrence Lebogue, *Sailmaker*
Mr. Samuel, *Clerk*
Robert Lamb, *Butcher*

John Smith  } *Cooks*
Thomas Hall

# CHAPTER I

This day my good friend William Elphinstone was laid to rest, in the Lutheran churchyard on the east bank of the river, not five cable-lengths from the hospital. Mr. Sparling, Surgeon-General of Batavia, helped me into the boat; and two of his Malay servants were waiting on the bank, with a litter to convey me to the grave.

Two others of our little company, worn out by the hardships of the voyage, and easy victims to the climate of Java, have preceded Elphinstone to the churchyard. They were men of humble birth, but Elphinstone should be well content to lie beside them, for they were Englishmen worthy of the name. Lenkletter was one of the *Bounty's* quartermasters, and Hall a cook. Mr. Sparling had dosed them with bark and wine, doing everything in his power to save their lives; but they had been through too much. Mr. Fryer, the master, Cole, the boatswain, and two midshipmen, Hayward and Tinkler, were rowed four miles up the river to attend the funeral.

After we had paid our last respects to the master's mate, I was grieved to learn that my friends had been informed by the Sabandar that they were to sail for Europe on the morrow, with the last of the *Bounty's* people, aboard the *Hollandia,* a ship of the Dutch East India Company's fleet. Grieved for myself, I must add, but glad for the sake of the others, whose longing for England, after an absence of nearly two years, was as great as my own. The deep ulcer on my leg, aggravated by the tropical climate, renders it imprudent to take passage at this time; in Mr. Sparling's opinion I shall be unable to travel for several months. I am grateful for the friendship of my Dutch colleague and sensible of the deep obligations he has placed me under, yet I am taking up my pen to ward off the sense of loneliness already descending upon me in this far-off place.

The seaman's hospital is a model of its kind: large, commodious, airy, and judiciously divided into wards, each one a separate dwelling in which the sick are accommodated according to their complaints. I am lodged with the Surgeon-General, in his house at the extremity of one wing; he has had a cot placed for me, on a portion of his piazza shaded by flowering shrubs and vines, where I may pass the hours of the day propped up on pillows — to read or write, if I choose, or to sit in idleness with my bandaged leg extended upon a chair, gazing out on the rich and varied landscape, steaming in the heat of the sun. But now that my shipmates will no longer be able to visit me, the hours will drag sadly. My host is the kindest of men, and the only person here with whom I can converse, but the performance of his duties leaves little time for idle talk. His lady, a young and handsome niece of M. Vander Graaf, the Governor of Cape Town, has been more than kind to me. She is scarcely twenty, and the Malay costumes she wears become her mightily: silk brocade and jewels, and her thick flaxen hair dressed high on her head and pinned with a comb of inlaid tortoise shell. Escorted by her Malay girls, she often comes of an afternoon to sit with me. Her blue eyes express interest and compassion as she glances at me and turns to speak with her servants, in the Malay tongue. I have been so long without the pleasure of female company that it is a satisfaction merely to look at Mme. Sparling; were I able to converse with her, the hours would be short indeed.

When we had buried Mr. Elphinstone, and I had asked the Surgeon-General for writing materials, it was his wife who brought me what I required. She took leave of me soon after; and since night is still distant, I am beginning to set my memories in order for the task with which I hope to while the hours away until I am again able to walk.

Of the mutiny on board His Majesty's armed transport *Bounty*, I shall have little to say. Captain Bligh has already written an account of how the ship was seized; and Mr. Timotheus Wanjon, secretary to the governor at Coupang, has translated it into the Dutch language so that the authorities in these parts may be on the lookout for the *Bounty* in the unlikely event that she should be steered this way. He questioned each of us fully as to what we had seen and heard on the morning of the mutiny; I should be guilty of presumption were I to set down an independent narrative based upon my own knowledge of what occurred. But of our subsequent adventures in the ship's launch I feel free to write, the more so since Mr. Nelson, the botanist, who informed me at Coupang that he meditated the same task, died in Timor, the first victim of the privations we had undergone.

Never, perhaps, in the history of the sea has a captain performed a feat more remarkable than Mr. Bligh's, in navigating a small, open, and unarmed boat — but twenty-three feet long, and so heavily laden that she was in constant danger of foundering — from the Friendly Islands to Timor, a distance of three thousand, six hundred miles, through groups of islands inhabited by ferocious savages, and across a vast uncharted ocean. Eighteen of us were huddled on the thwarts as we ran for forty-one days before strong easterly gales, bailing almost continually to keep afloat, and exposed to torrential rains by day and by night. Yet, save for John Norton, — murdered by the savages at Tofoa, — we reached Timor without the loss of a man. For the preservation of our lives we have Captain Bligh to thank, and him alone. We reached the Dutch East Indies, not by a miracle, but owing to the leadership of an officer of indomitable will, skilled in seamanship, stern to preserve discipline, cool and cheerful in the face of danger. His name will be revered by those who accompanied him for as long as they may live.

On the morning of April 28, 1789, the *Bounty* was running before a light easterly breeze, within view of the island of Tofoa, in the Friendly Archipelago. I was awakened a little after daybreak by Charles Churchill, the master-at-arms, and John Mills, the gunner's mate, who informed me that the ship had been seized by Fletcher Christian, the acting lieutenant, and the greater part of the ship's company, and that I was to go on deck at once. These men were of Christian's party. Churchill was armed with a brace of pistols, and Mills with a musket. I dressed in great haste and was then marched to the upper deck. It will be understood with what amazement and incredulity I looked about me. To be aroused from a quiet sleep to find the ship filled with armed men, and Captain Bligh a prisoner in their midst, so shocked and stupefied me that, at first, I could scarcely accept the evidence of my eyes.

There was nothing to be done. The mutineers were in complete possession of the ship, and those who they knew would remain loyal to their commander were so carefully guarded as to preclude all possibility of resistance. I was ordered to stand by the mainmast with William Elphinstone, master's mate, and John Norton, one of the quartermasters. Two of the seamen, armed with muskets, the bayonets fixed, were stationed over us; and I well remember one of them, John Williams, saying to me: "Stand ye there, Mr. Ledward. We mean ye no harm, but, by God, we'll run ye through the guts if ye make a move toward Captain Bligh!"

Elphinstone, Norton, and I tried to recall these men to their senses; but their minds were so inflamed by hatred toward Captain Bligh that nothing we could say made the least impression upon them. He showed great resolution; and, although they threatened him repeatedly, he outfaced the ruffians and dared them to do their worst.

I had been standing by the mainmast only a short time when Christian, who had been chief of those guarding Mr. Bligh, gave this business into the charge of Churchill and four or five others, that he might hasten the work of sending the loyal men out of the ship. It was only then that we learned what his plans were, and we had no time to reflect upon the awful consequences to us of his cruelty and folly. The ship was in an uproar, and it was a near thing that Bligh was not murdered where he stood. It had been the plan of the mutineers to set us adrift in the small cutter; but her bottom was so rotten that they were at last persuaded to let us have the launch, and men were now set to work clearing her that she might be swung over the side. Whilst this was being done, I caught Christian's eye, and he came forward to where I stood.

"Mr. Ledward, you may stay with the ship if you choose," he said.

"I shall follow Captain Bligh," I replied.

"Then into the launch with you at once," he said.

"Surely, Mr. Christian," I said, "you will not send us off without medical supplies, and I must have some cloathes for myself."

He called to Matthew Quintal, one of the seamen: "Quintal, take Mr. Ledward to his cabin, and let him have what cloathing he needs. He is to take the small medicine chest, but see to it that he takes nothing from the large one."

He then left me abruptly, and that was my last word with this misguided man who had doomed nineteen others to hardships and sufferings beyond the power of the imagination to describe.

The small medicine chest was provided with a handle, and could easily be carried by one man. Fortunately, I had always kept it fully equipped for expeditions that might be made away from the ship; it had its own supply of surgical instruments, sponges, tourniquets, dressings, and the like, and a hasty examination assured me that, in the way of medicines, it contained most of those specifics likely to be needed by men in our position. Quintal watched me narrowly while I was making this examination. I put into the chest my razors, some handkerchiefs, my only remaining packet of snuff, and half a dozen wineglasses, which later proved of great use to us. Having gathered together some additional articles of cloathing, I was again conducted to the upper deck. The launch was already in the water; Captain Bligh, John Fryer, — the master, — the boatswain, William Cole, and many others had been sent into her. Churchill halted me at the gangway to make an examination of the medicine chest. He then ordered me into the boat, and the chest and my bundle of cloathing were handed down to me.

I was among the last to go into the launch; indeed, there were but two who followed me — Mr. Samuel, the captain's clerk, and Robert Tinkler, a midshipman. The launch was now so low in the water that Mr. Fryer, as well as Captain Bligh himself, begged that no more men should be sent into her; yet there were, I believe, two midshipmen and three or four seamen who would have come with us had there been room. Fortunately for us and for them, they were not permitted to do so, for we had no more than seven or eight inches of freeboard amidships. There were, in fact, nineteen of us in the launch, which was but twenty-three feet long, with a beam of six feet, nine inches. In depth she was, I think, two feet and nine inches. Each man had brought with him his bundle of cloathing; and with these, and the supplies of food allowed us by the mutineers, we were dangerously overladen.

But there was no time, as yet, to think of the seriousness of our situation. The launch was veered astern, and for another quarter of an hour or thereabouts we were kept in tow. The mutineers lined the *Bounty's* rail, aft, hooting and jeering at us; but it was to Mr. Bligh that most of their remarks were addressed. As I looked up at them, I found myself wondering how a mutiny into which well over half the ship's company had been drawn could have been planned without so much as a hint of danger having come to the knowledge of the rest of us. I personally had observed no sign of disaffection in the ship's company. To be sure, I had witnessed, upon more than one occasion, instances of the rigour of Captain Bligh's disciplinary measures. He is a man of violent temper, stern and unbending in the performance of what he considers to be his duty; but the same may be said of the greater part of the ships' captains in His Majesty's service. Knowing the necessity for strict discipline at sea, and the unruly nature of seamen as a class, I by no means considered that Captain Bligh's punishments exceeded in severity what the rules and necessities of the service demanded; nor had I believed that the men themselves thought so. But they now showed a passion of hatred toward him that astonished me, and reviled him in abominable language.

I heard one of them shout, "Swim home, you old bastard!" "Aye, swim or drown!" yelled another, "God damn you, we're well rid of you!" And another: "You'll flog and starve us no more, you . . ." Then followed a string of epithets it may be as well to omit. However, I must do their company the justice to say that most of the jeering and vile talk came from four or five of the mutinous crew. I observed that others looked down at us in silence, and with a kind of awe — as though they had just realized the enormity of the crime they were committing.

They had given us nothing with which to defend ourselves amongst the savages, and urgent requests were made for some muskets. These were met with further abuse; but at length four cutlasses were thrown down to us, and for all our pleading we were given nothing else. This so enraged Captain Bligh that he stood in his place and addressed the ruffians as they deserved. Two or three of the seamen leveled their pieces at him; and it was only the superior force of his will, I believe, which prevented them from shooting. We heard one of them cry out: "Bear off, and give 'em a whiff of grape!" At this moment the painter of the launch was cast off, and the ship drew slowly away from us. I cannot believe that even the most hardened of the mutineers was so lost to humanity as to have turned one of the guns upon a boatload of defenseless men, but others of our number thought differently. The oars were at once gotten out, and we pulled directly astern; but the ship was kept on her course, and soon it was clear to all that we had nothing more to fear from those aboard of her.

At this time the *Bounty* was under courses and topsails; the breeze was of the lightest, and the vessel had little more than steerageway. As she drew off, we saw several of the men run aloft to loose the top-gallant sails. The shouting grew fainter, and soon was lost to hearing. In an hour's time the vessel was a good three miles to leeward; in another hour she was hull down on the horizon.

I well remember the silence that seemed to flow in upon our little company directly we had been cast adrift — the wide silence of mid-ocean, accentuated by the faint creaking of the oars against the thole-pins. We rowed six oars in the launch, but were so deeply laden that we made slow progress toward the island of Tofoa, to the northeast of us and distant about ten leagues. Fryer sat at the tiller. Captain Bligh, Mr. Nelson, Elphinstone, — the master's mate, — and Peckover, the gunner, were all seated in the stern sheets. The rest of us were crowded on the thwarts in much the same positions as those we had taken upon coming into the launch. Bligh was half turned in his seat, gazing sombrely after the distant vessel; nor, during the next hour, I think, did he once remove his eyes from her. He appeared to have forgotten the rest of us, nor did any of us speak to remind him of our presence. Our thoughts were as gloomy as his own, and we felt as little inclined to express them.

My sympathy went out to Mr. Bligh in this hour of bitter disappointment; I could easily imagine how appalling the ruin of his plans must have appeared to him at a time when he had every expectation of completing them to the last detail. We had been homeward bound, the mission of our long voyage — that of collecting breadfruit plants in Otaheite, to be carried to the West Indies — successfully accomplished. This task, entrusted to his care by His Majesty's Government through the interest of his friend and patron, Sir Joseph Banks, had deeply gratified him, and well indeed had he justified that trust. Now, in a moment, his sanguine hopes were brought to nothing. His ship was gone; his splendid charts of coasts and islands were gone as well; and he had nothing to show for all the long months of careful and painstaking labour. He found himself cast adrift with eighteen of his company in his own ship's launch, with no more than a compass, a sextant, and his journal, in the midst of the greatest of oceans and thousands of miles from any place where he could look for help. Small wonder if, at that time, he felt the taste of dust and ashes in his mouth.

For an hour we moved slowly on toward Tofoa, the most northwesterly of the islands composing the Friendly Archipelago. This group had been so christened by Captain Cook; but our experiences among its inhabitants, only a few days before the mutiny, led us to believe that Cook must have called them "friendly" in a spirit of irony. They are a virile race, but we had found them savage and treacherous in the extreme, as different as could be imagined from the Indians of Otaheite. Only the possession of firearms had saved us from being attacked and overcome whilst we were engaged in wooding and watering on the island of Annamooka. Tofoa we had not visited, and as I gazed at the faint blue outline on the horizon I tried, with little success, to convince myself that our experiences there might be more fortunate.

Many an anxious glance was turned in Captain Bligh's direction, but for an hour at least he remained in the same position, gazing after the distant ship. When at length he turned away, it was never to look toward her again. He now took charge of his new command with an assurance, a quiet cheerfulness, that heartened us all. He first set us to work to bring some order into the boat. We were, as I have said, desperately crowded; but when we had stored away our supplies we had elbowroom at least. Our first care was, of course, to take stock of our provisions. We found that we had sixteen pieces of pork, each weighing about two pounds; three bags of bread of fifty pounds each; six quarts of rum, six bottles of wine, and twenty-eight gallons of water in three ten-gallon kegs. We also had four empty barricos, each capable of holding eight gallons. The carpenter, Purcell, had succeeded in fetching away one of his tool chests, although the mutineers had removed many of the tools before allowing it to be handed down. Our remaining supplies, outside of personal belongings, consisted of my medicine chest, the launch's two lugsails, some spare canvas, two or three coils of rope, and a copper pot, together with some odds and ends of boat's gear which the boatswain had had the forethought to bring with him.

To show how deeply laden we were, it is enough to say that my hand, as it rested on the gunwale, was repeatedly wet with drops of water from the small waves that licked along the sides of the boat. Fortunately, the sea was calm and the sky held a promise of good weather, at least for a sufficient time to enable us to reach Tofoa.

Reliefs at the oars were changed every hour, each of us taking his turn. Gradually the blue outline of the island became more distinct, and by the middle of the afternoon we had covered well over half the distance to it. About this time the faint breeze freshened and came round to the southeast, which enabled us to get up one of our lugsails. Captain Bligh now took the tiller and we altered our course to fetch the northern side of the island. Not eighteen hours before I had had, by moonlight, what I thought was my last view of Tofoa, and Mr. Nelson and I were computing the time that would be needed, if all went well, to reach the islands of the West Indies where we were to discharge our cargo of young breadfruit trees. Little we dreamed of the change that was to take place in our fortunes before another sun had set. I now cast about in my mind, trying to anticipate what Captain Bligh's plan for us might be. Our only hope of succour would lie in the colonies in the Dutch East Indies, but they were so far distant that the prospect of reaching one of them seemed fantastic. I thought of Otaheite, where we could be certain of kindly treatment on the part of the Indians, but that island was all of twelve hundred miles distant and directly to windward. In view of these circumstances, Mr. Bligh would never attempt a return there.

Meanwhile we proceeded on our way under a sky whose serenity seemed to mock at the desperate plight of the men in the tiny boat crawling beneath it. The sun dipped into the sea behind us, and in the light that streamed up from beyond the horizon the island stood out in clear relief. We estimated the peak of its central mountain to be about two thousand feet high. It was a volcano, and a thin cloud of vapour hung above it, taking on a saffron colour in the afterglow. We were still too far distant at sunset to have seen the smoke of any fires of its inhabitants. Mr. Bligh was under the impression that the place was uninhabited. All eyes turned toward the distant heights as darkness came on, but the only light to be seen was the dull red glow from the volcano reflected upon the cloud above it. When we were within a mile of the coast, the breeze died away and the oars were again gotten out. We approached the rocky shore until the thunder of the surf was loud in our ears; but in the darkness we could see no place where a landing might be made. Cliffs, varying in height from fifty to several hundred feet, appeared to fall directly to the sea; but when we had coasted a distance of several miles we discovered a less forbidding spot, where we might lie in comparative safety through the night.

There was but little surf here, and the sound of it only served to make deeper and more impressive the stillness of the night. Our voices sounded strangely distinct in this silence. For all the fact that we had not eaten since the previous evening, none of us had thought of food; and when Bligh suggested that we keep our fast until morning, there was no complaint from any of the company. He did, however, serve a ration of grog to each of us, and it was at this time that I had reason to be glad of putting the wineglasses into my medicine chest, for we discovered that we had but one other drinking vessel, a horn cup belonging to the captain. The serving of the grog put all of us in a much more cheerful frame of mind — not, certainly, because of the spirits it contained, but rather because it was a customary procedure and served to make us forget, for the moment at least, our forlorn situation. Two men were set at the oars to keep the boat off the rocks, and Captain Bligh commended the rest of us to take what rest our cramped positions might afford. The light murmur of talk now died away; but the silence that followed was that of tired but watchful men drawn together in spirit by the coming of night and the sense of common dangers.

## CHAPTER II

THROUGHOUT the night the launch was kept close under the land. I had as my near companions Elphinstone, — the master's mate, — and Robert Tinkler, youngest of the *Bounty's* midshipmen, a lad of fifteen. The forebodings of the older part of our company were not shared by Tinkler, whose natural high spirits had thus far been kept in check by his wholesome awe of Captain Bligh. He had no true conception of our situation at this time, and it speaks well for him that when, soon enough, he came to an understanding of the dangers surrounding us, his courage did not fail him.

He had slept during the latter part of the night, curled up in the bottom of the boat with my feet and his bundle of cloathing for his pillow. Elphinstone and I had dozed in turn, leaning one against the other, but our cramped position had made anything more than a doze impossible. We were all awake before the dawn, and as soon as there was sufficient light we proceeded in a northeasterly direction along the coast. It was a forbidding-looking place, viewed from the vantage point of a small and deeply laden ship's boat. The shore was steep-to, and we found no place where a landing might have been made without serious risk of wrecking the launch. Presently we were out of the lee, and found the breeze so strong and the sea so rough that we turned back to examine that part of the coast which lay beyond the spot where we had spent the night. About nine o'clock we came to a cove, and, as there appeared to be no more suitable shelter beyond, we ran in and dropped a grapnel about twenty yards from the beach.

We were on the lee side here, but this circumstance alone was in our favour. The beach was rocky, and the foreshore about the cove had a barren appearance that promised nothing to relieve our wants. It was shut in on all sides by high, rocky cliffs, and there appeared to be no means of entrance or exit save by the sea. Captain Bligh stood up in his seat, examining the place carefully whilst the rest of us awaited his decision. He turned to Mr. Nelson with a wry smile.

"By God, sir," he said, "if you can find us so much as an edible berry here, you shall have my ration of grog at supper."

"I'm afraid the venture is safe enough," Mr. Nelson replied. "Nevertheless, I shall be glad to try."

"That we shall do," said Bligh; then, turning to the master, "Mr. Fryer, you and six men shall stay with the launch." He then told off those who were to remain on board, whereupon they slackened away until we were in shallow water and the rest of us waded ashore.

The beach was composed of heaps of stones worn round and smooth by the action of the sea, and, although the surf was light, the footing was difficult until we were out of the water. Robert Lamb, the butcher, turned his ankle before he had taken half a dozen steps, and thus provided me with my first task as surgeon of the *Bounty's* launch. The man had received a bad sprain that made it impossible for him to walk. He was supported to higher ground, where Captain Bligh — quite rightly, I think — gave him a severe rating. We were in no position to have helpless men to care for, and Lamb's accident was the result of a foolish attempt to run across a beach of loose stones.

The land about the cove was gravelly soil covered with coarse grass, small thickets of bush, and scattered trees. The level ground extended inland for a short distance, to the base of all but vertical walls covered with vines and fern. Near the beach we found the remains of an old fire, but we were soon convinced that the cove was used by the Indians only as a place of occasional resort.

Mr. Bligh delegated his clerk Samuel, Norton, Purcell, Lenkletter, and Lebogue as a party to attempt to scale the cliffs. Purcell carried one of the cutlasses, the others provided themselves with stout sticks. Thus armed, they set out; and were soon lost to view amongst the trees. They carried with them the copper kettle and an Indian calabash we had found hanging from a tree near the beach. The rest of us separated, some to search for shellfish among the rocks, others to explore the foreshore. Nelson and I bore off to the left side of the cove, where we discovered a narrow valley; but we soon found our passage blocked by a smooth wall of rock, thirty or forty feet high. Not a drop of water could we find, and the arid aspect of the valley as a whole showed only too plainly that the rainfall, on this side of the island at least, must be scant indeed.

Having explored with care that part of the cove which Bligh had asked us to examine, we sat down to rest for a moment. Nelson shook his head with a faint smile.

"Mr. Bligh was safe enough in offering me his tot of grog," he said. "We shall find nothing here, Ledward — neither food nor water."

"How do you feel about our prospects?" I asked.

"I have not allowed myself to think of them thus far," he replied. "We can, undoubtedly, find water on the windward side, and perhaps food enough to maintain us for a considerable period. Beyond that . . ." He broke off, leaving the sentence unfinished. Presently he added: "Our situation is not quite hopeless. That is as much as we can say."

"But it is precisely the kind of situation Bligh was born to meet," I said.

"It is; I grant that; but what can he do, Ledward? Where in God's name can we go? We know only too well what treacherous savages these so-called 'Friendly Islanders' are: our experiences at Annamooka taught us that. I speak frankly. The others I shall try to encourage as much as possible, but there need be no play-acting between us two."

Nelson talked in a quiet, even voice which made his words all the more impressive. He was not a man to look on the dark side of things; but we had long been friends, and, as he had said, there was no need of anything but frankness between us as we canvassed the possibilities ahead.

"What I think Bligh will do," he went on, "is to take us back to Annamooka — either there or Tongataboo."

"There seems to be nothing else he can do," I replied, "unless we can establish ourselves here."

"No. And mark my words — sooner or later we shall have such a taste of Friendly Island hospitality as we may not live either to remember or regret. . . . Ledward, Ledward!" he said, with a rueful smile. "Think of our happy situation a little more than twenty-four hours back, when we were talking of home there by the larboard bulwarks! And think of my beautiful breadfruit garden, all in such a flourishing state! What do you suppose those villains will do with my young trees?"

"I've no doubt they have flung the lot overboard before this," I replied.

"I fear you are right. They jettisoned us; it is not likely that their treatment of the plants will be any more tender. And I loved them as though they were my own children!"

We returned to the beach, where we found that the others had been no more successful than ourselves; but the exploring party had gotten out of the cove, although how they had managed it no one knew. Captain Bligh had found a cavern in the rocky wall, about one hundred and fifty paces from the beach; and the hard, foot-trampled ground within showed that it had been often used in the past. The cavern was perfectly dry; not so much as a drop of water trickled from the rocks overhead. One find we made there was not of a reassuring nature. On a shelf of rock there were ranged six human skulls which, an examination convinced me, had been those of living men not more than a year or two earlier. In one of these, the squamosal section of the temporal bone had been crushed, and another showed a jagged hole through the parietal bone. I was interested to observe the splendid teeth in each of these skulls; there was not one in an imperfect condition. These relics, gleaming faintly white in the dim light of the cave, were eloquent in their silence; and I have no doubt that they might have been more eloquent still, could they have conveyed to us information as to how they came to be there.

Shortly after midday the exploring party returned, utterly weary, their cloathing torn and their arms and legs covered with scratches and bruises. In the kettle they had about six quarts of water, and three more in the calabash. This they had found in holes amongst the rocks; but they had discovered neither stream nor spring, nor any sign of people. They had gone a distance of about two miles over rough ground where it was plain, they said, that no one had lived or could live. It was the opinion of all that the island was uninhabited. We then returned to the launch, for there appeared to be no chance of bettering ourselves here.

Again on the boat, we broke our fast for the first time since leaving the *Bounty*. Each man had a morsel of bread, a tasty bit of pork, and a glass of water. It was a short repast, and as soon as the last man had been served, we got in the grapnel and rowed out of the cove.

"We must try to get around to the windward side," said Bligh. "I fancy we shall find water there. Do you agree, Mr. Nelson?"

"It seems likely," Nelson replied. "As we were approaching yesterday, I observed that the vegetation appeared much greener to windward."

The wind was at E.S.E., and as we drew out of the shelter of the land it blew strong, with a rough, breaking sea. Close-hauled on the starboard tack, the launch heeled to the gusts, while water poured in over the lee gunwale and the people worked hard with the bails. Bluff-bowed, and deeply laden as she was, our boat buried her nose in each breaking wave, sending up great sheets of spray. Even Mr. Bligh began to look anxious.

"Stand by to come about!" he shouted, and then: "Hard alee!"

The launch headed up into the seas, while the halyards were slacked away and the gaffs passed around to the starboard sides of the masts. The sails slatted furiously as we bore off on the other tack.

Then, perceiving the danger in the nick of time, Bligh roared: "Over the side with you — those who can swim!"

It was no pleasant prospect, leaping into a sea so rough; but about half of our number sprang into the water to fend for themselves. The launch was so heavy that she answered her helm but sluggishly, and, though the foresail was backed, she was slow in bearing off. Caught directly in the trough of the sea, I am convinced that she would have foundered had we not obeyed Bligh instantly.

By the grace of God and the captain's skill, she bore off without filling. The swimmers scrambled in over the gunwales, the sails were trimmed once more, and we ran back to the shelter of the land.

We proceeded for several miles beyond the cove, and were presently rejoiced to see a clump of coconut palms standing out against the sky on the cliffs above us; but they were at such a height that we despaired of reaching them; furthermore, there was a high surf to make landing difficult. But young Tinkler and Thomas Hall were eager to make the attempt, and Bligh consented that they should try. We rowed as close to the rocks as we dared, and the two, having removed their cloathes, sprang into the sea, carrying with them each a rope that we might haul them back in case they came to grief. We might have spared ourselves the anxiety. They were as much at home in the water as the Indians themselves. We saw them disappear in a smother of foam, and when next seen, they were well out of danger and scrambling up the rocks. In less than an hour's time they returned to the shore with about twenty coconuts, which they fastened in clusters to the line, and we then hauled them to the boat.

We rowed farther along the coast, but, toward the middle of the afternoon, having found no shelter, nor any signs of water, Captain Bligh deemed it best to return to the cove for the night. We reached our anchorage about an hour after dark. It is hardly necessary to say that every man of us was now ravenously hungry. Captain Bligh issued a coconut to each person; and the meat of the nut, together with the cool liquid it contained, proved a most welcome, but by no means a satisfying, meal.

The following morning we made our third unsuccessful attempt to get round by sea to the windward side of the island. The sky was clear, but the wind was not diminished, and we were set to bailing the moment we were out of shelter of the land. This third experience made it only too clear that we could not hope to go counter to a heavy sea in our deeply laden boat, and we were thankful indeed that we had a refuge at hand. There was nothing we could do but return to the cove.

Bligh was determined that we should keep our meagre supply of food and water intact, and although, in view of the unsuccessful expedition of the day before, we had little hope of finding anything on this side of the island, we decided to try again. Therefore, Mr. Bligh, Nelson, Elphinstone, Cole, and myself set out to examine the cliffs once more, and we were so fortunate as to discover a way to and from the cove evidently used by the Indians themselves. In a narrow gully which had escaped earlier notice, we found some large, woody vines firmly attached in clefts of the rock and to trees overhead. We could see in the walls of the cliff footholds which the Indians had constructed to assist them in making the ascent. We stood for a moment examining this crude ladder.

"Shall I try it, sir?" Elphinstone asked.

"You stand an excellent chance of breaking your neck, my lad," Bligh replied; "but if the Indians can do it, we can."

Elphinstone climbed a little way until he could reach the vines, which were of the thickness of a man's forearm. Finding that they could easily support his weight, he proceeded, while we watched him from below. After an all but vertical climb of forty or fifty feet, he reached a ledge of rock that gave him a resting place, where he turned and called down to us.

It was, in all truth, a perilous climb, particularly so for Cole, who was a heavy man and encumbered with our copper kettle, which he carried over his shoulder. A series of gigantic natural steps brought us at last to the summit, between three and four hundred feet above the sea. The latter part of the climb had been less difficult; but, for all that, we little relished the thought of a return.

From this vantage point we had an excellent view of the volcano,

which appeared to rise from somewhere near the centre of the island.
The intervening country was much cut up by ridges and gullies, and
had an even more desolate look than when viewed from the sea.
Nevertheless, we set out in the direction of the central mountain, and
presently entered a deeper gully that appeared to offer a promise of
water; but all that we found were a few tepid pools amongst the rocks,
so shallow that it was tedious work scooping the water into the
kettle with our coconut-shell ladle. We collected in all three or four
gallons. Leaving our kettle here, we went on; and presently came to
some abandoned huts, fallen to ruin, and near them what had once
been a plantain walk, but so concealed by weeds and bushes that it was
a near thing we had missed it. We got three small bunches of plantains, which we slung to a pole, for carrying in the Indian fashion. We
continued inland for another mile, but the country became more and
more arid, covered in places by ashes and lava beds where only a few
hardy shrubs found nourishment. Evidently, we could hope for nothing more in this direction, so we returned, taking up our kettle on the
way, and it was near noon before we reached the cliffs above the
cove. Bligh, Nelson, and myself had each a bunch of plantains, fastened
across our backs with pieces of rope. Elphinstone and Cole took charge
of the kettle of water, and I still wonder that they were able to carry
it down without, I believe, the loss of so much as a drop of the precious
supply.

It was but natural that the thought of food should by this time be
uppermost in every man's mind. Realizing the need of sustaining our
strength, Captain Bligh allowed us the most substantial meal we had
yet enjoyed, consisting of two boiled plantains per man, with an
ounce of pork and a wineglass of water. We had combed the beach
all round the cove for shellfish without finding so much as a sea snail.
As it was impossible to leave the cove on account of the heavy sea,
another exploring party was sent out after dinner, but they returned
at sunset without having had any success. There yet remained one
direction in which none of our parties had gone — toward the northwest — and the following morning near half of our party, who had
spent the night in the cavern that they might have a more refreshing
sleep, were sent out in a last attempt to secure food and water. Mr.
Fryer was in charge of the expedition, and Captain Bligh ordered
him not to return until he was convinced that we had nothing to hope
for in that direction.

They were gone a full five hours, returning about ten o'clock, empty-handed, and with Robert Tinkler missing. He had become separated from the others, Fryer said, shortly before the decision to return was made. Bligh flew into a passion at this news.

"What, sir?" he roared at Fryer. "Do you mean to say that you, the ship's master, cannot keep a party of seven together? Damn your eyes! Must I go *everywhere* with you? Get you back at once and find him! Go, the lot of you, and don't come back without him!"

Silently the men set out; but they had not reached the foot of the cliffs when they heard a shout from above—and presently came Tinkler, carrying an Indian calabash containing about a gallon of water, and followed by an Indian woman and two men. The men had a cluster of husked coconuts on a pole between them.

This good fortune came at a time when it was needed, and I was glad to see that Bligh, who had been cursing the lad during his absence, forgot his anger and commended him warmly. Tinkler was pleased as only a boy can be who has succeeded in a matter in which his elders have failed. He had discovered the Indians near a hut in a small, hidden valley, and had made them understand that they were to come with him, bringing food and water.

The men were strongly made, bold-looking fellows, and appeared not at all surprised to find us there. They were unarmed, and naked except for a kirtle of tapa about the middle. The woman was a handsome wench of about twenty, and carried a child on her hip. They put down their load of coconuts and squatted near by, looking at us without the least sign of fear.

After our long sojourn at Otaheite, a good many of us had a fair knowledge of the Indian language as spoken there. We had already found that the speech of the natives of Annamooka, although allied to that of the Otaheitians, differed greatly from it; nevertheless, we could, after a fashion, converse with these people. Mr. Nelson was the best linguist amongst us, and he now questioned the men, asking first about the number of inhabitants on the island and the possibility of procuring food and water. One of them replied at length. Much of what he said was unintelligible, but we understood that there was a considerable population on the windward side of the island, and that little was to be had in the way of refreshment on this side.

Presently they rose, giving us to understand that they would fetch others of their countrymen. We were in no position to be lavish with gifts, but Captain Bligh presented them with some buttons from his coat, which they accepted stolidly and then departed.

As soon as they had gone, Mr. Bligh made a collection of whatever small articles we could spare from our personal belongings, to be used in trade with the Indians. We gave buttons, handkerchiefs, clasp knives, buckles, and the like. Mr. Bligh also prepared us for defense. Fryer and five others were to remain in the launch in readiness for any emergency. The master had one of our cutlasses, and the others were to be carried by Bligh, Purcell, and Cole, the strongest men of the shore party; the rest of us cut clubs for ourselves, but these were to be kept hidden in the cavern, and, if possible, our trading was to be done directly in front of the cavern, so that we should always have the Indians before us.

There were, then, thirteen of us on shore, with six men in the launch at a distance of one hundred and fifty yards. We should have been glad to keep the parties closer together, but Mr. Bligh thought best to have the shore party where it could not be surrounded, and we had the launch in view so we could watch over the situation there. Thus prepared, we waited with anxiety for the arrival of visitors.

They were not long in coming. I had often remarked, at Otaheite, with what mysterious rapidity news spreads among the Indians. So it was here; scarcely an hour had passed before twenty or thirty men had come down the cliffs; others came by canoes which they carried up the beach, and by the middle of the afternoon there were forty or fifty people in the cove. They were like the natives we had seen at Annamooka, well-set-up, hardy-looking men, with a somewhat insolent bearing; but we were relieved to see that they were unarmed, and their intent appeared peaceable enough. They were going back and forth continually, now squatting on the beach looking at the launch, now returning to the cavern to look at us. Of food and water they had little, but before evening we had bought a dozen of breadfruit, and several gallons of water. By means of Captain Bligh's magnifying glass we made a fire near the mouth of the cavern, where we cooked some of the breadfruit for our immediate needs, the natives looking on and commenting, in what appeared to be a derisive manner, on our method of doing so. No women were amongst them, nor any of their chief men, but they gave us to understand that one of these latter would visit us the next day.

Shortly after sunset they began to leave the cove, and the last of them had gone before darkness came on. This was an encouraging circumstance; for had they intended mischief, we thought, they would certainly have remained to attack us in the night. We supped upon a quarter of a breadfruit per man, and a glass of water, in better spirits than we had been at any time since the mutiny. A guard was set at the entrance of the cavern, and the rest retired to sleep, comforted by Captain Bligh's assurance that the morrow would be our last day in this dismal spot.

## CHAPTER III

CAPTAIN BLIGH had the enviable faculty of being able to compose his mind for sleep under almost any conditions. I have known him to go without rest for seventy-two hours together; but when a suitable occasion offered, he could close his eyes and fall at once into a refreshing slumber, though he knew that he must be awakened a quarter of an hour later. On this night he could hope for an undisturbed rest, and scarcely had he lain down when his quiet breathing assured me that he was asleep. As for myself, I was never more wakeful, and presently left the cavern to join the sentinels outside. They were stationed twenty or thirty yards apart, so that they might command a view in whatever direction. It was a beautiful night, and the cove, flooded with moonlight, seemed an enchanted spot. To the north lay the open sea, at peace now, for the wind had died away toward sunset. The long swells swept majestically in, breaking first along the sides of the cove, the two waves advancing swiftly toward each other and meeting near the centre of the beach, where the silvery foam was thrown high in air.

As I looked about me I was reminded of certain lonely coves I had seen along the Cornish coast, on just such nights, and I found it hard to realize how vast an ocean separated us from home.

Mr. Cole was in charge of the guard; he stood in the deep shadow of a tree not far from the cavern. I had a great liking for the boatswain; we had been friends almost from the day the *Bounty* left Spithead, and there was no more competent and reliable seaman in the ship's company. He was a devout man, with a childlike trust in God which only exceeded his trust in Captain Bligh. He never for a moment doubted the captain's ability to carry us safely through whatever perils might await us. It comforted me to talk to him, and when I returned to the cave it was in a more hopeful frame of mind.

I had a fixed belief in the treacherous nature of the misnamed Friendly Islanders, and fully expected we should be attacked during the night. I, of course, kept my misgivings to myself, and the following morning they seemed a little absurd. We were astir at dawn, and there was a feeling of hopefulness and good cheer throughout the company. We even looked forward with pleasure to the return of the Indians; knowing now our needs, we felt that they would supply them, and that we should be able to leave the cove by early afternoon.

The sun was two hours high before the first of the natives came down the cliffs at the back of the cove; and shortly afterwards two canoes arrived, with a dozen or fifteen men in each. We were greatly disappointed to find that they had brought only a meagre supply of provisions; we were, however, able to purchase a little water and half a dozen breadfruit. One of the canoe parties treated us with great insolence. They had with them half a dozen calabashes filled with water, — much more than enough for their own needs during the day, — but they refused to trade for any part of it. They well knew that we were on short rations of water, and taunted us by drinking deeply of their own supply while we stood looking on. Fortunately it was Nelson and not Bligh who was attempting to trade with this party. Bligh had little of the diplomat in his character, and had he been present his temper might have gotten the better of him; but Nelson remained cool and affable, and, seeing that nothing was to be gotten from these men, soon left them to themselves.

Upon returning to the cavern, we found Bligh trying to converse with a party, headed by an elderly chief, which had just arrived from inland. The chief was a stern-looking old man, well over six feet, whose robe of tapa cloth, draped in graceful folds about his person, proclaimed his rank; but had he been naked he could have been recognized at once as a man of superior station. In one hand he carried a spear of ironwood, barbed with bones of the stingray's tail, and tucked into a fold of his robe at the waist was what appeared to be a comb with long wooden teeth. Bligh looked around with relief at our approach.

"You have come in good time, Nelson; I was about to send for you. See what you can make of this man's speech."

Nelson then addressed him in the Otaheitian language, while most of our company and between thirty and forty of the natives stood looking on. The chief replied with a natural grace and eloquence common to the Indians of the South Sea, but there was a look of cruelty and cunning in his eye that belied his manner. I gave him close attention, but although I somewhat prided myself upon my knowledge of the Otaheitian tongue, I found it of little use to me in listening to the Friendly Island speech. Nelson, however, had a quick ear to detect affinities and an agile mind to grasp at meanings, and it was plain that he and the chief could make themselves fairly well understood. Presently he turned to Bligh.

"He has either seen us at Annamooka or had heard of our being there," he said. "I can understand only about half of what he says, but he wishes to know how we lost the ship, and where."

We were prepared for that question. Mr. Bligh had at first been undecided how to account for our presence here, in case Indians should be met with. We could not hope to be believed if we should say that the ship 'was at hand, for they could see for themselves that she was not; therefore, he instructed us to say that the vessel had been lost, and that we alone had been saved from the wreck. This, we knew, was a dangerous confession to make, but circumstances forced it upon us.

I watched the man's face while Nelson was relating the story, but he remained impassive, showing neither interest in nor concern for our plight. Nelson was puzzled for a time by the man's next inquiry, but at length grasped the meaning of it.

"He wishes to see the thing with which you bring fire from the sun," he said. Bligh was reluctant to bring forth his magnifying glass again, well knowing how the Indians would covet such a precious instrument; nevertheless, he thought it best to humour the chief. Some dry leaves were gathered and crumbled into a powder. Our visitors gathered round, looking on with intense interest whilst Bligh focused the rays of the sun upon the tinder; and when they saw smoke emerge, and the small flame appear, a murmur of astonishment ran through the crowd. The chief was determined to possess this wonder worker, and when Bligh refused him, his vexation and disappointment were only too apparent. He then asked for nails, the most acceptable article of barter with the natives of the South Sea, but the few parcels we possessed could not be parted with, and Nelson was instructed to tell him that we had none.

Whilst this conversation was taking place, other Indians were arriving, amongst them a chief whose rank appeared to be equal to, if not higher than, that of the first; he showed no deference to the older man, and we observed that the crowd of natives around us, immediately they saw him, opened a lane through their ranks so that he and his followers might approach. He was a man of about forty, of commanding presence. As he entered the open space where we stood, he glanced keenly from one to another of us. Then he walked up to Captain Bligh, but I noticed that he omitted, as the older chief had done, the ceremony of rubbing noses — a formal courtesy which had never been omitted heretofore, when we had the *Bounty* at our backs.

None of us could recollect having seen either of these chiefs at Annamooka. We learned that the name of the elder man was Maccaackavow, — at least, that is as near as I can come to the sound of the name, — and the other was called Eefow. We gathered that both came from the island of Tongataboo. When Bligh informed them that we proposed to go either to that island or to Annamooka, Eefow offered to accompany us as soon as the wind and sea should moderate. Bligh invited them into the cavern, where he presented each with a knife and a shirt.

It was at this time that I took up one of the skulls we had found there, and, bringing it to the chief Eefow, asked, in the Otaheitian dialect, whence it came. His face lit up at the question, and he replied: "Feejee, Feejee." He then went on, with great animation, to explain about them; and we understood that he himself had been the slayer of two of these victims. Captain Bligh was greatly interested in this narration, for when he had visited the Friendly Islands with Captain Cook he had gathered much information about a great archipelago, unknown to Europeans, called "Feejee" by the Indians, and which was not far distant from the Friendly Islands. He had Nelson question Eefow at length about Feejee, and was told the group comprised a vast number of islands, the nearest of which lay about a two days' sail from Tofoa. When we came out of the cavern, Bligh had Eefow point out their direction, and the chief showed him what bearings should be taken to sail toward them from Tofoa. The direction was to the west-northwest, which confirmed what Bligh had already been told.

This conference in the cavern had gone most prosperously, and we were encouraged to hope that our fears were groundless with respect to the Indians' intentions toward us. Another favourable incident occurred at this time: A man named Nageete, whom Mr. Bligh remembered having seen at Annamooka, came forward and greeted him in the most friendly manner. Although not a chief, he appeared to be a personage of some importance, and Bligh made much of him, taking care, however, to distinguish between his attitude toward Nageete and that toward the chiefs. With this man's help we were able to add considerably to our stock of water, enough for our immediate needs, so that we could keep the launch's stock intact; and we also purchased a few more breadfruit and a half-dozen large yams; but our scant supply of articles for trade was soon exhausted. Thereafter they would give us nothing; not so much as half a breadfruit would they part with unless payment were made for it.

Under these circumstances, we were at a loss what to do; we had parted with everything we could spare and were still in great need of food and water. Bligh appealed to the chiefs, again explaining our predicament. Nelson was as eloquent as possible, but the effect was negligible.

When he had finished, Macca-ackavow replied: "You say you have nothing left, but you have the instrument for making fire. Let me have that and my people here shall give you all they have."

But this request Bligh could not, of course, comply with; we had no flint and steel amongst us, and none of us was able to kindle fire by friction, in the Indian fashion. Macca-ackavow became sullen at our refusal to part with the magnifying glass.

Eefow then said: "Let us see what you have in your boat." But again Bligh refused, for the few tools and parcels of nails we had there were only less necessary than food itself.

So matters went until toward midday.

For our dinner we had each a small piece of cooked breadfruit, and sliver of pork. Bligh invited the chiefs to join our meal, which they did. It was a most uncomfortable repast. We were all sensible of a change in the attitude of the Indians: small groups conferred among themselves, and the two chiefs, whilst eating with us, conversed in what appeared to be some special and figurative speech, so that not even Nelson could understand a word that was said.

Fifteen of our company were on shore at this time; Fryer, with three men, remained with the launch, which still lay at a grapnel just beyond the break of the surf. We estimated that there were well over two hundred Indians around us, and not a woman amongst them. Fortunately, only the chiefs and two or three of their immediate retainers were armed.

The chiefs now left us and went amongst their people. Bligh took the occasion to inform us of his plans and to instruct us as to what our behaviour toward the natives should be throughout the afternoon.

"It is not yet clear," he said, "that they have formed a design against us, and we must act as though we had no suspicion of any such intent; but be on your guard, every man of you. . . . Mr. Peckover, you shall select three men and carry what supplies we have to the launch; but perform this business in a casual manner. Let there be no haste in your actions. We shall leave the cove at sunset, whether or no Eefow accompanies us, and make our way to Tongataboo, but I wish the Indians to be deceived on this point until we are ready to embark."

We had a fire going near the cavern, and the breadfruit had been cooked as we bought it. Peckover chose Peter Lenkletter, Lebogue, and young Tinkler to assist him, and they now began carrying down the supplies, a little at a time. This was dangerous work, for they had to run the gantlet of many groups of savages collected between us and the launch, and it was performed with a coolness deserving of high praise. Tinkler, who was no more than a lad, behaved admirably, and he was immensely proud that he had been chosen for the task over the other midshipmen. Meanwhile, Bligh sat at the mouth of the cavern, keeping a watchful eye upon all that went on and, at the same time, writing in his journal as quietly as though he were in his cabin on the *Bounty*. The rest of us busied ourselves with small matters, to make it appear that we expected to spend the night ashore. Nageete, who had strolled away after our midday meal, returned after a little time, apparently as well disposed as ever. He asked what our intentions were, and was told that we should wait until Eefow was ready to accompany us to Tongataboo, but that we hoped, in case the weather favoured, he would consent to go on the following day.

Nageete then said: "Eefow will go if you will give him the fire maker; and you should let him have it, rather than Macca-ackavow, for he is the greater chief."

Bligh might have resorted to guile, making a promise of the coveted glass, but this he refused to do, telling Nageete that under no circumstances could he part with it.

Presently the two chiefs rejoined us, and Bligh, with Nelson to interpret, questioned them further about the Feejee Islands, doing everything possible to keep our relations with them on a friendly and casual footing.

Whilst this conversation was taking place, an incident occurred that might easily have proved disastrous. There was a great crowd of Indians along the beach. Of a sudden, a dozen or more of them rushed to the line which held the launch to the shore and began to haul it in. We heard a warning shout from Peckover, who was just then returning with his party. Bligh, cutlass in hand, rushed for the beach, the rest of us, including the chiefs, following. His courage and force of character never showed to better advantage than on this occasion. We were vastly outnumbered, and might easily have been attacked and slain; but Bligh so overawed them by his manner that they immediately let go the rope, and Fryer and those with him hauled the launch back to its former position. This move of the Indians was made, I think, without the knowledge of the chiefs. However that may be, they at least ordered the men away from that vicinity, — Bligh having insisted upon this, — and all became quiet again.

It would have been well could we have embarked then and there; and Bligh would have had us make a rush for it, I think, had it not been that Cole and three others had been sent inland in the hope of finding a few more quarts of water. They had not yet returned, so we made our way back to the cavern to wait for them.

Then followed an anxious time. It became more and more apparent that we were to be attacked, and that the savages were merely biding a favourable opportunity. We were equally sure that the chiefs were of one mind about this and that they had informed their followers that we were to be destroyed.

"Keep well together, lads," said Bligh quietly. "See that none of them comes behind us. Damn their eyes! What are they waiting for?"

"I believe they're afraid of us, sir," said Fryer. "Either that, or they hope to take us by surprise."

We had not long to wait for evidence of their intentions. Savages, although they invariably recognize and respect the authority of their chiefs, lack discipline, and when a course of action is decided upon, are impatient to put it into effect. So it was here. Shortly after this, we heard, from a distance, an ominous sound: the knocking of stones together, which we rightly supposed was a signal amongst them previous to an attack. At first only a few of them did this, but gradually the sound spread, increasing in volume, to all parts of the cove; at moments it became all but deafening, and then would die away only to be resumed with even greater insistence, as though the commoners were growing increasingly impatient with their chiefs for withholding the signal for slaughter. The effect upon our little band may be imagined. We believed that our last hour had come; we stood together, a well-knit band, every man resolved to sell his life as dearly as possible.

It was late afternoon when Cole and his party returned with about two quarts of water which they had collected amongst the rocks. Mr. Bligh had kept a record of everything we had been able to secure in the way of provision, and the water we had either bought or found for ourselves had been just sufficient for our needs. We had added nothing to our twenty-eight gallons in the launch, but neither had we taken anything from that supply. Now that the shore party was again united, we waited only for a suitable opportunity before making an attempt to embark. Meanwhile, the clapping of stones went on, now here, now there, and yet it was necessary for us to keep up the pretense that we suspected nothing.

Nageete, who had been with us during this time, was becoming increasingly restless and was only seeking some pretext for getting away, but Bligh kept him engaged in conversation. We were all gathered before the entrance of the cavern in such a way that the Indians could not pass behind us. For the most part, they were gathered in groups of twenty or thirty, at some distance, and we saw the two chiefs passing from group to group. Presently they returned to where we stood, and I must do them the credit to say that they were masters at the art of dissembling. We asked them the meaning of the stone clapping, and they gave us to understand that it was merely a game in which their followers indulged to while away the time. They then attempted to persuade Captain Bligh and Nelson to accompany them away from the rest of us, as though they wished to confer with them in private, but Bligh pretended not to understand. We were all on our feet, in instant readiness to defend ourselves; nevertheless, I believe that we did succeed by our actions — for a time at least — in convincing the chiefs that we were ignorant of their intentions. Immediately they returned to us the clapping of stones had ceased, and the ensuing silence seemed the more profound.

Eefow then asked: "You will sleep on shore tonight?"

Captain Bligh replied: "No, I never sleep away from my boat, but it may be that I shall leave a part of my men in the cavern."

Our hope was, of course, that we could persuade the Indians of an intention to remain in the cove until the following day. I think there must have been a difference of opinion between the two chiefs as to when the attack upon us should be made, and that the elder one was for immediate action and Eefow for a night attack. They again conversed together in their figurative speech, of which we understood nothing.

Bligh said to us, very quietly: "Be ready, lads. If they make a hostile move, we will kill them both and fight our way to the launch."

We were, of course, in the unfortunate position of not being able to begin the attack, and yet we were almost at the point where action, however desperate, would have seemed preferable to further delay.

Eefow now turned again to Nelson. "Tell your captain," he said, "that we shall spend the night here. To-morrow I will go with you in your boat to Tongataboo."

Nelson interpreted this message, and Bligh replied: "That is good."

The chiefs then left us; but when they had gone a distance of fifteen or twenty paces, Macca-ackavow turned with an expression on his face that I shall not soon forget.

"You will not spend the night ashore?" he again asked.

"What does he say, Nelson?" asked Bligh.

Nelson interpreted.

"God damn him, tell him no!" said Bligh.

Nelson conveyed this message at some length, and in a more diplomatic manner than Bligh had used. The chief stood facing us, glancing swiftly from side to side amongst his followers. Then he again spoke, very briefly; and having done so, strode swiftly away.

"What is it, Nelson?" asked Bligh.

Nelson smiled grimly. "'*Te mo maté gimotoloo,*'" he replied. "Their intentions are clear enough now. It means: 'Then you shall die.'"

Bligh's actions at this time were beyond praise. To see him rise to a desperate occasion was an experience to be treasured in the memory. He was cool and clear-headed, and he talked quietly, even cheerfully, to us.

"It is now or never, lads," he said. "Hall, serve out quickly the water Mr. Cole has brought in."

The calabash was passed rapidly from hand to hand, for we knew it would be impossible to get the water to the launch; each man had a generous sup, and it was needed, for we had been on short rations for three days. All this while Bligh had kept a firm grip with his left hand on Nageete's arm, holding his cutlass in his right. He was determined that, if we were to die, Nageete should die with us. The man's face was a study. I have not been able to determine in my own mind, to this day, whether he was playing a part or was genuinely friendly towards us. I imagine, however that he had a heart as treacherous as those of his countrymen.

Bligh had already instructed us in what order we should proceed to the beach. Cole, also armed with a cutlass, took his station with the captain on the other side of Nageete; and the rest of us fell in behind, with Purcell and Norton bringing up the rear.

"Forward, lads!" said Bligh. "Let these bastards see how Englishmen behave in a tight place!"

We then proceeded toward the beach, everyone in a kind of silent horror.

I believe it was the promptness, the unexpectedness of our action alone that saved us. Had we shown the least hesitation, we must have all been slain; but Bligh led us straight on, directly toward one large group of Indians who were between us and the launch. They parted to let us through, and I well remember my feeling of incredulous wonder at finding myself still alive when we had passed beyond them. Not a word was spoken, nor was a hand lifted against us until we reached the beach.

Fryer had, of course, seen us coming, and had slacked away until the launch was within half a dozen paces of the beach, in about four feet of water.

"In with you, lads! Look alive!" Bligh shouted. "Purcell, stand by with me — you and Norton!"

Within half a minute we were all in the boat, save Bligh and the two men with him. Nageete now wrenched himself free from Bligh's grasp and ran up the beach. The captain and Purcell made for the boat, wisely not attempting to bring in the grapnel on shore; but Norton, who Bligh thought was immediately behind him, ran back to fetch it. We shouted to him to let it go; but either he did not or would not hear.

The Indians by this time had been roused to action, and they were upon Norton in an instant, beating out his brains with stones. Meanwhile we had hauled Bligh and Purcell into the boat and got out the oars. The natives seized the line which held us to the shore; but Bligh severed it with a stroke of his cutlass, and the men forward quickly hauled us out to the other grapnel and attempted to pull it up. To our dismay, one of the flukes had caught and two or three precious minutes were lost before it was gotten clear. It was fortunate for us that the savages were unarmed; had they been possessed of spears, or bows and arrows, the chance of any man's escaping would have been small indeed. The only spears amongst them were those carried by the two chiefs. Macca-ackavow hurled his, which passed within a few inches of Peckover's head and fell into the water a dozen yards beyond us.

But whilst they had no man-made weapons, the beach offered them an inexhaustible supply of stones, and we received such a shower of these that, had we not been a good thirty yards distant, a number of us might have met Norton's fate. As it was, Purcell was knocked senseless by a blow on the head, and various others were badly hurt. The speed and accuracy with which they cast the stones were amazing. We protected ourselves as well as we could with bundles of cloathing which we held before us. Meanwhile the men forward were hauling desperately on the grapnel, which at last gave way and came up with one fluke broken. Bligh, at the tiller, was in the most exposed position of any; that he escaped serious injury was due to the efforts of Elphinstone and Cole, who shielded him with floor boards from the stern sheets.

We now began to pull away from them, but the treacherous villains were not done with us yet. They got one of their canoes into the water, which they loaded with stones, whereupon a dozen of them leaped into her to pursue us. Our six men at the oars pulled with all their strength, but we were so heavily laden that the savages gained swiftly upon us. Nevertheless, we had got out of the cove and beyond view of the throng on the beach before we were overtaken. They now had us at their mercy, and began throwing stones with such deadly accuracy that it seemed a miracle some of us were not killed. A few of the stones fell into the boat and were hurled back at them; we had the satisfaction of seeing one of their paddlers struck squarely in the face by a stone cast by the boatswain. However, that was a chance shot: we should have been no match for them at this kind of warfare even had we possessed a supply of ammunition.

In the hope of distracting their attention from us, Mr. Bligh threw some articles of cloathing into the water; and to our joy they stopped to take them in. It was now getting dark, and, as they could have had but a few stones left in the canoe, they gave over the attack, and a moment later disappeared past the headland at the entrance to the cove. We were by no means sure that others would not attempt to come after us, so we pulled straight out to sea until we caught the breeze. With our sails set, we were soon past all danger of pursuit.

I was busy during the next hour caring for our wounded, of whom there were nine in all. Purcell was badly hurt. He had been struck a glancing blow on the head, which laid open his scalp and knocked him unconscious, but, by the time I was able to attend to him, he was again sitting up, apparently but little the worse for a blow that would have killed most men. An examination of the wound assured me pretty well that the skull had not been fractured. It was necessary to take half a dozen stitches in the scalp. Elphinstone had had two fingers of his right hand broken while protecting Captain Bligh, and Lenkletter had been deeply gashed across the cheek bone. The other wounds were bruises, the worst being that of Hall, who had been struck full on the right breast and nearly knocked out of the launch.

It can be imagined with what feelings of gratitude to God we watched the island of Tofoa dropping away astern. Now that we had time to reflect, a truer sense of the horror of the situation from which we had so narrowly escaped came home to us. The death of Norton cast a gloom upon all our spirits, but we avoided speaking of him then; the manner of his death was too clearly in mind, and it seemed that we could still hear the yells of the savages who had murdered him. Captain Bligh took his loss very much to heart and blamed himself that he had not thought to inform us, beforehand, to give no heed to the grapnel on shore. But he was by no means at fault. What the situation would be on the beach could not have been foretold, and poor Norton himself should have seen the folly of trying to save the grapnel. Nevertheless, his was an act of heroism such as few men would have been capable of attempting.

The wind, from the east-southeast, freshened as we drew away from the land; the darkness deepened, and soon Tofoa was lost to view save for the baleful glare from its volcano, reflected on the clouds above. Meanwhile we had gotten the boat in order and had taken the places Captain Bligh had assigned to us for the night. With respect to food, we still had our one hundred and fifty pounds of bread, short of a few ounces eaten at Tofoa, twenty pounds of pork, thirty-one coconuts, sixteen breadfruit, and seven yams; but both the breadfruit and the yams, which had been cooked on shore, had been trampled under our feet during the attack. Nevertheless, we salvaged the filthy mess and ate it during subsequent days. As already related, we still had twenty-eight gallons of water — the same amount we had carried away from the *Bounty* — but we had left only three bottles of wine, and five quarts of rum.

I am not likely to forget the conference we then held to determine our future course of action. We were running, of necessity, before the wind, in a direction almost the opposite to that of Annamooka or Tongataboo, and Fryer, who was the first to speak, earnestly begged Captain Bligh to continue this course — to proceed with us in the direction of home.

"We know what we have to expect of the savages, sir," he said. "Without arms, our experience at Tofoa will only be repeated on other islands, and we could not hope to come off so fortunate again."

Other voices were joined to the master's; there was no doubt as to the general desire of our company to brave the perils of the sea rather than those certain to be met with on land. Bligh was willing to be persuaded; in fact, I am sure that he himself would have proposed this change of plan had no one else spoken of it. Nevertheless, he wished us to be fully aware of the dangers ahead of us.

"Do you know, Mr. Fryer," he asked, "how far we must sail before we shall have any expectation of help?"

"Not exactly, sir."

"To the Dutch East Indies," Bligh went on; "and the first of their settlements is on the island of Timor, a full twelve hundred leagues from here."

A moment of silence followed. Not one of us, I believe, but was thinking: "Twelve hundred leagues! What hope, then, have we?"

"Even so," said Bligh, "our situation is by no means hopeless. Granted that every man of you gives me his full support, I believe we shall reach Timor."

"That you shall have, sir!" said Peckover. "What do you say, lads?"

There was a hearty agreement to this.

"Very well," said Bligh. "Now let me tell you, briefly, what we are likely to have in store. First, as to favouring elements: we are at a most fortunate time of year; we can count upon easterly winds for as long as we shall be at sea. The northwest monsoon should not commence before November, and long before that time we shall have reached Timor, or be forever past the need of reaching it. The launch is stoutly built; deeply laden as we are, we need not fear her ability to run before the wind. Her performance at this moment is a promise of what she can do. As to the perils we must meet — "

He paused while reflecting upon them. "Of those I need not speak," he went on. "They are known to all of you. But this I will say: If we are to reach Timor, we must live upon a daily allowance of food and water no more than sufficient to preserve our lives. I desire every man's assurance that he will cheerfully agree to the amount I shall decide upon. It will be small indeed, but we can be almost certain of replenishing our water many times before the end of the voyage. However, that remains to be seen, and I shall not anticipate doing so in deciding what each man's portion shall be. Mr. Fryer, have I your solemn promise to abide by my judgment in this matter?"

"Yes, sir," Fryer replied promptly.

Mr. Bligh then called each man by name, and all agreed as Fryer had done.

These matters having been decided, we fell silent, and so remained for some time; then Cole, who was seated amidships, said: "Mr. Bligh, we should be pleased if you would ask God's blessing upon our voyage."

"That I shall do, Mr. Cole," Bligh replied.

Never, I imagine, have English seamen been more sensible of the need for Divine guidance than the eighteen men in the *Bounty's* launch. We waited, our heads bowed in the darkness, for our leader to speak.

"Almighty God. Thou seest our afflictions. Thou knowest our need. Grant that we may quit ourselves like men in the trials and dangers that lie before us. Watch over us. Strengthen our hearts; and in Thy divine mercy and compassion, bring us all in safety to the haven toward which we now direct our course. Amen."

The watch for the early part of the night was now set, and the rest of us arranged ourselves for sleep as well as we could. The wind blew with increasing freshness, but the launch behaved well. The moonlit sea before us seemed to stretch away to infinity.

"Slack away a little, Mr. Cole," Bligh called.

# CHAPTER IV

THE sea was calm, though there was a fresh breeze at east. Now that Tofoa had been lost to view, every man in the boat, I believe, felt, for the first time since casting off from the *Bounty,* a faint thrill of hope. I was fully aware of the immense remoteness of the Dutch East Indies, and of the difficulties and dangers through which we should be obliged to pass were we to reach those distant islands; but Mr. Bligh's confident manner, and his calmness during our perilous escape from the savages, convinced me of our good fortune in being under his command.

Heavily laden as she was, and with only the reefed lug foresail set, the boat sailed fast to the westward. Mr. Bligh was at the tiller, with Peckover beside him; Fryer, Elphinstone, Nelson, and I sat in the stern sheets. The two midshipmen on the thwart were already asleep; but Tinkler, who had been chosen for Peckover's watch, was making prodigious efforts to keep awake. The gunner noticed the lad's yawns.

"Get you to sleep, Mr. Tinkler," he said gruffly; "I shan't need you to-night."

There was little talk among the men forward, though nearly all were awake. The slower-witted, I suppose, were only now arriving at a full realization of what lay before us. I heard frequent groans from those who were nursing bruises, and indeed my own injured shoulder was so painful as to preclude the possibility of sleep. It may be worthy of remark that the tincture of *Arnica montana,* of which I had a small supply, proved of great value to those of us who had been hurt.

Calm as the sea was, the launch was so deep that we shipped quantities of water as we ran clear of the land and began to feel the long roll of the Southern Ocean from east to west. Peckover set two men — Lebogue and Simpson — to bailing. Toward midnight, as the sea grew higher, they had all they could do to keep her clear of water, and became so fatigued that Peckover ordered others to relieve them. He pulled out his large silver watch, scrutinized it intently, and returned it to his pocket.

"What hour have you, Mr. Peckover?" asked the captain.

"I can't make out, sir."

Bligh glanced up at the stars. "Mr. Fryer, you have had no sleep?" he asked.

"Not yet, sir."

"Take the tiller, if you please; I shall try to rest, and I recommend you to do the same at four o'clock."

They changed places, moving gingerly in the pitching boat, and Bligh made himself as comfortable as possible. Hayward and Hallet rubbed their eyes as they were wakened to their turns at the bailing; they drew their jackets around them, shivering at the spray which flew constantly over the quarters.

Toward morning the wind chopped round from N.E. to E.S.E., and blew very cold, while the sea grew high and confused, breaking frequently over the stern of the launch. Mr. Bligh was aware of the change instantly, and took the tiller from the master's hands. Four men were now required to throw out the water, which came in sheets over the transom and quarters of the boat. At dawn the sky was overcast with low, dirty clouds, scudding fast to the westward, and the sun rose red and ominous. We were a sorry crew in the light of this Sunday morning; haggard-eyed, wet to the skin with salt spray, and so stiff that some could scarcely straighten their legs. Nelson tried to smile; his teeth chattered so violently that he stammered when he spoke.

Mr. Bligh's face looked drawn in the gray light, but his eyes were cool and alert. Each wave sent sheets of wind-driven spray into the boat; presently a sea greater than the others swung us high and curled over the transom. Above the roaring of the waves I heard faint cries and curses from the men as a rush of water swept forward in the bilges. Then, while I plied a coconut shell, snatched up in an instant, I heard Bligh's voice, audible in the calm of the trough. He was shouting to Hall, who sat with Lamb in the bows: —

"The bread! The bread!"

The man had been crouching with his head in his arms, shivering with the cold. He stared aft dazedly. Our bread had been stowed in the bow of the launch, the place least exposed to the driving spray. It was in three bags, and had been covered with the spare mainsail.

"Aye, aye, sir!" Hall shouted back, bending down to raise the canvas and examine what was beneath. A moment later he straightened his back. "One sack is wet, sir!" he shouted. "The lot will be spoiled if it's left here!"

Bligh glanced fore and aft. "Mr. Purcell!" he called.

The carpenter was plying a scoop close beside his chest. Another wave was passing beneath us, bringing fresh sheets of spray, but no solid water this time. He passed the scoop to the man behind him, who began to bail at once.

"Aye, sir," he said.

"Clear your chest of tools; place them in the bilges."

The carpenter removed the tray of small tools, and the heavier ones beneath.

"Now, lads, look alive!" Bligh shouted when all was ready. "Wait till I give the word. One sack at a time! Hall, you and Smith pull out the first and pass it to Lebogue! Then aft to the chest, hand to hand. Mr. Hayward, open the chest when the time comes. Mr. Purcell will cut the seizing and dump the bread in loose. Work fast! It'll be empty bellies otherwise!"

All but those bailing waited in suspense until the launch's bow shot up and she jogged back into the next trough.

"Now!" shouted Bligh.

Off came the sail; the sack was passed swiftly aft from hand to hand, cut open with a touch of the carpenter's clasp knife, and dumped into the open chest. Hayward closed the lid with a snap. The sail was safely tucked about the two remaining sacks before we felt the lift of the following wave. In the momentary lulls between succeeding waves, the other sacks came aft and their contents were safely stowed.

Every man in the boat, I believe, must have drawn a sigh of heartfelt relief. Small as our supply of bread was for such a voyage as lay before us, it was all that stood between us and certain death by starvation. It had been stowed in the chest not a moment too soon.

The seas grew so high that our scrap of sail hung slack from the yard when in the trough, filling with a report like a musket shot as the following sea raised us high aloft. Then the launch would rush forward dizzily, while water poured in over the quarters, and the straining sail, small as it was, threatened to snap the unstayed mast. Mr. Bligh crouched at the helm with an impassive face, turning his head mechanically to glance back as each rearing sea overtook us. Had he relaxed his vigilance for a moment, or made a false motion of the tiller, the boat would have broached to and filled instantly. All hands were now obliged to bail, those who had nothing better throwing out the water with coconut shells. We were greatly hampered by the coils of rope, spare sails, and bundles of cloathing in the bilges.

The force of the gale increased as it veered back to east and to northeast; it was soon apparent to all hands that our sail was too much to have set.

"We must lighten her, Mr. Fryer!" Bligh shouted above the roar of wind and sea. "Each man may keep two suits of cloathing — jettison the rest! And heave overboard the spare foresail and all but one coil of rope!"

"Aye, sir!" replied the master. "Can we not shorten sail? I fear we'll drive her under with but a single reef!"

Bligh shook his head. "No, she'll do. Over with the spare gear!"

His orders were carried out with an alacrity which showed that those under him realized the imminence of our danger. Though the weight of what we cast away would scarcely have exceeded that of a heavy man, the boat rode better for it, and the clearing of the bilges enabled six of us, bailing constantly, to keep her dry. A quarter of a cooked breadfruit, much dirtied and trampled during our naval engagement with the Friendly Islanders, was served out to each man with half a pint of water.

It was close on noon when the wind veered once more to E.S.E.; and as we could do nothing but run straight before it, the boat was now steered W.N.W. — in which direction, the Indians had informed us, lay the group of large islands they called Feejee. The sea was now higher than ever, and the labour of bailing very wearisome, but I was losing my dread of the boat foundering, for I perceived that since we had lightened her she rode wonderfully well, and was in little danger with a skillful hand at the helm. At twelve o'clock by the gunner's watch, Mr. Bligh had his sextant fetched out, and with two of us holding him propped up in the stern sheets, he managed to observe the altitude of the sun. Elphinstone was at the tiller, and I noticed with relief that he steered with confidence and skill. Our lives, from moment to moment, depended upon our helmsman. Had there been an awkward or timid man in his place, our chances would have been small indeed.

"We have done well," said the captain, when he had returned to the stern sheet. . . . "Ah, well steered, Mr. Elphinstone! Damme! Well steered!"

A great sea lifted us high and passed under the launch, roaring and foaming on both sides. As we dropped into the calm of the trough,

Mr. Bligh went on: "You see how she behaves, lads? She'll see us through if we do our part! By God, she will! Mr. Fryer, by my reckoning, we have run eighty-six miles since leaving Tofoa."

The wind was our friend as well as our enemy. Captain Bligh's feeling for the launch was shared by every man of us; we were beginning to love her, now that we knew something of her qualities.

"We must have a log," Bligh added. "Mr. Fryer, I count on you and the boatswain to provide us with a line, properly marked. Mr. Purcell, see what you can do to make us a log chip."

When we had eaten our dinner of five small coconuts, the carpenter took apart the tray from his chest; and from its bottom — a piece of thin oaken plank — he sawed out a small triangle, about six inches on a side. One side was weighted with a bit of sheet lead, and a hole was bored at each corner. The whole made what seamen call a "chip."

We had on board two stout fishing lines, each of about fifty fathoms length. One was kept towing behind the boat with a hook to which a bit of rag had been made fast. From the other, Fryer made a bridle for the log chip, measured off twelve fathoms, and marked the place with his thumb. The boatswain had been twisting some bits of a handkerchief; as the master held out the line, he rove a bit of the rag through the strands and knotted it fast. Then, with the carpenter's rule, Fryer measured off very carefully twenty-five feet. At this point the boatswain made fast another bit of rag, with a trailing end, in which he tied one knot. This was repeated, tying two knots, three knots, and so on until there were eight knots in the last rag.

"Will eight be enough, sir?" Fryer asked.

The captain was at the tiller, glancing back over his shoulder at the wave behind us. When it had passed under us, he replied in the sudden calm: "Aye, eight will do. Mr. Peckover, take your watch in the lee of the chest there, and practise counting seconds with Mr. Cole. You'll soon have the hang of it, I'll be bound!"

I heard them for a long time, as we sank into the troughs between the seas, counting monotonously: "One-an', two-an', three-an', four-an' . . ." At last the gunner called back: "Mr. Bligh!"

"Aye; are you ready?"

"We'll not be a second off, sir!"

"Then heave the log!"

Peckover coiled the line in his right hand to pay out freely, while the boatswain took his place at the starboard quarter. At a sign from the gunner he cast the log chip into the sea, and as the twelve-fathom mark passed through his fingers he began to count. At the fifteenth second he gripped the line and turned to Mr. Bligh.

"Four and a half, sir," he reported, beginning to pull in the line.

"Good! From now on, let the mate of the watch heave the log every hour. I shall reckon our longitude each day with the aid of Mr. Peckover's watch, and we can check the results by dead reckoning."

Crouched in the stern sheets, shivering and wet to the skin, I caught Nelson's eye as I turned my back to the spray. His thoughts, perhaps, like my own, were of the change in Bligh. He was above all a man of action, and seemed happy only in situations which demanded the exercise of his truly great qualities of skill, courage, and resourcefulness. He was born to lead men in peril or in battle, and now, in the boat, with the sea for enemy and his task the preservation of his men's lives, he was at his best — cheerful, kindly, and considerate to a degree I should have believed impossible a fortnight before.

The weather continued very severe during the afternoon and throughout the night; Captain Bligh held the tiller for eighteen hours. Though we had not yet begun to suffer greatly for lack of food, the night was a miserable one. At sunset the wind veered a little to the southward and blew so chill that I found it impossible to sleep. Laborious as the task of bailing was, we seized the scoops gladly when our turns came, for the hard work warmed us.

By nine o'clock the wind had blown the sky clear; the moon, sinking toward the west, cast a cold, serene light on the roaring sea. Each time the boat was flung aloft, we gazed out over miles of angry water, tossing, breaking, and ridged with great waves running to the west. Had not every bone in my body ached with the cold, I think I might have felt a kind of exultation at the majesty of the spectacle, and in the thought that our boat, small and frail as she was, could carry us safely over such a sea. And I was aware of what might be termed a cosmic rhythm in the procession of the waves. They passed under us with great regularity, the interval being about the time it took me to count ten, very slowly; they seemed to be about two hundred yards from crest to crest, and I estimated that they passed us at not less than thirty miles an hour. Hour after hour we alternated between fierce wind and spray and the roar of breaking water on the crests, and the calm of the black troughs, where the launch all but lost steerageway.

Mr. Bligh was silent during the night; his task was too exacting to permit of speech. He must have suffered more than any of us, for the movements required to steer the boat were too slight to warm his blood. The moon, sinking ever lower ahead of us, shone full on his face; his expression was calm and alert, though he could not suppress a strong shuddering.

At last the moon went down on our larboard bow. The stars shone with the cold light of an autumn evening at home. The waves roaring about us broke in sheets of pale fire, so that at times I could distinguish the faces of my companions in the eerie light.

Nelson and I had returned to the stern sheets after a long trick with the bails. We were in the calm between two seas at the time. Glancing over the side, I saw swift shapes of fire gliding back and forth alongside the boat: a dozen, a score of them — darting ahead, veering this way and that, disappearing under the boat. One of them ame to the surface within a yard of us, snorted loudly, and shot ahead.

"Porpoises!" Nelson exclaimed.

"Aye," said the captain; "my mouth waters at the thought of a porpoise steak, no matter how raw!"

Gripping the gunwales, we gazed over the side, thinking less of the beauty of the phosphorescent tracks than of the abundance of food so near at hand — food we were powerless to secure. The seas overtook us with a regularity that lightened Bligh's task at the tiller. He seemed not to feel the piercing chill of the air that penetrated our drenched cloathes. The splendid performance of the launch engaged his whole attention. Though trembling with cold, I caught something of his own exhilaration as I watched the great seas rearing their backs in the starlight and sweeping toward us.

"How well she rides!" said Nelson, between chattering teeth.

"I watched her building," Bligh replied proudly; "I inspected every strake and frame that went into her! A stancher boat was never built! Were she decked and reasonably laden, I could take her round the world."

When our turn came to bail once more, my legs were so benumbed that I had difficulty in getting forward, and Nelson had to be helped to his feet. The sky was turning gray when we were relieved once more.

The captain ordered a teaspoonful of rum to be served out. This revived us wonderfully, and we breakfasted on some bits of cooked yams found in the bottom of the boat. The weather was abating, although the sea would still have appalled a landsman, and the rising sun warmed us sufficiently to give us the use of our stiffened limbs.

By eight o'clock, when the boatswain hove the log, the wind had moderated to a fresh breeze, and so little spray was coming aboard that those forward were able to dry their cloathes. Captain Bligh glanced down at the compass and beckoned to Elphinstone.

"Take the helm," he said. "Keep her W.N.W. We should raise the land soon, unless the Indians are liars."

He flexed the muscles of his arm, stiffened by cold and his long night's work, and went on, addressing us all: "We have come through a bad night. In these latitudes, we may sail all the way to Timor without again being so sorely tried. You have borne up well, my lads, and we can depend upon the launch. My word for it! If we husband our provisions as agreed upon, we shall all reach home!"

"Never fear, sir," Cole ventured to remark. "We're with ye to a man. And thank God for Captain Bligh to lead us — eh, lads?"

There was a hearty chorus from the people: "Aye!" "Well spoken!" "Ye can lay to that!"

As the morning advanced we sighted several flocks of birds, hovering over shoals of fish — a sure indication of land. Once we passed through the midst of a school of tunnies, leaping and thrashing the sea into foam, yet none would seize our hook. We were now keeping a sharp lookout, and a little before noon land was discovered — a small flat island, bearing southwest, about four leagues distant. Other islands appeared, and by three in the afternoon we could count eight on the horizon, from south around through the west to north.

"The Feejee Islands," said Mr. Bligh, who had been awakened from a refreshing sleep by the first shout of *"Land!"* "We are the first white men to set eyes on them!"

"Can't we land here, sir?" asked the carpenter.

"Spoken like a fool, Mr. Purcell," said Bligh bluntly. "You've a short memory if you've so soon forgotten Tofoa! We could commit no greater folly than to land here. Captain Cook never saw these islands; but when I was master of the *Resolution,* in 1777, he learned much of their inhabitants from the Friendly Islanders. They are known to be fierce and treacherous, and eaters of human flesh. No. We shall keep well clear of these fellows!"

# CHAPTER V

Toward evening we raised three small islands to the northwest, about seven leagues distant, passing them at nightfall, when we snugged down to a reefed foresail. Had our circumstances been happier, I might have enjoyed more fully the emotion aroused by sailing an unknown sea, studded with islands on which no European had hitherto laid eyes.

Nelson was possessed of that most precious of gifts: an inquiring and philosophical turn of mind. Even in our situation, with not one chance in a thousand, as it seemed, of seeing England again, he was able to derive pleasure from the contemplation of the sea and the sky by day, and the stars by night. He regarded each island we passed, no matter how distant, with an inquiring eye, speculating as to whether it was of volcanic or of coralline formation, whether it was inhabited, and what vegetation might spring from its soil. When we passed shoals of fish, he named them, and the birds diving and hovering overhead. And what little I know of astronomy was learned from Nelson during the long nights on the *Bounty's* launch.

Though the wind freshened after dark and kept us pretty wet throughout the night, the sea was not rough and we managed to get a little sleep by putting ourselves at watch and watch, half of us sitting up, whilst the others stretched out in the boat's bottom. I found it a great luxury to be able to extend my legs, and, although shivering with cold, I slept for nearly three hours, and awoke much refreshed. At daybreak all hands seemed better than on the morning before. We breakfasted on a quarter of a pint of water each and a few bits of yam, the last of those we had found in the bottom of the boat.

During the early hours of the morning the wind moderated, and Mr. Bligh ordered the chest opened in order to examine the bread. One of the sacks was well dried, and the bread which had been wet on the first night was spread out in the sun. When it had been thoroughly dried, we carefully sorted our entire supply, placing all that was damaged or rotten in the sack, to prevent the rot from infecting what was still good. This damaged bread was to be eaten first.

After Captain Bligh had taken his observation at noon, he informed us that our latitude was eighteen degrees, ten minutes, south, and that, according to his reckoning, we had run ninety-four miles in the twenty-four hours past. It was cloudy to the westward, but Lebogue and Cole, old seamen both, believed that they could discern high land in that direction, at a place where the clouds seemed fixed.

We had been through so much since leaving the *Bounty* that I had scarcely given a thought to what I ate; now, casting up the total of what I had had in the seven days past, I perceived that the whole of it was no more than a hungry man, in the midst of plenty, would have eaten at a meal. Our scant rations had had their effect — cheeks were pinched and eyes unnaturally hollow and bright. There were no complaints of hunger as yet; the men were cheerful as they drank their sups of water and ate their bits of damaged bread.

It blew fresh from E.S.E. in the afternoon, and the sea began to break over the transom and quarters once more, forcing us to bail. Though choppy, the sea was flat, and old Lebogue stood on the bow thwart, shading his eyes with his hand as he gazed ahead. Suddenly he turned aft.

"Mr. Bligh!" he hailed in a subdued voice.

"Yes?"

"There's a monstrous great tortoise asleep, scarce two cable-lengths ahead! Let me conn ye on to him, sir, and I'll snatch his flipper! Many a one I've caught in the West Indies!"

Bligh nodded, with his eyes fixed on Lebogue. "Let no man make a sound," he said.

We were running at about four knots, and since the boat would almost certainly have filled had we turned broadside to the sea, there was no time to prepare a noose or to consult as to the surest method of capturing the tortoise. I knew that the slightest sound of our feet on the boat's bottom, or knock against her sides, would awaken the animal at once and send him away in alarm. Bligh was alert at the tiller, steering in accordance with the movements of Lebogue's arm. Not a word was spoken; we scarcely dared turn our heads. Once, glancing out of the corner of my eyes as the stern was lifted by a breaking wave, I caught a glimpse of the broad, arched back of the sleeping tortoise, close ahead on our starboard bow. Lebogue waved to starboard a little and then raised his arms as a signal to hold the course. Next moment he stepped softly down from the thwart and leaned far over the gunwale, whilst I heard the animal's powerful thrashing in the sea.

The tortoise was immensely heavy and strong, but Lebogue was a powerful man and determined not to let go. Before Smith or Lenkletter could seize his legs, — before any of us, in fact, could realize what was happening, — the tortoise had pulled him clean over the gunwale and into the sea.

A shout went up. With an oath, Mr. Bligh pushed the tiller into the master's hands and sprang to the side. "Hold me!" he shouted to Elphinstone, as he plunged his arms into the sea, straining every muscle to hold fast to Lebogue, whom he had seized by the collar of his frock. Three of us heaved the man in over the stern. He thought nothing of the wetting, but cursed his bad luck in not having captured the tortoise. Bligh praised his tenacity, and blamed the men seated near him for not holding fast to their mate.

"Had you acted promptly," he said, "instead of sitting there all agape, we should have had a feast to-night, and a supply of meat for many days! . . . Get forward, Lebogue. . . . Samuel, give him a spoonful of rum! He has earned it, by God!"

Warmed by his sup of spirit, Lebogue sat with Peckover and Cole, lamenting his lack of success, and planning what to do should another tortoise appear. "A monster," I heard him remark; "all of two hundredweight! Hold fast to my legs if we raise another — I'll never let go! Damn my eyes! To think of the grub we've lost! Did 'ee ever taste a bit of calipee?"

Bligh turned to Nelson. "Calipee!" he said, with a wry smile. "Were you ever in the West Indies, Mr. Nelson?"

"No, sir."

"I was four years in that trade, in command of Mr. Campbell's ship *Britannia*. By God, sir, those planters live like princes! When at anchor I was frequently asked to dine ashore. They used to disgust me with their stuffing and swilling of wine. Sangaree and rum punch and Madeira till one marveled they could hold it all. And the food! Pepper pot, turtle soup, turtle steaks, grilled calipee; on my word, I've seen enough, at a dinner for six, to feed us from here to Timor!"

Nelson smiled ruefully. "I could do with one of those dinners to-night," he said.

"I feel no great hunger," said Bligh, "though I would gladly have eaten a bit of raw steak."

A little before sunset the clouds broke, and we discovered land ahead — two high, rocky islands, six or eight leagues distant. The southerly island appeared of considerable extent and very high; though the light was too dazzling to see clearly, I thought it fertile and well wooded. Desiring to pass to windward of the smaller island, we hauled our wind to steer N.W. by N. At ten o'clock we were close in with the land, and could see many fires ashore. It was too dark to see more than that the island was high and rugged, and that it was inhabited; by midnight, much to our relief, we had left it astern.

We were cold and miserable during this night, and welcomed the exercise of bailing, but toward morning the wind moderated and the sea went down. At daybreak islands were in sight to the southwest, and from northwest to north, with a broad passage, not less than ten leagues wide, ahead of us. Our allowance for this day was a quarter of a pint of coconut water and two ounces of the pulp for each man. We now suffered thirst for the first time in the launch.

The islands to the southwest and northwest, between which we were steering, appeared larger than any we had seen in this sea. Though many leagues distant, their foreshores seemed richly wooded, and I thought I could perceive vast plains and far-off blue mountain ranges in the interior.

By mid-afternoon we were well between the two great islands. The wind now moderated to a gentle breeze from the east, and the sea became as calm as it is within the reefs of Otaheite.

Nelson could not take his eyes off the island to the south. "I would give five years of my life," he said regretfully, "for an armed ship and leisure to explore this archipelago."

"And I!" remarked the captain. "Yon island would make ten of Otaheite! And the land to the north seems larger still. 'Five' years! I would give ten for a ship! No such group has yet been discovered in this sea!"

Before sunset, we were amazed, on looking over the side, to perceive that we were sailing over a coral bank on which there was less than a fathom of water. Had there been the least swell to break on the shoal, we should have been aware of it long before and sailed clear. Since there was nothing to fear save grounding, we continued on our course, keeping a sharp lookout ahead. The launch moved slowly, through water clear as air; I could see every detail of the bottom. It was flat as a table, strewn with dead coral, and barren of life, seeming to extend for about a mile on either side of us. Twilight was giving way to dark when we came to the end of the shoal, which dropped off abruptly into deep water, as do nearly all of the coral banks in the South Sea.

A rain squall, that came on after dark, wet us to the skin and was over before we could catch more than a gallon of water. Then a cold breeze, like the night wind the people of Otaheite call *hupé,* blew down from the great valleys of the high land south of us. Though the sea was calm, we passed a wretched night, after a dinner of an ounce of damaged bread.

At daybreak our limbs were so cramped that some of the men could scarcely move. Mr. Bligh issued a teaspoonful of rum and a quarter of a pint of water, measured in his little horn cup. There was some murmuring when the morsels of damaged bread were served out. Purcell finished his bit at a single bite and a swallow, and sat shivering glumly on the thwart.

"Can't we have a bit more, sir?" Lamb begged in a low voice, of Fryer. "I'm perishin' with famine!"

"Aye!" put in Simpson. "I'd as soon be knocked on the head by cannibals as die slow the like o' this."

Bligh's quick ear caught their words. "Who's that complaining up forward?" he called. "Let them speak to me if they've anything to say."

There was an immediate silence in the bows.

"I wish to hear no more such talk," Bligh continued. "We'll share alike in this boat, and no man shall fare better than his mates. Mind you that, all of you!"

A fresh breeze was making up from the east. We set the mainsail and were running at better than five knots when they hove the log. Distant land of great extent was now visible to the south and west, and a small island, round and high, was discovered to the north. The great island we had left, which bore more the appearance of a continent than an island, was still in sight.

We had pleasant sailing that day. The roll of the sea from east to west seemed to be broken by the land behind us; though the breeze filled our sails and drove us along bravely, we shipped scarcely any water. I exchanged places with one of the men forward, and stationed myself in the bows, where I could watch the flying fish rising before the launch's cut-water.

These fish were innumerable in the waters of Feejee; I forgot my hunger, and our well-nigh hopeless situation, in the pleasure of watching them. The large solitary kind interested me most, for it was their custom to wait until the boat was almost upon them before taking flight. A few powerful strokes of the tail sent them to the surface, along which they rushed at a great pace with the body inclined upward and only the long lower lobe of the tail submerged. When they had gained sufficient speed, the tail left the water with a final strong fillip, while the fish skimmed away through the air, steering this way and that as it pleased.

The sun was hot toward noon, and, like the others, I suffered from thirst, thinking much of the quarter of a pint of water I was soon to enjoy. As I was turning to go aft, a flying fish rose in a frenzy within ten yards, just in time to escape some large pursuer. There was a dash of spray and a blaze of gold and blue in the sea. The flying fish sped off to starboard, while a swift cleaving of the sea just beneath showed where the larger fish kept pace with its flight. It fell at last. I saw a flurry of foam, and a broad tail raised aloft for an instant.

The boatswain was on his feet. "Dolphin!" he exclaimed.

We were in the midst of a small school of them; the sea was ablaze with darting blue and gold.

Cole went aft eagerly. "I'll put a fresh bit of rag on the hook, sir," he remarked to Mr. Bligh. He began to pull in the line as he spoke, and when the hook came on board, he opened his clasp knife and cut off the bit of dingy red rag which we had hoped for so long a fish might seize.

"Try this," said the captain, taking a handkerchief of fine linen from his pocket.

We watched eagerly while the boatswain tore the handkerchief into strips and seized them on to the shank of the hook, so that the ends would trail behind in the semblance of a small mullet or cuttlefish. When all was ready, he paid out the line, jigging the hook back and forth to attract the attention of the fish.

"Damn my eyes!" said Peckover in a low voice. "They've left us!"

"No, there they are!" I exclaimed.

A darting ripple appeared just behind the hook and sheered off. Cole pulled the line back and forth with all his art. The long dorsal fin of a dolphin clove the water like lightning behind the hook. The line straightened.

"I've got him!" roared Cole, while every man in the boat shouted at once.

The fish rushed this way and that, leaping like a salmon; but Cole's brawny arms brought him in hand-over-hand.

"Take care!" shouted Bligh; "the hook's nearly out of his mouth!"

Cole shortened his grip on the line and hove the fish aboard in one great swing. While still in the air, I saw the hook fall free; next moment the fish struck the floor of the shallow cockpit. Whilst Hallet, who sat closest, was in the act of falling on the dolphin with outstretched arms, it doubled up like a bow, gave a single powerful stroke of its tail on the floor, and flew over the gunwale and into the sea.

Tears came to Hallet's eyes. Miserably disappointed as I was, I could scarcely restrain a smile at the sight of Cole's face. Bligh gave a short, mirthless laugh. Those of the men who had risen to their feet to watch sat down in silence, and for a long time no one spoke. Cole let out his line once more, but the fish had left us, or paid no further attention to the hook.

Early in the afternoon, we hauled our wind to pass to the northward of the long, high island to the westward. It may have been one island, or many overlapping one another; in any case, it appeared of vast extent, stretching away so far to the southward that the more distant mountain ridges were lost in a bluish haze. The land was well wooded, and as we drew near I could distinguish plantations of a lighter green, regularly laid out. We were obliged to approach the land more closely than we desired, in order to pass through a channel that divided it from a small islet to the northeast.

When in the midst of this channel and no more than five miles from the land,—here distinguished by some high rocks of fantastic form, —we were alarmed to see two large canoes, sailing swiftly alongshore, and evidently in pursuit of us. They were coming on fast when the wind dropped suddenly, forcing us to take to our oars. The savages must have done the same, for they continued to gain on us for an hour or more. Then a black squall bore down from the southeast, preceded by a fierce gust of wind. It may convey some idea of the rain which fell during this squall when I say that in less than ten minutes' time, with the poor means of catching water at our disposal, we were able to replace what we had drunk from the kegs, to fill all of our empty barricos, and even the copper pot. While some of the people busied themselves with this work, others were obliged to bail to keep the water down in the bilges. The squall passed on, and a fresh breeze made up at E.S.E. We hastened to get sail on the launch, for as the rain abated one of the canoes was perceived less than two miles from us and coming on fast. She had one mast and carried a long narrow lateen sail, something like those of the large Friendly Island vessels we had seen at Annamooka. Had the sea been rough she would have overtaken us within an hour or two, but the launch footed it fast to the northwest, with her mainsail loosed and drawing well. I felt pretty certain, from the accounts I had heard, that if captured we should probably be fattened for the slaughter, like so many geese.

As the afternoon drew on, the canoe gained on us. Most of the people kept their eyes fixed on her anxiously, but Bligh, who was at the tiller, striving to get the most out of his boat, maintained an impassive face.

"They may wish to barter," he said lightly; "yet it is better to chance no intercourse with them. If the wind holds, night will fall before they can come up with us."

Nelson scarcely took his eyes off the canoe, though interest, and not fear, aroused him. The Indian vessel was at this time scarce a mile away.

"A double canoe," he remarked, "such as the Friendly Islanders build. See the house on the platform between. I spent a day at sea in such a vessel when I was with Captain Cook. They are manœuvred in a curious fashion; instead of tacking as we do, they wear around."

"I wish they would treat us to an exhibition of their skill," I replied.

"How many do you reckon are on board of her?"

"Thirty or forty, I should say."

Just before sundown, when the canoe had come up to about two cable-lengths astern of us, it fell dead calm. The land at this time bore S.S.W. about eight miles distant, with a long submerged reef, on which the sea broke furiously, jutting out to the north. We were not a mile from the extremity of this reef, with a strong current setting us to the west.

"Down with the sails, lads!" Bligh commanded. "To the oars!"

There was no need to urge the men; the halyards were let go in a twinkling, and the strongest amongst us — Lebogue, Lenkletter, Cole, Purcell, Elphinstone, and the master — sprang to the oars and began to pull with all their might.

The Indians had wasted no time. Instead of paddling, as I now perceived, they sculled their vessel in a curious fashion, standing upright on the platform between the two hulls, and plying long narrow paddles not unlike our oars, which seemed to pass down through holes in the floor. Only four men were at these sculls, but they were frequently relieved by others and drove the heavy double canoe, not less than fifty feet long, quite as fast as our six could row the launch. There

was now much clamour and shouting amongst the savages, those not
sculling gazing ahead at us fiercely. One man, taller than the others,
and with an immense shock of hair, stood on the forward end of the
platform, shouting and brandishing a great club in a kind of dance.
His gestures and the tones of his voice left no doubt as to their
intentions.

Our oarsmen pulled their best, for every man in the boat felt pretty
certain that it was a case of row for our lives.

At the end of half an hour, Mr. Bligh perceived that the master, a
man in middle age, was weakening. He made a sign to Peckover to
relieve him, and the gunner took the oar without missing a stroke. The
sun went down over the empty ocean on our larboard bow, and the
brief twilight of the tropics set in. The Indians were still gaining.

Working furiously at their sculls, they were driving their vessel closer
and closer to the launch. When twilight gave place to dusk, they were
not more than a cable-length astern. The tall savage, whom I took to
be their chief, now dropped his club and strung a bow brought forward
to him. Fitting an arrow to the string, he let fly at us, and continued his
practice for ten minutes or more. Some of the arrows struck the water
uncomfortably close to the boat. One fell just ahead of us and floated
past the side; it was nearly four feet long, made of a stiff reed, and
pointed with four or five truly horrible barbs, designed to break off
in the wound.

As I glanced down at this arrow, barely visible in the dusk, I heard
an exclamation from Nelson, sitting next to me, and turned my head.
The moon was at the full, and it was rising directly behind the Feejee
canoe, throwing into relief the black figures of the savages, some
sculling with furious efforts, others prancing about on her deck as they
shouted like a pack of devils.

Then, for no reason we could make out, unless he acted in accordance with some superstition concerning the moon, the chief turned to
shout unintelligible words to his followers. The scullers ceased their
efforts and began to row slowly and steadily; the canoe bore off, turned
in a wide circle, and headed back toward the land. Ten minutes later
we were alone on a vast, empty, moonlit sea.

# CHAPTER VI

On the morning of May the eighth, I awoke from a doze to find the sun half an hour high and rising in a cloudless sky. A more blessed sight could scarcely be imagined, for we had been drenched to the skin the whole of the latter part of the night. Nelson, who was beside me, was already awake, and motioned me to silence, nodding toward Captain Bligh, who was sleeping with his legs doubled under him on the floor in the stern sheets, his head pillowed on one arm, which rested on the seat. Fryer was at the tiller, with Peckover beside him, and Cole and Lenkletter sat forward by the mast. All the others were asleep. A gentle breeze blew; the launch was slipping quietly along, and before us stretched a great solitude of waters that seemed never to have known a storm.

Not a word was spoken. We basked in the delicious warmth, and we could see the huddled forms around us relax as they soaked it up in their sleep. Captain Bligh was having his first undisturbed rest since we had left Tofoa, and we were all desirous that he should have the full good of it. His cloathing was as bedraggled as ours, and his cheeks were covered with a ten days' growth of beard; but although his face was pale and drawn, it lacked the expression of misery which was becoming only too apparent upon the faces of the others.

Nelson whispered to me: "Ledward, merely to look at him makes me believe in Timor." I well understood what he meant. Waking or asleep, there was that about Bligh which inspired confidence. Had we been astride a log with him, instead of in the launch, I think we might still have believed in Timor.

He slept for the better part of three hours, and, by the time he awoke, most of the others were stirring, enjoying the precious warmth of the sun, but taking good care to say nothing of our luck. Even Nelson and I were seamen enough to know that the matter should not be spoken of: that to praise good weather is to tempt it to depart. As soon as we were thoroughly warmed and had dried our clothing, we set to work cleaning the boat and stowing our possessions away in better order than we had been able to do thus far.

Captain Bligh took the occasion to provide himself with a pair of scales for weighing our food. Thus far, our daily ration had been measured by guess, but a more exact method was necessary, both to prevent the grumbling of those who thought they had received an amount smaller than their share, and also to ensure that our food should see us through. Two or three pistol balls had been discovered under the battens in the bottom of the boat. The weight of these balls was twenty-five to the pound, and after a careful estimate of our entire amount of provisions, Bligh decided that each man's portion of bread at a meal should be equal to the weight of one ball. For scales the half shells of coconuts were used, carefully balanced against each other at the ends of a slender bar of wood to which a cord was attached, a little off the centre, as one of the coconut shells was a trifle heavier than the other. The carpenter made the scales, which served our purpose admirably, but it was a woeful sight to all to see how little of the bread was needed to balance the pistol ball. Our allowance of food was now fixed at one twenty-fifth of a pound of bread and a quarter of a pint of water per man, to be served at eight in the morning, at noon, and at sunset. What remained of the salt pork was saved for occasions when we should be in need of a more substantial repast. We still had several coconuts, and, while they lasted, used the meat of these in place of bread, and the liquid in the nuts instead of water; but, as I remember it, we ate the last of them on the tenth of May.

The method of serving our food was this: A portion of bread, of an amount about sufficient for the company, was taken from the chest and handed back in a cloth to Captain Bligh, who usually weighed out the eighteen rations, and they were then passed along from hand to hand. The water, which was stored amidships, was measured, usually by Fryer or Nelson or myself, while Mr. Bligh was weighing the bread, the cup used being a small horn drinking-vessel; and the water was then poured into one of the wineglasses, and handed to the men as they received their bread. It was curious to see the manner in which they accepted and dispatched their food. It was "dispatch" indeed, with most of them; their meal would be finished in an instant.

Purcell was among this number. No matter how miserable I might be, I found relief in watching him receive his tiny morsel. It was always with the same expression of amazement and injury. He would hold the bread in the palm of his huge hand for a few seconds, peering at it from under his shaggy eyebrows as though not quite certain it was there. Then he would clap it into his mouth with an expression of disgust still more comical, and roll up his eyes as though asking heaven to witness that he had not received his due allowance.

Some followed Mr. Bligh's example. He soaked his bread in a coconut shell, in his allowance of water, and then ate it very slowly so that he had the illusion, at least, of having enjoyed a meal.

Samuel, Bligh's clerk, followed a practice that did, in fact, provide him with what might be called the ghost of a meal. With the exception of his breakfast allowance of water, he would save his food and drink until the evening, when he had it all at once. This was, of course, a legitimate privilege, but I think Samuel's reason for exercising it was that he wished to gloat over his food while some of his near companions looked hungrily on. I must give him credit for his self-restraint; but in Samuel it did not, somehow, appear to advantage. I can still hear old Purcell's exasperated voice: "Damn your eyes, Samuel! Don't lick your chops over it! Eat and be done with it like the rest of us!"

Cole never failed to say grace before he partook of his food, however tiny the amount. His little prayer, delivered in a low voice, was audible to those who sat next him in the boat. I heard it, many's the time; and it was always the same: "Our Heavenly Father: We thank Thee for Thy ever-loving care, and for these Thy bounties to the children of men."

One might easily have imagined, from the simple, earnest manner of the old fellow, that he had just sat down to a table spread with all the good things of life, and that he considered such largess far beyond his deserts.

The afternoon continued fine, with the same gentle breeze carrying us smoothly in the direction we would go. At midday Bligh took our position. By our log we had sailed sixty-two miles since noon of the seventh, the smallest day's run we had yet made; but we were content that it should be so, for we had comfort from the sun's warmth and rest from the weary work of bailing.

We had sailed five hundred miles from Tofoa, nearly one-seventh of the distance to Timor; an average better than eighty miles per day. That number, somehow, encouraged us; we made much of it, passed it about in talk. Five hundred miles seemed a vast distance; but we were careful to avoid speaking of the more than three thousand miles that lay ahead.

On this day Mr. Bligh performed an act of heroism in having himself shaved by Smith, his servant. There was neither soap nor water to soften his beard. He sat on the floor in the stern sheets, his head held between Peckover's knees, while Smith crouched beside him cutting through the dry hair, stopping every moment to strop his razor. The task required the better part of an hour; and none of us, seeing Bligh's sufferings, was tempted to follow his example.

"By God, Smith!" he said when the ordeal was over. "I would run the gantlet of all the savages in the South Sea rather than go through this again. Were you ever shaved by the Indians, Mr. Nelson?"

"Once," Nelson replied. "Captain Cook and I both made the experiment on the island of Leefooga. The native made use of two shells, taking the hairs of the beard between them. It was a tedious task, but not so painful as I had imagined it would be."

Bligh nodded. "I've tried it myself; and I've heard that an Indian mother can shave her child's head with a shark's tooth on a stick, and make as close work of it as a man could do with a razor. But I'll believe that only when I've seen it done."

"They've great skill, the Indians," said Peckover; "but my choice is for our own way. I'd be pleased to be sitting this minute in the chair of the worst hairdresser in Portsmouth. I'd call it heaven, though he shaved me with a wood rasp."

"You'll see Portsmouth again, Mr. Peckover; never doubt it," said Bligh quietly.

A deep silence followed this statement. The men looked toward him, a pathetic, wistful eagerness apparent on every face. All wished to believe; and yet the chances against us seemed overwhelming. But there was no shadow of uncertainty in Bligh's voice or manner. He spoke with a confidence that cheered us all.

"And another thing we will see there," he went on: "Fletcher Christian hanging by the neck from a yardarm on one of His Majesty's ships, and every bloody pirate that joined him."

"It will be a long day, Mr. Bligh, before we have that satisfaction, if we ever do," Purcell replied.

"Long?" Bligh replied. "The arm of His Majesty's law is long, mind you that! Let them hide as they may, it can reach and take them by the neck. Mr. Nelson, where do you think they will go? I have my own opinion, but I should like yours."

This was the first time since we had lost the ship that Mr. Bligh had made more than a passing blasphemous reference to the mutineers, or would suffer any of us to speak of them.

"I can tell you where I think most of them will wish to go," Nelson replied: "back to Otaheite."

"So I think," said Bligh. "May God make them bloody fools enough to do it!"

"As they cast off the launch, sir, I plainly heard some of them shout 'Huzza for Otaheite!'" Elphinstone put in. "There was much noise at the time, but I couldn't have been mistaken."

"Whatever the others may decide to do," said Nelson, "there is one too wise to stop there long: Mr. Christian."

Bligh started as though he had been struck in the face. He glanced darkly at Nelson, his eyes blazing with suppressed anger.

"Mr. Nelson," he said; "let me never again hear a title of courtesy attached to that scoundrel's name!"

"I am sorry," Nelson replied quietly.

"Say no more," said Bligh. "It was a slip, that I know; but I could not suffer it to pass in silence. . . . I agree with what you say of him. He is too wily a villain to remain in a place where he knows he will be searched for. But you will see: the others will not follow him; and we shall have them, like that!" He opened his hand, closing it slowly and tightly as though he already had their several throats within his clutch.

"Aye," said Purcell sourly. "And the leader of 'em will go free. He'll never be found."

"Say you so?" Bligh replied with a harsh laugh. "You should know me better than that, Mr. Purcell. I pray I may be sent in search of him! There's not an island in the Pacific, charted or not, where he can escape me! No, by God! Not a sandy cay in the midst of desolation where I cannot track him down! And well he knows it!"

"Where do you think he might go, sir?" asked Fryer.

"We will speak no more of this matter, Mr. Fryer," Bligh replied, and there was an end to any discussion of the mutineers for many a day. Bligh felt keenly the humiliation of losing his ship, and although he rarely mentioned the *Bounty,* well we knew that the thought of her was always present in his mind.

That same afternoon he gave us an account of what he knew of the coastal lands of New Holland and New Guinea.

"This information is for you in particular, Mr. Fryer, and for Mr. Elphinstone," he said. "Should anything happen to me it will devolve upon you to navigate those waters, and you must know what I can tell you of the course to follow. That ocean is but little known; my knowledge of it I had from Captain Cook, when I was master of the *Resolution,* on his third voyage. Our task then was largely concerned with exploration in the Northern Hemisphere; but we had much time on our hands at sea, and Captain Cook was kind enough to inform his officers of his earlier explorations in the western Pacific, and of his passage through what he named 'Endeavour Straits.' I listened with interest, but I little thought I should ever have use for the information he gave us. Which only goes to show, young man," he added, turning to Hayward, "that knowledge of the sea never comes amiss to a seaman. Remember that. You never know when you may have occasion to use it."

"Is there any other passage between those lands save by Endeavour Straits?" Elphinstone asked.

"There may be," Bligh replied; "but if so, I've never heard of it. I need not go into the details of my recollection of the position as given by Captain Cook. You will find this marked on the rough chart I made from memory whilst we were in the cave at Tofoa. It is in my journal. That chart is all you will have to go by in steering through what Captain Cook considered the worst area of reef-infested ocean in the whole of the Pacific. This is the important thing to bear in mind now: Whether we will or no, with strong winds and a heavy sea we must run before them, very likely, farther to the north than we wish to go. Therefore, in case you are driven north of the twelfth parallel, take every opportunity to get to the south'ard, so that you may strike the great reef along the coast of New Holland in the region of thirteen south. It is thereabout, as I recall it, that Captain Cook found the passage which he named 'Providential Channel.' If you can strike it, you can coast to the north'ard with a fair wind, in tolerably quiet waters, till you round the northern cape of New Holland and pass through Endeavour Straits. You shall then have open sailing all the way to Timor."

"We shan't forget, sir," Fryer replied; "but God forbid that you should not be the one to see us through!"

"God will forbid it, I believe," said Bligh, gravely; "but in our situation it is best to provide for every possible mishap."

"Will there be islands, sir, inside the reef at New Holland, where we can go ashore?" Hayward asked.

"I have a clear recollection of Captain Cook speaking of various small lands scattered over the lagoons," Bligh replied. "He found none that were inhabited, as I remember, although he believed they were resorted to at times by the savages. We shall certainly stop at some of them to refresh ourselves."

"How far will New Holland be from where we are, sir?" Hallet asked.

"We will not speak of that, my lad," said Bligh in a kindly voice. "Think if you like of the distance we have come, but never let your mind run forward faster than your vessel. Lebogue is an old seaman. Ask him if that is good advice."

"Aye, sir, the very best," said Lebogue, nodding his shaggy head. "It's the only way for a quick passage, Mr. Hallet."

We fell silent again, watching Lebogue, who sat at our solitary fishing line, which he had kept in the water nearly all the way from Tofoa. We had no bait to spare, and Lebogue and the boatswain had tried every conceivable kind of lure that our means afforded. He was now using one made of the brass handle of a clasp knife and some bits of red cloth torn from a handkerchief. It trailed after the launch at a distance of forty or fifty yards, and was sometimes drawn closer that we might better observe it. There had been moments of breathless expectation when some fish of splendid size would rush toward it; but they invariably recognized it as belonging to nothing in nature, and sheered away. It was maddening to see fish around us — often great multitudes — and never to be able to catch one. But Cole and Lebogue were ever hopeful. They were continually changing the lure; but the result was always the same. On several occasions schools of small mulletlike fish had hovered alongside of us for a few moments. Had we been possessed of a hoop net we could, unquestionably, have caught some of them, they were in such quantities, but the attempt to seine them up with our few remaining hats had not been successful. For all our bitter disappointments, both the fish and the occasional sea birds we met with proved a boon to us. Attempts to catch them occupied our minds. Our bellies, however, felt differently about the matter, and would never agree that our unavailing attempts did more than add insult to injury.

We now had both sails up; they were drawing well, and the sea was so calm that we shipped no water. The sun went down, as it had risen, in a cloudless sky, and darkness came on swiftly. Presently the moon rose, flooding the lonely sea with a glory that transfigured our little boat and everyone in her. Purcell, with his dirty rags wound round his broken head, sat by the mast amidships, facing aft. He looked a noble, even an heroic figure, in that light. On the day of the mutiny, as we were rowing away from the *Bounty,* I wondered how long one small boat would hold two such men as Captain Bligh and himself before they would be at each other's throats. There had long been a feud between them on the ship. Purcell had a high opinion of his ability as a carpenter, and considered himself a monarch in his own department. He was as bullheaded as Bligh himself, but he had the good sense to know his place and to realize that the captain of a ship was, after all, in a position of higher authority than the carpenter. Secretly, as I knew, he gloried in the fact that Bligh had lost his ship, and considered it a just punishment for his tyrannical behaviour; and yet there was no man more loyal to his commander. On the morning of the mutiny there had not been a moment's hesitation in deciding where his duty lay. In the launch it interested me to observe his attitude toward Bligh, and Bligh's toward him. They hated each other; but, in Purcell's case at least, hatred was tempered by respect.

What a contrast the carpenter made to young Tinkler, who sat beside him! He loved this lad as much as he hated Bligh, and being an old seaman he invariably showed him great respect because of his rank as midshipman, never omitting to address him as "Mr. Tinkler." And Tinkler was worthy of respect as well as of affection. He was a plucky lad. There was never a time, no matter how desperate our situation, when he did not play his part like a man.

That night was the only one we had passed in any measure of comfort since leaving Tofoa. Our cramped positions were no pleasanter than they had been, but the boat, as well as our cloathing, was dry, and we were able to have some hours of refreshing sleep.

The ninth of May was just such a day as the eighth had been, with a calm sea and a light breeze from the east-southeast. Bligh had everyone roused at dawn, and as soon as we had worked a little of the stiffness out of our limbs, he set Cole to work, with some of us for helpers, in fitting a pair of shrouds for each mast. Others assisted the carpenter, who was employed in putting a weather cloth, made of some of our spare canvas, around the boat. The quarters were raised nine inches by means of the stern seats which were nailed to cleats along them, and the weather cloth was of the same width, so that, when the task was finished, the boat was as well prepared for rough weather as we could make her. This was the carpenter's day, and he made the most of it; and I will do him the justice to say that he did a thoroughly workmanlike job.

I was glad to hear Mr. Bligh remark: "That will do very well, carpenter."

It was high praise, coming from him; but Purcell would not have been Purcell had he not replied: "Begging your pardon, sir, it won't do well, but I can make no better with what we've got here."

At noon, on the ninth, we were sixty-four miles farther on our way. All of this day we saw neither fish nor bird.

Toward the middle of the afternoon, Nelson broke a silence that seemed to have lasted for hours. "I am constrained to speak, Mr. Bligh," he said, with a faint smile. "This sea is so vast and so quiet that I am inclined to doubt its reality and our own as well."

"That's a strange fancy, sir," Bligh replied; "but the sea is real enough; I can promise you that."

## CHAPTER VII

I REMEMBER Captain Bligh saying to Fryer, about noon on May the twelfth: "I think we've seen the worst of it."

"I am sure of it, sir," Fryer replied, but he believed no more than Bligh in the truth of the statement. It had fallen calm about half an hour before, but the sea, as viewed from the launch, was an awe-inspiring sight. Fryer had just relieved Bligh at the tiller, which he had held continuously for eighteen hours.

Our shrouds for the masts and the canvas weather cloth had been fitted none too soon; on the evening of that same day, — May the ninth, — at about nine o'clock, wind and rain had struck us together, and all through the night four men were continuously bailing, and there were times when every man of us save Bligh was so employed. The sky was concealed by low gray clouds scudding before the wind. So it remained all day and all night of the tenth, the eleventh, and till near midday of the twelfth; and now, although the wind had fallen, the sky was an ominous sight.

There was no break in the clouds, no signs of a lightening at any point in the heavy canopy that overhung us, so low that it seemed almost within reach. Nevertheless, it was calm, for the moment, at least, and the sky withheld its rain. Our sail was dropped into the boat.

"I want two men at the oars," Bligh said.

"I'll make one, sir," Lenkletter called out, and a dozen others at the same time. All were eager for a chance to warm their benumbed bodies. Lenkletter and Lebogue were first chosen, but there were reliefs every quarter of an hour so that the rest of us might enjoy the benefit of the exercise.

"Don't exert yourselves, men," said Bligh; "merely keep her stern to the swell."

The boat had never seemed so small to me as she did then, and I could imagine what a speck she would have appeared in that vast ocean could one have observed her with a sea bird's eye. The long swell, coming from the southeast, was of a prodigious height, but without the wind there was no menace in it. The seas moved toward us, rank after rank, with a solemnity, a majesty, that filled the heart with awe; cold and wretched though we were, we had a kind of solemn pleasure in watching them: seeing our little boat lifted high on their broad backs, to find ourselves immediately after in a great valley between them.

As a recompense for our sufferings, Captain Bligh issued an allowance of rum, two teaspoonfuls for each man; and for our dinner that day we had half an ounce of pork each, in addition to the bread. This made our midday meal seem a veritable feast, and the rum gave us a little warmth. It was the cold that we dreaded at this time, fully as much as the sea: the wind, penetrating cloathing perpetually drenched with rain, felt bitterly chill, as though it were blowing from fields of ice. Thanks to Captain Bligh, we now adopted a means of combating it that proved of inestimable service. He advised us to wring out our cloathing in sea water. It is strange that none of us had thought of this simple expedient before, but the fact remains that we had not. The moment we tried it we found ourselves wonderfully comfortable in comparison with our miserable plight before, the reason being that salt water does not evaporate in the wind so fast as fresh.

We passed the next two or three hours tolerably well; what between taking our turns at the oars and wringing out our cloathes from time to time, we broke the back of the afternoon, each man secretly watching all the while for any change that would give us reason to hope that better weather was in store; but the only change was that the dull light became duller yet, as the day wore on toward evening. And still there was no wind.

The silence made us uneasy. Our ears had been accustomed to the deep roar of the wind and the seething hiss of breaking seas. God knows, we wanted no more of such weather, but we did crave wind enough to carry us on our way. The great swells went under us noiselessly; the only sounds to be heard were the small human sounds within the boat — a spoken word, a cough, a weary sigh as someone shifted his position.

It must have been toward four o'clock in the afternoon that there was mingled with the vast quiet what was, at first, the very ghost of sound — and yet every man of us heard it. Elphinstone, who was lying in the bottom of the boat just before me, raised his head to look round. "What is that?" he said.

There was no need to reply. As we rose to the swell, every head was turned to the eastward; and there, not half a mile distant, we again saw approaching our remorseless enemy — rain.

It came on in what appeared to be a solid wall of blackness, faintly lighted by a dull grayish glow from the sky before it. There was no wind immediately behind; the slowness of its approach assured us of that; therefore, we waited in silence, while the sound increased and spread, now deadened as we fell into the trough, more loud as we rose to the crest of the next wave. Then, as though at the last moment it had leaped to make sure of us, we were in the midst of it — drenched, half drowned, gasping for breath, in a deluge such as we had never before experienced.

In an instant I lost sight of the men in the forward part of the boat. This, I know, will scarcely be believed by those whose experience of rain has been only in the northern latitudes, who know nothing of the enormous weight of water released in a tropical cloudburst. The fact remains that the launch vanished from my sight save for the after part of it where I sat, and the men immediately before my eyes were but shadows blurred by sheets of almost solid water. I heard Captain Bligh's voice, faintly, above the hiss and thunder of the deluge. The words were indistinguishable, but we well knew what we had to do. We bailed with the desperation of men who feel the water gaining upon them even as they bail; who feel it cover their feet and rise slowly toward their knees. And it was not sea water that we threw over the side. It was the pure sweet water of clouds, which men, adrift in a small boat in mid-ocean, so often pray for in vain, with blackening lips and swelling tongues; and we hurled it away from us with bailing scoops, coconut shells, the copper pot, with our hats, with our cupped hands, lest this precious fluid, which Captain Bligh had, rightly, doled out to us a quarter of a pint at a time, should be our death. There was irony in the situation, though we had no time to think of it then.

The darkness in the midst of the storm was almost that of night, but presently I could once more see the outlines of the boat and the forms of the men, and knew that the worst was over. We were a forlorn-looking crew: the water streamed from our cloathing, which was plastered against our bodies; from our hair and beards; and we were again chilled to the bone.

Mr. Bligh's voice sounded unusually loud against the ensuing silence. "Look alive, lads! Mr. Cole, close-reef the foresail, and get it on her. There'll be wind behind this."

"Aye, aye, sir," the boatswain called back. The rest of us, with the exception of the men at the oars, continued bailing, for there was a deal of water yet to be got rid of.

Lebogue was working beside me. "Aye," he muttered, at Bligh's remark about wind; "we've summ'at to come, I'll be bound."

We bailed her dry, and then had time, for a few moments, to know how cold we were. "Wring out your cloathes," said Bligh. We were not slow to obey, and the men nearest Lamb and Simpson performed this service for them, as they were too weak to do it for themselves. Meanwhile the foresail had been double-reefed and hoisted, Bligh again took the tiller, and we waited for the wind.

We saw it coming from afar. The oily swells, that had been smooth enough to reflect the gray light, were blackened under it. We saw it leaping from summit to summit; but whilst it came swiftly, there was no great weight of air at first. Our tiny bit of sail, heavy and dark with rain, bellied out, and the launch gathered steerageway once more. The dull light faded from the sky, and soon what was left of it seemed to be gathered on the surface of the sea, again streaked with foam and flying spray. Harder and harder it blew. No watch was set for the night. We well knew there was work and to spare at hand for all of us.

Nelson touched my arm and pointed overhead. A man-of-war bird, its great wings outspread, wheeled into the wind and hovered over us for a few seconds, seeming to stand motionless against that mighty stream as it looked down at us. Of a sudden it tipped, scudded away, and was lost to view.

Fryer was seated by Mr. Bligh, watching the following seas. "Stand by to bail!" he shouted.

I cannot recall the thirty-six hours that followed without experiencing something of the horror I felt at the time. Wind and rain, rain and wind, under a sky that held no promise of relief. Bad as the hours of daylight were, those of darkness were infinitely worse, for we could see nothing. It seemed a miracle to me that Mr. Bligh was able to keep the launch before the seas, the more so because the wind veered considerably at times, and he could not depend upon the feel of it at his back to tell him how the waves were approaching. He was helped to some extent by Fryer and Elphinstone, who crouched on their knees beside him, facing aft, peering into the darkness; but with the clouds of spray continually in their faces, they could see little or nothing until a sea was on the point of boarding us.

Never, I think, could the gray dawn have been welcomed more devoutly than it was by us on the morning of May the fourteenth; and, as though in pity of our plight, the wind abated shortly after. There was even a watery gleam of light as the sun rose, but our hopes and prayers for blue sky were unavailing. Nevertheless, the clouds were higher and the look of them less menacing than they had been for four days past.

As I looked into the faces about me I realized how frightful my own must appear. Lamb, the butcher, and George Simpson, the quartermaster's mate, appeared to be at the last extremity. They lay in the bottom of the boat, unable to do aught for themselves; throughout the night just past, the water we shipped continually had been washing around them, and it was as much as they could do at times to raise their heads above it. Nelson, too, was a pitiable sight. Never a strong man, the privations and hardships we had undergone had worn him down, but the spirit within the frail body was as tough as that of Captain Bligh himself. Never a groan or a word of complaint came from Nelson. Weak as he was, physically, he was a tower of strength in our company. The men who showed the fewest signs of suffering thus far were Purcell, Cole, Peckover, Lenkletter, Elphinstone, and the three midshipmen. Captain Bligh and the master, who had borne the brunt of our battle against the sea, were gaunt and hollow-eyed, but Bligh seemed to have an inexhaustible reserve of energy to draw upon. I must not omit to speak of Samuel, Bligh's clerk, who I had thought would be among the first to show the effects of hardship. He was city born and bred, with the pale complexion and the soft-appearing body usually found among men of sedentary occupations; nevertheless, he had borne up amazingly well, both in body and spirit. He was a man wholly lacking in imagination, and his belief in Captain Bligh was like that of a dog in its master. He could not, I am sure, conceive of any situation, however perilous, which Bligh was not more than equal to. I envied him this confident trust, particularly at night. Tinkler and Hayward were sturdily built lads, and youth gave them a great advantage over some of the rest of us. Hallet lacked their toughness of fibre, but for all that he played his part like a man, and deserved the more credit in that he was compelled to fight constantly against his terror of the sea. He was not the only one with this fear at his heart. I admit freely that my spirits were often far sunk because of it, although I did my best to conceal the fact.

There had been times, at night, when no man of us, unless it were Samuel, — no, not even Captain Bligh himself, — could have believed that we should see another dawn. The fact that we had survived the nights of the thirteenth and fourteenth gave us new courage. We knew, now, what our boat could do.

We were on a course, N.W. by W. Of a sudden the gray sky to the southwest lightened, and a few moments later there was a break in the clouds. We had all around us, as we thought, nothing but empty sea; but presently we saw, or thought we saw, pale-blue mountains that seemed to be floating high in air. Tinkler was the first to spy them, and before some of us could raise our heads to look, they had again vanished in the mists. Those who had not seen could not believe in the reality of the vision, but an hour later, there it was again; and this time there was no doubt in anyone's mind. Clouds of dense vapour lifted slowly, revealing a land of lofty mountains that stood in cold blue silhouette against the gray sky. At first we thought it one island; but as we approached we found there were four, which bore S.W. to N.W. by W., and distant about six leagues. The largest was, in Captain Bligh's judgment, about twenty leagues in circuit.

We altered our course to pass a little to eastward of the most northerly one. Bligh had only his recollection to serve him, but he believed them a part of the New Hebrides, which Captain Cook had named and explored during his second expedition to the South Sea, in 1774. All through the morning we were sailing at about two knots. The sea was now so calm that but two men were required at the bailing scoops. The rest of us feasted our eyes upon the land. Many an anxious and appealing glance was thrown in Captain Bligh's direction, but he gave no hint as to what his plan was. By the middle of the afternoon we had left the larger islands well astern, and were no more than two leagues distant from the northerly one. The wind was again blowing fresh, and our course was altered to approach still closer. We could see the smoke of many fires rising from the foreshore; the thought of their warmth increased our misery.

The land was of a horseshoe shape. A ridge of high mountains, falling steeply to the sea, enclosed a large bay with a northeasterly exposure. We passed the entrance to this bay not more than two miles off. In about half an hour we had rounded the northern cape, and were well in the lee.

No word had been spoken during this time. We waited with deep anxiety to learn what Captain Bligh's intentions were.

"Trim the sails," he ordered.

We headed up, approaching to within a quarter of a mile of a small cove that resembled, in a general way, the one at Tofoa; but here there was a smooth sandy beach instead of a rocky one, and the vegetation was of the richest green; indeed, the island seemed a paradise to our famished, sea-weary eyes. The sail was dropped and two men were set at the oars to keep us off the land.

"Now, Mr. Purcell," said Bligh, "we will repair our weather cloth. Look alive, for I wish to lose no more time here than is necessary."

Our weather cloth had been much damaged by the sea the night before.

A deep silence followed this order. Purcell remained where he was. Presently he raised his head, sullenly.

"Mr. Bligh," he said, "if you mean to go on from here without giving us a chance to refresh ourselves, I'm opposed; and there's more that feels as I do."

For all the stiffness in his legs, Bligh got to his feet in an instant. His lips were drawn in a thin line and his eyes were blazing with anger, but as he looked at the forlorn figures before him the expression on his face softened and he checked himself.

"There are more?" he asked quietly. "Who are they? Let them speak up."

"I'm one, sir," Elphinstone replied in a hollow voice; "and I'll ask you to believe I'm speaking for others more than myself."

"We are in a pitiful state, sir," Fryer put in. "A night of rest on shore might be the means of preserving the lives of some of us. There's sure to be food on so rich an island."

"There's coconut trees, sir," Lenkletter put in eagerly. "Look yonder, halfway up the slope."

A clump of coconut palms could, in fact, be seen, raising their plumed tops above the forests that covered the steep hillsides. Bligh looked from us to the land, and back again; presently he shook his head.

"Lads, we dare not risk it," he said. "You cannot suppose that I do not feel for your sufferings, since I share them with you. God knows I should be glad to rest here; but the danger is too great. We must not!"

"There's no Indians here, sir," said Purcell. "That's plain to be seen."

Bligh controlled himself with difficulty. "At the moment there are none," he replied; "but we have seen the smoke of many fires, and we were well within view as we passed the bay on the northern side. Make no mistake, we have been seen; and I will say this, which may cool your desire to go ashore: Captain Cook told me that the savages of the New Hebrides are cannibals of the fiercest sort. These islands must be a part of the same group."

"I don't fear them," Purcell interrupted, "whatever may be the case with yourself."

Bligh jerked back his head, as though he had been struck in the face. Purcell, always a cantankerous old rogue, had never before dared to speak in this fashion. Some allowance, perhaps, can be made for him under the circumstances. Although he had borne hardships well, it is possible that he felt the pangs of hunger more keenly than any of us.

Mr. Bligh behaved with a forbearance I had thought him incapable of exercising. Frequently, on the *Bounty,* I had seen him fly into a passion upon slight provocation. Now that he had ample cause for anger, he kept himself well in hand. The reason was, I believe, that he knew how desperately weary we were and how bitter our disappointment at being within view of what appeared to us Eden itself, and forbidden to rest and refresh ourselves there. No insult could have been more gross and unjust than that of the carpenter, and he well knew it.

For a moment Bligh did not trust himself to speak. Then he said: "Set about your work, Mr. Purcell. If you do not, by God you *shall* go ashore — with me, and with me alone."

The carpenter, knowing that he was in the wrong, obeyed at once. Those who had the strength assisted him; the rest of us kept watch on shore.

Presently Lebogue exclaimed: "Aye, sir, we've been seen, right enough! Look yonder!"

Half a dozen savages emerged from the thick bush and came down to the water's edge, gazing out toward us. We were directly opposite the entrance to the cove, and could see them plainly. They were naked save for short kirtles about the middle, and were armed with spears, bows, and arrows. About this same time, Tinkler and Hayward discovered a path leading up one of the hills at the back of the cove. At one point it was in plain view, where it rounded a grassy knoll. Keeping watch upon this place, we saw more Indians passing it as they hastened into the valley. The beach was soon thronged, and we could faintly hear their shouts as they ran this way and that, evidently in a state of great excitement. We had the entire half circle of the beach within view; no canoes were to be seen there, but we did not know what they might have concealed amongst the trees.

In view of Purcell's bold statement of half an hour before, it was interesting to observe his nervousness as the throng of savages increased. Many an apprehensive glance did he throw in their direction.

"Keep your eyes on your work, sir!" Bligh ordered. "Your friends ashore will wait for you."

Presently Tinkler, who had the keenest eyes amongst us, informed Bligh that he had seen three or four of the Indians running up the hill, evidently returning to the large bay on the other side of the mountains.

"They must be sending word to the people over there, sir," Fryer remarked, anxiously. "No doubt they have canoes in the bay, and mean to get at us by sea."

"I should think it more than likely, sir," Bligh replied, quietly. "Nevertheless, we shall have time to finish repairing our weather cloth."

Never, I fancy, had Purcell worked more earnestly than he did upon this occasion. Bligh watched him grimly and would allow him to skimp nothing.

Just as the work was finished, a large canoe, containing between forty and fifty savages, appeared round the northern promontory, about a mile distant. They had no sail, but, with ten or fifteen paddlers on a side, they came on swiftly.

"Now, Mr. Purcell," said Bligh; "is it your desire that we let them come up with us? You say you have no fear of them."

It was all but impossible for the carpenter ever to admit himself in the wrong; but upon this occasion he swallowed his stubborn pride at once.

"No, sir," he replied.

"Very well," said Bligh. "Get sail on her, Mr. Cole."

For all the stiffness of our limbs, the two sails were hoisted in an instant, and we drew away from the land. For the moment, at least, we forgot our hunger, our wet cloathing — everything was lost sight of in the excitement of the race. At first the savages gained rapidly, and it was plain from their actions that their intentions were anything but friendly: those who were not paddling brandished their weapons, and several of them shot arrows after us, some of which fell only a little distance astern. Then we caught the full force of the wind, and the space between us gradually increased. Presently they gave up the pursuit; we saw them enter the cove opposite which we had lain. We then stood away upon the old course.

Never, I think, during the whole of our voyage, were our spirits so low as upon this same afternoon. The sea stretched away, gray and solitary, and we dared not think of the horizons beyond horizons that remained to be crossed before we could set foot upon any shore. Most of us knew that we were still far from halfway, even, to the coast of New Holland. At the earliest we could not hope to reach it before another fortnight had passed.

I now come to an incident concerning which I am most reluctant to speak, and yet it must not be passed over in silence. There was, it seems, one man in our company so lost to all sense of his duty toward the others as to steal a part of our precious supply of pork. The theft amounted to one two-pound piece, and was committed during the night of this same day. With respect to the bread, Captain Bligh had put temptation beyond the power of anyone: it was kept under lock and key in the carpenter's chest. But the pork was not so guarded. It was stored, wrapped in a cloth, in the bow. We had passed a wretched night, with a strong northeast wind, a rough sea, and perpetual rain. There had been no sleep for anyone. At dawn the next morning,

Captain Bligh ordered a teaspoonful of rum and half an ounce of pork for our breakfast; and it was then that the theft was discovered. I well remember the look of horror in Mr. Cole's face as he reported it. "There's a piece missing, sir," he said.

I should not have supposed that any man guilty of such a crime against his comrades could have maintained an air of perfect innocence upon the discovery of the theft; but so it was, here. Captain Bligh questioned each of us by name, beginning with the master:—

"Mr. Fryer, did you take this pork?"

"No, sir," Fryer replied, with a sincerity that no one could doubt.

The question was repeated seventeen times, and the seventeen replies all carried conviction.

I remember having heard, or read, that men reduced to starvation in company sometimes lose all sense of moral responsibility, and that cases have been known where men of integrity, under normal conditions, have committed such crimes without any qualms of conscience, stoutly and indignantly denying them, no matter how damning the evidence against them might be. With us there was no evidence as to the possible culprit; most of our company had taken turns at bailing in the bow during the night, which was so black that one could not see one's next neighbour in the boat.

I shall say no more of this wretched affair except that the thief, whoever he may have been, must surely have despised himself. Captain Bligh brought home to him the enormity of the wrong he had done his fellow sufferers in words that he could never forget.

I believed, on the night of the fourteenth of May, that our company had suffered to the limits of endurance. "Another night as bad as this . . ." I had thought. And there were to be nine to follow — nine days and nights, during which time we were continuously wet and all but perished with cold. The wind shifted from southeast to northeast, now blowing half a gale, now dying away to a dead calm when the oars would be gotten out to keep the launch before the sea. There were moments of fugitive sunshine, but of such brief duration that they but added to our misery, for we were never able to dry our cloathes.

Our situation on the afternoon of May twenty-third was so like that of the twelfth that it seemed time had stood still. We rode the same mountainous seas, under the same lowering sky. What added to my confused sense that we were doomed to an eternity of misery was that

Mr. Bligh had again remarked to Fryer: "I think we've seen the worst of it."

We had been on starvation rations for twenty-one days past, and, during the whole of this time, wet to the skin and chilled to the bone. Our bodies were covered with salt-water sores, so that the slightest movement was agony, yet we were compelled to move constantly for the purpose of bailing. Many of us were now too weak to raise ourselves to our feet, but we crawled and pulled ourselves about somehow, and, knowing that our lives depended upon it, we could still manage to throw out water.

Never before had I realized what a torment the body could be. But I must add this: neither had I realized the toughness, the fineness, of the human spirit under conditions that try it to the utmost. The miscreant who had stolen the pork served only as a foil to the others, whose conduct was such during these interminable hours of trial as has given me a new and exalted opinion of my fellow beings. Whatever men may say in men's despite in the future, or whatever unfortunate revelations concerning them may come under my own observation, I shall think of the company in the *Bounty's* launch and retain my firm belief that, in their darkest hours, and in situations that bear upon them even past the limits of endurance, most men show a heroism that lifts them to heights beyond estimation. The cynic may smile at this. I care not. I know whereof I speak. I have seen the matter put to the proof in a company of eighteen whose members, with two exceptions, — Captain Bligh and Mr. Nelson, — were men such as one might find in any seacoast town in England.

I will not say that there had been no complaints, no urgent, piteous requests for additional food. There were. I can understand better now than I could then what strength Bligh needed to withstand the entreaties of starving men. He fed the weakest upon wine, a few drops at a time; but every demand for additional food was refused save upon the occasions when a tiny morsel of pork would be added to our mouthful of bread.

I have a vivid recollection of the events of the evening and the night of May twenty-third. Bligh had been continuously at the tiller for thirty-six hours, and he remained there until dawn the following morning. I sat in the bottom of the boat facing him, propped up against the thwart immediately forward of the stern sheets. Nelson lay beside me with his head on my knee. He was frightfully emaciated, and so weak that I believed he had not more than twenty-four hours to live. The strongest of our number were Mr. Bligh, Fryer, Cole, Peckover, Samuel, and the two midshipmen, Tinkler and Hayward. The two latter were at the oars as the last of daylight faded, keeping the launch before the sea.

It had been dead calm for more than two hours, but neither past experience nor the look of the sky gave us reason to expect that it would remain so. The last gray light faded quickly, and soon we were in the complete darkness that had been our portion during so many terrible nights.

About three hours after sunset I had fallen into a doze, and only a moment later, it seemed, I was awakened by the deep humming of the wind and the hiss and wash of breaking sea. I heard Bligh calling to Cole, whose station was forward by the reefed foresail, and immediately afterward solid water came pouring over our quarters. Never had we come so near to foundering as at that moment; indeed, for a few seconds I thought we were lost. Bligh shouted: "Bail for your lives!" and so we did. Not a man of us but realized that we were in the immediate presence of disaster.

The horror of that experience I shall not attempt to describe; but it had this good effect: that it aroused even the weakest from apathy, and called into play reserves of nervous force that we did not know we possessed. As for Captain Bligh, he displayed, throughout the whole of this night, a courage far above my poor powers to depict. Now and then his emaciated form would be clearly outlined for a second or two in a glare of lightning, then swallowed up in darkness. When I had said to Nelson, at Tofoa, that ours was a situation that Bligh was born to meet, I little realized how truthfully I spoke. Worn down though he was by hunger and hardship and lack of sleep, he showed no sign of weakening to the strain. Indeed, the more desperate our situation, the more he seemed to rejoice in it. I say this with no desire to exaggerate. He displayed on this night an exhilaration of mind the more striking in view of the peril of our situation. We passed through a series of violent squalls accompanied by thunder and lightning, and I shall never forget the vivid glimpses I had of him, one hand gripping the tiller, the other the gunwale, the seas that threatened to swamp us foaming up behind him and showering him with spray.

And I can still hear his voice in the darkness, heartening us all: "We're doing a full six knots, lads! Let that warm your blood if bailing can't do it — but don't stop bailing!"

Once, in a brief lull between storms, Fryer had suggested that a prayer be said. "No, Mr. Fryer," he replied. "Pray if you like, but to my way of thinking, God expects better than prayers of us at a time like this." It was in this same lull, I remember, that Cole called back, "Sir, shall I relieve you at the tiller?"

"Sit where you are, Mr. Cole," Bligh replied. "Do you think you can handle her better than myself?"

"I know very well I can't," Cole replied. "I was thinking how tired you must be."

A moment of silence followed; then we again heard Bligh's voice: "You are a good man, Mr. Cole, and an able man. I wish there were more like you in the service."

It was a handsome apology, and praise well deserved. I knew how it must have warmed Cole's heart.

The pause between squalls was of short duration. There was more, and worse, to come; and in the midst of it I saw Captain Bligh at the summit of his career.

There was a blinding glare of lightning, followed by a peal of thunder that seemed to shake the very bed of the deep. At that moment a great sea flung the launch into an all but vertical position. And there sat Bligh as on a throne, lifted high above us all, exalted in more than a physical sense.

"Bail, lads!" he shouted. "By God! We're beating the sea itself!"

## CHAPTER VIII

DURING the following night the severity of the weather relaxed; at dawn the sea was so calm that for the first time in fifteen days we found it unnecessary to bail. I had managed to sleep for two or three hours in a miserably cramped position. When I awoke, I lay without moving for some time, gazing in a kind of stupor at what I could see of the others in the boat.

Nelson lay beside me. His eyes were half opened, and with his parted lips, looking blue in the morning light, his hollow cheeks and sunken temples, I thought for a moment, until aware of some slight sign of breathing, that he must have died during the night. Captain Bligh sat in the stern, beside Elphinstone, who held the tiller. Although reduced, like the rest of us, to skin and bone, and clad, like ourselves, in sodden rags, there was nothing grotesque in his appearance. Wear what he might, he was still a noble figure, and suffering but added to the dignity and firmness of his bearing.

"Come up here in the sun, Mr. Ledward," he said. "It will make a new man of you."

I struggled to stand, but was unable to rise. Mr. Bligh helped me to the seat beside him. He made a sign to Hayward and Tinkler to help Nelson up. The botanist gave me a ghastly smile, designed to be cheerful.

"I feel better already," he remarked in a weak voice.

The captain now addressed all hands. "Luck's with us," he said; "we've left the bad weather behind. Off with your cloathes, before the sun gets too high, and give them a drying while you've the chance. The sun on our bare hides will be as good as a glass of grog. . . . Mr. Samuel, issue a teaspoonful of rum all round!" He glanced about at the people appraisingly, and then added: "We'll celebrate the good weather, lads! An ounce of pork with our bread and water!"

Our cloathing, reduced to rags by soaking in rain and wringing out in sea water, was hung along the gunwales to dry, and we now presented a strange and pitiful spectacle. Our skins, from long soaking in the rain, looked dead white, like the bellies of fish; some of the men were so reduced that I thought it a wonder they were able to stand. Nothing was more remarkable than their cheerfulness in bearing their afflictions. The warm sun, not yet high enough to scorch us, was exceedingly grateful, and our breakfast, enriched by a bit of pork, was a cheerful meal.

The morning was as beautiful as any I have known at sea. The breeze, at E.N.E., ruffled the sea to that shade of dark blue only to be seen between the tropics, and filled our sails bravely, without being boisterous enough to shower us with spray. The sky was clear save for the small, tufted, fairweather clouds on the verge of the horizon.

Mr. Fryer reached over the side and brought up a bit of coconut husk, on which the first green beginnings of marine growth appeared. He handed it to the captain, who examined it with interest.

"This has been removed by man," he remarked. "And look! It has not been overlong in the sea! We're close in with New Holland, not a doubt of it!"

Nelson took it shakily from Bligh's hand. "Aye, the nut was husked by Indians on a pointed stake. The growth of weed sprouts quickly in these warm seas."

"Look!" exclaimed Elphinstone, pointing off to starboard.

Our heads turned, and we saw a company of the small black terns called noddies, flying this way and that, low over the sea as they searched for fish.

"Now, by God!" said the captain. "The land is not far off!"

The birds swung away to the west and disappeared. They were of the size of pigeons, and their flight resembled a pigeon's flight.

"The worst of our voyage is over," said Bligh. "We shall be inside the reefs before the weather changes. You have borne yourselves like true English seamen so far; I am going to ask for further proofs of fortitude. I do not know certainly that there is a European settlement on Timor, and should there prove to be none, it would be imprudent to trust ourselves among the Indians there. For this reason, I think all hands will agree that we had best reduce our rations still further, in order to be able to reach Java if necessary. My task is to take you to England. To make sure of success, we must, from now on, do without our issue of bread for supper."

I glanced at the men covertly, knowing that some were so reduced that they might consider that Captain Bligh was cutting off the means of life itself. I was surprised and pleased, therefore, to see with what cheerfulness the captain's proposal was received.

"What's a twenty-fifth of an ounce of bread, sir?" asked old Purcell, grimly. "I've no complaint! I'd as soon have none as what we get. I reckon I could fetch Java with no bread at all!"

Bligh gave a short, harsh laugh. "I believe you might!" he said.

"Once inside the reefs," remarked Nelson, "we'll need little bread. There'll be shellfish, and no doubt we shall find various fruits and berries on the islets."

Tinkler smacked his lips, and grinned. Like the other midshipmen, he had withstood the hardships better than the grown men. Even Hallet seemed to have grown but little thinner.

I had violent pains in my stomach through this day and suffered much from tenesmus, as did nearly every man in the boat. Two or three were constantly at the gunwales, attempting what they were never able to perform, for not one of us, since leaving the *Bounty,* had had evacuation by stool. At nightfall I lay down in the bilges in a kind of stupor, till dawn. I was awakened by Bligh's voice.

"Don't move!" he said.

Then I heard the voice of Smith, from the bows: "I'll have him next time."

I opened my eyes and saw a small, black bird pass overhead, looking down at the boat. Nelson was already awake, and whispered weakly: "A noddy! Twice he's made as if to alight on the stem!"

"Hush!" said the captain, looking down at us.

The little tern passed overhead once more, set his wings, and slanted down in the direction of the bow. Next moment I heard a feeble shout go up from the people, and the sound of fluttering wings.

"Good lad!" said Bligh to the man forward. "Don't wring his neck!"

I managed to pull myself up to a sitting position while they were passing a wineglass to Smith, who held the bird while Hall cut its throat, allowing the blood to flow into the small glass, which was filled nearly to the brim.

"Now pluck him," said Bligh, while the glass was being handed aft. He motioned the midshipmen to help Nelson to sit up. "For you, Mr. Nelson," he went on, giving Tinkler the glassful of blood.

Nelson smiled and shook his head. "Lamb and Simpson need it more than I. Give it to them."

"I order you to drink the blood," said Bligh, with a smile that robbed the words of sternness. . . . "Mr. Hayward, hold the glass for Mr. Nelson while he drinks."

The botanist closed his eyes and took the blood with a slight grimace, raising a trembling hand to wipe his lips. The youngsters made him as comfortable as they could by propping his back against the thwart.

Fryer was at the tiller. The plucked noddy, no larger than a small pigeon, was now handed to Mr. Bligh, who laid it on the carpenter's chest, took a knife from his pocket, and divided the bird into eighteen portions. It was done with the utmost possible fairness, though a sixth portion of the breast was preferable to one of the feet, and I should have preferred the neck to the head and beak.

"Come aft, Mr. Peckover," said the captain. . . . "Face forward, Mr. Cole, and call out when Mr. Peckover gives the word."

The boatswain turned so that he was unable to see what went on. Peckover looked over the shares of raw bird and took up a choice bit of the breast.

"Who shall have this?" he called.

"Mr. Bligh!" replied Cole.

"No! No!" the captain interrupted. "There must be no precedence here, Mr. Cole: you will begin with anyone's name, at random. Should we catch another bird, the order must be changed. The purpose of this old custom is to be fair to all."

Peckover laid down the bit of breast and took up a wing. "Who shall have this?"

"Peter Lenkletter!"

The wing was handed to the quartermaster. When Bligh's turn came, he was so unfortunate as to get a foot with nothing on it but the web, and a shred or two of sinew where it had been disjointed, but he gnawed this miserable portion with every appearance of relish, and threw away nothing but the barest bones. The head and beak fell to me; and it amazes me, as I write, to recollect with what enjoyment I swallowed the eyes, and crunched the little skull between my teeth as I sucked out the raw brains. Small as the amount of nourishment was, I fancied that it brought me an immediate increase of strength. I was happy when Nelson got a rich, red morsel of the breast. He wished to share it with me, and when I refused, he lingered long over it. "The noddy eats well!" he said. "No pheasant at home ever seemed better flavoured!"

Lamb was one of those men who seem born to make the worst of every misfortune; he was unable to sit up, and had scarcely enough strength to complain of the pain in his bowels. When his turn came, he got the other foot; and Cole, who had just received a portion of breast, handed it to him. "Here," he said gruffly. "Ye need this more than me."

"Thankee, Mr. Cole, thankee!" said Lamb in a quavering voice as he stuffed the bit of flesh into his mouth.

The weather continued fair throughout the day, with a calm sea and a good sailing breeze at E.N.E. It was fortunate that we were not obliged to bail, for many of us could not have undertaken the task. Our log showed that we were making between four and four and a half knots. During the afternoon we passed bits of driftwood on which the barnacles had not yet gathered, and Elphinstone picked up a bamboo pole, such as the Indians use for fishing rods. It was slimy with the beginnings of marine growth, but could not have been more than two or three weeks in the sea. Purcell took the bamboo, dried and cleaned it, sawed off the ends square, and set to fitting and seizing a worn-out file into the large end, to make a spear for fish.

Toward evening, a lone booby appeared astern, and circled the boat for a long time, as if he desired to alight. We sat in suspense for ten minutes or more. The bird was not unlike our gannets at home, with a body as great as that of a large duck, and a five-foot spread of wings. I held my breath each time his shadow passed over the boat; I could hear Bligh's hearty, whispered curses when the bird came sailing in as if to alight and then slanted away.

At last young Tinkler whispered: "Let me try, sir — with the bamboo. I've seen the Indians at Otaheite take them so, by breaking their wings."

Bligh nodded. The bird had again turned away. The youngster crept forward, took the spear from Purcell, and stood on a thwart. The booby swung back toward the boat, while Tinkler waved his bamboo back and forth gently. It was strange, as the bird turned back toward the launch, to see how the moving spear aroused his curiosity. He came on with a rapid flap of wings, turning his head to see better, and passed over us very low, though still too high to be reached. Tinkler continued to move the rod gently.

This time the booby did not rise, but turned and headed back. The youngster held the spear with both hands, ready to strike. On came the bird, lower than ever, his wings held rigidly. Tinkler raised the rod to the full extent of his arms, and struck. The blow caught the booby where one of the wings joined the body, and with a grating cry he plunged into the sea.

"Hard up!" shouted Captain Bligh.

For the first time since leaving Tofoa, the boat was turned into the wind. Her sails fluttered as she luffed and lost steerageway; we made a board and came about on the other tack before we were able to pick up the bird.

"Mr. Tinkler," said the captain; "your fishing with the Indians was not wasted time!"

The launch shot up into the wind. Many eager hands went over the gunwale to pick up the wounded bird. Lebogue caught him and tossed him into the boat.

This time the blood was shared amongst Nelson, Lamb, and Simpson, who received a full wineglass each; and when the carcass — legs, head, bones, entrails, and flesh — was apportioned by the method of "Who shall have this?" our shares were of a size to make us feel that we were sitting down to a feast. Three flying fish, each about seven inches long, were found in the bird's stomach; they were fresh, and I was overjoyed when one fell to me. I had eaten the raw fish prepared by the Indians of Otaheite, and found it palatable when dipped in a sauce of sea water. I now opened my knife and scaled the flying fish gloatingly, before cutting it into morsels which I dropped into the salt water in my coconut shell. Nothing was wasted; I even ate the entrails, and quaffed off the bloody salt water in which the fish had soaked.

Though we sailed well, the weather remained serene that day and during the two days following. On Tuesday we passed fresh coconut husks and driftwood which appeared to have been in the water no more than a week. We had the good fortune to catch three boobies on this day; without their blood and raw flesh I am convinced that two or three of us must have succumbed. The sun was so hot at midday that I felt faint and sick. On Wednesday it was apparent to all that the land was close ahead. The clouds to the west were fixed, and there were innumerable birds about, though we could catch none. The heat of the sun again caused much suffering.

"Soak what rags you can spare in the sea, and make turbans of them!" said the captain, when he heard some of the people complaining of the heat. He laughed. "English seamen are hard to please! I'd rather be hot than cold any day, and dry than wet, for that matter! Wring out your turbans frequently. The cool water'll soon make you feel like fighting cocks. We should sight the reefs to-morrow, with this breeze."

The boatswain smacked his lips. "There'll be fine pickings, sir, once we find a passage. Cockles, and clams, and who knows what!"

"We'll find a way in, never fear. From our latitude, we should sight the land close to Providential Channel, through which Captain Cook sailed the *Endeavour*."

Nelson lay on the floor boards, listening to the talk as coolly as if dining with the captain aboard the *Bounty*.

"From what I have heard Captain Cook say," he remarked, "there must be many passages leading in to the sheltered water. No doubt we shall have several to choose from."

"So I believe," said Bligh.

At about nine o'clock that night, the captain lay down beside me to sleep.

"Keep a sharp lookout, Mr. Cole," he said; "we may be closer to the reefs than we suppose."

A swell from the east had set in, but the breeze was steady and light, and there were no whitecaps to wet us with spray. I lay half in a doze, half in a stupor, for several hours, listening to Bligh's quiet breathing. At last I fell asleep.

It must have been a little past midnight when I was awakened by the boatswain's voice: —

"Mr. Bligh! Breakers, sir!"

In an instant the captain was on his feet and wide awake. I heard a distant, long-drawn roar; and Bligh's abrupt command: "Hard alee!"

Three or four others were up by this time, ready for duty.

"Close-haul her!"

The moon was down, but the breakers were visible in the starlight as we clawed off.

"She lays well clear," remarked the captain. "By God! What a surf! Let it break! We'll find a way through when daylight comes!"

Many of us in the bottom of the boat were too weak or too indifferent even to raise our heads. Bligh noticed that I stirred.

"The reefs of New Holland, Mr. Ledward! We'll be sailing calm water soon, and stretching our legs ashore! You'll be feasting on shell-fish to-morrow, my word on it!"

I managed to turn on my side, and fell asleep once more, lulled by a new sound: the crisp slap of wavelets under the launch's bow as she stood off the land, close-hauled on the starboard tack.

At dawn, though the night had been warm and calm, most of the people were dreadfully weak. The birds we had eaten had merely prolonged our lives, without imparting any real strength. At the first signs of daylight, Mr. Bligh gave word to slack away to the west, but it was mid-morning before we again sighted the breakers. The wind had shifted to S.E. during the night.

Two teaspoons of rum were issued before we drank our water and ate our scant mouthful of bread. Heartened by the spirit and the prospect of smooth water and food, I struggled to a sitting position. Nelson was unable to sit up. Mr. Bligh had poured a few drops of rum between his lips, but he had shaken his head weakly when offered bread. I could see that the botanist, for all his courage, was at the end of his tether; unless we could secure fresh food for him, another day or two would see him dead. Lamb and Simpson were in a piteous state, and several others were nearly as bad.

Toward nine o'clock a line of tossing white stretched away as far as we could see to the north and south. The vast roll of the Pacific, broken by the coral barrier, thundered and spouted furiously.

Not more than a hundred yards beyond the first break of the seas, Bligh steered to the north, ordering Tinkler and Cole to trim the sheets.

"There, lads!" he said. "That should put heart in you! Never fear! We shall soon be inside!"

It was indeed a strange and heartening sight to men in our situation to see, just beyond the barrier of furious breakers, the placid waters of a vast lagoon, scarce ruffled by the gentle southeast breeze. And it seemed to me that I could perceive the outlines of land, blue and misty in the distance, far away across the calm water.

We had rounded a point of the reef and coasted for some distance in a northwesterly direction, when it fell calm for a few moments and the wind chopped around to east. Bligh bore up and ordered the sails trimmed once more, when we perceived that the reefs jutted far out to sea ahead of us.

"Forward with you, Mr. Cole!" said Bligh, and, when the boatswain stood in the bows with a hand on the foremast, "Can she lay clear?"

Cole gazed ahead intently for a moment before he replied: "No, sir! Can't ye point up a bit?"

Though close-hauled, the luff of the mainsail was shivering a little at the time. Bligh shrugged his shoulders. "Hard alee!" he ordered. "Let go the halyards and get her on the other tack!"

We had not sailed a quarter of a mile on the larboard tack, when it was evident that we were embayed. The east wind had caught us unaware, and we could not lay clear of the points to north or south. We turned the launch north once more.

"Who can pull an oar?" Bligh asked.

Lenkletter, Lebogue, and Elphinstone attempted to rise, and sank back ashamed of their weakness. Fryer, Purcell, Cole, and Peckover took their places at the thwarts. They pulled grimly and feebly; in spite of their courage, they had not sufficient strength to enable us to clear the point of reef about two miles ahead.

"Now, by God!" Bligh exclaimed. "We must weather the point or shoot the breakers — one of the two! . . . Mr. Tinkler! Are you strong enough to steer? Take the tiller and point up as close as you can!"

The captain set a tholepin on the lee side, ran out an oar, and began to pull strongly and steadily.

The prospect of shooting the breakers was enough to make the hardiest seaman pause. I could see, from time to time, the dark, jagged coral of the reef, revealed by a retreating sea. A moment later the same spot would be buried deep in foaming water, rushing over the reef with the thunder of a mighty cataract. It was incredible that our boat, small and deep laden, could live for an instant in such a turmoil. As I glanced ahead my heart sank. Then Tinkler shouted: —

"Mr. Bligh! There's a passage ahead, sir! Well this side of the point!"

Bligh shipped his oar and rose instantly. After a quick glance ahead, he turned to the men. "Cease pulling, lads," he said kindly. "Providence has been good to us. Yonder lies our channel; we can fetch it under sail."

## CHAPTER IX

THE passage was less than a mile ahead, and as we were now able to bear off a little and fill the sails, we were abreast of the opening in about a quarter of an hour. It proved to be a good two cable-lengths wide, and clear of rocks, with a small, barren islet just inside. We entered with a strong current setting to the westward; presently the roll of the sea was gone, and the launch sailed briskly over waters as calm as those of a lake at home.

I looked with longing at the islet close abreast of us. Though small and barren, it was at least dry land. Purcell's longing got the better of him.

"Let us go ashore, sir," he suggested, when it was apparent that the captain was going to sail on. "Cannot we land and stretch our legs?"

Bligh shook his head. "We should find nothing there. Look ahead, man!"

Two other islands, one of them high and wooded, were now visible at a distance of four or five leagues to the northwest; and close beyond, I could see the main of New Holland — valleys and high land, densely wooded in parts.

The afternoon was well advanced when we reached the first of the two islands — little more than a heap of stones. The larger island was about three miles in circuit, high, well wooded, with a sheltered, sandy bay on the northwest side. From this bay, the nearest point on the main was about four hundred yards distant. As there were no signs of

Indians in the vicinity, we beached the boat at once. For twenty-six days we had not set foot on land.

Mr. Bligh was the first to step on shore, staggering a little from weakness and the unaccustomed feel of firm ground. Fryer, Purcell, Peckover, Cole, and the midshipmen followed. All these could walk, though with difficulty. Hall, Smith, Lebogue and Samuel managed to get out of the boat, and either staggered or crawled to a place where the sand was soft and shaded by some small, bushy trees. The rest of us were in such a state as forced our stronger companions to help us ashore.

Mr. Bligh now uncovered, while those who were able knelt round him on the sand; and if ever men have offered heartfelt thanks to God for deliverance from the perils of the sea, surely we were those men.

After a brief silence, Bligh cleared his throat and turned to the master. "Mr. Fryer," he said, "take the strongest of the people and search for shellfish. There should be oysters or mussels on the rocks yonder. . . . Mr. Peckover, you will accompany me inland. . . . Mr. Cole, remain in charge of the boat. Take care that no fires are lit to-night."

Nelson and I had each had a small sup of wine, administered by the captain's hand. This, together with the prospect of something to eat and the delight of being once more on land, gave us fresh strength. We lay side by side. The sand was pleasantly warm, and a clump of dwarfish palms cast an agreeable shade.

We talked but little. We needed time to accustom ourselves to the fact that we were still alive, and to lie outstretched on dry land was a privilege so great that we could scarcely believe it ours.

"Can you realize, my dear Ledward, that our troubles are over?" Nelson asked, at length. "I have often heard Captain Cook speak of his passage inside the reefs of New Holland. Among these islands we shall find something to eat: shellfish, certainly, as well as berries and beans that are fit for food. There should be water on some of the larger islands."

"It is curious," I replied; "at present I feel not the slightest desire for food. I would not exchange the rest we are enjoying for the best meal that might be set before us."

"I feel the same," he said. "It is rest we need now above everything."

We fell silent again, and remained so for a long time. A flock of large birds, parrots of some sort, passed overhead with harsh cries and disappeared in the direction of the main. I saw Nelson's eyes roving this way and that as he studied the vegetation about us.

"These palms are new to me," he said; "yet I feel certain that their hearts, like those of the coconut palm, will provide excellent salad."

Presently the sun went down, and far along the beach we saw the foraging party returning. I knew how weary they must be, and felt ashamed of my own lack of strength.

"We're a useless pair, Nelson," I said. "Why were we not given stronger bodies?"

"Never fear," he replied. "We'll soon be taking our share of labour. I feel greatly refreshed already."

The captain and Peckover had their hats partly filled with fruits of two sorts.

"Have a look at these, Mr. Nelson," said Bligh. "By God! We've found little for the length of the walk. I observed that the birds eat freely of these berries. May we not do the same?"

"Aye, they look wholesome and good. I recognize their families, but the species are new to me. These palms, sir — cannot some of the people cut out a few of the hearts? We'll find them delicious, I'll be bound."

"There, Peckover!" Bligh exclaimed, turning to the gunner. "That shows the need for a botanist in every ship's company. We've walked miles for a few berries, and Mr. Nelson finds food for us within a dozen paces of the boat!"

"Aye," said Peckover. "I'd be pleased to have the knowledge inside Mr. Nelson's head. We've found good water, Mr. Ledward, and plenty of it. We can drink our fill while here."

Fryer and his men were coming up the beach — well laden, as I perceived at a glance.

"We shall feast to-night," he called. "We've found oysters galore! And larger and better tasting than those at home!"

"Come, lads," said Bligh; "let us turn to without waste of time."

I have never been averse to the pleasures of the table, and have had the good fortune to partake of many excellent meals; but never do I recollect having supped with more pleasure than on this night. Fryer had adopted the simple expedient of opening the oysters where they grew, without attempting to loose them from the rocks. Our copper pot held close to three gallons, and it was more than half full of oysters of an amazing size, soaking in their own juice. Some of the people had woven baskets of palm fronds, an art they had learned from the Indians of Otaheite, and in these they carried a supply of unopened oysters, prized off the rocks with a cutlass. The fruits were excellent, particularly one kind which resembled a gooseberry, but tasted sweeter; the palm hearts were like tender young cabbage, eaten raw.

I recommended Nelson, Lamb, and Simpson to eat of nothing but oysters that night, — a diet suitable to their distressed state, — and I myself refrained from anything else. The night was warm and clear. When we had supped, and drunk to our heart's content of the cool, sweet water of the island, I composed myself for sleep on the sand.

The firm ground seemed still to rock and heave. But it was wonderfully agreeable to stretch my legs out to their full extent; to lie on the warm sand and gaze up at the stars. I was sorry for some of the people, who had been ordered to anchor the launch in shallow water, near the sands, and to sleep aboard of her. Mr. Bligh thought it not unlikely that Indians might be about. Presently I closed my eyes to thank my Maker briefly for His goodness in preserving us; a few moments later I fell into a dreamless sleep.

I was awakened by the loud chattering of parrots, flying from the interior of our island, where they appeared to roost, to the main. Flock after flock passed overhead with a great clamour; the last of them had gone before the sun was up. My companions lay sleeping close by, in the attitudes they had assumed the night before. I saw the boatswain wade ashore from the launch and kneel on the wet sand while he repeated the Lord's Prayer in a rumbling voice, plainly audible where I lay. He rose, stripped off his shirt and ragged trousers, and plunged into the shallow bay, scrubbing his head and shoulders vigorously. Longing to follow his example, I managed to struggle to my feet, and was pleased to discover that I could walk.

Still splashing in the sea, Cole greeted me. "No need to ask how ye slept, Mr. Ledward! Ye look a new man!"

I felt one when I had bathed in the cool sea water and resumed my tattered garments, which a London ragpicker would have scorned to accept. The others were rising as I turned inland, walking with the uncertain gait of a year-old child.

Nelson managed to stand at the second attempt, but was forced to sink down again immediately, doubled up with a sharp pain in his stomach. "I've a mind to ask you to physic me," he said with a wry smile.

I shook my head. "It would be imprudent in our state of weakness. Our pain and tenesmus are due to the emptiness of our bowels."

Bligh joined us at that moment. "Sound advice, sir," he said; "if a layman may express an opinion. To physic men in our state would but weaken us still more. I have suffered from the same violent pains. We'll be quit of them once our bellies are filled." He turned to hail the boatswain. "Come ashore, Mr. Cole, the lot of you."

Fryer was sent out with a party to get oysters, and two men dispatched inland for fruit. Cole and Purcell were set to putting the boat in order, in case we should find savages about. I was among four or five whom the captain ordered to rest throughout the morning. Nelson lay beside me in the shade.

"What the devil is Cole up to?" he remarked.

The boatswain was wading about the launch, moving in circles and staring down into the water. After some time he came ashore with a long face. Bligh was writing in his journal, and glanced up as Cole addressed him.

"The lower gudgeon of the rudder's gone, sir," he said. "It must have dropped off as we was entering the bay. It's not on the sand — that I'll vouch for."

Bligh closed his journal with a snap, and stood up. "Unship the rudder. Are you sure it's nowhere under the boat?"

"I've made certain of that, sir."

"Then lend Mr. Purcell a hand." He turned to Nelson. "We've Providence to thank that this did not happen a few days ago! I had grummets fixed on either side of the transom, as you observed, in case we were forced to steer with the oars; but in severe weather it would have been next to impossible to keep afloat with them. We should have broached-to, almost certainly."

Presently the carpenter brought the rudder ashore.

"It's been under heavy strains, sir," he explained. "The screws holding the gudgeon to the sternpost must have loosened in the wood."

"Well, what can be done?"

Purcell held out a large staple. "I found this under the floor boards. It will serve."

"Do your best, and see that it is stoutly set. We must beach the boat and examine her bottom to-day."

The captain took leave of us and wandered inland to search for fruit. Purcell hammered at his staple on a rock, fitting its curve to the pintle of the rudder. I recommended the invalids to drink frequently of water, taking as much as they could hold, and set them an example by doing the same.

"It's grub I need, not water!" said Lamb, making a wry face as I handed him a coconut-shellful.

"You'll have plenty of that shortly, my lad!" I said.

Simpson crawled off for another useless attempt to perform the impossible. "Poor devil!" Nelson said. "I'll soon be doing the same."

A little before noon the oyster gatherers returned with a bountiful supply. Nelson and I had arranged a hearth of stones, and found strength to gather a quantity of firewood. Bligh was soon on hand to kindle the fire with his magnifying glass and supervise the making of the stew — our first taste of hot food since leaving Tofoa, nearly a month before. The people were gathered in a circle about our fireplace, staring at the pot like a pack of wolves.

When all the oysters had been opened, we found that they and their liquor filled the pot to within four inches of the brim. Captain Bligh ordered Samuel to weigh out a twenty-fifth of a pound of bread for each man, making three quarters of a pound in all. A pound of fat pork was now cut up very fine and thrown into the stew, already beginning to bubble over a brisk fire. I was sitting with Nelson on the lee side, inhaling savoury whiffs of steam that drifted past.

"Let us add a quart of sea water," said the master to Mr. Bligh. "It will serve as salt, and make the stew go further."

"No, Mr. Fryer. What with oysters and the pork, it will be salty enough as it is."

"We could add fresh water to make more of it. There'll not be enough to go round."

"Not enough, with a full pint each?" said Bligh impatiently. "If it will do for me, it will do for yourself, sir."

Fryer said no more.

Presently the stew was ready. It was served out in Bligh's own coconut shell, known to hold exactly a pint. My own shell held double that, and when I had been served I wished with the master that the amount might have been more. The crumbled bits of bread had boiled down to mingle with the liquor from the oysters and the fat pork, forming a sauce an alderman might not have despised. I tasted a small quantity with a little spoon I had whittled out of a bit of driftwood.

"Damme, sir!" said Bligh, turning to Nelson. "Many's the time I've eaten worse than this on His Majesty's ships."

"And many a better meal you have enjoyed less, I dare say," Nelson replied.

"I've served on ships," said Fryer, "where we'd not such a meal for six months together."

"Aye," said the captain. "Hunger's the only sauce. It was damn near worth starving for a month to have such a relish for victuals. . . . Do you mind what day it is, Mr. Nelson?"

"What day? I could not be sure of telling you within a week."

"It is Friday, the twenty-ninth of May: the anniversary of the Restoration of King Charles the Second. We shall call this Restoration Island, in his memory. The name will serve in a double sense. *We* have been restored, God knows!"

Employing some self-restraint, I managed to eat my share so as to take a full half hour to finish it. Fryer, I observed, gulped his down in an instant, and held out his shell for the few spoonfuls left over for every man. Purcell and Lenkletter played the gluttons as well, and I was forced to warn Simpson, still in a very weak state, against swallowing his food too fast.

Nelson and I felt so much revived after dinner that we set out for a tottering walk into the island. We found it rocky, with a barren soil, supporting a growth of stunted trees. There were many of the small palms whose hearts we had found good to eat; I recognized the *purau,* of Otaheite, in a stunted form; and there were other trees which Nelson informed me resembled the poisonous manchineel of the West Indies. About the summit of the island, not above one hundred and fifty feet in height, great numbers of parrots and large pigeons were feeding on the berries here growing in abundance, but though we tried to knock them down with stones, the birds were as hard to approach as partridges in England. We gathered a quantity of the better sort of berries, which eat very well indeed, and as we wandered toward the eastern side of the island we came upon two tumbled-down huts of the Indians. These were ruder than any Indian habitations I had seen. Nelson stooped over the blackened stones of a fireplace to take up a roughly fashioned spear, with the sharp end hardened in the fire.

At that moment I perceived in the sand the tracks of some large animal, unlike the footprints of any beast known to me. Nelson examined the tracks with interest.

"I think I can name the beast," he said: "Mr. Gore, Captain Cook's lieutenant, shot one at Endeavour River, south of here. It was as great as a man, mouse-coloured, and ran hopping on its hind legs. The Indians called it *kanguroo*."

"How could it have come here?" I asked. "Do they swim?"

"That I don't know. Perhaps; or it may be that the Indians stock these islands with young ones, where they may be easily caught when required."

"Is the flesh fit for food?"

"Cook thought it was good as the best mutton. The beasts are said to be timid, and to run faster than a horse."

As we approached the rocky shore on the east side of the island, Nelson chose himself a long, wide palm frond, and sat down, Indian fashion, to plait a basket. I admired the deftness of his fingers as they wove the leaflets swiftly this way and that; in ten minutes he had completed a stout basket, handle and all, fit to hold a full bushel.

"Now for the shellfish!" he remarked, as he rose shakily to his feet. "Gad, Ledward! I feel a new man to-day!"

I set to work with the cutlass, opening the oysters growing here and there on the rocks below highwater mark; with his Indian spear, Nelson waded among the pools. I soon had three or four dozen oysters in the basket. Nelson added two large cockles of the Tridacna kind to our bag: the pair of them a meal for a man. It was mid-afternoon when we took up our burdens and trudged back to the encampment, halting frequently to rest.

Our stew that afternoon was a noble one — oysters, cockles, and chopped-up heart of palm. This latter was added at Nelson's suggestion, and was the cause of some murmuring.

"Are we to have no bread, sir?" asked the carpenter sourly.

"No," replied Captain Bligh; "we shall save our bread. Mr. Nelson says these palm hearts are as good cooked as raw."

Fryer stood by with a gloomy face. "It will ruin the stew," he said. "The bread was the making of it at dinner time."

"Aye, sir," put in Purcell, "give us but half the full amount. It'll be poor stuff without the bread."

Bligh turned away impatiently. "Damn it, *no!*" he replied. "You're grown queasy as young ladies on the island here! Wait till you taste the stew, if you must complain."

Our meal was soon pronounced done, and each man received a full pint and a half. The sauce seemed to me even better than that we had eaten at dinner, and once the men tasted it all murmuring ceased.

At sunset, when it fell dead calm, we observed several columns of smoke at a distance of two or three miles on the main. Bligh ordered some of the people to pass the night in the boat, and a watch was kept on shore.

"We must be on our guard," he said; "though I believe there is small danger of the Indians visiting us to-night. Our fire made no smoke, and they cannot have seen the boat."

As darkness came on, Bligh went down to the beach, where Cole was on watch, and remained for a long time seated on the sand chatting with him, while the rest of us retired to our sleeping places.

Nelson was asleep almost at once; but returning strength had left me wakeful, and I lay for a long time gazing at the starlit sky. Purcell and the master lay close by, conversing in low tones. Perhaps they thought me asleep; in any event, I could not avoid overhearing what they said. After a time, I perceived that their talk had turned to the mutiny.

"Ungrateful?" the carpenter was saying. "Damn my eyes! What had they to be grateful for? Christian was treated worse than a dog half the time. I excuse none of 'em, mind! I'd be pleased to see every man of the lot swinging at a yardarm; but I'll say this: If ever a captain deserved to lose his ship, ours did."

"If that's your feeling, why didn't you join with Christian?" said Fryer.

"It's no love for Captain Bligh that kept me from it, I'll promise you that," said Purcell. "He's himself to thank for the mutiny, and so I'll say if we've the luck to get home."

"He has his faults," said Fryer. "He trusts none of his officers to perform their duties, but must have a hand in everything. But if you think him a Tartar, you should sail with some of the captains I've served under. There was old Sandy Evans! The last topman off the yard got half a dozen with a colt. He called it 'encouraging' them."

"I'd rather be flogged than cursed before my own men," growled Purcell. "You mind what he called me before my mates in Adventure Bay? And what he said to Christian, with all the people about, the day before they seized the ship?"

"He's overfree with his tongue," admitted Fryer. "But what captain is not? The Navy's no place for thin skins. Hard words and floggings are what seamen understand." He paused for a moment. "I've served under easier captains," he added. "He's a hard man to please. But where would we be without him now? Tell me that. Whom would you wish in his place in the launch?"

"I'm not saying he lacks his good points," the carpenter admitted grudgingly.

When I fell asleep at last, their voices were still murmuring on. I awoke feeling better than for many days past. Nelson was already up, and a party was setting out down the beach in search of new beds of oysters. Bligh was speaking to Purcell.

"I saw some good *purau* trees near the summit of the island," he said. "Take your axe and see if you can find us a pair of spare yards."

He turned to the boatswain. "Mr. Cole, see that the casks are all filled and placed in the boat."

I went off oystering with Nelson, both of us able to walk pretty well by now. When we returned, preparations for dinner were under way. Mr. Bligh held in his hand the last of our pork, a piece of about two pounds' weight, well streaked with lean. He handed it to Hall, motioning him to cut it up for the pot.

"We'll sail with full bellies," he remarked. "Since some villain robbed his mates of their pork, we'll put it out of his power to play that scurvy trick again."

He looked hard at Lamb as he spoke, and it seemed to me that the man hung his head with some slight expression of guilt.

With plenty of oysters, about a couple of ounces of pork for each man, and the usual ration of bread, we dined sumptuously; had we had a little pepper to season it, the stew would have been pronounced excellent anywhere. We had scarce finished eating when the captain spoke:—

"We shall set sail about two hours before sunset. With this moon coming on, we can avoid the danger of canoes by traveling as much as possible by night. Mr. Nelson and I will remain to guard the launch; the rest of you gather oysters for a sea store."

The master had just stretched out for a siesta after his dinner, and he sat up with a gloomy expression at Bligh's words.

"Can we not rest this afternoon, sir?" he asked. "None of us has his full strength as yet, and surely we shall find oysters at every landing place."

"Aye," growled Purcell. "You promised us we should touch at many islands before clearing Endeavour Straits."

"I did," said the captain; "but what assurance have you that we shall find oysters on them? We *know* that there are plenty here." He flushed, controlling his temper with some difficulty. "We've naught but bread now, and little enough of that. Fetch what oysters you wish, or none at all! I'm tired of your damned complaints!" He turned his back and walked away as if fearing to lose control of himself. Shamed into acquiescence, Fryer and the carpenter now joined the others setting out along the shore.

The captain's clerk was strolling southward with a basket on his arm, and I joined him, since Nelson was to remain with the boat.

"You know your Bible, Mr. Ledward," remarked Samuel, when we were out of earshot of the others. "Do you recollect the passage concerning Jeshurun who waxed fat, and kicked?"

"Aye; and it falls pat on Restoration Island!"

Samuel smiled. "Where would they be, where would we all be, without Captain Bligh? Yet they must murmur the moment their bellies are full! I've no patience with such men."

"Nor I." Glancing at the clerk's formerly plump body, now reduced to little more than skin and bones, and clad in rags, I could not repress a smile.

"Though we kick," I said, "none of us could be accused of waxing fat!"

Toward four o'clock we returned with what shellfish we had been able to secure, and found all in readiness to sail. We took our places in the launch, the grapnel was weighed, and we were getting sail on her, when about a score of Indians appeared on the opposite shore of the main, shouting loudly at us. The heads of many others were discernible above the ridge behind them; but, to our great content, they seemed to be unprovided with canoes. Owing to this fortunate circumstance, we were able to pass pretty close to them, with a fresh breeze at E.S.E. They carried long, slender lances in their right hands, and in their left hands some sort of weapon or implement of an oval shape and about two feet long.

These Indians were unlike any we had seen in the South Sea; they were coal black, tall, and remarkably thin, with long, skinny legs. Two of the men stood leaning on their spears, with one knee bent, and the sole of the foot pressed against the inside of the other thigh — an attitude comical as it was uncouth. Though too far off to distinguish their features clearly, they seemed to me quite as ugly as the natives of Van Diemen's Land.

The breeze freshened as we drew out of the lee, and the launch footed it briskly to the north, while the hallooing of savages grew fainter and finally died away.

## CHAPTER X

RESTORATION ISLAND had proved well worthy of its name. It might as truthfully have been called Preservation Island, for there is no doubt whatever that, had we been delayed a day or two longer in reaching it, several of our number must have succumbed. Nelson and I would have been two of these; we were drawing upon our last reserves of strength when we passed through the channel into the great lagoons of New Holland. But, after three days of rest and a sufficiency of food, we were wonderfully restored; so much so, that we could take interest and pleasure in the scenes before us.

Ours was, in fact, a great privilege, and I was grateful for the fact that I had recovered strength enough to recognize it. We were coasting the shores of a mighty continent, through waters and among islands all but unknown to white men. Indeed, in so far as I knew, Captain Cook alone had passed this way before us. On our left lay the main, stretching away, we knew not how many hundreds or thousands of leagues, and wrapped in a silence that seemed to have lain there since the beginning of time — a deep, all-pervading stillness like that of mid-ocean on a calm day. Not one of us, I think, but felt the vastness of this presence.

We had in view a low, barren-looking coast that appeared a complete solitude, uninhabited and uninhabitable; and yet we knew, from our experience of the day before, that a few bands of savages, at least, must find sustenance there. We saw more of them before we had sailed many miles.

A number of small islands were in sight to the northeast. Captain Bligh directed our course between them and the main. The strait was no more than a mile wide, and as we were passing through it, a small party of savages like those we had already seen came down to the foreshore on our left hand and stood regarding us.

"Now," said Bligh, "I mean to have a closer view of those fellows."

Accordingly, we steered inshore and laid the boat as close as was prudent to the rocks. Meanwhile, the savages, observing our intent, had run away to a distance of about two hundred yards.

Bligh shouted: "Come aboard, there!" and stood in the stern sheets waving a shirt aloft; but not a foot would they stir from their places. They were without a vestige of cloathing, and their bodies looked as black as ink in the clear morning light, against a background of sand and naked rocks. Their timidity was encouraging in our unarmed and weakened condition; we felt that we had little to fear from any small bands of these people.

"They'll never come," said Nelson, after we had lain at our oars shouting and beckoning to them. "It's a pity, too, for they seem harmless enough, and they must have ways of getting food that would be most valuable to us could we learn what they are."

"No, we may as well proceed," said Bligh. "I should like to see them near at hand. Sir Joseph Banks is most anxious to have a description of the savages of New Holland. He shall have to be content with the little I can tell him of their general appearance."

"That is a curious-looking instrument they carry in their left hands," I observed. "What can its purpose be?"

"In my opinion, it is some sort of a spear thrower," said Nelson. "One thing you can tell Sir Joseph," he added: "There are probably no savages in all the South Sea more ugly and uncouth than these. What a contrast they make to the Indians of Otaheite!"

We again hoisted sail, and steered for an island in view before us and about four miles distant from the main. This we reached in about an hour's time. The shore was rocky, but the water smooth. We made a landing without difficulty, and secured our boat in a little basin, where it rode in complete safety. We brought everything ashore, that the boat might be thoroughly cleaned and dried — putting our water vessels and the carpenter's chest, with its precious supply of bread, in the shelter of some overhanging rocks.

When we had scrubbed out the boat, Mr. Bligh told off two parties to go in search of shellfish. Purcell was placed in charge of one of these; the other members were Tinkler, Samuel, Smith, and Hall. These men stood waiting for the carpenter, who had seated himself on the beach with the air of one who meant to pass the day there. The other party, in Peckover's charge, had already gone southward along the beach. Captain Bligh, who had accompanied them a little distance, now returned to where the boat lay.

"Come, Mr. Purcell," he said brusquely; "set out at once with your men. We have no time to lose here."

The carpenter remained seated. "I've done more than my share of work," he said, in a surly voice. "You can send someone else with this party."

Bligh glared down at him. "Do you hear me?" he said. "Get you gone, and quickly!"

The carpenter made no motion to obey. "I'm as good a man as yourself," he replied; "and I'll stay where I am."

Nelson, the master, and myself, besides the members of the foraging party, were the witnesses of this scene. I had long expected something of the sort to happen, and had only wondered that an open break between Captain Bligh and the carpenter had not come before this time. There was a deep and natural antagonism between the two men; they were too much alike in character ever to have been anything but enemies.

Bligh strode across the beach to where the carpenter's chest had been placed, with two of the cutlasses lying upon it. Seizing the weapons, he returned to where Purcell sat and thrust one of them into his hand.

"Now," he said. "Stand up and defend yourself. Stand up, I say! If you are as good a man as myself, you shall prove it, here and now!"

There was no doubt of the seriousness of Bligh's intent. Despite the gravity of the situation, as I think of it now, there was something faintly comic in it as well. In the mind's eye I have the scene clearly in mind: The sandy spit of beach, backed by the naked rocks; the little group of spectators, their cloathes hanging in rags on their emaciated bodies, looking on at these two, who, despite starvation and hardships incredible, still had fight in them. At least, so I thought at first; but the carpenter quickly showed that his relish for it was faint indeed. He rose, holding his cutlass slackly, and gazed at Bligh with a frightened expression.

"Stand back, you others!" said Bligh. "Up with your weapon, you mutinous villain! I'll soon prove whether you are a man or not!"

He advanced resolutely toward the carpenter, who backed away at his approach.

"Fight, damn you!" Bligh roared. "Defend yourself or I'll cut you down as you stand!"

Purcell, although a larger man than Bligh, had little of the latter's inner fire and strength. Bligh was thoroughly roused; and had the carpenter tried to make good his boast, one or the other of them would, I am convinced, have been killed — and I have little doubt as to which would have been the victim. But Purcell made a complete about-face, and ran from his pursuer, who halted and gazed after him, breathing rapidly.

"Come back, Mr. Purcell!" he cried. "You have even less spirit than I gave you credit for! Come here, sir! . . . Now then; do you retract what you have said?"

"Yes, sir," Purcell replied.

"Very well," said Bligh. "Let me have no more of your insolence in the future. Get about your work."

It is to Bligh's credit that he never afterwards mentioned this incident. As for the carpenter, he was willing enough to have it forever put out of mind. He had, I believe, flattered himself that he was a match for his commander. From this time on, the relations of the two men were on a better footing.

The island upon which we had landed was of a considerable height. While the foraging parties were out, Mr. Bligh, Nelson, and myself walked inland to the highest part of it for a better view of our surroundings; but we could see little more of the main than appeared from below. In our weakened condition the climb had been a fatiguing one, and we took shelter in the shade of a great rock to recover our breath. The lagoons were miracles of vivid colouring in the clear morning light. We could plainly see the tiny figures of the foraging parties as they made their way slowly along the shallows, searching for shellfish. Almost directly below us was the launch, looking smaller than a child's toy in the bight where she lay.

"There she lies," said Bligh, gazing fondly at the tiny craft. "I love every strake of planking, every nail in her. Mr. Nelson, could you have believed that she could have carried eighteen men such a voyage as we have come? Could you, Mr. Ledward?"

"I was thinking of just that," Nelson replied. "We have been under God's guidance. It must have been so."

"Aye," said Bligh, nodding gravely. "But God expected us to play our part. We should not have had His help, otherwise."

"What distance have we come, in all, sir?" I asked.

"I have this morning reckoned it up," said Bligh. "I think I am not far out in saying that we have sailed, from Tofoa to the passage within the reefs of New Holland, a distance of two thousand, three hundred and ninety miles."

"God be thanked that we have so much of the voyage behind us," said Nelson, fervently. "This leaves us with one thousand miles ahead, does it not?"

"More than that," Bligh replied. "As nearly as I can recollect, we have between one hundred and fifty and two hundred miles to coast New Holland before we reach Endeavour Straits; but once again in the open sea, we shall have no more than three hundred leagues between us and Timor."

Nelson turned to me. "Ledward, how long can a man go, in the ordinary course of nature, without passing stool?"

"Ten days is a long period under more normal circumstances," I replied, "but our situation is anything but a usual one. We have had so little food that our bodies seem to have absorbed the whole of it."

"So I think," said Bligh. "There could have been nothing in our bowels until within a day or two past. You look another man, Mr. Nelson, now that you have had rest and better food. We shall all have time to gain new strength before we push off for Timor."

"I mean to survive," Nelson replied, smiling faintly; "if only to defeat the purpose of the wretches who condemned us to this misery."

"Spoken like a man, sir," said Bligh. A cold glint came into his eyes and his lips were set in a thin line. "By God! I could sail the launch to England, if necessary, with nothing but water in my belly, for the sake of bringing them to justice!"

He rose to his feet and strode back and forth across the little flat-topped eminence where we rested; then he halted before us. Pale, hollow-eyed, his shreds of cloathing hanging loosely upon his bones, he yet had within him a fund of energy that amazed me. Mention of the mutineers had stirred him as the call of a trumpet stirs an old cavalry horse. He laughed in his harsh mirthless way. "They flatter themselves that they have seen the last of me," he said; "the God-damned inhuman, black-hearted bastards! But Divine Providence sees them and will help me to track them down!"

Nelson threw a quick, quizzical glance in my direction. Bligh was quite unconscious of the mixture of blasphemy and reverence in his remark.

"Shall you endeavour to search for them yourself?" Nelson asked.

"Endeavour? By God, I shall more than endeavour! I shall sit on the doorstep at the Admiralty day and night until they give me command of the ship that is to search them out and bring them to justice. I have friends at home who will make my interest their own. I shall not draw a quiet breath until I am outward bound, on their trail."

"Your family may take a different view of the matter, sir," I said. "If we are fortunate enough to reach England, Mrs. Bligh will not wish to let you go so soon again."

"You know me little, Mr. Ledward, if you think I shall dawdle at home with those villains unhung. Not a day shall I spend there if I have my way. As for Mrs. Bligh, she is no ordinary woman. She will be the first to bid me Godspeed. . . . Let us go down," he added, after a moment of silence. "I grudge every moment that we are not proceeding on our way."

Nelson and I rose to follow him. Bligh stood looking toward a small sandy cay that could be seen at a considerable distance to the northward, and several miles farther from the main than the island upon which we then were.

"We shall go there for the night," he said. "It will be a safer resting place. The savages yonder must have seen us land here. They seem harmless enough; and yet, without weapons to defend ourselves, I mean to take no risks."

We went down by another way, to the northern side of the island, stopping now and then to examine the shrubs and stunted trees that grew out of the sand and among clefts in the rocks. We found nothing in the way of food except wild beans, which we gathered in a handkerchief.

"You are sure these are edible, Mr. Nelson?" Bligh asked.

"Yes, there is not the slightest danger," Nelson replied. "They are dolichos. The flavour is not all that might be wished, but the bean is a nourishing food. It is of the genus of the kidney bean to which the Indian gram belongs."

"Good," said Bligh. "Let us hope that the others have collected some as well as ourselves."

Upon reaching the beach, we discovered an old canoe lying bottom up and half buried in the sand. We dug away around it, but our combined strength was not sufficient to budge it, to say nothing of turning it over. It was about thirty feet long, with a sharp, projecting bow, rudely carved in the resemblance of a fish's head. We estimated that it would hold about twenty men.

"Here is proof enough," said Bligh, "that the New Hollanders are not wholly landlubbers. In view of this find, I am all the more willing to proceed farther from the main. We must keep a sharp lookout for these fellows. In our weakened condition they would find us an easy prey."

We were now joined by Purcell and his party of foragers, carrying our copper pot on a pole between them. They had had splendid luck — the pot was more than half full of fine, fat clams and oysters. Bligh put the carpenter at ease by greeting him in his usual manner.

"It couldn't be better, Mr. Purcell," he said. "Every man shall have a bellyful to-day. A stew of these, mixed with dolicho beans — many a ship's company will fare worse than ourselves this day."

I was pleased to find a healthy hunger gnawing at my stomach; nothing could have looked more succulent than the sea food, and every man of us was eager to be at the camp with the pot set over a good fire. It was high noon when we joined the others. Peckover's party had just come in with a supply of clams and oysters almost equal in amount to that in the pot. They had also found, on the south side of the island, an abundance of fresh water in hollows of the rocks — more than enough to fill our vessels. Every circumstance favoured us. The sun shone in a cloudless sky, so that Captain Bligh was able, with his magnifying glass, to kindle a fire at once. The oysters and clams were now dumped into the pot, together with a quart and a half of dolicho beans. The requisite amount of water was added, and to make our stew yet more tasty, each man's usual amount of bread was added to it. Smith and Hall, our cooks, had whittled out long wooden spoons with which they stirred the stew as it came to a boil, sending up a savoury steam that made the walls of our empty bellies quiver with anticipation. When the stew had cooked for a good twenty minutes, — the time had seemed hours to most of us, — the pot was set off the fire; and we gathered round with our half-coconut shells, while the cooks ladled into each man's shell all that it could hold of clams, oysters, beans, and delicious broth; and when all had been served, there was still enough in the pot for a half pint more, all round. The beans were not so tasty as we had hoped, but we made a small matter of that.

After our meal we rested for an hour in the shade of the rocks. I had just fallen into a refreshing sleep when Mr. Bligh aroused me. "Sorry to disturb you, Mr. Ledward," he said, "but we must push on. We are too close to the main here, and I have no desire for any night visits from the savages."

It was then about mid-afternoon. With a light breeze, we directed our course to a group of sandy cays which lay about five leagues off the continental shore. Darkness had fallen before we reached them and, as we could find no suitable landing place, we came to a grapnel and remained in the launch until dawn. All through the night we heard the cries of innumerable sea fowl, and daylight showed us that one of the cays was a place of resort for birds of the noddy kind. We found that we were on the westernmost of four small islands, surrounded by a reef of rocks, and connected with sand banks whose surface was barely above high tide. Within them lay a mirrorlike lagoon with a small passage, into which we brought the launch.

This place, so far from the main, seemed designed by nature as a refuge for men in our condition. Captain Bligh named it "Lagoon Island," and gladdened our hearts by informing us that he proposed to spend the day and the following night here. Unfortunately, the cays were little more than heaps of rock and sand, covered with coarse grass and a sparse growth of bush and stunted trees; but there were enough of these latter to protect us from the heat of the sun.

Our forces were divided so that some could rest while others searched for food. The lagoon abounded in fish; but try as we would, we could catch none. This was a great trial; after repeated unsuccessful efforts, we were forced to fall back upon oysters and clams and the one vegetable which these islands afforded — dolicho beans. Even the shellfish were not abundant here, and the party sent in search of them returned at about ten in the morning with a very small number, so that our dinner this day did little more than aggravate our hunger. During the long voyage from Tofoa we had been so cold and miserable the greater part of the time that the pangs of hunger were kept in check. Furthermore, the constant peril of the sea had prevented us from dwelling upon the thought of food. The case was altered now, and we thought of little else.

After our midday dinner, Elpinstone, with a party of four, was sent to the islet adjoining that at which we lay, to search for sea fowl and their eggs, for we had observed that the birds congregated at that place. The rest of us were glad enough to take our rest, crawling into the shade of bushes and overhanging rocks.

On this afternoon I enjoyed a long and undisturbed sleep which greatly refreshed me; indeed, I did not waken until near sundown, just as Mr. Elphinstone's party was returning. They came in all but empty-handed, having gotten no birds and only three eggs. This was, evidently, not the nesting season: they had found the islet practically deserted; the birds were away fishing for themselves, and the few they had seen were too wary to be caught.

"Nevertheless, we must try again," said Bligh. "They will soon be coming home with full gullets. We can be sure of catching them at night, and there will be a good light from the moon to hunt by. . . . Mr. Cole, you shall try this time. Go warily, mind! Let the birds settle for the night before you go amongst them."

"Aye, sir, we'll see to that," said Cole. Samuel, Tinkler, Lamb, and myself were told off to make up his party; and, having provided ourselves with sticks, we set out for the bird island.

It was a beautiful evening, cool and fresh now that the sun had set. There was not a breath of air stirring, and the surface of the lagoons glowed with the colours of the western sky. Our way led over a causeway of hard-packed sand, laid over the coral reef. It was scarcely a dozen paces across, and curved in a wide arc across a shallow sea filled with mushroom coral that rose to within a few feet of the surface. The bar connecting the islands was about two miles long. Tinkler and Lamb were soon far ahead; the boatswain, Samuel, and I followed at a more leisurely pace, stopping to examine the rock pools along the reef for clams and oysters, though we found nothing save a few snails, scarcely larger than the end of one's thumb. Nevertheless, we gathered them into the bread bag we had brought to carry back the birds.

Whilst in Mr. Bligh's company we had been careful to make no reference to the mutiny. On one occasion, I remember, young Tinkler had ventured to speak in defense of two of the midshipmen who had been left behind on the *Bounty;* but Bligh had silenced him in such a manner that no one else was tempted to bring up the subject in his presence. But now, the three of us, freed from restraint, fell naturally into talk of the seizure of the ship and of what had led up to it.

"What puzzles me," said Cole, "is that Mr. Christian could have made his plan without any of us getting wind of it."

"It was a sudden resolve on his part, I am fairly certain of that," I replied.

"That's my opinion," said Samuel. "No doubt the villain had plotted it long before, but he bided his time before opening his mind to the others."

Cole nodded. "Aye, it must have been so," he said. "What could have brought him to such a mad act, Mr. Ledward? Can you reason it out? He'd no better friend than Captain Bligh, and he must have known it in his heart." He shook his head, wonderingly. "I'd a liking for Mr. Christian," he added.

Samuel stopped short and gazed at the boatswain in a horrified manner.

" 'Liking,' Mr. Cole?" he exclaimed.

"Aye," said Cole. "He was hot-tempered and anything but easy under Mr. Bligh's correction; but I never doubted him a gentleman and a loyal officer."

"His Majesty can well spare gentlemen of Christian's kidney from his service," I replied. "You're too lenient in your judgments, Mr. Cole. Whatever else may be said of him, Christian is an intelligent man. He must have known that he was condemning us to all but certain death."

"Begging your pardon, Mr. Ledward, I don't believe he did know it. He must have been out of his mind. . . . This I will say: Mr. Christian will never again know peace. He'll have us on his conscience till the day of his death."

"He'll hang," said Samuel, confidently. "Hide where he may, Captain Bligh will find him and bring him to justice."

"Let that be as it will, Mr. Samuel," said Cole. "I'll warrant he's been punished enough as it is."

"Do you think God could forgive him, Mr. Cole?" I asked, out of curiosity more than for any other reason.

"He could, sir. There's no crime so black that God cannot forgive it if a man truly repents."

"Have *you* forgiven him?" I then asked.

He was silent for a moment as he pondered this question. Then, "No, sir," he replied, grimly. "He shall never have my forgiveness for the wrong he has done Captain Bligh."

We were now close to the bird island. Tinkler alone was awaiting us there.

"Where's Lamb, Mr. Tinkler?" Cole asked. "I told both of you to wait for us."

"He was here a moment ago. I ordered him to help me look for clams while we waited. I'm damned if I know where he's got to."

"It's your *place* to know, Mr. Tinkler," said Samuel shortly. "Captain Bligh shall hear of this if anything goes wrong."

"Now don't be a telltale, Samuel, for God's sake," said Tinkler anxiously. "What did you expect me to do — throw him down and sit on his head? He can't have gone far."

"The man's a fool," said Samuel. "He's not to be trusted out of sight."

"Aye," said Cole, "if there's a wrong way of doing a thing, Lamb will find his way to it. We may as well wait here. There's time enough."

No Lamb appeared, for all our waiting. The afterglow faded from the sky, and the moon, nearing the full, shone with increasing splendour, paling all but the brightest of the stars. The birds must have sensed the presence of enemies, for they were long in settling. They circled in thousands over the island, filling the air with their grating cries, but at last the deafening clamour died away and we ventured to proceed on our expedition. The island was, roughly, a mile long and about half as wide, and the birds appeared to have congregated for the night on the farthest part of it. We separated to a distance of about fifty yards and had gone but a little way when the air was again filled with their cries and the moon all but darkened by their bodies. I could guess what had happened: the precious Lamb, without waiting for us, had blundered in amongst the birds, to the ruin of our plans. I saw Tinkler and the boatswain break into a run. My own legs were not equal to the added exertion; indeed, I had so little strength that I had drawn to the limit of it in reaching the bird island, and it was all I could now do to walk, to say nothing of running. By pure chance I managed to knock down two noddies that circled low over my head. One of them was only slightly hurt, and fluttered away from me, but I at length managed to capture it. Having done so, I myself fell down, completely exhausted. Shortly afterward I felt an attack of tenesmus coming on, but to my surprise and relief I discovered that I was evacuating, for the first time in thirty-three days. Perhaps I should pass over this matter in silence; it is not, under ordinary circumstances, one to be referred to; but members of my own profession will understand

the interest I took both in the performance of a function so long delayed, and the result of it. The excrement was something curious to
see — hard, round pellets not so large as sheep's turds, and looking
perfectly black in the moonlight. The amount was woefully small, and
yet I believe that it was all my bowels contained at that time. It confirmed me in the opinion I had ventured to Mr. Nelson — that our
bodies had absorbed all but an infinitesimal amount of the little
nourishment they had received.

With my two precious birds, I now walked feebly on after my
companions, whom I at length found in one spot, gathered around the
crouching form of the recreant Lamb.

"Look at this wretch, Mr. Ledward!" Samuel shouted, his voice
trembling with rage. "Do you see what he has done?"

Cole said nothing, but stood with his arms folded, gazing at the
man. Overhead, the noddies circled about in thousands; but they were
far beyond reach. Their cries were all but deafening; we had to shout
to make ourselves heard.

But no words were needed to tell me the tale of what had happened.
Lamb's face and hands were smeared with blood, and around him lay
the gnawed carcasses of nine birds which he had caught and devoured.
I must do him the credit to say that he had made a good job of them;
scarcely anything remained but feathers, bones, and entrails. He was
making some whining appeal that could not be heard above the
tumult of birds' cries. Of a sudden the boatswain gave him a cuff
that knocked him sprawling at full length in the sand. Then Mr. Cole
bent over him. "Stop here!" he roared. "If you move from this spot,
you rogue, I'll thrash you within an inch of your life!"

We continued a quest that was now all but hopeless. The birds
were thoroughly alarmed, and although we waited for a full two hours,
they would not again settle. A few ventured down, but before we
could reach them they would take wing again. We caught but twelve
in all, though we should have returned with our bag filled.

We trudged back slowly, worn out with the fatigue of the journey
and reluctant to reach our camp, for we well knew how bitter would
be the disappointment of those awaiting our return. This was the first
bird island we had met with, and we had looked forward to a meal of
roasted sea fowl with an expectation that might have been laughable had
it not been so pathetic.

Mr. Cole carried the bag, driving Lamb on before him. The man persisted in his abject entreaties, begging that nothing be said of the matter to Mr. Bligh: —

"I was out o' me head, Mr. Cole. I was, straight. I was that starved — "

"Starved?" said Samuel. "And what of the rest of us, you bloody thief? Out of your head! You can tell that to Captain Bligh!"

The boatswain halted. "Mr. Samuel, we'd best not let him know the whole truth of it."

"What?" exclaimed Samuel. "Would you shield such a villain? When he's robbed some of us, it may be, of the very chance of life?"

"It's not that I'd shield him," said Cole, "but I'd be ashamed to let Captain Bligh know what a poor thing we've got amongst us."

"He knows already," Samuel replied. "Hasn't the man been a dead weight to us all the way from Tofoa? He's done nothing but lie and whine in the bottom of the boat all the voyage. We've him to thank, I'll be bound, for the stolen pork!"

"I didn't touch it, sir! I didn't!"

"You did, you rogue! It must have been you! There's none but yourself would have been such a cur as to steal from his shipmates!"

He was, in all truth, a wretched creature, the inestimable Lamb. I have little doubt that Samuel was right in surmising that he was the thief of the pork. But as that was gone, and the birds as well, I agreed with Cole that nothing was to be gained by disclosing Lamb's gorge of raw bird flesh. Tinkler sided with us, and Samuel at length agreed to keep that point a secret.

"But Captain Bligh shall know whose fault it was that the birds were frightened," he said.

"Aye," said Cole. "We owe it to ourselves that that should be told." And so it was agreed.

Captain Bligh was, of course, furious. He took the man's bird stick and thrashed him soundly with it; and never was punishment more richly deserved.

We were a sad company that evening. A fire of coals had been carefully tended against our return, when the fowls were to be roasted, and every man had promised himself at least two of the birds. But when Mr. Bligh saw the miserable result of our expedition, although the twelve birds were dressed and cooked, they were carefully packed away for future use; and we had for supper water, the handful of sea snails we had found, and a few oysters. Elphinstone and Hayward were then set at watch, and the rest of us lay down to sleep.

It seemed to me that I had no more than closed my eyes when I was aroused to find the island in a glare of light. The night was chill and the master had kindled a fire for himself at a distance from the rest of us. Some coarse dry grass which covered the island had caught from this, and the fire spread rapidly, burning fiercely for a time. It was the last straw for Mr. Bligh. We made a vain effort to beat out the flames, and when at last they had burned themselves out, he gave the company in general, and Mr. Fryer in particular, a dressing down that lasted for the better part of a quarter of an hour.

"You, sir," he roared at Fryer, "who should set an example with myself to all the rest, are a disgrace to your calling! You are the most incompetent bloody rascal of the company! Mark my words! We'll have the savages on us as a result of this! And serve you right if we do! What are you worth, the lot of you? A more useless set of rogues it has never been my misfortune to command! I send you out for birds, to an island where they congregate in thousands. You frighten them like a lot of children, and get none. I send you out for shellfish. You get none. I set you to fishing. You get none. And yet you expect me to feed you! And if I close my eyes for ten minutes, you're up to some deviltry that may be the ruination of us all! And you expect me to take you safe to Timor! By God, if I do, it will be thanks to none of you!"

He quieted down presently. "Get you to sleep," he said gruffly. "This may be our last night ashore till the end of the voyage, so make the most of it."

I lay awake for some time. Nelson, who was lying beside me, turned presently to whisper in my ear.

"What a man he is, Ledward," he said. "It comforted me to see him in a passion again. We'll fetch Timor. I did him a great injustice ever to doubt it."

I had precisely the same feeling, and I thanked God, inwardly, that Bligh and no other was in command of the *Bounty's* launch.

## CHAPTER XI

WE were astir before daylight, greatly refreshed by six or seven hours of sleep. Mr. Bligh awoke in the best of humours, intending to embark immediately, but was irritated when he found that Lamb was too ill to go into the launch.

"What ails the fellow, Mr. Ledward?" he asked, looking down at the man with an expression of disgust.

Lamb was doubled up with cramps from his gorge of the night before; there was no doubting the pain he suffered. I was tempted to let Bligh know the truth of the matter, for my impatience with this worse than useless fellow was equal to his own. I refrained, however, and was about to purge him when he was seized with a violent flux. Half an hour later he was carried into the boat and we proceeded on our way.

It was a beautiful morning, with cloudless sky, and a fresh breeze at E.S.E. This part of the coast of New Holland lies, as our sailors would say, "in the eye of the southeast trades"; and during the time we sailed within the reefs we had constantly a fine, fresh sailing breeze abaft the beam.

Mr. Fryer was at the tiller. Captain Bligh sat beside him with his journal open on his knees, engaged in his usual occupation of charting the coast. He glanced frequently at the compass to obtain bearings on the points, indentations and landmarks ashore; at short intervals, without raising his eyes from his work, he would order "Heave the log," and make a note of the launch's speed. Nelson had told me, what I could readily believe, that Captain Cook, in spite of Bligh's youth at that time, considered him among the most skilled cartographers in England. And I am confident that the officer who will one day be appointed to make a thorough survey of this coast will be amazed at the accuracy of Bligh's chart, drawn with only his sextant, a compass, and a rude log to aid him, in the stern sheets of a twenty-three-foot boat, sailing fast to the north with scarcely a halt.

All the time we sailed within the reefs of New Holland, Bligh was absorbed in this work, to such an extent that for hours at a time he seemed to forget our very presence. Mr. Bligh was an explorer born, but his interest was less in the strange people and natural curiosities to be found than in the charting of new coasts. I feel assured that there were entire hours within the reefs when he forgot the *Bounty,* forgot the mutiny, forgot that he was in a small unarmed boat, half starved, at the mercy of savage tribes, and hundreds of leagues from the nearest European settlement. His expression of interest and happiness at these times was such that it was a pleasure merely to look at his face.

We had sailed about two leagues to the northward when a heavy swell began to set in from the east, leading us to suppose that there must be a break in the reefs which protect most of this shore. The sea continued rough as we passed between a shoal, on which were two sandy cays, and two other islets four miles to the west. Toward midday we sailed past six other cays covered with fresh green scrub and contrasting with the main, which now appeared barren, with sand hills along the coast. A flat-topped hill abreast of us, Captain Bligh named "Pudding-Pan Hill"; and two rounded hills, a little to the north, he called "The Paps." At two hours before sunset we passed a large inlet, which Bligh longed to explore. It appeared to be the entrance to a safe and commodious harbour.

Three leagues to the northward of this inlet, we found a small island where we decided to spend the night. The sea was rough, the wind was now making up in gusts, and there was a strong current setting to the north. Though well wooded, with low scrub, the island appeared the merest pile of rocks, with only one poor landing place in the lee of a point. A shark of monstrous proportions swam alongside the boat for some time while we approached the land, and as we rounded the point, some of the people saw a large animal resembling a crocodile pass under the boat.

"Bigger'n the launch, he was," said Cole when the captain questioned him; "with four legs and a great long tail. A crocodile, ye can lay to that, sir."

It was a wretched anchorage, for the coral dropped in a vertical wall from the surface to a depth of two fathoms, and the bottom was very foul. The wind was making up, and the current swept in fast around the point.

Laying the boat alongside the rocks, Captain Bligh ordered Fryer and some of the people to spend the night on shore, since the anchorage was too uncertain for all to leave the boat in such weather. As we drifted fast to leeward, the grapnel was dropped. It dragged for a moment, and presently held as scope was paid out; then, as the weight of the launch fetched up against it, the line parted suddenly.

"Enough scope, you fools!" roared Bligh, not knowing what had happened. "Damn you, boatswain! What are you about, there?"

"We've lost the grapnel, sir!" Cole shouted.

"To the oars!"

The men ran out their oars and pulled with a will, for they realized as well as the captain the dangers of being blown off-shore on such a night. Their utmost exertions were just sufficient to gain slowly against current and wind. Bligh made his way forward where Cole was examining the broken line.

"A rotten spot, sir," said the boatswain; "the rust of the grapnel did it." He opened his clasp knife and cut away the rotten line.

Bligh was peering down into the water ahead. "Hold her here!" he ordered without turning his head.

There was something ominous about the place, and the wild red sunset; the thought of the monsters we had seen so short a time before would have deterred most men from doing what Bligh now did. He stripped off his ragged shirt and trousers, seized the end of the grapnel line, and plunged into the sea.

Cole gazed after him anxiously; then, seeing that the people had stopped rowing for a moment in their astonishment, he roared out: —

"Pull, I say! Do you want to drag the line out of the captain's hands? Pull, damn your blood!"

He was paying out line as he shouted, and gazing earnestly down into the water. Captain Bligh came to the surface, drew three or four long breaths, and dived once more. Nearly a minute passed before he reappeared. This time he swam to the stern of the boat and pulled himself aboard. For a moment or two he sat on the gunwale, breathing rapidly.

"By God, sir," I remarked. "I'm glad you did not ask *me* to dive."

He laughed grimly. "I was none too eager to go down; but I'll ask no one to do what I fear to do myself. The thought of the monstrous shark was never out of my mind." He shivered. "Nelson, what was that other thing we saw — a crocodile?"

"I've little doubt of it," Nelson replied. "Captain Cook saw what he believed were crocodiles in these waters."

Bligh shivered in spite of himself. "I'm as glad to be in the boat again," he said. "We are in a bad position here, and these currents are the devil; they seem to set four ways at once."

"You were fortunate to get down to the grapnel, sir," said Peckover.

"Aye, Mr. Peckover, the Indians of Otaheite are the men for that work. I managed to get the line rove through its ring before I had to come up to blow; but one of them would have stopped down to bend it on. We whites are good for nothing under water."

Dusk was setting in, and we profited by what remained of daylight to eat our small portions of the half-dressed birds left over from those obtained on Lagoon Island. In the strong wind and current, the boat rode uneasily to her grapnel, and we passed a wretched night. The moon, close on to the full, set sometime before daylight; in the first gray of dawn, Captain Bligh and some of the rest of us landed to see what we could obtain on shore, leaving Cole and Peckover in charge of the launch.

Nelson had passed a pretty comfortable night in the lee of some rocks; I found him awake, and he and I set out to explore the far side of the island. As we crossed through the scrub, we found the backs of many turtles, some of great size, and the fireplaces where the Indians had roasted the flesh. I was engaged in a futile search for clams on a small, sandy beach exposed to the east wind, when I heard Nelson shout.

I swung about, and saw him trying to turn over a turtle of immense size, which had just emerged from behind some bushes and was making her way to the water's edge.

"*Ledward!*" he shouted again, in an agonized voice.

In an instant I was at his side, but our combined strength was not enough to raise one side of the turtle from the sand. All the time we struggled to turn her, she was plying her flippers desperately, sending showers of sand over us and moving rapidly toward the sea, only a few yards distant. Her strength was prodigious; she must have weighed not less than four hundred pounds. Perceiving the impossibility of turning her, we gave up the attempt, and seized a hind flipper each, holding back with all our might. But she had reached the damp sand by now, where her powerful fore flippers could obtain a hold, and in spite of our utmost exertions she dragged us, little by little, into the sea. Through the shallows she went, while our grips weakened; then suddenly, as she plunged into deep water, we were forced to let go.

Panting, and wet from head to foot, we had barely the strength to make our way back to the sand. Once there, we sank down side by side. After a long silence Nelson looked up at me with a wry smile.

"That was tragedy! There was a fortnight's food in the beast, Ledward!"

"All of that," I replied. "She may have laid some eggs. Let us go and search."

Nelson shook his head. "No. I surprised her as she was beginning to dig. She had just come up from the sea, for her back was still wet."

We fell silent once more, and at last he said: "We'll say nothing of this to the others, eh, Ledward?"

We walked slowly back across the island, halting on a bit of rising ground to rest. A little to the left we could see the others gathered on the beach near the launch. Nelson lay back for a moment, his hands behind his head, and stretched out his legs at full length.

"You'd best follow my example," he said. "It may be the last chance we shall have."

"The last? Surely not!" I exclaimed.

"Bligh thinks we shall be clear of the coast by to-morrow or the day after."

I managed to smile somewhat dubiously. "Between ourselves, Nelson, I'll confess that no man in the boat can dread the prospect more than I."

"Dread it? I positively quake at the thought! God help us if we have any more nights like those on the way to New Holland!"

We found Bligh awaiting us. The others had obtained nothing, so he hailed the launch, and we soon set sail. The main at this place bore from S.E. to N.N.W. half W., and a high, flat-topped island lay to the north, four or five leagues distant.

On passing this island, we found a great opening in the coast, set with a number of mountainous islands. To the north and west the country was high, wooded, and broken, with many islands close in with the land. We were now steering more and more to the west, and Captain Bligh informed us that he was tolerably certain we should be clear of the coast of New Holland in the course of the afternoon.

Toward two o'clock, as we were steering toward the westernmost part of the main now in sight, we fell in with a vast sandy shoal which extends out many miles to sea, and were obliged to haul our wind to weather it. Bligh named the place "Shoal Cape." Just before dark we passed a small island, or rock, on which innumerable boobies were roosting. There was no land in sight to the north, south, or west.

Three hundred leagues of empty sea now lay between us and Timor.

The six days we had spent within the reefs of New Holland had allowed us to sleep in some comfort at night, and to refresh ourselves with what little the islands afforded. And, above all, the barriers of coral shielded us from the attacks of our old enemy, the sea.

But the sea had not forgotten us, and lay in wait, on the far side of Shoal Cape, armed with strong gales from the east and deluges of rain, unabated for seven days. On the misery of that week I shall not dwell.

On the morning of June tenth, I was lying doubled up in the stern sheets. Lamb, Simpson, and Nelson were in a state as bad as my own; and Lebogue, the *Bounty's* sailmaker, once the hardiest of old seamen, lay forward with closed eyes. His legs were swollen in a shocking manner, and his flesh had lost its elasticity; when it was pinched or squeezed, the impression of one's fingers remained clear.

The breeze was still fresh, though the sea had moderated during the night, and only two men were at the bails. Elphinstone was steering, with Bligh at his side. The countenances of both men looked hollow as those of spectres; but while the master's mate stared at the compass dully, the captain's eyes were calm. Our fishing line was made fast close behind Bligh. We had towed it constantly, day and night, for more than three thousand miles without catching a fish, though Cole and Peckover had exhausted their ingenuity in devising a variety of lures made from feathers and rags. Peckover had seized a new one on our hook the night before, employing the feathers of a booby Captain Bligh had caught with his own hands on the fifth — the only bird we had secured since leaving New Holland.

Bemused with weakness, I happened to glance at the line. We were sailing at not less than four knots at the time, and I was surprised to observe that the line, instead of towing behind us, ran out at right angles to the boat. For a moment I did not realize the significance of this. Then I said, in the best voice I could muster: "A fish!"

Mr. Bligh started, seized the line, rose to his feet, and began to haul in hand-over-hand, with a strength that surprised me.

"By God, lads," he exclaimed, "this one shan't get away!"

It was a dolphin of about twenty pounds' weight. The captain brought it in leaping and splashing, swung it over the gunwale, and fell to the floor boards, clasping it to his chest.

"Your knife, Mr. Peckover!" he called, never for an instant relaxing his hold on the struggling fish.

In an instant the gunner had cut the cord beneath the gills, but Mr. Bligh held fast to the dolphin while it blazed with the changing colours of death and its shuddering grew weaker, till it lay still and limp. The captain rose weakly, rinsed his hands over the side, and sat down once more, breathing fast. Peckover looked at him admiringly.

"No use his trying them jumping-jack tricks on you, sir!" he said.

"You've Mr. Ledward to thank," said Bligh. "We've towed so long without luck, that I'll be bound no other man would have noticed it!"

Peckover was gazing down longingly at the bulging side of the fish, and Bligh went on: "Aye, divide him up — guts, liver, and all."

Peckover knelt beside the fish, muttering to himself as he laid out imaginary lines of division, and then changed his mind. At last he began to cut. The people watched this operation with an eagerness which might have been laughable under happier circumstances. Only Elphinstone, at the tiller, had preserved an attitude of indifference throughout the affair, gazing vacantly at the compass and up at the horizon from time to time.

Under Bligh's direction, the gunner divided the fish into thirty-six shares, each of about half a pound. Eighteen of these were now distributed by our method of "Who shall have this?" A fine steak fell to me; the captain got the liver and about two ounces of flesh. Lebogue shook his head feebly when his share was offered him, and whispered: "I'm past eatin', lad."

I managed to turn on my side when Tinkler handed me my fish in a coconut shell, but I was now in such a state that the sight of raw flesh revolted my stomach. Seeing that Nelson felt the same, I did my best to make a pretense of eating before stowing my shell away out of sight. I am not of a rugged constitution, and it irked me to be so feeble when others were still able to bail and work the sails. Nelson was close beside me, and he said in a low voice: "Damme, Ledward, I cannot eat the fish."

"Nor I," I replied.

"No matter, we'll soon raise Timor."

"Mr. Samuel," said Bligh, "issue a spoonful of wine to those who are weakest."

He was eating the dolphin's liver, and I could see that he relished the food no more than I. But he forced himself sternly, mouthful by mouthful, to chew and swallow it.

Toward noon, the wind shifted from E.S.E. to nearly northeast, forcing us to lower our sails and raise them on the starboard tack. Then a black rain squall bore down on us, filling our kegs and permitting us to drink our fill. Those who were able wrung out their sodden rags in salt water, and performed the same office for their weaker mates. The sky was clouded over, and though there was a long swell from the east, the wind was light and we shipped little water over the stern. The boatswain was staring aft.

"Look, sir!" he exclaimed suddenly to Bligh.

Several of the people turned their heads; as I raised myself a little to look, I heard Hallet say: "What's that?"

Directly in our wake and not more than a quarter of a mile away, a black cloud hung low over the sea, with a sagging point that approached the water in a curious, jerking fashion. And just beneath, the surface of the sea was agitated as if by a small maelstrom. Little by little, the sea rose in a conical point, making a rushing, roaring noise that was now plainly audible; little by little, the cloud sagged down to meet it. Then suddenly the sea and cloud met in a whirling column which lengthened as the cloud above seemed to rise rapidly.

"Only a waterspout," said Bligh, after a glance aft. "Look alive, if I give the word."

For a time it seemed to remain stationary, growing taller and thicker as if gathering its force. Then it began to move, bearing straight down on us.

"Bear up," Bligh ordered the helmsman quietly. "Aye, so!" And, as the sails began to slat, "To the sheets, lads! Trim them flat!"

We changed our course not a moment too soon. The cloud, now overhead, was as black as ink, with a kind of greenish pallor at its heart; we had not sailed fifty yards, close-hauled, when the waterspout passed astern of us, a sight of awe-inspiring majesty.

All hands save Mr. Bligh stared at it in silent consternation. The column of water, many hundreds of feet high and thicker than the greatest oak in England, had a clear, glassy look and seemed to revolve with incredible rapidity. At its base, the sea churned and roared with a sound that would have made a loud shout inaudible. I doubt if any man in the boat was greatly afraid; we had gone through so much, and were so reduced by our sufferings, that death had become a matter of little moment. But even in my own state of weakness, I trembled in awe at this manifestation of God's majesty upon the deep. Not a word was spoken till the waterspout was half a mile distant and Bligh ordered the course changed once more.

"Ledward," remarked Nelson coolly, in a weak voice, "I wouldn't have missed that for a thousand pounds!"

"I have seen many of them," said Bligh, "though never so close. There's little danger, save at night . . ."

He shut his mouth suddenly and bent double in a spasm of pain. Next moment his head was over the gunwale while he retched and vomited. After a long time he rinsed his mouth with sea water, and sat up ghastly pale.

"Some water, Mr. Samuel," he managed to say. "Aye, a full half pint."

The water sent him to the gunwale once more, and during the remainder of the afternoon Mr. Bligh was in a pitiable state. I believe that the liver of the dolphin must have been poisonous, as is said often to be the case; though it may be that Bligh had reached the state I was in, in which the exhausted stomach can no longer accept food. Though constantly retching and vomiting, and suffering from excruciating cramps, he refused to lie down; he kept an eye on our course between his paroxysms, and directed the trimming of the sails. At sunset he took a spoonful of wine, which his stomach retained, and seemed better for it.

Though I no longer felt hunger or much pain, the night seemed interminably long. The moon came up at about ten o'clock, dead astern of us, and shone full in my face. I dozed, awoke, attempted to stretch my cramped legs, and dozed again. Sometimes I heard Nelson muttering in his sleep. The captain managed to doze for a time in the early hours of the night; when the moon was about two hours up, he relieved Fryer at the helm. The moon was at its zenith, from which I judged the time to be four in the morning, when Bligh roused Elphinstone, and again lay down to sleep. The wind was at east, and though the moonlight paled the stars, I could see the Southern Cross on our larboard beam.

I had said nothing to the others of my fears, but for a day or two past I had had reason to suspect that Elphinstone's mind was giving way under the strain. He was as little wasted in body as any man in the launch, yet his vacant eye, his lack of interest in what went on about him, and his strange gestures and mutterings were symptoms of a failing mind, although there was no reason to think him unequal to his duties. When Bligh took him by the shoulder to waken him, he said "Aye, sir!" in a dull voice, and took the tiller mechanically.

It was Peckover's watch; turning my head, I could see him seated with some others forward. His shoulders were bowed, and from time to time he nodded and caught himself, making heroic efforts to stay awake. A continual sound of faint groans and mutterings came from the men asleep in the bottom of the launch; dreamless sleep had been unknown to us for many days. Soon Bligh began to snore gently and irregularly.

Elphinstone sat motionless at the tiller, staring ahead with a vacant expression on his face. I could see his lips move as he muttered to himself, but could hear no sound. Then for a time I dozed.

It was still night when I awoke, though close to dawn. The master's mate was hunched at the helm, seeming scarcely to have moved since I glanced at him last. For a time I noticed nothing out of the way; then, looking over the gunwale, I perceived that the Cross was no longer on our beam. It was on the larboard bow; our course had been changed from west to southwest. Elphinstone leaned toward me.

"The land!" he whispered eagerly. "Yonder, dead ahead! Take care! Don't waken Mr. Bligh!"

I struggled with some difficulty into a position which enabled me to look forward. Peckover and the others sat sleeping, bowed on the thwarts. Ahead of the launch was only the vast moonlit sea, and an horizon empty save for a few scattered clouds.

"Timor," whispered Elphinstone, triumphantly. "God's with us, Mr. Ledward! He caused the wind to shift to the northeast, so we're dead before it still. You see it now, eh? The mountains and the great valleys? A fine island, I'll be bound, where we'll find all we need!"

He spoke with such sincerity that I looked ahead once more, beginning to doubt my own eyes; but I saw only the roll of the empty sea under the moon. Bligh stirred and struggled to a sitting position. He took in the situation at a glance.

"What's this, Mr. Elphinstone?" he said in a harsh voice. "Who ordered you to change the course?"

"The land, Captain Bligh! Look ahead! I steered for it when I sighted the mountains an hour ago."

Bligh swung about to stare over the sea. "Land?" he said, as if doubting the evidence of his own senses. "Where?"

"Dead ahead, sir. Can't you see the great valley yonder, and the high ridge above? It looks an island as rich as Otaheite!"

Bligh gave me a quick glance. "Go forward, Mr. Elphinstone," he ordered. "Lie down at once and get some sleep."

To my surprise, the master's mate said no more about the land, but gave the tiller to Bligh and made his way forward amongst the sleeping men. His face wore the mild, vacant expression of a man walking in his sleep.

"Mr. Peckover!" called Bligh harshly.

The gunner started a little and straightened his back slowly. "Aye, aye, sir!" he said.

"Don't let me catch you sleeping on watch again! You and those with you might have been the ruin of us all!" The other members of the watch were stirring, and the captain went on: "I'm going to wear. To the halyards! Get her on the starboard tack!"

When the halyards had been slacked away and the yards of our lugsails passed around to the larboard sides of the masts, Bligh bore up to the west, and the men trimmed the sails to the northeast wind.

This day, the eleventh of June, seemed the longest of my life. They had eaten the last of the dolphin the night before, and at sunrise a quarter of a pint of water and our usual allowance of bread were issued. I drank the water, but could not eat the bread. The captain made a grimace in spite of himself as he raised his morsel of bread to his mouth, but he munched it heroically, nevertheless, and contrived to keep it down. The boatswain had administered a spoonful of wine to Lebogue, and was coming to do the like for Nelson and me. Stepping over the after thwart with the bottle in his hand, he came face to face with Bligh, while an expression of horror came into his eyes.

"Sir," he said solicitously, "ye look worse'n any man in the launch. Ye'd best have a drop o' this."

Bligh smiled at the old fellow's simplicity, and said: "I'll pay you a handsomer compliment, Mr. Cole: you have lasted better than many of the younger men. . . . No, no wine for me. There are those who need it more."

Cole touched his forelock and turned to serve me, shaking his head.

I lay half dozing whilst the sun crawled interminably toward the zenith. Sometimes I opened my eyes after what seemed the passage of hours, only to discover that the shadow of the helmsman had shortened by no more than an inch. My whole life, up to the time we had left Tofoa, seemed but an instant beside the eternity I had spent in the boat, and on this day, after a long process of slowing down, I felt that time had come to a halt at last: I had always been sailing west before a fresh easterly breeze, with the sun stationary and low behind the launch, and would sail thus forever and ever, on a limitless plain of tossing blue, unbroken by any land. And Mr. Bligh would always hold the tiller — a scarecrow clad in grotesque rags, with a turban made of an old pair of trousers on his head.

\* \* \*

Noon came at last, and Cole took the tiller while the master and Peckover held Bligh up to take the altitude of the sun. Owing to his own weakness and that of the men supporting him, he had difficulty in getting his sight; though not breaking, the sea was confused, and the launch tossed and pitched uncertainly. After some time, he handed his sextant to the master and sat down to work out our position. Finally he looked up.

"Our latitude is nine degrees, forty-one minutes south," he said; "that of the middle portion of Timor. By my reckoning, we have traversed thirteen and one-half degrees of longitude since leaving Shoal Cape, — more than eight hundred miles, — and to the best of my recollection the most easterly part of Timor is laid down in one hundred and twenty-eight degrees east longitude, a meridian we must have passed."

"When shall we raise the land, sir?" the boatswain asked.

"During the night or early in the morning. We must keep a sharp lookout to-night."

Toward sunset, when I awoke from a long doze, there were great numbers of sea birds about. Lying on my back, I could see them passing and repassing overhead. Tinkler contrived to strike down one booby with the spare yard we had cut at Restoration Island, but the others took warning at this and avoided the boat. The bird was reserved for the next day, but I was offered a wineglass of its blood, which I managed to swallow only to vomit it up instantly. There was much rockweed around us, and coconut husks so fresh that they were still bright yellow in colour.

Darkness came, and still the wind held steady and fair. Every man able to sit up was on the thwarts, staring out over the tossing sea ahead, dimly visible in the light of the stars.

Like a sentient being, aware that the end of her long journey was at hand, the launch now seemed to surpass herself. With all sail set and drawing, she raced westward, shipping so little water that there was little need to bail. Sometimes the people were silent; sometimes I heard them speaking in low tones. I was aware of an undercurrent of new courage and confidence, of deep contentment that our trials were so nearly at an end. Not once during the long voyage had their faith in Mr. Bligh waned; he had declared that we should raise the land by morning, and that was enough.

It must have been nearly eleven o'clock when the moon rose, directly astern of the launch: a bright half-moon, sailing a cloudless sky. Hour after hour, as the moon climbed the heavens, the launch ran westward, whilst we listened to the crisp sound of water rushing under her keel.

Even old Lebogue revived a little at this time. No man of us had endured more grievous suffering, and yet he had borne his part in the work when others no weaker than himself lay helpless.

Bligh had taken the tiller at midnight, after an attempt to sleep; and toward three in the morning, when the moon was high above the horizon astern, young Tinkler stepped up on to the after thwart to peer ahead. He stood there for some time, swaying to the motion of the boat, with hands cupped above his eyes. Then he sprang down to face the captain.

"The land, sir!" he exclaimed in a shaking voice.

Bligh motioned Fryer to take the helm, and stood up. I heard a burst of talk forward: "Only a cloud!" "No, no! Land, and high land too!" Then, as the launch reared high on a swell, we saw the shadowy outlines of the land ahead: pale, lofty, and unsubstantial in the light of the moon, a great island still many miles distant, stretching far away to the northeast and southwest. The captain stared ahead long and earnestly before he spoke.

"Timor, lads!" he said.

# CHAPTER XII

THERE were some who doubted the landfall, who could not believe that the goal of our voyage was actually in sight. For all Mr. Bligh's quiet assurance, and the boatswain's repeated "Aye, lad! There's the land — never a doubt of it!" they dared not believe, lest day should come and the dim outlines melt into the shapes of distant clouds. We hauled on a wind to the northeast, and those who could stood on the thwarts from time to time, their confidence in what they saw increasing from moment to moment. Some could do no more than raise themselves to a sitting position in the bottom of the launch, clinging to the thwarts or to the gunwales as they stared ahead.

Veil after veil of moonlit obscurity was drawn aside, and at last, in the clear light of early dawn, there it lay: Paradise itself, it seemed, its lofty outlines filling half the circle of the horizon, bearing from S.W. to N.E. by E. The sun rose, its shafts of level, golden light striking across promontory after promontory. We saw great valleys filled with purple shadow, and, high above the coast, forests appeared, interspersed with glades and lawns that might well have been the haunts where our first parents wandered in the innocence of the world.

Our capacities for joy and gratitude were not adequate to the occasion. Mr. Bligh was, I believe, as near to tears as he had ever been in his life, but he held himself well under control. Others gave way to their emotion, and wept freely; indeed, we were so weak that tears came readily. Poor Elphinstone, alone of our company, was robbed of the joy of that never-to-be-forgotten morning; his sufferings had deprived him — temporarily, at least — of reason. He sat amidships, facing aft, scanning the empty sea behind us with an expression of hopeless bewilderment, an object of commiseration to all. Despite our efforts, we could not convince him that the land lay close ahead.

At the sunrise we were within two leagues of the coast. A land more green and fair has never gladdened seamen's eyes; scarcely a man of us did not long to go ashore at once. The coast was low, but on the higher regions beyond, we saw many cultivated spots. Near one of the plantations we observed several huts, but no people there or elsewhere. Purcell and the master ventured to suggest to Mr. Bligh that we land, in hopes of finding some of the inhabitants, who might inform us as to the whereabouts of the Dutch settlement.

"I can well understand your impatience, Mr. Fryer," said Bligh; "but we shall take no unnecessary risks. If my recollection serves me, Timor is all of one hundred leagues in extent. I have told you that I am by no means certain that the Dutch have a permanent outpost here. If they have, they may have subjected only a small part of the island to their rule. The inhabitants are, I believe, Malays, well known to be a cruel and treacherous race. We shall place ourselves in their power only as a last resort."

There was no disputing the wisdom of this decision. What we feared, of course, was that no European settlement existed on the island; but we did not permit ourselves to consider this melancholy possibility, and both Bligh and Nelson recollected that Captain Cook had been informed that the most easterly station of the Dutch was upon Timor.

We bore away again to the W.S.W., keeping close enough to the coast to avoid missing any opening that might exist; but throughout the morning neither cove nor bay did we see, nor any place where a landing might have been effected, because of the great surf breaking all along this windward shore.

At noon we were abreast of a high headland only three miles distant, and, having passed it, we found the land still bearing off in a southwesterly direction for as far as the eye could reach. Our dinner was the usual allowance: one twenty-fifth of a pound of bread, and a half pint of water — for Mr. Bligh was not the man to relax his vigilance until assured that the need for vigilance was past; but the bird we had caught the night before was divided in the customary manner. I received a portion of the breast, which, a week earlier, I should have considered a tidbit of the rarest sort; but now my stomach revolted at the sight and tainted smell of the raw flesh, and I could not eat it. I gave my portion to Peckover, and merely to see the relish with which he devoured it upset me the more, so that I fell to retching violently. Six or seven others were in as bad a state. Mr. Bligh gave the weakest of us a swallow of rum, of which we still had three quarters of a bottle.

All through the afternoon the weather was hazy, and we could see no great distance before us, but were close enough in to observe the appearance of the coast, which was low and covered with a seemingly endless forest of fan palms. At this time we saw no signs anywhere of cultivated spots, and, as we proceeded, the land had a more arid look. Captain Bligh said nothing of the matter; but I could see that he was worried lest we had gone beyond the habitable part of the island. I know not how many times during this day we had before us a distant promontory, beyond which nothing of the island could be seen; but always, upon rounding it, we found another far ahead, and the land still bearing away to the south. At sunset, we had run twenty-three miles since noon; and in the gathering dusk we brought to under a close-reefed foresail, in shoal water within half a league of the shore.

We did not know how near we might be to the end of all our troubles. Perhaps only a few miles farther, we thought, lay the Dutch settlement; but we dared not risk sailing on, lest we should run past it in the darkness. The excitement of the previous eighteen hours had exhausted our little strength, and, had it been possible, I believe that Captain Bligh would have landed here, if only to give us the refreshment of stretching out our cramped and aching limbs. The surf on shore was not great at this point, but we were too weak to have run our boat through it; so we lay huddled in the launch, most of us too far spent even for conversation. In my own case, much as I regret to admit it, I was in a weaker condition than any of the company save Lebogue, and I had a great ulcer on my leg that kept me in constant torment. We were all of us, in fact, covered with sores, due to the constant chafing of our emaciated bodies against the boards of the boat, and kept open and raw by the action of salt water. Nelson astonished me at this time; he looked like a dying man, but he seemed to have drawn, merely from the sight of Timor, a strength which he was, somehow, able to impart to others. Together, he and Bligh took over the office of looking after the sick, and I shall not soon forget their comforting, heartening words as they made their way amongst us, helping some poor fellow to change to a more comfortable position, and doling out a few drops of rum or wine from the last of our precious supply.

We were drawn together that night as never before. We had suffered so much that we seemed of one body. Antipathies, whether small or large, arising from our different characters, vanished quite away, and a rich current of sympathy and common feeling ran through our forlorn little company, making us, for that night at least, brothers indeed. I had observed many different aspects of Mr. Bligh's character, and, profoundly as I respected him, I had not supposed that he had in him any deep feeling of compassion for the men under his command. On this occasion he revealed a gentleness which quite altered my conception of his nature. The experience brought home to me the difficulty one has in forming a true notion of any of one's fellow creatures. They must be seen over a long period of time, and under many and varied conditions not often presenting themselves in sequence to a single observer. But some men are ever the same, unchanging and unchangeable as rock, no matter what the conditions. Cole, the boatswain, was one of these. Loyalty to his commander, devotion to duty, sympathy for those weaker than himself, and an abiding trust in God were the corner stones of his nature. All through that interminable night he was ever on the alert to do some suffering man a kindness.

About two in the morning, we wore and stood close along the coast till daylight. Seeing no signs of habitation, we bore away to the westward, with a strong gale against a weather current, which occasioned much sea and forced us to resume the weary work of bailing. This fell chiefly upon Fryer, Cole, Peckover, and two of the midshipmen, Tinkler and Hayward; others did what little they could, sitting propped up against the thwarts.

By this time every man of us — save Bligh, perhaps — had a feeling of mingled fear and hatred toward the sea: as though it were not a mindless force but a conscious one, bent upon our destruction, and becoming increasingly enraged that we had survived its cruelty and were about to escape. Even Bligh must have had something of the feeling, for I heard him say to the master: "She's not done with us yet. . . . Bail, lads!" he called. "I'll soon have you out of this."

Once more we had before us a low coast, with points opening to the west; and again we were encouraged to think we had reached the extremity of the island; but, toward the middle of the morning, we found the coast reaching on to the south a weary way ahead. Even the land, to my distorted fancy, appeared hostile — unwilling to receive us, tempting us on with false hopes only that we might be the more bitterly disappointed.

Presently we discerned, to the southwest, the dim outlines of high land, but in the moisture-laden air we could not be sure whether or no it was a part of Timor. Seeing no break between it and the coast we were following, Bligh concluded that it must be a distant headland of the island; therefore we stood toward it, and several hours passed before we discovered that it was a separate island — the island of Roti, as we afterward learned.

Shortly after Mr. Bligh had altered our course to return to the coast we had left, I lost all knowledge of what went on. The sun had been extremely hot, and we had no protection from its rays. It may be that I suffered a slight stroke, and this, combined with my other miseries, had proven too much for me. At any rate, I sank into a stupor which left me a dim consciousness of misery and of little else. Now and then I heard the confused murmur of voices, and I vaguely remember having been roused from frightful dreams, when I thought I was struggling alone in the sea and upon the point of drowning, to find that I was still in the launch, being raised up to escape the water that came over the side. I was, indeed, far gone, powerless to do aught for myself. Then followed a period of complete darkness, when I was nothing but an inert mass of skin and bones; and my next recollection was of someone repeatedly calling my name. Try as I would, I could not rouse myself sufficiently to reply. I heard Bligh's voice: "Give him the whole of it, Mr. Nelson. He'll come round."

And so I did. A quarter of a pint of rum was poured down my gullet. I remember how the heat and the strength of it seemed to flow into every part of me, clearing my brain and giving me a blessed sense of well-being; but oh! more blessed was the sound of Nelson's voice: "Ledward! Ledward! We're here, old fellow!"

It was deep night, the cloudless sky sprinkled with stars dimmed by the soft splendour of the waning moon. I found myself sitting propped up in the stern sheets. Nelson was kneeling beside me, and Cole supporting me with his arm around my shoulders. As I turned my head, Cole said: "That's what was needed, sir; he's coming round nicely."

I was conscious of a feeling of shame and vexation that I, the *Bounty's* surgeon, should be in such a deplorable state — an encumbrance instead of a help to the others.

"What's this, Nelson?" I faltered. "Damme! Have I been asleep?"

"Don't talk, Ledward," he replied. "Look! Look yonder! . . . Turn him a little, Mr. Cole."

The boatswain lifted me gently so that I sat half facing forward. The sail had been lowered, and there were six men at the oars, pulling slowly and feebly across what appeared to be the head of a great bay, so calm that the wavering reflection of the moon lay on the surface of the water. Outlines of the land were clearly revealed; not half a mile away I could see two square-rigged vessels lying at anchor, and beyond them, on a high foreshore, what appeared to be a fort whose walls gleamed faintly in the mild light.

"Easy, lads," Bligh called to the men at the oars, "don't exert yourselves"; and then, to me: "How is it with you, Mr. Ledward? I was bound you shouldn't miss this moment."

I could not speak. I hesitate to admit it, but I could not. I was weak as a six-months' child, and now, for the first time, tears gushed from my eyes. They were not tears of relief, of joy at our deliverance. No. I could have controlled those. But when I looked at Mr. Bligh, sitting at his old position with his hand on the tiller, there welled up within me a feeling toward him that destroyed the barriers we Englishmen are so proud of erecting against one another. I saw him then as he deserved to be seen, in a light that transfigured him. Enough. The deepest emotions of the heart are not lightly to be spoken of, and no words of mine could add to the stature of the captain of the *Bounty's* launch.

I managed at length to say: "I'm doing very well, sir," and left it at that.

The silence of the land seemed to flow down upon us, healing our weary hearts, filling us with a deep content that made all speech super-fluous. The launch moved forward as smoothly as though she were gliding through air, and the faint creak of the oars against the tholepins and the gentle plash of the blades in the water were sounds by which to measure the vastness of this peace.

It was then about three in the morning. Nearer we came and nearer to the little town hushed in sleep; not even a dog was astir to bay at the moon. As we drew in we saw that the two ships were anchored a considerable distance to the right of the fort and about a cable-length from shore. We made out a small cutter riding near them, and not a light showing in any of these vessels.

We turned then to approach an open space on the beach that ap-peared to be a point of embarkation for boats, and Mr. Cole made his way to the bow. A fishing line with a stone attached served as our lead line. At Mr. Bligh's order, Tinkler began heaving it. "Six fathoms, sir," he called. We moved slowly on into shallower water. In the moonlight we could now see the ghostly gleam of roofs and walls, embowered in trees and flowering shrubs whose perfume floated out to us with the cool, moist air that flowed down from the valley of the interior.

"Way enough!" said Bligh, and then: "Drop the grapnel, Mr. Cole."

The oars were gotten in; there was a light splash as the grapnel went over the side. The boatswain paid out the line and made fast. Our voy-age was at an end.

There were but eight of our company strong enough to sit upon the thwarts; the others were lying or sitting, propped up in the bottom of the boat.

"Let us pray, lads," said Bligh. We bowed our heads while he re-turned thanks to Almighty God.

We lay within thirty or forty yards of the beach. A little distance to the right, the walls of the fort rose from their ramparts of rock. All was silent there; not so much as a gleam of light appeared anywhere in the settlement. Captain Bligh hailed the fort repeatedly, with no result.

"Try your voice on 'em, Mr. Purcell," he said.

Purcell hailed, then the boatswain, then the two together; but there was no response.

"By God," said Bligh, "were we at war with the Dutch, I'll warrant we could capture the place, weak as we are, with nothing but four rusty cutlasses. They've not so much as a sentinel on the walls."

"We've roused someone at last," said Nelson. "Look yonder."

A strange-looking man was just emerging from the shadows of the trees lining the road that led to the beach. He was clad only in shirt and trousers, and had what appeared to be a white nightcap on his head. He was exceedingly fat, and walked at a waddling gait.

"Can you speak English, my good man?" Bligh called.

He came forward another pace or two, as though for a clearer view of us, but made no reply.

"I say, can you speak English? You understand?"

Whether it were astonishment, or fear, or both, or neither, that moved him, we were at a loss to know; but of a sudden he turned on his incredibly short legs and waddled away at twice the speed with which he had approached.

"Ahoy there!" Bligh called after him. "Don't go! Wait, I say!"

The man turned, shouted something in a deep, powerful voice, and disappeared under the shadow of the trees.

"Was it Dutch he spoke, Nelson?" Bligh asked.

"Undoubtedly," said Nelson; "but that is as much as I can say. . . . We shall fare well here, that's plain."

Bligh laughed. "Aye, so we shall, if that fellow is an average specimen of the inhabitants. Damn his eyes! What possessed him to run off like that?"

"Likely he's gone for help, sir. There may be English-speaking people here."

"Let us hope so, Mr. Fryer. Possess your souls in patience, lads. We must not go ashore without permission, and that we shall soon have, I promise you. Dawn is scarcely an hour off."

In a little time the Dutchman returned with another man dressed in a seaman's uniform.

"Ahoy, there! What boat is that?" called the latter.

"Who are you?" Bligh replied. "An Englishman?"

"Aye, sir."

"Is there an English ship here?"

"No, sir."

"Then how came you in these parts, my man?" said Bligh, with something of his old quarter-deck manner.

"I'm quartermaster's mate, sir, of the Dutch vessel yonder. Captain Spikerman."

"Good!" said Bligh. "Listen carefully, young man! Tell your captain — what's his name, again?"

"Spikerman, sir."

"Tell Captain Spikerman that Captain Bligh, of His Majesty's armed transport *Bounty,* wishes to see him at his very earliest convenience. Inform him that the matter is pressing. You understand?"

"Aye, aye, sir."

"Very well; carry him this message instantly. Don't fear to rouse him. He will thank you for doing so."

"Aye, aye, sir. He's sleeping ashore. I'll go this instant."

We must have waited a full three quarters of an hour, although the time seemed immeasurably longer. The delay, as we were to learn, was not Captain Spikerman's fault. He resided in a distant part of the town, and came as soon as he could dress.

Dawn was at hand, and the people in the town were stirring out of their houses, when we saw him approaching with two of his officers and the man who had carried our message. Captain Bligh stood up in the stern sheets. His clothing was a mass of rags revealing his frightfully emaciated limbs; his haggard, bony face was covered with a month's growth of beard; but he held himself as erect as though he were standing on the *Bounty's* quarter-deck.

"Captain Spikerman?" he called.

For a few seconds the little group on shore stared at us in silence. Captain Spikerman stepped forward. "At your service, sir," he replied.

"Captain Bligh, of His Majesty's armed transport *Bounty*. We are in need of assistance, sir. I will be grateful indeed if you will secure us permission to land."

"You may come ashore at once, Captain Bligh. I can vouch for the governor's permission. Your boat may be brought directly to the beach."

"Haul in the grapnel, Mr. Cole. Two men at the oars." Tinkler and Hayward hauled it in, Cole coiling the line neatly as they did so. Peckover and Purcell took the oars, and the launch proceeded on the last fifty yards of a voyage of more than three thousand, six hundred miles. "Easy, Mr. Cole! Don't let her touch!"

The boatswain fended off with our bamboo pole and attempted to leap out to hold her, but the poor fellow had forgotten his condition. His legs gave way and he fell into the water, holding on to the gunwale, until, with a grim effort, he managed to get his footing. Tinkler threw a line ashore which the English seaman of the Dutch ship took up. Captain Spikerman and his officers stood for a moment as though powerless to move. Then, taking in our situation, they themselves sprang into the shallow water to draw us alongside.

"God in heaven, Captain Bligh! What is this? From what place do you come?" Mr. Spikerman exclaimed.

"That you shall know in good time, sir," said Bligh; "but I must first see to my men. Some of them are in a pitiable state from starvation. Is there a place in the town where they may be cared for?"

"You may take them directly to my house. One moment, sir."

Captain Spikerman turned to one of his officers and spoke to him rapidly in the Dutch tongue. The young man made off at once, half running along the road to the town.

By this time a crowd of the townspeople had collected about us, and others came from moment to moment. They were of various nationalities, — Dutch, Malays, Chinese, and people evidently of mixed blood, — and they stared at us with expressions of mingled horror and pity. Meanwhile, those of us who could had gotten out of the launch; but more than half of the company had to be carried ashore. We were taken a little way up the beach, where mats were spread for us on the sand. There we waited the arrival of conveyances which were to carry us to Captain Spikerman's house, while the townspeople gathered in a wide circle, gazing at us as though they would never have done.

Of our people, Lebogue was in the most serious condition. The old fellow lay close beside me. He was no more than a skeleton covered with skin; but his was a resolute spirit, and, weak as he was, he yet had within him a strong will to live. Nelson, Simpson, Hall, Smith, and myself were in a plight only a little less grave. Nelson tried to walk ashore, but after a few steps his legs gave way and he was constrained to allow himself to be carried. Hallet was very weak, but managed to keep his footing. Poor Elphinstone's disabilities were, as I have said, mental rather than physical. His face still wore its vacant, puzzled expression, and he appeared to have no knowledge of his surroundings.

In a short while, Mr. Spikerman's lieutenant returned with litters and a score of Malay chair-men. They carried us into the town, Mr. Bligh and the stronger of the company following on foot. I have only a dim recollection of the way we went, past shops and warehouses, and along shaded streets, till we came to a pleasant house in an elevated situation where Captain Spikerman lived. He and his officers were kindness itself; I shall ever have a feeling of sincere liking for the people of the Dutch nation because of the humane treatment we received from those members of it who resided at Coupang. Such was the name of the haven — which I might better call "heaven" — at which we had arrived.

When we had been bathed with warm water our sores were dressed by Mr. Max, the surgeon of the town; whereupon we were placed in beds and given a little hot soup, or tea, which was all that our stomachs could receive at this time. I am speaking here of the greatest invalids amongst us, who were cared for in one room. Captain Bligh, when he had bathed and refreshed himself with food and a few hours' sleep, accompanied Captain Spikerman to the house of Mr. Timotheus Wanjon, the secretary to Mr. Van Este, the governor of the town. Mr. Van Este was at this time lying very ill, and incapable of transacting any business.

On this day I had the sweetest sleep I have ever enjoyed in my life. The cooling ointment with which my sores had been dressed, and the soft bed upon which I lay, lulled me to rest within half an hour. I was aroused, toward evening, to take a little soup and bread, but fell to sleep again immediately after, and did not waken until about ten of the clock the following morning.

After four days of complete rest, we were wonderfully restored, and all except Lebogue could rise from bed and walk a little in Mr. Spikerman's garden. His services to us were endless; he had put us under obligations we shall never be able to repay, but we did not, of course, wish to discommode him longer than was absolutely necessary. All his rooms were taken up by our company, and he was sleeping at the house of Mr. Wanjon. Captain Bligh found that there was but one available house in the settlement. Having examined it, he decided that we should all lodge there. Mr. Spikerman suggested that the house be taken by Captain Bligh for himself and his officers, and that the men be accommodated on one of the vessels lying in the harbour, but Captain Bligh was not willing at such a time to fare better than his men. Therefore, on our fifth day in Coupang, we removed to our new quarters.

The dwelling contained a hall with a room at each end, and was surrounded with a piazza. Above, there was a spacious, airy loft. One room was reserved to Captain Bligh; Nelson, Fryer, Peckover, and myself lodged in the other, and the men were assigned to the loft. The hall was common to all of the officers, and the back piazza was set aside for the use of the people. In order to simplify the matter of our victualing, the three midshipmen readily agreed to mess with the men. Through the kindness of Mr. Van Este, the house was furnished with beds, tables, chairs, settees — everything, in fact, of which we stood in need; and our food was dressed at his own house and brought to us by his servants.

Mr. Van Este expressed a desire to see Captain Bligh and some of his officers. It was therefore arranged that Mr. Bligh, Nelson, and myself should wait upon him, in company with Mr. Wanjon and Captain Spikerman. We found the governor propped up in bed, so wasted by his illness that he looked — as, indeed, he was — at death's door. His voice was exceedingly weak, but his eyes were full of interest. Captain Spikerman acted as our interpreter. He acquainted the governor with the circumstances of the mutiny. Mr. Van Este was not aware of the position of Tofoa and the Friendly Islands; in fact, I believe that he did not know of their existence. When he had been told that we had made a voyage in the ship's launch of above three thousand, six hundred miles, he raised a thin white hand and said but one word in reply. Captain Spikerman turned to Mr. Bligh.

"Mr. Van Este says 'Impossible,' Captain Bligh. You will understand that this is only a manner of speaking, to convey his astonishment. He does not doubt your word."

Bligh smiled faintly. "You may tell Mr. Van Este that he is right: it *was* impossible; nevertheless, we did it."

He then conveyed, through Mr. Spikerman, our gratitude for the kind and hospitable treatment we had received, and we took our leave. The governor was far too ill to bear the fatigue of a long conversation.

This day, June the nineteenth, was remarkable for still another reason. Mr. Max, my Dutch colleague, and I had agreed that our company need not be kept longer on a diet. Mr. Wanjon, who himself overlooked the matter of our victualing, had provided a feast equal to the greatness of the occasion; and he, Captain Spikerman, and Mr. Max readily consented to join us at table. On our way from the governor's house, we called for Mr. Max, and then proceeded to our residence, where the men were already at their dinner on the back piazza. Cole sat at the head of the table, with the midshipmen on either side and the others below. Even Lebogue had sufficiently recovered to be present. The table was loaded with food that would have gladdened any seaman's eyes; it was a pleasure to see the half-starved men stowing it away.

At Captain Bligh's entrance, they rose; but he at once motioned them to be seated.

"Eat hearty, lads," he said. "There's no need to wish you good appetites, that's plain."

"We're doin' famous, sir," Cole replied. A moment later, Captain Bligh retired with our guests to the hall, while Nelson and I remained for a little to look on at this memorable feast.

"I hope you'll not think we're goin' beyond reason, Mr. Ledward," said Cole. "Better vittles I never tasted!"

"And well you deserve them, every man of you," I replied. "Eat as much as you like."

"Aye, they'll do," said Purcell, grudgingly; "but I'd sooner set down to a good feed of eggs and bacon. All these rich faldelals . . . I don't well know what I'm eatin'."

"Trust old Chips to find fault," said Hayward.

"Here, Purcell; have some of the bread, if you don't like Dutch food," said Hallet. "Pass it along to him, Tinkler."

"Mr. Nelson and Mr. Ledward would like some, I'm sure," said Tinkler. "Try a little, Mr. Nelson."

He rose and took up a large platter, set high in the middle of the table on four tall water-glasses. Heaped on the platter was something that resembled nothing on earth save what it was: the bread of the *Bounty's* launch.

"Well, I'm damned!" said Nelson, with a laugh.

"Have just a crumb as an appetizer. We did, the lot of us," said Tinkler. "Mr. Ledward, what about you?"

"Wait!" Hayward exclaimed. "Don't you give 'em a ration, Tinkler, without weighing it. Where's Captain Bligh's scales?"

It warmed my heart to see them in such a merry mood, and the *Bounty* bread — the sight of it, at least — was indeed the best of reminders of misery past and done with.

"Is this all that was left in the launch, Tinkler?" Nelson asked.

"Yes, sir."

"We've been making an estimate, Mr. Nelson," said Hayward. "What you see on the platter would have lasted the eighteen of us another eleven days, had we not had the misfortune of finding Coupang."

"Save for our abominable luck in landing amongst the Dutch, we might even have got home on it," Tinkler added. "What do you think, boatswain?"

Cole looked up from his plate, holding his fork erect in his fist.

"I'll say this, Mr. Tinkler," he replied gravely. "If Captain Bligh was forced to take us all the way to England in the launch, with no more bread than what's on that plate, I'll warrant he could do it if we'd back him up."

At Cole's words there was a cheer, in which every man at the table joined heartily.

"But don't, for God's sake, suggest it, boatswain!" said Hayward in a low voice. "He might want to try."

The dinner at the captain's table proceeded more soberly. There was food, food, and more food: curried prawns with rice, baked fish with rice, roast fowl with rice, and many other dishes, with excellent wine and schnapps to wash all down. We of the *Bounty's* launch had been so long accustomed to thinking of wine and spirits as the most precious of commodities, to be taken only a spoonful at a time, that it was hard to convince ourselves that we need no longer be sparing of them. Captain Bligh, always a moderate drinker, was still sparing; but the rest of us did better justice to the good cheer; and our Dutch companions ate and drank with as much zest as though they had been members of our company all the way from Tofoa. Nelson threw a quizzical glance in my direction, toward the end of the meal, when they were attacking new dishes with undiminished appetite.

Our guests were naturally curious about the events of the mutiny, but they soon realized that it was a sore subject with Mr. Bligh, which he preferred not to discuss.

"You have our sworn affidavits, Mr. Wanjon," he remarked, at this time. "The facts are there, attested to by every one of my men. It is not likely that the villains will come this way, but should they do so, seize and hold them. Let not one of them escape."

"You may set your mind at rest on that score," Mr. Wanjon replied; and with this the discussion of the mutiny was dropped.

"I greatly desire to proceed homeward as soon as my men are fit to ravel," Bligh remarked. He laughed in a wry manner. "We are a company of paupers, Mr. Wanjon. We've not a shilling amongst us; not a halfpenny bit!"

"Do not let that worry you, Captain Bligh. Mr. Van Este has instructed me to provide you with whatever funds you may desire."

"That's uncommon kind of him. I shall draw bills on His Majesty's Government. . . . Captain Spikerman, is there a small vessel to be had hereabout — one fit to carry us to Batavia? I wish to arrive there in time to sail home with your October fleet."

"There is a small schooner lying in a cove about two leagues distant," Captain Spikerman replied. "She can be bought, I know, for one thousand rix-dollars."

"Pretty dear, isn't it?" said Bligh

"She's well worth it, I assure you. She is thirty-four feet long, perfectly sound, and would serve your purpose admirably. Should you care to look at her, I can have her here for your inspection within a day or two."

"Excellent," said Bligh. "I'll be greatly obliged to you."

The dinner was at an end, and presently our guests left us. Nelson was in a jubilant mood. He had asked permission to botanize the island in the environs of Coupang, and Mr. Wanjon not only agreed but had offered to provide servants to accompany him on his expeditions. Nelson was in no fit state to go abroad, and I demurred strongly against the plan. However, he had won Captain Bligh's consent and would listen to none of my objections. As a matter of fact, I would gladly have gone with him, had it not been that my ulcered leg made walking out of the question.

During the next ten days he was constantly away from Coupang, returning only occasionally to bring in his specimens. At first he appeared to thrive upon the work, but I soon realized that he was exerting himself far beyond his strength. Early in July he came down with an inflammatory fever which at last confined him to his bed, whether he would or no. Mr. Max and I both attended him, but his condition grew steadily worse. His weakened constitution had been tried too severely, and it was soon plain to both of us that he was dying.

He passed away on the twentieth of July, at one o'clock of the morning. I need not say how his loss affected our company. He was respected and loved by every one of us. In my own case, we had been friends from the day of our first meeting at Spithead, and I had looked forward to many years of his friendship. As for Mr. Bligh, Nelson was, I believe, one of three or four men whom he held in his heart of hearts. I think he would sooner have lost the half of his company than to have lost him.

We buried him the following day. His coffin was carried by twelve soldiers from the fort, dressed in black. Mr. Bligh and Mr. Wanjon walked immediately behind the bier; then came ten gentlemen of the town and the officers from the ships in the harbour; and the *Bounty's* people followed after. Mr. Bligh read the service, and it was as much as he could do to go through with it. The body was laid to rest be-hind the chapel, in that part of the cemetery set aside for Europeans.

I recall with little pleasure the remainder of our sojourn in Coupang. Mr. Bligh was constantly employed about the business of our de-parture, and the *Bounty's* people were daily aboard the schooner he had bought, making her ready for sea. In my own case, I was as useless now as I had been much of the time in the *Bounty's* launch. My ulcer would not heal, and I was forced to sit in idleness on the piazza of our dwelling, thinking of Nelson, and how gladly he would have lived to go home with us.

The schooner was a staunch little craft, as Captain Spikerman had assured us. Bligh named her *Resource,* and, as we were to go along the Java coast, which is infested with small, piratical vessels, he armed her with four brass swivels and fourteen stand of small arms, with an abundance of powder and shot.

On the twentieth of August, being entirely prepared for sea, we spent the morning in waiting upon our various Dutch friends, whose kindness had been unremitting from the day of our arrival at Coupang. Mr. Van Este, the governor, was lying at the very point of death, and Captain Bligh was not able to see him. Mr. Wanjon received us in his stead, and Mr. Bligh tendered him our grateful thanks for the in-numerable services he had rendered us. Mr. Max, the surgeon, who had cared for our people when I was unable to do so, would accept no remuneration for his attendance upon us, saying that he had done no more than his duty. His action was typical of that of others at Coupang who had been our hosts for more than two months.

Throughout the afternoon our hosts became our guests on board the *Resource,* and we showed them what small hospitalities our poor means afforded.

Captain Bligh looked his old self again. He was now cloathed as befitted his rank, and his hair was neatly dressed and powdered. As he stood on the after-deck, talking with Captain Spikerman and

Mr. Wanjon, I could not but remark the contrast between his appearance now and what it had been upon our arrival at Coupang. Nevertheless, as I observed him, I was conscious of a curious feeling of disappointment. It may be thought strange, but I liked him better as he was in the *Bounty's* launch: rags hanging from his wasted limbs, his hand on the tiller, the great seas foaming up behind him, and the low scud flying close overhead. There he was unique, one man in ten thousand. On the after-deck of the *Resource,* he appeared to be merely one of the innumerable captains of His Majesty's Navy. But well I knew in my heart the quality of the man who stood there. Forty-one days in a ship's boat had taught me that.

Toward four of the afternoon, the last of our guests returned to the shore. The breeze favouring, we weighed at once and stood off toward the open sea. The beach was thronged with people waving hats and handkerchiefs, and as we drew away the air quivered with the parting salute from the fort. Mr. Peckover, our gunner, was rejoiced to be employed for the first time this long while in his proper duties. Our brass swivels replied bravely to the Dutch salutation.

As for the *Bounty's* launch, she was towing behind, with Tinkler at the tiller, proud of the honour conferred upon him. Peckover and I were standing at the rail, looking down upon her in silence, thinking of her faithful service. We loved her, every man of us, as though she were a sentient being.

Presently Peckover turned to me. "How well she tows," he said. "She seems to want to come. Though we had no line to her, I'll warrant she'd still follow Captain Bligh."

"By God, Peckover," I said, "I believe she would!"

# EPILOGUE

On the first of October we cast anchor in Batavia Road, near a Dutch man-of-war. More than a score of East Indiamen were riding there, as well as a great fleet of native prows. The captain went ashore at once, to call on Mr. Englehard, the Sabandar — an officer with whom all strangers are obliged to transact their business; and on the same evening we were informed that we might lodge at an hotel, the only place in the city where foreigners are permitted to reside.

The climate of Batavia is one of the most unwholesome in the world. The miasmatic effluvia which rise from the river during the night bring on an intermittent fever, or paludism, often of great severity, accompanied by unendurable headaches. Weakened by our privations, some of us fell immediate victims to this disorder, which was to cost Lenkletter and Elphinstone their lives. The hotel, where I resided with the other officers, though situated in what is considered a healthy quarter of the city, and near the river bank, was intolerably hot, and so ill arranged for a free circulation of air that a man in robust health must soon have succumbed to its stifling rooms.

After one night in this place, Mr. Bligh was taken with a fever so violent that I feared for his life. I was unable to attend him, since I was suffering from a fever as well as from the ulcer on my leg, and Mr. Aansorp, head surgeon of the town hospital, was sent for. By administering bark of Peru and wine, this skillful physician so improved Captain Bligh that within a day he was able once more to transact the pressing business on his hands.

We had been four days at the hotel when Mr. Sparling, Surgeon-General of Java, had the kindness to invite Captain Bligh and me to be his guests at the seamen's hospital, on an island in the river, three or four miles from the town. This hospital is a model of its kind, large enough to accommodate fifteen hundred men. The sick receive excellent care and attention, and the wards are scrupulously clean. Mr. Sparling, who had been educated in England, listened with great interest to the account of our voyage, and insisted that Captain Bligh send for those of his people who were ill. Late one afternoon I was sitting on my colleague's shady verandah. He was smoking a long black *cigarro;* I lay on a settee with my bandaged leg stretched out on a stool. We were discussing the medical phases of our sufferings, Mr. Sparling expressing surprise that any man in the launch should have survived.

"You say that three of the people were forty-one days without evacuation?" he asked. "It is all but incredible!"

"So much so," I replied, "that I hope to write a paper to be read before the College of Surgeons. What little we ate appeared to be entirely used up by our bodies."

"It is a miracle that you are alive. But your constitutions have been too much impaired to withstand such a climate as this. I am concerned about Mr. Bligh. Should he stay long . . ." He shrugged his shoulders, paused for a moment, and went on: "I have never known a man of greater determination! With such a fever, most men would be on their backs. Yet he goes daily into the town to transact his business. I have spoken to the governor. Mr. Bligh will be permitted to take passage, with two others, on the packet sailing on the sixteenth of this month."

"You are kind indeed, sir! Mr. Bligh shared all of our sufferings, and, in addition, the entire responsibility was his. The strain has impaired his health gravely; I have feared more than once that he might leave his bones here."

"That possibility is by no means remote," said Sparling. "There is a high mortality here amongst Europeans. Mr. Bligh, I can see, is a man who will attend to his duty even to the serious prejudice of his health. Do what you can, Mr. Ledward, to urge upon him the necessity for caution."

"I have, sir," I replied; "you may be sure of that; but he cannot, or will not, take advice."

My colleague nodded. "He's a strong-headed man, that's plain. I should imagine that he was a bit of a tartar on the quarter-deck?"

At that moment a Malay servant appeared in the doorway, bowed, and spoke to his master. Mr. Sparling rose.

"Captain Bligh is disembarking now," he said, as he left me.

Presently he ushered Bligh to a chair and made a sign to the servant, who brought in a tray with glasses, and a decanter of excellent Cape Town wine.

"Let me prescribe a glass of wine," remarked Sparling. "There is no finer tonic for men in your condition."

"Your health, sir," said Bligh, "and that of our kind hostess, if I may propose it. I have had a hard day in the town; your house is a haven of refuge for a weary man."

His face was gaunt and flushed, and his eyes unnaturally bright, as he sat in one of Sparling's long rattan chairs, wearing an ill-fitting suit of cloathes, made by a Chinese tailor in the town.

"One of your men is very low," remarked the Surgeon-General presently; "the one we visited this morning. I fear there is little hope for him."

"Aye — Hall," said Bligh. "Poor fellow."

"The flux seems deadly in these parts," I observed.

"Yes," said Sparling. "Few recover from the violent form of the disease. He must have eaten of some infected fruits in Coupang."

We were silent for a time, while Bligh seemed to be brooding over some unpleasant thought.

"Ledward, I've had to part with the launch!" he exclaimed at last.

"You've sold her, sir?" I asked.

"Yes. And the schooner, too—but she meant little to me. As for the launch, though I am a poor man, I would gladly give five hundred pounds to take her home!"

"You could get no space for her on the *Vlydte?*"

"Not a foot! Damme! Not an inch! Not even for my six pots of plants from Timor."

Sparling nodded. "There are never enough ships in the October fleet," he remarked. "Every foot of space and every passage has been bespoken for months. It was only through the governor's influence that I got passage for you and your two men. Should my wife desire to send a few gifts of native manufacture to her uncle at the Cape of Good Hope, I declare to you it would be impossible at this time!"

"I had hoped to take the launch," said Bligh. "She should be placed in the museum of the Admiralty. A finer boat was never built! I love her, every frame and plank!"

"How did you fare at the auction?" asked Sparling.

Bligh laughed ruefully. "Damned badly!" he replied. "If I may remark upon it, sir, your method of conducting an auction strikes me as inferior to ours."

"Yes, from the seller's standpoint. I have attended your English auctions. Where the bids mount higher and higher, the bidders are apt to lose their heads."

"You should have been there, Ledward," said Bligh. "They set a high figure at first, which the auctioneer brings down gradually until someone bids. Small danger of losing one's head when there can be only one bid! Several Dutch captains were on hand; half a dozen Malays, a Chinaman or two, and some others—God knows what they may have been! There was one Englishman present besides ourselves, —Captain John Eddie, commanding a ship from Bengal. He'd come merely to look on, not to bid. The auctioneer put up the schooner first, at two thousand rix-dollars. The figure came down to three hundred, without an offer! By God, Mr. Sparling, a Scot or a Jew would starve to death in competition with your seafaring countrymen! At three hundred, an old Chinaman showed signs of interest, casting shrewd glances at a Dutch captain standing close by. At two hundred and ninety-five, Captain Eddie raised his hand. By God! I was grateful to him for that! The price was not a third of her value, but Eddie kept those bloody sharks from getting her. It warmed my heart to see their disappointment."

"What did the launch fetch?" I asked.

"Let us not speak of her. Cole and Peckover were with me; they felt as badly as I. If I could have left her here, in safe hands, until there was a chance to send her home . . ." He sighed. "It couldn't be arranged. It cost me dear to see her go!"

On the following day died Thomas Hall, our third loss since leaving the *Bounty*. He had endured manfully our hardships in the launch, only to succumb to the most dreaded of East Indian diseases. Lenkletter and Elphinstone, destined also to leave their bones in Batavia, were suffering with the same paludism that had attacked Captain Bligh.

At this time the Sabandar informed us that every officer and man must make deposition before a notary concerning the mutiny on board the *Bounty*, in order to authorize the government to detain her, should she venture into Dutch waters. Bligh considered this unlikely; but his determination to see the mutineers brought to justice was such that he left no contingency unprovided for.

On the morning of October sixteenth I was awakened long before daylight by sounds in Mr. Bligh's room, next to mine. He was to be rowed down the river to go on board the *Vlydte*, and I could hear him, through the thin wall, directing his servant, Smith, how to pack the large camphorwood box he had purchased some days before.

In the gray light of dawn, Mr. Bligh knocked at my door and entered the room.

"Awake, Ledward?" he asked. I struggled to sit up, but he motioned me not to move.

"I've come to bid you good-bye," he said.

"I wish I were sailing with you, sir!"

He laughed his short, harsh laugh. "Damme! I'm by no means sure you're not the luckier of the two! You may have the good fortune to go home on an English ship. Yesterday I called on Captain Couvret, aboard the *Vlydte;* we had some talk concerning the manner of navigation. They carry no log, and scarcely steer within a quarter of a point. No wonder they frequently find themselves above ten degrees out in their reckoning! The state of discipline on board is appalling to an

English seaman. It will be a miracle if we reach Table Bay; once there, I hope to transfer to an English ship."

"Permit me to wish you a good voyage, in any case."

At that moment Mr. Sparling called from the piazza: "Your boat is waiting, Captain Bligh!"

Bligh took my hand in a brief, warm clasp.

"Good-bye, Ledward," he said. "Don't fail to call on Mrs. Bligh when you reach London."

"I shall hope to see you, too, sir."

He shook his head. "It's not likely. If I have my way, I shall sail for Otaheite before you reach England."

He was gone — the finest seaman under whom I have ever had the good fortune to sail. From the bottom of my heart I wished him God Speed.

# THE RUN OF THE LAUNCH

*(From the Island of Tofoa to Coupang, on the Island of Timor)*

| Year 1789 | | No. of Miles | |
|---|---|---|---|
| May | 3 | 86 | |
| | 4 | 95 | |
| | 5 | 94 | |
| | 6 | 84 | |
| | 7 | 79 | |
| | 8 | 62 | |
| | 9 | 64 | |
| | 10 | 78 | |
| | 11 | 102 | |
| | 12 | 89 | |
| | 13 | 79 | |
| | 14 | 89 | |
| | 15 | (no record) | |
| | 16 | 101 | |
| | 17 | 100 | |
| | 18 | 106 | |
| | 19 | 100 | |
| | 20 | 75 | |
| | 21 | 99 | |
| | 22 | 130 | |
| | 23 | 116 | |
| | 24 | 114 | |
| | 25 | 108 | |
| | 26 | 112 | |
| | 27 | 109 | |
| | 28 | (no record) | Entered the Great Barrier Reef |
| | 29 | 18 | To Restoration Island |
| | 30 | — | At Restoration Island |
| | 31 | 30 | To Sunday Island |
| June | 1 | 10 | To Lagoon Island |
| | 2 | 30 | |
| | 3 | 35 | To Turtle Island |
| | 4 | 111 | Clear of New Holland |
| | 5 | 108 | |
| | 6 | 117 | |
| | 7 | 88 | |
| | 8 | 106 | |
| | 9 | 107 | |
| | 10 | 111 | |
| | 11 | 109 | |
| | 12 | (no record) | Sighted Timor |
| | 13 | 54 | Coasting Timor |
| | 14 | (no record) | Reached Coupang |

Total distance run, 3618 miles

# PITCAIRN'S ISLAND

*To*
ELLERY SEDGWICK

# THE PITCAIRN COMMUNITY

| *The "Bounty" Men* | *Their Women* |
|---|---|
| Fletcher Christian . . . . . . | Maimiti |
| Edward Young . . . . . . . | Taurua |
| Alexander Smith . . . . . . | Balhadi |
| John Mills . . . . . . . | Prudence |
| William McCoy . . . . . . | Mary |
| Matthew Quintal . . . . . . | Sarah |
| John Williams . . . . . . | Fasto (later Hutia) |
| Isaac Martin . . . . . . . | Susannah |
| William Brown . . . . . . | Jenny |

| *The Indian Men* | *Their Women* |
|---|---|
| Minarii . . . . . . . . | Moetua |
| Tetahiti . . . . . . . . | Nanai |
| Tararu . . . . . . . . | Hutia |
| Te Moa | |
| Nihau | |
| Hu | |

The vowels in the Polynesian language are pronounced approximately as in Italian; generally speaking, syllables are given an equal stress. The native names in this book should be pronounced roughly as follows: —

| | |
|---|---|
| Hu . . . . . . | Hoo |
| Hutia . . . . . | Hoo-tee-ah |
| Maimiti . . . . . | My-mee-tee |
| Minarii . . . . . | Mee-nah-ree |
| Moetua . . . . . | Mo-ay-too-ah |
| Nanai . . . . . | Nah-nigh |
| Nihau . . . . . | Nee-how |
| Tararu . . . . . | Tah-rah-roo |
| Taurua . . . . . | Ta-oo-roo-ah |
| Te Moa . . . . . | Tay-moa |
| Tetahiti . . . . . | Tay-tah-hee-tee |

# CHAPTER I

On a day late in December, in the year of 1789, while the earth turned steadily on its course, a moment came when the sunlight illuminated San Roque, easternmost cape of the three Americas. Moving swiftly westward, a thousand miles each hour, the light swept over the jungle of the Amazon, and glittered along the icy summits of the Andes. Presently the level rays brought day to the Peruvian coast and moved on, across a vast stretch of lonely sea.

In all that desert of wrinkled blue there was no sail, nor any land till the light touched the windy downs of Easter Island, where the statues of Rapa Nui's old kings kept watch along the cliffs. An hour passed as the dawn sped westward another thousand miles, to a lone rock rising from the sea, tall, ridged, foam-fringed at its base, with innumerable sea fowl hovering along the cliffs. A boat's crew might have pulled around this fragment of land in two hours or less, but the fronds of scattered coconut palms rose above rich vegetation in the valleys and on the upper slopes, and at one place a slender cascade fell into the sea. Peace, beauty, and utter loneliness were here, in a little world set in the midst of the widest of oceans — the peace of the deep sea, and of nature hidden from the world of men. The brown people who had once lived here were long since gone. Moss covered the rude paving of their temples, and the images of their gods, on the cliffs above, were roosting places for gannet and frigate bird.

The horizon to the east was cloudless, and, as the sun rose, flock after flock of birds swung away toward their fishing grounds offshore. The fledglings, in the dizzy nests where they had been hatched, settled themselves for the long hours of waiting, to doze, and twitch, and sprawl in the sun. The new day was like a million other mornings in the past, but away to the east and still below the horizon a vessel — the only ship in all that vast region — was approaching the land.

His Majesty's armed transport *Bounty* had set sail from Spithead, two years before, bound for Tahiti in the South Sea. Her errand was an unusual one: to procure on that remote island a thousand or more young plants of the breadfruit tree, and to convey them to the British plantations in the West Indies, where it was hoped that they might provide a supply of cheap food for the slaves. When her mission on Tahiti had been accomplished and she was westward bound, among the islands of the Tongan Group, Fletcher Christian, second-in-command of the vessel, raised the men in revolt against Captain William Bligh, whose conduct he considered cruel and insupportable. The mutiny was suddenly planned and carried swiftly into execution, on the morning of April 28, 1789. Captain Bligh was set adrift in the ship's launch, with eighteen loyal men, and the mutineers saw them no more. After a disastrous attempt to settle on the island of Tupuai, the *Bounty* returned to Tahiti, where some of the mutineers, as well as a number of innocent men who had been compelled to remain with the ship, were allowed to establish themselves on shore.

The *Bounty* was a little ship, of about two hundred tons burthen, stoutly rigged and built strongly of English oak. Her sails were patched and weather-beaten, her copper sheathing grown over with trailing weed, and the paint on her sides, once a smart black, was now a scaling, rusty brown. She was on the starboard tack, with the light southwesterly wind abaft the beam. Only nine mutineers were now on board, including Fletcher Christian and Midshipman Edward Young. With the six Polynesian men and twelve women whom they had persuaded to accompany them, they were searching for a permanent refuge: an island so little known, so remote, that even the long arm of the Admiralty would never reach them.

Goats were tethered to the swivel stocks; hogs grunted disconsolately in their pens; cocks crowed and hens clucked in the crates where several score of fowls were confined. The two cutters, chocked and lashed down by the bulwarks, were filled to the gunwales with yams, some of them of fifty pounds weight. A group of comely girls sat on the main hatch, gossiping in their musical tongue and bursting into soft laughter now and then.

Matthew Quintal, the man at the wheel, was tall and immensely strong, with sloping shoulders and long arms covered with tattooing and reddish hair. He was naked to the waist, and his tanned neck was so thick that a single unbroken line seemed to curve up from his shoulder to the top of his small head. His light blue eyes were set close together, and his great, square, unshaven chin jutted out below a slit of a mouth.

The light southwesterly air was dying; presently the ship lost way and began to roll gently in the calm, her sails hanging slack from the yards. Clouds were gathering on the horizon to the north. Quintal straightened his back and turned to glance at the distant wall of darkness, rising and widening as it advanced upon the ship.

Christian came up the ladderway. He was freshly shaven and wore a plain blue coat. The tropical sun had burned his face to a shade darker than those of the girls on the hatch. The poise of his strong figure and the moulding of his mouth and jaw were the outward signs of a character instant in decision, resolute, and quick to act. His black eyes, deep-set and brilliant, were fixed on the approaching squall.

"Smith!" he called.

A brawny young seaman, who had been standing by the mainmast, hastened aft, touching his turban of bark cloth.

"Clew up the courses, and make ready to catch what water you can."

"Aye, aye, sir!"

Smith went forward, shouting: "All hands, here! Shorten sail!"

A group of white seamen appeared from the forecastle. The brown men turned quickly from the rail, and several of the girls stood up.

"To your stations!" Smith ordered. "Fore and main courses — let go sheets and tacks! Clew lines — up with the clews!"

The lower extremities of the two large sails rose to the quarters of the yards, the native men and half a dozen lusty girls shouting and laughing as they put their backs into the work. Smith turned to the seaman nearest him.

"McCoy! Take Martin and rig the awning to catch water. Look alive!"

Christian had been pacing the quarter-deck, with an eye on the blackening sky to the north. "To the braces, Smith!" he now ordered. "Put her on the larboard tack."

"Braces it is, sir."

Edward Young, the second-in-command, was standing in the ladderway — a man of twenty-four, with a clear, ruddy complexion and a sensitive face, marred by the loss of several front teeth. He had gone off watch only two hours before and his eyes were still heavy with sleep.

"It has a dirty look," he remarked.

"Only a squall; I'm leaving the topsails on her. By God! It will ease my mind to fill our casks! I can't believe that Carteret was mistaken in his latitude, but it is well known that his timekeeper was unreliable. We're a hundred miles east of his longitude now."

Young smiled faintly. "I'm beginning to doubt the existence of his Pitcairn's Island," he remarked. "When was it discovered?"

"In 1767, when he was in command of the *Swallow,* under Commodore Byron. He sighted the island at a distance of fifteen leagues, and described it as having the appearance of a great rock, no more than five miles in circumference. It is densely wooded, he says in his account of the voyage, and a stream of fresh water was observed, coursing down the cliffs."

"Did he land?"

"No. There was a great surf running. They got soundings on the west side, in twenty-five fathoms, something less than a mile from the shore. . . . The island must be somewhere hereabout. I mean to search until we find it." He was silent for a moment before he added: "Are the people complaining?"

"Some of them are growing more than restless."

Christian's face darkened. "Let them murmur," he said. "They shall do as I say, nevertheless."

The squall was now close, concealing the horizon from west to north. The air began to move uneasily; next moment the *Bounty* lurched and staggered as the first puff struck her. The topsails filled with sounds like the reports of cannon: the sun was blotted out and the wind screamed through the rigging in gusts that were half air, half stinging, horizontal rain.

"Hard a-starboard!" Christian ordered the helmsman quietly. "Ease her!"

Quintal's great hairy hands turned the spokes rapidly. In the sudden darkness and above the tumult of the wind, the voices of the native women rose faint and thin, like the cries of sea fowl. The ship was righting herself as she began to forge ahead and the force of the wind diminished. In ten minutes the worst was over, and presently the *Bounty* lay becalmed once more, this time in a deluge of vertical rain. It fell in blinding, suffocating streams, and the sound of it, plashing and murmuring on the sea, was enough to drown a man's voice. Fresh water spouted from the awnings, and as fast as one cask was filled another was trundled into its place. Men and women alike, stripped to their kilts of tapa, were scrubbing one another's backs with bits of porous, volcanic stone.

Within an hour the clouds had dispersed, and the sun, now well above the horizon, was drying the *Bounty's* decks. A line of rippling dark blue appeared to the southwest. The yards were braced on the other tack, and the ship was soon moving on her course once more.

Young had gone below. Christian was standing at the weather rail, gazing out over the empty sea with an expression sombre and stern beyond his years. In the presence of others, his features were composed, but oftentimes when alone he sank into involuntary reflections on what was past and what might lie ahead.

A tall young girl came up the ladderway, walked lightly to his side, and laid a hand on his shoulder. Maimiti was not past eighteen at this time. Of high lineage on Tahiti, she had left lands, retainers, and relatives to share the dubious fortunes of her English lover. The delicacy of her hands and small bare feet, the lightness of her complexion, and the contours of her high-bred face set her apart from the other women on the ship. As she touched his shoulder, Christian's face softened.

"Shall we find the land to-day?" she asked.

"I hope so; it cannot be far off."

Leaning on the bulwarks at Christian's side, Maimiti made no reply. Her mood at the moment was one of eager anticipation. The blood of seafaring ancestors was in her veins, and this voyage of discovery, into distant seas of which her people preserved only legendary accounts, was an adventure to her taste.

Forward, in the shadow of the windlass, where they could converse unobserved, two white men sat in earnest talk. McCoy was a Scot who bore an Irish name — a thin, bony man with thick reddish hair and a long neck on which the Adam's apple stood out prominently. His companion was Isaac Martin, an American. Finding himself in London when the *Bounty* was fitting out, Martin had managed to speak with her sailing master in a public house, and had deserted his own ship for the prospect of a cruise in the South Sea. He was a dark brutish man of thirty or thereabouts, with a weak face and black brows that met over his nose.

"We've give him time enough, Will," he said sourly. "There's no such bloody island, if ye ask me! And if there is, it's nowheres here-about."

"Aye, we're on a wild-goose chase, and no mistake."

"Well, then, it's time we let him know we're sick o' drifting about the like o' this! Mills says so, and Matt Quintal's with us. Brown'll do as we tell him. Ye'll never talk Alex over; Christian's God Almighty to him! I reckon Jack Williams has had enough, like the rest. That'll make six of us to the three o' them. What's the name o' that island we raised, out to the west?"

"Rarotonga, the Indians said."

"Aye. That's the place! And many a fine lass ashore, I'll warrant. If we do find this Pitcairn's Island, it'll be nothing but a bloody rock, with no women but them we've fetched with us. Twelve for fifteen men!"

McCoy nodded. "We've no lasses enough. There'll be trouble afore we're through if we hae no more."

"In Rarotonga we could have the pick o' the place. It's time we made him take us there, whether he likes it or not!"

"Make him! God's truth! Ye're a brave-spoken fellow, Isaac, when there's none to hear ye!"

Martin broke off abruptly as he perceived that Smith had come up behind him unaware. He was a powerfully made man in his early twenties, under the middle stature, and with a face slightly pitted with smallpox. His countenance was, nevertheless, a pleasing one, open and frank, with an aquiline nose, a firm mouth, and blue eyes set widely apart, expressing at the same time good humour and self-confident strength. He stood with brawny tattooed arms folded across his chest, gazing at his two shipmates with an ironic smile. Martin gave him a wry look.

"Aye, Alex," he grumbled, "it's yourself and Jack Williams has kept us drifting about the empty sea this fortnight past. If ye'd backed us up, we'd ha' forced Christian to take us out o' this long since."

Smith turned to McCoy. "Hearken to him, Will! Isaac's the man to tell Mr. Christian his business. *He* knows where we'd best go! What d'ye say, shall we make him captain?"

"There's this must be said, Alex," remarked McCoy apologetically, "we're three months from Tahiti, and it's nigh three weeks we've spent looking for this Pitcairn's Island! How does he know there's such a place?"

"Damn your eyes! D'ye think Mr. Christian'd be such a fool as to search for a place that wasn't there? I'll warrant he'll find it before the week's out."

"And if he don't, what then?" Martin asked.

"Ask him yourself, Isaac. I reckon he'll tell 'ee fast enough."

The conversation was interrupted by a hail from aloft, where the lookout stood on the fore-topmast crosstrees.

"Aye, man, what d'ye see?" roared Smith.

"Birds. A cloud of 'em, dead ahead."

Pacing the after deck with Maimiti, Christian halted at the words.

"Run down and fetch my spyglass," he said to the girl.

A moment later he was climbing the ratlines, telescope in hand. One of the native men had preceded him aloft. His trained eyes made out the distant birds at a glance and then swept the horizon north and south. "Terns," he said, as Christian lowered his glass. "There are albacore yonder. The land will be close."

Christian nodded. "The ship sails slowly," he remarked. "Launch a canoe and try to catch some fish. You and two others."

The native climbed down swiftly to the deck, calling to his companions: "Fetch our rods, and the sinnet for the outrigger!"

The people off watch gathered while the Polynesian men fetched from the forecastle their stout rods of bamboo, equipped with handmade lines and curious lures of mother-of-pearl. The cross-booms were already fast to the outrigger float; they laid them on the gunwales of the long, sharp dugout canoe, and made them fast with a few quick turns of cord. They lowered her over the side, and a moment later she glided swiftly ahead of the ship.

The *Bounty* held her course, moving languidly over the calm sea. The canoe drew ahead fast, but at the end of an hour the ship was again abreast. One man was angling while the two paddlers drove the light vessel back and forth in the midst of a vast shoal of albacore. A cloud of sea birds hovered overhead, the gannets diving with folded wings, while the black noddy-terns fluttered down in companies each time the fish drove the small fry to the surface. Schools of tiny mullet and squid skipped this way and that in frenzied fear, snapped at by the fierce albacore below and the eager beaks of the birds. The angler stood in the stern of the canoe, trailing his lure of pearl shell far aft in the wake. Time after time the watchers on the ship saw the stiff rod bend suddenly as he braced himself to heave a struggling albacore of thirty or forty pounds into the canoe.

While the people of the *Bounty* gazed eagerly on this spectacle, one of the native men began to kindle a fire for cooking the fish. It was plain that there would be enough and to spare for all hands. Presently the canoe came alongside and two or three dozen large albacore were tossed on deck. Alexander Smith had relieved the man at the masthead, and now, while all hands were making ready for a meal, he hailed the deck exultantly: "Land ho-o-o!"

Men and women sprang into the rigging to stare ahead. Christian again went aloft, to settle himself beside Smith and focus his telescope on the horizon before the ship. The southerly swell caused an undulation along the line where sea met sky, but at one point, directly ahead, the moving line was interrupted. A triangle, dark and so infinitely small that none but the keenest of eyes could have made it out, rose above the sea. With an arm about the mast and his glass well braced, Christian gazed ahead for some time.

"By God, Smith!" he remarked. "You've a pair of eyes!"

The young seaman smiled. "Will it be Pitcairn's Island, sir?" he asked.

"I believe so," replied Christian absently.

The land was still far distant. The wind freshened toward midday, and after their dinner of fish all hands gazed ahead at the rugged island mounting steadily above the horizon. The natives, incapable of concern over the future, regarded the spectacle with pleased interest, but among the white men there was more than one sullen and gloomy face.

While the island changed form as it rose higher and higher before the ship, Christian sat in his cabin on the lower deck. With him were two of the Polynesian men, leaders of the others, whom he had asked to meet him there.

Minarii, a native of Tahiti, was a man of huge frame, with a bold, stern countenance and the assured, easy bearing of a man of rank. His voice was deep and powerful, his body covered with tattooing in curious and intricate designs, and his thick, iron-grey hair confined by a turban of white bark cloth. His companion, Tetahiti, was a young chief from Tupuai, who had left his island because of the friendship he felt for Christian, and because he knew that this same friendship would have cost him his life had he remained behind when the ship set sail. The people of Tupuai were bitterly hostile to the whites; good fortune alone had enabled the mutineers to leave the island without loss of life. Tetahiti was a powerfully made man, though of slighter build than Minarii; his features were more gently moulded, and his expression less severe. Both had been told that the *Bounty* was seeking an island where a settlement might be formed; now Christian was explaining to them the true state of affairs. They waited for him to speak.

"Minarii, Tetahiti," he said at last, "there is something I want you two and the other Maoris to know. We have been shipmates; if the land ahead of us proves hospitable, we shall soon be close neighbours ashore. For reasons of policy, I have not felt free to tell you the whole truth till now. Too much talk is not good on shipboard. You understand?"

They nodded, waiting for him to proceed.

"Bligh, who told the people of Tahiti that he was Captain Cook's son, lied to them. He was not a chief in his own land, nor had he the fairness and dignity of a chief. Raised to a position of authority, he became haughty, tyrannical, and cruel. You must have heard tales in Tahiti of how he punished his men by whipping them till the blood ran down their backs. His conduct to all grew unbearable. As captain, he drew his authority direct from King George, and used it to starve his crew in the midst of plenty, and to abuse his officers while the men under them stood close by."

Minarii smiled grimly. "I understand," he said. "You killed him and took the ship."

"No. I resolved to seize the ship, put him in irons, and let our King judge between us. But the men had suffered too much at Bligh's hands. For sixteen moons they had been treated as no Maori would treat his dog, and their blood was hot. To save Bligh's life, I put the large boat overboard and sent him into her, with certain men who wished to go with him. We gave them food and water, and I hope for the sake of the others that they may reach England. As for us, our action has made us outlaws to be hunted down, and when our King learns of it he will send a ship to search this sea. You and the others knew that we were looking for an island, remote and little known, on which to settle; now you know the reason. We have found the island. Minarii, shall you be content to remain there? If the place is suitable, we go no further."

The chief nodded slightly. "I shall be content," he said.

"And you, Tetahiti?"

"I can never return to my own land," the other replied. "Where you lead, I shall follow."

Four bells had sounded when Christian came on deck, and the *Bounty* was drawing near the land. At a distance of about a league, it bore from east-by-north to east-by-south, and presented the appearance of a tall ridge, with a small peak at either end. The southern peak rose to a height of not less than a thousand feet and sloped more gently to the sea; its northern neighbour was flanked by dizzy precipices, against which the waves broke and spouted high. Two watercourses, smothered in rich vegetation, made their way down to the sea, and midway between the peaks a slender thread of white marked where a cascade plunged over a cliff. The coast was studded with forbidding rocks, those to the north and south rising high above the spray of breaking seas. Clouds of sea fowl passed this way and that above the ship, regarding the intruders on their solitude with incurious eyes. Everywhere, save on the precipices where the birds reared their young, the island was of the richest green, for vegetation flourished luxuriantly on its volcanic soil, watered by abundant rains. No feature of the place escaped the native passengers, and exclamations of surprise and pleasure came from where they were grouped at the rail.

The leadsman began to call off the depths as the water shoaled. They had thirty fathoms when the northern extremity of the island was still half a mile distant, and Christian ordered the sails trimmed so that the ship might steer southeast along the coast. The wind was cut off as she drew abreast of the northern peak; the *Bounty* moved slowly on, propelled by the cat's-paws that came down off the land. The shore, about four cables distant, rose steeply to a height of two hundred feet or more, and there was scarcely a man on board who did not exclaim at the prospect now revealed. Between the westerly mountains and others perceived to the east lay a broad, gently sloping hollow, broken by small valleys and framed on three sides by ridges and peaks. Here were many hundreds of acres of rich wooded land, sheltered on all sides but the northern one.

The sea was calm. Before an hour had passed, the sails were clewed up and the *Bounty* dropped anchor in twenty fathoms, off a cove where it seemed that a boat might land and the steep green bluffs be scaled.

Standing on the quarter-deck, Christian turned to Young. "I fancy we shall find no better landing place, though we have not seen the southern coast. I shall take three of the Indians and explore it now. Stand offshore if the wind shifts; we can fend for ourselves."

The smaller canoe was soon over the side, with Tetahiti and two other men as paddlers. Christian seated himself in the bow, and the natives sent the little vessel gliding swiftly away from the ship. Passing between an isolated rock and the cape at the eastern extremity of the cove, the canoe skirted the foot of a small wooded valley, where huge old trees rose above an undergrowth of ferns and flowering shrubs. The pandanus, or screw pine, grew everywhere above the water's edge, its thorny leaves drenched in salt spray and its blossoms imparting a delicious fragrance to the air. Presently they rounded the easternmost cape of the island, which fell precipitously into the sea, here studded with great rocks about which the surges broke.

As the canoe turned westward, a shallow, half-moon bay revealed itself to Christian's eyes. The southerly swell broke with great violence here, on a narrow beach of sand at the foot of perpendicular cliffs, unscalable without the aid of ropes let down from above. A cloud of sea fowl hovered along the face of the cliffs, so high overhead that their cries were inaudible in the lulls of the breakers.

"An ill place!" said Tetahiti, as the canoe rose high on a swell and the beach was seen, half-veiled by smoking seas. "No man could climb out, though a lizard might."

"Keep on," ordered Christian. "Let us see what is beyond."

The southern coast of the island was iron-bound everywhere, set with jagged rocks offshore and rising in precipices scarcely less stupendous than those flanking the half-moon bay. On the western side there was a small indentation where a boat might have effected a landing in calm weather, but when they had completed the circuit of the island Christian knew that the cove off which the ship lay at anchor offered the only feasible landing place.

The sun was setting as he came on board the *Bounty;* he ordered the anchor up and the sails loosed to stand off to windward for the night.

## CHAPTER II

At dawn the following morning the island bore north, distant about three leagues. Close-hauled, on the larboard tack, the ship slid smoothly through the calm sea, and toward seven o'clock she passed the southeastern extremity of the island. About half a mile to the northwest, after rounding this point, was the shallow indentation where the *Bounty* had been anchored the previous day. Sounding continuously, with lookouts aloft and in the bows, she approached the land and again came to anchor half a mile from the beach, in seventeen fathoms.

Christian and Young stood together on the quarter-deck while the sails were clewed up and furled. With his spyglass Christian examined the foreshore carefully. Presently he turned to his companion.

"I shall be on shore the greater part of the day," he said. "In case of any change in the weather, heave short and be ready to stand off."

"Yes, sir."

"We are fortunate in having this southwesterly breeze; I only pray that it may hold."

"It will, never doubt it," Young replied. "The sky promises that."

"Be good enough to have one of the Indian canoes put into the water."

This order was quickly complied with, and a few minutes later Christian, taking with him Minarii, Alexander Smith, Brown, the gardener, and two of the women, Maimiti and Moetua, set off for the beach. Minarii sat at the steering paddle. The bay was strewn with huge boulders against which the sea broke violently. To the right and left, walls of rock fell all but sheer to the cove, but midway along it they discovered a ribbon of shingly beach, the only spot where a boat might be landed in safety. Steering with great skill, directing the movements of the paddlers and watching the following seas, Minarii guided the canoe toward this spot. They waited for some time just beyond the break of the surf, then, seizing a favourable opportunity, they came in on the crest of a long wave, and, immediately the canoe had grounded, they sprang out and drew it up beyond reach of the surf.

Directly before them rose a steep, heavily wooded slope, the broken-down remnant of what must once have been a wall of rock. Casuarina trees, some of them of immense size, grew here and there, the lacy foliage continually wet with spray. Coconut palms and the screw pine raised their tufted tops above the tangle of vegetation, and ferns of many varieties grew in the dense shade. For a moment the members of the party gazed about them without speaking; then Maimiti, with an exclamation of pleasure, made her way quickly to a bush that grew in a cleft among the rocks. She returned with a branch covered with glossy leaves and small white blossoms of a waxlike texture. She held them against her face, breathing in their delicate fragrance.

"It is the *tefano,*" she said, turning to Christian. Moetua was equally delighted, and the two women immediately gathered an armful of the blossoms and sat down to make wreaths for their hair.

"We shall be happy in this place," said Moetua. "See! There are pandanus trees and the *aito* and *purau* everywhere. Almost it might be Tahiti itself."

"But when you look seaward it is not like Tahiti," Maimiti added wistfully. "There is no reef. We shall miss our still lagoons. And where are the rivers? There can be none, surely, on so small an island that falls so steeply to the sea."

"No," said Christian. "We shall find no rivers like those of Tahiti; but there will be brooks in some of these ravines. What do you think, Minarii?"

The Tahitian nodded. "We shall not lack for water," he said. "It is a good land; the thick bush growing even here among the rocks proves that. Our taro and yams and sweet potatoes will do well in this soil. We may even find them growing here in a wild state; and there are sure to be plantains in the ravines."

Christian threw back his head, gazing at the green wall of vegetation rising so steeply above them. "We shall have work and to spare in clearing the land for our plantations," he said.

"I'll take to it kindly, for one," Smith replied warmly. "It does my heart good to smell the land again. Brown and me is a pair will be pleased to quit ship here, if that's your mind, sir. Eh, Will?"

The gardener nodded. "Shall we stop, sir?" he asked. "Is this Pitcairn's Island, do ye think?"

"I'm convinced of it," Christian replied. "It is far off the position marked for it on Captain Carteret's chart, but it must be the island he sighted. Whether we shall stay remains to be seen."

The women had now finished making their wreaths. They pressed them down over their thick black hair, which hung loosely over their shoulders. Christian gazed at them admiringly, thinking he had never seen a more beautiful sight than those two made in their kirtles of tapa cloth, with flecks of sunlight and shadows of leaves moving as the wind would have it across their faces and their slim brown bodies. Maimiti rose quickly. "Let us go on," she said. "I am eager to see what lies beyond."

The party, led by Minarii, was soon toiling up the ridge, the natives, Smith among them, far in advance. Christian and Brown followed at a more leisurely pace, stopping now and then to examine the trees and plants around them. The ascent was steep indeed, and in places they found it necessary to pull themselves up by the roots of trees and bushes.

Two hundred feet of steady climbing brought them to a gentler slope. Here the others were awaiting them.

Before them stretched a densely wooded country that seemed all but level, at first, after the steep climb to reach it. Far below was the sea, its colour of the deepest blue under the cloudless sky. In a southerly direction the land rose gently for a considerable distance, then with a steeper ascent as it approached the ridge which bounded their view on that side. To the northwest another ridge could be seen, culminating at either end in a mountain peak green to the summit, but the one to the north showed sections of bare perpendicular wall on the seaward side. The land before them was like a great plateau rather than a valley, traversed by half a dozen ravines, and lying at an angle, its high side resting upon the main southern ridge of the island, its lower side upon the cliffs that fronted the sea. The ridges to the west and south rose, as nearly as they could judge, five or six hundred feet above the place where they stood.

"That peak to the southwest must be all of a thousand feet above the sea," said Christian.

"Aye, sir," Smith replied. "We'll be high and safe here, that's sure. Ye'd little think, from below, there's such good land."

At a little distance before them the ground fell away to a small watercourse so heavily shaded by great trees that scarcely a ray of sunlight penetrated. Here they found a tiny stream of clear water and gladly halted to refresh themselves. Christian now divided his party.

"Minarii, do you and Moetua bear off to the left and climb the main ridge yonder. Smith, you and Brown follow the rise of the land to the westward; we must know what lies beyond. I will proceed along this northern rim of the island. Let us meet toward midday, farther along, somewhere below the peak you see before us. The island is so small that we can hardly go astray."

They then separated. Keeping the sea within view on the right, Christian proceeded with Maimiti in a northwesterly direction. Now and then they caught glimpses through the foliage of the mountain that rose before them, heavily wooded to the topmost pinnacle, but descending in sheer walls of rock on the seaward side. Save for the heavy booming of the surf, far below, the silence of the place seemed never to have been broken since the beginning of time; but a few moments later, as they were resting, seated on the trunk of a fallen tree, they heard a faint bird-call, often repeated, that seemed to come from far away. They were surprised to discover the bird itself, a small dust-coloured creature with a whitish breast, quite near at hand, darting among the undergrowth as it uttered its lonely monotonous cry. They saw no other land birds, no living creatures, in fact, save for a small brown rat, and a tiny iridescent lizard scurrying over the dead leaves or peering at them with bright eyes from the limbs of trees. Of a sudden Maimiti halted.

"There have been people here before us," she said.

"Here? Nonsense, Maimiti! What makes you think so?"

"I know it," she replied gravely. "It must have been long ago, but there was once a path where we are now walking."

Christian smiled incredulously. "I can't believe it," he said.

"Because you are not of our blood," the girl replied. "But Moetua would know, or Minarii. I felt this as we were climbing up from the landing place. Now I am sure of it. People of my own race have lived here at some time."

"Why have they gone, then?"

"Who knows?" she replied. "Perhaps it is not a happy place."

"Not happy? An island so rich and beautiful?"

"The people may have brought some old unhappiness with them. It is not often the land that is to blame; it is those who come."

"You can't be right, Maimiti," Christian said, after a moment of silence. "What could have brought them so far from any other land?"

"It is not only you white men with your great ships who make long voyages," she replied. "There is no land in all this great ocean that people of my blood have not found before you. Even here they have come."

"Perhaps. . . . Don't you think we shall be happy here?" he asked presently. "You're not sorry we came?"

"No . . ." She hesitated. "But it is so far away. . . . Shall we never go back to Tahiti?"

Christian shook his head. "Never. I told you that before we came," he added gently.

"I know. . . ." She glanced up with a wistful smile, her eyes misted with tears. "You must not mind if I think of Tahiti sometimes."

"Mind? Of course I shall not mind! . . . But we shall be happy here, Maimiti. I am sure of it. The land is strange to us now; but soon we shall have our houses built, and when our children come it will be home to us. You will never be sad, then."

The relationship between Christian and this daughter of Polynesian aristocrats was no casual or superficial one. It was an attachment that had its beginning shortly after the *Bounty's* first arrival at Tahiti, and which had deepened day by day during the months the vessel remained there, assembling her cargo of young breadfruit trees. During the long sojourn on the island, Christian had made a serious effort to learn the native speech, with such success that he was now able to converse in it with considerable fluency. The language difficulty overcome, he had discovered that Maimiti was far more than the simple, unreflecting child of nature that he had, at first, supposed; but it was not until the time came when it was necessary for her to choose between him and giving up, forever, family and friends and all that had hitherto made life dear to her that he realized the depth of her loyalty and affection. There had been no hesitation on her part in deciding which it should be.

Presently she turned toward him again, making an attempt to smile. "Let us go on," she said. She took Christian's hand, as though for protection against the strangeness and silence of the place, and they proceeded slowly, peering into the thickets on either side, stopping frequently to explore some small glade where the dense foliage of the trees had prevented the undergrowth from thriving. Of a sudden Maimiti halted and gazed overhead. "Look!" she exclaimed. "*Itatae!*"

Coming from seaward, outlined in exquisite purity against the blue sky, were two snow-white terns. They watched them in silence for a moment.

"These are the birds I love most of all," said Maimiti. "Do you remember them at Tahiti? Always you see two together."

Christian nodded. "How close they come!" he said. "They seem to know you."

"Of course they know me! Have I never told you how I chose the *itatae* for my own birds when I was a little girl? Oh, the beautiful things! You will see: within a week I shall have them eating out of my hand."

She now looked about her with increasing interest and pleasure, pointing out to Christian various plants and trees and flowers familiar to her. Presently a parklike expanse, shaded by trees immemorially old, opened before them. On their right hand stood a gigantic banyan tree whose roots covered a great area of ground. Passing beyond this and descending the slope for a little way, they came to a knoll only a short distance above the place where the land fell steeply to the sea. It was an enchanting spot, fragrant with the odours of growing, blossoming things, and cooled by the breeze that rustled through the foliage of great trees that hemmed it in on the seaward side. Beyond, to the north, they looked across a narrow valley to the mountain which cut off the view in that direction. Christian turned to his companion.

"Maimiti, this is the spot I would choose for our home."

She nodded. "I wished you to say that! It is the very place!"

"All of our houses can be scattered along this northern slope," he added, "and we are certain to find water in one of these small valleys."

Maimiti was now as light-hearted as she had been sad a little time before. They sat down on a grassy knoll and talked eagerly of plans for the future, of the precise spot where their house should stand; of the paths to be made through the forests, of the gardens to be planted, and the like. At length they rose, and, crossing the deeply shaded expanse above, they came to a breadfruit tree which towered above the surrounding forest. It was the first they had seen. Another smaller tree had sprung from one of its roots, and by means of this Maimiti climbed quickly to the lower branches of the great one, which was loaded with fruit. She twisted off a dozen or more of the large green globes, tossing them down to Christian.

"We shall have a feast to-day," she called down. "Did you bring your fire-maker?"

Christian brought forth his flint and steel; they gathered twigs and leaves and dry sticks, and when the fire was burning briskly they placed the fruit in the midst of it to roast. When the rough green rinds had been blackened all round, they left the breadfruit among the hot ashes and again set out to explore further. Upon returning, an hour later, they found Minarii and Moetua squatting by the fire roasting sea birds' eggs which they had collected along the tops of the cliffs beyond the southern ridge. And Minarii had brought a cluster of green drinking coconuts and a bunch of fine plantains he had found in the depths of the valley.

"We shall eat well to-day," he said. "It is a rich land we have found. We have no need to seek further."

"So I think," Christian replied. "Did you climb the ridge to the south'ard?"

"Yes. There is good land beyond, better even than that in this valley. I was surprised to find it so; but on this side is where we should live."

"That is good news, Minarii," Christian replied. "I, too, supposed that the sea lay directly below the southern ridge. How wide are the lands beyond?"

"In some places they extend for all of five or six hundred paces, sloping gently down from the ridge to the high cliffs that front the sea."

"Have you found any streams?"

"One. It is small, but the water is good."

"We shall not lack for sea fowls' eggs," said Moetua. "All the cliffs on that southern side are filled with crannies where they nest. I collected these in little time, but there is danger in gathering them; it made my eyes swim to look below."

It was now getting on toward midday, but the lofty trees spread for them their grateful shade, and the breeze, though light, was refreshingly cool. While preparations for the meal went forward, Christian again strolled to the seaward side of the plateau, where he had a view of the full half-circle of the horizon. Far below, to the east, he could see the *Bounty,* looking small indeed under the cliffs, against the wide background of empty sea. Her anchors were holding well. Having satisfied himself that the ship had maintained her position, he seated himself with his back to a tree, hands clasped around his knees, and remained thus until he heard Maimiti's voice calling him from above. He rose and went slowly back to the others.

Their meal was under way before Smith and Brown appeared. Both were enthusiastic over what they had found.

"It's as fine a little place as ever I see, Mr. Christian," Smith said, warmly. "We climbed to the top of that peak, yonder."

"How much land is there beyond the western ridge?"

"Little enough, sir, and what there is, is all rocks and gullies."

Christian turned to Brown. "What have you found in the way of useful plants and trees?"

"I needn't speak of the coconut palms and the pandanus, sir. Ye've seen for yourself that there's more than enough for our needs. Then there's *miro* and sandalwood, and the *tutui* . . ."

"The candlenut? There is a useful find indeed!"

"There's a good few scattered about; and the *miro,* as ye know, is a fine wood for house-building. As for food plants, it's as well we've a stock on board. We've found wild yams and a kind of taro, but little else."

"You could overlook the whole of the island from the peak?"

"Aye, sir," Smith replied.

"What would you say of its extent, judging roughly?"

"It can't be much over two miles long, sir, if that; and about half as wide. What do ye think, Will?"

"Aye, it's about that," the gardener replied. "There's a fine grove of breadfruit on the shelf of land ye can see from here, sir, but I'm as glad we brought some young trees with us. We've varieties I didn't see, here, in looking about this morning."

"Have you found any evidence that people have been here before us?"

"To say the truth, sir, I never even thought of that," Brown replied.

"Ye don't mean white men, Mr. Christian?" Smith asked.

"No. We are the first, I am sure, who have ever landed here; but Maimiti thinks Indians have once inhabited the place."

"If they did, it must have been long ago. Never a trace did we see of anything of the kind."

Christian now turned to Minarii, addressing him in the native tongue. "Minarii, is it possible, do you think, that Maoris have ever visited this land?"

"*É*," he remarked, quietly. "There has been a settlement here, where we now are. It is the place that would have been chosen for a village, and that great banyan tree has been planted. The breadfruit as well."

Maimiti turned to Christian. "You see?" she said. "Did I not tell you so?"

Christian smiled, incredulously. "I have great respect for your judgment, Minarii," he said, "but in this case I am sure you are wrong. Before us sea birds alone have inhabited this land."

Minarii inserted his hand into the twist of tapa at his waist and drew forth a small stone adze, beautifully made and ground to perfect smoothness. "Then the sea fowl brought that?" he asked.

It was late afternoon when the party returned to the ship. Smith and Brown went forward, where they were surrounded at once by the other seamen, eager for a report of conditions ashore. Christian retired to his cabin and supped there, alone. Toward sunset he joined Young on deck. For some time he paced up and down, then halted by his companion, who stood at the rail gazing at the high slopes before them, all golden now in the light of the sinking sun.

"We will call this 'Bounty Bay,' Mr. Young, unless you have a better suggestion?"

"I was thinking that 'Christian's Landing' would be a suitable name, sir."

Christian shook his head. "I wish my name to be attached to nothing here," he said, "not even to one of those rocks offshore. Tell me," he added, "now that we have found the place, how do you feel about it?"

"That we might have searched the Pacific over without having discovered a more suitable one."

"There is no real anchorage here," Christian went on. "The place where we lie is the best the island affords. You can imagine what this cove will be in a northerly blow. No ship would be safe for ten minutes in such an exposed position. You realize what a decision to remain here means? Our voyages are over until our last day."

"That is of course, sir," Young replied, quietly.

"And you are content that it shall be so?"

"Quite."

Christian turned his head and gave him a swift, scrutinizing glance. When he spoke again it was not as the *Bounty's* captain addressing an inferior officer. There was a friendly gleam in his eyes, and a note of appeal in his voice.

"Old friend," he said, "from this time on, let there be no more ship's formality between us. The success or failure of the little colony we shall plant here depends largely upon us. I shall need your help badly, and it may be that you will need mine. Whatever happens, let us stand by each other."

"That we shall," Young replied warmly, "and there is my hand upon it."

Christian seized and pressed it cordially. "We have rough men to handle," he continued. "It was to be expected that the more unruly ones should have come here with me. . . . Tell me frankly, why did you come? There was no need. You took no part in the mutiny; you might have remained on Tahiti with the other innocent men to wait for a ship to take you home. Once there, a court-martial would certainly have vindicated you."

"Let me assure you of this," Young replied, "I have never regretted my decision."

Christian turned again to look at him. "You mean that," he said, "I can see that you do. And yet, when I think what you have given up to throw in your lot with me . . ."

"Do you remember Van Diemen's Land," Young asked, "where Bligh had me seized up at one of the guns and flogged?"

"I am not likely to forget that," Christian replied, grimly.

"I was a mutineer at heart from that day," Young went on. "I have never told you of this, but, had there been an opportunity, I would have deserted the ship before we sailed from Tahiti — for home, as we then thought. As you know, I slept through the whole of the mutiny. When I was awakened and ordered on deck, the thing was done. Bligh and those who went with him had been cast adrift, and the launch was far astern. Had I known in advance what you meant to do . . ." He paused. "I will not say, Christian, that I would have given you my active support. I think I should have lacked the courage . . ."

"Let us speak no more of that," Christian interrupted. "You are here. You little know what comfort that thought brings me. . . . I was thinking," he added presently, "what a paradise Pitcairn's Island might prove, could we have chosen our companions here. We have an opportunity such as chance rarely grants to men — to form a little world cut off from the rest of mankind, and to rear our children in complete ignorance of any life save what they will find on this small island."

Young nodded. "Whom would you have chosen, could you have had your wish, from the *Bounty's* original company?"

"I prefer not to think of the matter," Christian replied, gloomily. "We must do what we can with those we have. The Indians are fine fellows, with one or, perhaps, two exceptions. I have few regrets concerning them. As for the men of our own blood . . ." He broke off, leaving the sentence unfinished.

"Brown and Alex Smith might have been chosen in any event," Young remarked.

"I should have excepted them. They are good men, both."

"And their respect and admiration for you are very near idolatry," Young added, with a faint smile. "That of Smith in particular; you've a loyal henchman there."

"I'm glad you think so. I've a great liking for Smith. What do you know of him? Where does he come from?"

"I've learned more about him these past three months than I did during the whole of the voyage out from England. He was a lighterman on the Thames at the time Bligh was signing on the *Bounty* men, but he hated the business and was only waiting for a suitable opportunity to go to sea again. He has told me that his true name is Adams, John Adams, and that he was born and reared in a foundling home near London."

"Adams, you say? That's curious! Why did he change his name?"

"He volunteered no information on that score, and I didn't feel free to question him."

"No, naturally not. Well, whatever scrape he may have been in, I'll warrant there was nothing mean or underhanded in his share of it."

"I'd be willing to take my oath on that," Young replied, heartily. "He's rough and uncouth, but you can depend upon him. He hasn't a tricky or a dishonest bone in his body."

"There is a decision we must make soon," Christian said, after a moment of silence. "It concerns the vessel."

"You mean to destroy her?"

"Yes. Do you agree to the plan?"

"Heartily."

"There is nothing else we can do, the island being what it is; but I want the suggestion to come from the men themselves. They must soon see the necessity, if they have not already."

"Supposing there were a safe anchorage?"

"Not even then should I have wanted to keep her. No, we must burn all bridges behind us. I fancy there is not a lonelier island in the Pacific, and yet the place is known, and there is always the possibility of its being visited. A ship can't be concealed, but once we are rid of the *Bounty* we can so place our settlement that no evidence of it will appear from the sea. The landing is a dangerous one and not likely to be attempted by any vessel that may pass this way; certainly not if the place is thought to be uninhabited. We shall have little to fear, once we are rid of the vessel."

"May I make a suggestion?"

"Please do. Speak your mind to me at all times."

"The men are impatient, I know, to learn of your plans. Would it not be well to tell them, to-night, how the island impresses you?"

Christian reflected for a moment. "Good. I agree," he said. "Call them aft, will you?"

He paced the quarter-deck while Young was carrying out this order. The men, both white and brown, gathered in a half-circle by the mizzenmast to await Christian's pleasure. The women assembled behind them, peering over their shoulders and talking in subdued voices. It was a strange ship's company that gathered on the *Bounty's* deck to listen to the words of their leader.

"Before anything more is done," he began, "I wish to be sure that you are satisfied with this island as a home for us. You were all agreed that we should search for the place, and that, if we found it suitable, we should settle here. You will have learned from your shipmates who went ashore with me what the island has to offer us. Remember, if we go ashore, we go to stay. If any object, now is the time to speak."

There was an immediate response from several of the men.

"I'm for stopping, Mr. Christian."

"It's a snug little place. We couldn't wish for better, sir."

Mills was the first of the dissenting party to speak.

"It's not my notion of a snug little place."

"Why not?" Christian asked.

Addressed thus directly by his commanding officer, Mills shifted from one foot to the other, scowling uneasily at his companions.

"I've spoke my mind, Mr. Christian; it ain't my notion of a place, and I'll stand by that."

"But that's no reason, man! You must know why you're not satisfied. What is it that you object to?"

"He'd be satisfied with no place, Mr. Christian; that's the truth of it," Williams, the blacksmith, put in.

"You prefer Tahiti. Is that it?" Christian asked.

"I'm not sayin' I'd not go back if the chance was offered."

Christian regarded him in silence for a moment.

"Listen to me, Mills," he proceeded. "And the rest of you as well. I have spoken of this matter before. I will repeat what I've said, and for the last time. We are not English seamen in good standing, in our own ship, free to do as we choose and to go where we choose. We are fugitives from justice, guilty of the double crime of mutiny and piracy. That we will be searched for, as soon as the fact of the mutiny is known, is beyond question."

"Ye don't think old Bligh'll ever reach England, sir?" Martin interrupted.

Christian paused and glanced darkly at him.

"I could wish that he might," he said, "for the sake of the innocent men who went with him. As matters stand, it is not likely that any of them will ever again be heard of. Nevertheless, His Majesty will not suffer one of his vessels to disappear without ordering a wide and careful search to be made, to learn, if possible, her fate. A ship-of-war will be sent out for that purpose, and Tahiti will be her destination. There she will learn of the mutiny from those of our company who remained on that island. The Pacific will then be combed for our hiding place; every island considered at all likely as our refuge will be visited. Should we be discovered and taken, death will be the portion of every man of us. For my own part, I mean never to be taken."

"Nor I, sir!" Smith put in. Others of the mutineers added their voices to his. There was no doubt as to the general feeling concerning the necessity for a safe hiding place.

"Very well," Christian continued. "It is agreed, apparently, by all, or most of you, that you have no wish to swing at a yardarm from one of His Majesty's ships-of-war. What, then, is best to be done? Surely it is to seek out some island unlikely to be visited for as long as we may live. We have found such an island; it lies before us. We are distant, here, more than a thousand miles from Tahiti, and far from the tracks of any vessel likely to cross the Pacific in whatever direction. It is a fertile and pleasant place; that you can see for yourselves. Our Indian friends, whose judgment I trust more than my own in such matters, say that it is capable of supplying all our needs. There are no inhabitants to molest us; our experiences at Tupuai will not be repeated here. To me it seems an ideal spot, and Mr. Young agrees that we might have searched the Pacific over without having found one better suited to men in our position. Now, then, reflect carefully. Shall we make our home here or shall we not? And those who are opposed must give better reasons than that of Mills."

"Is this to be for good, Mr. Christian?" McCoy asked.

"Yes. Let there be no mistake about that. I have already said that if we go ashore we go to stay."

"Then I don't favour it."

"For what reason?"

"The place is too sma'. We'd do better for ourselves on that island we raised after the mutiny, on our way to Tupuai."

"Rarotonga, you mean."

"Aye. It's a likelier place."

Christian reflected for a moment.

"I will say this, McCoy. I seriously considered taking the vessel to

Rarotonga, but there are the best of reasons why I decided against the plan. The place is known to those of the *Bounty's* company who remained on Tahiti, and amongst them are men who will be sure to speak of it to the officers of whatever vessel may be sent in search of us. Furthermore, it is but little more than a hundred leagues from Tahiti. We could never feel safe there. . . . Have you anything further to say?"

He waited, glancing from one to another of the mutineers. Mills avoided his gaze and stood with his arms folded, scowling at vacancy. Martin looked at Quintal and kicked him with his bare foot as though urging him to speak, but no further objections were offered.

"Very well, then. Those who favour choosing Pitcairn's Island as our home, show hands."

Five hands were lifted at once. McCoy, after a moment of hesitation, joined the affirmative vote. Martin followed.

"Well, Mills?" said Christian, sharply.

The old seaman raised his hand with an effort. "I can see it's best, Mr. Christian, but I deem it hard to be cut off for life on a rock the like o' this."

"You would find it harder still to be cut off at a rope's end," Christian replied, grimly.

"What's to be done with the ship, sir?" Martin asked.

"Burn her, I say." It was Smith who spoke.

"Aye, burn and scuttle her, Mr. Christian," said Williams. "There's no other way."

There was immediate dissent to this proposal on the part of both Martin and Mills, and for a moment all the seamen were shouting at once. Christian waited, then gave an order for silence.

"Not a man of you but is seaman enough to know that we can't keep the ship here," he said, quietly. "She must be dismantled and burned. What else could we do with her?"

The matter was discussed at some length, but it was plain to all that no other possibility offered itself, and when the question was put to a vote the show of hands was again unanimous.

"I have only one other thing to add," Christian said. "In matters of importance that concern us as a community, every man, from this day on, shall have his vote. All questions shall be decided by the will of the majority. Are you agreed to this?"

All were in favour of the proposal, and Christian, having admonished them to remember this in the future, dismissed them. When they had gone, Young turned to his commander.

"For their own good, Christian, you have been too generous."

"In granting them a voice in our affairs?"

"Yes. I think ultimate decisions should rest with you."

"I well realize the danger," Christian replied; "but there is no alternative. I alone am the cause of their being here. Had I not incited them to mutiny, the *Bounty* would now be nearing England — home." He broke off, staring gloomily at the land. "That thought must be often in their minds."

"They were your eager assistants," Young replied. "Not one of them joined you against his will."

"I know. Nevertheless, I swept them into action on the spur of the moment. They had no time to reflect upon the consequences. No, Edward, I owe the meanest man among them whatever compensation is now possible. Justice demands that I give each of them a voice in our affairs; yes, even though I know it to be to their own hurt. But you and I, together, can, I hope, direct them to wise decisions."

The sun had now set and the silence of the land seemed to flow outward to meet the silence of the sea. High overhead, sea birds in countless numbers floated to and fro with lonely cries in the still air, their wings catching the light streaming up from beyond the horizon. The *Bounty* rocked gently over the long smooth undulations sweeping in from the open sea.

At length Christian turned from the rail. "It is a peaceful spot, Edward," he said. "God grant that we may keep it so!"


## CHAPTER III

THE *Bounty's* people were astir with the first light of day, and preparations for disembarking supplies went rapidly forward. The mutineers, with the exception of Brown, the gardener, were to remain on board under Young's charge, sending the supplies ashore. This done, they were to proceed with the dismantling of the vessel. The native men and most of the women were to constitute the beach party, transporting cargo to the landing place by means of the ship's cutters and two canoes brought from Tahiti. As soon as a path had been made, they were to carry the stores on to the site above the cove selected for the temporary settlement. Williams, the blacksmith, had converted some cutlasses into bush knives by filing off the upper part of the long blades. Provided with these, and with axes, mattocks, and spades, Minarii and two of his native companions were soon hard at work on shore, hacking through the dense thickets and digging out a zigzag trail to the level ground above.

Although the *Bounty's* stores had been shared with the mutineers who remained on Tahiti, there was still a generous amount on board: casks of spirits, salt beef and pork, dried peas and beans, an abundant supply of clothing, kegs of powder and nails, iron for blacksmith work, lead for musket balls, and the like. There were also fourteen muskets and a number of pistols. The livestock consisted of half a dozen large crates of fowls, twenty sows, two of which had farrowed during the voyage, five boars, and three goats. The island being small, it was decided to free both the fowls and the animals and let them fend for themselves until the work of house-building was under way.

The weather was all that could be desired; the sky cloudless, the breeze light and from the southwest. So it remained for five days. By the end of that time the precious stock of plants and animals had been carried ashore as well as most of the ship's provisions, and shelters made of the *Bounty's* spare sails had been erected on a spot overlooking the cove.

An incident occurred at this time which aroused intense excitement among the Maori members of the company. It was an immemorial custom, among the Polynesians, when migrating from one land to another, to carry with them several sacred stones from their ancestral *maraes,* or temples, to be used to consecrate their temples in a new land. The Tahitians had brought with them two such stones from the *marae* of Fareroi, on the northern coast of their homeland. Minarii, the chief in whose charge they were, had brought them on deck to be taken ashore, and Martin, seeing them at the gangway and knowing little and caring less of their significance to the natives, had thrown them overboard. The native men were all ashore at the time, but Martin's act had been witnessed by some of the women, who were horrified at what he had done. One of them leaped overboard and swam to the beach, informing the men of what had happened. They returned in all haste, and the white seamen, forward, resolved to brazen out the sacrilegious act performed by Martin. A pitched battle was averted only by the quick-wittedness of Maimiti and the tactfulness of Young, who had the liking and respect of the native men. Fortunately, the stones could still be dimly seen lying on the white sand below the vessel, and it was the work of only a few minutes to dive, secure them with lines, and draw them up. This done, peace was restored and the natives returned to their work ashore.

On the morning of the fifth day the wind shifted to the northeast and blew freshly into the cove. All had agreed that the vessel was to be beached as soon as the wind favoured, and Young now put everything in readiness for the *Bounty's* last brief voyage. Christian, who had spent the night ashore, returned at once. Most of the native women were aboard at this time and the mutineers were at their stations, waiting, talking in low voices among themselves. Christian clambered over the rail, glanced briefly around, and went to the wheel.

"It could not have happened better for us, Ned," he said quietly. "There's been no trouble aboard?"

"Thus far, no," Young replied. "We'll have her ashore before Mills gathers his wits together. I've kept Martin working aft with me until a moment ago."

Christian called to the men forward. "Stand by to back the fore-top-mast staysail!"

"Aye, aye, sir!"

"Break out the anchors.

The men at the windlass heaved lustily, their sunburned backs gleaming with sweat. The stronger of the women assisted at this task, while others ran aloft to loose the fore-topsail. With her staysail backed, the vessel swung slowly around, the topsail filled, and, while the anchors were catted, the ship gathered way and drove quietly on toward the beach.

The spot selected for running the vessel ashore lay under the lofty crag, later called Ship-Landing Point, on the left side of the cove. Yielding the wheel to Young, Christian now went forward to direct the vessel's course. It was a tense moment for all the *Bounty's* company; men and women alike lined the bulwarks, gazing ahead across the narrowing strip of water. Martin, McCoy, and Quintal stood together on the larboard side.

Martin shook his head, gloomily. "Mark my word, mates! Many's the time we'll rue this day afore we're done!"

Quintal thumped him on the back. "Over the side with 'ee, Isaac, and swim back to Tahiti if ye've a mind that way. I'm for stoppin'."

"Aye, ye was easy won over, Matt Quintal," Martin replied. "It's all for the best, is it? We'll see afore the year's out. . . . God a mercy! There's bottom!"

The vessel, still a quarter of a mile from shore, struck lightly. The rock could be seen, but it was at such a depth that it no more than scraped the hull gently; in a few seconds she was clear of it, but her end was near. Riding more and more violently to the onshore swell, she approached two rocks, barely awash and about four fathoms apart. A moment later the ground swell carried her swiftly forward, lifting her bow high, and she struck heavily.

The impact was both downward and forward; with her own movement and the sea to help her, she slid on until her bow was lifted two or three feet. There, by a lucky chance, she stuck, so firmly wedged that the sea could drive her no further. The broken water foamed around her, and now and then a heavier swell, breaking under her counter, showered her decks with spray.

No time was lost in making the vessel as secure as possible. The rocks where she struck lay at about thirty yards from the beach, and were protected in a southeasterly direction by the cliff that formed that side of the cove. Two hawsers were now carried from the bow to the shore and made fast to trees. The vessel remained in the position in which she had struck, canted at a slight angle to starboard. Christian, having satisfied himself that she was as secure as he could make her, set the men to work at once at the task of dismantling.

There was no respite for anyone during the following week. The topgallant masts were sent down as soon as the ship was beached. The topmasts now followed, whereupon the fore, main, and mizzenmasts were cut into suitable lengths for handling and for use as lumber ashore. Most of the men were employed on board, and the women, excellent swimmers, helped to raft the timbers through the surf. So steep was the slope above the landing beach that it was necessary to dig out the hillside and bank up the earth so that the timbers and planking might be stacked beyond reach of the sea until such time as they could be carried on to the settlement. Realizing the need for haste, all worked with a will. Fortunately, the shift in wind had been no forerunner of heavy weather. The breeze remained light and the sea fairly calm.

At length the vessel had been gutted of cabins, lockers, and storerooms, the deck planking had been removed, and the men were ripping off the heavy oaken strakes. Their task being so nearly finished, a day of rest was granted, and for the first time since the *Bounty* had left England, no one was aboard the vessel. An abundance of fish was caught during the morning, and with these, fresh breadfruit, plantains, and wild yams the native men had found, the *Bounty's* people made the most satisfying meal they had enjoyed since leaving Tahiti. Never before had they eaten together, and the feeling of constraint was apparent to all. Christian and Young tried to put the men at ease, but the meal passed in silence for the most part. The women, according to Polynesian custom, waited until the men had finished before partaking of the food. Their hunger satisfied, the men drew apart and lay in the shade, some sleeping, some talking in desultory fashion. Early in the afternoon, Martin, Mills, and McCoy, who had seen little of the island thus far, set out to explore it with Alexander Smith as their guide.

They toiled slowly on into the depths of the valley, making their way with difficulty through the dense forests and vine-entangled thickets. An hour had passed before they reached the ridge overlooking the western side of the island. The breeze was refreshingly cool at that height, and they seated themselves in a shady spot overlooking the wild green lands below. No sound was heard save their own laboured breathing and the gentle rustling of the wind through the trees that shaded them. Mills sat with his arms crossed on his knees, gazing morosely into the depths of the thickets beneath them.

"And this is what Christian's brought us to!" he said. "There's what we can see from here, and no more."

"There's room enough," said McCoy.

"Room? Ye're easy pleased," Martin put in, gloomily. "A bloody rock, I call it!"

"Aye, Tahiti's the place," said Smith, scornfully. "Ye'd have us all go back there to be took by the first ship that comes out from England. Ye're perishin' to be choked off at a rope's end, Isaac. None o' that for me!"

McCoy nodded. "It's no such a grand place for size, this Pitcairn's Island; but Christian's right — it's safe. We'll never be found."

"And here we'll bide to our last day!" said Mills. "Have 'ee thought o' that, shipmates?" He smote his horny palms together. "God's curse on the pack of us! What fools we've been to break up the ship!"

McCoy sat up abruptly. "Hearken to me, John. Ye and Isaac had

your chance to stay at Tahiti, but I mind me weel ye was all for comin'
awa' with the rest of us to a safer place. And now we've found it, ye'll
nae hae it. And what would ye hae done with the ship? Hoist her three
hunnerd feet up the rocks? Where could we keep her?"

"It's as Christian says," Smith added. "We're not free to go where
we like."

"And whose fault is that?" Mills replied. "If he'd minded his own
bloody business . . ."

"Aye," said Martin, "we'd ha' been home by now, or near it. We've
a deal to be thankful for to Mr. Fletcher Christian!"

"I'd like well to hear ye tell him that," said Smith. "Ye'll be sayin'
next he drove us into the mutiny. There was no man more willin' than
yerself, Isaac Martin, to seize the ship."

"That's truth," said McCoy. "Give Christian his due. We was all of a
mind, there."

"The man's clean daft. Is there one of ye can't see it?"

"Daft! . . ."

"Sit ye quiet, Alex. So he is, and we've all been daft with him. He's
queer by nature, that's my belief, and since we took the ship he thinks
the world ain't big enough to hide him and us in. He's a master talker
when he's a mind to talk; that I'll say, else he'd never coaxed a man of
us off Tahiti. What if a ship did come there? Couldn't we ha' hid in
the mountains? There's places a plenty where God himself couldn't
ha' found us. Or if we was afeared o' that, we'd only to take a big
Indian canoe and sail to Eimeo or one of them islands to leeward, a
good hundred miles from Tahiti. We could ha' played hide-and-seek
with a dozen King's ships till they got sick o' the chase and went off
home. Then we'd live easy for ten or fifteen years till the next one came.
Ain't that common sense? Speak up, Will!"

"Aye," McCoy replied, uneasily. "Like enough we might hae
done it."

"Might! Damn my eyes! I've spoke o' ships because Christian's got
ships on the brain, but I'll warrant tnem as stayed on Tahiti is as safe
as we'll be here. Bligh'll never get home; Christian himself knows
that. Does anyone but him think they'll send a ship out from England,
halfway round the world, to see what's become of a little transport?
Bloody likely! They'll mark her down as lost by the act o' God, and
that'll be the end of it."

"Damn your blood!" said Mills, scowling at him. "Why couldn't ye ha' spoke like this to Christian? What's the good o' talkin' of it now?"

"Didn't I say we was daft, the lot of us? He's made us believe what he told us, and now we're done for."

"I'd like to see ye with a rope around your neck, waitin' to be hoisted aloft," said Smith. "It's not Christian ye'd be callin' daft then."

"Leave all that, lads," said McCoy. "We're to stop here now, and there's an end of it."

"And Christian's always to have his way, is he, whatever's done?" Martin asked.

"No, damn my eyes if he is!" Mills exclaimed. "We're jack-tars no longer, mates! Don't forget it! We're to have a say here as good as his own. He's promised it."

"There's no need to fash yersel'," said McCoy. "Wasn't it Christian that made the offer? And he'll bide by it; that we know."

"Who's sayin' he won't? But I want us to mind what he's said. . . . There's the rum, now. He's promised us our grog as long as it lasts, and we've had none these two days."

"Curse ye, John, for mindin' us o' that," said McCoy with a wry smile.

"And how would we have it with us workin' aboard and the spirits ashore?" said Smith.

"Aye, we're no settled yet," said McCoy. "Gie him time. We'll have our tot afore the evening."

"There's Alex would a had us go without altogether," said Mills.

"Ye've a thick skull, John. I was for makin' it last a good few years, and, as Christian says, ye can't do that and claim seamen's rations now. How much do we have? Ye know as well as myself, there's but the two puncheons — that's 164 gallons — and the three five-gallon cags."

"There's but eight of us to drink it, Alex. Brown's an abstainer."

"Aye," said McCoy, fervently. "God be thanked for Brown and the Indians! If they was fond o' grog . . ."

"Like it or not, none the Indians would have. We could see to that," said Mills.

"What I say is this," Smith continued. "Christian's give ye yer choice with the rum, and ye was all for yer half-pint a day. With eight of us to drink it, there's three and a half gallons a week. Afore the year's out, where'll we be for grog? And mind ye, there's no Deptford stores here. When it's gone, it's gone, and we'll do without for the rest of our lives."

"We'll no think of that, Alex," said McCoy. "We'll just relish what we've got and thank God it's no less. Mon, but I'd like my dram this minute!"

"What would ye say, messmates, to better than a dram for the four of us within the half-hour?" Martin asked. McCoy turned his head quickly.

"What's that ye say, Isaac? How should we hae it, and the rum stored in Christian's tent?"

"Oh, it's rum ye must have, is it?" Martin replied, with a sly smile. "Ye wouldn't look at brandy, I doubt? And fine old brandy, too?"

"What are ye drivin' at, man?" asked Mills, harshly. "Can't ye speak out plain? There's no brandy in the stores."

"Have I said it was in the stores?"

"Hark 'ee, Isaac! If ye've been thievin' from the medicine chest . . ."

"I've done no such thing. I'll tell 'ee, mates," he proceeded, leaning forward with his elbows on his knees. "A few days back while we was rippin' out the cabin partitions, I found eight quarts o' brandy under what was Old Sawbones's bed-place. I reckon he'd hid it away for his own use on a thirsty day. Anyway, there it was, packed careful in a canvas bag. Sez I when I found it: 'This'll belong to nobody but Isaac Martin. It's not ship's stores, it's finder's luck'; so I hid it away, and last night, after we'd come ashore, I found a safe place to stow it. But I'd no mind to be greedy with it. Ye'll allow that, for I've told what there was no need to tell if I'd meant to keep it."

"That's plain truth, God bless ye!" said McCoy. "If I'd found it I doubt but I'd been hog enough to drink the lot of it on the sly."

"Ye would so, Will," said Mills. "Ye've your good points, but sharin' anything in the way o' grog's not one of 'em. Where's this brandy now, Isaac?"

"We passed where I hid it on the way up here. It's a good piece from the camp. We can drink it somewheres thereabout and the rest none the wiser. What do ye say, Alex? Must I give it up as ship's stores?"

"That's no called for," McCoy put in earnestly.

"To my thinkin' it belongs to the ship and calls to be shared by all."

"There's three of us to say no to that," said Mills.

Smith rose. "Do as ye please," he said, "but it's a bad beginning ye're makin'. I'll go along and leave ye to it."

For a moment his companions looked after him in silence; then Martin called out, "If we're asked for, Alex, tell 'em we're walkin' the island and will sleep the night out."

Smith turned and waved his hand. A moment later he was lost to view in the forest, below.

McCoy shook his head admiringly. "He's a grand stubborn character. And there's no man fonder of his grog; there's the wonder of it."

"If we'd the brandy with us we could ha' won him over for all his fine notions o' what's fair to the rest," Martin replied. He rose to his feet. "Well, shipmates?"

"Aye, lead on, Isaac," said McCoy, eagerly. "We'll no be laggin' far behind."

Once below the ridge they lost the breeze and sweat streamed from their half-naked bodies as they pushed their way through the tall fern into the thickets below. At length they reached the depths of the valley, where the air was moist and cool. Martin led the way, walking in the bed of a small stream. Presently he stopped and looked about him uncertainly. McCoy gave him an anxious glance. "Ye've not lost yer bearin's, Isaac?"

"It's somewhere hereabout," said Martin.

"Curdle ye, Isaac! Don't ye *know*? What like was the place where ye hid it?" said Mills.

"It was by just such a tree as this. There was a hollow by the roots and I put it there. . . . No, it'll be a step farther down."

They proceeded slowly, Martin glancing from side to side. Presently his face lighted up. "Yon's the one," he said, hurrying forward. A widespreading hibiscus tree that looked as ancient as the land itself overhung the stream, its branches filled with lemon-coloured blossoms. Martin knelt by the trunk and reached to his arm's length among the gnarled and twisted roots. The eyes of his companions glistened as he drew out, one by one, eight bottles. He sat back on his heels, glancing triumphantly up at them.

"God love ye, Isaac!" McCoy exclaimed, in an awed voice.

"And it's old Sawbones's best brandy, mind ye that! Whereabout shall we go to drink it? We can't sit comfortable-like here."

McCoy and Martin carrying three bottles each, and Mills with two, they proceeded down the valley for another fifty yards until they came to a little glade carpeted with fern and mottled with sunlight and shadow. At this point the tiny stream made a bend, and in the hollow against the further bank was a pool of still water, two or three yards wide. Here they seated themselves with grunts of satisfaction. Martin, taking a heavy clasp knife which he carried at his belt, knocked off the neck of a bottle with one clean even blow.

"Ye needna be so impatient as all that," said McCoy. "Bottles'll be handy things here."

Martin took a long pull before replying. "If there was one, there was fifteen dozen empties took ashore from the spirit room," he said. His companions were not far behind him in enjoying their first drink. McCoy, replacing the cork in his bottle, leaned it carefully against the tree beside him.

"Isaac, I'll never forget ye for this," he said. "It fair sickens me to think I could nae hae done the same if I'd found the brandy."

"Enjoy yourself hearty, Will. There's plenty for all. I'll be blind drunk afore I've finished my second."

"We needna be hasty, there's a blessing," McCoy replied. "We've the night before us, and there's water close by to sober us up now and again."

"I'm as willin' Matt Quintal's not with us," said Mills.

"Aye," Martin replied. "There's a good shipmate when he's sober, but God spare me when he's had a drop too much!"

McCoy nodded. "There's no demon worse. D'ye mind his wreckin' the taproom at the Three Blackamoors the week we left Portsmouth? When it took five of us to get him down?"

"Mind! I've the marks on me yet," said Mills. . . . "God strike me! What's this?"

A tiny bouquet of flowers and fern, attached to a slender ribbon of bark, came dropping down through the foliage of the tree that shaded them. After dangling in front of Mills's nose for a moment, it was jerked up again. A ripple of laughter was heard, and, looking up quickly, they could see an elfin-like face peeping down from among the green leaves.

"It's your own wench, Mills! Damme if it's not!" said Martin.

Mills's rugged face softened. "So it is! Come out o' that, ye little witch! What are ye doin' here?" he called.

The girl descended to the lowest branch and perched there, out of reach, smiling down at them.

"She's a rare lass for roamin' the woods and mountains," said Mills, fondly. He held out his arms. "Jump, ye little mischty!" The girl leaped and he caught her in his arms. She was dressed in a kirtle of bark cloth reaching to her knees, and her thick hair fell in a rippling mass over her bare breasts and shoulders. Mills held her off at arm's length, gazing at her admiringly.

"Ye've spoke truth, John," said Martin. "She's a proper little witch."

"Aye," said McCoy, "ye've the prettiest lass o' the lot. I wonder she'd come awa' from her kinfolks and a' with a dour old stick the like o' yersel'."

Mills stroked her hair with his great rough hand. "Ye'll allow this, Will: ye've not seen her weepin' her eyes out for Tahiti like some o' the women."

"Nay, I'll grant that," said McCoy. "She seems a contented little body."

"I'd be pleased to say the like o' my wench, Susannah," said Martin, glumly. "She was willin' enough to come away with us, but now we're here she's fair sick to be home again. I've had no good of her since we beached the ship."

"It's in reason she should be, Isaac," McCoy replied. "My woman's the same way. Gie 'em time; they'll joggle down well enough. Mills's lass here'll learn 'em how to make the best of things, won't 'ee, Prudence?"

The girl's lips parted in a ready smile, revealing her small white teeth.

"How d'ye manage with her, John?" Martin asked. "Ye're the dumbest o' the lot for speakin' the Indian lingo. Is it sign talk ye use with her?"

"Never ye mind about that," Mills replied gruffly. "I've no call to learn their heathen jabber. Prudence takes to English like a pigeon picks up corn."

"They're a queer lot, all these Indian wenches," said Martin. "Why is it, now, they make such a fuss about cookin' the food?"

"It's against their heathen notions," said McCoy. "Young's told me how it is. Indian men won't have their womenfolks fussin' with their vittles. It's contrary to their religion, he says."

"I'll learn mine better'n that, once we're settled," Martin replied. "She'll bloody well do as I tell her."

"There's no need to beat it out of 'em, Isaac. They'll come around well enough, once they see how it is with us."

"Aye, give 'em time; they'll follow our ways," said Mills. "It ain't in reason to expect it at the start."

"And the men with 'em, if they know what's good for 'em."

"Ye'll go easy there, Isaac," said McCoy, "else we'll have a fine row on our hands one o' these days. Minarii and Tetahiti's a pair not to be trifled with."

"Say ye so, Will?" Mills replied grimly. "They'd best learn at the start who's masters here."

"Christian and Young treat 'em like they was as good as ourselves," said Martin.

"There's three we can do as we like with, but mind the others!" said McCoy. "Will the lass ken what we say, John?"

"She's not that far along. Will 'ee sing 'em a song, Prudence?" he asked.

The girl laughed and shook her head.

"It strikes me she knows more 'n she lets on," said Martin.

"I've been learnin' her one," Mills went on proudly. "Come, now, lass: —

> We hove our ship to when the wind was sou'west, boys,
> We hove our ship to for to strike soundings clear . . .

Ye mind how it goes? Come, there's a good wench."

After considerable urging the girl began singing in a soft, clear voice and a quaint pronunciation of the English words that delighted her listeners. She broke off and they cheered her heartily.

"Damme if that ain't pretty, now!" said Martin. "Give her a sup o' brandy; there's nothin' better to wet the whistle."

"Will 'ee have a taste, sweetheart?" said Mills, holding out the bottle. Prudence shook her head. "She don't fancy the stuff," he said, "and I ain't coaxed her to relish it."

"And it's right ye are," said McCoy, "seeing there's none too much for oursel's. If the women learned to booze we'd be bad off in no time for grog."

"What! A wench not drink with her fancy-man?" said Martin. "That's not jack-tar's fashion. Give her a sup."

"Aye, ye're right, Isaac," Mills replied. "It ain't natural on a spree. Come, lass, just a drop now."

He put his arm around her shoulders and drew her to him, holding the bottle to her lips. Thus urged, the girl closed her eyes and took two or three resolute swallows. Choking and sputtering, she pushed the bottle away and ran to the near-by stream. The three men laughed heartily.

"Fancy a dolly-mop at home makin' such a face as that over good brandy," said Martin.

"My old woman could drink her half-pint in two ticks, not winkin' an eye," said McCoy. . . . "There's an odd thing," he added; "I doubt I've thought of her twice this past twelve-month."

"Was ye wedded to her, Will?"

"Aye; all shipshape and Bristol-fashion. I liked her well enough, too."

"If I know women she'll not be sleepin' cold the nights ye've been away," said Mills.

"Aye, she'll hae dragged her anchor long afore this," McCoy replied. He raised his bottle. "Well, here's luck to her wherever she is."

Prudence returned from the brook and seated herself again at Mills's side.

"How is it with ye, lass?"

She laughed and pointed to the bottle. "More," she replied.

"There's a proper wench, John," said Martin, admiringly. "Damn my eyes if she won't make a proper boozer, give her time. All she needs is a sup o' water to follow."

Mills smiled down at her, proudly. "She'll do," he said. "Here, darlin', drink hearty."

"Ahoy there, mates!"

The three men looked up quickly to find Quintal standing behind them.

"God love us! It's Matt himself," said McCoy, uneasily.

"Come aboard, Matt; we was wishin' for ye," Martin put in with an attempt at heartiness.

Quintal squatted on the balls of his feet, his brawny hands on his knees, and grinned at them accusingly. "I've no doubt o' that," he said, "and searchin' for me far and wide. And where did ye find all this?"

"Never ye mind, Matt. We ain't thieved it. It's private stock. Would ye relish a taste?"

Quintal looked longingly at the bottle. "Ye know damned well I would. No, don't coax me, Isaac. I'd best leave it alone."

"That's common sense, lad," said McCoy. "Ye ken yer weakness. We'll no think the less o' ye for standin' out against it."

Quintal seated himself in the fern with his back to a tree. "Go on with your boozin',", he said. "What's this, Mills? The little wench ain't shakin' a cloth?"

"She's havin' her first spree," said Mills. "She's took to brandy that easy. Where's Jack Williams?"

"I've not seen him these two hours."

"Not alone, I'll warrant, wherever he is. And it won't be Fasto that's with him."

"Aye, he's fair crazed over that — what's her name? Hutia?"

"Why can't he keep to his own?" Mills growled.

"Where's the need, John?" Martin asked. "I mean to take a walk with Hutia myself, once we're well ashore."

"Aye, ye'll be a proper trouble-maker, Isaac, give ye half a chance," said Quintal. "The Indians can play that game as well as ourselves. I'm with John. Let each man keep to his own."

"Aye, aye, to that!" said McCoy. "Once there was trouble started 'twixt us and the Indians, there'd be the deil and a' to pay. We've the chance, here, to live quiet and peaceful as ever we like. I say, let's take it and hold fast by it."

"And how long will the Indians hold by it, think ye?" asked Martin. "There's three without women. They'll be snoopin' after ours, fast enough."

"They'll leave mine alone," said Mills. "That I'll promise!"

"Say ye so, John? She'll be amongst the first. I'll warrant some of 'em's had her before now."

Mills sprang to his knees and grasped Martin by the shoulders, shaking him violently.

"What d'ye say, ye devil? Speak up if ye've seen it! Tell me who, or I'll throttle ye!"

"Let me go, John! God's name! I've seen naught! I was only havin' a game wi' ye."

Mills glared at him suspiciously, but upon being reassured by the others he released him and resumed his place.

"Christian's gone aboard again," said Quintal; "him and Young."

"There, lads, we can take it easy," said McCoy in a relieved tone. "Prudence, will 'ee gie us a dance?" He turned to Mills: "Ye don't mind, John? It's a joy to see her."

"Mind? Why should he?" said Martin. "Come, Prudence, up wi' ye, wench!"

The fumes of the brandy had already mounted to the girl's brain and she was ready enough to comply. The men well understood the quick rhythmic slapping of hands upon knees that marked the time for the dances of the Maori women. Prudence danced proudly, with the natural abandon of the young savage, pausing before each of the men in turn, her slim bare arms akimbo, gazing tauntingly into their eyes as she went through the provocative movements of the dance. Of a sudden she broke off with a peal of laughter and ran lightly away into the thickets.

The men cheered heartily. "Come back, ye little imp," Martin called. "We'll have more o' the same."

"That we will," said McCoy. "John, I'll trade wenches wi' ye any day ye like."

"Keep your own," said Mills, with a harsh laugh. "I'm well pleased with what I got. Come back, ye little mischty! We've not done wi' ye yet."

The girl feigned reluctance for a moment; then, running back to Mills, she seized the bottle from his hands and drank again. Quintal watched her with fascinated eyes, nervously clasping and unclasping his great hairy hands. By this time the others were in the mellow state of the first stages of a spree.

"Matt Quintal," Martin exclaimed, "I'll see no man sit by with a dry gullet! Ye're perished for a drink, that's plain. Come, have a sup."

He passed over a bottle which Quintal accepted, hesitatingly. "Thank 'ee, Isaac. I'll have a taste and no more."

It was a generous taste that called for another, and yet another, freely offered by Mills and Martin. A few moments later Quintal reached across and seized the partly emptied bottle at McCoy's side.

"Damn yer blood, Matt!" McCoy exclaimed anxiously. "Easy, now! There's but eight quarts for the lot of us!" Quintal held him off with one hand while he drank. "D'ye grudge me a drink, ye hog?" he said, grinning. "Ye've another full bottle beside ye. I'll take that if ye'll like it better."

"It's nae that I grudge ye a drink, Matt, but there's enough in the bottle wi' what ye've had to make ye mad drunk, and well ye know it."

"Aye," said Mills. "Drink slow, Matt, and water it a-plenty. It'll last the night if ye do that."

The afternoon was now well advanced, and the shadow of the high ridge to the westward had already crept beyond the little glade where the men were seated. They drank and lolled at their ease. There was no need, now, to urge Prudence to dance. Martin, Quintal, and McCoy slapped their knees and cheered her on as her gestures and postures became more and more wanton and provocative, but the expression on Mills's face was increasingly sullen. "That'll do, lass," he said, at length. "Off wi' ye, now. Go back wi' the others." But the girl laughed without heeding and, as though with intent to enrage him, passed him by without a glance, dancing before Quintal, gazing into his eyes with a sultry smile. Of a sudden Quintal seized her by the arm, pulling her into his lap, and gave her a bearlike hug, kissing her heartily. Mills sprang to his feet.

"Let her go, damn yer blood! Let her go, I say!"

The girl, sobered a little, began to struggle, but Quintal held her fast. He turned to Mills with a drunken leer. "She knows who's the best man, don't 'ee, wench?" Pinioning her arms, he kissed her again and again, but as Mills strode forward he got to his feet just in time to receive a blow in the face, delivered with all the strength of Mills's arm. The blood streamed from his nose and he staggered back, but recovered himself. An insane light came into his closely set blue eyes. He tossed the girl aside and clenched his enormous fists.

"Ye bloody bastard! I'll kill ye for that!" He gave Mills a blow on the chest that knocked him full length, but he was up again in a second. Rushing forward, he grappled Quintal around the waist. McCoy and Martin were both on their feet by this time, looking anxiously on.

"Stop it, lads!" McCoy called, earnestly. "Matt, think what ye do."

Glaring wildly, Quintal turned his head and gave McCoy a backhanded blow that sent him sprawling. Mills, for all his strength, was no match for the younger man, and in a moment Quintal had him down, with a knee on his chest and his fingers around his throat. Mills's eyes started from their sockets and his tongue protruded from his mouth.

"He'll kill him, Isaac! Pitch in!" McCoy shouted. The two men sprang upon his back, tugging and straining with all their strength. Quintal loosed one hand to seize Martin's arm, giving it such a wrench that he cried out with pain. Meanwhile, with the pressure partly relieved from his throat, Mills gave a desperate heave and, with the others to help him, managed to topple Quintal over. The three men were upon him at once, but their combined strength was not sufficient to keep him down. Breaking Mills's hold on his legs, he struggled to his feet, the others clinging to him desperately.

"God be praised! Here's Alex," McCoy panted. "Quick, mon!"

Before Quintal had time to turn his head, Smith's burly form was upon him with the others. He fought like a demon, but the odds were now too great. Presently he lay helpless, breathing heavily, his face streaming with sweat and blood, his eyes glaring insanely. "Will ye give in, ye devil?" said Smith. With a bellow of rage Quintal resumed the struggle, and his four antagonists needed all their strength to hold him. "Is there a bit o' line amongst ye?" Smith panted. "We must seize him up." "Prudence!" Mills called; "fetch some *purau* bark!" The girl, who had been looking on in terror, understood at once. Running to a near-by hibiscus tree, she bit through the tough smooth bark of some of the low-hanging branches and quickly ripped it down, in long strips. After a prolonged struggle the four men had Quintal bound, hand and foot. Presently his eyes closed and he fell into a heavy sleep.

"Ye was needed, Alex," said McCoy, in a weak voice. "He'd ha' done for the three of us. . . . Ye'll not let on ye've seen us?" he added. "We can booze quiet now Matt's asleep."

"I was sent to look for ye," said Smith. "Mr. Christian's decided to burn the ship. Ye can stay, or go to see her fired, as ye've a mind; but he wanted ye to know."

"Burn and be damned to her, now," said Mills.

"He reckons what timbers there is left in her will be more trouble to get out than they're worth."

"I could ha' told him that three days back," said Martin. "See here, Alex! We've a good sup o' brandy left. Ye'd best stay and have a share."

He held out a bottle while Smith stood irresolutely, looking from one to another of them. Of a sudden he threw himself on the ground beside them. "So I will, Isaac!" he said, as he seized the bottle. "We're hogs for drinkin' it on the sly, but away with that!"

Dusk deepened into night. Quintal was snoring loudly, and Martin had now reached the maudlin stage of drunkenness. His thoughts had turned to home and he blubbered half to himself, half to his companions, cursing Christian the while, and the hard fate that had left them stranded forever on a rock in mid-ocean. Smith and McCoy, having vainly tried to quiet him, at length gave it up and paid no further heed to him. Mills drank in silence; when deep in his cups he became more and more dour and taciturn. Prudence was asleep with her head in his lap.

"Ye're a marvel for drink, Will," Smith was saying. "I'll warrant ye've had twice as much as Martin, but there's none would know it from yer speech."

"I've a good Scotch stomach and a hard Scotch head," McCoy replied. "Ye maun go north o' the Tweed, mon, if ye'd see an honest toper. We've bairns amangst us could drink the best o' ye English under a table, and gang hame to their mithers after, and think nae mair aboot it."

Smith grinned. "Aye, ye're grand folk," he replied, "and well ye know it."

"We've reason to, Alex; but aboot this burnin' o' the ship . . ."

"Christian's aboard of her now, with Young and Jack Williams. They'll be firin' her directly."

Presently a faint reddish glow streamed up from behind the seaward cliffs to the east. It increased from moment to moment until the light penetrated even to where they sat.

Smith got to his feet. "We'd best go and see the last of her, Will. I'll cut Matt loose; there's no harm in him now. What'll ye do, John, stay or come with us?"

Mills rose and took the native girl up in his arms. "Go past the tents," he said. "I'll leave her there."

Martin was asleep. McCoy took up the bottle beside him and held it up to the light. "Isaac's a good sup left here, lads."

"Leave that," Mills growled. "It's his, ain't it?"

"Will it be safe, think ye? Matt might wake . . ."

"So he might; there's a good Scotch reason," said Smith. "Pass it round, Will."

Having emptied the bottle, they left it at Martin's side, and the men proceeded slowly down the valley, Smith leading the way. They found no one at the tents; Mills left Prudence there and they went along the roughly cleared path to the lookout point above the cove. The ship was burning fiercely, flames and sparks streaming high in the air. In the red glare they could plainly see the other members of the *Bounty's* company seated among the rocks on the narrow foreshore.

"She makes a grand light," said McCoy, glumly.

"Aye," said Smith.

They were silent after that.

# CHAPTER IV

A DEEPER awareness of their isolation from the world of men now came home to them. The empty sea walled them round, and the ship, burned to the water's edge but still lying where she had been driven upon the rocks, was an eloquent reminder to all of the irrevocable nature of their fate. For some of the white men, in particular, the sight of the blackened hulk, washed over by the sea, had a gloomy fascination not to be resisted. In the evening when work for the day was over, they would come singly, or in groups of two or three, to the lookout point above the cove and sit there until the last light had left the sky, gazing down upon all that remained of the vessel as though they could not yet realize that she was lost to them forever.

Among the mutineers, Brown was the one most deeply affected by the nature of their fate. He was a small, shy man of thirty years, with a gentle voice and manner, in marked contrast with those of some of the companions chance had forced upon him. Curiously enough, his presence among them was due to that very mildness of his character, and to his inability to make immediate decisions for himself. He had sailed in the *Bounty* in the capacity of assistant to Mr. Nelson, the botanist of the expedition, and had spent five happy months on Tahiti, studying the flora of the island and helping to collect and care for the young breadfruit trees. Upon the morning of the mutiny he had been shaken from sleep by Martin, who had thrust a musket into his hands and ordered him on deck. There he had stood with his weapon, during the uproar which followed, completely bewildered by what was taking place, appalled by what he had unwittingly done, and incapable of action until the opportunity for it had been lost. Christian had been as surprised as grieved when, later, he discovered Brown among the members of his own party; and Brown of necessity transferred to Christian his dependence for the protection and guidance furnished up to that time by his chief, Mr. Nelson. He knew nothing of ships or the sea, but he had a profound knowledge of soils and plants, and his love of nature compensated him, in a measure, for hours of desperate homesickness.

He suffered no more from this cause than did many of the women of the *Bounty's* company. They longed for the comfort of numbers; for the gaiety of their communal life at Tahiti; for the quiet lagoons lighted at night by the torches of innumerable fishermen; for the clear, full-running mountain streams where they had bathed at evening. They longed for the friends and kindred whom they knew, now, they could never hope to see again; for the voices of children; for the authority of long-established custom. Conditions on this high, rock-bound island were as strange to them as the ways of their white lords, and the silence, the loneliness, awed and frightened them.

Two only of their numbers escaped, in part, the general feeling of forsakenness: the young girl whom Mills had taken, and whom he had named, with unconscious irony, "Prudence," and Jenny, the consort of Brown. Jenny was a slender, active, courageous woman of Brown's own age, with all the force of character he lacked. She was the oldest of the women, but she was sprung from the lower class of Tahitian society, and, although of resolute character, she maintained toward Maimiti and Taurua, the consorts of Christian and Young, the deference and respect which their birth and blood demanded that she should. To Moetua, as well, the same deference was extended; for she too was of the kindred of chiefs, and her husband, Minarii, had been a man of authority on Tahiti.

Gradually the sense of loneliness, common at first to all, gave place to more cheerful feelings, and men and women alike set themselves with a will to the work before them. A tract of land near the temporary settlement was chosen for the first garden, and for the period of a week most of the company was engaged in clearing and planting. This task finished, the garden was left to the charge of Brown and some of the women, while the others, under Christian's direction, were occupied with house-building.

The site chosen for the permanent settlement lay beneath the mountain which they called the "Goat-House Peak," a little to the eastward of a narrow valley whose western wall was formed by the mountain itself. By chance or by mutual agreement they had divided themselves into households, and all save Brown and Jenny, who wished to live inland, had chosen sites for their dwellings on the seaward slope of the main valley. Christian's house was building below the gigantic banyan tree where he and Maimiti had halted to rest on the day of their first visit ashore. The second household was that of Young and Alexander Smith, with their women, Taurua and Balhadi. Mills, Martin, and Williams formed the third, with Prudence, Susannah, and Fasto; Quintal and McCoy, Sarah and Mary, the fourth; and the native men, the fifth. This latter was the largest household, of nine members: Minarii, Tetahiti, Tararu, Te Moa, Nihau, and Hu, with the wives of the three first, Moetua, Nanai, and Hutia. Te Moa, Nihau, and Hu were the three men unprovided with women.

The white men, with the exception of Brown, were erecting wooden houses made partly of the *Bounty* materials and partly of island timber, and the roofs were to be of pandanus-leaf thatch. The dwelling for the native men was situated in a glade a quarter of a mile inland from Bounty Bay. Quintal and McCoy lived nearest to the landing place. The houses of the other mutineers were closer together, but hidden from one another in the forest that covered the valley.

The native men, helped by the stronger of the women, were allotted the task of carrying the supplies to the settlement while the white men were building a storehouse to contain them. Christian, with the general consent, grudgingly given by some of the men, took the stores into his own charge and kept the keys to the storehouse always on his person.

He ruled the little colony with strict justice, granting white men and brown complete liberty in their personal affairs so long as these did not interfere with the peace of the community. An equitable division of labour was made. Williams was employed at his forge, with the native, Hu, as his helper. Mills and Alexander Smith had charge of the saw pit; Quintal and McCoy looked after the livestock, building enclosures near the settlement for some of the fowls and the brood sows. Brown was relieved of all other employment so that he might give his full time to the gardens. The native men were employed as occasion demanded, and during the early months of the settlement it was they who did the fishing for the community and searched for the wild products of the island — plantains, taro, candlenuts for lighting purposes, and the like. Christian and Young had general supervision of all, and set an example to the others by working, with brief intervals for meals, from dawn until dark. As for the women, they had work and to spare while the houses were building, in collecting and preparing the pandanus leaves for thatch. These had first to be soaked in the sea, then smoothed and straightened and the long, thorn-covered edges removed; after which they were folded over light four-foot segments of split canes and pinned thus with slender midribs from the leaves of palm fronds. Some two thousand canes of these *raufara,* as they were called, each of them holding about forty pandanus leaves, were needed for the thatching of each dwelling.

From the beginning Christian had set aside Sunday as a day of rest, in so far as the community work was concerned. Neither he nor Young was of religious turn of mind, and the other white men even less so; therefore no service was held and each man employed himself as he pleased.

Late on a Sunday afternoon toward the end of February, Christian and Young had climbed to the ridge connecting the two highest peaks of the island. It was an impressive lookout point. To the eastward the main valley lay outspread. On the opposite side the land fell away in gullies and precipitous ravines to the sea. Several small cascades, the result of recent heavy rains, streamed down the rocky walls, arching away from them, in places, as they descended. Small as the island was, its aspect from that height had in it a quality of savage grandeur, and the rich green thickets on the gentler slopes, lying in the full splendour of the westering sun, added to the solemnity of narrow valleys already filling with shadow, and the bare precipices that hung above them. The view would have been an arresting one in the most frequented of oceans; it was infinitely more so here where the vast floor of the sea, which seemed to slope down from the horizons, lay empty to the gaze month after month, year after year.

The ridge at that point was barely two paces in width. Christian seated himself on a rock that overhung the mountain wall; Young reclined in the short fern at his side. Sea birds were beginning to come home from their day's fishing far offshore. As the shadows lengthened over the land their numbers increased to countless thousands, circling high in air, their wings flashing in the golden light. The two friends remained silent for a long time, listening to the faint cries of the birds and the thunder of the surf against the bastions of the cliffs nearly a thousand feet below.

The spirit of solitude had altered both of these men, each in a different way. Brief as their time on the island had been, the sense of their complete and final removal from all they had known in the past had been borne in upon them swiftly, and had now become an accepted and natural condition of their lives.

Christian was the first to speak.

"A lonely sound, Ned," he said at length. "Sometimes I love it, but there are moments when the thought that I can never escape it drives me half frantic."

Young turned his head. "The booming of the surf?" he asked. "I have already ceased to hear it in a conscious way. To me it has become a part of the silence of the place."

"I wish I could say as much. You have a faculty I greatly admire. What shall I call it? Stillness of mind, perhaps. It is not one that you could have acquired. You must have had it always."

Young smiled. "Does it seem to you such a valuable faculty?"

"Beyond price!" Christian replied, earnestly. "I have often observed you without your being aware of the fact. I believe that you could sit for hours on end without forethought or afterthought, enjoying the beauty of each moment as it passes. What would I not give for your quiet spirit!"

"Allow me to say that I have envied you, many's the time, for having the reverse of my quietness, as you call it. There is all too little of the man of action in my character. When I think what a sorry aide I am to you here . . ."

"A sorry aide? In God's name, Ned, what could I do without you? Supposing . . ." He broke off with a faint smile. "Enough," he added. "The time has not come when we need begin paying one another compliments."

They had no further speech for some time; then Christian said: "There is something I have long wanted to ask you. . . . Give me your candid opinion. . . . Is it possible, do you think, that Bligh and the men with him could have survived?"

Young gave him a quick glance. "I have waited for that question," he replied. "The matter is not one I have felt free to open, but I have been tempted to do so more than once."

"Well, what do you think?"

"That there is reason to believe them safe."

Christian turned to him abruptly. "Say it again, Ned! Make me believe it! But, no. . . . What do I ask? Could nineteen men, unarmed, scantly provided with food and water, crowded to the point of foundering in a ship's boat, make a voyage of full twelve hundred leagues? Through archipelagoes peopled with savages who would ask nothing better than to murder them at sight? Impossible!"

"It is by no means impossible if you consider the character of the man

who leads them," Young replied, quietly. "Remember his uncanny skill
as a navigator; his knowledge of the sea; his prodigious memory. I
doubt whether there is a known island in the Pacific, or the fragment
of one, whose precise latitude and longitude he does not carry in his
head. Above all, Christian, remember his stubborn, unconquerable
will. And whatever we may think of him otherwise, you will agree that,
with a vessel under him, though it be nothing but a ship's launch,
Bligh is beyond praise."

"He is; I grant it freely. By God! You may be right! Bligh could do
it, and only he! What a feat it would be!"

"And it may very well be an accomplished fact by now," Young replied. "Nelson, Fryer, Cole, Ledward, and all the others may be approaching England at this moment, while we speak of them. They
would have had easterly winds all the way. They may have reached
the Dutch East Indies in time to sail home with the October fleet."

"Yes, that would be possible. . . . If only I could be sure of it!"

"Try to think of them so," Young replied earnestly. "Let me urge
you, Christian, to brood no longer over this matter. You are not justified in thinking of them as dead. Believe me, you are not. I say this
not merely to comfort you; it is my reasoned opinion. The launch, as
you know, was an excellent sea boat. Think of the voyages we ourselves
have made in her, in all kinds of weather."

"I know . . ."

"And bear this in mind," Young continued: "there are, as you say,
vast archipelagoes known to exist between the Friendly Islands and the
Dutch settlements. It is by no means unlikely that Bligh has been able
to land safely, at various places, for refreshment. How many small uninhabited islands have we ourselves seen where a ship's boat might lie
undiscovered by the savages for days, or weeks?"

He broke off, glancing anxiously at his companion. Christian turned
and laid a hand on his shoulder. "Say no more, Ned. It has done me
good to speak of this matter, for once. Whatever may have happened,
there is nothing to be done about it now."

"And if Bligh reaches home?"

Christian smiled, bitterly. "There will be a hue and cry after us such
as England has not known for a century," he replied. "And the old
blackguard will be lifted, for a time at least, to a level with Drake. And
what will be said of me . . ."

He put the palms of his hands to his eyes in an abrupt gesture and kept them there for a moment; then he turned again to his companion. "It is odd to think, Ned, that you and I may live to be old men here, with our children and grandchildren growing up around us. We will never be found; I am all but certain of that."

Young smiled. "What a strange colony we shall be, fifty years hence! What a mixture of bloods!"

"And of tongues as well. Already we seem to be developing a curious speech of our own, part English, part Indian."

"English, I think, will survive in the end," Young replied. "Men like Mills and Quintal and Williams have a fair smattering of the Indian tongue, but they will never be able to speak it well. It interests me to observe how readily some of the women are acquiring English. Brown's woman and that girl of Mills's are surprisingly fluent in it, even now."

"Do you find that you sometimes think in Tahitian?"

"Frequently. We are being made over here quite as much as the Indians themselves."

"I feel encouraged, Ned, sincerely hopeful," Christian remarked presently. "Concerning the future, I mean. The men are adjusting themselves surprisingly well to the life here. Don't you think so?"

"Yes, they are."

"If we can keep them busy and their minds occupied . . . For the present there is little danger. That will come later when we've finished house-building and are well settled."

"Let's not anticipate."

"No, we shan't borrow our troubles, but we must be prepared for them. Have you noticed any friction between ourselves and the Indian men?"

"I can't say that I have. Nothing serious, at least, since the day when Martin chucked their sacred temple stones into the sea."

Christian's face darkened. "There is a man we must watch," he said. "He is a bully and a coward at heart. The meanest Maori in the South Sea is a better man. Martin will presume as far as he dares on his white skin."

"It is not only Martin who will do so," Young replied; "Mills and Quintal have much the same attitude toward the Indians."

"But there is a decency about those two lacking in Martin. I have explained him to Minarii and Tetahiti. I have told them that Martin belongs to a class, in white society, that is lower than the serfs among the Maoris. They understand. In fact, they had guessed as much before I told them."

Young nodded. "There is little danger of Martin's presuming with either of them," he said. "It is Hu and Tararu and Te Moa whom he will abuse, if he can."

"And his woman, Susannah," Christian added. "I pity that girl from my heart. I've no doubt that Martin makes her life miserable in countless small ways." He rose. "We'd best be going down, Ned. It will be dark soon."

They descended the steep ridge to the gentler slopes below and made their way slowly along, skirting the dense thickets of pandanus and rata trees, and crossing glades where the interlaced foliage, high overhead, cut off the faint light of the afterglow, making the darkness below almost that of night.

In one of these glades two others of the *Bounty's* company had passed that afternoon. Scarcely had Christian and Young crossed it when a screen of thick fern at one side parted and Hutia glanced after the retreating figures. She was a handsome girl of nineteen with small, firm breasts and a thick braid of hair reaching to her knees. She stood poised as lightly as a fawn ready for flight, all but invisible in the shadows; then she turned to someone behind her.

"Christian!" she exclaimed in an awed voice. "Christian and Etuati!"

Williams was lying outstretched in the thick fern, his hands clasped behind his head.

"What if it was?" he replied gruffly. "Come, sit ye down here!" Seizing her by the wrist, he drew her to him fiercely. The girl pushed herself back, laughing softly. "*Auē,* Jack! You want too much, too fast. I go now. Tararu say, 'Where Hutia?' And Fasto say, 'Where my man?'"

Williams took her by the shoulders and held her at arm's length.

"Never ye mind about Fasto, ye little minx! Which d'ye like best, Tararu or me?"

The girl gave him a sly smile. "You," she said. Of a sudden she slipped from his grasp, sprang to her feet, and vanished in the darkness.

# CHAPTER V

A PATH, growing daily more distinct, and winding picturesquely among the trees, led from Bounty Bay along the crest of the seaward slopes as far as Christian's house, at the western extremity of the settlement. Close to his dwelling a second path branched inland, along the side of a small valley. This led to Brown's Well, a tiny, spring-fed stream which descended in a succession of pools and slender cascades, shaded by great trees and the fern-covered walls of the ravine itself. The uppermost pool had been transformed into a rock cistern where the drinking water for the settlement was obtained. A larger one, below, was used for bathing, and during the late afternoon was reserved for the exclusive use of the women. This was the happiest hour of the day for them.

At the bathing pool they cast off, with the strange English names bestowed on some of them by the mutineers, the constraint they felt in the presence of the white men. But in the midst of their laughter and cheerful talk there were moments when a chance remark concerning Tahiti, or a passing reference to something connected with their old life there, would cast a shadow on their spirits, passing slowly, like the shadow of a cloud on the high slopes of the valley.

One afternoon several of the women were sunning themselves on a great rock which stood at the brink of the pool. Their bath was over and they were combing and drying their hair, while some of them twined wreaths of sweet fern. Moetua had spoken of the *tiare maohi,* the white, fragrant Tahitian gardenia.

"Say no more!" said Sarah, her eyes glistening with tears. "We know that we shall never see it again. Alas! I can close my eyes and smell its perfume now!"

"Tell me, Moetua, if all were to do again, would you leave Tahiti?" Susannah asked.

"Yes. Minarii is here, and am I not his wife? This is a good land, and it pleases him, so I must be content. Already I think less often than I did of Tahiti. Do not you others find it so?"

"Not I!" exclaimed Susannah bitterly. "I would never come again. Never! Never!"

"But we were told before we left that the ship was not to return," remarked Balhadi quietly. "Christian made that known to all of us."

"Who could have believed it!" said Sarah. "And Mills and the others said it was not so, that we would surely return. . . . Do you remember, you others, the morning after we set sail from Matavai, when the wind changed and the ship was steered to the westward?"

"And we passed so close to the reefs of Eimeo?" Susannah put in. "Do I not remember! Martin stood with me by the rail with his arm tight around me. He knew that I would leap into the sea and swim ashore if given the chance!"

"Quintal held me by the two hands," remarked Sarah, "else I should have done the same."

"Why did the ship leave so quickly?" asked Nanai. "No one in Matavai knew that she was to sail that night."

"They feared that you would change your minds at the last moment," Moetua replied.

"That is how I was caught," said Prudence. "Mills went to my uncle with his pockets filled with nails, the largest kind; he must have had a score of them. My uncle's eyes were hungry when he saw them. 'You shall spend the night on the ship, with the white man,' he told me. So he was given the nails and I went with Mills. When I awoke at daybreak, the vessel was at sea."

"And you like him now, your man?" Hutia asked.

Prudence shrugged her shoulders. "He is well enough."

"He is mad about you," said Susannah. "That is plain."

"He is like a father and a lover in one," the girl replied. "I can do as I please with him."

"For my part," observed Moetua, "I would not change places with any of you. I prefer a husband of our own race. These white men are strange; their thoughts are not like ours. We can never understand them."

"I do not find it so," said Balhadi. "My man, Smith, might almost be one of us. I can read his thoughts even when his speech is not clear to me. White men are not very different from those of our blood."

"It may be so," replied Moetua, doubtfully. "Maimiti says the same. She seems happy with Christian."

"It is different with Maimiti," Sarah put in. "Christian speaks our tongue like one of us. The others learn more slowly."

Prudence had finished combing her hair and was beginning to plait it rapidly, with skillful fingers. She glanced up at Sarah: "How is it with you and Quintal?" she asked.

"How is he as a lover, you mean?"

"Yes, tell us that."

Sarah glanced at the others with a wry smile. "Night comes. He sits with his chin on his great fists. What are his thoughts? I do not know. Perhaps he has none. He is silent. How could it be otherwise when he is only beginning to learn our speech? He pays no heed to me. I wait, well knowing what is to come. At last it comes. When he is wearied, he rolls on his back and snores. *Atira!* There is no more to tell."

Prudence threw back her head and burst into laughter. The others joined in and the glade rang with their mirth. Sarah's smile broadened; a moment later she was laughing no less heartily than the rest.

"What a strange man!" said Nanai, wiping the tears of mirth from her eyes.

Sarah nodded. "He thinks only of himself. I shall never understand his ways."

"What of the men who have no wives?" asked Moetua, presently.

"How miserable they are!" said Hutia, laughing. "Who is to comfort them?"

"Not I," remarked Balhadi. "I am content with my man, and will do nothing to cause him pain or anger."

"Why should he be angry for so small a thing?" asked Nanai.

"You know nothing of white men," said Prudence. "They consider it a shameful thing for the woman of one man to give herself to another. Nevertheless, I will be one of those to be kind to the wifeless men."

"And I!" exclaimed Susannah. "I fear Martin as much as I hate him, but I shall find courage to deceive him. To make a fool of him will comfort me."

"This matter can be kept among ourselves," said Moetua. "The white men need never know of it."

"Christian would be angry, if he knew," remarked Balhadi gravely. "It is as Prudence says: the white men regard their women as theirs alone. Trouble may easily come of this."

"Then Christian should have brought more women, one for each," replied Moetua. "He must know that no man can be deprived of a woman his life long."

"He knows," said Susannah. "He is a chief, like Minarii, and would protect me from Martin, if it came to that."

"And it *will* come to that," observed Prudence.

"Yes," put in Nanai. "You should go to Christian now, and tell him how you are treated. Martin is a *nohu*."

"He is worse than one," Susannah replied gloomily. "I believe that he has not once bathed since we came here. I can endure his cruelty better than his filth. . . . Alas! Let us speak of something more pleasant. I try to forget Martin when here with you."

All of these women were young, with the buoyant and happy dispositions common to their race. A moment later they were chatting and laughing as gaily as though they had not a care in the world.

The garden was now in a flourishing condition. The red, volcanic soil was exceedingly rich, and the beds of yams, sweet potatoes, and the dry-land taro called *tarua* gave promise of an early and abundant harvest. The pale green shoots of the sugar cane were beginning to appear, and young suckers of the banana plants were opening in the sun. An abundance of huge old breadfruit trees had been found in the main valley, but Brown had, nevertheless, carefully planted the young trees brought from Tahiti, clearing a few yards of land here and there in favoured spots.

Like the plants, the livestock loosed on the island throve well. The hogs grew fat on the long tubers of the wild yam, and the place was a paradise for the fowls, with neither bird nor beast of prey to molest them, and food everywhere to be had for the picking. The small, brown, native rat had, as yet, no taste for eggs and did not harm the young chicks. The fowls began to increase rapidly, and the cheerful crowing of the cocks was a welcome sound, relieving the profound silence which had been so oppressive to all during the first days on shore. On the further side of the high peak, to the west of the settlement, a house and a pen had been made for the goats, where they were fed and watered each day.

From the main ridge of the island to the cliffs on the southern side the land sloped gently, forming an outer valley as rich as that on the northern side. This was named the Auté Valley, from the circumstance that the first gardens of the *auté,* or cloth-plant, fetched from Tahiti, were set out here.

Brown had chosen to live on this southern slope, remote from the others; his little thatched house stood in a sunny glade, embowered in the foliage of lofty trees and near a trickle of water sufficient for one family's needs. He and Jenny had cleared a path through the thickets behind and above them, over the ridge and down to join another path which led through the heart of the Main Valley to the settlement.

Jenny, Brown's girl, though small and comely, had all the resolution the gardener lacked. They had lived together on shore during the long months at Tahiti while Captain Bligh was collecting his cargo of bread-fruit plants, and the thought of returning to her had been Brown's only solace after his involuntary part in the mutiny. Her feeling toward him was that of a mother and protectress, for Jenny was one of those women of exceptionally strong character who choose as husbands small, mild men, in need of sterner mates.

Like Brown, Minarii had a deep love of nature and of growing things. Nearly every evening he came to exchange a word with Jenny and to mark the growth of the young plants; little by little, a curious friendship sprang up between the stern war-chief and the lonely English gardener. A man of few words in his own tongue, Brown was incapable of learning any other, but Jenny spoke English by this time, and with her as interpreter he spent many an evening listening to Minarii's tales of old wars on Tahiti, and of how he had received this wound or that.

One evening late in February, Minarii and Moetua, his wife, came to Brown's house. The native set down a heavy basket, and his grim face relaxed as he took Brown's hand.

"We have been down over the southern cliffs," Moetua told Jenny. "The birds are beginning to lay. Here are eggs of the *kaveka* and *oio,* which nest on the face of the cliff. You will find them good. Minarii made a rope fast at the top and we clambered down. Fasto came as well."

"Thank them," Brown put in to Jenny. "I shudder to think of any man, to say nothing of women, taking such risks!"

Minarii turned to his wife. "Go and eat, you two, while I prepare our part."

While Brown went to fetch some wild yams, Minarii kindled a fire, heated several stones, and dropped them into a calabash of water, which began to boil at once. Eggs were then dropped in till the calabash was full, and the yams hastily scraped and roasted on the coals. The two men made a hearty meal.

The moon came up presently and the visitors rose to leave. When they were gone, Jenny spread a mat before the doorstep and sat down to enjoy the beauty of the night. She patted the mat beside her, and

Brown stretched himself out, with his head on her knee. The night was windless; the moonlight softened the outlines of the house and lay in pools of silver on the little clearing. Smoothing Brown's hair absently, Jenny recounted the gossip of the settlement.

"I have been talking with Moetua," she said. "There is trouble coming, and Williams is the cause of it. Do you know why he sent Fasto with them to-day?"

"I suppose he wanted some eggs," said the gardener, drowsily.

"Perhaps he likes eggs, but he likes Hutia better. He meets her in the bush each time he can get Fasto out of the way. And Tararu is a jealous husband, though a fool. Jealous! Yet he would like to be the lover of Mills's girl!"

"Of Prudence? That child?"

"Child!" Jenny gazed down at him, shaking her head wonderingly. "You yourself are only a child," she said. "You understand only your plants and trees."

John Williams was working alone on his house, while Martin and Mills carried plank up the path from Bounty Bay. The framing of the two-story dwelling was now finished, and he was sawing and notching the rafters. The three women had worked well in preparing the thatch, and he planned to finish the roof before beginning on the walls and floor. It was close to midday and the sun was hot in the clearing. Williams was naked to the waist; the sweat streamed down his chest, matted with coarse black hair. He put down his saw and dashed the perspiration from his eyes.

"Fasto!" he called.

A short, dark, sturdy woman stepped out of the shed where their cooking was done. She was of humble birth, silent, docile, and industrious. Williams appreciated to the full her devotion to him, as well as her skill in every native pursuit.

"Dinner ready?" he asked. "Fetch me a pail of water."

She dashed the water over his head and shoulders, while he scrubbed the grime from his face. Then she brought his dinner of roasted breadfruit, yams, and a dozen tern's eggs, spreading broad green leaves for a tablecloth beside him on the ground. He squeezed her arm as she leaned over him. "Hard as nails! Sit ye down and eat with me, old girl." She shook her head. "Oh, damn yer heathen notions! . . . Any more eggs? No?"

Ignorant of the native tongue, which he held in contempt, Williams had forced the woman to learn a few words of English. Tears came into her eyes, for she felt that she had been remiss in her wifely duty. Struggling to express herself, she murmured: "Fetch more eggs, supper."

"Aye. There's a good lass. Work hard and eat hearty, that's Jack Williams."

As he rose, he gave her a kiss and a pat on the back. Fasto smiled with pleasure as she went off to the cookhouse with the remnants of the meal.

Toward mid-afternoon, when he paused once more in his work, the blacksmith had put in nine hours on the house and accomplished much. Fasto had gone off an hour earlier with her basket, toward the cliffs on the south side of the island. Martin and Mills were still engaged in their task at the cove. Scrubbing himself clean, Williams hitched up the kilt of tapa around his waist and glanced quickly up and down the path. Sounds of hammering came from McCoy's house, but no one was in sight. Crossing the path, he disappeared into the bush.

A quarter of a mile south of the settlement, in the midst of the forest, an old pandanus tree spread its thorny leaves to the sun. Its trunk, supported on a pyramid of aerial roots, rose twenty feet without a branch. Hutia was descending cautiously, taking advantage of every roughness of the bark. The ground was littered with the leaves she had plucked for thatch. She sprang down lightly from the tree and began to gather up her leaves in bundles, working mechanically as she glanced this way and that and stopped to listen from time to time. Then suddenly she dropped her work and stepped into the shadow of a thick-spreading *purau* tree close by. Williams appeared, walking softly through the bush. He glanced aloft at the pandanus tree and down at the bundles of leaves on the ground. Peering about uncertainly, he heard the sound of soft laughter. Next moment the girl was in his arms.

"Where is Fasto?" she asked apprehensively.

"Never ye mind about her; she'll not be back till dark."

While Williams lingered in the bush and his mates toiled up from the cove with the day's last load of plank, Prudence sat by the house, stripping thorns from a heap of pandanus leaves beside her. She was scarcely sixteen, small of stature and delicately formed, with a pale golden skin and copper-red hair.

She turned her head as she heard the sound of a footfall on the path. From the corner of her eye she saw Tararu approaching. Bending over her work as if unaware of his coming, she gave a little start when he spoke.

"Where are the others?" he asked.

"*Aué!* You frightened me!"

Tararu smiled, seating himself at her side. "Afraid of me? I must teach you better, some day when Mills is not so close. . . . Where are the other women?"

"Collecting leaves."

"You have worked well. How many reeds of *raufara* are needed?"

"Two thousand," said Prudence. "One thousand eight hundred and seventy are done."

With eyes cast down upon her work, she began to sing softly, a rhythmic and monotonous little melody sung in Tahiti by the strolling players of the *arioi* society. Tararu bent his head to listen, chuckling silently at the broad double-meaning in the first verse. She began the second verse, and as he listened to the soft, childish voice, the man regarded her intently.

> "A bird climbs the cliffs,
> Robbing the nests of other birds,
> Seeking eggs to feed her mate.
> But the mate is not building a nest. No!
> He is hiding in a thicket with another bird."

Prudence sang on as if unaware that she had a listener, making no further mention of the doings of birds. After a futile attempt to catch her eye, Tararu rose and walked away inland. Like many philanderers, he felt the most tender solicitude concerning the virtue of his own wife.

Hutia was making her way down to the settlement with a heavy bundle of leaves on her back. She moved silently through the bush, with eyes alert, and was aware of her husband a full ten seconds before he knew of her approach. Her gait and posture changed at once, and she looked up wearily as the man drew near.

"Lay down your burden," Tararu ordered.

She dropped the bundle of leaves with a sigh. "It was good of you to come."

Tararu gazed down at her without a smile, but she returned his glance so calmly that his suspicions were shaken. He was deeply enamoured of her, though always ready for a flirtation with another girl, and he desired nothing more than to be convinced of her inno-

cence. No guilty wife, he thought, could meet her husband so fearlessly.
He smiled at last, took up the bundle, and led the way to the settlement.

One evening in early March, Hutia was making her way to the
bathing pool. She had had words with Tararu, who had knocked her
down while two of the native men stood by, and, wishing to nurse her
anger alone, she had delayed her bath until an hour when the other
women should have returned to the settlement.

She had no eyes for the beauty of the glade. Hedged in by thick
bush, which made a green twilight at this hour, the place was deserted
save for Prudence at her bath. The girl stood knee-deep in the water,
her back to Hutia and enveloped to the waist in her unbound hair. She
had a small calabash in her hand and was bending to take up water
when Hutia spoke.

"Make haste!" she said harshly. "I wish to bathe by myself."

Prudence glanced coolly at the other girl. "Who are you? Queen of
this island? Am I your servant, me, with a white man for husband?"

"Husband!" exclaimed Hutia angrily. "Aye, and you'd like to have
mine as well. Take care! I have seen you looking at him with soft
eyes!"

"Keep him!" Prudence said jeeringly, turning to face the other.
"Keep him if you can!"

"What do you mean?"

"What I say!" Prudence laughed softly. "*You* keep him! A black-
haired loose woman like you!"

She was of the *ehu,* or fair Maoris, and her words stung Hutia to
the quick. "Red dog!"

"Sow!"

Hutia sprang on the smaller girl fiercely, seized her by the hair, and
after a short tussle succeeded in throwing her down in the pool. There,
astride of her enemy's back and with hands buried in her hair, she held
her under water, jerking at her head savagely till the younger girl was
half drowned. At last she was satisfied. She stood up, turned her back
scornfully, and began to bathe.

Prudence rose from the pool, donned her kilt and mantle with
trembling hands, took up her calabash, and disappeared into the bush.
Stopping to compose herself and to arrange her hair before she reached
the settlement, she went straight to·the cookhouse where she knew that
Fasto would be at work.

"There is something I must tell you," she said to the elder woman, who sat on a little three-legged stool as she grated a coconut for her fowls. "You have been kind to me. I am young and you have been like a mother. Now I must tell you, before the others begin to mock."

"Aye, child, what is it?" said Fasto.

This simple and industrious woman had a soft heart, and the girl's youth appealed to the mother in her. She took her hand and stroked it. "What is it, child?" she repeated.

Prudence hesitated before she spoke. "It is hard to tell, but will come best from one who loves you. Open your eyes! Williams is a good man and loves you, but all men are weak before women's eyes. Hutia has desired him long. Now they meet each day in the bush, while you and Tararu are blind. . . . You do not believe me? Then go and see for yourself. Hide yourself near the great pandanus tree at the hour when Williams goes inland to bathe. Your man will come, and Hutia will steal through the bush to meet him."

Fasto sat in silence, with bowed head and eyes filling with tears as she continued to stroke the girl's hand.

"I cannot believe it, child, but I will do as you say. Should I find my husband with that woman . . . There will be no sleep for me this night."

When the moon rose on the following evening, Williams was striding along the path that led to McCoy's house. Most of the inmates were already in bed, but Mary sat cross-legged on the floor, plaiting a mat of pandanus by the light of a taper of candlenuts. She was a woman of twenty-five, desperately homesick for Tahiti. Williams called to her softly.

"Mary! Eh, Mary! Is Will asleep?"

McCoy rose from his bed of tapa and crossed the dim-lit room to the door. "Jack? I was only resting. We're dead beat, Matt and me."

"Come outside. . . . Have 'ee seen Fasto?"

"No. What's up?"

"She went off to fetch eggs; before I had my bath, that was, and not a sign o' her since. I was cursing her for a lazy slut at supper time, but, by God, I'm afeared for her now! Her lazy! The best wench on the island, pretty or not!"

"I've seen naught of her," said McCoy. "Wait, I'll ask Mary."

He went into the house, and Williams heard them whispering together. Presently he returned. "Aye, Mary's seen her; she passed this way late in the afternoon. Mary gave her a hail, but she never turned her head. She'd her egging basket. Like enough she was making for the Rope."

The blacksmith stood irresolute for some time before he spoke. "Thank 'ee, Will. I'll be getting home. If she's not back by morning, I'll make a search."

His heart was heavy and his thoughts sombre as he trudged home through the moonlit bush. Though he lay down on his sheets of clean tapa, smoothed by Fasto's hands, he could not sleep.

At daybreak he set out with Martin and one of the native men. They launched the smaller canoe and ran her out through the breakers. The morning was calm, with a light air from the west, and as they paddled around Ship-Landing Point, they scanned the declivities above. Beyond the easternmost cape of the island, flanked by jagged rocks offshore, they entered the half-moon cove at the foot of the Rope. As the canoe rose high on a swell, the native gave an exclamation and pointed to the beach of sand at the base of the cliffs, where something lay huddled beneath a small pandanus tree.

"Steer for the shore!" the blacksmith ordered gruffly.

They had a near thing as a feathering sea swept them between two boulders, but Williams paddled mechanically, face set and eyes staring at the beach ahead. He was out of the canoe before it grounded; while the others held it against the backwash, he hastened across the narrow beach to the pandanus tree.

The cove was a lonely, eerie place, hemmed in by precipices many hundreds of feet in height. The western curve of the cliffs lay in full sunlight, which glinted on the plumage of a thousand sea fowl, sailing back and forth at a great height. Williams came trudging back, took from the canoe a mantle of native cloth, and returned to spread it gently over the bruised and bloodstained body of Fasto. He knelt down on the sand beside her. Hearing Martin's step behind him, he motioned him away.

The others stared in silence for a moment, then walked quickly away along the foot of the cliffs. After a long interval, Williams hailed them. He was standing by the canoe with Fasto's body, wrapped in tapa, in his arms. He laid her gently in the bilges; at a word from the native steersman, the little vessel shot out through the surf. Williams dropped his paddle and sat with shoulders bowed, silent and brooding, while the canoe rounded the cape and headed northwest for Bounty Bay.


## CHAPTER VI

A FEW days after the burning of the *Bounty,* Minarii had chosen a site for the temple he and the other Polynesian men were to build. A homeless wanderer might worship kneeling in the wash of the sea, the great purifier and source of all holiness, but settled men must erect a temple of their own. The six native men were worshipers of the same god, Ta'aroa, and their *marae* would be dedicated to him.

Sometimes alone, sometimes in company with Tetahiti, Minarii had made a leisurely exploration of those parts of the island least likely to attract the whites, and at last, on a thickly wooded slope to the west of the ridge connecting the two peaks, he had found the spot he was searching for. He was alone on the afternoon when he began his clearing, and had not long plied his axe when he perceived that other worshipers had assembled here in the past. As he made his way through the dense undergrowth he discovered a platform of moss-grown boulders, set with upright stones before which men had once knelt. Close by, on rising ground, stood two images of gross human form and taller than a man, and before one of them was a slab of rock which he stooped to raise. The task required all of his strength, but he was rewarded by the sight of a skeleton laid out in the hollow beneath, with hands crossed on the ribs and the mouldering skull pillowed on a large mother-of-pearl shell.

"*Ahé!*" he exclaimed under his breath. "A man of my own race, and from a land where the pearl-oyster grows!"

He gazed at it for some time, then replaced the heavy slab carefully and descended from the *marae.* Religion entered into every act of a Polynesian's life, and save in time of war they held the dead and the beliefs of others in deep respect. The bones would lie in peace, and no stone of the old temple would be employed to build the new.

Minarii chose another site that lay a stone's throw distant, and measured off a square six fathoms each way. There was a plentiful supply of boulders in the ravine below. Here the leisurely task began, all six of the natives working at it whenever they had an hour to spare. Little by little the temple of Ta'aroa took form — a rocky platform set with kneeling stones and surrounding a small pyramid three yards high, made sacred by the two stones brought from the ancestral temple at Tahiti. The clearing was shaded by majestic trees, and a neat fence enclosed the whole, bordered with a hedge of flowering shrubs.

On a morning early in April, Minarii and his companions were sweeping the pavement and tidying the enclosure in preparation for the ceremony of awakening the god. The shoulders of all six were bared in sign of respect. Presently while the others waited in deep silence, Minarii stepped aside to put on the sacred garments of his office. The flush of dawn was in the east when he returned, clad in flowing lengths of tapa, dyed black. His companions knelt by their stones, their faces now clearly revealed in the increasing light, while their priest turned toward the still hidden sun, holding his hands aloft as he chanted: —

> "The clouds are bordering the sky; the clouds are awake!
> The rising clouds that ascend in the morning,
> Wafted aloft and made perfect by the Lord of the Ocean,
> To form an archway for the sun.
> The clouds rise, part, condense, and reunite
> Into a rosy arch for the sun."

Bowing his head, he awaited in silence until the sun began to touch the heights with golden light. He then made a sign to Tetahiti, who stepped behind the little pyramid and returned with a small casket, curiously carved and provided with handles like a litter. This was the dwelling place of the god, now believed to be present. Minarii addressed him solemnly: —

> "Hearken to us, Ta'aroa!
> Grant our petitions.
> Preserve the population of this land.
> Preserve us, and let us live through thee.
> Preserve us! We are men. Thou art our god!"

The chanting ceased, and a moment of profound silence followed; then the priest concluded: "O Ta'aroa, we have awakened thee. Now sleep!"

The ceremony was over. The casket had been conveyed to its niche at the base of the pyramid, and Minarii had returned to the small hut near by to resume his customary garments, when voices were heard from the thicket and a moment later Mills and McCoy appeared at the edge of the clearing. They halted at the sight of the native men and then came forward to the fenced enclosure. McCoy gazed at the stone-work admiringly.

"A braw bit o' work," he remarked. "And the six of ye built this, Tetahiti?"

The native regarded him gravely. "This is our *marae*," he explained, "where we come to worship our god."

"What's that he says?" Mills asked, contemptuously. Without waiting for a reply, he passed through the gate and stood surveying the *marae*. He was about to mount the stone platform when Minarii, who had now returned, laid a hand on his arm.

"Your shoulders! Bare your shoulders before you set foot there!"

Knowing scarcely a dozen words of the native tongue, Mills shook him off and was about to proceed when McCoy called out anxiously: "Are ye horn-mad, John? Bare yer shoulders, he says. It's their kirk, mon! Would ye enter a kirk wi' a covered head?"

Mills gave a harsh laugh. "Kirk, ye call it? It's a bloody heathen temple, that's what it is! I'll have a look, and I'll peel my shirt for no Indian!"

Before he had mounted three steps Minarii seized him by the arm and threw him to the ground so fiercely that he lay half stunned.

"Ye fool!" McCoy exclaimed. "Ye've slashed a het haggis now!"

Minarii stood over the prostrate Englishman threateningly, his eyes blazing with anger. The faces of the other native men expressed the horror they felt at this act of desecration. Fortunately for Mills, McCoy, who spoke the native tongue with considerable fluency, was able to smooth matters over.

"Let your anger cool, Minarii," he said, rapidly. "You are in the right, but this man meant no harm. He is ignorant, that is all."

"Take him away!" ordered Minarii. "Come here no more. This is our sacred place."

Mills struggled to his feet, dazed and enraged, and stood with clenched fists, eyeing the native while McCoy spoke.

"Pull yersel' together, John! Say naught and get out o' this afore there's blood shed! Come along, now. They've right on their side, and he's an unchancy loon to meddle with."

Mills was in middle age, and Minarii's stern face and gigantic figure might have intimidated a far younger man. He turned aside and permitted McCoy to lead him away. The natives gazed after them in silence as they climbed the ridge and disappeared on the path leading to the settlement.

"Go you others," said Minarii, "and let no more be thought of this. The man was ignorant. As McCoy said, he meant no desecration."

Tetahiti remained behind and the two men lingered outside the enclosure surveying their handiwork with deep satisfaction.

"The building was auspicious," said Minarii, after a long silence. "The sacredness is in the stones."

Tetahiti nodded. "Did you not feel the god lighten the heavy boulders as we worked?" he asked.

"They were as nothing in our hands. Ta'aroa is well pleased with his dwelling place. Here we can offer prayers for our crops and for fishing, and dedicate the children who will come. Now for the first time my heart tells me that this is indeed my land — our land."

Minarii was silent for some time before he asked: "You know these white men better than I; have they no god?"

"Christian has never spoken to me of these things and I do not like to ask; but I would say that they worship none."

"It is strange that they should be godless. Captain Cook came three times to Matavai; I remember his visits well. He and his men were of the same race as these, but they worshiped their god every seventh day, in ceremonies not unlike our own. They bowed their heads; they knelt and listened in silence while one of them chanted. Our white men do none of these things."

"It must be that they have no god," Tetahiti replied.

Minarii shook his head gravely. "Little good can come to godless men. It would be well if we were alone here with our women. The ways of these whites are as strange to us as our ways to them."

"There are good men among them," said Tetahiti.

"Aye, but not all. Some yearn for Maori slaves."

"Martin, you mean? *Tihé!* He is slave-born!"

"It is not Martin alone," Minarii remarked, gravely. "Humble folk like your man Te Moa and my Hu rely upon us to protect them, and yet already Quintal and Williams and Mills treat them as little better than slaves. We want no bad blood here. We must be patient for the good of all, but the day may come . . ." He broke off, gazing sombrely before him.

"Christian knows nothing of this," said Tetahiti. "Shall I open his eyes?"

"It would be well if he knew, but these things he must learn for himself. We must wait and say nothing."

For a month or more after the burial of Fasto, Williams had seen nothing of Hutia. The girl was fond of him, in her way, and was wise enough to bide her time. Strive as he might, the blacksmith could not rid his mind of the thought that Fasto had learned of the intrigue, and that in her chagrin she had thrown herself from the cliffs. Though rough and forthright, he was by no means an unkindly man. For a time he had gone about his work in silence, without a glance at Hutia when she passed, but little by little his remorse was dulled, and the old desire for the girl overpowered him. Once more their meetings in the bush had begun, conducted, on her part at least, with greater discretion than at first.

But Williams was far from satisfied; he wanted the girl for his own. What had begun as mere philandering gradually became an obsession. On many a night he lay awake far into the morning hours, torturing his brain in attempts to conjure up some means of obtaining Hutia. Now at last he felt that he could endure no more. One afternoon when he was working with Mills at the forge he put down his hammer.

"Stand by for a bit, John," he said.

Mills straightened his back with a grunt. "What's up?" he asked, incuriously.

"I can't go on the like o' this. Every man of ye has his woman. I've none."

"Ye'll not get mine," growled Mills. "Take a girl from one of the Indians."

"Aye, Hutia'd do."

The other gave a dry laugh. "Ye should know! A pretty wench, but an artful one, Prudence reckons."

"I'm thinkin' what Christian would say; and Minarii . . ."

"Damn the Indians! Call for a show of hands. Ye've the right. Where'd we be without Jack Williams and his forge?"

Christian's house was the most westerly in the settlement, and stood on rising ground close to the bluffs, which sloped more gently here than at Bounty Bay. To the west, a deep ravine led the waters of Brown's Well to the shingle, three hundred feet below. A belt of trees and bush along the verge of the bluffs screened the house from the sea.

The dwelling was of two stories, heavily framed and planked with the *Bounty's* oaken strakes; the bright russet of its thatch contrasted pleasantly with the weathered oak. The upper story was a single large, airy room, with windows on all sides, which could be opened or closed against the weather by means of sliding shutters. It was reached by an inside ladder which led through a hatchway in the floor. It was here that Christian and Maimiti slept.

A partition divided the lower floor into two rooms. One was reserved for Christian's use. A roughly fashioned chair stood by a table of oak which held a silver-clasped Bible and a Book of Common Prayer, the *Bounty's* azimuth compass, and a fine timekeeper by Kendall, of London. Christian wound the instrument daily, and checked it from time to time by means of lunar observations, taken with the help of Young.

Christian had finished his noonday meal and was seated with Maimiti on a bench by the door, on the seaward side of the house. The sun was hot, and the sea, visible through a gap in the bush below, stretched away, calm, blue, and lonely, to the north. Looking up, presently, Christian observed Williams approaching.

The blacksmith touched his forelock to Christian, and saluted Maimiti as though she had been an English lady. "Might I speak with ye a moment, sir?" he asked.

"Yes. What is it, Williams? Do you wish to see me alone?"

"Aye."

The blacksmith remained standing, after the girl had gone, and hesitated for some time before he spoke.

"I doubt but ye'll think the less of me for what I have to say, but I must out with it. Men are fashioned in different ways — some hot, some cold, some wise, some fools. I reckon ye'll admit I'm no laggard and know my trade; but I've a weakness for the women, if weakness that be. . . . It's this, sir: I've lost my girl, and must have another."

He waited, clasping and unclasping his hands nervously. Christian reflected for a moment and said, slowly: "I foresaw this. It was bound to come. I don't blame you, Williams; your desire is a reasonable one. But surely you can see that no man is likely to give up his woman to you. What I propose might seem abhorrent at home, but the arrangement was an honourable one in ancient times. Have you no friend who would share his girl with you?"

Williams shook his head. "It won't do, sir; I'm not that kind. I must have one for myself."

"Which would you have?"

"Hutia."

"Tararu's wife? And what of Tararu?"

"He's but an Indian, and should give way."

"He's a man like ourselves. Consider your own feelings, were the situation reversed."

"I know, sir," Williams replied stubbornly, "but I must·have her!" He clenched his fists and looked up suddenly. "Damn the wench! I believe she's cast a spell on me!"

"Well, it has come, with a vengeance," Christian said, as though to himself. He raised his head. "Your seizure of another man's wife might have the gravest consequences for all of us. My advice is, do nothing of ·the kind."

"Ye're right, sir; I know that well enough. But I'm past taking advice."

"You mean that you would seize the woman regardless of the trouble you may cause the rest of us? Come, Williams! You're too much of a man for that!"

"I can't help it, Mr. Christian; but I'll do this, if ye'll agree. Put it to a vote. If there's more say I shan't have her, I'll abide by that."

"You've no right to ask for a show of hands over such a matter," Christian replied, sternly; "the less so since you are not denied the favours of this woman as matters stand." He paused to reflect. "Nevertheless, this is a question that does concern us all, and I will do as you ask. We'll have it out to-night. Fetch the others here when you have supped."

The evening was windless, after the long calm afternoon, and the stars were bright as the mutineers assembled before Christian's house. Brown was the last to arrive. When he had joined the group, Christian rose and the murmur of conversation ceased.

"Williams, have you told the others why we are gathered here?"

"No, sir; I reckoned that would come best from ye."

Christian nodded. "A question has arisen that concerns every man and woman on the island. Williams has lost his girl. He says that he must have another." He paused, and a voice in the starlight growled, "He'll have none of ours!"

"He wants Hutia," Christian explained, "Tararu's wife."

"He's had her times enough," Quintal put in.

Williams sprang up, angrily, and was about to speak when Christian checked him.

"That is no business of ours. He wants her in his house. He wishes her to leave her husband and live openly with him, and has asked me to put the question to a vote. His desire for a woman is a natural one; under other circumstances it would concern him alone, but not as we are situated. Differences over women are dangerous at all times, and in a small community like ours they may have fatal consequences. The girl's husband is a nephew of Minarii, whom you know for a proud man and a chief among his own people. Is it likely that he would stand by while Tararu's wife was seized? And what of Tararu himself? Justice is universal; the Indian resents injustice as the Englishman does. We are of two races here; so far there has been no bad blood between us. To stir up racial strife would be the ruin of all."

He paused, and a murmur of assent went up from the men on the grass. But Mills spoke up for his friend.

"I'm with Jack. Ain't we to be considered afore the Indians?"

"Aye, well spoke!" said Martin.

"Well spoke?" said McCoy. "I winna say that! I'm wi' Mr. Christian. It's no fault o' Jack's there's not been trouble afore now. I'm nae queasy. I'll share my Mary wi' him."

"Keep your Mary!" growled Williams.

"Are you ready for the vote?" Christian said. "Remember, this is to decide the matter, once and for all. We are agreed to abide by the result. Those who would allow Williams to take Tararu's wife, show hands." He peered into the darkness; the hands of Mills and Martin alone were lifted.

"We're six to three against you, Williams," said Christian. "I believe you'll be glad of this one day."

"I'll abide by the vote, sir," the blacksmith replied in a gruff voice.

May passed and June ushered in the austral winter, with cold southwest winds and tempestuous seas. The evenings grew so chill that the people were glad to remain indoors after sundown, natives and whites alike.

Those evenings were far from cheerful in the blacksmith's house. Since the night of the meeting he had become more and more gloomy and taciturn. Mills tried in vain to draw him into talk; at last he gave up and turned to Prudence for company. Williams avoided Hutia. He had given his word, and he knew that if he were to keep it their meetings must cease. He found no peace save in the exhaustion of hard work.

In the dusk of a morning late in June, Mills rose to find Williams already up and gone. He felt mildly surprised, for the blacksmith brooded and paced the floor so late that he seldom wakened while it was still dark. Williams had been busy with a pair of the *Bounty's* chain plates, converting them into fish spears for the Indian men, and during the early forenoon, while Mills worked at clearing a bit of land not far off, he was again surprised, as he rested from his labour, to hear no cheerful clink of hammer on anvil. Toward nine o'clock his vague feeling of uneasiness grew so strong that he wiped the sweat from his face and dropped his axe. Martin limped out of the house as he approached. For a moment Mills forgot the blacksmith.

"Damn 'ee!" he exclaimed. "Ye've done naught but lie abed, I'll warrant!"

"It's all I can do to walk, man!" said Martin. "Work? With an old musket ball in me leg, and the nights perishin' cold? Let the Indians work! That's what we fetched 'em for."

"Where's Jack?" Mills asked.

"That's what I want to know."

"Ye've not seen him?"

"No. And the large cutter's gone. Alex Smith came up from the cove an hour back. He and Christian are on the mountain now. Not a doubt of it: Jack's took the boat and made off."

Mills turned to take the path that led past Christian's house and on to the Goat-House Peak. Halfway to the ridge he met the others coming down. "Is it true that Jack's made off with the boat?" Christian nodded, and led the way down the mountainside at a rapid walk.

They halted at Christian's house while he acquainted Maimiti with the situation and sent for some of the Indian men. He then hastened on to the landing place. The little crowd on the beach watched in silence while Christian had the larger of the two canoes dragged to the water's edge. With Minarii in the stern, they shot the breakers and passed the blackened wreck of the ship, wedged between the rocks. Christian waved to the northeast, took up a paddle, and plied it vigorously.

The wind had died away two hours before, and the sun shone dimly through a veil of high cloud. The sea was glassy calm, with a gentle southerly swell. Before an hour had passed, Minarii pointed ahead. The cutter's masthead and the peak of her lugsail were visible on the horizon, though the boat was still hull-down.

Williams sat on the cutter's after-thwart, his chin propped in his hands. From time to time he raised his head to glance back toward the land. He feared pursuit, but hoped the wind might make up before it came. It was useless to row, he had discovered; with only one man at the oars, the heavy boat would scarcely move.

One of the *Bounty's* compasses lay in the stern sheets, with Williams's musket, a small store of provisions, and several calabashes filled with water. The blacksmith had some idea of where Tahiti lay, and knew that he would have a fair wind, once he could work his way into the region of the trades. But the thought that obsessed him was to get away from Pitcairn; as a destination, any other island would do. He might fetch Tahiti, he thought vaguely, or pick up one of the coral islands which they had passed in the *Bounty*. He cared little, in fact, where he went, or whether he died of thirst or was drowned on the way.

Presently he stood on a thwart, peering ahead with narrowed eyes for signs of wind. Then, turning to glance backward, he perceived the canoe, scarcely a mile away. He stepped down from the thwart, took up his musket, measured a charge from his powderhorn, and rammed the wad home. With sombre eyes, he selected a ball from his pouch.

The canoe came on fast. When it was half a cable's length distant, the blacksmith stood up and leveled his piece. "Stop where ye are!" he ordered, hoarsely.

Christian rose to his feet, waving the paddlers on. "Williams!" he ordered sternly, "lay down your musket!"

Slowly, as if in a daze, the black-bearded man in the boat obeyed, slumping down on the thwart with shoulders bowed. The canoe lost way, riding the swell lightly alongside, and Christian sprang aboard the cutter.

"Are you mad?" he asked, with the sternness gone from his voice. "Where could you hope to fetch up?"

"Aye, Jack," put in Mills, "ye must be clean daft!"

"Leave be, Mr. Christian," muttered Williams. "I'll not go on as I have. Where I fetch up is my own concern."

Christian seated himself beside him. "Think, Williams," he said kindly. "This boat is common property. And how would we fare without a blacksmith? Tahiti lies three hundred leagues from here. You would be going to certain death. . . . Come, take yourself in hand!"

Williams sat gazing at his bare feet for a long time before he spoke. "Aye, sir, I'll go back," he said reluctantly, without raising his head. "I've done my best. If trouble comes o' this, let no man hold me to account."


# CHAPTER VII

FROM now on Williams spent most of his time away from the settlement. On a lonely wooded plateau, on the western side of the island, he set to work to clear a plot of land and to build a cabin. Through the cold months of July, August, and September, he left the house each morning before the others were awake, returning at dusk. Mills respected his silence, and Martin, after one or two rebuffs, ceased to question him. In early October he announced that he was leaving for his new home, and, with Mills to help him, he carried his belongings over the ridge and down to the distant clearing where his cabin stood.

Though small, the cabin was strong and neatly built, with walls of split pandanus logs, set side by side. The floor alone was of plank, and the few articles of furniture had been put together with a craftsman's skill. Mills had not seen the place before. He glanced around admiringly.

"Ye've a snug little harbour here, Jack," he said as he set down his burden. "All Bristol-fashion, too! So ye're bound to live alone?"

"Aye."

Mills shrugged his shoulders. "I've no cause to meddle, but if it's Hutia ye're still pinin' for, why don't ye take her and be damned to the Indians?"

"I've no wish to stir up trouble. Christian's been fair with us. I'll do what I can to be fair in my turn. I'll try living alone away from the sight of her, but I'm not sayin' how this'll end. Thank 'ee for the lift, John," he added. "Tell the lads I'll come over when there's work for the forge."

The shadows were long in the clearing, for it was late afternoon. Grass was already beginning to hide the ashes about the blackened stumps. As he sat on the doorstep of his house, the slope of the ground to the west gave Williams a view of the sea above the tree-tops. Snow-white terns, in pairs, sailed back and forth overhead. It was their mating season and they were pursuing one another, swooping and tumbling in aerial play. No wind was astir; the air, saturated with moisture, was difficult to breathe. Williams rose, cursing the heat, went to the small cookhouse behind his cabin, and kindled a fire to prepare his evening meal. At last the sun set angrily, behind masses of banked-up clouds, dull crimson and violet. It was not a night for sleep. The blacksmith was on foot before dawn, and the first grey of morning found him crossing the ridge, on his way to Christian's house.

Alexander Smith wakened at the same hour. Like Williams, he had tossed and cursed the heat all night, between snatches of fitful sleep. He opened the door, rubbed his eyes with his knuckles, stretched his arms wide, and yawned.

The moon, nearly at the full, was still up, though veiled by clouds in the west. The big red rooster in the *purau* tree flapped his wings, crowed and regarded the ground with down-stretched neck and deep, explosive cackles. With a prodigious noise of wings, he left his perch and landed with a heavy thump. One after the other, the hens followed, and each in turn was ravished as she touched the ground. The last hen shook herself angrily, the cock made a final sidewise step with lowered wing, and glanced up at his master as if to say: "Well, *that's* over with! Now for breakfast!" Smith grinned.

The fowls followed him in a compact little flock to the cookhouse, where the coconut-grater stood. Seating himself astride the three-legged stool to which the grater of pearl shell was lashed, he began to scrape out the coconut meat, a crinkled, snowy shower that soon filled his wooden bowl.

He stopped once to fill his own mouth, and chuckled, as he munched, at the impatience of the fowls, standing in a wistful circle about the bowl. He rose, calling, as the natives did, in a high-pitched, ringing cry, and while the fowls came running with outstretched wings he scattered grated coconut this way and that.

Hearing the familiar call, the pigs in their sty under the banyan tree burst into eager grunts. "*Mai! Mai! Mai!*" responded Smith, gruntingly, and strolled across to empty the half of his coconut into their trough. He had the seaman's love of rural things.

It was now broad daylight. Balhadi came to the door, greeted her husband with a smile, and went to the cookhouse to prepare his breakfast. Smith stripped off his shirt and dipped a large calabashful from the water barrel for his morning wash. After scrubbing his face vigorously with a bit of tapa, he made the morning round of his plants. A fenced enclosure, of about half an acre, surrounded his house, and he derived keen pleasure from the garden he had laid out inside, with its stone-bordered paths and beds of flowering shrubs. Spring was coming on fast. He walked slowly, stooping often to examine the new growth or to inhale the perfume of some waxen flower. Now and again, as he straightened his back, he paused to glance at his newly completed house. Young was not a strong man, nor clever with his hands, and Smith had put up the building almost alone. He still derived from the sight of his handiwork a deep and inarticulate satisfaction. It was a shipshape job — stoutly built, weatherproof, and sightly, with its bright new thatch. The Indians said that such thatching would last ten years.

Balhadi was calling him to eat. She was a short, strongly made woman, wholesome and still youthful, with a firm, good-humoured face. Smith felt a real affection for her, expressed in robust fashion. He pulled her down to his knee, gave her a resounding kiss, and fell to on his breakfast. Ten minutes later he shouldered his axe and strode away to his morning's work in the bush.

"Alex! Alex O!"

Tetahiti was hailing him from the path. He and Smith were good friends, and both loved fishing. "I came to fetch you," said the native. "Can you leave your work till noon? There is wind on the way, but the morning will be calm. I have discovered where the albacore sleep."

Smith nodded, and stood his axe against the fence. He followed Tetahiti down the path that led to Bounty Bay. They passed Mills's house, and McCoy's, and halted at the dwelling of the natives, not far from the landing place. The men had gone to their work in the bush; Smith chaffed with Moetua while his companion fetched the lines. Hutia was nowhere to be seen.

"Look," said Tetahiti, "we've octopus for bait. I speared two last night."

The sea was fairly calm in the cove, sheltered from the westerly swell. The native selected a dozen longish stones, weighing three or four pounds each, and tossed them into the smaller of the two canoes. They were soon outside the breakers and paddling to the northwest, while Tetahiti glanced back frequently to get his bearings from the land. At a distance of about a mile, he gave the word to cease paddling.

"This is the place," he said, as the canoe lost way and floated idly on the long, glassy swell. "I have been studying the birds for many days; this is where the fish cease to feed on the surface, and go down to sleep in the depths."

Each man had a ball of line two hundred fathoms or more in length. One end was tied to the outrigger boom; to the other, running out from the centre of the ball, the hook was attached. They now baited their hooks and made fast their sinkers, with a hitch that permitted the stones to be released by a sharp jerk.

"Let us try at one hundred fathoms," said Tetahiti.

Smith lowered his sinker over the side and allowed the line to run out for a long time, until a knot appeared. He pulled sharply and felt the hitch unroll and the release of the sinker's weight. Then, moving his line up and down gently, to attract the attention of the fish six hundred feet below, he settled himself to wait.

The sun was well up by now, but the horizon to the north was ominous. There was not the faintest breath of wind; even at this early hour the heat was oppressive.

"We shall have a storm," remarked the native. "The moon will be full to-night."

Smith nodded. "Christian thinks so, too."

"Your ears are opened," said Tetahiti. "You are beginning to speak our tongue like one of us!"

"I have learned much from you. What day is this — what night, I mean?"

"*Maitu.* To-night will be *hotu,* when the moon rises as the sun sets."

Smith shook his head, admiringly. "I can never remember. We whites have only the names of the seven days of our week to learn. Your people must learn the twenty-eight nights of the moon!"

"Yes, and more; I will teach you the sayings concerning *maitu:* 'A night for planting taro and bamboo; an auspicious night for love-making. Crabs and crayfish shed their shells on this night; albacore are the fish at sea. Large-eyed children and children with red hair are born on this night.' . . . *Mau!*"

He shouted the last word suddenly as he struck to set the hook and allowed his line to run hissing over the gunwale. Smith watched eagerly, admiring the skill with which Tetahiti handled the heavy fish. Next moment it was his turn to shout. For a full half-hour the two men sweated in silence as they played their fish. Smith's was the first to weaken. It lay alongside the canoe, half dead from its own exertions — a huge burnished creature of the tunny kind. Holding his tight line with one hand, Tetahiti seized the catch by the tail while Smith clenched his fingers in the gills. A word, a heave in unison, and the albacore lay gasping in the bilges — a magnificent fish of a hundred pounds or more. Smith clubbed it to death before lending Tetahiti a hand.

The sea grew lumpy and confused as they paddled back to the cove. A swell from the north was now rolling into Bounty Bay, making their landing a difficult one. Minarii was awaiting them on the shingle. He helped them pull the canoe up into the shade.

"You come none too soon," he said. "The sea is making up fast. You are weary; let me carry your fish."

He fastened the tails of the albacore together, hoisted the burden of more than two hundredweight to one shoulder, and led the way up the steep path.

It was nearly noon. The workers had returned from the bush, and smoke went up from the cookhouses of the little settlement. Minarii set down his burden at the native house, and made a sign to his man Hu to cut up the fish. The women gathered about, exclaiming at sight of the catch. There was neither buying nor selling among the Polynesians. When fish was caught, it was shared out equally among all members of the community, high and low alike, a custom already firmly rooted on Pitcairn.

"I will carry Brown's share to him," said Minarii. Hu and Te Moa slung the remaining shares between them on a pole, and walked up the path, followed by Smith. McCoy's Mary stood before her house. She was great with child and had trouble in stooping to take up the cut of fish dropped on the grass at her feet.

"Hey, Will!" called Smith. "Here's a bit of fish for 'ee."

McCoy and Quintal appeared in the doorway. "Thank 'ee, Alex, ye're a lucky loon. Albacore!"

"Aye," put in Quintal. "Next best to a collop of beef!"

After a stop at the house of Mills, Smith dismissed the two natives at his own door and went on to Christian's house, Balhadi accompanying him. She carried a gift of a taro pudding, done up in fresh green leaves.

"For Maimiti," she explained. "This may tempt her to eat."

"When does she expect her child?"

"Her time is very close — to-day or to-morrow, I think."

Christian met them at the door and Balhadi carried the fish and her pudding to the cookhouse.

"A fine albacore, Smith!"

"I reckon he'd go a hundredweight, sir!" said Smith with a fisherman's pride. "And Tetahiti got one might have been his twin brother. All hands'll have a feed of 'em."

"Stop to dine with us."

"I hate to bother ye, sir, at a time like this."

Christian shook his head. "No, no! Jenny's here, and Nanai, to lend a hand. They'll make a little feast of it, with your girl. They're funny creatures, brown or white; birth and death are what they love. Come in."

"Thank 'ee, sir. I've a cut of fish for Jack; I'll just hang it up in the shade."

"He left not ten minutes gone. Come in and rest before we dine. They'll be giving us some of your fish. Do you like it raw, in the Indian style?"

"Aye, sir, that I do!"

"And I, when prepared with their sauce of coconut. We think of the Indians as savages, yet we have much to learn from them."

"I don't know what we'd do without 'em, here. We'd get no fish without the men to teach us how to catch 'em, and as for the girls, I reckon we'd starve but for them!"

They were sitting by the table in Christian's room, for Maimiti could no longer climb the ladder to the apartment upstairs, and the dining room was set aside for her use. The two men were silent for a time while the chronometer beside them ticked loudly and steadily. Christian glanced at its dial, which registered the hour in Greenwich, and the sight set his thoughts to wandering back through the past — to his boyhood in Cumberland and on the Isle of Man, to his early days at sea.

"Had that old timekeeper a voice," he remarked, "it could tell us a rare tale! It was Captain Cook's shipmate on two voyages, traveling thousands of leagues over seas little known even now. It began life in London; now it will end its days on Pitcairn's Island."

Smith nodded. "Like me, sir!" he said.

"Were you born in London? I took you for a countryman."

"Aye, Mr. Christian; born there and reared in a foundling's home. I'm under false colours here. My real name is John Adams; the lads used to call me 'Reckless Jack.' I got into a bit of trouble and thought best to sign on as Alexander Smith."

Christian nodded, and asked after a brief pause: "Tell me, Smith, are you contented here?"

"That I am, sir! My folk were countrymen, till my dad was fool enough to try his fortune in London. It's in my blood. Happy? If ye was all to leave, and give me the chance, I'd stop here with my old woman to end my days."

Christian smiled. "I am glad, since I fetched you here. It would be curious, were we able to look ahead twenty years. There will be broad plantations, new houses, and children — many of them — I hope."

"And yours'll be the first-born, sir!"

Jenny appeared in the doorway, carrying a platter of fish. She smiled at the two men, and beckoned Balhadi in to help set the table. An hour later Smith rose to take his leave.

"Ask Williams to come down to the cove this afternoon," said Christian. "We shall need all hands to get the boats up out of reach of the sea."

A heavy swell from the north was bombarding the cliffs as Smith made his way over the ridge. The heat was sultry, though the sky was now completely overcast, and he knew that the wind could not be far off. Williams met him at the cottage door.

"Come in, Alex. Set ye down. What's that — fish? A monster he must have been, eh? Here, let me hang it up; Puss has smelt it already."

The blacksmith's cat, a fine tabby whose sleekness proved her master's care, was mewing eagerly, and Williams paused to cut off a small piece for her.

"She's spoiled," he remarked. "D'ye think she'd look at a rat? But I hate rusty tools and scrawny living things."

As they entered the cottage, Smith observed, on the floor close to the bed, a round comb of bamboo, such as the women used. Next moment, out of the corner of his eye, he saw Williams kick it hastily under the bed. He glanced about the neat little dwelling appreciatively.

"Ye've the best-built house of the lot," he said, "and the prettiest to look at. Aye, it's small, but all the better for that."

"What d'ye think of the weather, Alex?" Williams asked.

"It'll be blowing a gale by night. I'd best be getting back. Mr. Christian wants all hands at Bounty Bay. He's afeared for the boats."

The blacksmith nodded. "I'll come along with ye," he said.

The wind was making up from the northwest, with heavy squalls of rain, and before the two men reached the cove it hauled to the north, blowing with ever-increasing force.

It was late afternoon when the people began to straggle back, up the steep path to the settlement. The boats and the two canoes had been conveyed to the very foot of the bluff, far above where they were usually kept, and it seemed that no wave, no matter how great, could reach them there.

But at nightfall the gale blew at hurricane force. The deep roar of the wind and the thunder of breaking seas increased as the night wore on. The rocky foundations of the island trembled before the onslaught of wind and wave. There was little sleep for anyone, and there were moments when it seemed that only a miracle could preserve the houses from being carried away. Daybreak came at last.

Toward seven o'clock Smith went trudging up the path to Christian's house. The wind was abating, he thought, though the coconut palms along the path still bent low to the gusts, their fronds streaming like banners in the gale. Smith glanced up apprehensively from time to time as a heavy nut came whacking to the ground. Once, in a place where the path was somewhat exposed, he staggered and leaned to windward to keep his feet. Each time a great comber burst at the foot of the cliffs, he felt the ground tremble underfoot. At last he reached Christian's house.

The sliding shutters on the weather side were closed, but the door was open in the lee. Smith found Christian in the room, with Jenny and Taurua.

"Balhadi is with her," Christian said, drawing the newcomer aside and raising his voice to make it heard. "The pains have begun. What of the boats?"

"Gone, sir, all but the large cutter," replied Smith regretfully. "The sea's higher 'n ye'd believe! All was snug an hour back. Then a roarin' great sea came in and carried away both canoes and the small cutter. And when the wind had cleared the air of spray, we looked out, sir, and the old *Bounty* was gone!"

Christian paced the floor nervously for a minute or two, stopping once to listen at the door of the other room. Then, halting suddenly, he addressed Taurua: "Go in to her, you and Jenny; say that I am going down to the landing place and shall not be long." He turned to Smith. "Come, there is nothing I can do here at such a time."

They found Young and a group of men and women at the verge of the bluffs, crouching to escape the full force of the wind while they watched with fascinated eyes the towering seas that ran into Bounty Bay. Speech was impossible, but Young took Christian's arm and pointed out to where the blackened hulk of the ship had lain wedged among the rocks. No trace of her remained.

The waves were breaking high among the undergrowth at the foot of the path, and during the brief lulls, when the spray was blown ashore, Christian saw that the cove was a mass of floating rubbish and uprooted trees, and that avalanches had left raw streaks of earth where the sea had undermined the steep slopes toward Ship-Landing Point.

The gale was abating when at last the three men turned to make their way back to Christian's house. At the door they heard faintly, between gusts of wind, the wail of a newborn child. The door of the other room opened, and Jenny and Taurua came in, with the smiles of women who have assisted at a happy delivery. Balhadi appeared behind them. She beckoned to Christian.

"*É tamaroa!*" she said. "A man-child!"

As she closed the door behind him, Christian saw Maimiti on a couch covered with many folds of tapa; and close beside her, swathed to the eyes in the same soft native cloth, an infant who stirred and wailed from time to time. Maimiti looked pale and worn, but in her eyes there was an expression of deep happiness. Balhadi pulled back the tapa that muffled the baby's face.

"Look!" she said proudly. "Was ever a handsomer boy? And auspiciously born! You know our proverb: 'Born in the hurricane, the child shall live in peace.'"

Young smiled when Christian came out of the room. "It is fitting that your child should be our first-born," he remarked, as he held out his hand. "What shall you name him?"

"Nothing to remind me of England," replied Christian. "Smith, Balhadi has proven herself a true friend to-day. You shall be the child's godfather. Give him a name."

The seaman grinned and scratched his head. "Ye'll have naught to remind 'ee of England? I have it, sir. Ye might name him for the day, if ye know what day it is."

The father smiled grimly as he consulted his calendar. "It's a good suggestion, Smith. The day is Thursday, and the month October. Thursday October Christian he shall be!" He glanced out through the doorway. "Here come the others; set out the benches."

The other mutineers and their women were approaching the house. One after another, the men shook Christian's hand, while the women filed in to seat themselves on the floor by Maimiti's couch. When the benches were full, Christian raised his voice above the roar of the wind.

"There's a question that calls for a show of hands. Shall we issue an extra grog ration to-day, and drink it here and now?"

Every hand went up, but McCoy asked anxiously: "How much ha' we left, sir?"

Christian drew a small, worn book from his pocket and turned the pages. "Fifty-three gallons."

McCoy shook his head gloomily. "A scant four months' supply!"

When the glasses were full, the men toasted the child in the next room: —

"A long life to him, sir!"

"May he be as good a man as his father!"

McCoy was the last to drink. He watched the filling of his glass with deep interest, and sniffed at the rum luxuriously before he took a sip.

"I'll nae drink it clean caup out," he said apologetically, and then, as he held the glass aloft, "Tae our first bairn! I've run 'ee a close race, sir. My Mary'll hae her babe within the week!"

## CHAPTER VIII

With the warm spring rains of November, the planting of the cleared lands began. The weather was too sultry for hard work when the sun was overhead; the men went out to their plantations at daybreak, rested through the hot noon hours, and worked once more from mid-afternoon till evening dusk.

Smith, Young, and Christian had joined forces in clearing a considerable field in the Auté Valley. Now the rubbish had been burned and the smaller stumps pulled, and the volcanic soil, rich and red, lay ready to nourish a crop of yams.

On a morning toward the middle of the month, the three men set out well before sunrise, taking the path that led south, up the long slope of the plateau, and over the ridge. No wind was astir, a light mist hung over the tree-tops, and the fresh spring verdure was beaded with dew. A party of women, ahead, took the path that branched off to the east. Presently, with Christian leading the way, the men toiled up the steep trail to the ridge, and came to a halt. Dropping the heavy basket of lunch, Smith was the last to seat himself. The place commanded a wide prospect to the north — over the rich plateau, christened the Main Valley, to the misty greyish-blue of the sea beyond. It was a custom, well established by now, to rest here for a few minutes each morning before descending to work in the Auté Valley.

The upper rim of the sun was touching the horizon, gilding the small, fluffy, fair-weather clouds. The clearings in the Main Valley were not as yet extensive enough to be visible from the ridge. From the sea to the bare summits of the ridges, virgin forest clothed the land. Here and there, the silvery foliage of a clump of candlenut trees contrasted with the dark green of the bush, and scattered coconut palms curved up gracefully to their fronded tops, sixty or seventy feet above the earth.

In the valley below, the women were at work beating out bark cloth. Each tapa-maker had her billet of wood, fashioned from the heart of an ironwood tree, and adzed flat on the upper surface. They varied from a fathom to a fathom and a half in length, and were supported on flat-topped stones set in the earth, so spaced that no two beams gave forth the same note when struck. They were, in fact, rude xylophones; the women derived great pleasure from the musical notes of their mallets, and the measured choruses produced when several of them worked together. "Tonk, tink, tonk, tonk; tinka-tonk, tink!" — the deliberate notes were sweet, measured, and musical. Young loved the sound of them, which expressed to him the very spirit of rustic domesticity, of the dreamy happiness of the islands, of morning in the dewy bush.

Presently the men rose and made their way down the slope of the Auté Valley, to the glade where Brown's cottage stood. The seed yams, fetched from Tahiti, had been planted early in February in a good-sized clearing near by. The gardener and Jenny had tended them till they were ready to be dug, weeding the rows carefully, and watering the young plants in times of drought. They had been left in the ground until October, and stored on platforms in the shade, out of the reach of rats and wandering swine.

A slender column of smoke rose from Jenny's cookhouse. The gardener was on his knees, absorbed in potting a young breadfruit plant which he had just severed from the parent tree. Christian approached so softly that Brown started at the sound of his voice. He rose stiffly, dusting the earth from his hands. "Morning, sir." He smiled at Young and gave Smith a friendly nod. "What's to be planted to-day, Mr. Christian?"

"Have you many more of the long yams? The *tahotaho?*"

"Aye. There's a-plenty. To my way of thinking, they're the best of the lot."

He led the way to a large raised platform, under a spreading tree. It held two or three tons of sprouted yams, all of the same variety, and averaging no less than fifty pounds in weight. While Christian chatted with the gardener, his companions went to the cookhouse and returned with half a dozen bags of coarse netting and three carrying poles. Each bag was now filled with yams, handled gently in order not to injure the sprouts. Young's load was made light, but Smith and Christian balanced a hundredweight at either end of their poles. In a land where wheels and beasts of burden were unknown, no other method of transport was possible.

Christian squatted, settled the stout pole on his shoulder, raised himself upright with a grunt, and led the way to the new clearing. It lay about four hundred yards distant from Brown's cottage, in a westerly direction, and the feet of the three men had already worn a discernible path through the bush. The land sloped gently to the south, hemmed in by high green walls of virgin forest. Christian dashed the sweat from his eyes when he had set down his load.

The hills were to be about a yard apart, and all had been well lined and staked the day before. Young set to work at cutting up the yams, so large that many of them sufficed to plant twenty-five or thirty hills. Side by side on two rows, Christian and Smith began to ply their mattocks, digging a hole at each stake, filling it in with softened earth and decaying vegetation. Their companion was soon planting the sprouted bits of yam, pressing the earth down carefully over each.

The two men worked doggedly till nearly ten o'clock, striving to keep ahead of Young, never halting, save to spit on their hands and take fresh grips on their mattock hafts. They had cast their shirts aside, and the sweat streamed from their shoulders and backs. The sun was high overhead when Christian flung down his mattock and wiped his face with his bare forearm.

"Avast digging!" he said to Smith.

"Aye, sir; I've had enough."

Young followed them to a shady spot where they sluiced their bodies with water from a large calabash. Smith wandered away into the bush and was back before long, with a cluster of drinking coconuts and a broad leaf of the plantain, to serve as a cloth for their rustic meal. He drew the sheath knife at his belt, cut the tops from a pair of nuts, and offered them to his companions.

Christian threw back his head and finished the cool, sweet liquor at a draught. He smiled as he tossed the empty nut away.

"We've a rare island," he remarked, "where grog grows on the trees!"

"What have the girls given us to-day?" inquired Young, glancing at the basket hungrily. Smith spread the plantain leaf on the ground and began to remove the contents of the basket, displaying a large baked fish, the half of a cold roast suckling pig, cooked breadfruit, scraped white and wrapped in leaves, and a small calabash filled with the delicious coconut sauce called *taioro*. The three men seated themselves on the grass and were beginning their meal when Jenny appeared, carrying a large wooden bowl which she set down before them.

"A pudding," she explained. "I made two."

When she was gone, they fell to heartily, dining with the relish only hard work can impart. The fish disappeared, and the crisp, browned suckling pig; the pudding of taro and wild arrowroot, covered with sweet coconut cream, soon went the same way. Smith sighed.

"I'm for a nap, sir," he said, as he rose to his feet with some difficulty; "I've stowed away enough for three!"

Five minutes later he was snoring gently in the shade of a *purau* tree, a stone's throw distant. Christian turned to Young.

"There's a good man, Ned," he remarked.

"Yes. I've come to know him well. Had he been reared under more fortunate circumstances . . ."

Christian nodded. "He's a fine type of Englishman, and a born leader, I suspect. Life's wasteful and damned unjust! What chance has a man in the forecastle? Who can blame him if he diverts himself with trollops or dulls his mind with drink? Not I! Smith deserved a better chance from life. He has the instincts of a gentleman."

They fell silent. The sun was now directly overhead, and presently they moved to a place of dense shade where they could sit with their backs to the trunk of an ancient candlenut tree. "Seamen are a strange lot," Christian remarked, presently. "You and I have been together since the *Bounty* left Spithead, and now we shall pass the remainder of our lives on this morsel of land. Yet I know nothing of you, nor you of me! Where was your home, Ned? Tell me something of your life before you went to sea."

"I was born in the West Indies, on St. Kitts, and lived there till I was twelve years old."

"I've been there! It was eight — no, nine years ago. We cast anchor at Basseterre to load sugar, and I had a run ashore. I was only a lad at the time."

"We lived just outside the town, at the foot of Monkey Hill. I loved the island, and was unhappy when sent away to school. Here in the South Sea I feel more at home than in England."

"Odd that we should both be islanders! My own boyhood was passed on the Isle of Man. My first speech was the Manx, not unlike the Gaelic of the Highlanders." Christian smiled, half sadly. "I can still hear the voice of our old nurse, singing the lament for Illiam Dhone."

"Who was he?"

"William Christian, my ancestor — 'Fair-Haired Illiam' in our language. He was executed in 1663, for high treason against the Countess of Derby, then Queen of Man. He was innocent."

For two hours or more, till Smith wakened, they chatted idly of the past. Then, as the shadows began to extend eastward, the three men fell to work once more. It was dusk when they laid down their mattocks and filed homeward, past Brown's cottage and over the ridge.

The summer proved warm and rainy and the yams grew well. They were ready for digging when autumn had dried out the soil and June ushered in the winter of 1791.

Midway of the settlement, near the house of Mills, the communal storage platforms, called *pafatas,* had been set up. Supported on stout posts higher than a man's head, and floored with a grating of saplings laid side by side, the four large platforms were designed to hold twenty tons or more of yams. As with the fish, so with the fruits of the earth; all hands were to share alike.

As the yams were dug, the men fetched them in on their carrying

poles and passed them up to the women, one by one, to be stowed aloft.
The long yams were laid crisscross, to allow a free circulation of air;
day after day the piles grew higher, till at last, toward the middle of
the month, it was announced that another day's work would see the
harvest home.

Four large hogs were killed that night, scalded, scraped, and hung
from the branches of a banyan tree. There was a sense of rejoicing in
the houses, of deep satisfaction with a communal task performed, of
happy anticipation of well-earned rest.

At daybreak the people began to assemble by the platforms, exchanging good-natured banter as they eyed the preparations for their
evening feast. Hu and Te Moa had been appointed cooks, and were
already engaged in scraping out pits for two large earth ovens, one for
baking the hogs and one for ti roots, yams, taro, and other vegetables.
McCoy slapped the smooth white flank of one of the hogs.

"Ye're forbid to Jews, and no true Scot'll eat 'ee, but bide here till
Will McCoy comes back!" He turned to Quintal: "Vivers for all
hands, Matt! Gin we'd ilk a tass o' grog!"

Quintal grinned, and at that moment Christian came around the
turn of the path. He was carrying his small boy, now eight months
old, and Maimiti followed him. McCoy caught his eye.

"Can't 'ee spare a sup o' grog for to-night, sir? Just a wee tassie all
round?"

Christian shook his head. "We've but four bottles left. It was agreed
to save that for medical stores."

"Aye, sir," replied McCoy regretfully. "So it was, I mind me; I'll
say nae mair."

Presently the men took up their poles and bags of netting; several
of the women accompanied them to lend a hand as they scattered to
the different parts of the island where their plantations were situated.
Christian handed young Thursday October to his mother, shouldered
his pole, and took the path with Smith and Young to the Auté Valley.

All day long the yams came in and were stowed aloft, without a halt
for dinner or a rest at noon. At sunset the *pafatas* were bending under
their loads, and every soul on Pitcairn's Island, save Minarii and his
wife, was there by the ovens, still covered with heaps of matting and
breadfruit leaves.

Minarii had cleared and planted the largest field on the island, and
his crop was the heaviest of all. Aided by Moetua, he had toiled like

a Titan throughout the day. Now, in the dusk of evening, they were fetching in the last load. A shout went up from the natives as they came in sight. Minarii was in the lead, half running, half walking, with bent knees. His carrying pole was a mighty bludgeon of hard-wood, but it curved and swayed with the man's movements, for no less than two hundredweight of yams was suspended from either end. Behind him came Moetua, trotting under a load Young or McCoy could not have lifted from the ground.

As the couple set down their burdens, several of the natives, men and women, sprang forward to lend a hand. Prudence and Nanai swarmed up the posts of the nearest *pafata* and squatted, clapping their hands. Up went the yams, of forty, fifty, and sixty pounds weight, to be stowed amid shouting and much good-natured mirth. Tararu was about to heave up the last of them when Minarii laid a hand on his arm.

"For the god," he said. "Ta'aroa will be content with his first fruits."

Christian nodded to the two cooks. "Open the ovens!" he ordered.

When Minarii and his wife returned, bathed like the others, and the woman with a wreath of flowers on her hair, the feast had been spread on a stretch of level lawn. Christian sat at the head of the rustic table, and below him the men faced each other in two lines. The women had their meal at a little distance, and a bright fire of coconut husks burned between.

Two hours later, when the last of the broken meats had been gathered up and the natives were drumming and dancing in the firelight, Christian took leave of the company. Maimiti followed him, with her sleeping child on her arm.

"A happy day," he said, as they strolled homeward in the starlight. "We have begun well here. Your people and mine were like brothers to-night!"

It was past midnight when the fire was allowed to die out and the people straggled back to their houses to sleep. The new day began to brighten the eastern sky, and one by one the fowls fluttered down from the trees. Still the doors of the houses remained closed, and the people slept. Only Minarii was afoot.

In the first grey of dawn he had taken the path to the *marae,* bear-ing a little offering of first fruits for his god. Uncovering his shoulders reverently, he had climbed to the rude platform of stone and laid the basket of food on Ta'aroa's altar. Then, after a brief prayer, supplicating the acceptance of the offering and the continued favour of the god, he had set out to return to his house, where he meant to rest throughout the morning.

Upon reaching the summit of the Goat-House Ridge, he seated himself on a flat rock to rest. The sun was above the horizon now; the sky was cloudless, and there was a light, cool breeze from the west. No music of tapa mallets came up from the wooded depths of the Main Valley; all was still save for the occasional long-drawn crowing of the cocks. He drew a deep breath. Life was good, he thought, and this island, to which the white captain had led him, was a good land. The fish from this sea were sweet; pigs throve here without attention; as for yams, who in Tahiti had seen the equal of these? He had had many wives, but Moetua was the best of them, though she had never borne him a child. A fine, strapping girl, a fit mate for a man like himself! And she had no eyes for the other men. He rose, stretching his arms wide as he turned, and glanced casually and half instinctively around the half-circle of horizon to the west. Suddenly his easy pose became rigid. For a full minute or more he gazed westward, hands shading his eyes. Then he turned and plunged down the steep path toward Christian's house.

Christian, clad only in a loin cloth, was scrubbing himself by the water cask at the rear of the house when Minarii arrived. He hailed the native man cheerily, then paused, with the calabash in his hand, to give him a keen glance. "What is it, Minarii?" he asked.

"I have been on the ridge. Chancing to glance westward, I saw that something broke the line where sea and sky meet. It gleamed white when the rising sun shone upon it. Christian, it is a sail!"

Christian's face was impassive. "You are sure?" he asked.

Minarii nodded: "It is a white man's ship. Our sails of matting are brown."

"Is she steering this way?"

"I could not make out."

"Find Smith," said Christian. "Tell him to come to me at once."

Maimiti sat on the doorstep, suckling her eight months' boy. Christian stopped for a moment to caress her hair and to gaze down tenderly at his son. When he came out of the house, spyglass in hand, Alexander Smith was striding up the path. "We are going to the Goat-House," Christian told the girl.

As they walked away briskly, he informed Smith of Minarii's news.

"We'll stop on the mountain till we make certain of her course. It is too early for a ship sent out from England to search for us, but a British vessel may have put in at Matavai by chance and learned of the mutiny from the others there. She would be on the lookout for us."

Both men were panting when they reached the summit, and both turned their eyes westward, where a speck of white broke the line of the horizon. Christian rested his glass in the fork of a scrubby tree, focused it, and gazed out to the west. Three or four minutes elapsed before he lowered the glass.

"She's hull and courses down," he said. "I can make out topsails, topgallants, and royals when they catch the sun."

He handed the glass to Smith, who scrutinized the distant vessel long and earnestly. "She's steering this way, sir," he said at last. "Look again. Ye'll see her foretopmast staysail."

Christian soon convinced himself of the truth of Smith's words, and they turned to go.

"With this westerly wind, she'll come on fast, sir," remarked Smith.

"Aye," replied Christian grimly, as he picked his way down the steep path. "She should be close in by one o'clock."

He said no more till they were approaching the house. Halting at the door, he turned to Smith. "Go at once to Brown and Williams, and tell any others you meet on the way. Every fire must be put out. I want all hands, men and women, to assemble at McCoy's house. Tell them to waste no time."

"A ship is coming," he told Maimiti, when Smith was gone. "Unless they make a landing, we have nothing to fear. I am going to warn the others. Do you stop here and gather together everything we possess from the ship — plates, knives, axes, tools. All must be well hidden. Should they land, we will conceal ourselves in the bush till they are gone."

At Young's house, Christian stopped to explain the situation and to give his orders. Half consciously, he had taken command of the island as if it had been a ship. All fires were extinguished and the mutineers set to work with their women collecting every article of European manufacture, in preparation for flight to the bush. When all were assembled before McCoy's house, Christian revealed his plan.

"She is making direct for the island," he said. "If the wind holds, she will fetch the land within a few hours. From the cut of her sails she is a small English frigate. She cannot have been sent out in search for us, but it is possible that she touched at Tahiti and learned of the mutiny there. Our course is clear in any case. If they pass without making a landing, they must not know that the island is inhabited. Should they land, we must take to the bush and remain hidden there, with everything that might betray us as white men." He paused, and the men spoke rapidly in low voices among themselves. "Williams and Mills," Christian went on, "I leave the smithy to you. See that the bellows, the forge, and the anvil are safely hidden, and every trace of Williams's work removed. Young, the path leading up from Bounty Bay must be wiped out and masked. Take the Indian men. Yours is the most important task of all! Pile stones in a natural manner here and there on the path, and plant young ironwood trees between; their foliage will not wilt for a day or two. McCoy, take charge of the houses, and see that nothing remains to betray us. Smith, you shall be our lookout, and report instantly should the ship change her course. And remember, no fires! If they land, we shall repair at once to the grove of banyan below the Indian temple. They will never find us there."

Mills slapped the stock of the musket in his hand. "Find us or not," he growled, "I don't mean to be taken. Not while I've powder and lead!"

"Are ye daft?" asked McCoy. "One shot'd be the ruin of us all!"

"Aye," said Christian sternly, "McCoy is right!"

The people dispersed to their tasks and Christian walked back to set his own house in order. Smith followed and stopped at the door while the spyglass was fetched.

Less than two hours had passed when Smith returned. "She's an English man-of-war, sir, not a doubt of it! A frigate of thirty-two, I reckon, and coming straight on for the land."

By early afternoon Christian's orders had been carried out, and the people were assembled not far from McCoy's house and a quarter of a mile from the landing place. The path leading up from the cove had been masked so skillfully that no trace of it was visible, and after a final inspection by Christian the workers had made their way separately up the bluff.

The ship was now close in; Smith was stationed on a point that jutted out beyond a small ravine, to hail the others when she rounded the northern cape. Christian was admonishing the group of men and women on the grass.

"She is a man-of-war, and there will be a dozen spyglasses trained on shore. When she comes in sight, the women must remain here. Maimiti, you will see to that! The men shall go with me to the point, but once there, we must take care not to be seen."

There was a rapid murmur of conversation as he ceased to speak, broken by a hail from Smith. The ship had rounded Young's Rock and was now little more than a mile from Bounty Bay, and at a distance of about three cable lengths from shore. Her courses were clewed up; she came on slowly under her topsails, before the fair westerly wind. At a sign from Christian the men followed him down to Smith's lookout point.

The place was well screened by bush and about three hundred feet above the beach; the rise to the plateau was steep enough here to merit the name of cliff. Each man chose for himself a peephole through the foliage, and seated himself to watch the progress of the ship. There were exclamations from the mutineers: —

"She's English, not a doubt!"

"A smart frigate, eh, lads?"

Nearly an hour passed while the vessel coasted the island slowly, sounding as she approached the cove. The men peering through the bush could see the red coats of marines, and a stir and bustle amidships as she drew abreast of Bounty Bay. A boat was going over the side; presently, with two officers in the stern and a full crew at the oars, she began to pull toward the cove, while the frigate tacked and stood offshore.

Though the wind was westerly, there was a high swell from the north, and one of the officers astern rose to his feet as the boat drew near the breakers. At a sign from him, the men ceased rowing, and the cutter rose and fell just beyond the first feathering of the seas.

"They'll never chance it!" muttered Young. Christian nodded without taking his eyes from the boat.

"She's been to Tahiti," growled Mills, "ye can lay to that! Thank God for the swell!"

The taller of the officers, a lieutenant from his uniform, was raising his spyglass to scan the rim of the plateau. For a long time the glass moved this way and that while the officer examined the blank green face of the bush. At last he snapped his telescope together and made a sign to the rowers to return to the ship. Hove-to under her topsails, she was a good mile offshore by now, and the cutter was a long time pulling out to her. Through his glass Christian watched the falls made fast, and the sway of the men at the ropes as the boat went on board. Presently the courses were loosed and the frigate slacked away to bear off to the east.


# CHAPTER IX

By the end of the year, the swine had multiplied to an extent which made it necessary to fence all the gardens against their depredations. The fowls, wandering off into the bush, had gone wild and regained the power of flight lost in domesticity. The women caught as many as they required in snares, baited with coconut; when a man wished to eat pork, half an hour's tramp with a musket sufficed to bring a fat hog to bag. Sometimes they shot a fierce old sow, ran down the squeaking pigs, and fetched them in to be tamed and fattened in the sties.

During the breadfruit season, from November till May, the trees planted by the ancient inhabitants of the island produced more than enough to feed all hands. The pandanus abounded everywhere; its nuts, though somewhat laborious to extract, were rich, tasty, and nourishing. The long, slender, wild yams grew in all the valleys, and in the natural glades, where the sunlight warmed the fertile soil, were scattered patches of ti — a kind of dracæna, with a large root, very sweet when baked. *Pia maohi,* or wild arrowroot, indigenous to all the volcanic islands of the Pacific, was here, valuable for making the native puddings of which the white men soon grew fond. The coconuts would have been enough for ten times the population of the island. At the proper season, the cliffs provided the eggs and young of sea birds, the latter, when nearly full grown, being fat, tender, and far from ill-flavoured. Shellfish and crustaceans were to be gathered on the rocky shores when the weather was calm, and fish abounded in the sea. Once their houses were built, and the land cleared for plantations of yams and cloth-plant, the mutineers found themselves able to live with little labour.

There were two small Christians now — Thursday October and the baby, Charles; McCoy was the father of a boy and a girl, and Sarah had presented Quintal with an infant son. The adult population numbered twenty-six, now that Fasto was dead, and their island would have supported in comfort at least five hundred more. There had been little friction during the two years past, for the hard work together, the sense of sharing a common task, had bred good feeling between whites and Polynesians. Now, as the second anniversary of their settlement on the island approached, all began to take life more easily. Minarii and Tetahiti spent much time at sea in the cutter, fishing for albacore; certain of the white men took to loafing in the shade, while they forced the humbler natives to perform the daily tasks too heavy for womenfolk. Williams was seldom seen at the settlement, and McCoy, once the most sociable of men, was frequently absent from his house.

No one knew where he spent so many hours each day, and none cared save Quintal, who grumbled incuriously at times when he wished to chat with his friend. Mary suspected that her husband was tired of her and had found consolation elsewhere, but his absence brought her more relief than jealousy, for he had been a trial to her since the daily grog ration had ceased; his cuffs were far more frequent than his caresses. With two small children to occupy her, Mary would have been content had her husband moved away for good.

With the secretiveness of a Scot, and unknown to all the others, McCoy was conducting certain experiments in a narrow gorge on the unfrequented western slope of the island. In his youth he had been apprenticed to a distiller, and, while acquiring a rough knowledge of the distiller's art, he had also acquired an inveterate love of alcohol. Unlike most British seamen of his day, McCoy cared little for sprees and jovial drinking bouts, and under ordinary circumstances never went to excess. What he loved was the certainty of an unfailing supply of grog, the glow and gentle relaxation of a quiet glass or two by himself. When the last of the *Bounty's* rum was gone, save for the small amount preserved in case someone fell ill, McCoy's moods of gaiety had ceased, and he had grown silent and morose.

The idea had come in a flash, one afternoon when he was alone at Williams's forge. He was searching for a bit of wire, or a nail, to make a fishhook, and as he turned over the odds and ends of metal fetched from the ship he came on a few yards of copper tubing, coiled up and made fast with a bit of marline. A coil! With a coil, cooled in water, it would be no trick at all to set up a small still!

Hiding the tubing carefully, he strolled home deep in thought. The copper pot from the ship would be the very thing, but it was at Christian's house and not to be had without awkward explanations.

There were a number of kettles which had been placed on board for trade with the Indians; he had two of his own, but they were too small to make more than a pint a day; yet a pint a day would be ample for one. It would be best to keep the matter to himself. He suspected that Christian would scent danger and put an immediate stop to it. He might let Matt Quintal in. . . . No, Quintal always went mad when enough grog was on hand. What could he use? Sugar cane was not plentiful, and all of the people were fond of chewing it. He could never get enough without exciting suspicion. Why not ti? The roots would have to be baked to make them sweet, then mashed in water and allowed to ferment. There was plenty of ti; nearly everyone was heartily tired of it.

Deliberately, and with the greatest secrecy, McCoy went about his preparations. Musket on his arm, as if pig-hunting, he wandered about the island casually till he found a spot that suited him. Far off from Williams's cottage, and below the upper slopes frequented by the increasing flock of goats, he found a narrow, walled-in gorge, where a trickle of water wandered down from the peak. Little by little, carrying his light loads before sunrise or in the dusk of evening, he accumulated what he needed there — a kettle, the coil, a supply of the roots, a native pestle of stone for mashing them, and a keg in which to ferment the mash afterwards. Then, still without arousing curiosity, he fetched several bags of coconut shells, which burn with an intense and smokeless heat.

The kettle was of cast iron, and held about two gallons. McCoy set it up carefully on three stones, inserted one end of his coil in the spout, and made the joint tight with a plaster of volcanic clay. He bent the flexible coil so that it passed into a large calabash sawed in half, and out, through a watertight joint, after a dozen turns. A dam of stones and mud across the watercourse formed a little pool, from which the cold water could be dipped to fill the calabash. When all was ready, he cooked a large earth oven of the roots, mashed them with his pestle on a flat rock, and stirred up the mash with water in his keg.

The month was January, and the weather so hot that fermentation was not long delayed. When McCoy lifted the lid of his keg, thirty-six hours after the first stirring, a yeasty froth covered the mash. He stirred it once more, replaced the lid, and strolled homeward, killing a fine yearling hog on the way.

He was so obsessed with his plans, so eager to see and to taste the results of the experiment, that he scarcely closed his eyes all through the night. Long before the others were awake, he took up his musket and stole out, past Mary, sleeping peacefully, with her two children at her side. The stars were bright overhead; the day promised well.

Striding along the starlit path, McCoy passed the house of Mills, passed Young's house, and turned inland along the near bank of the ravine that led down from Brown's Well. He halted for a moment to drink, where the rivulet ran into the upper end of the pool. Starlight was giving place to dawn as he climbed to the small plateau above and toiled up to the summit of the Goat-House Ridge.

Lack of breath forced him to rest for a moment here, where another man might have lingered to admire the wide prospect of land and sea. Beyond the sleeping settlement and the jagged peak of Ship-Landing Point, the sea stretched away, misty and indistinct in the morning calm. But in the east the sun announced its approach in a glory of colour among the low scattered clouds — blended gold and rose, shimmering like mother-of-pearl. McCoy shouldered his musket and took a dim goat-path leading down to the west.

He found the mash working powerfully; there was a rim of froth on the ground about the keg. He put a finger into the mess, tasted, and spat it out. Then, after a thorough stirring, he ladled the kettle full with half a coconut shell. Unwrapping his tinder carefully, he ignited the charred end with a stroke of flint on steel and blew up the dried leaves beneath the kettle to a flame. Soon a hot, smokeless fire of coconut shells was burning brightly.

The lid of the kettle was of heavy cast iron, and fitted tightly, but McCoy now plastered it about with clay before he filled his sawn calabash with water and stood a pewter half-pint on a rock, where it would catch the drip from the coil. The kettle sang, and began to boil at last, while he poured more cool water over the coil from time to time. A drop formed at the end of the copper tube, grew visibly, and fell into the half-pint. Another drop formed and fell; another and another, while the man watched with eager eyes.

When there was an inch or more of spirit in the pot McCoy could wait no longer. He built up his fire, replenished the mash in the kettle, and substituted his half coconut shell for the pewter pot. Then, after ladling more cool water into the calabash, he seated himself with his back to a tree. He passed the half-pint under his nose, sniffing at the contents critically.

"I've smelt waur!" he muttered, and took a preliminary sip.

McCoy made a wry face and swallowed violently. He opened his mouth wide and blew out his breath with all his force.

"Ouf! There's nae whiskey in Scotland can touch her for strength! I've tasted waur — het from the still, that is."

He took a more substantial sip this time, coughed, sputtered, and rose to his feet. "It's water she needs just now. Gie her time! Gie her time! Ouf! A glass o' this'd set old Matty daft!"

Mixed with a small measure of water, the spirit proved more palatable, though McCoy made many a wry face as he sipped. All through the morning he kept his fire going and the kettle full, drinking the raw spirit as fast as it condensed in the coil. The sun was overhead when he allowed the fire to die out and stretched himself to sleep in the shade, with flushed face and laboured and irregular snores.

He awoke late in the afternoon, and, though his head ached unmercifully, he made his way back to the settlement in deep content.

McCoy's supply of ti had been obtained from a natural glade not far inland from the house where Martin lived with Mills. The plant, more or less rare elsewhere on the island, grew in great plenty here, and at the suggestion of the natives the glade had not been set out to yams, though it lay close in and there was no clearing to be done. In the beginning both natives and whites had eaten the sweet baked roots with relish, but the ti proved cloying after a time and the plants were allowed to flourish undisturbed.

Returning to his house in the cool of late afternoon, McCoy glanced through the scattered bush and perceived Martin in the distant glade, plying a mattock side by side with Hu. He left the path abruptly, and was surprised and displeased to see that they were grubbing up the roots of ti and casting them aside.

"What're ye up to, Isaac?" he asked angrily.

Martin halted in his work, and the native rested on his mattock-haft. "Get on with yer work, ye lazy lout!" exclaimed Martin. "Did I tell 'ee to rest?" He turned to McCoy.

"What's that to you?"

"Damn yer eyes! Ye're grubbing up all the ti!"

"It's no more yours than mine! Who wants it, anyway? I'm going to make a yam patch here."

"I want it! There's others on the island beside yersel'! Yams? Ye've the whole place to plant 'em on."

"Aye. And walk half a mile out to work. If ye'd a musket ball in your leg like me, ye'd think different."

McCoy controlled his temper with difficulty. "Listen, Isaac," he said, "I've a tooth for sweets; not a day but I grub up a root or two. There's nae patch of ti on the island the like o' this. Ye've scarce made a start; be a good lad and plant the yams elsewhere!"

After considerable persuasion, Martin agreed to leave the glade undisturbed. He summoned the native in a manner brutal and contemptuous, and led the way to the house, mumbling his discontent. McCoy picked up his musket and went home.

Late the same evening he was reclining with Quintal on a mat spread before the doorstep. The women and children had gone into the house to sleep. McCoy had been brooding over his argument with Martin. Sooner or later, he feared, someone more intelligent than Martin might preempt the ti patch, and put him in a position from which he would be unable to extricate himself without disclosing the secret of the still.

"Matt," he said, breaking a long silence, "did 'ee ever think o' dividing the land? We live like Indians here — sharing all hands alike; it ain't in white human natur to keep on so."

Quintal nodded.

"When I clear a bit o' land," McCoy went on, "and put in yams, or plantains, or what not, I'd like to think it's mine for good, and for little Sarah and Dan when I'm underground. Ye've young Matty to think on, and there'll be more bairns coming along."

"Aye," said Quintal, "I'm with 'ee there."

"Let every man gang his ain gait! If ye fancy yams, plant 'em for yersel'. Gin it's taro ye want, though it's nae white man's vivers to my mind, why, plant taro, and damn the rest! That's a Scot's way, and an Englishman's too."

Slow in thought and with no gift of words, Quintal had a high opinion of McCoy's sagacity. "Aye, Will," he said, "the land would divide up well. There's enough and to spare, for the nine of us. We could make a common of the west end, for the goats."

"Nine, ye swad! And the Indian men?"

Quintal grunted contemptuously. "Never mind them! Give 'em land, and they'll not work for us."

McCoy gave his companion a quick glance. "Matt! Ye're nae dowff as ye look! Aye . . . there's summat in that. But we must no put their beards in a blaze!"

One morning, about a fortnight after Quintal's talk with McCoy, Tararu was fishing from the rocks below Christian's house. The sea was calm, for this part of the coast was sheltered from the southerly swell.

Tararu was the nephew of Minarii, and well born in Tahiti, though neither his person nor his character was such as was usual among the native aristocracy. He was of low stature and slight build, and there was more cunning than determination in his face. An idle fellow, who preferred the company of women to that of men, he spent much of his time in solitary fishing excursions, which gave him an excuse to be absent when there was hard work to be done. The tuna-fishing offshore was too strenuous for his taste, and, though the others jeered at him for following a sport usually relegated to women, they were always glad to share his catch.

He squatted on a weed-covered rock, beside a shallow pool left by the receding tide. The water was deep, close inshore, at this place. Tararu's line was made of native flax, twisted on his naked thigh; his barbless hook was of pearl shell, and his sinker a pear-shaped stone, pierced at its small end to allow the line to be made fast. He baited his hook with a bit of white meat from the tail of a crayfish, whirled the sinker about his head, and cast out. The coiled line flew from his left hand, the sinker plunged into the sea twenty yards away. He drew in a fathom or two tentatively, till he felt the line taut from his stone, and squatted once more to wait for a bite.

The birds were beginning to nest, and many hundreds of them came and went about their business over the calm sea. The morning was so still that he could hear, very faintly, the clink of Williams's hammer at the forge, and the bleating of young goats on the ridge to the west. The sun was not yet high enough to be unpleasantly warm. Though his eyes were open, Tararu seemed to doze, as motionless as the black rock beneath his feet, and scarcely more animate.

But he was on the alert when at last a fish seized his bait. He did not strike as a white fisherman would have done; his incurved hook of pearl shell did not permit of that. Tararu kept a taut line, allowing the fish to run this way and that, while the hook turned and worked ever deeper into its jaw. It was a large, blue-spotted fish of the rock-cod kind, called *rod,* and weighing ten pounds or more — a rare prize. Presently, he swung it up out of the sea, disengaged the hook, and slid the fish into the pool beside him, where it sank to the bottom with heaving gills. Slowly and methodically he baited his hook once more.

The sun was high overhead and the pool well stocked with fish when Tararu coiled his line and laid it on a ledge above him to dry. The last wave but one had wet him to the ankles and streamed hissing into the pool. He opened his knife, and began to sharpen it on a flat pebble. The blade was half worn away by long use.

"Tararu! Tararu O!"

One of his countrymen was approaching, clambering down over the rocks. Tararu greeted him with a lift of the eyebrows, and held out his knife.

"Look," he said, pointing to the pool, "I have been lucky! Clean and string them while I rest."

Hu was a small, humble, dark-skinned man, whose ancestors for many generations had been servants to those of Minarii. He grunted with pain and put a hand to his side as he stooped over the pool.

"Are you hurt?" asked Tararu. "Have you had a fall?"

"Not a fall," replied the other, beginning to clean the first fish that came to hand. "Martin again."

"Did he beat you?"

"Aye . . . with a club."

"What had you done?"

Hu shook his head. "Done? How can I say? Nothing I do pleases him. We went together to the yam field. He sat in the shade and directed me at the work. The holes I dug were not deep enough, or too deep. I put in too many dead leaves when I filled them; I cut up the seed yams too fine! I am your man, and your uncle's — not Martin's slave! I told him so; then he beat me."

His hands trembled as he worked, and he caught his breath in a sob of anger. "What can I do? Will you not protect me, you or Minarii?"

Tararu reflected for some time with downcast eyes. "There is only one way," he said at last. "I dare not stir Minarii too deeply, for if trouble comes with the whites, they will take their muskets and shoot us all. Kill Martin! Kill him in a way that none will suspect."

"*Mea au roa!*" exclaimed Hu, looking up from his task with gleaming eyes. "But how is it to be done?"

Tararu leaned over the pool, fumbled among the fish remaining there, and drew forth an odd creature, about a foot long, with a small mouth and a strange square body, checkered in black and white. "With this!" he said.

"A *huéhué*," remarked the other. "I have heard that there is poison in them."

"The flesh is sweet and wholesome if the gall bladder is removed entire. The gall is without colour and has no strong taste, yet four drops of it will kill a man. Squeeze out the bladder on a bit of yam or on a pudding. He will be dead before the setting of the sun."

Hu shook his head. "Leave poisoning to wizards and old women. Not even Martin could I kill in that way!"

Tararu shrugged his shoulders, and the other went on: "But it might be done on the cliffs. He has ordered me to go with him to the Rope this afternoon. The birds are beginning to lay."

When the fish were cleaned and scaled, Hu shouldered the heavy string and followed Tararu in the stiff climb to the plateau.

Toward mid-afternoon, Martin and Smith sauntered down the path to the house of the natives. They carried egging baskets and coils of rope, and found Hu waiting to accompany them. Smith led the way to the ridge, and a short walk brought them to the verge of the cliffs hemming in the little half-moon bay. The Rope was exposed to the full force of the southerly swell, and the thunder of the breakers came up faintly from far below. Sea birds in thousands sailed back and forth along the face of the cliff.

Smith peered over the brink and dropped the coil of two-inch line from his shoulder. Making fast one end to the trunk of a stout pandanus tree, he tossed the coils over the cliff, slung his basket about his neck, and began to reconnoitre the ground. There were many nests in the scrub pandanus bushes that stood out almost horizontally from the wall of rock. Birds sat in some of them; in others, deserted temporarily during the heat of the day, he perceived the clutches of eggs. Martin was making fast his rope at a place about thirty yards away. It was his custom to take one of the natives on these egging excursions, to perform the task he had no stomach for.

Smith gripped the rope with both hands and scrambled over the brink of the cliff, pressing the soles of his bare feet against the rock.

Little by little he lowered himself to a jutting rock fifty feet below, where he could rest at ease, and where he had spied two well-filled nests within reach. He had transferred the eggs to his basket when the sounds of a scuffle and angry shouting reached his ears. Smith listened for a moment, set his lips, and began to climb the ropes rapidly, hand over hand, aiding himself with his feet. At the summit, he set down his basket before he rose from his knees. Then, half running through the scrub, he made for the sound of Martin's angry voice.

"Kill me, would 'ee? Take that, ye Indian bastard! And that, God damn 'ee!"

Martin stood over the bloody and prostrate form of Hu, kicking him savagely at each exclamation. He swung about as he felt Smith's hand on his shoulder, and said, still shouting: "The bastard! Tried to rush me over the cliff, he did!" He made as if to kick the native once more, but Smith's powerful grip held him back.

"Avast, Isaac!" ordered Smith, and then, glancing down, he asked: "Is this true?"

"Aye," groaned the prostrate man, who could scarcely speak, "it is true."

Martin wrenched himself free and aimed another kick at Hu. Smith sprang on him and pulled him back roughly. "I'll not stand by and see the like o' this!" he exclaimed.

"Damn your blood, Alex!" said Martin angrily. "I tell 'ee, he tried to push me over the cliff!"

"D'ye think I'm blind, man? Ye've given him cause, and to spare!"

Anger got the better of Martin's customary caution. Smith had released him, and now stood between him and the native, who was rising painfully to his feet.

Martin clenched his fists. "This is my lay! Stand by! Or d'ye want a clout on the jaw?"

Next moment, with a light of insane rage in his eyes, he sprang forward and struck Smith a heavy blow. The smaller man grunted without flinching, put up his hands, and lowered his head. The fight was over in two minutes; Martin lay on the ground with a bruised jaw and breathing heavily through his nose. When he sat up dazedly at last, Smith spoke.

"We'll say no more of this. . . . It's best so. Mind what I say, Isaac, it'll go hard with ye if I catch ye bullying this man again. And Hu, —

though I can't say I blame ye much,—remember, no more such murderin' tricks!" He touched his lips. "*Mamu's* the word!"


## CHAPTER X

It was a calm night in February 1792; the sky was cloudless and the rising moon low over the sea. The natives had supped and were reclining on the grass before their house, gossiping in subdued voices, broken by the occasional soft laughter of the women. Minarii lay in silence, hands behind his head. Tararu stood alone at some little distance, gazing up the moonlit path. Though they spoke lightly of other things, one thought was in every mind, for Hutia had not returned.

In their love of decorum, the Polynesians resemble the Chinese; to their minds, an action is often less important than the manner in which it is performed, and the appearance of virtue more so than virtue itself. Like the others, Tararu had long known where the girl spent so many hours each day, but hitherto she had conducted her affairs with discretion, taking care to put no affront upon her husband's dignity. Now at last the persuasions of Williams had overcome her fear of a scene. Turning his head slightly Minarii perceived that Tararu was gone. He sat up, seemed to reflect for a moment, and lay down once more, his lips set in a thin, stern line.

The moon was well up when Tararu emerged from a thicket near the lonely cottage of Williams. Stepping lightly and keeping to the shadows, he reached the open door and listened for a moment before he peered into the house. His wife was asleep on a mat just inside, her head pillowed on the blacksmith's brawny arm. For an instant, passion overcame his fear of Williams; had he carried a weapon, he would have killed the blacksmith as he lay. Hutia's small naked foot was close to the door, and Tararu stretched out a shaking hand to rouse her. At first she only murmured incoherently in her sleep, but when he had nearly pulled her off the mat, she opened her eyes.

"Come outside!" he whispered fiercely.

Williams sat up. "What do you want?" he growled.

"My woman!" exclaimed Tararu, in a voice that broke with anger. "My woman, you white dog!"

The blacksmith sprang to his feet. His fists were clenched and his short black beard bristled within an inch of Tararu's chin. "She's my woman now! Clear out!"

Williams looked so formidable, so menacing, that the native cast down his eyes, but his sense of dignity would not permit him to turn away quickly enough to please the other man. As he turned slowly, trembling with anger and humiliation, a kick delivered with all the strength of the blacksmith's sturdy leg sent him sprawling on all fours. He rose with some difficulty while Williams stood over him. "Now will you go?" he asked truculently.

Tararu clenched his teeth and limped away up the moonlit slope.

Though the others had gone into the house to sleep, Minarii still lay outside, wide awake, when Tararu returned. He sat up to listen impassively to a torrent of whispered words, and when the other fell silent his reply was a grunt of contempt.

"You call yourself a man," he remarked after a short pause, "and come to me with this woman's tale! *Atira!* If you want the woman, rouse her and fetch her home."

Tararu hesitated. "I did waken her," he admitted. Then emotion got the better of him, and he went on incoherently: "My words roused Williams — he kicked me and knocked me down!"

Minarii's deep voice interrupted him. "Were you not my sister's son . . ." He rose, with an expression of stern displeasure on his face. "*Tihé!* To think that I should take a hand in such affairs! Wait for me here; perhaps soft words will right the wrong. If not . . ." He shrugged his great shoulders as he turned away.

The night was warm and Alexander Smith was working in the little garden before his house. Young and Taurua had gone early to bed; Balhadi had been helping her man to water some ferns planted the day before, but drowsiness had overcome her, and she too had retired. The moon was so bright that Smith watered and raked and weeded as if it had been day. It was late when he stopped and sat down on the rustic bench by the path. He had been fishing with Tetahiti the day before, and a long siesta in the afternoon had left him with no desire to sleep.

The moon was nearly at the zenith when he raised his head at the sound of a step on the path. It was Minarii, and Hutia walked behind him, bowed and sobbing. He halted at sight of Smith.

"It is fortunate that you are awake, Alex," he said. "There is trouble — trouble that may lead to graver things." He went on to recount the happenings of the night.

"Where is Williams?" Smith asked.

"On the floor of his house," replied Minarii grimly. "He fought like a man. . . . Look!" He pointed to a great black bruise on his jaw.

Smith thought for a moment before he spoke. "We must act quickly. Only Christian can handle this. Stop here while I rouse him."

When he was gone, Minarii seated himself with his back to a hibiscus tree and the girl crouched beside him. Presently his hand fell on her shoulder in a grip that made her wince. Concealed in the deep shadow of the tree, they watched the blacksmith move down the path toward the house of Mills.

Williams was in no mood for half-measures. He limped painfully, and halted from time to time to spit out a mouthful of blood. When he had wakened Mills, they walked side by side to the house of McCoy.

"Damn him, he was too much for me!" said the blacksmith, thickly. "Had you or Matt been there, we'd have murdered him!"

Mills grunted sympathetically. "Here we are," he remarked. "I'll go in and fetch 'em."

A moment later he came out with McCoy and Quintal, rubbing the sleep from their eyes. They listened attentively to what the blacksmith had to say.

"Where are they now?" asked Quintal.

"At the Indian house, I reckon."

McCoy smiled sourly. "This'll mean a fight. Curse ye, Jack! Ye have yer woman week days and Sabbaths to boot; must ye stir up the whole island because ye can nae sleep wi' her nights?"

Williams turned away angrily. "Then stop where ye are. Come along!" he said to Mills. "We'll fetch the muskets."

"Ne'er fash yersel', Jack," put in McCoy. "We'll help ye fast enough, but it's an unchancy business for all that!"

"We'd best get it over with," said Mills. "Teach the bloody Indians their place. . . . Who's this?"

Christian was striding rapidly down the moonlit path, followed by Smith and Minarii. Hutia brought up the rear, half trotting to keep pace with the men. She longed to slip into the bush and escape, but dared not. Williams moved forward truculently when he perceived Minarii, only to fall back at sight of Christian's face.

"What is all this?" Christian asked sternly, coming to a halt.

"I made up my mind last night, sir," Williams replied with a mingling of defiance and respect. "I told my girl to stop with me and leave her Indian for good. He came to fetch her when we were asleep. I woke and kicked him out. Then Minarii came." He drew a deep breath and spat out a mouthful of blood. "He was too much for me. When I came round, he was gone and my girl with him. What could I do but make haste down to the settlement and fetch the others to lend a hand?"

Minarii stood with head high and arms folded on his bare chest. His face was impassive and sternly set. Christian turned to him. "Shall I tell you what Williams says?"

"He has not lied."

Christian glanced down distastefully at Hutia, cowering on the grass with her head in her arms. "Is the peace of this land to be broken because of a loose girl and two men who forget their manhood?"

"Well spoken!" said Minarii. "On that point we see alike. But I cannot stand by while my sister's son is shamed before all, and cursed and kicked by a commoner, even though he be white."

"Then fetch Tararu. He must come at once."

As Minarii walked toward the natives' house, Christian turned to the four mutineers. "I'm going to settle this matter here and now!" he said. "We have had more than enough of it. The woman shall choose the man she wishes to live with, and there is to be no murmuring afterward. Let that be understood."

"I'm with ye, Mr. Christian!" exclaimed McCoy.

"Aye," muttered Quintal. "That's the way to settle it."

When Minarii returned, followed by his nephew, Christian spoke once more. "Tararu," he said, "stand forth! The woman shall choose between you. And let the man rejected keep the peace."

"Stand forth, Williams," he went on. "Minarii, tell her that she is to make her choice and abide by it."

The girl was still crouched on the grass, face hidden in her arms. Minarii spoke to her in a harsh voice before he pulled her roughly to her feet. With eyes cast down, but without a moment of hesitation, she walked to the blacksmith and linked her arm in his.

Autumn came on with strong winds from the west, and fine rains that drizzled down for days together. In early April the weather turned so cold that the people spent much of the time in their houses. Situated more than seven degrees of latitude to the south of Tahiti, Pitcairn's Island lay in the region of variable westerly winds, and its climate was far colder and more invigorating than that of the languorous isles to the north.

One night in April, the wind shifted from west to southwest and blew the sky clear. While the stars twinkled frostily, the sleepers in the house of Mills stirred with the cold, half wakening to pull additional blankets of tapa up to their chins.

Mills and Prudence slept in the room upstairs, on a great standing bed-place filled with sweet fern and covered with many layers of soft bark cloth. Prudence lay on her side, her unbound hair half covering the pillow, and one arm thrown protectingly over the tiny child who slumbered between her and the wall.

Presently the open window on the east side of the room became a square of grey in the dawn. The old red cock from Tahiti, roosting in the *tapou* tree, wakened, clapped his wings loudly, and raised his voice in a long-drawn challenging crow. Prudence stirred and opened her eyes. The baby was already awake, staring up gravely at the thatch. The young mother roused herself, leaned over to sniff fondly at the child's head, on which a copper-red down was beginning to appear, and sat up, shivering. Taking care not to waken Mills, she threw a sheet of tapa over her shoulders, picked up the child, and stepped lightly over the sleeping man.

With her baby on one arm, the girl climbed nimbly down the ladder, crossed the room where Martin snored beside Susannah, opened the door softly, and went out. It was broad daylight now and the glow of sunrise was in the east. Save for mare's-tails of filmy cloud, the sky was clear; the trees swayed as the strong southwest wind hummed through their tops. Prudence drew a long breath and threw back her head to shake the heavy hair over her shoulders.

In the maturity of young motherhood, she was among the handsomest of the women. Her brown eyes were set wide apart under slender, arched brows; though small, her figure was perfectly proportioned; her beautiful hair, of the strange copper color to be found occasionally among Maoris of unmixed blood, fell rippling to her knees. Her race was the lightest-skinned of all brown folk, and the chill, damp winds of Pitcairn's Isle had brought the glow of young blood to her cheeks.

Mills was deeply attached to her, in his rough way; she had been happy with the dour old seaman since the birth of their child. Eliza raised her voice in a wail and Prudence smiled down at her as she walked to the outdoor kitchen.

"There!" she said, as she deposited the baby in a rude cradle Mills had made, and tucked her in carefully. "Lie still! You shall have your meal presently."

As if she understood, the child ceased to cry and watched her mother gravely as she struck a spark to her tinder and blew up the flame among some chips of wood. When the fire was burning well, Prudence filled the pot from the barrel of rain water and set it on to boil. She took up Eliza, seated herself on the stool used for grating coconuts, and teased the child for a moment with her breast, offered and withdrawn. Soon the baby was suckling greedily; after a time, before the kettle had boiled, her eyelids began to droop, and presently her mother rose to place her in the cradle once more, sound asleep.

Prudence now took some eggs and half a dozen plantains from a basket hanging out of reach of rats, and dropped them into the boiling water. From another basket she took a breadfruit, cooked the day before. She heard Mills at the water barrel, washing his face, and turned to greet him as he appeared at the kitchen door. He stooped over the cradle and touched the sleeping baby's head with a stubby thumb.

"Liza, little lass," he said, "ye've a soft life, eh? Naught but eat and sleep."

Prudence set food before him, and stood leaning on the table as he fell to heartily. "I am hungry for fresh meat," she said. "See, the weather has changed. Take your musket and kill a hog for us."

Mills swallowed half of an egg and took a sup of water before he replied. "Aye, that I will, lass. Fire up the oven, for I'll not fail. Ye must eat for two, these days."

When he was gone and she had eaten her light breakfast of fruits, she spread a mat in the shelter of the banyan tree by the forge, and fetched her sleeping child and an uncompleted hat she was weaving for Mills. Susannah was stirring in the kitchen, but Martin would not be on foot for another hour or two.

Prudence glanced up from her work at the sound of a footstep and saw Tararu approaching, an axe on his shoulder. She had scarcely laid eyes on him since the trouble with Williams; he had ceased his former gossiping and flirtatious way with the women, and spent most of his time in the bush. He caught her eye and made an attempt to smile. Polynesian etiquette demanded that some word be spoken, and he asked, in a hoarse voice: "Where is Mills?"

"Gone pig-hunting," she replied.

The *Bounty's* grindstone stood close by, near the forge. Tararu took the calabash from its hook, filled it at the water barrel, and replaced it so that a thin trickle fell on the stone. Picking up his axe, he set to work. Prudence bent over her plaiting, glancing at the man from time to time out of the corner of her eye. He ground on steadily, first one side of the blade and then the other, halting occasionally to test the edge with his thumb. An hour passed.

Something in Tararu's manner, and in the meticulous care with which he worked, struck the girl as out of the ordinary. He was a lazy, shiftless fellow as a rule.

"Never have I seen an axe so sharpened!" she remarked. He grunted, intent on his task, and she went on: "What is your purpose?"

He looked up and hesitated for a moment before he replied. "I have been clearing a field for yams. Yesterday I found a *purau* tree, tall, straight, and thick. To-morrow I shall fell it, and begin to shape a canoe."

As he went to work once more, Prudence's quick mind was busy. Canoe-building was practised in Tahiti only by a guild of carpenters called *tahu'a,* which included men of all classes, even high chiefs. Minarii was an adept, but Tararu knew no more of the art than a child of ten. Yet why should he lie to her?

After a long time the axe was sharpened to Tararu's satisfaction, bright and razor-edged. He shouldered it, gave Prudence a surly nod, and walked away into the bush. The girl took up her child, gathered her work together absently, and went into the house, deep in thought.

When she reappeared, a mantle of tapa was thrown over her shoulders, and she carried her child, warmly wrapped against the wind, on one arm. She had plaited her hair in two long, thick braids, twisted them around her head, and pinned them in place with skewers of bamboo. Walking with the light and resilient step of youth, she took the path that led past Smith's house and Christian's, and up, over the summit of the Goat-House Ridge. Half an hour later, she was approaching Williams's lonely cottage. At some distance from the door she halted and gave the melodious little cry with which a Polynesian visitor announced his presence to the inmates of a house.

Hutia appeared at the door and greeted the other without a smile.

"Where is your man?" asked Prudence.

"At work in the bush."

"Hutia," said the younger girl earnestly, coming close to her old enemy, "you and I have not been friends, but should anything happen to Williams, my man would never cease his mourning, for the two are like brothers."

"Come into the house," Hutia said, her manner changing. "The wind is over cold for *aiu*."

She took the baby from the younger girl's arms and covered the little face with kisses before she closed the door. "Now tell me what is in your mind," she went on.

Prudence recounted at length how Tararu had sharpened his axe, how he had replied to her question, and her own suspicions. The other girl's expression turned grave.

"Aye," she said at last, "I fear you are right. He is a coward at heart and will come by night if he comes."

"So I think," replied Prudence. "Who knows? I may be wrong, but you will do well to warn your man."

"Guard him, rather; I shall tell him nothing. He would only mock me for a woman's fears. If I convinced him of danger, he would go in search of Tararu, bringing on more trouble with Minarii. No. We have two muskets here. I can shoot as straight as any man!"

Prudence stood up after a time and took her child. "I must return to light the oven," she remarked. "Mills has gone to shoot a pig."

"Let us be friends from now on," said Hutia. "There is no room for bad blood on this little land."

When the young mother was gone, Hutia set about her household tasks, and greeted Williams with her usual cheerful and casual manner at dinner time. But when he had supped that evening, and stretched himself out, dead-tired, she waited only until certain that he was in a sound sleep before making her preparations. In the light of a taper of candlenuts, smoking and sputtering by the wall, she loaded the two muskets, measuring the powder with great care, wadding it with bits of tapa, and ramming the bullets home with patches of the same material, greased with lard. The last skewered nut was ablaze when the task was finished, giving her time to see to the priming and wipe the flints carefully before the light flickered and winked out. With a heavy musket in each hand she stepped softly across the room and out into the starlit night. Like many of the women, Hutia understood firearms thoroughly.

The house had only one door. Shivering a little in the chill breeze, she stationed herself in a clump of bushes, one musket across her knees, the other standing close at hand. Even in the dim starlight, no one would be able to leave or enter the house unperceived, and she knew that two hours from now she could count on the light of the waning moon.

A long time passed while the girl sat alert and motionless. At last the sky above the ridge began to brighten and presently the moon rose, in a cloudless sky, over the wooded mountain. The shadow of the house took form sharply; the clearing was flooded with cold silvery light, bounded by the dark wall of the bush.

It was nearly midnight when Hutia turned her head suddenly. Pale and unsubstantial in the moonlight, the shadowy figure of a man was moving across the cleared land. The girl cocked her musket as she rose. Tararu approached the cottage slowly and softly. When he was within a dozen yards of her, Hutia stepped out into the moonlight.

"*Faaea!*" she ordered firmly, in a low voice. He gave a violent start and endeavoured to conceal his axe behind him. "Come no closer," she went on, "and make no sound. If you waken Williams he will kill you. I know why you are here."

Tararu began to mumble some whispered protestation of innocence, but she cut him short, scornfully. "Waste no words! It is in my mind to shoot you as you stand."

Hutia's hands were shaking a little with anger. Her former husband was only too well aware of her high temper and determined reckless-ness when roused. With a suddenness that took her aback, he sprang to one side and bounded away across the clearing, axe in hand. She raised the musket and took aim between his shoulders. For five seconds or more she stood thus, her finger on the trigger she could not bring her-self to pull. She lowered the weapon, watched the runner disappear into the bush, and turned toward the cottage.

When Williams rose next morning, he found Hutia up before him as usual and his morning meal ready.

"Ye've a weary look, lass," he remarked. "Sleep badly?"

"Aye — I had bad dreams." She looked up from her work. "The sea is calming down. I shall go fishing this morning, in the lee."

The blacksmith nodded. "Good luck to ye. I could do with a mess of fish!"

Toward noon of the same day, Tararu was at work on a small clear-ing in the Auté Valley. None of the men, save Martin perhaps, had a deeper dislike of work; his chief object in clearing the little yam field was to be alone. He was beginning to hate the house of the natives, where he now spent as little as possible of his time. Their ideas of courtesy prevented an open display of contempt, but Minarii treated him coldly, and he could not face the disapproval in Tetahiti's eye. The morning was cool, and he plied his axe with more diligence than usual.

Tararu's basket of dinner hung from the low branch of a *purau* tree at the edge of the clearing, and he was working at some distance, unaware that he was not alone. Peeping through a screen of leaves, Hutia had reconnoitred the cleared land and was now approaching the basket cautiously, unseen and making no sound. She glanced at the man, whose back was turned to her, reached into the basket, took out a large baked fish, done up in leaves, and unwrapped it, crouching out of sight. Glancing up warily once more, she squeezed something which had the appearance of a few drops of water into the inside of the fish, holding it carefully to give the liquid time to soak in. A moment later the fish was wrapped up and returned to the basket, and Hutia disappeared, as quietly as she had come.

Ten minutes had passed when Tararu glanced up at the sun and dropped his axe. As he strolled across to where his basket hung, he heard a cheerful hail and saw Hu.

"You've not eaten?" asked the newcomer. "That is well. I've brought you some baked plantains; the women said you had none."

"Fetch a banana leaf to spread the food on, and you shall share my meal."

The servant was the only one of his countrymen whose manner toward him had not changed; Tararu was grateful for the little attention and glad of his company. They ate with good appetites, gossiping of island trivialities, and when the last of the food was gone both men lay down to sleep.

## CHAPTER XI

ONE afternoon Christian was trudging up the path that led to the Goat-House Ridge. Toiling to the summit, he left the path and turned north along the ridge, to make his way around to the seaward slope of the peak. His path was the merest cranny in the rock, scarcely affording foothold, but he trod the ledge with scarcely a downward glance. Deeply rooted in the rock ahead of him, two ironwood trees spread gnarled limbs that had withstood the gales of more than a century; a goat would have been baffled to reach them by any way other than Christian's dizzy track.

Reaching the trees, he lowered himself between the roots to a broad ledge below and entered a cave. It was a snug little place, well screened by drooping casuarina boughs — ten or twelve feet in depth, and lofty enough for a tall man to stand upright. Half a dozen muskets, well cleaned and oiled, stood against the further wall; there was a keg of powder, a supply of bullets, and two large calabashes holding several gallons of water.

The cave was a small fortress, where a single resolute man might have held an army at bay so long as he had powder and lead. It was here that Christian spent an hour when he wished to be alone, lost in sombre reflections as he gazed out over the vast panorama of lonely sea and listened to the booming of the surf many hundreds of feet below. For the situation of the mutineers and the native men and women with them he felt a deep and tragic sense of responsibility, and since the passing of the frigate he had realized that sooner or later their refuge was certain to be discovered. He had resolved not to be taken alive when that day came.

Christian now took up his muskets, one after the other, and concealed them with his powder and ball among the roots of the further ironwood tree. When nothing but the calabashes of water remained in the cave, he made his way back to the ridge and took the path to the settlement, walking rapidly. He found Maimiti with her baby, Charles, seated on a mat in the shade of a wild hibiscus tree. Nanai, the wife of Tetahiti, was beside her. Thursday October Christian, a sturdy boy of two, had trotted down the path to Young's house, where he spent much of his time with Balhadi and Taurua, childless women who loved the small boy dearly.

"Come with me," said Christian to his wife. "There is something I wish to show you. You'll look after the baby, eh, Nanai?"

"Shall we be gone long?" Maimiti asked.

"Till sunset, perhaps."

She followed her husband up the trail to the ridge and along the breakneck path to the ironwood trees. When he lowered himself to the ledge before the cave and held up his arms for her, she gave an exclamation of surprise.

"*Ahé!* No one knows of this place!"

"Nor shall they, save you. I want no visitors here!"

He seated himself on the ledge, with his back to the wall of rock, while Maimiti examined the cave with interest. Presently she sat down beside him and they were silent for a time, under a spell of beauty and loneliness. Sea birds hovered and circled along the face of the cliff below, the upper surfaces of their wings glinting in the sun and their cries faintly heard above the breakers. The wind droned shrilly through the foliage of the ironwood trees, thin, harsh, and prickly. At length Christian spoke.

"Maimiti, I have brought you here that you may know where to find me in case of need. I love this place. Sometimes, in its peace and solitude, I seem to be close to those I love in England."

"Where is England?" she asked.

He pointed in a northeasterly direction, out over the sea. "There! Across two great oceans and a vast island peopled by savage men. Such an island as your people never dreamed of, so wide that if you were to walk from morning till night each day it would take three moons to cross!"

"*Mea atea roa!*" she said wonderingly. "And Tahiti — where is my island?"

"Yonder," replied Christian, pointing to the northwest. "Are you no longer homesick? Are you happy here?"

"Where you are, my home is, and I am happy. This is a good land."

"Aye, that it is." He glanced down at her affectionately. "The cool weather is wholesome. Your cheeks grow pink, like an English girl's."

"Never have I seen boys stronger and better grown than ours."

"All the children are the same. And since we came here not a man or a woman has been ill. Were not some of the fish poisonous, our island would be like your *Rohutu Noanoa,* a paradise."

"Do you believe that Hu and Tararu died of eating a fish?"

He turned his head quickly. "What do you mean?" he asked. "Surely they died of poisoning; they were known to have eaten a large fish declared to be poisonous in Tahiti."

"The *faaroa* is harmless here; I have eaten many of them."

"What do you mean?" he repeated, in a puzzled voice.

She hesitated, and then said: "It was whispered to us by one who should know. The others suspect nothing. What if Tararu hated Williams more bitterly than we supposed? What if he sharpened an axe expressly to kill him by night, and found Hutia waiting with a loaded musket, outside the door? I think she made it her business to poison Tararu's dinner, and that Hu partook of the food by chance!"

Christian knew that suspicion was foreign to Maimiti's nature, and the seriousness of her words made him look up in astonishment. "But have your people poisons so subtle and deadly?" he asked.

"Aye, many of them, though they are not known to all. Hutia's father was a sorcerer in Papara, an evil man, often employed by the chiefs to do their enemies to death. The commoners believe that such work is accomplished by incantations; we know that poison is administered before the incantations begin."

Christian remained silent, and she went on, after a pause: "The others suspect nothing, as I said."

He sighed and raised his head as if dismissing unpleasant thoughts from his mind. "It is ended," he said, rising to his feet. "Let us speak no more of this."

Three years had passed since the arrival of the *Bounty* at Pitcairn, and the little settlement presented the appearance of an ordered and permanent community. The dwellings had lost their look of newness and now harmonized with the landscape as if they had sprung from the soil. Each house was surrounded by a neat fence enclosing a small garden of ferns and shrubbery, and provided with an outdoor kitchen, a pigsty at a little distance, and an enclosure for fattening fowls. As in Tahiti, it was the duty of the women to keep the little gardens free of weeds, and to sweep the paths each day.

Winding picturesquely among the trees, well-worn trails led to the Goat-House, to the western slope where Williams lived, to the Auté Valley where the principal gardens of the cloth-plant had been laid out, to the yam and sweet-potato patches and plantain walks, to the rock cisterns Christian had insisted on building in case of drought, to the Rope, and to the saw pit, still used occasionally when someone was in need of plank.

The smithy, under the banyan tree by the house of Mills, looked as if it had been in use for many years. The vice and anvil bore the marks of long service; the bellows had been mended with goatskin, to which patches of hair still clung; there was a great pile of coconut shells close to the forge, and another of charcoal made from the wood of the *mapé*. The ground underfoot was black with cinders for many yards about.

The life of the mutineers had become easy, too easy for the good of some. Quintal, Martin, and Mills had taken to loafing about their houses, forcing most of their work on Te Moa and Nihau. Happy with the girl who had given him so much trouble in the past, Williams saw little of his friends. Smith and Young worked daily, clearing, planting, or fishing for the mere pleasure of the task.

For more than a year McCoy had kept the secret of the still. Only a Scot could have done it, one gifted with all the caution and canny reserve of his race. Little by little he had exhausted the principal supplies of ti, and for many months now he had been able to obtain no more than enough to operate his still twice or, rarely, three times each week. A small stock of bottles, accumulated one by one, were hidden where he concealed the still when not in use; by stinting himself resolutely, he managed to keep a few quarts of his liquor set aside to age. In this manner, which had required for some time a truly heroic abstinence, McCoy was enabled to enjoy daily a seaman's ration of half a pint of grog.

His temperament was an unusual one, even among alcoholics. When deprived of spirits, he became gloomy, morose, and irritable, but a glass or two of rum was sufficient to make him the most genial of men. Mary had been astonished and delighted at the change in him. He conversed with her for an hour or more each evening, laughing and joking in the manner the Polynesians love. He romped with two-year-old Sarah and took delight in holding on his knees the baby, Dan. With his grog ration assured, there was no better father and husband on the island than McCoy.

He longed to make a plantation of ti, but decided after much thought that the risk was too great. Explanations would be lame at best, and the sharper-witted among his comrades would be certain to suspect the truth. Meanwhile, he realized with a pang that the island produced only a limited supply of the roots, bound to be exhausted in time. Even now, fourteen months of distilling had so diminished the ti that McCoy's cautious search for the roots, scattered here and there in the bush, occupied most of his waking hours. He took the work with intense seriousness, and though by nature a kindly man, not inconsiderate of others, he now joined heartily with Quintal in forcing Te Moa to perform their daily tasks in the plantations and about the house. If the native was remiss in weeding a yam patch or chopping firewood, McCoy joined his curses to Quintal's blows. The unfortunate Te Moa was rapidly sinking to the condition of a slave.

After Hu's death, Martin had similarly enslaved Nihau, and Mills, seeing that his neighbours were comfortable in the possession of a servant who did nearly all their work, soon fell into the same frame of mind. The natives resented their new status deeply, but so far had not broken out in open revolt.

On a morning in late summer, McCoy set out on one of his cautious prowls through the bush. He took care to avoid the clearings where others might be at work, and carried only a bush knife and a bag of netting for the roots. Making for a tract of virgin bush at the western extremity of the Main Valley, where he had formerly spied several plants which should be mature by now, he was surprised and displeased, toward eight o'clock, to hear the strokes of a woodsman's axe not far ahead. He concealed his bag, which contained three or four smallish roots, and moved forward quietly, knife in hand and a frown on his face.

Tetahiti was a skilled axeman who loved the work. He was felling a tall candlenut tree, and each resounding stroke bit deep into the soft wood. Warned by a slight premonitory crackle of rending fibres and the swaying of branches overhead, he stepped back a pace or two. A louder crackling followed; slowly and majestically at first, and then with a rushing progress through the air, the tree which had weathered the gales of many years succumbed to the axe. McCoy had just time to spring aside nimbly as it crashed to earth.

"Who is that?" called Tetahiti, in dismay.

"It is I, McCoy."

"Had I known you were there . . ."

McCoy interrupted him. "*Eita e peapea!* It was my fault for approaching unannounced." He was irritated, but not on account of the tree. "What are you doing here?" he asked.

The native smiled. "You have heard the men of Tahiti call me 'Tupuai taro-eater.' We love it as the others love their breadfruit. I never have enough, so I am clearing this place, where the soil is rich and moist."

"Aye," said McCoy sourly, as he caught sight of several splendid ti plants hitherto concealed by the bush, "the soil is good."

Tetahiti pointed to where he had thrown together several roots larger than any McCoy had seen. "Where the ti flourishes as here, taro will do well." Seeing the other stoop to examine the roots with some show of interest, he went on: "These are the best kinds; the *ti-vai-raau,* largest of all, and the *mateni,* sweetest and easiest to crush."

"Are you fond of it?"

"No, its sweetness sickens me. But I thought I would fetch in a root for Christian's children."

"Then give me the rest."

The native assented willingly, and before long McCoy was trudging over the ridge and down toward his still, bent under a burden far heavier than usual. His thoughts were gloomy and perplexed as he prepared a ground oven to bake the roots.

It was late afternoon when he returned to the house. He found Quintal alone, sitting on the doorstep with his chin in his hands. His expression was morose, and he seemed to be thinking, always a slow and painful process with him.

"What's wrong, Matt?" asked McCoy.

"The Indians, damn their blood!"

"What ha' they done?"

"It's Minarii. . . . I'd a mind to put Te Moa to work on my valley — ye know the place, a likely spot for the cloth-plant. I took a stroll up that way and found Minarii clearing the bush. 'Chop down as many trees as ye like,' said I, 'but mind ye, this valley is mine!' He looked at me cheeky as a sergeant of marines. 'Yours?' he says. 'Yours? The land belongs to all!'"

"Did ye put him in his place?"

Quintal shook his head. "There'd been bloodshed if I had."

"Aye, he's a dour loon."

"We was close enough to a fight! It was the thought of Christian stopped me; I want him on my side when the trouble comes."

McCoy nodded slowly. "Ye did right; it's a fashious business, but we'll ha' peace gin we divide the land."

"How'll we go about it?"

"We've the right to a show of hands. I'll see Jack Williams, and Isaac, and Mills; we'll be five against the other four. Then we'll go to Christian."

Quintal brought his huge hand down resoundingly on his knee. "Ye've a level head! Aye, let every Englishman have his farm, and be damned to the rest!"

"Ilka cock fight his ain battle, eh?" said McCoy, with a complacent grin.

Late the next evening Tetahiti was trudging up the path from the cove. He had been fishing offshore since noon, and carried easily, hanging from the stout pole on his shoulder, nearly two hundredweight of albacore. At the summit of the bluff he set down his burden with a grunt and seated himself on a boulder to rest for a moment. He glanced up at the sound of a step on the path, and saw that Te Moa was approaching at a rapid walk.

"I was hastening down to help you," said the man apologetically.

"Let us stop here while I rest," Tetahiti replied; "then you can carry my fish to the house. There is enough for all."

"I must speak!" said Te Moa after a short silence. "I can endure no more!"

"Are the white men mistreating you again?"

"They take me for a dog! Quintal sits in his house all day, like a great chief. McCoy is always away in the hills; I think he has secret meetings with some of the women. In the beginning I did not dislike these men; I shared their food as they shared in the work, and McCoy smiled when he spoke, but they are changed, and little by little I have become a slave. Have you noticed Quintal's eyes? I fear him — I believe he is going mad."

"Aye, I have seen him on his doorstep, talking to himself."

"What can I do? If I displease him, he beats me, both he and McCoy."

Tetahiti flushed. "They are dogs, beneath a chief's contempt! Let them work for themselves. Cease going to their house."

"I fear Quintal. He will come and fetch me."

"Let him try!" Tetahiti's deep voice was threatening. "I will deal with him. We have been patient, hoping to avoid bad blood. Once he affronts you in public, Christian will put an end to all this."

He rose and helped the other to shoulder the heavy load of fish.

Half an hour later, stopping at Quintal's house to give Sarah a cut of albacore, Te Moa found the women alone. "They are gone to Christian's," Mary explained, "on some business that concerns them all. Best wait till morning to distribute your fish."

The sun had set, and in the twilight, already beginning to lengthen with the approach of spring, the mutineers were seated on the plot of grass before Christian's house. He and Young sat on a bench facing the men. Williams was the last to arrive. The hum of talk ceased as McCoy rose to his feet.

"Mr. Christian," he said, "there's a question come up that's nae to be dismissed lightly. Ye've bairns, sir, as have I, and John Mills, and Matt Quintal here. We've them to think on, and the days to come. A man works best on his ain land. The time's come, I reckon, to divide up the island, giving each his share."

Christian nodded. "Quite right, McCoy!" he said heartily. "Mr. Young and I were speaking of the same thing only last week. As you say, a man works with more pleasure when the land is his, and the division will leave no grounds for dispute after we are dead. The island can be divided so that each will have a fair share; I have already given the matter some thought. A show of hands is scarcely necessary. Are there any who disagree?"

"Not I, sir!" said Alexander Smith, and there was a chorus: "Nor I! Nor I!"

"Then it only remains to survey the place and see that all are dealt with fairly. Mr. Young and I will undertake the task, and propose boundaries for the approval of all hands. Let us meet again one evening, say a fortnight from now."

"Ye've an easy task, sir," remarked McCoy; "John Mills and I was talking of it an hour back. The island'll divide itself natural into nine shares."

"Nine!" exclaimed Christian. "Thirteen, you mean."

"Surely ye're nae counting the Indians, sir?"

"Would you leave them out?"

"There's nae call to share with 'em."

Christian controlled his temper with an effort. "Is this your idea of justice, McCoy?" he asked quietly. Alexander Smith spoke up.

"Think of Minarii, Will! Think of Tetahiti! How would they feel if we did as ye propose? There's land and to spare for five times our numbers! We'd be fools to stir up bad blood!"

"We've oursel's to think on, Alex," replied McCoy stubbornly. "Oursel's and our bairns. The Indians can work our lands and share what they grow."

"That's my notion!" put in Martin approvingly.

"I'm with 'ee, lad!" remarked Quintal, and Mills exclaimed: "Aye! Well spoke!"

"Listen!" ordered Christian quietly. "Think of the consequences of such a step. All of you know something of the Indian tongue. They have a word, *oere,* which is their greatest term of contempt. It means a landless man. Two of our four Indian men were chiefs and great landowners on their own islands. Would you reduce them to the condition of *oere* here? Attempt to make them slaves, or dependents on our bounty? We have land and to spare, as Smith says. To leave the Indians out of the division would be madness! Their sense of justice is as keen as our own. Do you wish to make enemies of them, who will brood over their grievances and hate us more bitterly each day? Make no mistake! I would feel the same were I treated as you propose to treat these men who have been our friends!"

McCoy shook his head. "I can nae see it that way, sir. We've oursel's to think on, and we've the right to call for a show of hands — ye promised that!"

"Mr. Christian is right," said Young. "Such a course would be madness. Bloodshed would come of it — I'm sure of that!"

Brown ventured to remark, "Well spoken, Mr. Young," but he shrank before the black look Martin turned on him.

"We want a show of hands, sir," growled Mills, "and we want it now!"

"You're in the right," Christian said sternly. "See that you don't misuse it! McCoy's proposal is folly of the most dangerous kind! So be it. . . . Shall we divide the island into nine shares, leaving the Indians out?"

McCoy raised his hand, as did Quintal, Mills, Williams, and Martin. They were five against the other four.

"One thing I must insist on," said Christian, after a moment's pause. "The decision is so serious, so charged with fatal consequences, that you must give it further thought. We shall meet again, the first of October. I trust that one or more of you will change his ideas on reflection, for the step you propose would be the ruin of our settlement. Yes, the ruin! Think it over carefully, and before you go each man is to give me his promise to say nothing of this to the Indians."

Young and Christian remained seated on the bench after the others were gone. Neither man spoke for some time. The evening was warm and bright with stars.

"They hold the Indians in increasing contempt," said Young, "and would make slaves of them, were it not for you."

Christian smiled grimly. "Make a slave of Minarii? Or of Tetahiti? For their own sakes I hope they attempt nothing so mad!"

"They are no better and no worse than the run of English seamen, but a life like ours seems to bring out all that is bad in them. They are better under the stern discipline of the sea."

"They'll get a taste of it if they persist in this folly! McCoy is at the bottom of this! Unless he has changed his mind when we meet to settle the matter in October I shall be forced to take stern measures, for his own good!"

"Aye, we are facing a crisis. I fear it was a mistake to give them the vote. You'll have to play the captain once more, to save them from their own folly!"

Young rose to take his leave. When he was gone, Christian entered the house and climbed the ladder to the upper room. The sliding windows were open and the starlight illuminated the apartment dimly. He crossed the room on tiptoe to the bed-place where Maimiti and her two boys slept under blankets of tapa. Maimiti lay with her beautiful hair rippling loose over the pillow; the younger boy slept as babies sleep, with small fat arms thrown back on either side of his head.

Presently Christian descended the ladder and lit a taper of candlenuts in the lower room. The *Bounty's* silver-clasped Bible lay on the table; he took up the book and began to read while the candlenuts sputtered and cracked. He read at random, here and there, as he turned the pages, for he could not sleep and dreaded to be alone with his thoughts. The Bible, which had brought comfort to so many men, brought none to Christian that night.

"And the Lord passed by before him," he read, "and proclaimed, The Lord, The Lord God, merciful and gracious, long-suffering, and abundant in goodness and truth, keeping mercy for thousands, forgiving iniquity and transgression and sin, and that will by no means clear the guilty; visiting the iniquity of the fathers upon the children, and upon the children's children, unto the third and to the fourth generation."

The man sighed as he turned the pages, and presently he read: "I will punish you seven times more for your sins. . . . I will scatter you among the heathen, and will draw out a sword after you. . . . And upon them that are left alive of you I will send a faintness into their hearts in the lands of their enemies; and the sound of a shaken leaf shall chase them; and they shall flee, as fleeing from a sword; and they shall fall when none pursueth."

Christian closed the book slowly and set it down on the table at his side. He covered his face with his hands, and sat bowed, elbows on his knees. The last of the candlenuts burned down to a red glow and winked out, leaving the room in darkness, save for the faint starlight that found its way through the window.

Though the bearing of the five trouble-makers grew more arrogant with the assurance that the land would soon be theirs and the Maoris their bondsmen, three weeks passed without an open break. Minarii and Moetua were building a house in the small valley Quintal considered his own; the native had disregarded with contempt Quintal's warning that he was a trespasser and only McCoy's dissuasion had prevented a serious quarrel between the two. "Bide yer time, mon," the Scot admonished him more than once. "Ye've only to do that and we'll put him off all lawfu' and shipshape." Quintal watched the building with an increasing dull anger. "Bide the devil!" he would growl in reply. "Wait till his house is finished. . . . I'll show him who owns the land!" McCoy would shrug his shoulders impatiently. "It's nae beef nor brose o' mine, but ye told Christian ye'd bide!"

Minarii's house was small, since only he and his wife were to live there, but it was handsomely and strongly built, with a thatch of bright yellow pandanus leaves and a floor of flat stones chinked with sand. It stood in the new clearing, on a slope of Quintal's valley.

Tetahiti had helped the builders with the ornamental lashings of the ridgepole, and on the morning when the house was finished, toward the end of the month, he strolled up to admire the completed work. Minarii was sprinkling sand from the watercourse into the chinks of his stone *paepae,* and straightened his back as he perceived the other approach.

"Come in!" he called.

"It is finished, eh?" remarked Tetahiti, glancing critically about the single lofty room. "You two have worked well. A pretty house! You of Tahiti are more skillful carpenters than the men of my island."

"It is but a bush hut. Nevertheless we shall soon come here to live. It is in my mind to make a large enclosure for the breeding of swine."

Tetahiti nodded. "Aye. Pigs thrive on this island."

"Let us go inland together. I was about to set out when you came. Yesterday, in the Auté Valley, I marked down a sow with eight young pigs of an age to catch."

The other shook his head. "I am going back to the house to sleep. It was dawn when I came in from the night fishing."

The sun was overhead when Tetahiti awoke from his siesta. He lay on a mat in the shade of a *purau* tree near his house, and for a moment, while he collected his thoughts confused by dreams, he stared up wild-eyed at the broad, pale green leaves which made a canopy overhead. Hearing his wife's footstep, he sat up, yawning.

Nanai was approaching with a basket of food. She smiled at her husband as she set down his dinner beside him on the mat.

"Have you slept well?" she asked. "Nihau prepared your meal. There's a joint of cold pig, and baked plantains, and fish of your own catching with coconut sauce."

She retired to a little distance while he ate, and fetched him a calabash of water to rinse his hands when the meal was done.

"Tetahiti," she said earnestly, "there is something I must tell you while we are alone. You must know, though I cannot believe it true." He nodded to her to go on, and she continued: "Susannah told me, swearing me to secrecy. Martin told her, she said. When I tell you, you will understand why I break my word."

"*Faaite mai!*" ordered Tetahiti, a little impatiently.

"Susannah says that the whites have had a meeting, unknown to us, and have decided to portion out the land, setting stones on the boundaries of each man's share."

"You cannot believe it?" he interrupted. "Why not? It is our ancient custom and would avoid dissension here."

"Aye, but let me finish. She says that the Maori men are to be left out of the division, that you will be *oere* from now on, slaves to work the lands of the whites."

Tetahiti laughed scornfully. "A woman's tale!" he exclaimed. "You know little of Christian if you suppose he would allow such a thing!"

"I told you I did not believe it!" said Nanai.

She left him, a little piqued in spite of herself at his reception of the news. The man lay down once more, hands behind his head. Though incredulous of Susannah's tale, he could not dismiss the thought of it, and little by little, as he reflected on certain things that had seemed without significance hitherto, and on the increasingly overbearing attitude of the whites, the seed of suspicion took root in his mind. He rose slowly and took the path to Martin's house.

He found the woman he sought alone. Mills was at work in the bush, and Martin lay snoring in the shade of the banyan tree. Though dark and by no means pretty, Susannah had once been a pleasant, light-hearted girl. Three years of Martin had broken her spirit. She went about her household duties mechanically, and rarely smiled. She gave a start at the sound of Tetahiti's voice. He beckoned her to the doorway, and asked in a low voice: —

"The tale you told Nanai . . . is it true?"

"She told you?" asked Susannah nervously.

"Aye. It was no more than her duty. Did you invent this woman's story?"

"I told her only what Martin told me."

He glanced at her keenly, perceived that she was speaking the truth. "Why should he invent such lies?"

"Lies?" said Susannah, shrugging her shoulders. "Who knows? Perhaps it is the truth!"

Martin awakened suddenly, perceived Tetahiti at the door, and sprang to his feet. He came limping across to the house. "What d'ye want here?" he asked, unpleasantly.

Tetahiti turned slowly and looked at the black-browed seaman with stern disdain. "To learn the truth. I think your words to this woman were lies!"

"Aué! Aué!" moaned Susannah, wringing her hands.

"What words?" asked Martin, unable to return the other's glance.

"That you white men have portioned out the land among you, un-known to us, and that we are to be left landless! Did you tell her that?"

Martin stood with downcast eyes. "No," he muttered after a mo-ment's pause; "she must have invented the tale."

The native took one stride, seized him by the neck, and shook him angrily. "You lie! Now speak the truth lest I choke it out of you!" He released Martin, who stood half crouched, his knees trembling visibly. "Have you agreed to portion out the land?"

Reluctantly the seaman met the angry native's eyes. "Aye," he re-plied, sullenly.

"And *we* are to be left out of the division?"

Martin nodded once more, and Tetahiti went on still more fiercely: "Did Christian consent to this?"

"Aye."

Without further speech Tetahiti turned on his heel and strode off rapidly in the direction of Christian's house. Pale and badly shaken, Martin stood watching him till he was out of earshot, before he entered the house, seized Susannah by the hair, and began to cuff her brutally.

Christian had taken a brief nap after his dinner, and when he awakened Maimiti was standing in the doorway, a basket of tapa mallets in her hand. Balhadi stood outside. Seeing that he had opened his eyes, Maimiti said: "We are going to Brown's Well to beat the cloth."

He sat up with a sharp twinge, for he had had a headache since dawn and felt irritable and out of sorts. "Let Balhadi go. Don't work to-day. Who knows at what moment the pains may begin!"

"Our child will not be born before night."

"Then work at something here if you must work. It is madness to go inland at a time like this."

Usually the most affectionate and docile of wives, Maimiti was now in one of the perverse humours which accompany her condition. She shook her head stubbornly. "I desire to go, and I am going. Men do not understand these things!"

He said no more as the two women turned away and walked down the path. He was thinking, in a mood of dejected irritation, of the gulf which divided Polynesians and whites. No man respected the good qualities of the natives more, but they seemed willful as children, believing that the wish justified the act, and living so much in the present that they were incapable of worry, of plans for the future, or of ordered thought. He rose and stood in the doorway, with a hand on his aching head.

The short, burly figure of Alexander Smith appeared beneath the trees. He was coming down the path from the Goat-House, and perceiving Christian at the door, he approached, holding up a rusty axe.

"I found it, sir!" he announced.

"Good! Where?"

"On the ridge. Where Tetahiti was felling that *tapou* tree."

Christian sighed as he took the axe and felt its edge absently. "It's the best I have left. The Indians! When they finish a bit of work, no matter where, they drop their tools and forget where they've left 'em. . . . They're all alike!"

Smith grinned. "Ye're right, sir! D'ye think I can learn my old woman to put things back where they belong? Not if we was to live in the same house for a hundred years!"

"Aye, there are times when they would try a saint."

Presently Smith took leave of Christian, who went into the house once more and lay down on his settee. The violent throbbing of his headache moderated as he closed his eyes; he was drifting into a troubled sleep when the sound of rapid steps aroused him.

Never in his life had Tetahiti entered any man's house — chief's or commoner's — without the customary hail and pause for the invitation from within; to do so was a most flagrant breach of the first law of Polynesian courtesy. But now he entered Christian's garden, strode up the path without a halt, and in through the open door.

Christian opened his eyes. Before he could speak the man was standing over him with a scowl on his face, blurting out in a voice vibrant with anger: "Is it true? True that you whites have held a secret meeting? That you have dared to divide the land among you, leaving us as *oere,* as slaves?"

Taken completely by surprise, Christian said: "Who told you this?"

"No matter!" replied Tetahiti furiously. "Is it true?"

"Yes . . . no . . . let me explain to you . . ."

"I knew it!" the other cut him short.

Christian controlled his temper with an effort. "Sit down, Tetahiti. I will explain."

"Explain! There is nothing to explain. It is shame I feel that I should have regarded you as my friend! A chief? You are no better than Quintal! Aye, no better than Martin, that base-born hog!"

The white man sprang up and faced the other so sternly that he recoiled a pace. Then, composing himself with a violent effort, he went on: "Sit down! You must know . . ."

The native interrupted him fiercely: "Enough!" He spun on his heel and flung himself out through the door. "Wait!" called Christian in a voice anxious and peremptory. There was no reply.

Tetahiti strode down the path to Bounty Bay, glancing neither right nor left, nor returning the salutations of his countrywomen in the houses of the mutineers. He found his wife awaiting him at the door. She had been watching his approach with anxious eyes.

"Where is Minarii?" he asked gruffly.

"Is it true?"

"Where is Minarii?"

"He has not been here; I think he is at his new house in the bush. Is it true?"

He made no reply; Nanai took his arm and gazed up anxiously at his face. He shook her off without a word and turned away as abruptly as he had come.

It was mid-afternoon; a still, warm day in early spring. The trees shadowing the lower parts of Quintal's valley were beautiful with the pale green of new foliage; a clear, slender brooklet, revived by recent rains, trickled down the watercourse. While still at some distance from the house of Minarii, Tetahiti became aware of a faint scent of burning wood; glancing up, he perceived that a column of smoke rose above the tree-tops ahead. As he reached the edge of the clearing, he gave a deep exclamation of astonishment.

Only a pile of smouldering embers marked the spot where the newly completed house had stood. Close by, with arms folded, and head bent as if deep in brooding thought, he perceived the gigantic figure of the chief. Minarii turned his head as the other approached.

"What is this?"

"I did not see it done. It is Quintal's work!"

They were silent for a time, both staring at the embers with sombre eyes. At last Tetahiti said: "Let us sit down, Minarii. There is something you must know."

# CHAPTER XII

THE house of Quintal and McCoy had long been in darkness. Their sleeping rooms were on the upper floor, divided by a partition of matting. The ground floor was used as a common room and was furnished with two tables, some roughly made chairs and benches, and a cupboard used for food and to contain various household utensils. Some time after midnight, Minarii stole silently out of this dwelling and proceeded in the direction of Christian's house. A light was burning there, for Maimiti was in labour with her third child, and a number of the women were gathered to assist Balhadi, who was the most skillful midwife among them. Minarii advanced with the greatest caution and halted at the edge of the clearing, where he crouched for some time, listening and watching. It was a clear, starlit night, and he could make out the forms of Christian and Young walking back and forth across

the grassplot on the north side of the house, and those of various
women seated on the bench by the open doorway.

Withdrawing as noiselessly as he had come, he crossed the belt of
forest land, skirting some of the nearer gardens of the settlement until
he came to a footpath leading over the western ridge. Crossing the
ridge and descending the slope for some distance, he struck into another
path which entered the ravine which the white men called Temple
Valley by reason of its having been set aside by Christian for the use
of the native men in the practices of their religion. This valley, narrow
and rocky, was, in fact, little more than a gorge, and near the head
wall, in a cleft not a dozen paces across, the natives had erected the
stone platform that served as their *marae*. The path leading to it was
steep, winding over the roots of great trees and among rocks that had
fallen from the heights above; but Minarii was familiar with every
foot of the way, and, dark as it was, he proceeded without hesitation.
Mounting steadily, he came at length to a huge boulder that all but
blocked further passageway. Here he halted.

"Tetahiti?" he called, in a low voice.

"*É, teié,*" came the reply, almost at his side.

The darkness was intense; scarcely a gleam of starlight penetrated
the foliage of the great trees overarching the ravine. Minarii seated
himself with his back to the rock. "The others have come?" he asked.

"We are here," a voice replied.

"Listen well," said Minarii. "In the house of Quintal and McCoy
there were, as you know, two muskets. I have taken these, and the
powder and ball kept by them. You have done what was agreed,
Tetahiti?"

"I have the muskets from Young's house, and Nihau has those of
Mills and Martin. We have powder and ball for twenty charges."

"Will not the weapons be missed?" Nihau asked.

"That is a chance that must be taken," said Minarii.

"I have my ironwood club," said Nihau. "I care not whether I carry
a musket."

"You speak foolishly," Minarii replied. "We have not to do with men
of our own race, here. Our purpose is to kill them, and quickly. I have
my club, but I shall carry a musket as well, and you shall do the same."

"It must now be decided whether any are to be spared," said Tetahiti.
"I am thinking of Christian."

"Wait," said Minarii. "Let us first consider the others. Five I can kill with joy in my heart — Quintal, Williams, Martin, Mills, and McCoy."

"We waste words in speaking of these," Tetahiti replied.

"I long to see them dead," Nihau added, fiercely, "and their bodies trampled in the mud!"

"Good. Four remain. We must be of one mind about them. Tetahiti, speak now of Christian."

"You ask a hard thing, Minarii. He is a brave and good man, and our friend."

"Our friend?" There was scorn in Minarii's voice. "Does a friend insult his friends? He is a chief in his own land. He knows you and me to be chiefs in ours. And he has agreed to divide the land among his own men, leaving us with nothing, as though we were slaves! Had he spit in our faces, the shame could not have been greater."

"Your anger is just," Tetahiti replied, "but what he has done was not meant to shame us, this I know."

"And how do you know?"

"This is what he once told me: his men must have a voice here, equal with his own. Those who are strongest in numbers have their will, even against the desire of their chief."

"That is a lie!" Minarii replied. "One of two things must be true: either he is no chief, as we have believed, or he wishes to shame us. The first cannot be so. Would he be ruled, then, by pigs of men such as Quintal and Mills and Martin? Would he bow to them in a thing so important as the division of our lands if he did not wish us ill?"

"I have nothing to reply," said Tetahiti. "My mind is as dark as your own; yet I cannot believe that Christian wishes to shame us."

"Why, then, should he do so?" Minarii asked. "A chief does what he wills. Christian and Young shall both be killed," he continued, quietly. "Let their deaths be at my hands. Even though it were as you have said, do you not see that they must die? The blood of their countrymen would cry out for ours. Christian and Young are men. They would take their just revenge upon us."

Tetahiti was long in replying. "It is true," he said at length. "There is no other way. But understand this, Minarii: he who kills Christian shall call me friend no longer."

"Let that be as it will," Minarii replied, grimly. "The island is large enough. You can go with your women to one side. I will go with mine to the other."

"Minarii," said Tetahiti, "Brown is your friend. Is he to be spared?"

"He is like my brother, a younger brother. He has nothing but good in his heart. He will see us coming and suspect nothing. Who could strike him down?"

"It can be done," said Te Moa. "Let him be among the last when our blood is hot and the lust for killing upon us all. I could do it then."

"If Christian is not to be spared, Brown shall die," said Tetahiti.

"I see that it must be so," Minarii replied; "but you shall not touch him, Te Moa! Tetahiti shall kill my friend, since I am to kill his. But see that you do it swiftly, you man from Tupuai!"

"My hand shall be as steady as your own. His death shall be as swift as you make that of Christian."

"It remains to be seen whether this land will seem as large as I thought, with the white men dead," said Minarii. "It may be too small to hold us two."

When Tetahiti replied, the anger was gone from his voice. "Enough, Minarii. Let there be no hot words between us. I see that my friend must die. Can you be blind to the need of death for your own? His life, alone, among the slayers of his countrymen would seem to him worse than death. Do you not see this?"

"I see it," Minarii replied, coldly. "Let no more be said of him."

"One remains to be spoken of. What of Smith?"

"A brave and good man who has done none of us harm," said Nihau. "Evil is the need that calls for his death."

"There is no other way," said Minarii. "It must be as Nihau says."

They were silent for some time; then Minarii again spoke. "I say this for you, Nihau, and Te Moa. We four have nine to kill. There must be no blundering, and you must do exactly as we say."

"So it shall be," Nihau replied.

"The plan shall be in your hands, Minarii," said Tetahiti. "It falls to you of right as the older man."

"I am content," Minarii replied, "and I must be obeyed as you would obey a chief in war."

"It is agreed," said Tetahiti.

"This is not war, and it will be a shame to us forever that we must kill men as hogs are killed for the oven; yet it must be done."

"If we used no secrecy in this affair, Minarii, but challenged those five to fight us four?" asked Tetahiti.

"That is spoken like a chief," said Minarii. "It is what I, myself, would most desire, but Christian would never allow them to accept such a challenge; then our purpose would be known and our chance for killing them gone."

"We could wait," said Nihau, "making a pretence of friendship until their minds were again at rest. When they believed we had forgotten we could fall upon them as we plan to do now."

"Speak no more of this," said Minarii, sternly. "Could you wait in patience for such a time? If I have my way they shall all be dead before another sun has set."

"If it is willed," said Tetahiti. "That must first be known."

"It is willed that they shall die; that is certain," said Minarii. "Whether or not it shall be in the coming day we shall soon know."

The strip of sky above them was now suffused with a faint ashy light, sifting like impalpable dust into the gloom of the ravine. Soon the dim outlines of trees and rocks and the crags above them could be discerned, and the forms of the men, who had long been only voices in the darkness, were revealed to each other. Minarii sat by the boulder where he had first halted. He was a man of commanding presence. Naked, save for the strip of bark cloth about his loins, he seemed equally unconscious of the chill dampness of the night air and of the long fatigue of his motionless position. Tetahiti sat near him, his back to a tree and his legs outstretched. The thick mantle of tapa around his shoulders was wet and limp with the heavy night dews. Nihau and Te Moa were seated on the lowest of the roughly laid stone steps that led to the *marae*. The ravine was extremely narrow at this point, and beyond the stone platform the fern and moss-covered head wall rose toward the ribbon of sky in a series of giant steps of basaltic rock.

Presently Minarii rose. Nihau and Te Moa made way for him as he mounted the stone staircase to the platform of the *marae*. Tetahiti removed his mantle and followed, the other two bringing up the rear. They waited in silence at the summit of the staircase while Minarii retired to a small thatched house at one side of the *marae*. He appeared a moment later in his ceremonial robes, whereupon Tetahiti proceeded to the rocky recess where the casket containing the god was kept. This was brought to the altar stone in the centre of the platform. All four now took their places at the kneeling stones and the ceremony of awakening the god was carried out. A moment of deep silence followed; then Minarii made his prayer

"Our God, who listens: hear us!
Judge, Thou, if we have summoned Thee amiss.
Judge, Thou, if our wrongs are great and our cause just.
Known to Thee is the cause before tongue can speak;
Therefore it is told.
If our anger is Thy anger, let it be known!
If the time favours, speak!"

A few moments later the four men filed down from the *marae,* and as soon as they were beyond sacred ground Minarii halted and turned to face his companions.

"Our success is sure," he said, "and now we must not rest until they are all dead."

"What is first to be done?" asked Tetahiti.

"You and I should return to the village," said Minarii. "Our absence may be wondered at, but if we two go down they will suspect nothing."

"I have promised to obey you," said Tetahiti, "but this thing I cannot do. Maimiti's child must now have come. I cannot face her and Christian, knowing what we have to do."

"That was to be expected, and we shall not go down," Minarii replied. "Nihau alone shall go."

"What shall I do there?" Nihau asked.

"Tell the first woman you meet that I am hunting pig, with Williams, and that you three will be fishing until evening from the rocks below the western valley. Go now and return quickly."

The path from the settlement to the western valley crossed the high lands a little below the Goat-House Peak. Here it branched, a second trail leading southward along the ridge to the partially clear lands of the Auté Valley. The ridge was bare at the junction of the two paths, and at this point was a rustic bench used as a resting place on journeys across the island. Not far to the right rose a small heavily wooded spur which commanded a view of the ridge and of the valleys on either side. Here Minarii, Tetahiti, and Te Moa now lay concealed, awaiting the return of Nihau.

The sun had not yet risen, but a few ribbed clouds, high in air, glowed with saffron-coloured light. A faint easterly breeze was blowing, fragrant with the breath of sea and land. The summit of the spur was only a few yards in extent. Tetahiti and Te Moa, their muskets beside them, lay at a point directly above the junction of the two paths. Minarii watched the steep approach from the settlement. That people were astir there was evident from the threadlike columns of wood smoke that rose straight into the air above the forests until caught by the breeze, which spread them out in gossamer-like canopies above the dwelling houses. The houses themselves were hidden from view; not even the clearings, some of them of considerable extent, could be seen from above. Save for the smoke, the island, in whatever direction, presented the appearance of a solitude that had never been disturbed by the presence of man.

Half an hour passed. Minarii crept back to where the others were lying. A moment later Nihau appeared; he crossed the open space by the rustic bench and plunged into the thicket to the right. When he had joined them the four men crouched close, talking in low voices.

"They suspect nothing," said Nihau. "I met Nanai, Moetua, and Susannah on their way to the rock cistern. They will be making tapa to-day."

"You saw Christian?" asked Tetahiti.

"No. He and Young are still at Christian's house. Maimiti's child was born just before the dawn."

"Is the child a boy or a girl?"

"A girl."

"What men have you seen?" asked Minarii.

"Only Smith, carrying water down from the spring to Christian's house."

"Minarii, it is a hard thing to kill Christian on this day when his child is born," said Tetahiti.

"It is a hard thing," Minarii replied, "nevertheless we shall do as we have planned, and now two of us shall go quickly to Williams's house and not return to this place until he is dead."

"Then he shall fall at my hands," said Tetahiti. "Christian may work in his yam garden to-day. He may be the first to come this way and I would not be the one left to meet him here."

"That is as it should be," said Minarii. "Te Moa shall go with you. See that Williams's woman is not allowed to escape. Take her and bind her. Carry her to the lower end of the small valley behind Williams's house. She must be left there until we come to release her."

"It shall be done," said Tetahiti.

He grasped his musket and was about to rise when Minarii laid a hand on his arm. A moment later Hutia appeared on the path leading from Williams's house. She carried a basket with a tapa mallet projecting from it, and was humming softly to herself as she sauntered along the path. Upon reaching the bench she seated herself there for a moment to examine a scratch on her leg. She wet a finger and rubbed the place; then she held her small pretty hands out before her, regarding them approvingly as she turned them this way and that. The valley was all golden now in the light of the just-risen sun. The girl rose and stood for a moment looking down over the forests. Still singing, she went lightly down the path and disappeared among the trees.

"It is plain from this that our god was not awakened unwisely," said Minarii. "He is ordering events to suit our purposes and now none of you can doubt that this is the day appointed for what we must do."

"I see it," said Tetahiti. "Wait here. We shall soon return."

Followed by Te Moa, he made his way through the thick bush below the spur, and was soon lost to view.

"It will be well if Christian comes now," said Nihau.

"Nothing shall be done here," said Minarii. "If any turn into the path for the Auté Valley, we will follow. If they go down into the western valley, we will wait here until Tetahiti returns. Now watch and speak no more."

Christian and Young were seated in a small open pavilion on the seaward side of Christian's house. Christian held his eldest child, now a sturdy lad of three years, on his lap.

"You must make haste, Ned," he was saying, "else I shall have such a start as you will never be able to overcome."

Young smiled. "Taurua and I are both envious of you and Maimiti," he replied. "The poor girl is beginning to fear that we are to have no children."

"Taurua? Nonsense! She'll bear you a dozen before she's through. What a difference children will make, here, in a few years' time! What a change they have brought already!"

"What are we to do in the matter of their education? Have you considered the matter at all?"

"Mine shall have none, in our sense of the word," Christian replied.

"You shan't teach them to read and write?"

"What end would it serve? Consider the difficulty we should have in trying to give children, who will know life only as they see it here, a

.conception of our world, our religion. Let their mothers' religion be theirs as well. Save for the cult of Oro, the war god, the Indian beliefs are as beautiful as our own, and in many respects less stern and savage. We believe in God, Ned; so do they. It would be a mistake, I think, to mingle the two conceptions."

"You may be right," Young replied, doubtfully; "and yet, when I think of the future . . ."

"When our children are grown, you mean?"

"Yes. What would our parents think, could they see their grand-children, brought up as heathens, worshiping in the Indian fashion?"

Christian smiled, bleakly. "There's small chance of their ever knowing of these grandchildren."

They were silent for some time. Christian sat stroking the thick black hair of the solemn little lad on his lap. "If the chance were offered, Ned, of looking into the future, would you accept it?"

"I should want time to consider the matter," Young replied.

"I would; whatever it might reveal, I should like to know. What would I not give to see this boy, twenty years hence, and the second lad, and the little daughter born this morning! God grant that their lives may be happier than mine has been! It is strange to think that they will never know any land but this!"

"We can't be certain of that."

"Not completely certain, but chances are strongly against any other possibility. We must make it a happy place for them. We can and we shall," he added, earnestly. "But get you home, Ned, and sleep. Your eyes look heavy enough after this all-night vigil."

"They are, I admit. And what of yourself? Why not come to my house for a little rest? We shan't be disturbed there."

"No, I feel thoroughly refreshed, now that Maimiti's ordeal is over. This evening I shall call the men together. Whether they will or no, the division of land shall be altered to include the Indians and on equal terms with ourselves."

"It is a wise decision, Christian; one we shall never regret, I am certain of that."

Christian accompanied his friend a little distance along the path. Returning to the house, he tiptoed to the door of Maimiti's chamber and opened it gently. Balhadi sat crosslegged on the floor by the side of the bed. The newly born infant lay asleep in a cradle made of one of Christian's sea chests. He crossed the room softly and stood for a moment looking down at Maimiti. She opened her eyes and smiled wanly up at him. "I knew you had come," she said. "I heard you in my sleep."

He knelt down beside the bed, stroking her hair tenderly. She took his other hand in both of hers.

"*Aué,* Christian! Such a time this little fledgling gave me! Her brothers came so easily, but I thought she would never come."

"I know, dear. Are you comfortable now?"

"Yes; how good it is to rest! Does she please you, this little daughter?"

"She will be like you, Maimiti. Balhadi and Taurua both say so. Already I love her."

"There — I am content. Balhadi, let me have her. . . . Oh, the darling! How pretty she is!"

Balhadi laid the sleeping child in the mother's arms, and a moment later Maimiti herself had fallen into a profound slumber.

On the spur overlooking the ridge, Minarii and Nihau were still waiting, so well concealed that no scrutiny from below could have revealed their hiding place; nevertheless, they had a clear view of the ridge and of the bench there which faced eastward, a little to the left of the path. The sun was well above the horizon when the sound of voices was heard from below, and shortly afterwards Mills appeared, followed by Martin. The men were bare to the waist and wore well-patched seamen's trousers chopped off at the knee. Their heads were protected by handkerchiefs knotted at the four corners. Upon reaching the summit of the ridge they halted. Martin walked to the bench and sat down.

"Do as ye like, John," he said, "I'll have a blow."

"Aye," said Mills, "ye'd set the day long if ye could have yer way."

"Where's the call for haste? Come, set ye down, man, and cool off. There'll be time enough to sweat afore the day's done."

Mills joined his companion, and for a time the two men had no further speech.

"Have ye seen Christian this morning?" Martin asked, presently. Mills shook his head. "My woman was over half the night. This bairn's a girl, she says."

"Aye; that makes seven, all told, for the lot of us, and three of 'em Christian's."

"And where's yours?" Mills asked. "What's wrong with ye, Marty, that your woman's not thrown a foal in three years?"

"Ye've no great call to boast, with the one," Martin replied. "The fault's Susannah's — that I'll warrant."

"Aye, lay it to the woman," Mills replied scornfully.

"And why not? I board her times enough. If she was a wench from home, now, she'd be droppin' her young 'un a year, reg'lar as clockwork. She's bloody stubborn, is Susannah."

"Is she takin' to ye better now?"

"She's not whimperin' for Tahiti all the while, the way she was. I've beat that out of her. . . . What's that? A shot, wasn't it?"

"Aye. That'll be Williams. Huntin' pig, I reckon."

"I've a mind to go myself this afternoon; there's a fine lot o' pig runnin' wild in the gullies yonder. What do ye say we invite ourselves to dinner with Jack? I've not seen him this week past."

"I'm willin'; but come along now. We've work and to spare, to get through afore dinner time."

"Damn yer eyes, John! Can't ye set for half an hour? The day's young yet."

"Dawdle if ye like, ye lazy hound! I'm goin'."

"Fetch my axe from the tool-house; I'll be along directly," Martin called after him. Mills went on without replying and was lost to view below the crest of the ridge.

Nihau turned slightly and slipped his musket forward, glancing at Minarii as he did so. The chief, without turning his head, stretched out a hand to stay him. In the stillness of the early morning the crowing of the cocks could be heard and the rhythmical sound of tapa mallets in the valley below. Martin sat leaning forward, his elbows on his knees, his hands clasped loosely, gazing vacantly at the ground between his bare feet. Presently he turned to look down the path along the ridge to his right. Tetahiti and Te Moa were approaching, their bodies half hidden by the fern on either side of the path. After a casual glance, Martin turned away again. At sight of him, Tetahiti stopped short, then came quickly on, changing his musket from his right hand to his left. As they neared, Martin again turned his head slightly to give them a contemptuous glance.

"So ye're pig-hunters, are ye?" he said, derisively. "And where's the bloody pig? Safe enough, I'll warrant! Which of ye missed fire? I heard but the one shot."

The two natives stood before him without speaking.

Martin rose, lazily. "Give me yer piece," he said, to Te Moa. "I'll learn ye how to put in a charge, and much good may it do ye."

He stepped forward, holding out his hand for the musket. With the quickness of a cat, Tetahiti seized him by the wrist. At the same moment Minarii and Nihau appeared from the bush at the side of the ridge. Passing his musket to Te Moa, Nihau stepped forward and seized Martin by the other arm, and before the white man could again speak he was half pushed, half dragged along the path leading to the Auté Valley. For a few seconds he was too astonished to offer resistance; then he held back, making violent efforts to wrench himself free.

"What's the game?" he cried, hoarsely. "Let me go, ye brown bastards! Let me go, I say! . . . John! John!"

"Loose him," said Minarii.

Tetahiti and Nihau released their holds. Minarii reached forward and grasped him by the back of the neck. Martin howled with pain in the powerful grasp of the chief, who held him at arm's length, with one hand. "Don't 'ee, Minarii!" he cried, in an anguished voice. "Don't 'ee, now!" The chief dropped his hand. "Walk," he said.

About one hundred yards beyond there was a broad slope of partially clear land. They turned off here. They had gone but a little way when Martin again halted and turned toward Minarii. His eyes were dilated with terror. He glanced quickly from one to another of the four men. "What do ye want?" he cried in a trembling voice. "Te Moa! . . . Nihau! . . . For God's sake, can't ye speak?"

Minarii again reached forward to grasp him. Of a sudden Martin's legs went limp and he fell to his knees. They lifted him up and he fell again. "Carry him," said Tetahiti. Nihau and Te Moa grasped his arms, lifting him, and carried him along with his legs dragging on the ground. At a sign from Minarii they dropped him at a spot where a great pile of brush had been heaped up for burning. Martin fell prone. He turned his head, his eyes glaring wildly. Minarii motioned to Te Moa, who stepped back, unloosing the long bush knife fastened by a thong to his belt. Martin struggled to his knees. "Oh, my God! Don't 'ee, lads! Don't 'ee kill me!" With an awful cry he sprang to his feet, but Nihau was upon him at once, and, throwing out his leg, tripped him and sent him sprawling. "Be quick," said Minarii in a contemptuous voice. As Martin again rose to his knees, Te Moa swung the long, keen blade with all his force, taking off his head at a blow.

The air seemed to be ringing still with the last despairing cry of the murdered man. The head, which appeared to leap from the body, had rolled a little way down the slope. Te Moa ran after it and held it aloft with an exultant shout, letting the blood stream down his arm. Scarcely had he done so when Mills appeared, axe in hand, at the edge of the clearing. At sight of Te Moa, whose back was toward him, he stopped short; then with a bellow of fury he rushed upon him. Te Moa turned and leaped aside just in time to save himself.

The impetus carried the white man past him, and before he could again turn and raise his axe, Minarii, concealed from his view by the brush pile, sprang out, and with a quick blow of his club broke Mills's arm and sent the axe flying from his hand. The boatswain lurched to one side, and Nihau, swinging his club at arm's length, brought it down with crushing force on the man's head.

They dragged the two bodies into the thicket beyond the clearing, where Nihau, with a clean stroke of his knife, severed the head of Mills from the trunk. Te Moa cut a small straight branch from an ironwood tree, shaving it down and rounding it, sharpening it to a needle's point at one end. Laying Martin's head on the ground, he drove the ironwood splinter through it, from ear to ear. A thong of bark was pulled through with it, and he then fastened the head at his hip, to his belt of sharkskin. Nihau did the like with Mills's head. Minarii and Tetahiti squatted near by, watching.

Minarii rose. "Come," he said. He grasped his club and his musket and made his way noiselessly through the bush toward the ridge. The others followed. They came to a little hollow under the western side of the ridge, well screened by fern and not more than a dozen paces below the junction of the paths. Here Minarii halted, and the others crouched beside him. Minarii turned to Nihau. "Watch there," he said, pointing to the spur above them. "If any come, throw a handful of earth here where we wait."

Nihau took his musket and disappeared in the fern.

"This plan was well made," said Tetahiti.

"There is no honour in killing men so; yet it must be done," said Minarii. They spoke no more after that.

Presently there was a light patter of earth and small pebbles among the fern that sheltered them. Minarii lay on his belly, and drew himself forward a little way. Several minutes passed; then they heard the light tread of bare feet along the path in front of them, and a slight rustling and rasping of the bushes on either side. Minarii pushed himself back to where Tetahiti lay. He waited for a few seconds, then rose to his knees and glanced to left and right over the top of the fern.

"Who passed?" Tetahiti asked.

Minarii avoided his glance. "You have agreed to obey me this day as you would obey a chief in war. Wait here, then — you and Te Moa."

Tetahiti rose to his knees and looked down over the thickly wooded land below them, but there was no one to be seen. Stooping, he seized Minarii's musket and thrust it into his hand. "Your club shall be left here," he said. "Go quickly."

Two hundred yards from their hiding place, on a shaded knoll, a combined tool- and store-house had been erected for the common use. Minarii crept forward until he could command a view of this house. He saw Christian appear with an axe in his hand and go on down the path. Minarii then examined carefully the charge in his musket. He waited where he was until he heard the clear steady sound of axe strokes in the forest beyond. Taking up his musket, he proceeded in that direction.

Several small clearings had been made on these upland slopes. Minarii halted opposite the second one. Christian was at work a short distance from the path, hewing down a large *purua* tree. He swung his axe steadily, with the deliberate measured strokes of a skilled woodsman. His back was toward Minarii, who approached stealthily, his musket held in one hand, until he was not ten paces distant.

"Christian," he called, quietly.

Christian turned his head. Seeing who it was, he leaned his axe against the tree. "Oh, Minarii." He straightened his back and flexed the muscles of his shoulders, turning toward the native as he did so. Of a sudden the faint smile on his face vanished. "What is it?" he asked.

For a second or two they stood regarding each other, Minarii grasping his musket in both hands. An expression of amazement, of incredulity, came into Christian's eyes, then one of sombre recognition of his danger. He stepped back quickly, reaching behind him as he did so toward his axe. With a swift movement, the chief raised his musket to his shoulder and fired. Christian staggered back against the tree; then sank to his knees, his head down, swaying slightly. Of a sudden he fell forward and lay still.

# CHAPTER XIII

ALEXANDER SMITH's taro garden lay in swampy ground within a five-minute walk of the settlement. He had been at work there for some time, knee-deep in mud, clearing the weeds and water grass from around the young plants. Having reached the end of a row, he waded to firm ground, cleaned his muddy hands on the grass, and sat down to rest. Rising presently to resume his work, he stopped short, hearing his name called. For a moment he saw no one; then Jenny appeared from behind a covert and ran headlong toward him.

"What is it, Jenny?"

"Come quickly!" she said, in an agonized voice. She ran ahead of him into the forest beyond the clearing. Halting there, she was unable to speak for a moment, holding out her hands, which were smeared with blood. Then she burst into a torrent of words. "It is Brown's blood, not mine, that you see! Tetahiti has killed him! Have you heard no shots?"

"Yes, but . . ."

"Tetahiti has killed him, I tell you! They are all together — Tetahiti, Minarii, Nihau, and Te Moa. They have muskets, clubs, and knives. Three are already dead. Where is Christian?"

"He has gone to the Auté Valley."

"Then he too must be dead! Come quickly! Arm yourself!"

"Wait, Jenny! You say . . ."

"Will you come?" she cried, wringing her hands. "Mills's head I have seen! It is hanging at Nihau's belt! They are seeking you now!"

Faintly, from far to the eastward, the sound of a shot was heard.

"There! Will you believe me? It is not pig they are shooting, but men!"

She turned and sped down the slope toward the settlement. Smith ran after her and seized her hand.

"Maimiti must know nothing of this, Jenny! You understand? Now do as I tell you! Young is asleep in his house. Go and warn him. Tell him I will meet him there. I must fetch Christian's musket."

The woman nodded and sped on down the path.

All was silent in Christian's house. The door stood open. Smith entered softly. Balhadi lay asleep on the floor by the door leading to Maimiti's chamber. Smith shook her gently by the shoulder. She sat up quickly, rubbing her eyes. "*Aué!* Oh, it is you, Alex. Shh! We must not disturb Maimiti. She is having a good sleep. She needs it, poor child!"

"Where is Christian's musket, Balhadi?"

"His musket? Let me see. Yes, it is hanging on the wall in the other room."

"Fetch it, with the powder flask and the bullet pouch."

Smith returned to the door and looked out. The little glade lay peaceful and deserted. Balhadi returned with the musket. "What is it, Alex?" she asked, in a low voice. Motioning her to follow him, Smith went around the dwelling to a small outbuilding used as a storehouse.

"Listen, Balhadi, what you feared has happened. The Maoris are killing the white men . . ."

"*Aué!*"

"I have met Jenny. Three are already dead, she says. She has seen Nihau with Mills's head at his belt. Te Moa has Martin's. Brown is dead. Christian may be, but that is not known. Where is Young?"

"At his house, I think. Go quickly, Alex!"

"You must stay with Maimiti. Say nothing to her . . ."

"No, no! Do you think you need to tell me that? Go! Make haste!"

Save for the clearings made for the houses and the path to the cove, the forests of the island had been little disturbed along the seaward slope of the plateau. Smith ran across the path into the heavily wooded land, making his way with great caution toward Young's house. Jenny, Prudence, and Taurua were standing in the dooryard. Smith revealed himself at the edge of the clearing. Taurua ran toward him at once.

"Ned is not here, Alex," she said, in a trembling voice. "He came home to sleep — that I know. I left Maimiti only a little time ago. Ned was not in the house when I came, and we can't find him."

"You *must* find him!"

"We shall if he is alive, but we are afraid to call out. Two shots have been fired in the direction of Quintal's plantation."

"I heard them. Fetch my musket, and the powder and ball. Run!"

Taurua returned, bringing only a cutlass. Jenny followed her.

"The muskets are gone, both yours and Ned's," she said. "They must have taken them in the night."

"Then you must keep this one for Young," he said, handing her the weapon. "Give me the cutlass."

"What shall you do?"

"I must find Christian, if he is alive. Now go, all three of you, and search for Young. I shall make my way to the Auté Valley. If I find that the others are dead, I shall hide near the Goat-House. Tell Young to come there."

He then reëntered the forest and was lost to view.

The three women separated and continued their search. Taurua, having hidden the musket, went along the seaward slope, examining every hollow among the rocks, every clump of bushes. Presently she found Young, stretched out on a grassy slope, asleep. She roused him and clung to him a moment, unable to speak; then she quickly informed him of what had happened. He gazed at her in silence for a moment.

"Ned! Are you awake?" she cried. "Do you understand what I say?"

"Only too well. Christian is dead, I fear. You say Alex left his musket for me? Why did you let him, Taurua?"

"Why? Because he is stronger than you! He can defend himself well with a cutlass."

Young rose. "I must find him at once," he said. "Where is the musket?"

Taurua went ahead. A moment later she beckoned Young to follow. Prudence and Jenny had returned to the house. There was a window at the eastern end of the dwelling overlooking the path in the direction of the cove. Prudence, her child in her arms, kept watch there. Jenny watched from the window at the opposite end of the house. Taurua brought the musket from the bushes where she had hidden it. The powder flask was half filled, and there were only four balls in the bullet pouch. Young had just seated himself to charge the musket when Prudence called softly from the window: "Hide, Ned! . . . Minarii!"

Taurua seized him by the arm and pulled him into the room adjoining. Two large chests stood there, near the bed. Young crouched between them and Taurua threw over him a large piece of tapa. Jenny concealed herself behind the curtains of the bed-place. Prudence remained at the window, crooning softly to her child. Taurua reëntered the common room and quickly seated herself on a stool in one corner, resuming a task, interrupted some time before, of grating coconut meat into a bowl. She had herself well in hand. A moment later Minarii appeared in the doorway. He now carried only his musket. He greeted them casually. Taurua looked up, smiling. She did not trust herself to speak at first.

"Where are you going, Minarii?" Prudence asked. "Is it you who has been shooting pig this morning?"

"*É,*" he replied, "Williams and I. We wounded a large boar on the ridge. He ran down into the Main Valley. We have not yet found him. Where is Young, Taurua?"

"Fishing, at the cove. He went early this morning."

Minarii glanced around the room.

"If you pass Brown's house," said Prudence, "will you tell Jenny that I have the bundle of reeds for her? I'll carry it up this afternoon."

"I'll tell her if I see her." He took up his musket, nodding to the two women as he turned away.

"*A noho, orua.*"

"*Haere oé,*" they replied.

He turned and went back the way he had come. Prudence remained at the window. "We have fooled him, Taurua. He thinks we know nothing."

"Is he keeping to the path?"

"Yes. . . . He is out of sight now."

Taurua rose and went quickly into the other room. A moment later Young, waiting his chance, ran out of the house and disappeared into the forest.

It was getting on toward mid-morning. Young had been gone for some time. The three women sat on the bench by the doorstep, talking in low voices.

"Minarii would have saved Brown?" Taurua was saying.

"He could easily have killed him had he meant to do so," Jenny replied. "This happened: We were weeding the yam garden near the house. Minarii found us there. 'There is little time for words,' he said. 'Three of the white men are dead. Tetahiti, Nihau, Te Moa, and I have killed them. They shall all die except Brown. Him I will save if I can. When I shoot my musket over his head he must fall to the ground and lie as dead. He must not move till the others have passed; then let him hide in the woods. It is his only chance.' Then he fired into the air and pushed Brown and sent him sprawling. 'Go into the house!' he said to me. 'Go at once and stay there! The others are close behind.'

He went on into the forest. Soon came the other three. I watched from a tiny hole in the thatch. They halted when they saw Brown lying on his face. They walked toward him and stopped again. Brown could not have heard them. He moved, turning his head a little. Tetahiti was not ten paces from him. He raised his musket and shot him through the head. When I saw what he would do, I ran from the house and sprang on him from behind, but it was too late. Then the three of them bound my hands and feet and carried me into the house. As soon as I could free myself I ran to warn Alex."

"I see how it was," said Taurua. "Minarii must have killed Christian. They must have quarreled over who should die, and . . ."

"The beast! The vile dog!" Jenny exclaimed, her eyes blazing. "Tetahiti shot my man as he lay on the ground! *Aué! Aué!*"

She put her head in her arms, rocking back and forth on the bench; but she made no further outcry. The time for weeping had not come. All three women were too stunned for tears.

"Nanai must have known of this," said Prudence, fiercely. "Both Nanai and Moetua must have known of what was to happen to-day, and they gave us no warning."

"You are wrong, Prudence," Taurua replied. "Minarii and Tetahiti would never have told their wives of such a plan."

"I shall hate them forever!"

"That can be understood," said Taurua, "but they are not to be blamed. I saw them both early this morning. Had they known, I could have guessed it at once. No, they are as innocent as ourselves."

They talked in low voices, waiting, listening, hearing nothing save the crowing of cocks in the forest and the soughing of the wind through the trees. Prudence's child awoke and began to cry. She reëntered the house and took it up, nursing it in her arms as she walked the room. Taurua laid a hand on Jenny's arm. "Listen!" The two women turned their heads at the same moment. At the turn of the path below the house Mary and Sarah appeared, half running, half walking, carrying their children in their arms. Taurua and Jenny ran forward to meet them. Mary was weeping hysterically. "You know, Taurua? They have been here?" she cried.

"Tell us quickly — are your men dead?"

"They must be! Minarii . . ."

"Hush, Mary," said Sarah. "We don't know that they are dead."

"They must be! McCoy has only his bush knife. Quintal has nothing to defend himself with. How can they escape? *Aué*, Prudence! Are you here? Do you know that your man is dead? Ours will be next!"

The moment they had entered the house, Mary sank to the floor and lay there, her head buried in her arms. Taurua took up her child. "What has happened, Sarah?" she asked.

"You heard the shots?"

"Yes."

"They were fired at Quintal. He and McCoy were to make a fence to-day, and Quintal had gone up the valley to carry down some posts he had cut. He left me to sharpen his axe. I was carrying it up to him when Minarii and Te Moa stepped out from behind some bushes. Te Moa was covered with blood and he had Martin's head hanging at his belt. Minarii took the axe from me and told me to go back to the house. Just then I saw my man come out of the bush with a bundle of poles on his shoulder. I shouted to him. Minarii and Te Moa ran toward him. Both fired, but they must have missed, for Quintal ran back into the forest."

"What of McCoy?"

"He was still at the house. I ran down to warn him, and before any of them came to look for him he had time to escape."

"Had the muskets at your house been taken?" Jenny asked.

"Yes. I must have looked at the very hooks where they hung, early this morning, without wondering why they were not there."

"Who came to search the house?"

"Tetahiti and Nihau. McCoy had just gone. I asked Tetahiti if they had killed Quintal. He would say nothing, but as they went out again Nihau stopped at the door. 'You want to know if your man is dead?' he asked. 'Yes,' I replied. 'I will tell you this,' he said; 'you will be one of my women to-morrow, and Te Moa shall have Mary.' Then he ran on after Tetahiti."

"Which way did they go?"

"Inland, up the valley. What of Ned, Taurua? And Christian and Alex?"

"They are dead! They must be by this time!" Mary cried in a terrified voice. Again she broke out in hysterical weeping. She clutched and held fast to Taurua's legs. Jenny took her roughly by the shoulders. "Hush, Mary!" she said. "What a coward you are! Stop, I say! Have you no spirit?"

"Could there be a more worthless woman?" said Prudence, in her soft voice. "Leave her, Jenny; there is nothing to be done with such a thing as she is."

They tried in vain to quiet her. She became more and more hysterical, clinging to Taurua with all her strength. Sarah was, herself, on the verge of panic, but controlled herself. Of a sudden, Mary raised her head. Her eyes were dilated with terror.

"Come," she said, in a low gasping voice. "We must hide! They will kill us, too! Yes . . . they will kill us all! Shhh! Do you hear anything?"

She sprang to her feet, gazing wildly toward the door; Taurua spoke to her soothingly. "Be silent, Mary. You are in no danger. None of the women will be killed."

"Yes! Yes! You have not seen them! They are like sharks maddened with blood!"

Prudence stepped forward and struck her across the face with her open hand. "Will you be silent?" she said. The sharp blow, better than words could have done, quieted the terrified woman. She sank down again, whimpering in a low voice. Taurua lifted her up. "Come, Mary; lie you down in the other room. We will watch. No one shall harm you." The others waited in silence. Presently Taurua returned. "The poor thing has worn herself out," she said. "She will sleep, I think."

"May she sleep well," said Jenny. She held Mary's two-year-old boy on her lap. "What will this son be like," she added, "if he has his mother's nature?"

Taurua went to the door and stood for a moment looking into the forest beyond the path. "I must return to Maimiti," she said. "Balhadi is alone there. Stay here, you three."

"And wait, doing nothing, while all our men are killed?" Jenny asked. "Not I!"

"What would you do?" Sarah asked.

"One thing at least I can do. My man lies on the ground before our house, a prey to the ants. His body shall be left there no longer. Prudence, will you come with me?"

"No, no, Prudence! Stay!" Sarah begged. "Don't leave me alone with Mary!"

"Sarah, no possible harm can come to you here," Taurua said. "If they had meant to kill us, do you not think that they would have done so before now? Jenny is right. Something may be done to help our men. Listen, Jenny, this you shall do: Find Hutia; she may be at the rock cistern. She will go with you. When you have cared for your man's body, then learn if you can what ones are dead; if you can find Alex and Young, let them know that we think McCoy and Quintal are still living. Or, if you will, stay with Maimiti and I will go in your place. Prudence has her child; she must remain here with Sarah and Mary."

"Stay you with Maimiti," Jenny replied. "I will go."

So it was decided, and the two women set out on the path to Christian's house.

It was late afternoon. Prudence sat alone on the bench before Young's house. Sarah and Mary remained within doors, their children around them, talking in whispers. Mary was quiet now. Three hours had passed and nothing had been heard, nothing seen. Prudence turned her head. "Taurua is returning," she said. The other two women rose and came to the door, waiting anxiously. Taurua was alone.

"Jenny has not come?" she asked.

Prudence shook her head. "We have seen no one since you left," she replied. "Who are at Christian's house?"

"A little time after I went there, Susannah came. She was at the rock cistern with Hutia. They knew nothing until Jenny brought them word. Both have gone with Jenny. We must wait."

Taurua went to the outdoor kitchen, returning with some cold baked yams and plantains, which she placed on the table. "Here is food," she said, "for those who need it. Prudence, you and Mary should eat for the sake of your babies." She prepared some food for the two older children, who seized it greedily, but the women themselves ate nothing.

Now that Taurua had come, Mary and Sarah ventured to the bench by the doorstep, and the four women sat there, talking little, peering into the forest beyond the path, streaked through with shafts of golden light.

"Maimiti has not been told?" Prudence asked.

"She had just wakened when I went back," Taurua replied. "She is so happy with her little daughter. She said to me: 'Now, Taurua, I have nothing more to wish for.' Every little while she would send Balhadi or me to the door to look for Christian. How could we tell her? How? Who could do it?" Her eyes filled with tears. "*Aué*, Maimiti '*ti é!*'" In a moment all the women except Prudence, who sat dry-eyed, forgetting themselves and their own sorrows, were weeping together for the mother of the newly born child. "What will she do, Taurua?" Sarah asked, at length.

"We must not think of it now," Taurua replied, drying her eyes. "And we do not yet know that he is dead. Let us hope while we can."

The sun had disappeared behind the western ridge before Jenny returned. Hutia and Susannah were with her. Their kirtles of tapa were torn and soiled and their arms and legs covered with cuts and bruises. As soon as they had entered the house, Taurua closed the doors and the wooden shutters to the windows. "Now, Jenny?" she asked.

The women were breathing hard. "Give us some water," Jenny said. "Our throats are dry with dust." They drank greedily. "We have seen Minarii and Nihau, but no one else," Jenny began. "They passed almost within arm's length of where we lay hidden in the fern."

"If we had had muskets we could have killed them both," Hutia added.

"They must have gone again to the Auté Valley, for they were coming down from the ridge. As soon as they had passed we went on. We went first to Hutia's house. Williams's body was lying in the doorway. He had been shot through the head. We carried him inside. Then we went to Christian's new clearing just below the ridge. We found an axe leaning against a tree half cut through. There was blood on the ground close by, but what happened there we do not know. We searched everywhere, but could not find his body.

"You saw Mills's body?" Prudence asked.

Jenny hesitated, glancing quickly at Hutia. "No," she said, "it must have been hidden."

"And you saw none of our men, Jenny? No one at all?" Sarah asked, in a trembling voice.

Jenny shook her head.

"That is not strange," Taurua said, quietly. "They lie concealed."

"They are dead!" Mary cried, burying her face in her hands.

"Hush, Mary! What a foolish woman you are! They may be together now, all of them. It must be so."

"But if they are, Taurua, what can they do without weapons?"

"Ned has a musket. Alex Smith has a cutlass. Quintal is a man as strong of body as Minarii. He will cut him a club in the bush. We have reason to hope, I tell you!"

"Do you think that Minarii will rest until they are all dead? Never!

He well knows that his own life will not be safe until all the white men have been killed."

"It is true," Sarah said, wretchedly. "We shall never know peace now until one party or the other are all dead."

"And who wishes for peace until those four are killed?" Jenny exclaimed. "I saw Tetahiti shoot my man as he lay helpless on the ground. Do you think I shall rest until he himself is dead?"

"Let us speak no more of this," said Taurua. "There has been bloodshed enough . . ."

She broke off. The report of a musket shot was heard close by. Mary ran into the house, her hands pressed to her ears. The other women rose quickly and looked at one another.

"Let us go in," said Taurua, "and make ready the house. Some of our men may have to come here to defend themselves."

"And one of them may be lying dead within sound of our voices," said Jenny. "I must know what has happened. You others prepare the house." Without waiting for a reply, she ran across the path and plunged into the forest.

She quickly crossed the wooded land bordering the path. Beyond this, and not more than one hundred and fifty yards from Young's house, there was half an acre of cleared ground planted to sweet potatoes and yams. The report of the musket shot had come from this direction. Jenny halted within the border of the woodland and looked out across these gardens. She saw no one. She skirted the plantations and was about to proceed farther into the valley, when she came upon a cutlass lying half hidden by a clump of plantains. There was fresh blood on the dead leaves near by and she discovered naked footprints in the moist earth of the plantain walk a little way beyond. She had proceeded but a short distance farther, when she came upon Alexander Smith lying face down, groaning feebly. She knelt beside him, and, putting her arms around him, lifted him to a sitting position with his head resting against her shoulder. He opened his eyes drowsily. "Jenny?" he said. She examined him swiftly. The ball had entered at his shoulder and had come out at the neck. "Alex, could you walk with me to help?" He nodded. With one arm around her shoulders, he struggled to his feet, but they had gone only a few steps when his body went limp. With both arms around him, she held him for a moment and then let him sink gently down. She ran back to Young's house and returned with

Taurua and Hutia. Smith was a solidly built man and it was all the three women could do to lift and carry him, but a quarter of an hour later they had him in Young's bed. He was breathing heavily and had lost much blood.

"It is a clean wound; the ball has passed through," said Taurua. "The great artery has not been touched — that is certain. Otherwise he would be dead."

The women worked quickly and in silence. Susannah carried water while Taurua and Jenny staunched the flow of blood from Smith's wound and bound it well. He was now unconscious and his face ghastly pale. Hutia kept watch by the door and Prudence by the window. The sun had set and the shadows began to deepen in the room.

"They left him for dead — that is clear," said Jenny. "Did Minarii know that he still lives, mad with killing, as he now is, he would come and club him as he lies."

"Yes," said Taurua, "and we must be prepared if they come here. I shall go now for Balhadi. Keep watch, you two. If you see any of them coming, cover Alex at once with the tapa mantle as though he were dead and kneel all of you by the bed, wailing and crying. They will believe and not molest you. When Balhadi comes she can be prepared to gash herself with a *paohino*. Seeing her face streaming with blood, they will be sure to think her man dead."

"The plan could not be better," said Jenny. "Make haste, Taurua; we shall do as you say. Balhadi must lose no time in coming."

Taurua set out for Christian's house. It was a lonely way between the two dwellings, with ancient forest trees overarching the path. She had gone about half the distance when she heard her name called, and halted. Nanai came out from behind a screen of bushes and beckoned to her, earnestly. Taurua went to where she stood and regarded her coldly, waiting for her to speak. Nanai was deeply agitated, but controlled herself.

"Hate me if you will, Taurua, for what my man has done this day," she said, "but believe, if you can, what I say: I knew nothing of their plans, and Moetua is as innocent as myself."

"I am willing to believe it," Taurua replied, "but this will not give life to murdered men. Speak quickly if you have more to say, for I have little time to spend here."

"Your man lives . . ."

Taurua grasped her by the arm. "You know this? Where is he?"

"On the Goat-House Peak, hidden in a spot where they will never be able to find him. It was I, Taurua, who told him of the place and led him there."

Taurua gazed at her searchingly. "We have long been friends," she said. "You would not deceive me — that I could never believe."

Nanai's eyes filled with tears. "You are like my own sister, Taurua, and Ned has been as a brother. Ask your heart if I could act basely toward you. But this I ask in my turn. If Ned is spared, he must put thoughts of revenge from his heart. Tetahiti is my husband."

"Though he and those with him were killed, the dead cannot breathe again. I cannot promise that his word will be given, but I shall do what I can to bring this about."

"It is enough, Taurua. Minarii is terrible in anger, but the desire for killing is short-lived. Ned has only to remain hidden. His life will be spared. Tetahiti will wish it — of that I am sure. Moetua and I will stand with you all in this."

"Alex is badly hurt. We have carried him to our house. We know nothing of Christian."

"Listen, Taurua. Moetua is close by. We shall go together in search of him. Perhaps we can help him if he still lives. Whatever has happened, I will bring you word when we know. Do what can be done to soften the hearts of the others toward us two. What our men have done is done. That cannot be forgiven, but let them know that Moetua and I are blameless."

"That I shall do," Taurua replied, "but keep well aloof from them until a later time, and most of all from these three — Jenny, Hutia, and Prudence. Their men have been murdered by your husbands. Their anger toward you can be understood."

"They shall not see us," Nanai replied.

"Now I must hasten to Maimiti," said Taurua. "Go, and good go with you for your kindness to me."

Nanai clung to her for a moment; then she turned and disappeared in the shadows of the forest.

Balhadi had seen Taurua approaching. She came quickly to the door and the two women spoke in whispers. "He will live, Balhadi, this I believe," Taurua was saying. "I would not tell you so if I thought there was no hope. But do as I have said if Minarii or the others come. Cover Alex as you would cover a corpse, and all of you wail over him as for one dead. They will believe and not molest him."

A moment later she was alone in the room. She went to the door of Maimiti's bedroom and halted there, listening; then she returned to a bench near the table, and seated herself, her chin in her hands, staring unseeingly out of the window. Her eyes brimmed with tears, and for a time she wept silently.

Presently she heard Maimiti's voice calling Balhadi. Drying her eyes quickly, she entered the room where the mother was lying.

"Balhadi has gone to her house, Maimiti."

"Oh, is it you, Taurua? Christian has not come?"

"Not yet. Shall I light a taper?"

"There is no need. I love this dim light of evening. Such a good sleep I have had! Look, Taurua, how she sucks! She is like a little pig. Where can Christian be? He told me he would come early in the afternoon, and here it is past sundown!"

"He will come soon."

"Go up the path to meet him, dear. He must surely be coming now. What a strange father he is! You would think he had a little daughter born to him every day! Go quickly, Taurua. Tell him to hasten."

Taurua nodded and turned hastily away. She stood for a moment outside the door gazing up the path now barely discernible in the dim light of evening. A moment later she seated herself on a bench there and buried her head in her arms.

## CHAPTER XIV

In the rich little valley between Ship-Landing Point and the easternmost cape of the island, Tetahiti and Nihau lay in the fern where they had slept, conversing in voices inaudible a few yards away. The moon had set long since, but the first faint grey of dawn was in the east. Nihau sat up, shrugged his shoulders, and spat.

He began to count on his fingers. "Nine muskets we have; fourteen were landed from the ship. Five are missing, though Young may have taken that which always stood in Christian's house."

Both men started and seized their weapons at the sound of a footfall close by, but relaxed at a low hail from Minarii. He was followed by Te Moa, who carried a bunch of ripe plantains on his back. He set down the fruit, as well as four drinking nuts fastened together with strips of their own fibrous husk, and Tetahiti reached into the fern behind him for a basket of baked yams.

They ate quickly and in silence. When the meal was over, Tetahiti remained for some time deep in thought. "Minarii," he asked, "will you not consent to spare Young? Quintal and McCoy must be hunted down, but Young . . ."

"He too must die! Speak no more of this! They must all be killed, and quickly!"

"Where can the others be?" said Nihau.

"Wherever they are, they shall not live to see the end of this day."

Minarii rose, taking up his musket as he spoke. "Go with Nihau and search the western slopes," he went on. "Waste no more powder at long range. With Te Moa, I shall comb this end of the island, so that a rat could not escape our eyes. Let us meet a little after nightfall in the thicket close to Quintal's house."

Minarii beckoned to his follower, and led the way up to the head of the valley and across the ridge. It was a stiff climb and both men were panting as they skulked along the ridge to the brink of the curving cliffs called "the Rope." Their feet made no sound on the rocky path, and, though the stars were only beginning to pale, Minarii moved with the alert caution born of years of bush warfare. He halted in a clump of pandanus at the very edge of the cliff.

"I had not thought of this place," he said to Te Moa in a low voice. "Keep watch while I scan the beach below. It will soon be day."

He set down his musket and stretched himself out at full length to peer down the dizzy face of the precipice at the narrow strip of beach many hundreds of feet below. Though the morning was windless, a southerly swell had made up during the night, and great seas came feathering and smoking into the shallow bay, to burst with long-drawn roars that seemed to shake the solid rock. The spray of the breakers hung in the air, oftentimes veiling cove and beach from the eyes of the watcher above. Sea fowl wheeled and soared before their nesting places.

The light grew stronger. Presently the sun's disc broke the horizon to the east. Peering down through a tangle of thorny pandanus, Minarii gave a sudden low exclamation. He beckoned over his shoulder to the other man.

"I see him!" exclaimed Te Moa in a whisper. "There by the big rock! Ah, he is gone!"

"Who is it?"

"I could not tell for the drifting spray."

Minarii reached for his musket, measured the distance with his eye, and shook his head. Some time passed before Te Moa whispered rapidly: "Look! At the eastern end of the sands!"

"McCoy or Young," said Minarii. "Quintal is a span wider in the shoulders."

The fog of salt spray closed in again; when it dispersed, the man or men on the beach had disappeared. Minarii backed away from the verge of the cliff and crouched in the pandanus thicket. "What think you?" he asked. "Your eyes are younger than mine. Are there two, or one?"

"Two, I think. Quintal and McCoy."

"Perhaps. Yet one man might have walked the distance in the shelter of the scrub."

"Whether one or two, they are trapped," said Te Moa. "No man could climb the cliffs nor enter those breakers and live."

"And safe from us," remarked Minarii, musingly. "This sea is a *miti vavau,* sprung from a distant storm. It made up quickly and will calm down as fast. I will keep watch here. Go you to the landing place and lash the outrigger on our canoe. Go softly. When the work is done, hide yourself near the path at the top of the bluff. If the swell goes down, I will hasten across to you. If not, we shall meet as appointed, near Quintal's house."

When Te Moa was gone, Minarii settled himself to watch. He lay as immobile as the basalt crags of the ridge. Twice during the hours of the morning he had glimpses of a figure below, but the swell grew heavier as a south wind made up; the cove was now one smother of foam, half invisible under the wind-driven spray. The sun reached its zenith and began to decline. In spite of the south wind, it was warm in the shelter of the scrub. Minarii grew drowsy as the afternoon advanced. He was stifling a yawn when his quick ear caught the sound of a footstep not far off. He took up his musket, cocked it noiselessly, and turned his head to peer out through the matted leaves.

Twenty yards to the west, the low scrub parted and Matthew Quintal stepped out into the open, glancing this way and that. He wore a knotted handkerchief on his head, and a pair of trousers cut off roughly at the knee. His eyes were bloodshot and his great arms crisscrossed with scratches beneath the growth of coarse red hair. He came to a halt, crouching to avoid showing himself against the sky line, and began to gaze intently at the ridges and hillsides to the westward, one hand shielding his eyes from the sun.

Firearms — even bows and arrows — were regarded as cowards' weapons by the men of the island race, and Minarii hated Quintal so fiercely that he yearned to kill him with his bare hands. He set down the musket softly beside his club, and stepped out of the thicket, a look of sombre rejoicing in his eyes. Flexing the huge biceps of his left arm, he smote the muscle a resounding blow with his right hand; the native challenge to combat. The blow rang out like a pistol shot. Quintal spun on his heel; then he rushed toward Minarii.

They came together crouching, with their hands low. Minarii feinted and lashed out with his right fist, a mighty blow that drove home smacking on the other's jaw. Only Quintal's great bull neck saved him; he blinked, staggered, and rushed in under the native's guard, seizing him beneath the arms in a hug that might have cracked the ribs of an ox. Minarii grunted as he was lifted off his feet; next moment he drove his thumbs deep into his enemy's throat. With eyes starting from his head, Quintal brought his knee up sharply, and as the other released his grip and staggered back, grunting with pain, the white man sprang on him and brought him to the ground. They grappled, twisting fiercely as each strove for a throttling hold on the other's neck. Then suddenly, as they had fallen, they were up again, but this time Quintal had his left arm braced on the native's chest, and a grip on Minarii's great sinewy right wrist. A breath too late, the warrior realized his danger. As they turned in a half-circle, his battering fist rained blows on Quintal's head, but the Englishman held on doggedly, exerting all of his enormous strength.

Next moment, with a loud snap, the bone broke. Grunting with pain and anger, Minarii wrenched himself free and got in a blow that caught Quintal unaware. His head flew back; as he stood swaying with vacant eyes, the native's uninjured hand shot up under his chin and closed on his throat. Both men were bleeding from a score of deep scratches, for they were fighting in the thorny pandanus scrub on the very brink of the cliff.

With huge fingers sunk in his enemy's neck, Minarii dragged him toward the precipice. Dazed, throttled, and in great pain, Quintal reached up feebly, felt for a finger, and bent it back with all the strength that remained to him. As the clutching hand at his throat let go, he struggled to his feet. At that moment Minarii aimed a mighty kick at his chin. Had the toughened ball of the warrior's foot found its mark, the fight would have been over; but, as it chanced, the crumbling rock on which he stood gave way. He staggered, waving his left arm in an effort to regain his balance. The white man sprang forward, seized the upraised foot of his enemy, and hurled him backward.

Quintal craned his neck and saw the warrior's body rebound from a crag a hundred feet down, crash through a thicket of dwarf pandanus standing out horizontally from the cliff, and plunge on and down, to fetch up against a stout palm-bole, five hundred feet below.

The Englishman was scarcely able to stand. One eye was swelling fast, he was scratched and bruised from head to foot, and his throat bore the red imprints of the dead man's fingers. He swallowed with difficulty, coughed, spat out a mouthful of blood, and felt his neck tenderly. Then, after a long rest with head in his arms, he set out at a limping shuffle, across the ridge and down into the valley to the west.

Only the bent and torn pandanus leaves and a sprinkle of blood here and there on the rocky ground bore witness to the combat. The sea fowl still soared before their eyries on the Rope, with the afternoon sun glinting on their wings. The sun went down at last behind the western ridge, and the bowl of the Main Valley began to fill with shadows.

In the thick bush, well back from the settlement, Tetahiti and Nihau were making their way cautiously toward the place of rendezvous. All through the day they had searched the western half of the island, without a glimpse of the men they sought. Tetahiti was in the lead. He halted as they came to one of the paths that led inland; then he seized Nihau's arm and pulled him back into the bush. Next moment Moetua came into view. She was unaccompanied.

Tetahiti called to her in a low voice: "Moetua O!"

As she turned, he beckoned her to follow him into the bush. "Where is Minarii?" she asked.

"With Te Moa, searching for the white men."

She was nearly of his own stature, and now she looked him squarely in the eyes, without a smile. "Tetahiti," she said earnestly, "have you not had enough of killing? Will you spare none?"

"All must die. Those are your husband's words. Have you seen Quintal or McCoy?"

"No. As for Young, if I knew where he was concealed I would not tell you!"

Tetahiti shrugged his shoulders. "I am of the same mind, yet Minarii is right; it is the white men or ourselves. None shall be left alive."

"Blood! Blood!" she said in a low voice as she turned away. "Men are wild beasts. To-day I hate them all!"

Te Moa was awaiting them at the rendezvous, an area of unfelled bush not far from Quintal's house. He told Tetahiti of what they had seen at the Rope, and of the chief's instructions to him.

"Here is food," he said. "You two are weary and I have done nothing all day. Sleep when you have eaten. Minarii will soon be here. I will keep watch and arouse Nihau when I can stay awake no longer."

Prudence and Hutia sat close together on the floor of Mills's house. The smaller girl caressed, from time to time, the head of the sleeping baby on her knees. The door opened softly. Hutia called in a low voice not without a slight quaver: "*Ovai tera?*"

"It is I, Jenny!"

She closed the door and felt her way across the darkened room. "Listen!" she whispered rapidly. "Our chance has come! Have you courage to seize it?"

"Courage for what?" asked Prudence coolly.

"To kill the slayers of our men!"

Prudence rose, set down her child on a bed, and came back to Jenny's side. "Now tell us what is in your mind."

"I have found Tetahiti and Nihau and Te Moa asleep. Te Moa lies with his back to a tree at some little distance from the others. His musket is between his knees. They must have posted him as a sentinel, but sleep has overcome him. We have an axe and two cutlasses. Are your hearts strong? Will your arms not falter?"

"Not mine!" said Hutia grimly.

"I claim Nihau," remarked Prudence, in her soft voice.

"Aye," said Jenny, "and Tetahiti is mine!"

Hutia slapped her knee softly. "*Eita e peapea!* I will bear my part, so that the three die. . . . But Minarii, where is he?"

"He may come soon," said Jenny. "We must make haste. The moon will set before long. Take the cutlasses and let me have the axe."

They rose and took up their weapons. Prudence bent over her sleeping child for a moment before she left the house.

An hour passed and the moon hung low over the western ridge. Quintal was making his way down toward the settlement. He walked with a limp, slowly and cautiously, keeping in the shadows of the bush. Passing the blackened platform of stones where Minarii's house had stood, he began to reconnoitre the thicket which separated him from the cleared land surrounding his own deserted house. He was about to emerge into the moonlight when he caught his breath suddenly, halted, and whispered: "Christ!" Next moment he stooped to take up the severed head of Te Moa, and turned the face to the moon. McCoy's old cat, fetched from Tahiti, was a great night wanderer in the bush. He rubbed his back against Quintal's leg, turned away, and began to lap at something on the ground. Fiercely and noiselessly, with his bare foot, Quintal kicked him away.

He glanced this way and that, walked to a tree that stood at a few yards' distance, and came to a halt before the bodies of Tetahiti and Nihau. "All dead!" he muttered. "And a good job, too! Who could ha' done this?"

With three muskets under his arms, Quintal now took the path to the settlement.

The candlenuts were alight in the house of Mills, but the windows and doors were barred. Quintal whistled softly outside, and after a moment's pause Jenny called, "Who is it?" in an uncertain voice. He made himself known. Presently the door was unbarred and he entered the house. Prudence was on the floor, suckling her child; Hutia started to her feet nervously at sight of him.

"Where is Minarii?" asked Jenny, closing and fastening the door.

"Dead. I killed him. What Englishmen are dead? I found Jack killed by a musket ball, and the headless bodies of Martin and Mills."

Jenny told him briefly all that she knew, and he asked: "Where is Will McCoy?"

She shook her head. "Who killed the men I found yonder in the bush?" he went on.

The three women exchanged glances, and at last Jenny spoke: "If I tell you, will you keep the secret? *Parau mau?*"

"Aye!"

"They were the murderers of our husbands," said Jenny slowly. "We killed them as they slept."

Quintal blinked bloodshot eyes as his slow mind considered this information. "Damn my eyes!" he exclaimed. "Women's work, eh?"

"Listen," Jenny said. "It was our right and duty to kill these men. But their wives may have other thoughts. They must not know the truth. There has been trouble enough on this unhappy land. Will you tell the others that you killed those three?"

"Aye, if you wish it; why not?"

"You will tell no one, not even Sarah?"

"No. Where is she?"

"At Young's house."

Prudence covered her breast and laid the sleeping child on Mills's bed. "We are glad to have you here," she remarked. "We feared Minarii, and the spectres of the newly dead!"

Quintal limped across to Mills's bed-place and lay down. Hour followed hour while the three women whispered nervously and lit fresh tapers of candlenuts. At last the stars paled before the light of dawn. When the last of the fowls had fluttered down from the trees, Hutia slipped out of the house. Jenny was moving about in the outdoor kitchen, and Prudence sat astride a rude little three-legged stool by the door, grating coconuts. Presently the basket was full and she stood up.

"*Pé! Pé! Pé!*" she called, ringingly, while the fowls began to run with outstretched wings, increasing their speed as the girl flung out handful after handful of the crinkled snow-white flakes. She upturned the basket, dusted her hands, and entered the house. Quintal still slept heavily, face turned to the wall. Prudence bent over her child, her lips caressing the cool little forehead. She took a comb of bamboo from the shelf above the bed, seated herself on the doorstep, and began to undo the long and heavy plait of her hair. Shaking her head impatiently, she raised a hand to dash the tears from her eyes.

Mary and Sarah were approaching the house, leading McCoy's children and Quintal's boy. As Prudence glanced up, Sarah asked, "Where is he?"

"He still sleeps."

Without rising, she moved a little to let the older girl pass into the house. Mary stood before her, her eyes red with weeping. McCoy's two children clung to the folds of her kirtle.

"Has Matt seen my man?"

Prudence shrugged her shoulders. She felt only contempt for this soft, unready woman who became hysterical when it was time to act.

Sarah was kneeling at Quintal's side. He turned uneasily and opened his eyes. His two-year-old son was trying to climb on to the bed. The father's eye brightened and he smiled.

"Up, Matty!" He lifted the child to his side. "There's a stout lad! Eh, Sarah, old wench!"

"Where is McCoy?" she asked.

"Dead, like enough. We must search for him."

He rose, stretching his muscles gingerly, limped out through the back door to the water barrel, and dashed a calabash of water over his head. His injured leg had stiffened during the night, and he found it next to impossible to walk. Sarah spread a mat for him close to the door and fetched him a breakfast of half a dozen ripe plantains. He ate half-heartedly, for he was only beginning to realize the full extent of the catastrophe. Will McCoy dead, no doubt, and Christian, too. And Jack Williams . . . old John Mills. Murdering bastards, those Indian men. Damn their blood, why couldn't they have kept the peace? Alex Smith would probably die, from what the women said. Quintal drew a deep breath and raised his head. The woman beside him leaned forward at sight of his gloomy face.

"Ye must help me," he said, "I can scarce walk. There's naught to hurt ye in the bush; take Mary and make a search for Will. The children can stop with me."

"Where shall we search?"

"Try the eastern cape. Let Mary follow the ridge west above Tahutuma. If ye don't find him, there, work down the Main Valley. He may be living; hail him, from time to time, on the chance."

Sarah nodded as she rose, but Mary would not go until Jenny agreed to accompany her. Sarah set out to the east, while the other two crossed the Main Valley to the ridge.

The sea had calmed during the night. The sun was about an hour up and the morning cool and cloudless. Sarah glanced fearfully this way and that as she walked. Now and then she stopped and hailed: "Will! Will O! Will McCoy!" but for some time her clear hails died away without a response in the morning calm.

When she had turned inland and was gazing down over the broad wooded bowl of the plateau, she heard a faint rustle in the bushes and a hoarse voice.

"Sarah? Are ye alone?"

"Yes."

"Duck down off the sky line! Where's Matt?"

McCoy was close to her now, and she started as the leaves were pushed aside and his haggard face appeared, ugly with a three days' growth of red stubble. He stared wildly at her, as though doubting her word.

"Where's Matt?" he asked again, in a low voice.

"At the house. Come back with me. They are all dead."

"Who are dead?"

"All of the Maori men."

"And the Englishmen?"

"Come back with me. Quintal will tell you."

"Are ye speaking truth?"

"Yes!" replied Sarah impatiently.

Some rat or lizard made a slight rustling sound among the dead leaves a few yards off. McCoy gave a violent start and peered about him in terror. The shirt and ragged trousers he wore were wet with salt water. He scrutinized the woman suspiciously.

"Fetch Matt. I'll believe it when he tells me."

Sarah shrugged her shoulders wearily. "There is nothing to fear. Yet I will fetch him if you wait."

"Be off!"

When she was gone, he moved cautiously through the bush to higher ground, where he could overlook the rendezvous without being seen.

While McCoy awaited the coming of his friend, Taurua was walking rapidly along the western side of the plateau, toward Christian's yam plot. From time to time she called softly: "Moetua! Nanai!" At last, in a thicket near the steep path leading to the ridge, she found those she sought.

The two girls sat by a litter of *purau* saplings lashed with bark. Christian lay on this rude couch, ghastly pale and with a stubble of black beard on his chin. His eyes were closed; only his rapid, shallow, and laboured breathing showed that he lived. Moetua and Nanai sat cross-legged by the stretcher, moistening bits of tapa with cool water from a calabash and laying them on the wounded man's forehead. His fever, perilously high, dried the cloths fast.

Moetua looked up at the newcomer with the slight smile courtesy demands of her race, but the sight of Taurua caused her to rise instantly.

"What is it, Taurua?" she asked, with a tremor in her voice.

Nanai stood up, twisting her hair hastily into a knot and scanning Taurua's face anxiously. "Aye, speak out!" she said.

The other girl cast down her eyes and drew a long breath. "I would that another might have told you," she said slowly. "I am the bearer of ill tidings. . . ."

"Speak!" commanded Moetua.

"Your husbands . . . both are dead, and Te Moa and Nihau."

Moetua's face turned pale. After a long time she said, "The gods have forgotten. There is a curse on this unhappy land." Nanai stood with bowed head. The taller girl put a hand on her shoulder, and turned to Taurua once more. "Who killed Minarii?"

"Quintal has killed them all."

"Young had no hand in it?"

"No."

Moetua's eyes were full of tears as she looked Taurua straight in the face. "You are sure?"

"Sure! I swear it!"

Taurua turned away and sank down on her knees beside Christian. "The fever consumes him," she said to Moetua. "We must carry him to Young's house."

"Go back to Maimiti. We will fetch him down," said Moetua.

When she was gone, the two girls sat for some time in silence, with bowed heads and stony eyes. At last Moetua rose and made a sign to Nanai to take up one end of the litter. Carrying their burden easily, and still in silence, they took the path to Young's house.

They found Young with Balhadi in the room. Alexander Smith lay in the bed on the seaward side, unconscious and with closed eyes. Though he had lost much blood, his face was flushed with fever. Balhadi sat beside him on a stool. She looked up at the sound of foot-steps outside the door.

Without a glance or a word of greeting, the two girls carried the litter into the room, set it down by the bed opposite Smith's, and lifted Christian's unconscious body on to the fresh spread of tapa. Young rose as they entered and was about to speak when he caught sight of Moetua's face. Still without a word, she turned and beckoned Nanai to follow her out through the door.

Young crossed the room hastily to Christian's side. He listened to the wounded man's breathing, opened his shirt with gentle fingers, re-moved the dressing of native cloth, and examined the wound. As he rose from his knees his eyes met Balhadi's anxious glance.

"Can he live?" she asked.

"He must!" he replied, in a low voice. "He must and he shall!"

# CHAPTER XV

THE American sealing vessel *Topaz* was steering west-by-south with all sail set, before a light air at east. The month was February and the year 1808. Her captain, Mayhew Folger, was one of the first Yankee skippers who were beginning to round the Horn, venture into the Spanish waters off the American coast, and steer west into the vast and little-known South Sea, in search of sealskins, whale oil, or trade.

The *Topaz* was ship-rigged, and, although small, she had the sturdy weather-beaten look of a vessel many months outbound and well able to find her way home. The coast of Peru was now more than a thousand leagues behind her and she sailed a sea untracked by any ship since 1767, when Captain Carteret's *Swallow* had passed that way.

When Folger had taken the sun's altitude, at noon, he went below to make his calculations and to dine. Turning to go down the companionway, he caught the mate's eye.

"Keep her as she is, Mr. Webber," he said.

The mate was an Englishman of thirty, or thereabout, with a clear, ruddy complexion and an expression firm, reserved, and somewhat serious. He stood with arms folded, not far from the helmsman, glancing aloft from time to time to see that the sails were drawing well. It was midsummer in the Southern Hemisphere; the sky was cloudless, and the sun, tempered by the east wind, pleasantly warm. The ship rolled lazily to an easy swell from the northeast.

Two bells sounded, and shortly afterward the man in the crow's nest hailed the deck. He had sighted land, distant thirty-five miles or more. A moment later the captain appeared, wiping his lips with the back of his hand and holding an old-fashioned spyglass which he extended to the mate.

"Get aloft, Mr. Webber, and see what you make of it."

Folger strode the deck until the other returned and handed him the telescope.

"A high, rocky island, sir, from the look of it. The bulk of the land is still hull-down. It bears sou'west-by-west."

"Hmm! A likely place for seals, I should think. You can alter the course to steer for it."

When Webber had given the necessary orders, the captain addressed him once more. "A discovery, sure as I'm a Yankee! There's nothing charted hereabouts save Pitcairn's Island, and Carteret laid that down a good hundred and fifty miles to the west."

The *Topaz* approached the land slowly, for the wind was dying to the lightest of light airs. At sundown the land was still far distant; it was not until past midnight that the ship was put about to stand off and on. Shortly after daybreak the land bore south — a small island, high and wooded to the water's edge, with a heavy surf breaking all along shore.

Captain Folger came on deck in the grey of dawn. As he was focusing his leveled telescope, the mate, standing at his side, gave an exclamation of astonishment.

"Smoke, sir! Yonder, above the bluffs!"

The captain peered through his glass for a moment before he replied. "Aye, so it is. The place is inhabited, without a doubt. I can see the smoke of four different fires." He sighed as he lowered his glass. "Well, there go our hopes of seals — and half our water casks empty. They'll be Indians, of course, apt to be hostile in this sea."

"Inhabited or not," remarked the mate, "no boat could land on this side. She would be dashed to pieces."

"And all hands drowned," Folger added, once more peering through his glass. "There's not a sign of a beach, and the coast is studded with rocks, offshore. . . . Bless me! Here's some of 'em now! Three, in a canoe!"

Webber's unassisted eye soon made out the tiny craft, appearing and disappearing as it approached over the long swell. The ship was allowed to lose what little headway she had, and within a quarter of an hour the canoe was close by — a long, sharp, narrow craft, with an outrigger on the larboard side. Her crew backed water at a distance of about thirty yards from the *Topaz,* and sat, paddle in hand, as though prepared to flee back to the land as swiftly as they had come. They regarded the ship with looks of wonder and awe, not unmingled with apprehension. In spite of repeated hails to come on board, they neither spoke nor came closer for some time. The mate gazed at these strange visitors with the keenest interest, observing that they were lads, the eldest no more than eighteen or nineteen. If Indians, they were, certainly, lighter in complexion than any he had seen. Their faces were bronzed by a life in the open air, but scarcely darker than those of white seafaring men. The stern paddler, who wore a straw hat of a curious shape, ornamented with feathers, seemed somewhat reassured by his scrutiny.

"You are an English ship?" he called, in a strong, manly voice.

"What in tarnation!" Folger exclaimed under his breath. And then: "No. This is an American vessel."

The three youths looked at one another and spoke together briefly in low voices.

"Who are you?" Folger called.

"We are Englishmen."

"Where were you born?"

"On the island yonder."

"How can you be English?" asked the captain.

"Because our father is an Englishman," came the quiet reply.

"Who is your father?"

"Alex."

"Who is Alex?"

"Don't you know Alex?"

"Know him? God bless me! How should I know him?"

The lad in the canoe regarded the captain earnestly, then turned to his companions again for another low colloquy in an unintelligible dialect. At length he said, "Our father would make you welcome on shore, sir."

"Come aboard first, my lads. You've nothing to fear from us," Folger replied in a kindly voice.

The steersman glanced at his companions, and, after a moment of hesitation, they dashed their paddles into the water and drew alongside. A line was dropped to them and made fast, and the three young islanders swarmed on deck with rare agility. The captain stepped forward to greet them, a smile on his kindly, weather-beaten face.

"I am Captain Folger," he said, extending his hand to the tallest lad, "and this is Mr. Webber, the mate."

"My name is Thursday October, sir. This is my brother, Charles, and this is James."

The spokesman, for all his youthful appearance, was a full six feet in height, and magnificently proportioned, with a handsome, manly countenance and a ready smile. All were barefoot, bare-chested, and bare-legged, and dressed in kilts of some strange cloth which reached to their knees. Their manner was easy and they showed no further signs of timidity, though they stared about them in round-eyed wonder at what they saw.

"What a huge, great ship, sir!" remarked Thursday October in a voice of awe. "We've heard of them from our father, but have never seen one before."

The people of the *Topaz* were crowded as far aft as convention allowed, regarding their visitors with glances as interested as those the three lads bestowed on the ship.

"You shall be shown over her, presently," said the captain, "but I want to ask you about your island, first. Is there a landing place on the other side?"

"Only one, and that dangerous. We land and embark in the cove yonder."

Folger glanced toward the land and shook his head. "Our boats could never risk it. You have plenty of fresh water here?"

"Yes, sir."

The captain pointed to the scuttle-butt, outside the galley door. "We've a score of casks like that one. Could they be landed in your bay?"

"That would be easy, sir," Thursday October replied, quickly. "If you would tow them to the edge of the breakers, we could swim them in, one by one."

"And you could fill them, once on shore?"

"Yes, sir; though we would have to fetch the water down in calabashes."

"How long would it take?"

"Brown's Well is the nearest water." The lad thought for a moment, measuring with his eye the cask by the galley. "With all of us at work, I'll warrant we could do it in two or three days."

"And you'd be willing to lend us a hand?"

The lad's face lighted up. "To be sure we would, sir! There's a plenty of us ashore to help."

"Good! Never mind the work, young man. You shall be well rewarded. Now the boatswain will show you over the ship, above decks and below. Keep your eyes open and choose what will be most useful to you. Within reason, it shall be yours for filling my casks."

As the three lads followed the boatswain forward, Captain Folger turned to the mate. "The weather has a settled look, Mr. Webber; yet I don't feel free to leave the ship. Will you go ashore and see that no time is wasted in filling the casks?" Webber's expression of pleasure was so transparent that Folger went on without waiting for a reply. "I envy you! Who can they be? There's a mystery here; you must solve it."

"I'm to go in the canoe, sir?"

"Yes, and you'd best stay ashore until the work's done. We'll tow the casks in with the longboat. Tell Mr. Alex, or whoever he is, that we'll be off the cove, ready to work, by noon."

When the young islanders had finished their tour of the ship, they proved reluctant to make known their wants. Being urged, they at length informed the captain that a couple of knives, an axe, and a copper kettle would be more than ample compensation for watering the ship. Folger, who had taken a great fancy to the lads, gave them the kettle at once, and then forced upon them half a dozen each of large clasp knives and axes.

"And what style of man is Mr. Alex?" he asked, as they were handing down their things into the canoe. "Is he tall or short?"

"Like yourself, sir," Thursday October replied. "Short and strong-made."

Folger went below and returned with a new suit of stout blue broadcloth on his arm.

"Take this to Mr. Alex with my compliments."

Thursday October's eyes lit up with pleasure. "God will reward you for your kindness, Captain! We have no such warm clothes as these. Our father is no longer young and often feels the cold in the wintertime."

The three then shook hands warmly with Folger and the boatswain, waved to the others, and sprang down into the canoe, followed by the mate. A moment later they had cast off and were paddling swiftly toward the cove, now about three miles distant.

Webber was seated amidships, and as they drew near to the land he forgot his curiosity in admiration of the sixteen-year-old lad who sat on the forward thwart. Never, he thought, as he watched the play of muscles on the paddler's back and shoulders, had he seen a nobler-looking boy. His countenance, when he turned his head, had the open, fearless look of a young Englishman, yet there was something at once pleasing and un-English in his swarthy complexion, his black eyes, and the thick black hair falling in curls to his shoulders.

They were close in with the land now, to the east of the little cove, where a huge rock, rising high above the waves, stood sentinel off-shore. A bold and lofty promontory, falling away in precipices to the sea, gave the cove some shelter from the southeast winds; the swell, rising as it approached the land, rushed, feathering and thundering, into the caverns at the base of the cliffs, each wave sending sheets of spray to a great height. The cove itself was studded with jagged rocks, black and menacing against their setting of foam. It seemed incredible, at first glance, that even skilled surfmen could effect a landing at such a place. The cove was iron-bound, save at one spot where Webber now saw a tiny stretch of shingly beach, at the foot of a steep, wooded slope. A score or more of people were gathered there, staring at the approaching canoe. To reach the shingle, Webber perceived, the little craft would have to be steered with the greatest nicety, through a maze of rocks that threatened instant destruction. Yet the young paddlers seemed wholly unconcerned and approached with an air of complete confidence.

They halted briefly on the verge of the breaking seas, and then, at a word of command from Thursday October, all three dashed their paddles into the water at once. A great feathering sea lifted the canoe and bore her forward as swiftly as a flying fish on the wing. She turned, flashed between two boulders, and was swept high on to the little beach. Half a dozen sturdy lads rushed into the surf to hold her against the backwash; the paddlers sprang over the side to seize the gunwales, and with the next comber they carried her high up on the shingly sand.

The little crowd on the beach, Webber observed with some surprise, was made up of boys and girls who might range from ten to eighteen years of age. Not a grown man or woman awaited the canoe. Where were the parents of all these youngsters? Thursday October had said that they had never before seen a ship. It seemed remarkable indeed to the mate of the *Topaz,* if Alex, the father, were truly an English-man, so long cut off from humankind, that he and the other adults should show so little interest in visitors from the outside world.

The young people seemed shy, almost apprehensive. None stepped forward to greet the stranger; they seemed rather to shrink from him, whispering together in little groups and regarding him with bright eyes which expressed curiosity and wonder. The boys, like the three who had come out to the vessel, all wore kilts of figured cloth; the girls were neatly clad in the same materials, and most of them wore chaplets of sweet-scented flowers. Some of the girls would have attracted attention anywhere, though their beauty was more of the Spanish than of the English kind. When they whispered together, they spoke in some jargon unknown to the visitor.

The three paddlers now returned from a long thatched shed, well above high-water mark, where they had carried their canoe. The youngest, known as James, carried the suit of clothes, and now the boys and girls clustered around him, feeling of the cloth and exclaiming softly in wonder and admiration. Thursday October touched Webber's arm.

"Come this way, sir," he said.

The land rose steeply from the beach to the sloping plateau above, in a wooded bluff perhaps two hundred feet in height. A zigzag path led to the summit, and the lads and lasses were already trooping upward and were soon lost to view. Webber followed his guide, envying the agility of the lad, who strode along freely and without a halt, while he himself panted with his exertions and was obliged from time to time to cling to the roots of trees, bushes, or tufts of grass. At length they reached the summit, where the mate halted to regain his breath. The young islander then led the way along a well-footed path that followed the seaward bluffs, winding this way and that among great trees whose deep shade felt deliciously cool. After crossing two small valleys, or ravines, they reached a kind of village, consisting of five houses scattered far apart along a stretch of partially cleared land which sloped gently toward the sea.

The houses were of two stories and thatched with leaves of the pandanus. They looked old and weather-beaten, but were strongly timbered, and three of them were planked with oak which Webber recognized as the strakes of a shipwrecked vessel. As they passed the first house he saw a dark, gypsy-looking woman peering out at him, and, at another open window-place, a second, somewhat younger, with a handsome face and thick rippling hair of a copper-red color the Englishman had never seen before. He caught glimpses of several other women at the farther dwellings, but they were no more than glimpses. Faces vanished from view the moment he looked toward them.

Presently they came to an ancient banyan tree on the seaward side of the path. Its huge limbs, from which innumerable aerial roots depended, like hawsers anchoring the tree still more firmly to the earth, seemed to cover half an acre or more. Directly opposite, on the inland side of the path at a distance of about thirty yards, stood a dwelling, delightfully pleasant and neat like all of the others, with a green-sward dappled with sunlight and shadow and bordered with flowers and flowering shrubs.

A man of about fifty stood in the doorway. He was short and powerfully built, clad in the same strange cloth the others wore, but neatly cut and sewed into the form of frock and trousers, after the fashion of the old-time British tar. His grey hair fell upon his shoulders, and his features and the glance of his eye expressed strength tempered with benevolence.

"Welcome, sir," he said, stepping forward and extending his hand.

"My name is Webber. I am mate of the ship yonder."

With a word of apology to the visitor, Thursday October now stepped forward and spoke rapidly and briefly to the old man, in the same curious jargon the mate had heard on the beach — a language in which certain words of English were discernible, but whose sense was unintelligible to him. Presently the old man dismissed the lad with a nod and ushered the Englishman into the house.

"Dinah!" he called. "Rachel! Where are ye, lasses?"

Two little girls not yet in their teens appeared at the door, regarding the stranger with bright-eyed timidity.

"Fetch some coconuts for the gentleman," their father went on, "and what fruit ye can find."

The children dashed away without replying, while their father brought forward a chair. "Sit ye down, sir, and rest, and taste of what our island affords. Ye've been long at sea, I take it?"

"Three months and more," the mate replied. "Little we thought there was land anywhere hereabout. What is the name of your island?"

"It's Pitcairn's Island, sir. No doubt ye've been misled by the chart. Captain Carteret laid it down a hundred and fifty miles west of its true position."

"But he called it uninhabited."

"Aye, so it was in his day. . . . Ye need water, the lad says. We've plenty here, but it'll be a three-day task at best to get it down to the beach. Can ye bide the time?"

"We've no choice. Scarcely a spit of rain have we had since we left the coast of Peru. Most of our casks are empty."

"And what might your errand be in these parts?"

"We're a sealing ship," Webber replied. "We were bound to the westward when we raised your island. Are there seals hereabout? In that case we'd like well to fish here, if you've no objection."

The islander shook his head. "Ye'd have no luck, Mr. Webber. I've seen a few of the animals on the rocks at rare times. The last was all of ten years back."

The old man fell silent, elbows on the rude table and chin in his hands. Webber had a slightly uncomfortable feeling that he was being studied and appraised. His curiosity concerning the inhabitants of this seagirt rock was so intense that once or twice he drew breath to put the direct question, but he thought better of it each time. His host was, plainly, a man of intelligence, who would realize how strange this little community must appear to a man from the outside world. If he had reasons for keeping silent, they should be respected. If willing to satisfy a stranger's curiosity, he would do so in his own good time.

"Ye're an Englishman, I take it?" said the islander at last.

"Yes. But the ship is American. She hails from Boston, in New England."

The old man gave him a keen glance. "Say ye so!" he replied. "Then there's still peace between us and the Colonies?"

"Aye, and a brisk trade, too."

The old man sighed and paused for a moment before he spoke. "Close on to twenty years I've been here, Mr. Webber. Ye're the first man to set foot on shore in all that time."

Webber looked up in astonishment. "Twenty years!" he exclaimed. "Then you've heard nothing of what's happened in the world — of the revolution in France; of old Boney, of Trafalgar, and all the rest!"

The children now returned, bringing drinking nuts and a dozen great yellow plantains in a wooden bowl, together with other fruits which were strange to the mate. He partook of them with the relish of a sailor long at sea, and, while he ate, narrated briefly the events of the stormy years at the end of the eighteenth century and the beginning of the nineteenth. The old man displayed little interest in political happenings and battles on land, but the account of England's naval victories brought a flush to his cheek and a sparkle to his eye. Yet all the while he seemed to labour under a baffling and unnatural reserve, maintaining a silence concerning himself out of keeping with a countenance as frank and open as that of John Bull himself.

The sun was high when Thursday October returned to escort the visitor down to the beach. "I'd take it kindly, sir," said the old man as he rose to his feet, "if ye'd stop with me whilst the watering is done. Or will your captain come ashore?"

"He'll want to stretch his legs before we leave," the mate replied, "but he will remain on board till the work is finished. I shan't put you out if I accept?"

The islander laid a hand on his arm. "Put me out, Mr. Webber? God bless ye, sir, never in the least! Ye'll be welcomed, and hearty, by one and all — that I promise ye!"

The longboat was towing the first of the barrels into the cove when the mate arrived at the beach. All the young people engaged in the task of swimming them in through the surf, shouting and sporting in the breakers, where they seemed as much at home as on land. Webber had never seen such swimmers; they appeared and disappeared in the swirling white water among the rocks, guiding the great, clumsy casks to the landing place, where they were beached without the slightest mishap. Soon all the first lot were ashore and rolled to a piece of level land that had been dug out of the hillside, while the longboat pulled back to the ship, now two miles distant.

Toward the close of the afternoon, Webber went for a ramble about the plateau, with some of the younger children as his guides. They led him first to a rock cistern in the depths of the valley and retired while he refreshed himself with a bath. No man could have asked for merrier companions, once their shyness had worn off. They brought him fruits and flowers, and spoke freely, even eagerly, of the trees and plants of the island, of the wild swine, the goats and fowls; but, for all their childlike faith and trust in him, Webber was aware of the same reserve so noticeable in the man they called father. They seemed to be partakers in a conspiracy of silence concerning their history; and it was silence the guest respected, however much his curiosity was aroused.

Toward sunset he returned to the house where he had been bidden to sup and spend the night. He found his host seated on a bench outside the door with half a dozen of the smaller children seated on the grass around him. He was giving them an exercise in dictation, and the mate observed that he read from the Bible — a copy so worn and well thumbed that it was falling to pieces. He read slowly, a phrase at a time, while the children, with lips pursed and chubby fingers clasped round their pencils, — the blunt spines of a kind of sea-urchin, — set down the words as he pronounced them. For slates they used thin slabs of rock ground smooth on both sides.

"Avast!" said the old man as he perceived his guest. "That'll do for to-day, children. Rachel, run and tell Mother we're ready to sup. Come in, Mr. Webber. Ye've an appetite, I hope? I must tell ye, sir, ye've filled my old head so full of republics, and battles, and what not, I've been woolgathering all the afternoon!"

As they were about to seat themselves at the table, a woman of forty or forty-five came in through the back door, bearing a large platter containing baked pig and heaped up with sweet potatoes, yams, and plantains, all smoking hot. She had a pleasant homely face and the mate perceived at once that she was not of white blood.

"This is Balhadi, Mr. Webber, the mother of the little girls yonder." The mate stepped forward to greet her, and as he did so, his host spoke to her in the curious speech the islanders used among themselves. As soon as he had finished, she stepped forward and took the stranger's hand in both of hers, caressing it as a mother might do, her eyes glistening with tears as she peered up at him; then she turned and withdrew.

The two men seated themselves, and when the old man had heaped their plates he bowed his head, and, quietly and reverently, asked God's blessing on the food of which they were about to partake. Webber was a religious man in the fine sense of the word; cant and snuffling were hateful to him, and he felt his heart touched and uplifted by the simplicity and the deep sincerity of the brief prayer.

Twilight was fading to dusk by the time they had finished the meal. While they were still at the table the mate had observed, through the open doorway, small groups of people turning in at the gateway and gathering on the grassplot before the dwelling. His host now led the way outside and for a few moments they remained seated on the bench by the door, looking on in silence at the scene before them. All the inhabitants of the island seemed to have assembled there. They sat in groups on the grass, speaking in soft voices among themselves. They were clothed in fresh garments and the younger women wore newly made wreaths of fern and flowers pressed lightly down over their loose dark hair. The visitor gazed about him with the keenest interest, thinking that he had never seen a group of healthier, happier-looking children. Counting them idly, he found that the young people numbered four-and-twenty, and seated among them were eight or nine women of middle age, the mothers, evidently, of this little flock. It was clear that they were all of Indian blood. But where were the fathers? With the exception of his host and himself, not a man of mature age was present.

Presently the old man rose to his feet, and at a sign from him the older women came forward to greet the visitor. The first to take his hand was a tall and slender woman of forty; the Englishman thought he had never seen a face at once so sad and so maturely beautiful.

"Mr. Webber," said his host, "let me make ye known to Maimiti, Thursday October's mother."

She greeted him in a soft, low voice, making him welcome in a few words of English spoken with a strange accent, very pleasant to hear. Following her came a woman of commanding presence, a head taller than the mate himself, whom his host introduced as Moetua. In her fine carriage, the poise of her head, most of all in the proud spirit that looked out of the dark eyes, Webber was reminded of some mother of the heroic stage, or of some queen of the Amazons capable of performing deeds worthy to be handed down in the legends of primitive races.

Next came four women with English names, — Mary, Susannah, Jenny, and Prudence, — although they were evidently of the same race as the others. It was Prudence whose handsome face and copper-red hair he had admired at the window of the house he had passed on the way from the cove. These were followed by three more with strange Indian names which he found it impossible to keep in mind. Some greeted him in silence, merely shaking his hand; others spoke to him in the English tongue, though in a manner which revealed that they were little accustomed to the common use of it; but, whether silent or not, all made him feel, by the simple sincerity and kindliness of their manner, that he was indeed a welcome guest.

Meanwhile, some of the younger people had brought a small table and two chairs from the house which they placed on the greensward, and a moment later Dinah appeared carrying her father's Bible, and Rachel with a kind of taper made of a dozen or more oily nuts threaded like beads on the midrib of a coconut leaflet which was stuck upright in a bowl of sand. The topmost nut was burning brightly, with hissings and sputterings, while a slender column of smoke rose from it, ascending vertically in the still air. The little company now seated themselves on the grass before the table, and the murmuring of voices ceased. The old man turned to his guest.

"This is the hour for our evening worship, sir," he said. "We should be pleased to have ye join with us."

A chair was placed for the visitor at one side of the group, whereupon his host seated himself at the table and opened his silver-clasped Bible, holding the volume close to the flickering light. He turned the pages slowly with his large, rough fingers. Presently, clearing his throat, he began to read.

"I say then, Hath God cast away his people? God forbid."

Webber felt himself carried back to his boyhood, twenty years before. His grandfather, a white-bearded yeoman farmer, had read a chapter from the Bible each evening, in just such a quiet, earnest voice, after the same admonitory clearing of the throat; but how different a scene was this to the one he so well remembered in the north-country farmhouse of his childhood! The old man read on, his finger slowly following the lines, while the members of his little congregation listened with an air of the deepest interest and respect. When the lesson was at an end, all knelt and repeated the Lord's Prayer in unison, and as the guest listened to the voices of youths and maidens mingling with the clear, childish accents of the little children, he felt that here indeed was worship in purity of heart, in simple unquestioning trust in God's loving-kindness toward His children. It was as though all felt His presence there among them.

The service over, old and young came forward to bid the stranger good-night before dispersing to their various homes. When the last of them had gone, it seemed to Webber that his host looked at him with even more kindness and with less reserve than hitherto.

"It's plain that ye've a great love of children, Mr. Webber," he said. "Ye've some of your own, I take it?"

"That I have; three of them, the oldest about the age of the lad I had on my knee a moment ago. Whose child is he?"

"My own, though he's living with his foster mother just now. . . . It's over early for bed, sir. Would ye relish a bit of a walk? I've a bench not far off, overlooking the sea. It's a pretty spot and the moon will be up directly."

He led the way along the path toward the cove, but turned off in a moment on another leading through the groves to a rustic seat placed at the very brink of the cliff which fell steeply to the sea.

"Many's the time I come here of an evening, Mr. Webber," he explained, as they seated themselves. "Ye may think me fanciful, but there's times when the breakers seem the very voice of God — comforting at a time like this, wrathful on a night of storm. . . . Look! Yon she comes!"

The moon, a little past the full, was rising above the lonely horizon, flashing along the white crests of the breakers far below and glinting along the motionless fronds of the coconut palms.

The islander turned to his guest, hesitated, and said at last: "No doubt ye've wondered at my not naming myself. Smith's my name — Alexander Smith."

He watched his companion's face closely, as though to divine what effect the mention of the name might produce. As there seemed nothing to say, Webber remained silent.

"And ye must have wondered about other things," the old fellow went on, after a long pause. "Who we are, set down on this bit of land so far from any other."

The mate smiled. "I should have been more or less than human had my curiosity not been aroused."

His companion sat leaning forward, elbows on his knees, his hands clasped loosely, as he gazed out over the moonlit sea.

"Ye're an honest man, that's sure," he said, at length, "and a kind-hearted man. . . . I'd never believe ye could wish harm to me and mine?"

"Harm you? God forbid!" the mate replied, earnestly. "Set your mind at rest there, my friend. I would as soon harm my own little family as this flock of yours."

"What happened, Mr. Webber, was long ago — more than twenty years back. . . ." Of a sudden he turned his head. "Did ye ever hear of a ship called the *Bounty?*"

The words came to Webber like a thunderclap — like a blaze of lightning where deep darkness had reigned a moment before. In common with most seamen of his day, he had heard of the notorious mutiny on board the small armed transport sent out from England to fetch breadfruit plants from the island of Tahiti to the West Indies. He remembered clearly the principal events in that affair. The fate of the *Bounty* and those who had been aboard her constituted one of the mysteries of the sea.

The mate turned to his companion and said, with emotion in his voice, "Then you're . . ."

"Aye," Smith interrupted quietly, "one of Fletcher Christian's men, Mr. Webber. It was here we came."

A hundred questions crowded into Webber's mind, but his companion was now more eager still.

"What can ye tell me of Captain Bligh?" he asked, anxiously. "Was he ever heard of again?"

"Indeed he was! He got home, at last, with most of his men, after the greatest open-boat voyage in the history of the sea."

Smith brought his hand down resoundingly on his knee. "Thank God for that!" he exclaimed, reverently. "You've done me a great service, sir. Now I'll sleep better of a night. And the men we left on Tahiti? What became of them?"

"I've read a book or two on the subject," Webber replied; "and the tale is well known. A ship-of-war was sent out to search for the *Bounty*. Let me see . . . *Pandora*, I think she was called. They found a dozen or fifteen of the *Bounty's* company on Tahiti. The *Pandora* seized them and they were being taken home in irons when the vessel was wrecked off the coast of New Holland. A number of her company and several of the prisoners were lost, and the rest of her people were forced to take to the boats. They reached England nearly a year later, as I remember it, when the prisoners were tried by court-martial. Three or four, I believe, were hung."

Smith had been listening with an air of almost painful eagerness. "Ye don't recollect the names of the lads was hung?" he asked.

Webber shook his head, as he was forced to do when his companion asked after numerous men by name.

"I'm sorry; I can tell you the fate of none of them," he replied. "Of the *Bounty's* company I remember only Captain Bligh, and Christian, the officer said to have led the mutiny."

"It was Mr. Christian's son, Thursday October, that brought ye ashore."

"And where is Christian, and the others who came with you? As I remember it, there were a dozen or more in all."

"Nine," said Smith. "That is, nine of us white men. Besides, there was six Indian men and twelve women that came with us from Tahiti. The women ye met this evening are the mothers of these lads and lasses."

"But where are the fathers?"

"There's none left, save me."

"You mean they've gone elsewhere?"

Smith shook his head. "No. They're dead, sir."

The mate waited for him to proceed. The old fellow sat staring before him. At length he said: "Are ye a patient man, Mr. Webber? Could ye listen to a story 'twould take me a couple of evenings to tell?"

"An account, you mean, of what has happened here?"

"Aye."

"I should like nothing better! Why, man, there are scores in England would travel a hundred leagues to hear the tale from your lips! Have no fear! You'll find me a patient listener, I promise you!"

"I've no wish to tell it, God knows," Smith continued, earnestly. "And yet, if so be as I could . . . it would ease my heart more than I could well say. I've little learning — that ye can see for yourself; but I've forgot nothing that's happened here. Ye shall have the truth, Mr. Webber. I'll keep nothing back, but I'll ask ye to bear in mind that the Alex Smith who speaks is not the Smith of the *Bounty* days.

"Well, sir, to begin at the beginning . . ."

As he listened, the mate of the *Topaz* was lost to the present moment. He felt himself carried, in an all but physical sense, into the past. In place of Alexander Smith — stout, middle-aged, and fatherly — he saw a rough young seaman in the midst of as strange a company as ever sailed an English ship. He was conscious of the heave of the *Bounty's* deck beneath his feet, of the hot suns, the wind and weather of bygone days. He found himself looking on at old unhappy scenes, sharing the emotions and hearing the voices of men long since dead — voices that had broken the silence of this lonely sea and still lonelier island, nearly twenty years before.

## CHAPTER XVI

WHERE was I, sir? (Smith proceeded, on the following evening). Aye, if ye recollect, Mr. Christian and me was lying wounded in the house. Save for what I learned afterwards, I can tell ye nothing of the time that followed. Ye can fancy the state the women was in. Moetua and Nanai went off into the bush by themselves after they'd fetched Mr.

Christian. Jenny and Taurua stopped with Mrs. Christian, who kept asking for her husband and wondering why he didn't come back. Ye'll recollect that she'd been brought to bed of a daughter on the morning the killing began.

Hutia stopped with Balhadi to care for us. Mr. Christian had lost so much blood, he lay quiet as a dead man. I'd a high fever; for three days without a let-up, they told me, I babbled, and cursed and raved. The rest of the women, with McCoy's children and little Matt Quintal and Eliza Mills, gathered in one house. They was that dazed and listless they might have starved, I reckon, if they'd not had the little 'uns to think on. They sat huddled on the floor the day long, with scarce a word exchanged, some of 'em crying softly with heads covered, as Indians do. The days was bad enough; it was the nights they dreaded most. They've strange notions, not like ours. They reckon that the spirits of the new dead, no matter if dear friends or husbands in life, are fierce, ravening things, hating the living. Of a night, the women in Mills's house would bar every door and window, and huddle with the children by their candlenut torch, quaking at every little sound outside.

Quintal stopped alone at his place, sitting on the doorstep most of the time, with his chin in his hands, and he'd speak to no one. I've no notion what was going on in his mind. It may be he felt the loss of Mills and Jack Williams, or was thinkin' of the fix Mr. Christian was in, and how he'd brought the trouble on by burning Minarii's house.

The killing started at dawn, as ye know. September twenty-second, it was, 1793, a date I'll not forget. The last of the Indians was killed on the night of the twenty-third. Next morning, when Moetua and Nanai was gone, Taurua came across from Mr. Christian's house to speak to my old woman. She told her Mrs. Christian was in such a state it was all they could do to keep her in bed. It was agreed by all she'd have to be told.

Mr. Young said, long afterwards, he'd as soon face the hangman as live through that morning again. They tried to soften the news to Mrs. Christian, but she guessed what they held back.

Up she got, in her kirtle, threw a mantle over her shoulders, took up her newborn babe, and went out the door without a word. When they reached our house, she went straight to the bed-place, motioning Hutia away.

Mr. Christian's eyes was closed and his fever was high. Hutia took the child, and his wife settled herself at the head of the bed-place to keep the cloths on his forehead wrung out cool and fresh. Ye know what a shock the like of that will do to a woman. Mrs. Christian's milk had begun to flow strong and good that morning; by nightfall her breasts was dried up. When the baby cried, Balhadi fed it on what the Indians call *ouo,* the sweet jelly they scrape out of young coconuts. Aye, and she throve on it; for the next year she'd naught else.

All that night, through the next day and the night following, Mr. Christian and I lay there, tended by the women and Mr. Young. He'd told Mrs. Christian what had happened; after that she scarce spoke a word. It must have been the morning of the third day when the fever left me and I opened my eyes.

Here I was in my own house, weak as a cat and bad wounded. My left shoulder and my neck was all stiff and sore. When I tried to move, it pained me cruel. My head was light from the fever and it was a good bit afore I could set my thoughts in order. It came back slow — how Jenny'd come to my taro patch, how I'd climbed the Goat-House, hoping to meet up with Mr. Young, and hid myself alongside the path in the Main Valley, on the chance of cutting down one of the Indians and getting his musket. Towards sunset I'd crept down to Mr. Young's plantain walk, for I'd had naught to eat all day. Then I recollected Te Moa, and Nihau, with Mills's head at his belt, stepping out sudden as I was reaching up for some ripe fruit, and the shot that knocked me down; how I'd scrambled up and made a run for it; then something to do with Jenny, and no more. Three was killed, she'd told me at the taro patch. That was all I knew.

My bed-place was on the north side of the room, by an open window. It was a calm, sunny morning, with scarce enough breeze to move the tree-tops. Here and there, where the screen of bush was thin, the sea showed blue through the trees. Beautiful, it was, and peaceful; ye'd never have thought men could plot murder in such a place. I set my teeth and turned my head the other way.

I saw someone on the other bed, across the room, but couldn't make out who it was. Mrs. Christian sat on the floor beside him with her back to me, and I could see neither her face nor his. He never moved, and I took a notion he was dead. Taurua and my old woman was feeding a tiny baby on a mat, and Mr. Young stood near by. I called out to him.

Balhadi sprang up, baby and all; and Mr. Young came across to me. "Hush, Alex!" said he. "Thank God ye're better, now the fever's down!" My old woman tried to smile at me, and nodded with a hand on my head.

"Who's that yonder?" said I.

"Mr. Christian."

"Is he living?"

"Aye."

Mrs. Christian came over and spoke to me kindly.

When she'd gone back to sit by Mr. Christian, I had a glimpse of his face. One look was enough. There's no mistaking a dying man. Mr. Young signed to Balhadi to take the baby away, and sat on a stool close by.

"Ned," I whispered, "tell me what's happened, else ye'll have me in a fever again."

When he had, I lay there thinking on it and wondering what the outcome'd be. It was a black business. Ye won't wonder I felt bitter toward Quintal and McCoy. They'd done more'n anyone else to bring on trouble with the Indians, and come through scot-free. God meant this island to be a little Garden of Eden, and we'd made a hell of it. Mr. Christian had done all a man could. Now he lay dying for his pains. Knowing him as I did, I reckoned he'd be glad to go. We'd had our chance, and we'd failed. Why? It wasn't the Indians' fault; they'd had cause enough for what they'd done. I thought of Tetahiti, who'd been my friend; and of Minarii — both high chiefs on their own islands. Because their skins wasn't white, McCoy and Quintal and Martin and Mills reckoned they wasn't fit to own land. I went back to the beginning, to the day we landed here, trying to make out how we'd got on the wrong course. No, it was no fault of the Indians. All the men asked was to be treated like men; they'd have been our best friends had we met 'em halfway. As for the girls, ye'd travel far to find a better lot. Real helpmates, they was, ready to take their share in all that was going. And none o' your sour, scolding kind. *We* was to blame, and no one else. In the first place, we should have seen to it, afore ever we left Tahiti, that each man had his girl, with some to spare. That might have kept Williams out o' mischief. *Might,* I say, for ye could never tell with a man like Jack. He and his precious Hutia was the start o' the trouble. But it was bound to come, girls or no girls. There was them amongst us reckoned the Indians was made to be used like dogs. That's the first and last of it, sir, in few words.

I slept most of the morning. I felt a deal better when I woke up again, and grateful just to be alive. Maimiti was still at the foot of Mr. Christian's bed, watching him with a look on her face would have melted a heart of stone. All at once I saw her eyes light up; she came quickly and softly to the head of the bed and knelt down beside him, taking his hand. The fever had left him and he was conscious.

He looked at her in a puzzled way at first. "What's this, Maimiti?" said he. "Where are we?"

"In Ned's house."

She fetched him some water, and I could see by the look in her eyes that hope was springing up in her. He drank a little and said no more for a bit; then he asked, "Is Ned here?"

Mr. Young was at the door. He came in and stood at the foot of the bed. He didn't trust himself to speak.

"What is it, Ned? What has happened?"

"Don't worry or try to talk just now," said Mr. Young.

"Where is Minarii?"

"He is dead."

"And the other Indian men?"

"All dead."

Mr. Christian turned his head slow on the pillow and saw me. "Are ye hurt, Smith?"

"Aye, sir, but not bad," said I.

His voice was stronger when he spoke next.

"Ye must tell me the whole of it, Ned. I want to know."

There was no getting out of it. Mr. Young told him, quick and short. However he felt, he gave no sign; just lay there, a-starin' up at the ceiling; then his eyes closed, and Mr. Young tiptoed out o' the room.

Mrs. Christian never moved from her place at the foot of the bed, where she could watch his face. She was blind to what I could see. Trust a good woman to hope. It was afternoon when he came round again and drank a little of the water she offered him. Then a long time passed without a word said. It was well on toward eight bells when young Thursday October came to the door. He was three at the time, and ye never saw a handsomer little lad. He'd a finger in his mouth as he stood in the doorway, looking into the room with his round eyes. At last he came in on tiptoe, half afraid, even after he'd made his father out. Mr. Christian turned his head and saw the little fellow. Desolate, his face was; such a look as I hope never to see another man wear.

"Take the child out," said he.

His wife took up the lad and set him down outside the door. She was gone for a minute or two; I think it took her that long to get herself in hand.

The afternoon wore through. Balhadi fed me a bit of sweet coconut water now and again. I could look out the window, as I told ye. A fine breeze had made up; the trees was swaying, and there was white-caps out at sea. All the womenfolk was gathered outside, waiting. Mr. Christian was conscious this while, but he spoke no more than a word or two. He knew he was dying, most like, and felt glad to go. All he'd touched was ruined, he'd be thinking: the *Bounty's* voyage, the men set adrift with Captain Bligh in the launch, those who'd stopped on Tahiti, and now our little settlement, where he'd hoped for so much. Aye . . . I'll warrant there was never a man waited his end with greyer thoughts than Mr. Christian. My heart bled for him.

The breeze died away after sundown, as it often does here. I don't recollect a stiller, more beautiful evening. It was spring in these parts, as ye'll remember, and the twilight came on slow. Mrs. Christian gave her husband a sip of water, set down the cup, and stopped where she was, seated on the bed beside him. He put a hand on hers and looked up with a faint smile. Then he turned his head, slow.

"Alex," he said.

"Sir?"

When he spoke again it took me by surprise, and I'm not certain of the words to this day. He said, "There's a chance, now," or "There's still a chance" — one or the other.

He seemed to expect no reply, so I made none, but lay there trying to make out just what he meant. If he'd said, "There's a chance, now," the words was the bitterest ever spoke, for he must have meant that with him dead and out of the way there might be hope for us. I can scarce believe he spoke so, but it may have been.

After a long time I heard his voice again: "Never let the children know!" and those was the last words I heard him say.

I must have dozed off then, and when I opened my eyes it was dark in the room.

It was Mrs. Christian's low, hopeless cry that woke me. I couldn't see her, or Mr. Christian, but I knew the end had come.

## CHAPTER XVII

THE month that followed was a sorry time, with the silence of death over all. I was afeared, at first, that Mrs. Christian might lose her reason. She wasn't one to weep, and that stony kind of grief ain't natural in a woman. Tears would have helped but none came. It made my heart sore to see her going about the house with that dazed, dead look on her face, like as if the truth hadn't come home to her yet. And there was nothing ye could do to help. She had to fight it through alone. Sometimes a whole day'd pass without her speaking a word.

Aye, it was a numb, hopeless time for all, and I'll never forget how lonesome it seemed with so many gone. There was one, Martin, I'd have had no wish to see back. We was all of a mind about him: he was better dead; but the others, whites and Indians alike, was sore missed, and most of all, of course, Mr. Christian. We could see better, now, the man he'd been, and the deep need we had for him. There was no one could take his place. We was like sheep without a shepherd.

Mr. Young was the hardest hit of any of the men, I reckon; ye'd scarce believe the change that came over him. He'd sit on the bluffs for hours at a time, lookin' out over the sea, or wander about the settlement like a man walkin' in his sleep. There'd been no one fonder of a joke in the old days, but after Mr. Christian's death I never again heard him laugh. My bein' hurt and needin' a bit of care was a help to him. When Maimiti or Balhadi wasn't settin' by me, he was, and I'd try to get his mind on other things: plans for the future — how we'd divide ourselves up, now, amongst the houses, the new gardens we'd make, and the like. He'd try to show interest, but it was plain he had no heart for anything.

But Mrs. Christian wouldn't give in, and having the children to see to and the other women to comfort was a godsend to her. Little by little she became more like her old self, and she'd hearten the others with her quiet ways. I don't know what some would have done without Maimiti.

One day when she and Mr. Young was by me in the house, she spoke of Moetua and Nanai. Ye'll mind that they was the wives of Minarii and Tetahiti. They'd not been near the settlement since the day they brought Mr. Christian down, but lived by themselves in Jack Williams's old house on the other side of the island. Some believed they must have known their men meant to kill all the whites, and there might have been a war and a massacre amongst the womenfolk if it hadn't been for Maimiti and Taurua; they knew well enough that Moetua and Nanai had naught to do with it and was as innocent as themselves.

Well, Mrs. Christian asked Mr. Young to go across and coax 'em down, if he could. "Tell 'em to come for my sake, Ned," said she.

All the women liked Mr. Young; they'd do anything he said. Inside of an hour he was back, and they with him. He came in first and they stood at the door. Ye've seen Moetua, sir; ye can picture what she was in her young womanhood. I've seen thousands of Indian women, whilst on the *Bounty*, on islands scattered all over this ocean, but none to match Moetua for strength and beauty. She was like a young oak tree. I can't say better than that she was a fit wife for Minarii. It'd done my heart good just to see them two going about together.

It wasn't fear of Prudence and Hutia or all the womenfolk together that kept her away from the settlement at this time. She'd have been more than a match for the lot of 'em. But she knew Quintal had killed her husband, and she was afeared she might take her revenge on him. She'd not his great brute strength, but, with the fire of hate in her heart, I'll not say she couldn't have mastered him and put him to death.

Nanai had a softer nature. She was of the best Indian blood: ye could tell at a glance the difference there was between her and women the like o' Jenny or Hutia. She was gentle. She needed someone to cling to, and it was a blessing she had Moetua, after Tetahiti was killed. Half crazed as some o' the women was, after the killing, I reckon they might have found a way to murder Nanai if she hadn't been with Moetua.

As I've said, they stood at the door, waiting. The minute she saw 'em, Maimiti came across and took 'em by the hands and brought 'em in. "Moetua," said she, "what our men have done is done. It may be that your husband killed mine; now both lie dead. Nanai, Christian and Tetahiti were friends. We have been like sisters in the past. I have nothing but love in my heart for ye two. Will ye come here and live with me?"

I can tell ye what was said, but not how it was said. Never a woman lived with a more kind, gentle nature than Mrs. Christian. Moetua took her in her arms and held her close. She had a beautiful husky voice, near as deep as a man's. "Aye, that we will!" said she. Then the three of them wept together, with their arms round each other. Glad I was to see that meeting. It was the first time Mrs. Christian had shed tears.

As soon as I was able to walk, she asked me if I'd let her have my house and move over to hers. I knew how it was with her: she'd a terror of setting foot in the house where she and Mr. Christian had lived. So we moved down there — my old woman, and Hutia, and Prudence, who was to live with us. Mr. Young took Mills's house, with Taurua and Jenny. Quintal and McCoy stopped where they always had, with their own two girls and Susannah.

My wound healed slow. I was able to walk by the end of October. But it was close to Christmas before I had any use of my left arm. I was good for little this while and had to stop indoors. It was a quiet time, but desperate lonesome, as I've said. Quintal and McCoy kept clear o' me, and I was glad they did, for my heart was bitter towards both. I knew we'd mostly them to thank for bringin' trouble to a head with the Indians. I wouldn't have cared if I'd never set eyes on either of 'em again.

Ye'd have said, sir, that God had give us that time to mind us of the past and the mistakes we'd made, and to make sure of our ways for the days to come; but some of us was too ignorant to profit by it, and the rest too weak or stubborn. I'm speakin' of the men. What followed was no fault o' the women. Them that went our ways did it because we led 'em or forced 'em to it.

I've spoke of McCoy's still. He had it going long afore the killing started, but he was that close about it not even his crony, Matt Quintal, knew what he was up to. There's no better way to show ye what a sly clever man Will McCoy could be. On this mite of an island, where there was so few of us, he'd been able to make spirits, enough for his own use, and none of us knew.

It wasn't till later I learned all that went on. McCoy had been shook bad by the days he was in the bush with the Indians after him.

A time or two they all but had him; they'd passed within a few feet of where he lay hid, and he'd seen Mills's bloody head, and Martin's, hangin' at their belts. Aye, he'd been near daft with fear, and, when all was over, the women who went in search of him couldn't coax him back to the settlement. He'd not even believe Mary, his own girl, and it wasn't till Quintal came and showed him the Indians' dead bodies that his mind was set at rest. Then off he went again, no one knew where.

Quintal was crazed himself, in a different way. There'd always been something a little queer about Matt; I'd noticed it in the old days on the *Bounty*. It wasn't often, but now and again something he'd say or do would show ye the man wasn't quite right in his head. The trouble got worse, after the killing. He'd set on his doorstep muttering to himself, the women said, and act so queer, most of the time, they was afeared of him. For all that, he began to work about his place again, chopping wood, doing a bit o' weedin' in the gardens, and the like. Then it came over him, of a sudden, that McCoy had quit the house. Slow and dogged, Quintal began to search for him, and found him at last in one of the gullies on the west side of the island. McCoy had made him a hut, close by his still, a dry, cozy little place with a soft bed of fern inside.

"So this is where ye hide out!" said Matt. "What's come over ye, Will, and what's all this gear ye've got?"

McCoy saw he'd have to tell, and he was glad, in a way, that Quintal'd found him. "Set ye down, Matt," said he. He pulled a bottle out of the fern, and a pewter half-pint he had by him.

"Taste that," said he, and he poured him out a big dollop of spirits.

Quintal took a sniff and then poured it down. "It ain't bad, not by a long way," said he; "but what is it? Where'd ye get it from?"

"I made it," said McCoy, "out o' ti roots."

Then he told Quintal how it was done. They got the *Bounty's* big copper kettle. The other McCoy had was too small to make spirits for more than one; with the big one they could brew any amount and set some of it aside to age. A new still was set up, and so new trouble started.

In the beginning they went at their drinking quiet-like. It was noticed, of course, that they'd be off together somewheres, but the womenfolk was glad to have 'em gone, and took no thought of what they might be up to. After a few weeks they'd bring their grog to the house, and they teached their girls and Susannah to drink with 'em. It wasn't long till Prudence and Hutia took to goin' there of an evening, and sometimes even Jenny would go. That's how I first got wind of it.

I'll say this for myself, sir, and it's the one right thing I did in all that time: I tried to hold Hutia and Prudence back, at first. But they'd found that grog could make 'em forget the troubles we'd had. Once they knew that, there was no keepin' 'em away from McCoy's house; but the women I've spoke of was the only ones that ever touched the stuff. The others would have naught to do with it.

One evening before I was able to get about much, Mr. Young came in to see me. He was like a new man, and it was easy to guess where he'd been.

"Alex," said he, "I've brought ye what will do ye a world of good."

"What's that?" said I, knowing well enough what it was.

He'd a bottle under his arm, which he set on the table.

"Will McCoy's sent this along to ye, with his hearty good wishes," said he; "and it's grand stuff, Alex. Ye'd scarce know it from the best London gin."

"Ye've had a good sup already, Ned," said I. "That's plain to be seen."

"I have so," said he. "Where's the sense of our holding out against a tot o' good grog now and again? It's a sad lonesome life we lead here. God knows a little good cheer won't harm us."

"Ned," said I, "I'll not say I don't wish I had a cag o' the same, but have ye reckoned what this might lead to? Ye've never seen Quintal in his cups. I have. He's the devil himself!"

"He was quiet and pleasant as ye please to-night," said Mr. Young.

"That may be," said I. "There's times when he's harmless enough; but ye never know when he'll be the other way."

"Quintal or no Quintal," said he, speakin' a little thick, "I'm for the grog! I've not felt like this in months, lad. My idea is that a little o' this — seamen's rations, mind ye, like we had in the old days — will harm none of us."

I said naught for a bit. Of a sudden he looked at me in a sober way, and got up from his chair.

"God forgive me, Alex!" said he. "If ye wish to abstain, I'd cut off my right hand before I'd be the one to urge ye!" He grabbed up the bottle and was about to go, and, fool that I was, I begged him to set down again. I'd been away from spirits for so long, I could just as well have kept off it; and I knew how it would be once I started again. No seaman ever loved his rum more than myself. I'd been used to it from the time I was a mere lad, and words can't say how I coveted a share o' that bottle.

Well, sir, the long and the short of it was that I fetched a couple of half-pints and a calabash of water, and between us we finished the whole bottle. And Mr. Young was right: it did me a world of good. I'd been low-spirited enough, but after a few drinks everything was bright and sunny. Balhadi looked on at the two of us, pleased as anything to see us so cheerful again. At this time none of the women-folk knew the harm there was in drink. In years past there'd been a spree or two in the bush, but these they'd not seen, and for the most part we'd drunk our grog rations from the old *Bounty's* supply quiet and peaceable till all was gone. So the womenfolk, bein' ignorant, made no fuss at all, at first, about the still. Most wouldn't drink because they couldn't abide the taste o' spirits, but they didn't mind us doing it.

As soon as I was able to get about, I took to joinin' the others at McCoy's house. At first there was no harm in any of us. We'd agreed each man was to have his half-pint a day and no more. It was even less at the start, because we hadn't enough to make up a half-pint around, but that was soon mended. We'd never worked harder in the old days than we did now at clearing land for ti-planting. Quintal and me took charge o' that, and Mr. Young and McCoy minded the still. They soon had a cag o' spirits set by to age and started filling another. We hunted the island over for wild ti roots whilst them we'd planted was coming along. The food gardens was left to the womenfolk.

Ye can guess what followed, sir. We was young seamen, save Mr. Young, and the eldest of us scarce five-and-twenty. As soon as there was a good store of spirits set by, no more was said about half a pint a day, though Mr. Young held fast to that at first. The rest of us drank as much as we'd a mind to, and the five girls with us. There was Sarah Quintal, and McCoy's Mary, and the three others I've spoke of —Susannah, Hutia, and Prudence. These last had no men o' their own, and the grog made 'em as wild and hot-blooded as ourselves. Ye'll not need to be told how it was with us. We took no thought o' wives or anything else.

There was trouble a-plenty afore many weeks. Mrs. Christian wasn't long in seein' the truth o' things. She'd come to Mr. Young and me and beg us to leave off for the children's sakes if for naught else. And we'd be shamed to the heart and promise to do better; but, a few days after, back we'd go and all would be as before. It got so as Mrs. Christian and the other decent women would have naught to do with us. She gathered the children away from McCoy's house, and she fitted bolts and bars to her house, well knowing what a dangerous man Quintal was, at times, when he was drunk. One night, when the rest of us was too far gone to stop him, he near killed Sarah. She and Mary both had more than enough bad treatment. They'd have been only too glad to leave the house, but didn't dare to, for fear o' what their men might do.

So it went with us for another three months; then a thing happened that brought even such brutes as we'd become to our senses.

The four of us men was at McCoy's house, drunk as usual, with Prudence and Hutia and Susannah. Mary and Sarah had got to the place where they was more afraid to stay than to go, and Mrs. Christian had taken 'em in at her house. Quintal had been of a mind to fetch 'em back, but the rest of us had talked him out o' that and got him quieted down. McCoy didn't mind Mary going, for he still had some decency in him and he knew she'd be best away with the children.

I came stumbling back to my own house about midnight and Balhadi got me into bed. She'd stayed by me all this while, and Taurua had done the like by Mr. Young, which only goes to show how patient and long-suffering good women can be. But they was near to the end of their patience, as I'm about to tell ye.

It seemed to me I'd scarce closed my eyes when I was shook awake by Balhadi. "Quick, Alex!" said she. "Rouse the others and come! Quintal's just gone by toward Maimiti's house! He means mischief!"

I set out at a run for McCoy's house and roused him and Mr. Young, who was sleeping there. Before we'd come halfway back, we heard Quintal batterin' at the door of Mrs. Christian's house. The sound of it sobered us, I can promise ye!

The moon was about an hour up. Quintal was at the door with a fence post he'd picked up, and all but had it battered down by the time we got there. McCoy yelled at him, but he gave no heed. We could hear the children crying indoors, and then Mrs. Christian's voice, cool and quiet. "I've a musket here," said she. "I'll shoot him if he sets foot inside. Stand away, ye others!"

McCoy was the only one of us who could ever manage Quintal with words. He ran up low and took hold of his arm. "Matt, are ye mad?" said he. Quintal turned and gave him a shove that threw him clear across the dooryard. "I want Moetua," said he.

I dragged him back, and Will was at his legs and Mr. Young tried to hold one of his arms. The three of us was no match for him, and that's the truth. Then the women took a hand.

Balhadi pitched in with us; then what was left of the door was broke down and out came Moetua. Hating Quintal as she did, she was better than two men. She got her fingers round his throat and would have killed him if it hadn't been for Maimiti. We tied him up and carried him, half dead, back to McCoy's house.

That was the last straw for the women. Even Prudence and Hutia left us, wild young things that they was in those days, and they took Susannah with 'em. They joined the others at Mrs. Christian's house. We'd bound Quintal hand and foot, so he couldn't move, and had to keep him so all the next day, for he was like a wild animal. Nothing we could say would quiet him.

That same morning, Balhadi went down to Mrs. Christian's and was gone till afternoon. There was a scared, sober look on her face when she came back. I noticed it, though I was still muddled and sleepy with the drink I'd had. She'd a mind to tell me something, — I could see that, — but she held off, and I didn't coax her to come out with it, whatever it was. The fact is, I was ashamed and disgusted with myself, thinking how I'd used Balhadi all these months, and I was short and surly with her to hide how I felt. Around the middle of the afternoon I told her to fetch me a bite to eat, which she did. When I'd finished I lay down for a nap, and having had no sleep the night before, I didn't wake till daylight the next morning.

Balhadi was nowhere about. It was a day of black squalls, makin' up out of the southeast, with hot calm spells betwixt 'em. I went to the edge of the bluffs, as I always did of a morning, for a look at the sea and sky. While I was there, a squall came down so sudden I'd no time to run to the house, and squatted in the lee of a clump o' plantains, takin' what shelter I could. It was over in ten minutes, and I was looking out to the eastward when I saw something afloat about a mile offshore. For all my bleary eyes, it looked like a capsized boat. I rubbed and looked again and made out what I thought was people in the water alongside, and some up on the keel.

I'd no notion of the truth, but ye'll know the start it gave me to see a capsized boat, with men clinging to it, in this lonely ocean. In all the years we'd been here we'd sighted but the one ship I've told ye of. I scanned the horizon all round, as far as I could see, for the ship this boat belonged to, but there was none in view; then I ran to McCoy's house to get the spyglass.

Him and Mr. Young was there, still asleep. I shook 'em out of it and the three of us hurried down to the lookout point above the cove. Ye know how it is when ye get a glass on something far off — it jumps right up to your eye. What I saw was our cutter, upside down, and all our womenfolk around it, some swimming, some clinging to the boat as best they could, while they held their little ones up on the keel.

Ye'll know the shock it gave us — such a sight as that. Even with it there before our eyes, we was hard put to believe it was real. We ran back to McCoy's house to fetch Quintal. He was snoring fit to shake the place down. We pulled him out of the bed-place tryin' to waken him. "Rouse him out of it," said I to Will. "Kick him awake somehow! Let him know young Matt's out there like to drown!" Then Mr. Young and me ran to the cove.

We dragged the biggest of the canoes down into the water. By good luck there was no great amount of surf and we was soon beyond it. We made the hafts o' them paddles bend, I promise ye!

Afore we was half a mile out, another black squall bore down on us — solid sheets of water, and wind fit to blow the hair off your head. It passed, quick as it had made up, and there was the cutter, not a cable's length off.

Had the girls been women from home, more than one of the children would ha' been drowned that day; but these knew how to handle themselves in the sea. Prudence and Mary came swimmin' to meet us, and passed up their babes afore they clambered aboard. Next minute we was alongside, and took little Mary from Mrs. Christian. Then the older ones they had on the keel was passed over to us.

McCoy and Quintal was on the way by this time in the other canoe. Quintal was in the stern. He made the water boil and no mistake!

"Is Matt safe?" he yelled when he was still a quarter of a mile off.

"Aye, safe!" I hailed back. "And all hands!"

Mary was in our canoe, with their two little ones, half drowned, in her lap, and I'll not forget the look on Will's face when he saw 'em. We was takin' the other women on board, Mrs. Christian the last. The two canoes held the lot of us. We took the cutter in tow and made for the cove.

Some of the women was weeping, but not a word was spoke all the way. Mrs. Christian sat on a thwart with little Mary in her arms. She'd a look of hopelessness and despair that'll haunt me to my last day.

We ran the breakers and got the women safe ashore, and them with the children hurried on to the settlement. The others helped us get the cutter righted and bailed out and back in the shed. We had no words with 'em or they with us. We was too shocked and sobered by what they'd tried to do to have a harsh word for any of 'em.

Will ye believe it, sir? They'd meant to sail off with the young 'uns in that bit of a cutter! Mrs. Christian understood the compass, and they minded some low islands we'd passed in the *Bounty* on the way from Tahiti. That's where they was bound, if so be as they could find 'em. Unbeknownst to us, Mrs. Christian had got 'em together, provisioned the cutter, and set sail to the north. Had they not made the sheet fast and capsized in a squall, they'd all ha' been lost, as certain as sunrise!

But this'll show ye how desperate they was. They was sickened to the heart's core of men, and they'd come to hate the island where there'd been so much bloodshed and misery. We'd drove 'em to the point where they'd sooner chance death by drowning, or thirst and starvation, than live with us and have their children brought up by such fathers as we'd become.

That evening the four of us got together, but not to drink. It was McCoy himself that spoke first. "Mr. Young," said he, "I'm done with it! I know how much blame falls to my share in all that's passed. I'll be the cause o' no more trouble. We've children and good women here. I'm for a decent life from now on."

"I'm with ye, Will!" said I, standin' up, "and there's my hand on it!"

We was all of a mind, Quintal as hearty and earnest as the rest. There was to be no more distilling, that was agreed on and swore to, and we went to our beds sober and peaceable for the first time in many a day. Aye, we thought we was turning a new leaf that evening. There was to be naught but peace and quiet in the days to come.

# CHAPTER XVIII

Now, sir, I'll pass over three years. It was a time I don't like to think about. I said I'd tell ye the truth of what's happened here, and so I will, but ye'd not want to hear the whole of it. There's little to be said about those years save that we went from bad to worse. Not all at once. For two or three months after the womenfolk tried to leave the island we kept our word, and not a drop of spirits was touched. We did try, the four of us, to make a new start; then it was the old story over again: our solemn promises was broke, and the end of it was that Maimiti left the settlement with her three children and went over to the Auté Valley to live, and Moetua and Nanai went with her. They built a house with no help from any of us, and not long after, Jenny and Taurua, Mr. Young's wife, joined 'em, and they gathered all the children up there, away from us. I was glad they did. The settlement was no place for children, that's the truth of it.

Balhadi had stayed by me all this while, hoping I'd come to my senses, and Mary had done the like by McCoy, but little heed we gave to either of 'em. Four of the women — Hutia, Susannah, Prudence, and Sarah, Quintal's girl — stayed on with us, for the most part, and we lived together in a way it shames me to think of.

Mr. Young made one with us in this. Ye'll wonder he could have done it. He was a gentleman born. How did it come he could join with men the like of Quintal, McCoy, and myself? My belief is he'd lost all heart and hope, seein' how things went. He was never a man to lead. He must have thought we could never be made to go his way, so he went ours. But it was plain he hated himself for doing it. Never have I seen a sadder face than Mr. Young's at this time. It was a blow to him when Taurua left to join Maimiti, but he didn't change his ways. He took to drinking harder than ever, like as if he wanted to kill himself. For all that, he was a gentleman in whatever he did. I knew well enough it was only the grog that made him able to abide the rest of us.

So things went till the end of 1797. I mind me well of a spree we had in the fall of that year. We'd started by killing a pig and making a feast. There was the four of us and the women I've spoke of. It happened that Jenny and Moetua had come down to the settlement that day. They found us in a carouse that was the worst, I reckon, we'd ever had up to that time. McCoy recollected that it was four years to the very week from the time when the last of the Indian men was killed. He was so drunk he cared for naught, and he told the women we'd made the feast to mind us o' that. Then Quintal made him brag before Moetua, who'd been Minarii's wife, about how he'd thrown her husband over the cliff at the top of the Rope. I was far gone in drink myself, then, and I've no doubt I did my part to make the women hate us the more.

I've little recollection of what happened after, but I know the women was horror-struck at our brute ways. There was fighting 'twixt Quintal and McCoy and some o' them, but I was too drunk to take part in it. I was awake early next morning and found I'd climbed to the loft, somehow. Mr. Young was asleep on a bed on the other side of the room. I went down the ladder and found Quintal and McCoy sprawled out on the floor, and a precious-looking pair they was! McCoy was scratched and bruised all over his body, and he had every stitch of clothing torn off him. Quintal's face and beard was smeared and caked with blood from a deep gash on his head; one of the women must have given him an awful knock. The benches and tables was upset, and glass from broken bottles was scattered all over the floor.

I went along home for a bit, but there was no one about, or in any of the other houses. I went on to Mr. Christian's old place where Prudence and Susannah lived at this time. Maimiti had never set foot there — or in the settlement, for the matter of that — since the day she'd moved to the Auté Valley.

The *Bounty's* chronometer was at Mr. Christian's house. He'd kept it going from the time the ship was seized from Captain Bligh to the day he was killed. Mr. Young minded it after that, till he took to drinking so hard; then I'd looked after it, and if I did nothing else I saw that it was never allowed to run down. I don't know why I did it, for time meant nothing to us and we'd the sun to go by. Likely it was because the clock was a link with home and minded me of the days before we'd brought so much misery on ourselves. Anyway, I never missed a day in winding it, and I took charge of Mr. Christian's calendar. He'd said to me once: "Alex, if anything happens to Mr. Young or me, see that ye keep my calendar going; else ye won't know where ye are."

Ye might have thought the four of us would sober up now, after such a spree as we'd had, but it wasn't the way with us then. We was at it again all that day, and the next, but on the third morning I'd had enough. It was then I began to suspicion something was amiss with the womenfolk. Not one had come near us, and we'd nothing left to eat in the house save a bunch of plantains. Quintal and McCoy and me made out a meal with 'em, and I carried some up to Mr. Young, who was lying down in the loft. He always kept to himself as much as he could. He'd come down now and again, but he said not a word more than was needed to any of us. I told him about the women, but he was in a black mood and begged me to go away and leave him alone.

McCoy and Quintal had lost track of the days; they didn't know how long we'd been drinking steady and they didn't care. The two of them was in a stupor again when I left the house about the middle of the morning.

The settlement was empty, just as it had been the past two days. I went along to the pool below Brown's Well; there was hardly an hour of the day but ye'd find some of the women at the spring, but there was none that morning, so I went along the trail that goes along the western ridge and into the Auté Valley from that side.

When we first came here, all that high land was covered with forest, but we'd cleared bits of it here and there. It was as pretty a place as ye could wish to see, high and cool, with rich little valleys running down to the north, and paths amongst the trees, and open places where we'd made gardens. We'd left the forest standing round about.

For three months past none of us men had set foot in the Auté Valley. As I've said, we'd hardly drawn sober breath in all that time; the work was left to the womenfolk. Balhadi and Taurua had kept Mr. Young and me supplied with food, and Mary and Sarah had done the like for the other two. Hutia and Prudence and Susannah would come to McCoy's house now and again, but we'd seen little enough of the others. They kept away, and we'd not lay eyes on 'em for weeks together.

I went along the old trail, amongst the woods and fields, till I came to open sunny land that stretched south to the cliffs above the sea. And there I stopped.

All the land here was cleared and laid out in gardens, and the women was at work amongst them, and they'd made pens for fowls and pigs to one side. But what made me stand and stare was a kind of stockade, beyond, and close against the cliffs to the south'ard. It was made of the trunks of trees set close together deep in the ground and all of a dozen feet high. I judged it to be about twenty yards square.

I could see it was new built, and it was as strong a little fort as men could have made.

I was so took aback that I stood stock-still for a bit; then I went on, slow, till some of the women spied me, and four of 'em came up to meet me.

Mrs. Christian was in front. Moetua and Prudence and Hutia came with her, and each one carried a musket. They halted and waited for me, and when I was about a dozen yards off Maimiti said, "Stand where ye are, Alex! What is it ye want?"

I didn't know what to say, I was that surprised, and I was ashamed to meet Maimiti face to face, knowing what she must think of such a drunken useless thing as I'd become. The last time I'd seen her was a day long before, at Brown's Well. She spoke about Mr. Christian, and how well he'd thought o' me. She begged me to take hold of myself, and I'd give my solemn promise I would. Three days after I was back at McCoy's house, and things went on just as they had before.

A man who's lost his self-respect will try, like as not, to brazen it out, if he can, and so I did.

"Where's Balhadi?" said I. "I want her to come home."

Mrs. Christian looked me straight in the eyes; then she said, very quiet: "Go back where ye've come from. Balhadi wants nothing more to do with ye."

"Let her tell me that herself," said I. I knew well enough it was so. For three years Balhadi and me had lived together as happy as heart could wish, and I knew she'd been as fond of me as I was of her. But after the still was started everything fell to pieces. At last she let me go my own way.

Maimiti beckoned to the others, who'd gathered in the gardens below and stood looking toward us. They came to where we stood. Balhadi was amongst them, and when Maimiti asked if she wanted to go back with me she said, "No."

Then Maimiti said, "Now go ye back, Alex, and mind ye this: Ye're to stay on the other side of the island. Ye may do as you please there; but from this day, if any of ye set foot in the Auté Valley, it will be at your peril. We have all the muskets here, and the powder and ball, and the lead for making more. Ye know that the half of us can shoot as well as any of ye men, so get ye gone to your friends and let them know what I've said."

"Do ye think, Maimiti," said I, "that we'll rest with matters in this state? Our wives had best come back if they know what's good for 'em."

Then Taurua spoke up. "Say ye so, Alex? We've give ye chances enough, and ye're worse than pigs, the lot of ye. Not one of us shall go, and ye'd best let us alone."

They was in dead earnest; I could see that. In my heart, I was proud of their spirit and well knew they had all the right on their side; but the badness in me came to the front, and I said things I was ashamed of even as I said 'em. I began to threaten and bluster and talk big, and I was mean enough to tell Sarah that Quintal would half kill her as soon as he could lay hands on her. She had a deathly fear of Quintal, and with reason. Many's the time he'd beat her in the past.

The old scared look I'd seen so often came into her face; it was like as if she saw Quintal behind me. Mrs. Christian put an arm around her shoulders as a mother might have done. She had a gentle, womanly nature, but no man could better Maimiti in courage. There, before the others, she told me what miserable things the four of us was. She didn't raise her voice, but what she said struck home. "And let Quintal know this," she went on in her quiet way. "We keep watch here day and night. If he or any of ye try to molest us, I promise it shall be for the last time. Now be off, for we've no more to say to ye."

I went back the way I'd come, and the women stood watching until I was out of sight in the forest. When I'd reached the ridge below the Goat-House Mountain I sat down on a bench we had there and looked out over the land, all so peaceful and quiet and sunny. I thought of the times I'd rested in the place with Mr. Christian as we'd go back and forth from the settlement. He'd tell me about his hopes and plans, and ask my advice about this and that. He was always thinking of ways to do us good and make us more happy and contented as time went on. I never heard him speak of the mutiny, but I knew he thought he'd ruined the lives of all of us, and felt bound to do what he could to make up for it. He planned and worked with that in mind, and if we'd backed him up the way we should have, not a drop of blood would ever have been spilt here.

Little comfort I had from my thoughts that morning. I saw no light ahead, and I didn't care what happened. I've no mind to defend myself. I knew right from wrong, but I'd a reckless streak in me that made me take to the bad at this time as though to spite myself.

I went down to the village and searched through the houses. The women had took every musket and pistol, as Mrs. Christian said, and all the powder and ball and lead was gone from the storehouse. They'd carried away their own things as well, but none of ours was touched save the weapons. Mr. Young and me had some fowls penned up near the house. I'd clean forgot 'em and the poor things was half dead. I fed and watered them and went along to join the others.

Quintal and McCoy was still dead drunk; I couldn't have roused 'em if I'd wanted to. Mr. Young wasn't in the house, but I found him on the slope to seaward. I could see from the look he gave me that he'd no wish for company, but I thought I'd best tell him what had happened. When I had, he smiled in a bitter way. "It's what we might have expected," he said. "The wonder is they haven't all left us long since."

"What's to be done now?" said I. I could see how little heart he had for anything.

"What's to be done? Nothing, Alex. I mean to leave 'em alone. The rest of ye can do as ye've mind to," and with that he got up and went off amongst the trees, home. I would have liked well to go with him, but I knew he wanted to be alone, so I stayed where I was.

Before I go on, I'd best tell ye something more about Quintal and McCoy. McCoy was a good neighbor when he was sober. He was quiet and hard-working and fond of his wife and children, but there was an ugly streak in him that showed now and again. It wasn't often ye'd see it, and then it was best to leave him alone. I've known him to beat Mary black and blue, and be so sorry for it, after, there was nothing he wouldn't do to make it up to her. He'd more brains than the rest of us seamen together, but spirits was a thing he couldn't resist. Once the still was set going, he thought of naught but that. He would drink more than any two of us, and I often wondered how long he could keep it up at that rate.

Quintal was a big man — not tall, but thick through and strong as a bull, and slow-witted as he was strong. He'd sit for hours at a time, saying nothing, and ye'd wonder if he ever had a thought in his head. There was little harm in him, sober, but all the women except Moetua had a mortal fear of him, drunk. Maimiti he'd never laid hands on, but the others whose men had been killed he thought of as his own property to do as he liked with. Moetua was near as strong as Quintal himself. He'd tried to handle her, but she taught him a lesson or two he didn't forget. All the womenfolk hated him except his Sarah. They'd come to think of him as worse than a wild beast, which wasn't far from the truth.

In the afternoon, when McCoy and Quintal woke up, I told 'em what the women had told me.

"It couldn't have happened better," said McCoy. "Let 'em go their way and we'll go ours."

"What!" said Matt. "And have naught to do with 'em for the rest of our lives?"

"Rest ye patient," said McCoy. "D'ye think they'll stop as they are for long? They'll come to heel soon enough if we take 'em at their word. It's Maimiti and Taurua's put 'em up to this, with two or three more to back 'em. Leave 'em alone. We'll have our cronies back soon enough."

Quintal was in one of his ugly spells. "'I'll not leave 'em alone," said he. "They'll play none o' their games with me. I'll fetch a pair of 'em down."

"Ye'll do naught o' the kind, Matt," said McCoy. "Don't be a fool. They've all the muskets, and there's a good half-dozen can shoot as well as any of us. They're in no way to be trifled with now, that's plain; but if we set quiet here we'll have 'em back of their own wish."

"Set quiet if ye like," said Quintal. "I'm going." Up he got and off he went, out of the house and across the valley, without another word.

"What d'ye think, Alex?" said McCoy. "Will they try to harm him?"

For all Maimiti had said, I didn't believe they would. We'd had our way so long, doing as we pleased and giving no heed to any of 'em, that we'd come to fancy we could keep on using 'em as we'd a mind to.

"They'll not shoot," said I, "unless he tries to climb their stockade, and he'll not do that, for it's all of a dozen feet high."

"We'd best go and see what happens," said McCoy. "I'd like well to have a look at the fort they've made."

So we followed across the valley to the southern ridge. We didn't catch sight of Quintal till we'd reached the upper side of the Auté Valley. He was standing at the edge of a thicket, staring down at the fort. "God bless me!" said McCoy when he saw the place. The three of us stood for a bit, looking out across the valley. Some of the women was at work in the gardens about a hundred yards away, and others farther on. They didn't see us, for we kept hid amongst the trees.

"When could they ha' done all this?" said Quintal. The pair of 'em was surprised as I'd been at sight of the fort; for all I'd told them, they wasn't expecting to see such a strong-made place.

"There's no matter o' that now," said McCoy. "Ye see it, Matt, and if ye're not daft ye'll come back with Alex and me. Ye'll only make things worse if ye try any hard usage with 'em. Come along down, man, and leave 'em alone."

But there was no talking Quintal over, once he got a notion into his head. He'd a great conceit of his strength, and was too thick-witted to believe the women would dare to hold out against him, even with muskets in their hands.

"Stand ye here and watch," said he. "I want none o' yer help, if that's what ye're afeared of."

Quintal hadn't washed himself for days, and he had a great bushy beard that half covered his chest. He'd no clothes on save a bit of dirty bark cloth about his middle, and with his club in his hand he looked worse than any naked savage I've ever laid eyes on.

All that piece of land down from the ridge had been cleared; the women had seen to that, so as they could have a view of anyone coming. The minute Quintal showed himself out of the forest there was a conch shell blown by someone on watch on a platform inside the stockade. Those at work in the gardens had spied him at the same time. There was half a dozen outside, and instead of running back to the fort, as we'd expected, they spread out in a line and waited for Quintal to come on. I saw Moetua and Prudence in the centre. Moetua carried a cudgel and Prudence had a musket. Mrs. Christian was off to one side, with Hutia; and Balhadi and Taurua stood on the other side.

Moetua got down on her knees, and Prudence, who was a little thing, but as good a shot as any man, stood behind with the musket resting on Moetua's shoulder. Mrs. Christian knelt down behind a boulder and rested her piece on that. They'd not been twenty seconds in getting ready for Quintal. He was a good sixty yards off when he halted; then he went on, slow and steady, like the thick-skulled simpleton he was. Afore he'd gone three steps farther, Maimiti blazed away at him, and we saw Quintal half swing round and go down. He gave a bellow and leaped up again, and at that, Prudence fired. Quintal waited for no more. He ran back up the slope as fast as he could go, with the women after him, Moetua in the lead. He came crashing into the thickets and on he went down into the Main Valley. McCoy and I didn't wait to see what the women meant to do. We followed Quintal.

He was on a bench by the door, holding his hand over his left shoulder, and with blood streaming down one side of his face. Maimiti's shot had torn through the muscles of his shoulder, but Prudence had meant to kill, and a near thing it was for Quintal. The ball had all but took off one of his ears. McCoy and I was busy for the next hour getting him bandaged.

We'd no more doubt that the women was in earnest. Quintal had learned the only way he could — by being hurt; he had to lay up for near two months while his wounds was healing. He was in an ugly temper all this while, and it was as much as we could do to get a word out of him. Whether it was drink, or lonesomeness, or both together, I don't know, but McCoy and I could see he was getting more queer in his head every day. He'd talk to himself, even with us in the room, and half the time ye could make naught of what he'd say.

Things went on quiet enough for a while. Quintal and McCoy worked on at making spirits, and before they was through they filled up every bottle we had, with a cag or two beside. I kept clear of 'em as near as I could. I did some gardening again, and with that and fishing I was busy most hours of the day. But when night came I'd set me down to drink with 'em, hating myself all the while for doing it.

McCoy was sure some of the women would come back. "Rest easy, Matt," he'd say to Quintal. "There'll be no need to chase after 'em. We'll have a two-three of 'em down here before the week's out." But two months went by and not one came near us.

We saw little of Mr. Young. As I've said, he went off home the day I told him about the women leaving, and he came no more to McCoy's house. And never again, to his last day, did he touch a drop of spirits. I was worried about his health. The year before, he was took with what looked like asthma trouble, and it was getting worse. He needed someone to look after him, but he was bound to do for himself, and he wouldn't hear to my letting the women know he was sick. He was always friendly when I went along to see him, but I knew he wanted to be alone and that made me slow to bother him. Not a word did he say about my keeping on with Quintal and McCoy, but I was sure how he felt.

By the time Quintal's wounds was healed, him and McCoy decided they'd had enough of waiting. They'd come to think the right of things was on our side now. I was strong against makin' any move, but they was bound to stir up more trouble.

"What'll ye do?" said I to Will. "Fetch Mary back, willing or not?"

"Mary?" said he. "I'd not have her now if she was to crawl on her knees, beggin' me. There's a-plenty besides her, and one of 'em I'll take!"

Quintal was gettin' more ugly every day, and he was of the same mind. I knew I couldn't keep 'em quiet for long, and I had the notion to go across and warn Mrs. Christian. I should have done it, but, as I've said, I had a stubborn streak in me. I'd been told to keep away from the Auté Valley, and so I did.

One day Quintal was bound to go. There was no use arguing with either of 'em, so I tried another plan. I fetched out a bottle of spirits, hopin' to get 'em so dazed with grog they'd not be able to move.

"There'll be the devil to pay now," said I, "so we may as well have a good spree afore trouble starts." They was agreeable, and didn't go that day, but early next morning, when I was away, they set out across the island. They was still drunk, but able to take care of themselves, and they'd sense enough left to recollect the women could shoot. They'd no mind to go marchin' down amongst 'em the way Quintal had.

I was told what happened, afterward. When they got to the top of the ridge they hid themselves so as they could look across the gardens to the stockade. Some of the women was at work outside and they still carried muskets. They'd waited a good two hours when they saw Nanai and Jenny come out of the fort. They'd baskets on their arms, but no weapons, and they went off to the westward.

There's a steep little valley runs down to the sea below the mountain on the southern side. They waited till they was sure that was where Nanai and Jenny was bound; then they back-tracked and came round to the west side of the Auté Valley, and hid themselves close to the path that goes down this ravine. They'd only to wait to catch the women as they came up.

"I'll take Jenny and you can have Nanai," said McCoy. Jenny was Mrs. Christian's right hand. McCoy believed we had her to thank for coaxin' Prudence and Hutia away from us. He was glad to have this chance to get back at her.

Presently they spied Nanai comin' up amongst the trees, below. It was a stiff climb and she had a carrying pole, with a bunch of plantains at one end and a basket of shellfish on the other. Nanai was about twenty-three at this time. She'd been Tetahiti's wife, if ye remember. There was none had a greater fear of Quintal.

When she reached level ground she set down her load to rest not three steps from where they was hid. Out Quintal jumped and grabbed her. She was so terrified she made no struggle at all, and they had her tied hand and foot in a minute. They stuffed leaves in her mouth with a strip of bark tied across it, to make sure she wouldn't cry out.

Jenny wasn't far behind, and they had her before she knew where she was. She was small, but wiry as a cat, and she fought like one, tooth and nail. It was as much as Quintal could do to hold her while McCoy put a gag over her mouth. He got the palm of his hand bit through doing it. When they had her tied he took her over his shoulder, and Quintal came after, with Nanai.

I'd come back to the house, in the meantime, and found no one there. I guessed what Quintal and McCoy was up to, but I didn't believe they'd be able to get at the women. In case they had, I didn't want to be mixed up in it. So I went along to Mr. Young's house and spent the night there. I said naught to him about the others.

They brought the girls to the house and Nanai was loosed, but Jenny was kept tied at first. Then McCoy began to crow over Jenny, but she had a fiery spirit and gave him as good as he sent. "Lay hands on me, Will McCoy, and I won't rest till I've killed ye," said she. "Where's Alex and Ned Young?"

"Leave Ned out o' this," said McCoy. "He has naught to do with us. He's been a sick man this long while; yet, betwixt ye, ye've kept Taurua away from him."

Then he told her I was off on a woman hunt of my own and would be along with another of 'em directly.

Nanai was crouched in a corner, with Quintal on a bench in front of her. All at once she made a spring for the door, but Quintal grabbed her by the hair and dragged her back. Ye'll not wish to hear what went on after this. First they tried to force the girls to drink with 'em, and in the end they abused both in a shameful way. In the night, when Quintal and McCoy was asleep, they got away. When I came down from Mr. Young's next morning I could see there'd been a fight in the house. McCoy was nursing his bit hand with a rag tied round it. But not a word was said of what had happened. They was a glum surly pair, and no mistake!

## CHAPTER XIX

THE next day Mr. Young came along to see us. He was having one of his bad attacks of asthma and it was all he could do to speak. When we'd set a chair for him he broke in a fit of coughing was pitiful to see. It wasn't till that morning that it came in to me what a state Mr. Young was in. He'd wasted down to little more than skin and bone. When his coughing spell was over he told us what he'd come for.

"I've been asked to bring ye a message from the women," said he. "Maimiti says the three of ye must leave the island. They're all agreed on this. Ye can take the cutter and what ye need in the way of supplies, but ye must clear out."

"Clear out!" said I. "Where to?"

"I don't know. Tahiti, I suppose. Where ye like, so long as it's away from here. They'll give ye three days to make plans."

"And do they think we'll be fools enough to go?" said McCoy.

"Maimiti says ye must," he replied, almost in a whisper. He had to fight for breath every few words he spoke. "Ye'd best do it. I'll go with ye."

"Go with us?" said I. "That ye won't, Ned. D'ye think we'd allow it, sick as ye are?"

He held up his hand. "Wait, Alex. . . . It's no matter what happens to me. I want to go. . . . Get away from here. . . . We could fetch some island to the westward; one o' them we passed on the way from Tahiti. Try it, anyway."

"And if we won't go, what then?" said McCoy.

"Maimiti means what she says. They'll take action."

Quintal laughed. "Let 'em try!" said he.

My heart went out to Mr. Young. He'd no wish to go, I knew that well enough; but he was the only one could use a sextant, and he knew we could never fetch up any place without him. Even with him our chances would be poor enough. But he was thinkin' of the women and children more than us. He wanted them to have a chance to live quiet decent lives.

"What are ye for, Alex?" said Quintal. "Ye'll wish to give in to the bitches, I'll warrant — let 'em drive us out. Damn yer eyes! If it'd not been for yerself and Will, we'd ha' learned 'em who's masters here long afore this."

"Aye, ye made a brave show, Matt, a while back," said I, "runnin' up the hill with the lot of 'em at yer heels. They've had right enough on their side, the womenfolk, and well ye know it! It'll be yerself and Will has drove 'em to this."

"Drove 'em, did we?" said McCoy. "We've not been near 'em till yesterday, and much good it's done us to keep clear. But there'll be some drivin' now, I promise ye!"

Mr. Young shook his head. "Take care!" said he. "They mean what they say."

"Sit ye down, Will," said I. "Let's talk this over quiet, and see what's best to be done."

But neither of 'em would listen to reason and was all for doin' something straight off. Mr. Young could have been no more sick of 'em than I was.

Presently he got up, shaky and weak, and made ready to go. "I've done all I can," said he. "Now look out for yourselves!"

"Never ye mind about us," said Quintal. "We'll do that and more!" I wanted to help Mr. Young along the path, home, but he wouldn't hear to it and went off alone.

McCoy was uneasy about the still, and nothing would do but it must be hid away. Quintal helped him carry it to a place in the valley where they'd never be able to find it. As I've said, we'd spirits enough on hand to last us for months, and that was stowed away as well, in a safe place.

I didn't know just what to do. Ye may think it strange, but I still had a soft spot in my heart for Will and Matt. We'd been shipmates so long, and I'd the wish to stand by 'em, come what might. And wasn't I as much to blame, or near as much, as themselves? For all that, I wanted bad to follow after Mr. Young and talk things over with him. I'd the notion the pair of us should see Mrs. Christian and try to patch things up; join with the women, mebbe, if they'd have us, and leave McCoy and Quintal to go their own way. But, when I thought it over, that seemed to me a dangerous thing for all. It would oppose us men, two and two, and might lead to the killing of one side or the other. What I wanted above all was for us to keep clear of any more bloodshed. And there was another thing. It shames me to say it, but I couldn't abide the thought of bein' without drink. So the end of it was I did naught, but waited to see what would come.

That day McCoy and Quintal got as drunk as I'd ever seen 'em, and stayed so, and lucky it was that Matt was in none of his ugly spells. He drank himself to sleep with scarce a word said. I had my share, but not so much but I was up and about, doin' my chores. But I mind how low-spirited I was, thinkin' of the lonesome unnatural life we had, when there was no need for it. And all this time I missed the children and craved to see 'em. What fools we was to think more of our grog than we did of them!

The three days went by, but there was no sign of the women. That didn't surprise us, for we'd no idea they'd do anything. After we'd et, at midday, we had our sleep, as usual. It was towards the middle of the afternoon when I woke up; I could see the streaks of sunlight slanting down through the chinks in the windows. The house had four shutters, two on each side. I got up to open 'em. As I was sliding the first one back, a musket was fired from the edge of the forest, and the ball sang past within an inch or two of my head. I ducked down and slammed the window shut. McCoy was asleep on the floor by the table. He raised up his head. "What's that?" said he, and he'd no more than spoke when another ball splintered through the boards of the shutter I'd just closed. That roused Quintal; he sat up and glared at the two of us. I motioned 'em to keep quiet, and crawled to a knothole in one of the planks that gave me a view across the strip of cleared land, which was about twenty yards wide.

At first I saw naught but a bit of the forest; then I made out the barrel of a musket was pushed through the bushes and pointing at the door, and another farther along. A minute later I had a glimpse of Hutia behind a tree. We'd been caught, right enough, and was still so muddled with sleep, it took us a quarter of an hour to get our wits together. While I was spying out the valley side of the house, Quintal opened the door a wee crack on the other side. Two shots was fired the minute he did it. One grazed his hipbone, breaking the skin. We knew, then, the place was surrounded, and the women meant to kill us if they could. McCoy called out for Mrs. Christian, but there was no answer save another shot through the wall.

For all their warnings, we'd not believed they'd take any such action as this. We'd no mind to give in, now, but all we could do was to keep well hid. Every little while shots would be fired through the windows or doors; we had to lay flat on the floor. There was fourteen muskets amongst 'em, and half a dozen pistols, and the women who couldn't shoot kept the extra ones loaded for the others. Quintal and I was for making a rush out, but McCoy was against this. "Don't be fools," said he. "That's what they hope we'll do, and it's little chance we'd have to get clear by daylight. We'd best wait till dark, unless they take it into their heads to rush us before." So we stayed as we was, with the doors blocked with the benches and tables and some bags of yams and sweet potatoes. We didn't speak above a whisper all this time.

We'd little fear they would try to come to grips with us in the house. They'd keep well off and trust to the musket; but they was bound to get us into the open afore dark, and so they did. Some of 'em slipped up to the ends of the house with torches of dry palm fronds and set fire to the thatch.

In a couple of minutes the whole place was in a blaze. There was no time for anything except to get out as quick as ever we could, and a chancy thing it was. Quintal was so thick-headed as to clear away the benches we'd piled in front of the door. I heard the women on that side shooting at him as I went out one of the windows on the seaward side. I dodged around the cookhouse as one of them fired at me. She was hid behind a rock, and before any of the others could shoot I was across the bit of open ground and amongst the trees.

As soon as I was well out of view I slowed down to a walk, for I was sure they'd not scatter and try to follow us. I went up the western ridge and on to the Goat-House Peak. It was near dark by that time; the house was still in a full blaze, but it soon burnt itself out. I heard no more shots; all was as quiet as though there was no one but me on the island. I knew the women would do no more prowling round at night; they'd keep together and go back to the fort, so I waited till moonrise and then went down to Mr. Young's house.

I made certain there was no one about, and slipped inside. Mr. Young was gone. Afterward I learned that some of the women had come down the day before, with a litter they'd made, and carried him up to their place so's they could look after him. I got a scare and jumped halfway across the room when something brushed against my leg, but it was only one of the *Bounty's* cats was born on the ship on the way out from England. He was a great pet of mine. I went out to the cook-shed to scratch up a coconut for him, and whilst I was at it I heard McCoy's voice calling out for Ned.

He was hid under the banyan tree below the house. He'd been shot through the fleshy part of the leg and had lost a good deal of blood. Moetua had chased him, he said, but he'd managed to get clear of her in the forest. Quintal he'd not seen.

It was a painful wound he had. I cleaned the place and bound it up. As soon as that was done he was all for moving on. He was scared bad. "They mean to kill us, Alex; I take that as certain," said he. "Like enough they've done for Quintal."

"That may be," said I, "but they'll not come in the night. We can rest here till daylight, and then hide out till we know what they're up to."

We went off next morning while it was still dark. McCoy was too lame to go far, but I hid him in a thicket where they could never have found him. I kept watch on the settlement and no one came near it. Not a sign of Quintal did we see in all that time, though I searched far and wide for him. We was both sure he was dead.

We kept away from the settlement for ten days; then we moved into Mr. Young's house. We felt none too easy at first, not knowing but the women might be spying on us and making ready for another attack; but after three weeks we felt certain they meant to leave us alone as long as we didn't molest them. McCoy was laid up this while; I spent a good piece of my time getting food and searching for Quintal's body. It was a lonesome life. I can't say we relished it.

It was in March 1797 that the women burned the house. After that McCoy and I let up on the drinking. We'd have a sup together now and again, but there was no swilling it down the way we'd done before.

One day McCoy was away from sunup, and when he came back he told me he'd seen his girl, Mary. He'd met her in the forest, without the others knowing.

"What did she say of Quintal?" I asked him.

"They thought they'd hit him," said he, "but they couldn't be sure what happened."

"Did ye tell Mary we'd not seen him?"

"Aye. He's dead, Alex, for certain. Who knows but he may have lingered on for days, past helping himself, and us knowing nothing about it?"

"What else did Mary tell ye?" I asked. "How did they know but what we'd been killed as well? And yet none of 'em came near to see."

"They've known. They kept watch of us for a fortnight, Mary says. They reckoned Quintal had been bad hurt and we was nursing him."

"There's a thing I'd like well to know," said I. "Did Mary and Balhadi come down with the rest the day they burned the house?"

"They did not; and I'll tell ye more, Alex. They was against the others coming, and Sarah Quintal with 'em. Bad as we'd used 'em, they had no wish to see us dead."

"And what's the mind of the rest about us now?"

"We'll not be troubled, Mary says, as long as we let 'em alone."

"It's a wonder to me, Will, ye didn't try to coax Mary back," said I.

"So I did, but she'll not come. They've had enough of us, Alex. That's the truth of it."

"Will," said I, "could we break up the cursed still and be sober again? It would be desperate hard at first, but like enough we could do it."

Many's the time I've thought, since, of what might have happened if he'd said, "So we can, Alex! We'll not rest till it's done!" I was in the mind, and if I'd made an honest try I might have coaxed McCoy. But the truth is I was half afraid he'd agree.

"I couldn't, Alex," said he. "God forgive me, I couldn't! Where'd we be, in such a lonesome shut-off place, without a drop to cheer us up now and again?"

"It's right ye are," said I. "I was daft to think of it," and there was an end o' that.

"How is it with Ned Young?" I asked him.

"He's been desperate sick, Mary says, and he's still in his bed."

"It's little we'll see of Ned from now on," said I. "He'll never come back to us, and it'll be better so for all hands. And now I'll tell ye, Will, what I mean to do. Ye can go as you've a mind to, but I'll keep clear of the women if so be as I can. There's been trouble enough here. I'll be the cause of no more."

"There'll be no need o' that," said he. "I'll be seeing Mary again, and I'll have a word with her whenever ye say. I'll warrant there's a two-three of the women will be willing enough to come down and pass the time o' day with ye."

But I told him I'd go it alone for the present.

The next day we roamed the Main Valley over on a last hunt for Quintal's body. There wasn't a place he might have crawled into that we hadn't searched, but we tried once more. By the middle of the afternoon we was ready to give up. We'd come out on the western ridge, and McCoy thought we ought to hunt through the gullies on that side, but I was sure no man as bad hurt as Quintal must have been would crawl that far to die. There'd be no sense in it.

"But it's what Quintal might do, for all that," said McCoy. "There was no sense in *him,* poor loon! We'd best look, anyway. I'll feel better when it's done."

I was willing, for I hated to think of poor Matt's body lying unburied; but before we went down on that side we climbed the Goat-House Peak for a look around. And there, close to the top, where the cliffs made a straight drop to the sea, we found an axe handle leaned up against a rock. It was one of them had been in McCoy's house the day it was burned. It gave us a shock to see it, for we knew that Matt himself had carried it there. It was stained with dried blood, and we saw what we thought was blood on the rock itself. It's a chancy place, the Goat-House Peak; the footing is none too sure for a well man; and the axe handle was resting not three feet from the edge of the seaward cliffs. McCoy crawled to the edge and looked over, but there was nothing to see save the surf beating up against the rocks. We looked no farther. We couldn't guess why Matt had come there, but we knew he had, and there'd be no body to find. He might have lost his balance, but, knowing Matt, we thought he must have been so bad hurt he'd thrown himself off to make an end.

We went down without a word. He was a rough, hard man, was Quintal. Ye'll think, sir, from what I've said of him, that he was naught but a great brute we might be glad to think was dead. A brute he was, in his strength, — I've never seen his equal there, save Minarii, — and dangerous bad, times, when drunk. But there'd been a side to him I've not brought out the way I should have. There was none but liked the old Matt Quintal that first came to Pitcairn, and it was that one I was thinking about as we went back to the settlement.

It hit McCoy harder than it did me, for they'd been cronies ever since the *Bounty* left England, and they'd lived together here. Quintal thought the world and all of McCoy, and when he was sober would do whatever he said; but these last years, when he was growing so queer, not even McCoy could manage him.

That night it set in to raining and blowing hard from the east, and it kept on for three days. There was nothing we could do but stay in the house. We started drinking again, McCoy on one side of the table and me on the other. Before half the night was over he'd finished two quarts of spirits, but for all that he'd no mind to leave off. He'd took it into his head he was to blame for all the misery there'd been on the island, and he'd talk of naught but that.

"It's the truth I'm speaking, Alex," he'd say. "I was the first to want the land divided, and talked it up and egged the others on to stand out against Christian. That's what started the killing. There's not a murdered man, Indian or white, but that has me to thank for his death."

And so he went on, the night through, till I was half crazed with hearing the same thing over and over again. Finally I could stand it no more.

"Ye'd best go to bed, Will," I said, and with that I went out of the house. The night couldn't have been wilder or blacker. I lost my way and fell down a dozen times before I reached Mr. Christian's house. All wet and slathered in mud, I rolled into his old bed-place and went to sleep.

It was past midday when I woke up, and raining harder than ever. I went out in it for a bath and to feed my pigs and fowls. When I'd cleaned up the muddy mess I'd made in Mr. Christian's house, I went to the out-kitchen and boiled me some yams and cooked some eggs; had my own breakfast and carried some up to McCoy. He was settin' at the table, wide awake, just as I'd left him. He'd finished what was left in the bottle I'd been at the night before, but he spoke to me as sober as though he'd been drinking nothing stronger than water. There was no more weeping talk. I tried to coax him to eat a bite, but he wouldn't touch what I'd brought him.

"Leave me alone," said he. "Go back to Christian's house, or wherever ye've been. I'm wanting no company."

"I can manage without yours," said I, and left him there. It rubbed me the wrong way to have him speak like that when I'd taken the trouble to cook his breakfast and bring it to him.

The wind shifted to the north and blew a gale; low grey clouds was scudding past not much over the trees. I went down the cove to see if the *Bounty's* old cutter was safe. We had it in a shed above the landing place. Not that we ever used it much. I don't think it had been out of the shed since the time the womenfolk tried to go off in it. We might as well have broken it up, for any good it was to us, but we'd patch and caulk it, none of us knew why, exactly.

I've never but once seen a heavier surf in the cove than there was that day. It was an awesome sight to watch the great seas piling in, throwing spray and solid water halfway up to the lookout point. The shed was gone and the cutter with it, and the wreckage was scattered far out across the cove. We had two Indian canoes, but they was safe. We'd lost canoes before, and when we made the last ones we took care to dig out a place for 'em well above the reach of any sea that might make up.

I went back to Mr. Christian's house, and for two days I kept away from McCoy. Then I got a bit worried about him, and after I'd had my supper I went along to see him whether he wanted me to or not.

The wind had gone down, but it was still cloudy, unsettled weather.

McCoy had all the doors and the windows shut. I called out to him, but there was no answer, so I pushed open the door and went in.

It was so dark inside that I could see naught at first. "Will! Where've ye got to?" said I. Then I heard his voice from the corner of the room. "Is it yourself, Alex? Quick, man! Shut the door!"

I slammed it to in spite of myself, he spoke in such a terror-struck voice. "What is it, lad?" I said. I didn't know but what the women might have changed their minds about leaving us alone; but when he begged me to make a light I knew it couldn't be that.

We kept a supply of candlenut tapers ready for lighting on a shelf, along with a flint and steel and a box of tinder. The tinder had got damp with the rainy weather and I was a quarter of an hour getting a taper alight. I found McCoy huddled down in a corner with the table upset and pulled up close, to hide behind. The minute I saw him I knew what was wrong. He had the horrors coming on, for the first time since I'd known him.

"Alex!" said he, "Alex!" — and that was as much as he could get out at first. He was a pitiful sight, shakin' and shiverin', with his knees under his chin and his eyes staring up at me like a wild man's.

"What's all this, Will?" said I, in as easy a voice as I could manage. "What's this game ye're playin' on me?" And whilst I spoke I righted the table and pulled it back into the middle of the room. "Come aboard, lad! D'ye still hate the sight of an old shipmate?"

He kept his eyes on the door, with a look on his face I'll not forget. Then up he sprung, and in three steps he was beside me on the bench, and gripped my arm with both his hands, so tight that the marks of his finger nails was there for days.

"Don't let him touch me!" said he, in a voice it sickened me to hear. Then he slid down to the floor under the table and held me fast by the legs.

"What ails ye?" said I. "What are ye afeared of?"

"Minarii," said he, in a whisper. "There by the door!"

"Will, ye daft loon! There's no Minarii here. Don't ye think I could see him if there was? Come, have a look for yourself."

He got up slow to his knees and turned himself till he could look toward the door.

"Are ye satisfied now?" said I. "There's none here but ourselves."

"Aye, he's gone," said he, in a weak, shaky voice. "Ye've scared him off."

"He's never been here," said I. "It's naught but your fancy. I'll show ye."

I tried to get up, but he held me fast and wouldn't let go.

"Don't leave me, Alex! Stay close here!"

I got him up on the bench again, but he kept tight hold of my arm. I'd seen a man or two with the horrors before. McCoy's was just coming on and I knew what I was in for. I coaxed him to loose me, after a bit, and I got a carrying pole was standing in a corner, and laid it on the table.

"I'll let no one touch ye, Will; ye can lay to that!" said I. "I'll knock 'em silly with this afore they know where they are."

That quieted him some, but try as I would I couldn't get him to bed. He was afeared to lie down. There was eight empty bottles scattered about the room. One I'd about finished the last night we was together. The rest McCoy had emptied alone, and I wouldn't have believed it unless I'd seen it.

He got worse as the night went on. He babbled wild and I couldn't make sense of it; but what he'd see was Minarii, with the heads of the murdered white men, and he was possessed with the notion that he'd come for ours. Time and again he'd be certain Minarii had opened the door, and I'd grab up the carrying pole and rush at naught, making out I'd drove him off. McCoy would think I had, and rest quiet for half an hour, maybe; then it would be the same thing over again.

So it went till long past midnight. I kept a light going until I'd burned all the tapers we had in the house. It had been bad enough before; ye can fancy what it was when the light was gone. I was twice McCoy's heft, and three times as strong, or so I'd believed; but it was all I could do to hold him when the terror was on him, and the screams he let out was like nothing human. Once he got loose and dashed his head so hard against the wall that it knocked him out for a bit. That gave me a chance to get him on to the bed and there I held him to daylight. He was in convulsions at the last, and if ever ye've held a man in that state, ye'll know what I went through.

It was just beginning to get light in the room when his body went limp under me and I saw he'd dozed off. I was done up and no mistake. It was as much as I could do to walk to the table and set down. Every muscle of me was tired and I was famished for sleep. I put my head on my arms and knew no more till I was roused by another yell, and before I could get my wits together McCoy was out of the door and running down the path toward Mr. Christian's house.

I followed, but the path's no easy one to race over, especially after such rains as we'd had. I slid and fell and got up again, and stumbled over the roots of trees, and by the time I got to Mr. Christian's house McCoy was making straight for the bluffs above the sea. I yelled, "Will! Come back!" But he never turned his head, and down he went, out of sight.

The sea was higher if anything than it had been the day before. When I reached the edge of the bluffs where I could look over, McCoy was halfway down. Whether he jumped or fell I don't know, but all at once he made a fearsome drop and struck amongst the rocks far below, just as a great sea came roaring in and took him, throwing up spray as high as where I stood. Another came directly after, and I caught a glimpse of his body being washed down and under it. I stood there for a half an hour, but I saw him no more.

# CHAPTER XX

I found his body the next afternoon. It had been washed to the mouth of the little valley west of Mr. Christian's house, and it was so battered and crushed 'twixt the rocks and the sea, ye'd scarce have thought it was anything human. Ye'll know how I felt when I had to take it up, but take it up I did, and buried it.

Then, sir, I went straight to the place where we'd hid our store of spirits. It was in a hole amongst the rocks on the seaward side of McCoy's old house. And I bashed in the two small cags and emptied 'em, and I took the rest, bottle by bottle, and broke every one into a thousand pieces against the rocks. Then I went to the place where we'd hid the still, and I took the copper coil and ran back to the bluffs, and I threw it as far as ever I could; and when I saw it splash in the sea I said, "God be thanked, there's an end of it!"

What with watching over McCoy and searching for his body all the next day, I was knocked up. I felt I could sleep for a week, but I couldn't bring myself, then, to go back to Mr. Christian's house, or to any of ours. I went to the place where the Indians had lived. It was in a pretty glade not far from where the path goes down to the cove. Many an evening I'd spent in that house afore there was any trouble amongst us. I'd a great liking for the Indians, and for Minarii and Tetahiti in particular. You'd go far to find two better men, brown or white. I'd been with 'em, day after day, and to say the truth, I'd found more pleasure with them than with my own mates. I'd puzzled now and again to think why they'd wanted to kill the lot of us. I knew they hated some, but I wouldn't have believed they'd have wanted all of us dead. But when ye come to think of it, they wouldn't dare leave any of us alive, once they'd started killing. There could be no friendship after that. It would have been us or them till one side or the other was wiped out.

I'd not been near their house in months, and it was a sorry-looking place now. The trail was grown over with bushes and the house going to rack and ruin. It gave me a lonesome feeling to see it, but I went in, and laid me down, and was asleep in five minutes.

I slept till daylight, and the first thing I thought about when I woke up was how bad I wanted a good stiff tot o' grog. I tried hard to put the notion out o' my head, but the more I tried the worse it got, and the end of it was I hurried along to the place where we'd kept the spirits to see if I mightn't have missed a bottle the day before. I found I hadn't, and I rested there, looking down at all them bits of broken glass shining on the rocks below, and cursing myself for the fool I'd been. There was no shame in me for being such a weak thing. I could think of naught but that I must get me a drink, some-how. Then I was minded of the bottles McCoy had emptied, and I thought I might find a drop left in one of 'em. A drop was all there was. I suppose I drained out a couple of spoonfuls from the lot, and then I washed out each bottle with a sup o' water so's to have it all. But that was only a torment, and I didn't rest till I'd searched all the houses in hopes of finding a bottle put by somewhere. I found one that had about a half-pint in it, in the tool-shed, and went near daft with joy at the sight of it.

Ye'll understand, sir, if ye've been a toper and left off sudden, the state I was in. There'd not been a day in four years I hadn't had my two or three tots o' grog, and most days there'd been a sight more taken. I'd got so as I needed spirits more than food or sleep or anything else, and if there was ever a sorry man it was me, that day, thinking how I'd thrown the copper coil into the sea. We'd nothing else would serve to distill spirits with. Then I minded how McCoy had made some beer, once, with ti roots. He'd made a mash and let it ferment. It was bitter stuff, and fair gagged ye to get it down, but it was strong.

I'd no sooner thought of it than I set off with a mattock over my shoulders for McCoy's ti plantation. I wanted to get a mess of roots to baking straight off; but before I got to the place I stopped. I could take ye to the very spot, sir, and show ye the rock I set on whilst I fought the thing out with myself. I thought of all the misery we'd brought on the womenfolk and ourselves those last years. I thought of the children. I knew that if I digged up them ti roots I was lost; I'd finish the way McCoy had. "Never!" said I. "Back with ye, Alex Smith, and make an end, once and for all!"

And so I did, though I went through torments for a fortnight. I couldn't sleep, I couldn't eat, and I wasn't sure but I'd have the horrors myself afore I was done. But I held fast.

Little by little things got easier for me. I could have my rest at night; there was no more walking up and down till I was so beat I could scarce stand. At times when it was hardest, I set my mind on Mr. Christian, and it would strengthen me to think how pleased and comforted he'd be if he could know the fight I was makin'. I'd never forgot the hopeless look on his face the day he died. It was when his lad, Thursday October, had walked into the room. I remembered him saying, "Take the child out," to Mrs. Christian. There's no father could have loved children more. He couldn't bear to see the lad, that was it, thinking what might happen once he was gone. A blessing it was he couldn't see what did happen.

It was a rare thing to get back my self-respect. I'd wake of a morning with a feeling of peace in my heart, and there wasn't a day long enough for the work I had in hand. I cut off the beard I'd let grow, and shaved regular, like I used to, and kept myself clean and tidy. I moved back into my old house where I'd lived with Mr. Young, and made everything shipshape there; then I went through the other houses and set them to rights as well as I could, working alone, though why I did it I couldn't say. I might have had the notion in the back of my head that the women would want to come back some day.

I was bound not to go too near 'em, for I had my pride. If they wanted to keep clear, they could for all of me, and Mr. Young with 'em. I'd not be the one to make the first move.

I had work and to spare, days, but night was a lonesome time. There was little I could do after dark but set and think. When I was redding up the houses, I found the *Bounty's* old Bible and Prayer Book. They'd been Mr. Christian's, before. After his death Mr. Young took charge of 'em, and I'd often see him reading in one or the other, though he wasn't what ye'd call a religious man. But these was all we had in the way of books, and I reckon they helped him pass the time. I found a couple of the *Bounty's* spare logbooks that he'd filled with writin', but what it was I couldn't make out. Little schooling I'd ever had in my young days. It was as much as I could do to write my name, but I'd got far enough along to spell out words of print. I thought, maybe, with the Bible to help, I could bring back what I'd been teached as a lad, but I had to give up. It was all gone clean out o' my head.

One day — it was around a month after I'd buried McCoy — I was weeding a bit of garden I'd made near the house. I'd set me down to rest when I heard a rustlin' in the bushes behind me. I looked round, and there was my old woman.

Not a word was spoke. In three steps she was down on her knees beside me. She put her arms around me and her head on my shoulder, and began to weep in the soft quiet way the Indian women do. I was touched deep, but I sat lookin' straight in front of me. After a bit, when I was sure I had myself in hand, I said: "Where's your musket, Balhadi? Ain't ye afeared to go roamin' without it? I might do ye a mischief."

She said naught, but only held on to me the tighter. I reached up and took hold of her hand, and we rested so for a good ten minutes. I'll not go into all that was said. It was like the old days afore any trouble was started. I told her about McCoy and she had her cry over that, not being a woman to nurse hard feelings towards anyone, and Will was a good man, well liked by all when he'd been sober. She cried more, for joy, when I told her I'd destroyed the still and the spirits. I felt paid a hundred times over for the misery I'd suffered in getting myself in hand. I'd been hurt that Mr. Young hadn't come near me, but Balhadi said it was because he was too sick to come. He'd been in his bed all this while.

"I'd like well to see him," said I.

"Then come, Alex," said she, taking hold of my hand. "There's not been a day but he's spoke of ye, and what ye've told me will do him more good than any of us women can. Ye'll be welcomed hearty, that I promise, and there'll be none gladder to see ye than Maimiti."

So I started along with her, but afore we'd gone a dozen yards I stopped.

"No, Balhadi," said I. "I'll rest here in the settlement. Ye can tell Maimiti and the others how it is with me now. If they want to see me, they know where they can find me, and they can do as they've a mind about coming back. I'll not be the one to coax 'em."

So off she went, alone. That was the middle of the morning, and three hours later here they came, all the womenfolk, some carrying children or leading 'em, some with baskets and bundles, — all they could manage at one time, — Maimiti in the lead, and Moetua with Ned Young pickaback, as though he'd been a child. Some of the young ones I'd never seen; others I'd hardly laid eyes on for three years. Thursday October was a fine lad, now, past eight years, and his brother Charles was six, and little Mary Christian five, who was born the very day the killing began. There was eighteen children, all told, two of 'em mine, and it shames me to say that neither of these was Balhadi's. When I saw that little flock, as pretty, healthy children as a man could wish to look on, I was grieved past words, thinking of the fathers of so many dead and buried, never to have the joy of their own. It was hard to believe that the four of us that was left after the massacre had been such crazed brutes when we'd all these little ones to cherish and care for. Whatever had come over us? There's no·way to explain or reason it out. We was stark, staring mad, that's all there is to say.

The women came along one by one to greet me kindly. Not a word was said of what was past. I could see Mrs. Christian's hand there. Better women never breathed than herself and Taurua, Mr. Young's girl. Both had courage would have done credit to any man, but they'd no malice in their hearts. I began to see from that morning the change that had come over all the women. The time that had gone by had something to do with it, but what they'd been through was the main reason. It aged their hearts and sobered 'em beyond their years. Prudence and Hutia, in particular, had been wild young things when the *Bounty* came to the island, up to any kind of mischief, and enough they'd made, one way and another. But they'd grown to be fine women, and good steady mothers to their children.

We divided ourselves up into households like we had before. Mrs. Christian with her children, and Sarah and Mary with theirs, moved into the house where Mr. Young and me had lived before. Moetua, Nanai, Susannah, and Jenny went to the Christians' house; Mr. Young, with Taurua and Prudence and their children, lived where Mills and Martin had; Balhadi, Hutia, and me took ours to the Indians' old place.

In a few days all their things was moved down from the Auté Valley. It did my heart good to see the houses that had stood empty so long filled with women and children, and the paths and dooryards cleared, and the gardens new made. Mr. Young was like a different man. I never heard him laugh or joke the way he had in the days afore trouble came, but he'd found peace again. The old hopeless look was gone out of his face. His strength was slow in coming back, and he'd set in his dooryard, watching the children come and go, and taking deep comfort, as I did, in the sight of 'em.

Thursday October was a son any father might have been proud to own—as handy a lad as I've ever seen, and bright and active beyond his years. He'd a deal of his father's nature in him and his mother's as well. There couldn't have been a finer cross in blood than theirs. Next to him was Sarah McCoy, only a few months younger; than came her brother Dan, who was seven, and after him a pair of stout lads, young Matt Quintal and Mr. Christian's second boy, Charles. These five followed me about as close as my shadow, and words couldn't tell how I joyed to have 'em with me. None of the children knew what had happened here in the past, whilst they was little, and we was all of a mind they should never know.

One morning I set off with the five I've spoke of for a day of roaming on the west side of the island. That part, as you've seen, sir, is all steep gullies and ravines, with bits of open land between, good for nothing in the way of gardens. Even if it had been good land we'd not have bothered with it, having enough and to spare in the Main Valley. I hadn't been down there in months, nor any of the womenfolk, and the children had never set foot in it.

It was a bright cool morning, quiet and peaceful; we could hear the cocks crowing far and wide through the forests. I mind how it came to me, as we was climbing the western ridge, that this place was home to me at last. Ye may wonder I'd not thought of it so long since, seeing we'd no means of leaving it. I liked the island fine in the beginning, but after a year or so I always had the notion in the back of my head that some day a ship would come—not an English ship, in search of us, but a Spanish one, likely, or a ship from the American colonies.

It was in my mind to change my name and go off in her, and make my way back to England in the end. But now I was thinking of Pitcairn's Island as home. There's no better way to show ye the change that come over me, and it was the children that brought it to pass.

When we got on the ridge to the south of the Goat-House Mountain, I set me down to rest, and little Sarah McCoy with me. The lads was eager to go on, and down they ran into the western valleys, as sure of foot as the goats that roamed wild there. I let 'em go, knowing they couldn't lose themselves. Sarah and I followed, after a bit. She was a quiet little mite, as pretty as a picture, with dark curly hair like her mother's. It made my heart sore to think her father couldn't have lived to see her as she was then.

There had been a path down to the western shore, but it was all grown over now, it had been so long since any of us had gone that way. We came out on an open spot overlooking the sea and waited there. The lads had gone roaming off in every direction, into the little valleys and down the rocks to the bit of beach on that side. I'd no mind to follow, knowing they was well able to take care of themselves. The fowls had increased wonderful the years we'd been on the island; hundreds ran wild through the bush. The boys loved to hunt for their eggs; they'd find enough in half an hour for all the settlement, and there was even more to be had in this wild part of the island. We'd not waited long before Thursday October and the two youngest lads came back with a basket full of 'em, and some fine shellfish they'd found amongst the rocks. Little Matt Quintal had gone off by himself, and, after waiting half an hour or thereabouts, I went in search.

I'd not gone a quarter of a mile when I spied him below me, scrambling through the thickets as fast as he could go. I thought he was chasing one of the wild roosters, but when I called out he came runnin' towards me, so terrified he couldn't speak. I grabbed him up and he held fast around my neck with his face pressed tight against my shoulder.

I set him down on my knee. "What's this, Matty?" said I. "Was ye tryin' to run away from yer shadow?"

He held on to me like he'd never let go. I talked quiet and easy to him, and finally he got so's he could speak. He told me he'd seen a *varua ino*. That's what the Indians call an evil spirit. There's not one of the women but believes to this day in ghosts and spirits of all kinds, good and bad. Many's the time they claim to see or hear 'em. It's always tried my patience the way they talk o' such things at night, and tell the young 'uns tales about 'em. I've wished often enough to put a stop to such foolishness, but ye might as well try to change the colour o' their skins. I wouldn't mind if it was only to do with the mothers, but the children listen with all their ears and believe every word they're told.

The lad was half crazed with fear, and shivering all over, but at last I got him to say what he thought he'd seen. It was a huge great man, he said, a-settin' on a rock.

"Did he see ye?" I asked.

"No; he had his back towards me," said he.

"I'll tell ye what ye saw, lad," said I. "There's some old stone images yonder where ye've been. They was made by folk that lived here long ago. They're ugly things, bigger'n a man and made to look like men, but they're naught but stone, and there's no more harm in 'em than there is in this rock we're a-settin' on."

"I saw it move," said he.

"Ye saw naught o' the sort, Matt," said I. "Ye fancied ye did, I don't doubt . . ."

"No, no! I did! I saw it move!" said he, and he stuck to that. I couldn't coax him out o' the notion, so I took him on my shoulder and carried him back to where the other children was.

Brought up as they'd been, they was all sure that little Matt must have seen an evil spirit. But they wasn't afeared of it with me there. So I told 'em to wait where they was while I chased that ghost clean off the island. "If there is one yonder," said I, "as soon as he sees me he'll go flyin' off beyond the cliffs, and that'll be the last o' *him*. He'll never come back again."

They set there as quiet as mice and made no fuss whatever. They all believed Father Alex could do anything he was a mind to, and that even *varua inos* was afeared o' him.

What I reckoned to do was go off a piece, out of sight of the children, and then come back and tell 'em the spirit was gone, for good and all. But when I'd gone about as far as I thought was needed, I spied something that gave me a shock. In a bit of soft ground I saw the tracks of bare feet, half again as big as my own.

I'd seen them tracks before, many's the time, but I couldn't believe these was real, even as I looked at 'em. I crossed over the place and went along a dry gully for about fifty yards, makin' no noise, till I came to a wall of rock that slanted under, where I'd sheltered from the

rain more than once in the old days. The Indians had used it for a
camp when they fished on that side of the island; half a dozen could
sleep dry there, and well sheltered from the wind. I pushed by the
bushes and peered through. There sat Matt Quintal with his back to
me, just as his own lad had seen him.

He'd nothing on save what was left of a pair of seaman's trousers;
it was the same pair he'd worn the day the women burned us out of
the house. Under the rock was a bed he'd made of fern and dry grass,
and he was squatting in the Indian fashion, close by, cracking fowl's
eggs and drinking 'em down. There was the carcass of a wild pig to
one side, all torn apart, and the bones of others was scattered around
where he'd thrown 'em. The smell of the place was enough to sicken
a dog.

If I'd had my wits about me, I'd have backed off without a word,
but I called out, "Matt!" afore I could stop myself. He turned his head
slow, looking this way and that, and then he spied me. When I saw
his face I felt the chills go up and down my back. Ye never saw such
a pair of eyes outside of a madhouse; and he'd a great beard, now, that
reached to his waist, and bushed out the width of his chest.

I tried to be easy and natural. "Matt, ye rogue," said I. "Where have
ye hid yourself this long while? God's truth! We thought ye was dead!"

I'd no more than got this out when he grabbed up a club thick as
my arm and made a rush at me with a bellow that was like nothing in
nature, brute or human. I ran for my life, jumping over rocks and
dodging amongst the trees; then I caught my foot in some vines and
pitched for'ard. I turned my head as I fell, thinkin' he was right at
my heels, but he'd stopped thirty or forty yards back; and there he
stood, with his great club in one hand, looking around in a puzzled way,
like as if he wasn't sure I'd been there. I lay flat amongst the bushes,
and I didn't move till he'd gone back the way he'd come.

When I'd shook myself together I hurried along to the children,
and glad they was to see me again. They'd heard the roar Quintal let
out, but they'd not seen us, and I thought best to say it was me that
made the noise to scare off the evil spirit.

"Did ye see it, Alex?" Dan'l McCoy asked.

"Nay, lads," said I; "but if there was one, I reckon I scared him so he'll
bother us no more. But I want none of ye to come down to this side of
the island till I've had a good hunt through it, for I saw a great wild
boar in the gully yonder. He might do one of ye a mischief."

We went home, then, and Sarah McCoy and little Matt kept tight hold of my hands all the way.

I told Mr. Young what I'd found. The only way we could reason it out was that Quintal had got so crazed he'd clean forgot there was anyone on the island save himself. He couldn't have been roaming the Main Valley or he'd have been seen.

"It's not likely he's ever been across the island since he went down there," said Mr. Young; "but now that he's seen ye, Alex, there's no telling what he may do." He shook his head in a mournful way. "I thought we'd got to the end of our troubles at last," said he, "and here's another sprung up. We must be under a curse."

I was anxious enough, myself, and it was hard to say what was best to be done. One thing was certain: the women would have to be told; so we called 'em together, and I gave 'em the full truth of what I'd seen. They was horror-struck, especially Sarah, who'd been Quintal's woman. For all that, she wouldn't hear to a hand being lifted against him. Jenny wanted us to shoot him and be done with it, and Prudence and Hutia backed her up, but Mrs. Christian and the rest was against this.

"Haven't we had trouble enough here, Jenny," said I, "without hunting down a poor crazed man to shoot him in cold blood?"

"Better that," said she, "than leave him free to harm us and the children. And that he'll do, sooner or later. The time will come, Alex, when ye'll wish ye'd done as I say."

It came sooner than we feared it would. Two days later I was giving some of the women a hand at mending fence at Mr. Christian's house. There was Jenny and Susannah and Moetua, and, natural enough, we had Quintal on our minds. I'd seen to the loading of all the muskets, and there was two or three in every house, ready for use in case of need. Jenny had a sharp, bitter tongue when she'd a mind to use it, and she was trying to make out to the others I was afeared of Quintal. I let her run on, paying no heed to her woman's talk, and whilst she was in the midst of it we heard screams from the direction of the Christians' house. Directly after there were shots fired. I ran there as fast as I could and found the women in a terrible state. Little Sarah McCoy had gone to Brown's Well for water, and whilst she was dipping it up she saw Quintal coming down the path from the ridge. The minute he spied her he chased after her. Mrs. Christian heard the screams and rushed out with a musket. Quintal had all but caught the lass when Mrs. Christian fired over his head. At the sound of the shot he stopped short and ran off into the bush.

Sarah was old enough to remember Quintal, but she thought it was his ghost she saw. It made my heart sick to see her shivering and shaking in her mother's arms. She didn't get over the shock for days after.

We didn't dare rest, any longer, scattered as we'd been. Half of the women and children moved into Mr. Young's house, and the rest came with me. Mr. Young was too poorly to leave the village, but that same afternoon I took a musket to protect myself and went into the valley to spy out Quintal, if I could, but not a sign of him did I see. Then I climbed the mountain, where I could overlook the island. I had the *Bounty's* spyglass with me and I searched the western valleys bit by bit. There was little ye could see, below, because of the trees and thickets, but at last I spied him as he was climbing down amongst the rocks to go to the beach. I felt easier after that, and ye can imagine the relief it was to the womenfolk to know that he'd gone to his old place. They scarce left the houses after that, not knowing how soon he might take it into his head to come back.

Every day I'd go to the ridge with a musket and the spyglass to keep watch, and most times I'd have a glimpse of him. Once I saw him with the carcass of a wild pig acrost his shoulder, and it sickened me to think of him eating the raw flesh. He'd no way of making fire, but he seemed to care naught about that. Another time I'd a good view of him for near a half-hour. He was stark naked, settin' on a rock. The spyglass brought him as close as though he was within speakin' distance. He was talkin' to himself, and going through queer motions as a crazed man will.

One afternoon I'd no sight of him. It was getting on towards sundown and I was ready to come away when I spied Hutia and Prudence running along the ridge towards where I was. When they saw me they beckoned in a desperate way, but they didn't call out. It didn't take me long to reach 'em.

Quintal was in the Main Valley, but that wasn't the worst of it. He'd come all the way round, by the Auté Valley, more than likely, and he'd rushed out of the forest on Sarah, his own woman, and Mary McCoy. They was not over a hundred yards from the house. Mary told what happened. Quintal had passed her by and chased after Sarah. The poor woman was so terrified she'd run away from the house instead of towards it. Then she saw she was trapped, and the only way she could go was towards the crag we call Ship-Landing Point, that shuts in the east side of the cove. Quintal was close behind. Sarah went on to the very top of the crag, and when she could go no further she threw herself off, sooner than let him catch her.

Mr. Young had gathered all the women and children at my house by the time I got there. Three had gone down to the cove to search for Sarah's body. No one knew where Quintal had got to. Mary was the only one had spied him and she'd run to the house without waiting to see what he'd do next. I was on my way to the landing place when I met the women coming up. Moetua had Sarah in her arms. She was still breathing, but she died within the half-hour.

It was dark by that time. The women laid Sarah's body out and covered it with a cloth, and some of 'em was crouched down beside it, wailing and crying as the Indians do when there's death in the house. Mr. Young and me tried to quiet 'em, but they was past listening to reason. The children took fright from the mothers, and most of them was crying as well. Mrs. Christian and Taurua was the only ones kept themselves in hand. Mr. Young stood guard on one side of the house and me on the other, and it was as much as we could do to stop there with the women carrying on as they did.

About an hour after Sarah's body was brought up, Susannah was found missing. There was only one candlenut taper burning in the house, and with the light so dim, and so many there, none had noticed that Susannah wasn't amongst 'em. I couldn't believe, at first, that anything had happened to her, for I'd seen her with the others just before I'd gone down to the cove to help bring Sarah's body up. We knew she'd not go roaming off alone, after what had happened. Then one of the children said he'd seen someone going to the out-kitchen, which was about twenty yards from the house. It was getting dark and he couldn't be sure who it was. We'd no doubt, then, that Quintal had been hiding near by, waiting for such a chance, and that he'd grabbed Susannah.

Some thought he might have carried her to one of the other houses; so, dark as it was, I made a search, and glad I was when I'd finished. Wherever Quintal had gone, there was nothing more we could do till daylight. Ye can fancy the night we put in; never was there a longer one. Jenny came out to where I stood guard to tell me it was my fault Sarah was lying dead. "And Susannah will be dead by this time," said she. "If ye'd been half a man, Alex Smith, ye'd have killed the brute the day ye found him." The poor woman was half crazed herself, after all that had happened. I couldn't blame her for letting out at me.

Mr. Young and me set out in search at the crack o' dawn. He was in no fit state to come, but he was bound to do it. We each had a musket and I carried a hand axe in my belt in case of need. We knew we'd got to kill Quintal, and ye can fancy how we felt. We took the path through the settlement and past Brown's Well, and when we got up on the ridge Mr. Young was so tired he had to rest. I've never felt more sorry for anyone than I did for him that morning. It was only his spirit gave him the strength to go on.

We both thought Quintal would go back to his old place in the gully, and it was there we meant to look first. "Alex," said he, "if we see him alone, no matter if his back is turned, we must both shoot, and shoot to kill." That was all the speech we had.

I led the way when we got down into the western valley. We went slow, stopping every few yards to listen. When we got close I whispered to Mr. Young to watch that side whilst I went forward to look.

I crawled through the bushes without making the least noise; then I came to the place. Susannah was lying on her back, without a rag to her body, with her feet tied together and her arms bound to her side with long strips of bark that went round and round her. Quintal was nowheres in sight. I made sure of that, then came out quick as ever I could, and I had her free in five seconds. She was in a terrible state, all covered with scratches and bruises, and one of her ears had been bit clean through, but I thanked God she was alive. She made no sound as I cut her loose. I whispered, "Get ye back yonder, Susannah. Ned's there. Where's he gone?" She motioned that he was somewhere on the far side of the place. I lifted her up; she was scarce able to stand, but she managed to do as I told her.

I looked to the priming of my musket and went for'ard. Quintal was asleep behind some bushes not a dozen steps farther on. As soon as I saw him I backed off to the far side of the gully and raised my piece; but I couldn't pull the trigger. I've never felt worse in my life than I did that minute. I stood lookin' at him, thinking of the Matt Quintal I'd known on the *Bounty*. Then I minded me of the women and children and of Sarah lying dead, and I knew I had to go through with it.

I picked up a handful of pebbles and tossed it on him. He was lying on his back and saw me the minute he raised his head. His club was there beside him. He grabbed it and up he sprang, and as he came for me I pulled the trigger, but the musket missed fire. I'd only time to dodge to one side and grab my hand axe. He made such a rush that he went past me. I ducked under the blow he aimed at me and threw out my leg, and he went sprawling his full length. Then, sir, as he got to his knees, I brought the axe down on his head with all my strength.

## CHAPTER XXI

It was a merciful quick death, sir. He was killed on the instant, without a cry from his lips. I set me down for a bit, shook to the heart; then I put by the axe and went back to where Mr. Young was waiting. Maimiti had give us a tapa mantle to fetch for Susannah, fearin' the state she might be in, dead or alive. She'd put this over her and was crouched there beside him.

"Go ye back with her, Ned," said I. "The women will be half crazed till they know she's safe. Ye can tell 'em it's done. He'll trouble us no more."

I didn't know my own voice as I spoke, and Mr. Young said never a word. He was not a man of strong nature, even in health, and there's none hated strife and bloodshed more than him who'd had to share in so much. I knew the horror he'd have of seein' Quintal's body. I was bound to spare him that.

Bruised and hurt as she'd been, Susannah had more strength left than him, and it was her took his arm and helped him up the steep rocky way. Slow they went, and I watched till they was out of sight amongst the trees and appeared again, high above, and crossed over the ridge to the Main Valley. Then I went back to where Quintal lay, and digged his grave with the axe I'd killed him with. It was hard, slow work, but I did it, and laid him in the place and smoothed over the ground, and covered it with leaves and moss so that none could tell where it was. Then I went down to the sea and threw the axe far out, and washed myself, and walked back across the island.

We buried Sarah the same day. She'd no kin amongst the women, and three was chosen to act as such and mourn her in their fashion, weeping and wailing, gashing their faces and breasts cruel with little sticks they called *paohinos,* set with sharks' teeth. Ye wouldn't have known 'em in that state; it was like as if they was out of their senses.

Such things brought home to me how little we understood our women-folk for all the years we'd lived with 'em. Sometimes they'd seem no different from women at home; then of a sudden ye'd see the gap there was between our ways and theirs. As I've said, they had a mortal terror of the new dead, especially them they'd been afeared of in life. For a week they was all huddled into my house at night, women and children together, with tapers burnin' from sundown to sunup. Not even Moetua would set foot outside the door after dark. But that passed. In the end Mr. Young and me coaxed 'em back to their own houses, and we lived as we had before.

And now, at last, sir, I've reached the end of the evil times. From that day we've had peace here, and, with God's help, so it shall be through all the years to come. Quintal had to be put to death — that I believe. The lives of none would have been safe with him roamin' the island, crazed brute he'd become, ready to spring out on women and children. But it was little comfort I took from thinkin' so as I stood, that day, over his grave. Ye'll know how I felt, after all the blood had been spilt here. I wished I was dead and buried with him.

Aye, peace followed, but there was none in my heart for many a long day.

Mr. Young had used up what little strength he had and was in his bed for a fortnight. Then he began to mend, and I thought he was on the way to full health again. He saw how it was with me, though I never spoke Quintal's name, and made out as well as I could to seem easy in mind. But he knew, and it was thanks to him and the children that I got through the worst of that time.

No words could tell the blessing the children was to all. They made a new life for us, as different from the old as day from night. There was twenty-one at this time, all the way from nine years to a pair of newborn babes. Three was Christians, seven Youngs, three McCoys, two Mills, four Quintals, and there was two of my own. None, so far as I know, belonged to the Indian men; they was all ours of the *Bounty*. So the women said, but the truth is we didn't know for certain who was the fathers of some. There was no doubt about Mrs. Christian's, but the others of one name was not always by the same mothers. Ye'll bear in mind the rough, wild way we lived; and the past six years there'd been more than twice the number of women there was men. Some without men of their own wanted children as bad as the rest. Aye, for all their hate of us at that time, they still had the great wish for

children. It gave 'em something to live for. If they'd not cleared out
of the settlement, sickened of our drunken ways, I'll warrant there'd
have been half again as many. Ye may think it strange, but, now that
all was peace, it was the wish of Balhadi and Taurua, our own two
girls, that Mr. Young and me should be fathers of babes to any that
wanted 'em. And when I recollect the need there was for children, and
the blessings they've brought, and the way we've lived these last years,
like one big family of kind and loving hearts, I can't feel it was a
wrong way of life. It seems to me it was the right way, and the only
way for that time.

None of the children, God be thanked, was old enough to recollect
the time of the murders. Four or five remembered McCoy and Quintal,
but they soon forgot, as children do, and we never spoke the names of
any that was dead. We was bound that no memory of that time should
be carried on to them.

And they healed our hearts, sir, and in the end made this small island
like a heaven on earth. That's a strong way to put it, but so it was.
There was scarce an acre of ground but had some sad or shameful thing
joined with it, and at first they'd come to mind as I'd go from place
to place. I'd have a horror of walking about. But the children mended
that. They made the earth sweet and clean once more. Before another
year was gone they overlaid the whole island with so many new and
happy memories that had to do with them alone, the old ones all but
faded out beneath 'em.

They took after the Indian ways and spoke their mothers' tongue,
as it was natural they should. A happier set of children never grew up
together. There was no strife amongst 'em, and that seemed strange
to me when I'd recollect the fightin', wranglin' 'uns I'd been brought
up with in London, and the bloody noses I got and give from the time
I was five years old. I thought it must be so with all children, but
amongst these there was never a blow struck or a harsh word spoke.
Aye, it was a joy to see 'em.

Ye'll know the comfort Mr. Young and me took to be with 'em
from day to day, watchin' 'em grow and blossom out in new ways. If
I was partial towards any of the lads, it was to Thursday October and
little Matt Quintal, but the truth is I loved every one as though they
was my own flesh and blood. I'd take a walk of an evening, after
supper, which we always had afore sundown. The mothers would be in
the dooryards with the little ones on their laps and the older lads and

lasses playin' their games close by; and I'd be struck to the heart with pity that Mr. Christian couldn't have lived to see 'em as they was then.

Now I must tell ye of a thing happened close after Quintal's death, for it's the greatest blessing has come to me all the years of my life, though I didn't know it at the time. As a usual thing I'd go along to Mr. Young's house of an evening, for I couldn't abide to be alone with my thoughts. One evening I'd gone late. The women and children was already abed, and Mr. Young was at his table, writin' in one of the old *Bounty's* logbooks. I'd often seen him at that. He gave me a nod and went on with it, and I set me down to wait till he was through.

"What is it ye write there so often, Ned?" I asked him. "Is it a journal ye're keepin'?"

"Aye," said he. "I've a record here of births and the like, but that's not the whole of it." Then he told me he'd write down whatever he could recollect out of books he'd read in past years. It was Mr. Christian had first put him in the way of it. About a year after we'd come here they begun doing it in their spare time, and they'd filled pages and pages. After Mr. Christian's death, Mr. Young had left off, but now he'd took it up again in earnest. He'd been a great reader from the time he was a lad, and there could have been little he hadn't mastered and kept in mind.

He read me a bit from a story called *The Pilgrim's Progress,* as he'd recollected and set it down. I was taken clean out of myself and begged him to go on, which he did, from one piece to another he had there. Mind ye, sir, I was naught but an ignorant seaman, with no more knowledge of the joy to be had from books than the pigs that run wild here. I didn't even know the names of our English writers, not a blessed one! Mr. Young told me about 'em. I could have listened the night through.

"Was ye never teached to read and write, Alex?" said he.

"A little, when I was a mite of a lad," said I, "but it's all gone from me now."

"How would ye like to take it up again?" said he. "I'll help. Ye've a taste for it, that's plain."

"I'd like it well enough," said I, "but ye'd soon sicken of the bargain, Ned, for I'm dismal ignorant. Hard work ye'd have tryin' to pound learnin' into my head."

"I'll chance that," said he, "and if ye're willin' we'll begin afore we're a day older."

Little I thought anything would come of it, but I was only too pleased to say aye to that. I was in desperate need of something to keep my mind off Quintal. Whether I could be teached or not didn't matter so much. I could try, anyway, and pass the evenings, which was the worst time of day for me then.

That was the start of it. The next day Mr. Young took me in hand, and slow work he had at first. But he was that patient he could have teached a stone image, and I'll say this for myself: I was bound to learn. And once I had a thing, it was mine. I never forgot.

He began to read to me out of the Bible. In the foundling home where I was raised, I'd heard bits from the Bible, but I was a wild young lad and gave no heed. It was different, now. I listened with all my ears, careful and patient, and Mr. Young was a master reader. We started with the Book of Genesis. Every evening when my lesson was over he'd go through half a dozen chapters, and I'd have that to think over till the next evening.

Our life went on as peaceful as heart could wish. Mornings, as a usual thing, we was all at work in the gardens. Two or three times a week, afternoons, the women would be at their tapa-making below the rock cistern. There was a pretty sight to see, sir. Many's the time I'd go up to look on. There'd be four or five beatin' out the bark at once — they took turns at it — whilst the others looked after the babes and the little ones. They'd be scattered amongst the rocks with the sunlight flickerin' down on 'em through the trees, the mothers combing the children's hair after their baths, and makin' wreaths of ferns for their heads and garlands of flowers to hang around their necks. They could do wonders with blossoms; they'd spend hours stringin' 'em together in different ways, and whilst they was at it they'd sing their Indian songs. There'd been no laughter or singin' for years till after Quintal's death, and it warmed my heart to see such a blessed change in the womenfolk. Their homesickness for Tahiti was gone at last. They'd talk of it, of course, but not in the old heartsick way, with tears in their eyes. Pitcairn's Island was home, now, to all.

Midday, after we'd had our dinners, was a time of rest, the Indian fashion. For two hours, or thereabouts, ye'd hear no sound; then all would be astir again to do as they'd a mind to. That was the time I'd take the older lads and lasses to roam the hills and valleys; or we'd go offshore, when the season was right, in the canoes, to fish. The Indians had showed me how and when to fish in these waters. There's a

skill to it I wouldn't have believed in the old days; and some of the
*Bounty* men was that stubborn they'd never acknowledge that the
Indians knew better about such matters than themselves. But I learned
by goin' out with 'em, and I've passed on all I've learned to the children.
But it's little they've got from me compared to what their mothers has
teached 'em, or what they've picked up, natural. They know the use of
every plant and tree and flower on the island. They know the winds and
the seasons and the nesting times of the birds. If there's anything they
don't know about this island I'd be pleased to hear what it is. They
learned to swim near as soon as they learned to walk. I used to be
afeared to let the little ones go into the water, but bless ye, I soon got
over that! Birds ain't more at home in the air than these lads and
lasses are in the sea. In these days the older ones swim all the way
around the island for the fun of it. To see 'em sport in the breakers
ye'd think they was born amongst 'em.

But there's no need to tell ye all this, sir, for ye can see for yourself
how it is with us. It's the same now as it was then, save that the little
tots has grown up more. But I like to mind me of the days when it was
all new and we could scarce believe in the peace that had come at last.

I had my lessons with Mr. Young late of an afternoon, and evenings
as well. Some of the children took to comin' in to watch, and it wasn't
long till I found they was gettin' the hang o' things just from listenin'
to what Mr. Young would tell me. Not their letters, of course, but the
way of speakin' English. They'd carry away any amount of it in their
heads. One day I spoke to Mr. Young about this.

"They're as bright as new buttons, Ned," said I. "If ye was to teach
them along with me, I'll warrant they'd soon catch the meaning and
go on full sail, leagues ahead of the place I've reached."

"Aye," said he, "I've thought o' that." He got out of his chair and
walked up and down the room for a bit, turning the thing over in his
mind.

"But where'd be the good of it, Alex? We want to do what's best
for them. I'd come to think Mr. Christian was right. It was his wish
they should have their mothers' ways and their mothers' beliefs. No,
let's keep 'em as they are. If I was to teach 'em to read, they'd have
naught but the Bible for their lesson book, and what they'd find there
would only puzzle and upset their minds."

I believed then he had the right of it, and no more was said. Mr.
Young had brought me along as far as the Book of Leviticus, and I

didn't know what to make of a good part of what I'd listened to, myself. I could fancy how it would have puzzled the children. There was the story of the children of Israel, and God favouring them and hardening Pharaoh's heart so Moses could bring plagues on the Egyptians: rivers of blood, and swarms of vermin and frogs, and diseases for their cattle, and the like. If it was God had hardened Pharaoh's heart, I couldn't see that Pharaoh was to blame; and I wondered about the innocent people amongst the Egyptians, for there's always good as well as bad in any land. Why should they be made to suffer for the evil ones amongst 'em? Mr. Young told me it was a story the Israelites had wrote for themselves, to show their side of things. That's how it looked to me, but I took a powerful interest in the Bible for all that. Many's the night we sat over it till the small hours, for Mr. Young was as pleased to read as I was to listen.

We went on so for nine months, and slow but sure I learned to read. I couldn't well say how pleased and proud I was when I found I'd got the way of it; and I worked at writin' as well. What I'd lost as a lad came back, but it was hard work that brought it. Not a day passed without my lesson, and I'd study by myself for hours together.

Then Mr. Young's health give way again. He'd never got back his strength, and the old asthma trouble came on worse than ever. We had a long spell of cold rainy weather, and that may have brought it. The women tried all their Indian medicines of herbs and poultices and the like, but this was a thing they'd never seen before, and they couldn't find a cure for it. If ye've ever watched a man drown, sir, powerless to help him, ye'll know how it was with us. He'd be took bad four or five days together and fight for his breath in a way was pitiful to see. And all that time he was getting weaker. So it went for three long months, but we never give up hope.

We tried all ways we could think of to give him a little ease. One afternoon we had him propped up with pillows in a chair I'd made for him. He'd been better that day, but I saw a look in his face that told me he knew he was dying. He didn't talk much — just sat with his hands in his lap, lookin' through the trees to seaward. We was alone in the room.

Presently he turned his head.

"Alex," said he, "there's a thing or two I want to speak of, while I can."

My heart smote me, the way he said it. He wanted so bad to live.

There was a time, after Mr. Christian's death, when he'd no wish to go on, but the children had changed that. He wanted to grow old amongst 'em, along with me, and see 'em reared to manhood and womanhood.

"If ever a ship should come," said he, "and it's likely there will, soon or late, ye'd best tell who ye are. If there's a good man aboard of her — one ye can trust — I'd make a clean breast to him, Alex, of what's happened here. Let him know the truth."

"I will so, Ned," said I.

"It's yourself has been spared of all of us to bring up the children. It's a great trust and a sacred one. Guard it well. Be faithful to it. I know ye will."

He took my hand and held it. "That's all," said he. "I'd have liked well to stay on with ye, lad. But it's not to be."

I couldn't speak, sir. All I could do was to hold his hand in both of mine, with the tears streamin' down my face. Then Mrs. Christian and Taurua came in. I couldn't bear to set with him longer. I had to leave the room.

He died that same night, the three of us by him, and we laid him to rest the following day. Words can't say how we missed him. For all he was so far above me in blood and rearing, I loved him as if he'd been my own brother. He had the most kind and gentle nature. If ever ye could have laid eyes on him, ye'd have known at first sight he was a good man, one ye could love and trust. When we lost him we was that stunned and grief-stricken there was naught we could take up with the least relish or pleasure. It seemed as if we couldn't go on without Mr. Young.

Aye, it was a dark, lonesome time that followed. But lonesome's not the word. It was worse than that for me. It was as if I'd been told that of all the *Bounty* men that sailed from England together there was none left save myself. I walked the island with a heart heavy as lead. I thought of the mutiny and the part I'd played in it, and how I'd helped to set Captain Bligh and eighteen innocent men adrift in a little boat, in the middle of the ocean. As I lay in bed at night I'd see the launch riding the waves, and them in it dead of thirst or starvation; or a picture would come to mind of the lot of 'em bein' murdered by savages on some island where they'd landed. I'd think of the blood spilt here, and Quintal's face would come before me; night and day I'd see it, until I was near desperate, not knowing how I was to live with such memories behind me.

The children was no help to me, then. I was struck with fear at the very sight of 'em, thinking of what might happen when they was grown men and women. I minded what Mr. Young had read to me once: that the sins of the fathers would be visited on the children for generations. I'd come to believe that. I believed it was God's law them innocent babes should be punished for our sins, and us through them. I tried to pray to Him, but I didn't know how, and ye'll mind I thought of Him, then, as a God of wrath and vengeance. I'd heard naught and read naught of a God of forgiveness and love. But that was to come. I was to be led into the way of peace at last; but it was a long way, sir, and I can't tell ye the torment I suffered through afore I found it.

Aye, if ever a man felt lost and desperate, it was Alex Smith, sir. I couldn't believe there was any hope for me. It may have been because I was alone, with no other man I could open my heart to. However it was, I believed the blood of all the innocent men that had died since the mutiny was on my head. I believed it was meant I should be made the scapegoat for the guilty ones and be punished for 'em. By thinkin' so much over the past, I'd come to believe it was God's will I should be destroyed, by my own hand. One day — it was around two months after Mr. Young's death — I went to the great cliff on the south side of the island with the intent to throw myself off. I was out of my mind, sir — that's the truth of it.

Ye've been to the top of the Rope. Ye know what a fearsome place it is, with a straight drop to the sea, hundreds of feet below. It was there Quintal and Minarii had battled with their bare hands, when Minarii was pushed to his death over the cliff. I reached the place not knowing how I got there, stumbling along like a blind man, with my heart bitter as gall. It was midday when I crossed the island. I thought all the women and children was in the settlement having their usual rest, but I wasn't more than half a dozen steps from the brink of the cliff when I spied three of the children curled up there, asleep, like kittens in the sunshine. There was little Matt Quintal, and Eliza Mills, and Mary, Mrs. Christian's youngest, who was seven years old at that time. Matt had a little pole beside him he'd cut from the bush, with a basket of yams on one end and a small bunch of plantains on the other. The lasses had their eggin' baskets filled and put away in the shade close by; and afore they'd gone to sleep they'd made garlands of blossoms to hang around their necks.

I stepped back and stared at 'em like a man has been waked out of a horrible dream, and all at once there flowed into my heart a flood of hope and joy and love I could never explain. It must have been God's mercy that showed me that pretty innocent sight, for as sure as ye hear me, sir, if they hadn't been there I'd have flung myself off the cliff. I sank down on my knees beside 'em. The tears ran down my cheeks, and a voice inside me spoke as plain as words, tellin' me I was to live for them children, and love and cherish 'em, and think no more of evil times past and done with.

Ye'd have said Mary heard that voice. She opened her eyes and looked at me in a puzzled way. The next minute she jumped up and had her little arms around my neck.

"Alex! What is it?" says she, but my heart was so full I couldn't speak. All I could do was hold her close. Presently I said, "Never mind, darlin'. I'm weepin' for joy, if ye wish to know, and the love I have for ye lads and lasses."

Our voices roused up the other two, and they didn't know what to make of seein' me in such a state. Eliza came on the other side and I gathered her in with Mary and held the two of 'em so; and Matty stood on his knees in front of me with a look of wonder on his face. He hadn't a trace of his father in him. He'd gone all to the mother's side, as handsome a lad as ye could hope to see, with dark curly hair and great brown eyes, true and trustful like them of a dog.

"Alex, are ye hurted?" says he.

"Nay, lad," says I, "but ye've give me a turn, the three of ye, lyin' asleep so close to the edge of the cliff. You might have rolled off it."

Then Eliza's face brightened up and she laughed at me, and the others with her. "Was ye weepin' for *that*, Alex?" says she. "Why, we've climbed down there many's the time."

"What!" says I. "Not over the Rope?"

"Aye," says she; and afore I could think, the lad jumped to his feet. "I'll show ye, Alex," said he, and over he went. I was scared out of my wits. The cliff is all but sheer, and a missed handhold or foothold would send ye to your death, hundreds of feet below; and there went Matt, like a crab down a wall of reef! I called and begged him to come back, scarce darin' to breathe, and when he'd gone down, twenty-five feet or so, to show how easy he could do it, up he climbed again, as cool as ye please. In my heart I was proud of his pluck, but I didn't let on. Many a fright the children has give me since, the lot of 'em, the way they clamber down cliffs and along ridges that would scare a goat, but they never come to grief, and I've got used to seein' 'em now, in a way. They're as much at home on the rocks and ledges as they are in the sea.

I like to mind me of that day. I wasn't a Christian man, Mr. Webber, I don't know if I'll ever merit to be called one, but if it wasn't God's love that saved me, what could it have been? It must have been that! He must have seen and took pity on me for the children's sakes. He had work for me to do. There's no explainin' it, else. And somehow the load of misery was lifted from my heart so that I never felt it again so sore and heavy as at that time.

I'd left off my study at readin' and writin' when Mr. Young was took sick. Now I went at it again, though why I did I couldn't have said for certain. I think I had the notion to go on so as I could read the bits Mr. Christian and Mr. Young had wrote down in the old *Bounty's* logbooks. I took more interest in them than I did in the Bible, and I got to the place where I could read and understand the most part. But all this while, sir, I was bein' led. I know that, now. God was bringin' me to a knowledge of His love in His own way.

I went back to the Bible, takin' it up where Mr. Young had left off readin' to me. If I'd known what I know now, I'd have gone straight to the New Testament, but like enough it was best I should have burrowed along, slow and patient, like a mole in the dark. I did that for three years. I didn't read all. There was parts too knotty for me and I'd have to pass them by; but others, like the Psalms and the Proverbs, I'd come back to again and again till I got so I knew most of 'em by heart.

I've heard tell of men bein' led all of a sudden, in a day or a week, to the knowledge of God. It wasn't so with me. I was brought to it little by little, but when I came to the Life of Jesus, my heart began to open like doors swingin' apart. Once I was sure God was a loving and merciful Father to them that repent, it seemed to me I could feel His very presence, sir, and I grew more sure every day of His guiding hand. And I knew, in the end, that I'd come to the way of Life — the only way. I'll say no more of this, for it's a sacred, holy thing, but I was certain I'd found it because of the peace that came to me and has never left me since.

But I was troubled about the children. Not as they was then, but over what might happen when they was grown men and women. They had their fathers' blood in their veins. How could I know something wouldn't happen to lead 'em into our old ways? For all Mr. Young had said, I couldn't believe it was God's wish they should be kept in ignorance of His Holy Word. The more I thought about it, the more strong it came in to me that I'd been led so as I could lead them. It seemed to me I could hear the very voice of Jesus: "Suffer little children to come unto me, and forbid them not, for of such is the kingdom of Heaven." And I did, sir. I brought 'em to Him, and their mothers with 'em.

Ye'll wonder an ignorant seaman could have done it. I couldn't have, alone. It was God showed me the way. I began with the mothers. I'd gather them together of an evening and tell them the story of the Bible. Not the whole of it, of course. There was a deal I didn't know, but I had the main parts well in mind. It was a joy to see the interest they took. It was the story they fancied in the beginning, but they soon got to see there was more to it than that. What made it easier for me was that they was all young women at the time we left Tahiti and their minds was not hardened into the Indian beliefs; and I taught 'em in a way that surprised me. I'd never have thought I could do it so well. It seemed as if I was told what to say, and I'd have an answer ready for every question they'd ask. It was God's doing, the whole of it.

If it was a joy to teach the mothers, ye'll know what it was when I started with the children. Their little hearts was so eager and open and ready to receive there was times I was afeared to speak, lest I'd have God's teaching wrong. They'd believe without the least question of doubt. That made me slow and careful. I said naught about sin, for they didn't know what it was, and I saw no need to put any idea of it into their hearts. I teached 'em what I believed Jesus would wish 'em to be teached: to love one another, to speak truth and act it, to honour their mothers and do as they'd be done by.

All this was in the Indian language, which I'd learned to speak near as well as themselves. But as I went on I saw I'd got to do more. I looked to the years to come, when I'd be gone and they left without the skill to read God's Word for themselves. They might forget what they'd heard from me and drift into evil ways as we had. I saw I had to teach 'em their letters. Aye, it was a sacred duty. Once I was sure of that, I didn't rest till I'd started a school for the older ones.

As ye know, likely, the Indians has no letters of their own. Theirs is naught but a spoken tongue, and it would have puzzled a better head than mine to know how to go about such a task. Mr. Young would have known, and sorry I was I hadn't pleaded with him till he'd agreed to teach the children along with me. There was times I thought I'd have to give up. It wasn't the children's fault. They was bright and quick. Often they'd see what I was drivin' at afore I was sure of it myself. All I had on my side was the deep wish to teach 'em and a stubborn streak in me that wouldn't let me give in till I'd showed 'em what letters meant, and how they was put together to make words. Their knowin' bits of English was a great help, but if ever a man sweat blood over a thing was past his skill, that man was myself.

But they got the notion of it at last, and, once they had, it would have amazed ye to see how fast they went on. Thursday and Charles Christian and Mary McCoy was the best, but there was little to choose amongst the five I took into the first school. I'll not forget how proud they was when they got so as they could read a few lines and write little messages to one another. Their mothers thought it was the wonder of the world, and when ye come to look at it, there's few things to equal the wonder of writin'. I'm blessed if I can see how men ever came to the knowledge of it in the first place.

There was a writin' chest had belonged to Captain Bligh, with a good store of paper in it, and ink, and pens. I cherished them sheets of paper as if every one was beat out of gold. When the ink was gone I made some that did famous out of candlenut ash, and pens we had a-plenty, with all the fowls there is on the island. When the last of the paper was gone, I made slates for the children out of slabs o' rock. There's a kind of rock here ye can chip off in thin layers. They's what we used for slates, and we still do; but it's hard to grind it down and make it smooth.

The school was a pride to the children as much as it was to me. I didn't have to coax 'em into it. Bless ye, no! They all wanted to learn their letters. I took the young ones in as fast as they came to an age, and the older ones was a great help with them. And the questions they'd ask, once they learned to read a bit! They'd make my old head swim! I didn't let 'em read the Bible for themselves. There was parts would only have puzzled 'em, as Mr. Young said. I picked out the chapters, and the most of it was Christ's teaching to His disciples. And they'd take it to their hearts, sir, and keep it there — aye, and live by it.

And now I'm near to the end of the story. I might go on for another night, or a week of nights, for the matter of that, tellin' ye what's happened these past five years; but I've no wish to try ye past the limit of patience. Ye can see how it's been. Our life has gone by as quiet as a summer's day. There's never been the least strife amongst us since the day Quintal was killed. We've lived for the children. Their mothers and me has never had a thought save how we can make their lives as happy as ours was miserable in the old days. They're good mothers, for all they was heathens before, and still are, in some of their ways. But there's heathen ways, sir, us white men could study to our profit. I have. There's been time for it here. I've learned more from these Indian women than ever I've been able to teach them.

Aye, it's a quiet life and a good life we've had here these nine years. I doubt if ye could find anywhere a family of human beings that lives together with more kindness and good will. We're at peace, in our lives and in our hearts. There's the sum of it, in few words.

Now and again, when I go out to fish, I pass over the place where the hulk of the *Bounty* lies. I look down at her and mind me of the times I trod her decks. I mind me of the day we put out from Portsmouth, all of us so eager for the voyage ahead, and thinkin' what we'd see amongst the islands we was bound for. Little we knew what was to come! Little we guessed how soon we was to be scattered far and wide, and the ends some of us was to meet!

We did a cruel wrong when we set Captain Bligh adrift with all them innocent men. He was a hard man and an unjust man. But, no matter how sore we was tried, we should never have seized the ship, and none knew it better than Mr. Christian when it was too late. Ye'll know from what I said that he never had a moment's pleasure or peace of heart from that time to the day of his death. Aye, it was a cruel, lawless deed, and all that can be said for us is that the mutiny wasn't a cold-blooded, planned-out thing. It was the matter of half an hour and was over with afore it came in to us what we'd done. Then it was past mending. We was punished for it as we deserved, but I'll say no more o' this, for it's over and ended.

Ye'll never know the joy it's give me to hear that Captain Bligh and his men won through to safety. I can be truly at peace from this time on. That knowledge was the one thing needful, and I never thought to have it.

Now I've done what Mr. Young wished I should do: told ye the story from start to finish, and kept nothing back. I'd have told ye, regardless, Mr. Webber, for it's been a burden on my heart all these years. I thank ye kindly that ye've let me ease the weight of it.

It's a late hour. Ye'll be ready for bed, and we'll go along to the house.

The last of the casks is filled, Thursday says, and ready to be towed out. It's been a rare treat to the children to be of service to ye. They've a sea stock on the beach will last ye halfway home, I shouldn't wonder — pigs and fowls and fruits and vegetables. We've food and to spare here. Bless ye! We could fill a score of ships like the *Topaz* and never miss it in the least.

There's one thing more I'd like to speak of. It's about the children. If only I could keep 'em as they are, Mr. Webber — ignorant of the world, and the world ignorant of them! That would be my heart's wish! Maybe ye'll say it's a foolish wish; but if ye could be in my place, see and be with 'em from day to day, ye'd feel as I do. Aye, ye would so — I'm certain of it. They've missed so much that children outside is laid open to, almost from babyhood. I'd not have ye think they're perfect, without flaw or blemish. They're human. But I do believe ye might search the world around without finding children more truly innocent and pure-minded than these.

When I think they was sprung from rough, hard seamen, for the most part, mutineers and pirates, I can scarce believe they're our own flesh and blood. It's a miracle! There's no other name for such a thing! Never a night passes that I don't thank God that He's let these Indian mothers and me live to see it.

Aye, if only we could keep 'em so! I'll not forget the morning the *Topaz* was sighted. It was Robert Young spied ye first. We was in the school when he came runnin' up from the bluffs. "Alex," said he, "there's a great canoe comin' over the sea!"

There was an end of lessons. The lads had never seen a ship, though I'd told 'em there was such things. I had to, for they'd seen what's left of the old *Bounty*. We rushed to the bluffs, and when I saw the vessel, Mr. Webber, my heart sank. Shall I tell ye what I wished to do? Ye was still miles off and couldn't have seen the smoke of our fires. I wanted to put 'em out, gather the womenfolk and the lads and lasses — every chick and child — and hide with 'em in the forest, in the deepest part of the valley. It wasn't that I was afeared for myself. I was thinkin' of the children. I wanted to keep 'em clear of all knowledge of the world their fathers was raised in. I wished sore to do it! But they was so stirred up and eager, it would have broke their hearts if I'd not let 'em go off to ye and ask ye ashore.

And now ye've found us, it'll soon be known we're here. I've no doubt it'll cause a bit of a stir, outside, when Captain Folger tells that he's found the hiding-place of the old *Bounty's* men. I wouldn't try to coax him or yerself to keep silent about us, Mr. Webber. It's your duty to report us — that I know. And other ships will come, once it's known that Pitcairn's Island is summat more than a lonely rock for sea birds. . . . Aye. Soon or late they'll come, as Mr. Young said. . . . Well . . .

But God bless me! I mustn't keep ye up longer. Ye'll be perished for sleep. I'll warrant I could talk the night through, it's been so long since I've had a seaman to yarn with. Good night, sir, and rest well. I'll be astir bright and early to meet Captain Folger.

## EPILOGUE

AT sunset on the following day, Alexander Smith was seated with half a dozen of the children on the highest pinnacle of the crag, Ship-Landing Point, overlooking Bounty Bay. Below them, at various places along the seaward cliffs, were the other members of the Pitcairn colony, all steadfastly gazing eastward. The *Topaz,* with all sail set, under a fresh westerly breeze, had drawn rapidly away from the land and was now far out, looking smaller than a child's toy vessel against the lonely expanse of blue water.

The hush of early evening was over land and sea. The ravines and valleys were filled with purple shadow, deepening momentarily, and, in the last level rays of the sun, crags, ridges, mountain peaks, and the lofty cliffs that bounded the island on the west stood out in clear relief, bathed in mellow golden light.

The old seaman turned to a little girl at his side, who was weeping softly, her head in her arms.

"There, lass! Comfort ye now. Bless me! Ye'll have the lot of us weepin' with ye directly."

The girl raised her head, making an attempt to smile through her tears.

"It's sad to have them go so soon," she replied. "Will they never come back?"

"That I couldn't tell ye, darlin'. But who knows? They might."

"But where is it they're going, Alex?" one of the boys asked.

"Home . . . a long way . . . thousands of leagues from where we are."

"What is a league?"

"A league? Well, let me think. . . . If the land here was half again as big as it is, ye'd have just about a league from one end to the other."

"And they have thousands of leagues to sail before they reach their home?"

"Aye — thousands, the way they'll go."

"Then we'll never see them again!"

"Now, Mary, lass! Don't ye start weepin' along of Rachel! Wouldn't ye have Captain Folger see his dear ones? And there's Mr. Webber with three children, the oldest the age of yourself, waitin' for him in his own land. Think of the joy there'll be the day he comes home!"

"I want them to go home; it isn't that. But I want them to come back. And if it's so far . . . they do hope to come again, don't they?"

"Aye; and mebbe they will. But ye can't never tell about ships — where they'll be off to next."

"Where is their home?"

"Off yonder."

"Is it like ours?"

"Aye, in a way, but in some ways it's nothing like. It's a great country they live in. Ye could put together hundreds of lands the size of ours — thousands of 'em — and it wouldn't make one as big as theirs. And it's cold in the winters. It's that cold the water freezes in the brooks and streams."

"What does that mean — freezes?"

"Well, I don't know as I can tell ye, exactly. It gets colder and colder, and the end of it is the water in all the streams is froze till it's hard like rock, and ye can walk on it."

"Alex! It couldn't be so! You can walk on the water as Jesus did?"

"Nay, Robbie, it's not the same. Jesus walked on water like we have here. But in them perishin' cold places . . . well, it freezes and gets hard, like I said. Anybody can walk on the froze water. I've done it myself."

Another of the lads turned to him eagerly.

"I'd like to see it! Alex, if they come again, couldn't I go with them to their land?"

"Would ye wish to go?"

"Aye."

A girl of twelve years seized the boy's arm.

"You wouldn't go, Dan! We'd never let you go!"

"I'd come back."

"I've no doubt ye'd wish to come back," said Smith; "but ye might be away years and years. Ye might never have the chance to come home again. Think how lonesome ye'd be, Dan, and all of us, without ye. Nay, lad, bide here, whatever comes. Never any of ye leave home. Ye don't know how it is out yonder."

"But we want to know! All of us do! Why have you never told us of the other lands?"

"It's been so long since I've seen 'em I'd most forgot there was such places."

"But you'll tell us about them now?"

"Aye, Alex, do!"

"Will you tell us to-night?"

Taking their eyes, for a moment, from the distant ship, all turned to him eagerly.

"There, now. We'll see. . . ."

"No, Alex! Promise you will!"

"Not to-night, children. But like enough I will, one of these days, if ye've still the wish to hear. There's Thursday and Matt comin' in. Run down and help 'em up with the canoe, Dan — ye and John and Robbie. . . . Rachel, ye lasses had best go home, now, afore it's dark. Tell Mother I'll be along directly."

The sun had set and the last light faded swiftly from the sky. In the east the first stars appeared. The ship was now but a mere speck almost on the verge of the horizon. Motionless, his chin in his hands, elbows on his knees, the old seaman gazed after her till she was lost to view in the gathering darkness. At length he rose and turned away, slowly descending the steep northern slope of the crag to the path which led to the settlement.